TWISTED IN CHAOS

DESTRUCTIVE DEVASTATION SERIES BOOK TWO

ALY BECK

Cover Design: Pretty in Ink Creations

Dev Editing: Steph Rawlins

Editing: Jenni Gauntt

Formatting: Jenni Gauntt

INTRODUCTION

Welcome to Twisted in Chaos.

This is a book on the darker side of things with several Red Flags that may tick your yays or nays. Please see the next page and visit my website www.authoralybeck.com to view the full list to ensure you know what you're jumping into.

And if you happen to come across something that needs to be added, please email me at alybeck1129@gmail.com

Thank you so much for once again reading my work! I appreciate you all so much and I hope you like the conclusion of Journey's thiccccc story! Ha.

RED FLAG SHOPPING LIST

Please note that Twisted in Chaos does dabble in darker themes and has situations that might be uncomfortable....

- Violence.
- KABOOMS (Could be Orgasms or Firepower. It's up to you to decide.)
- *Potential spoiler**
- Pregnancy.

Check out www.authoralybeck.com for the full list.

PREVIOUSLY ON TWISTED IN OBSESSION

JOURNEY WEST, OUR BELOVED FMC, HAS BEEN UNDER HER monster—Gabriel Viotto's, thumb for years since she saved her sister, Sunshine, from being assaulted by Thomas Mondelli. Journey stabs him, and he dies.

Gabriel sent her sister Sunshine to a hospital because of her heart condition and only let Journey talk to her through written correspondence and the occasional video chat while he trained Journey for 6 months to become his spy.

Enter....the Devil's of Briar Cove. The mafia heir, Jericho, and his besties, Arrow and Sheppard. (Our MMCs).

They stalk Journey to a party, wear masks, and rock her world. From there, they stalk her more, forcing her to live with them and be their girl by signing a contract.

They chase her through the woods, fuck some more. She meets Arrow's pet lions—Max and Nova... and you guessed it... fuck some more.

Arrow removes her IUD without her knowledge. Jericho marries her without her knowledge. Come to think of it, I think Shepp is the only angel out of the three of them... Oh, our sweet, mute painter.

Oh! And they fuck some more... without the IUD. *wink*

At the end of TIO, they attend their mafia initiation night where Journey is sold to Shadow, the mysterious villain who has been attacking the Viotto Crime family.

And surprise! He's Thomas Mondelli (Shepp's father and also, the man Journey murdered.)

BUM BUM BUMMMMM!!!!

Now are you ready to jump back in?

CHARACTER LIST

Main Characters:

Journey FMC

Jericho MMC

Shepp MMC (Only uses ASL to converse since his father cut his tongue out).

Arrow MMC (also, slightly unhinged)

Side characters:

Gabriel Viotto- Jericho's father.

Grace Viotto- Jericho's mother

Thomas Mondelli- Shadow. Also, he's supposed to be dead.

Elias White- leader of the blue spider gang

Jenni- Journeys BFF

Sunshine- Journey's little sister.

CHAPTER ONE
Journey

"You," I breathe.

Vomit churns in my stomach at the sight of him hovering above me with that same menacing smile that haunts my memories. It lurks in the shadows of my mind, surfacing during my darkest moments.

In those bleak hours, he is always there, taking what isn't his. And then, my knife appears, slicing through him again and again. I leave no part of him unmarked—torso, face, limbs, hands, feet. I stab him relentlessly for daring to harm my sister and me.

Blood drips from every inch of him, and his howls of pain fill the trailer, pulling me back from the blackness that had consumed my vision.

How he survived to become a never-ending nightmare, I'll never know.

And that was only the beginning.

He's the catalyst of my darkness. Thomas Mondelli. Shepp's father.

"Me," he says with glee, clapping his hands together.

The man who was second-in-command to my monster—Gabriel Viotto. The man who made my life a living hell for murdering the man before me.

Only, he's not dead, given the fact he's standing right in front of me, eyeing the emotions crinkling my face.

Shadow—my monster's greatest adversary.

All the pain. All the torture I endured at the hands of Gabriel was for nothing. The guilt that gnawed at me for years. Wasted. Was my sister safe? Yes. But me? Am I okay?

No.

Never again.

Did my monster know he was alive? Was he in on the plan to let Shadow freely roam as a new man until he could make this deal to send Sunshine and me away?

I'll never be the same fucking person I was four years ago when I was just trying to survive and provide for my sick sister.

The familiar darkness swirls inside me, starting low in my belly and spreading like dark tendrils, encapsulating every inch of me, swallowing me whole, and taking my fear and rendering it useless.

Like me.

I'm useless. I keep fucking up and getting myself bound to chairs and stuck in cages because men in power deem it so.

Long before, as a child, literal sunshine made up my insides. Happy. Carefree. Living my life the best way I knew how. Sure, I had a shitty childhood filled with a mother who didn't give a shit if I ate or had clothes. As long as she had the men coming in and out and the drugs they brought her to fill her veins, that's all that mattered.

Not me. Or my sister, Sunshine.

Then it happened. That fateful day when I snuck out to hang with my friends and left my little sister locked behind her bedroom door. Even though I knew the dangers, my mom brought men back to our trailer day in and day out. Nothing new. Except this time, my mother sold her own damn kid to get the drugs she was aching for.

And me? Well, I stabbed a man to stop him from molesting

my sister. Then, my mother sold me to a monster without caring for my well-being.

It was there in the depths of my monster's basement when Gabriel Viotto tortured me into submission that my darkness was created from my misery. It started as nothing more than a tiny black dot blocking the trauma and feelings.

Then, it transformed into its own damn entity, covering my insides and suppressing the torture and murders I was forced to take part in.

After months of living in a small dirty cage, in blood-stained clothes, my darkness never left me. It grew like a parasite clinging to my soul and darkening me day by day.

Until he freed me from the confines of that cage and sent me back to my trailer with strict instructions on how I could make up for my indiscretions.

But I wasn't truly free.

And I never will be.

"You," I gasp again like a broken record, unable to say anything but the obvious.

"Yes, me," Shadow confirms, tilting his head as he looks me up and down from head to toe.

Shots of denial pour through me in waves. My stomach sloshes with nausea. My throat burns. I force my eyes shut, counting to ten in my head. Panic consumes me, slowly eaten by my darkness.

He's not here. Can't be! Why? Because I killed him three years ago.

Heaviness pushes on my chest. I gasp for oxygen, begging it to fill my lungs. Every breath I suck in becomes painful, like razor blades tearing through tissue and refusing to inflate.

This can't be happening. I can't be facing the man I stabbed. He's supposed to be dead and buried. That's what they said. That's what Shepp said. His own son. That's why I was taken to my prison. He's dead. He's fucking dead!

Just tonight. Last night? Today? Fuck. My sense of time

withers away. How long have I been in Shadow's clutches, rotting away in the chair?

Minutes? Days? Weeks?

How long has it been since Gabriel sold me out and pushed me into the stairwell where men took me hostage?

Pain pulsates through my skull the more I try to search my memories for the time gap, but I come up empty-handed. It's like it's all vanished, swallowed by a time thief.

Only the faint memories of our night starting at the initiation ball, celebrating my guys' leap into manhood within the Viotto Crime Family, remain.

However long ago, I was securely in Jericho, Arrow, and Shepp's protective arms, enjoying the wine and snacks. Well, as safe as I could be, surrounded by the entire gun-toting Viotto family. They are the most notorious crime family on the West Coast, controlling parts of California and expanding their empires through gambling, gunrunning, and whatever else they do to make ends meet.

I inwardly groan, remembering Arrow admitting to removing my birth control and Jericho marrying me without my knowledge. They're truly walking, talking red flags. And I somehow got myself entangled with them. Technically, though. It wasn't my doing. They kidnapped me, forced me to sign a contract, binding me to them, and handcuffed me to their wrists.

And where did that all land me?

Here. Tied to a chair.

I grit my teeth, throwing my eyes open. Stay alert. Take in the scene. Form a plan to get everyone out. My eyes wander around the room, avoiding Shadow looming over me with a curious gaze. Judging by the cave-like space we've been thrust into; I'm not digging my way through the thick rock walls. Makeshift lights barely illuminate the small cavern. There are no windows. Only a singular door. One way in. One way out.

Wonderful.

How the hell am I supposed to get Shepp, Sunny, and myself out of here in one piece?

No, I am leaving this goddamn prison with my life intact. Sunny. Me. Shepp. We're all getting out of here. No matter what.

Pain ricochets through me as the memories of the night before flood in. The distinct sound of gunshots popping off and three bodies thumping loudly against the stage. Gabriel sold Sunny and me to Shadow for money. My money. Something I had only known about for a short time.

Greed makes the world evil.

But why does he even need my twenty-million-dollar inheritance? He's rich enough without it. Gabriel owns Briar Cove without lifting a damn finger. He could bark an order, and anyone in a fifty-foot vicinity would jump into action.

His greed leaves me with nothing but confusion.

My eyes stagger to Shepp, bloodied and on the ground to my left. He hasn't moved an inch since they tossed him there. Through the low light of the room, I carefully eye his chest, watching as it shakily expands and deflates. He's breathing. Alive! But not conscious, either. My heart aches thinking about his demise. Or Jericho. Or Arrow. Are they okay? Did they get shot? Hurt? God damn it. I need to know if they're alive or dead.

I swallow hard, bringing my gaze back to the smug man in front of me. It takes every ounce of courage to look into his blank eyes. On instinct, I want to recoil when I notice the thick scars surrounding his left eye. Scars I must have given him.

He resembles an evil-looking villain, hellbent on ending my life.

He must notice where my mind travels to because his grin grows impossibly large and cartoonish. Evil radiates off him again, like the first time I saw him in our trailer manhandling my baby sister like he owned her after my mom fucking sold her to him.

Fuck.

I need to remain calm to process this entire situation with a level head. There's no room to lose my cool or let the swarming panic take me under.

"No," I rasp, swallowing the bile again, trying to keep my damn composure. "No. Fuck no!" I hiss out, showing every damn emotion inside me, rattling my chair with my frantic movements.

Yeah, way to stay cool and collected, Journey. Way to face him like a woman. Now, raise your chin. Buck the fuck up and face your ghost like the brave woman you are.

My darkness swarms every inch of me, dampening the panic clogging my throat. I breathe and count to ten, getting myself under control again.

Despite my monster being the biggest dickbag on the planet, he gave me a plethora of good lessons to defeat an enemy. Any enemy. Mine. His. Whoever. Months of torture broke me down until I was the perfect puppet. And now, I need to remember who he made me into.

I'm a badass bitch, capable of so many things Shadow can't fathom.

I take a deep breath, calming the raging storm inside me. The boys' encouraging voices echo in my mind, offering me the strength I'm desperate for.

I discreetly pull at my restraints, wincing when they tighten around my wrists and ankles, binding me to the rickety chair, creaking with every move.

"Believe it or not, I'm still here. Always have been." Shadow's grin sends shivers down my spine.

Fear sparks deep inside me, flickering to life when his attention falls on Sunny, sitting rigidly in her chair. My fear has never been for me. My desperation to live has never been solely on my shoulders. It's always been for Sunshine and her safety.

"How wonderful to see both of you again. I've been aching

to get my hands on you. But you've always been so protected."
He tsks at that, putting his hands behind his back.

My heart aches at the movement, reminding me of something Jericho often does when he's deep in thought.

"Why?" I croak, attempting to bring his attention back to me.

Sunny doesn't deserve this.

He snorts. "So, I can thank you for the freedom you bestowed upon me."

Everything inside me stops all at once. What did he say? I blink several times when a menacing chuckle vibrates through him.

"Freedom?" I bravely ask.

"Freedom," he repeats with a nod. "Imagine the hell I lived in under Gabriel's rule." He spits at the ground. "Dying allowed me to build this." He holds his hands out, gesturing to the stuffy, dim room. "A man of the family must die before his soul is released from the binds of his duty. I died. Therefore, I was released to build my empire in the shadows beneath that backstabber's nose. He'll pay for ever betraying the men around him, including me."

Right. Of course. The blood oath of the family. Something Gabriel forced me to do, too. The night I fell on my knees and bared my chest, leaving behind a scar of memories I can never forget.

I am a part of the family. Therefore, my death is the only thing that will release me from its binds.

"But no matter," he says, shaking his head. "There are so many things you don't know." He grins. "So many secrets left to be answered."

"What are you talking about?" I question, watching his every move as he steps back. Not bothering to elaborate on what he means.

"Come on, you. You're coming with me," he grunts, digging a knife out of his pocket and flicking it open.

My breath stalls when he cuts the ties around Sunny's wrists and ankles. My darkness swirls before my eyes, cutting off any rational thought.

"No. What are you doing?" I growl, pulling at my restraints when he forcefully pulls Sunny to her feet.

She stumbles slightly, but he rights her with his tight grip.

"Please," Sunny gasps, clutching her chest and yanking her arm. "You can't."

My heart pounds against my ribs when her gaze flicks to me. Terror lives in the depths of her deep green eyes, filling with fat tears, threatening to spill over. She shakes her head at me, warning me off while attempting to fight for her life against him. Her long brown locks hang over her slim shoulders, swaying with every jerk of her body. Her sickness has made her vulnerable. Weakening her entire being. Fighting against him will only cause her more harm than before.

Fear grabs me when Sunny suddenly droops in his grip, deflating completely. Sunny's chin juts and tightens. She eyes me, maybe for reassurance. Or maybe to let me know she's about to do something stupid. Something a fourteen-year-old shouldn't do.

Fuck.

"I'll be fine," she mouths to me in a stark turn of events.

The fuck she will.

"Get your hands the fuck off her," I shout, thrashing in my seat.

I pull at the restraints more, begging God or whatever deity above to set me free and save my damn sister once and for all. I just got her back.

It's been three years of hell, viewing her through a screen. Or begging for scraps of her words in vague letters, which I could only do every few months.

The thick air of the room compresses down on me. My lips pop open. Shadows dance across the dimly lit room as chaos grips my mind, holding me hostage as the scene unfolds in front of me. And there's nothing I can do about it.

My sister is being taken away again, and I'm strapped to a goddamn chair.

I'm a failure of epic proportions. I promised to keep her safe the moment my drugged-up mom brought her home from the hospital and laid her in my arms. She was mine to protect from anything or anyone who wanted to harm her.

And I've let her down.

Again.

"I fucking can!" he snarls, tightening his fingers around her upper arm.

More than likely, leaving thick bruises behind as he continues to drag her beside him.

"She's my concern." Shadow taps on the door a few times until it opens. "We're going up. Take her," he grunts and stills when the guard moves in and whispers something in his ear. Shadow's entire demeanor changes, and he narrows his eyes at the guard, snarling something under his breath that I can't quite hear. "Right. I'll be right there," he hisses, shoving Sunny roughly back into the room and slamming the door in her bewildered face.

"Sunny," I gasp, with tears pooling in my eyes. "Sunny, come here." Desperation leaks into my voice, wishing I could reach out and grab her, but I'm still bound to the damn chair.

"J," she whimpers, running toward me and wrapping her arms around my neck.

The entire world freezes the moment her skin touches mine. Her warmth radiates into me like pure sunshine, awakening my blackening soul. It's been too long without her. The world felt so dark and gloomy without her by my side, where she belonged. So dismal and not worth living. Now that she's right before me, I never want her to let me go.

"You'll be okay," I vow. "We'll get out of here."

Some way. Somehow.

Sunny sucks in several breaths before she pulls back and gazes at me. There's something there—a feeling—hiding in the backs of her eyes that I can't decipher yet.

"You're going to be okay," I whisper through the tears flowing down my cheeks. "I'll never let anyone hurt you ever again."

That's a promise—a vow I won't break again.

Sunny's face relaxes, and she wipes away any tears on her cheeks. "He's going to take me," she says abruptly with determination. "It's going to happen. And there's nothing you or I can do about it."

Yeah, okay, Liam Neeson. Cool story. But it's not going to happen. I'll battle my way out of this room with my body strapped to this chair. They can put me down before I officially give up.

All to save Sunny and Shepp.

"No. I won't let him!" Denial smacks me in the face. "This can't…"

It can't happen. He'll hurt her. Again. She doesn't understand who she's up against. He already tried to ruin her once. What will he do when he has her alone?

"It is," Sunny says with a tight smile, resting her forehead against mine. "You've been my hero for so long, Journey. To keep me healthy and safe, you have made so many sacrifices. You got me on the transplant list. He made you do so much to keep me safe," she hiccups, shaking against me.

"And I'd do it over and over again to ensure you were okay," I whisper, letting the tears escape from my eyes. "You're my little sister. I'm supposed to protect you."

"And you're my big sister. Sisters do anything for each other. It's my turn." She pulls back slightly. Confidence rests in her eyes as she gently wipes my tears away. "It's my turn to keep you safe. Whatever I have to do, J."

"Sunny."

"Journey," she mocks playfully with a hiccup.

"Sunny, untie me. Let me fix this. Let me…" Desperation roars through me when a defiant streak sparkles in her eyes. "No! Set me free. We can work together. We can…"

"No," Sunny says, stepping back and folding her arms. "He's going to take me, J. He's going to do it, and there's nothing we can do about it."

"Yes, there is!" I plead. "We can work together. We can… We can…" I struggle to find the right words to say. Take him down? Murder him without a weapon? What can we do? Anything! "We have to fight." It's my last resort and the only thing I know how to do to get us out of here. Maybe ambush him when he walks in. Knock him over the head, and then we can all run.

But Shepp…. He's still unconscious and probably too heavy to carry.

Desperation claws at me from the inside out, begging me to find a way to keep Sunshine out of Shadow's grasp.

She shakes her damn head, letting her brown locks flutter in the thick air resting between us. She steps back. Determination settles on her shoulders, pulling them back. For someone so damn small and sick, she has the stubbornness of a mule.

There's no changing her mind.

More tears trail down my cheeks. "You don't understand what you're up against," I whisper, pulling at my restraints again until the rope is cutting through my flesh.

"I will," she says, raising her chin with defiance.

"They're monsters," I choke out with desperation. "Remember what he did to you! To us." I suck in a breath when her chin drops an inch, and worry takes over her expression. "Remember what he tried to take…" I trail off. "Please, Sunny. Please don't."

"I know how to pretend," she says, stepping forward with a little smirk resting on her lips. "You were my hero for so long, J. I'm grateful for what you did for me. You protected me in the best possible way. Now, it's my turn to protect you."

"What if he hurts you again? What if he... You need surgery! What about your meds?" I'm grasping at straws, barely hanging on and keeping my composure.

I'm suffocating. More panic breaks through the darkness, festering inside me and clawing at my flesh to break free and scream some sense into her.

But it's useless.

Like me.

My gaze flickers to Shepp, still unconscious on the ground. Unmoving.

"I'll be fine." is all she says before wandering close to Shepp and bending down. She gently looks him over and checks his pulse, giving me a nod. "He's still alive. I'll make sure you're both okay. I love you, Journey."

A hint of relief slams through me the moment she checks him over, but it doesn't last long. Sunshine is saying goodbye. Again. Ready to take on the monster who destroyed our lives with his careless act.

The urge to shout and scream her into submission gnaws at my throat, but I tamp it down. What choice do I have? I can't force him to leave her here.

"I love you, too," I sob. "Promise me you'll be safe."

"Pinky swears and promises," she whispers, holding her pinky in the air for me to see.

"Pinky swears and promises," I gasp out, nearly sobbing when she leans over for my hand and wraps her pinky with mine.

I squeeze my eyes shut, attempting to get ahold of myself, when the binds around my wrists loosen just as the door smashes open.

"Take her up," Shadow hisses with agitation, basically tossing my tiny sister into the arms of the young-looking guard, who nods in compliance.

My entire being fills with numbness as the last of my sister disappears through the door, and then the inevitable happens.

Shadow stands before me with a knife, sporting a sinister smile that could peel the flesh off any mortal.

It's time to steel my spine and face the manic man prowling toward me maliciously.

"Looks like you and I need to have a little chat," he says, stepping forward and leaning down. "It's been long overdue since you stabbed me."

CHAPTER TWO
Journey

DIM LIGHT HALOS OVER THE MAN STANDING ABOVE ME, smirking at me when his words fully register in my mind. Shadows form over his face, only giving me glimpses of his deranged smile and beady eyes.

Shivers roll through me as everything sinks in, weighing heavily on my shoulders.

Oxygen slips away through my parted lips as the sweeping panic swarms through my veins. Reminding me of the pain in the back of my head, throbbing in tune with my frantic heart.

I squeeze my eyes shut, stupidly taking my eyes off the enemy for a split second, getting my panic under control.

"This was never going to end well for you, Little Snake. I kept you alive this long to get what I wanted," Gabriel says, nodding to the men behind me. *"Tell Shadow I send my regards and have faith he'll deliver what belongs to me."*

"So, you're Shadow," I say again, tears glistening as I wait for more confirmation, laughing slightly. "Of course you are."

"I am," he says with pride, leaning down and exposing his entire face to me.

Scars. So many mar his skin—all the result of my transgressions.

"What did you do, Journey? What did you do?" My mother's shrill cries roar through my mind on repeat.

Like always, when I think about the time, I thrust a knife over and over again into the man who tried to steal my sister's innocence.

And mine.

So many questions go through my mind when his fingers play with the sharp edge of the knife he's gripping. Blood drips from his fingertip, trailing down his bare forearms. He doesn't seem to mind. Chills spread throughout my body as he hums a song beneath his breath, waiting to strike me.

I'm going to die here tonight. I feel it in my aching bones.

"How are you still alive?" I bravely ask.

If he's about to end my life, I at least deserve the answers owed to me.

He has my sister. He'll use me just like my monster did and hold her health over my head.

It's a vicious cycle of bullshit. My life is nothing but season after season of a TV show, recycling their storylines with new villains popping up every year for me to defeat.

But what if I can't? What if I can't continue facing these monsters and keeping Sunny safe?

What if this is the straw that breaks the camel's back? And I'm about to crash, burn, and spiral into the depths of my darkness.

"By pure dumb luck," he chuckles. "Being stabbed twenty times should have killed me. But thanks to the quick thinking of my partner in crime, I was able to recover in the darkness and rise like a fucking phoenix into a new man." He grins, proud of himself, as he paces.

"So, you're the one who has been coming after Gabriel?" I swallow hard at the name I once refused to say.

Shadow tilts his head. "Aren't you full of questions?" he asks with a lazy grin, continually playing with the knife. "I suppose I can answer them. Just this once."

"Please don't hurt my sister," I whisper with desperation, but it's the only thing I know right now. My sister needs me to protect her, whether or not she believes it. "She has a heart condition. She needs a transplant."

"I'm well aware of what your sister has been up to," he scoffs, prowling forward. My neck wrenches back when he hovers above me, aiming the knife at my throat. "Look at how easy it would be for me to slice your throat right here. Fitting, right? Considering that's how you murdered me." Obviously, I didn't aim high enough because the bastard is still kicking. And somehow, better than ever. How irritating.

I swallow the lump in my throat, barely avoiding the sharpened edge of the knife.

"What's stopping you, then?" I provoke him, steeling myself for the inevitable. Why would he keep me alive? Not after I hurt him so badly.

He grins again, dragging the sharp edge of the knife over my throat. My flesh burns as he slowly drags it an inch and then stops, watching with intent as warm blood trickles down my flesh.

"A lot of things are stopping me," he says, tilting his head. "Although, ripping out your throat and watching you gasp for breath like you did to me would be quite satisfying."

The imagery works through my mind as he utters those dreadful words. I'm truly at his mercy. Sure, my hands are loosened. But what good would it do? I'd rile him up, and surely, my life would be over for good.

"Why? Don't you want to get your revenge on me?" I ask, lifting my chin until I'm staring deep into his lifeless eyes. "I killed you."

Sure, Journey. Keep digging your grave further. By the time you're done asking your questions, he'll have sliced you up like a Thanksgiving turkey.

Stupid. Stupid.

Internally, I berate myself for antagonizing him. I learned years ago with my monster to hold my tongue. He lashes out, inflicting pain when I ask questions or even open my mouth.

Shadow licks his lips, staring me up and down, holding nothing but darkness. Nothing resides there like so many monsters before him. He's a mass of a man with no soul.

He yanks the knife away from my throat with a calculated smirk pulling at his lips. His greasy, long brown hair hangs near his chin as he brushes it behind his ears with jerky movements.

"Maybe I will. Maybe I won't." He shrugs, standing tall. "You ever wonder how your little sister came about?" He inquires, tilting his head. A tune emanates from his throat again as he taps his chin a few times.

"What about her?" I ask slowly, watching him as he wears a path into the stone floors in front of me, going back and forth. "What about my sister?" My voice rises a little, giving way to the worry sitting heavily on my chest.

"That woman you call mom has been working the streets for a long time. Gabriel loved to throw her drugs and men from his inner circle. She was the best of the best, offering herself up to beast after beast without protest. She had a debt to pay, too. But you don't know that bit, do you?"

"A debt?" I ask, furrowing my brows. "What kind of debt?"

What the hell is he going on about in his classic villain monologue? I swear all the bad guys pace in front of their captured prey, spouting all their secrets and plans. I mean, what do they have to lose? In their minds, their victim will never get out, or they'll die trying. Maybe that's what's happening here, and I should milk him for all he's worth while I've still got a pulse. The more information I know, the better off I'll be.

Knowledge is power, after all.

"Of course, you don't know. Old Gabe kept you in the dark about a lot of stuff happening right under your little nose," he says with a knowing grin, sending shivers down my spine. How much didn't I know about my mom? A lot, apparently.

"She wasn't just some drugged-up whore Gabriel kept around. She owed him a lot of money and time."

Well, that's news to me.

"Why would he want to keep her around if she owed him?" It doesn't seem like his style. He's more of a *kill now and get rid of the problem* kind of guy. Hell, I'm shocked he kept me.

"He took a real liking to your mama," he chuckles, rubbing at his chin and smearing blood across his flesh. "She reminded him of someone he used to know. Stupidly, he trusted her, and then he learned his lesson. Such a shame; she was a good woman, too." He shakes his head in what seems like disappointment. This is something I'll have to dissect later.

"I don't understand," I whisper, the effects of being whacked in the back of the head coming in full force with a pounding headache. Who knows how long I've been out or been locked away in here. My vision slightly burns as he stops right in front of me again.

"What a shame it would be for me to tell you all these secrets he's kept from you for all these years, huh? When the man himself could tell you."

"What secrets?" My breath stalls momentarily in my lungs when he stops dead in front of me.

"I'll tell you all the little secrets Gabriel kept from you when you tell me every little detail of what you did for him. I will test your loyalties." He offers me one last smile. "Now, I'm going to spend some quality time with my daughter. Thanks for keeping her safe all these years. Your sacrifices won't go to waste by the time I'm done with her."

Everything in the room comes to a grinding halt, including my damn breaths. They stall in my throat until I'm wheezing and begging for air.

"What?" I gag out, shaking my head. "Daughter?"

He said that, right? Daughter? As in, my sister Sunny is his flesh and blood. There's no goddamn way. He wasn't... My mom wasn't... Wait... In unison, my mouth slackens, and my eyes widen at his confession. There's no way. Is that why he took us? Am I only here because I was associated with his child? Am I...

I blink several times. "Are you fucking kidding me? Your..." my whisper trails off when he cackles in delight. "No!" I say with more oomph this time, thrashing my head from side to side until I'm panting with the realization of it all.

Shadow is Sunshine's father. I guess there was a reason he was never on the birth certificate. Sable never wanted anyone to know. But how did he know about her? And why did he touch his own goddamn daughter? Not to mention Shepp.

Disgust rolls through me. I want to vomit on the ground at the facts ping-ponging inside my brain.

He points a finger at me. "She's my best-kept secret." Then the terrible man fucking winks at me with delight. "Imagine my surprise when I got the call years ago from your mom. She was drugged out of her gourd, confessing it was mine." His eyes roll toward the ceiling, and he mutters a few choice words under his breath. "But that's not important."

My mind reels with the information, and I shake my head. The denial is strong inside me. "No. Sunny can't be yours. She's..."

Well, I don't know who her father is. I suspected a random John who came to visit and fucked her without a condom.

"Mine," he says in a low voice. "And now we're all together as a big, happy family. She's going to be my greatest asset." His laugh sends my mind reeling with the possibilities. Maybe there's more to why he wanted us here besides wanting her in his grasp. I can only hope it's not to finish what he started all those years ago when I stabbed him violently.

But why Shepp? The poor man has been through enough at the hands of Thomas Mondelli. He took his voice from him by removing his tongue. Among other horrible things he's done. To us. To Shepp. Who else has Shadow harmed with his perverted ways and wandering hands? I can't let

him get his hands on my sister again. Or Shepp. Or—
fuck, me.

Now, my sister has volunteered as a willing victim in his
games, putting herself in his sights.

"She's sick," I plead with his humanity. "She needs..."

"Doctors, nurses, meds, and all that other shit. I'm aware
of her failing heart. Gabriel isn't the only leader with connections around the state of California. You'd be surprised who
I've got in my back pocket."

"What... What about us?" I ask, risking a look at Shepp,
who is still passed out on the cold, hard ground. He hasn't
moved, but his chest continues to rise and fall like he's in a
deep sleep.

My body sags with relief for only a moment.

Shadow's vacant stare lands on Shepp's unmoving body,
and he shrugs. "He wasn't a part of the deal." He rubs his chin
with no genuine emotion attached to his words.

"What deal?" I whisper. "You made a deal for Sunny
and me?"

Shadow watches me closely. "A little tit for tat. I gave
Gabriel the wife he wanted back, and he gave me what I
wanted—my daughter. It was a win-win. Shepp was just the
extra cherry on top of it all."

"So, he knows about you?" I gape, shaking my head. "He
knows about you and continues to..." I roll my lips together as
my stomach sloshes uncomfortably, threatening to send the
contents of my stomach—or lack thereof—to the ground.

"No," Shadow barks. "I have my ways." He levels me with
a glare. "I have pretenders and messengers—people who
conduct my meetings in my stead. We're all Shadow under the
moonlight. Not just me. Only my most loyal know me as I am.
My followers. What a great system, though, right?"

None of what he's saying relieves the ache in my chest.
Thomas Mondelli never died at my hands. Yet, I paid the price
for his death as he lived in the shadows of Briar Cove, building

an empire. Day after day, I experienced torture. Whether I killed for Gabriel or spied for him, I was under his thumb because I killed his second-in-command.

But I didn't, really.

Because the proof is right in front of me.

Gabriel Viotto's second-in-command has been alive and thriving this entire time. And now I'm his captive.

"So, you'll be good little captives and stay here until I decide what I want to do with you. Kill you? Torture you? Throw you to the fucking sharks? Or maybe you'll become useful for my cause. Tell me, what did Gabriel do to you after he dragged you away for your crimes?" He leans in with curiosity, like he doesn't have a fucking clue what happened to me in the depths of that basement.

Shit. Maybe he doesn't. Why would he care? He got away scot-free from his duties by bleeding out in my trailer. Going on to build his own empire.

I lick my lips with reluctance, hesitating to detail what happened to me. What other choice do I have? If I relay what happened, maybe he'll take it easier on us, and we can break free.

"He tortured me," I say, raising my chin. "Starved me. Left me for dead." I conveniently leave out the part about my money being the primary influence for my captivity and training.

"Child's play," he scoffs, rolling his eyes.

"He trained me, too," I say with calculation, watching interest sparks in his eyes.

He grins. "Training? Hmm. Interesting," he trails off.

"You're going to prove yourself to me, Little Snake. I want to know my time is worth the effort of keeping you alive."

"Yes, sir. How can I prove myself?" I ask, gazing at the wall in front of my face rather than looking at my monster standing in front of me.

It's one of the first times he's allowed me out of the cage to eat and use the restroom. He's finally taken a little mercy on me. Slowly but surely, I'm figuring out how to appease his demands.

"I'm going to train you just like the boys of the family," he says with a smirk when my gaze snaps to him.

"Just like the boys?" I stupidly ask and wince when his fingers wrap around my throat.

"Just like the boys," he whispers, leaning in as his fingers squeeze the breath from my lungs and I'm left gasping for oxygen. "By the time I'm done with you, you'll be so broken down that I can build you into the perfect little spy. Who would suspect you? You're just the daughter of a whore who will never make anything of herself." His jaw tenses before he tosses me to the ground.

The hard basement floor collides with my back and ass, sending spiraling pain through my entire body. I cry out on instinct, sucking in a breath as he looms over me with malicious intent.

"This will be a good first lesson for you, Little Snake." He rolls his white dress-up shirt over his muscular forearms and cracks his knuckles. "In the face of torture, never reveal the truth or cry out in pain. You hold in your pathetic cries. Viotto's do not beg."

My breaths come in short pants when I refocus on the new dangers around me. Unlike Gabriel, Shadow hasn't moved from his spot in front of me to punish me for my emotions. He observes me as I shake away the pain. It's then that I decide to grab my future by the balls and comply with whatever Shadow wants.

He holds all the cards in his hands. And he fucking knows it.

"I'll do whatever you want as long as Sunny and Shepp are safe." I lift my chin, hoping to lure Shadow to my side. My loyalties lie with the three men who now own my heart in every way. But the enemy of my enemy is now my friend. I'll do or say anything to keep my sister, Shepp, and me safe. "Gabriel used me as his spy. I know a lot. I've seen a lot. You and I could help each other out."

His dark, lifeless eyes inspect my face, and he nods. "See? One big happy family," he says as his lips split into a manic grin. "Now, get comfortable. You'll be here for a while."

I blink several times when he saunters through the door and shuts it behind him without another word, and a lock clicks into place, sending my heart into a frenzy. It's like my time in the basement all over again.

Panic crawls up my throat, closing it as I gasp for air. Tears track down my cheeks. I was free. I survived. I fucking fought for my life repeatedly, doing what I had to do to get back home. All for Sunshine. I huff in several breaths, attempting to collect myself. It's no use. I'm too strung up on all the emotions warring inside of me. Sadness. Fear. Regrets. Fuck. I need to swallow them down so I can wade through this with my head held high, but I'm drowning in the abyss.

Five minutes. That's all I'll give myself to freak out before I swallow my emotions forever. I'll pull my big girl panties up and start planning our escape. Or how we're going to get through this with our lives intact.

What's he doing to my sister? Is she okay? At least in the hospital setting, I knew she was being cared for. Despite sparse letters and video calls, I saw her face shining back at me.

Now? What am I going to get?

I'm jumping into the unknown with a new villain.

My pulse quickens when the lights in the room dim more, leaving me in the shadows with barely any light to see. The only noise present is my heart beating like a loud drum in my ears. Over and over again, drowning out any other noises. Darkness creeps in, taunting me with the fear I've collapsed in before. Deep breaths, Journey. Fucking breathe through the terror shaking your fucking bones.

You're not in that cage. You're in a chair. Sure, you're still locked down. But you'll be fine. Now, get your shit together. You're nineteen years old; you shouldn't be this afraid of the damn dark. Don't let it rule you now.

Fuck Shadow.

There weren't any actual answers to my questions. Not even the one about why we're here and what he wants with Shepp and me. Obviously, he wants Sunny for something nefarious. I just haven't figured it out yet. After all this time, why is he coming after his daughter? Why now? Why not when she was in the hospital?

I'm so fucking confused. My brain aches from all the shit that's happened today. But I can't focus on that right now. I need to get myself out of these loosened ropes and help Shepp. He needs me right now.

I take a deep breath, centering myself and finally letting my darkness cloud my thoughts. Every ounce of worry and despair disappears the moment it decides to show its beautiful face. Relief spills through me. If for only a moment.

"Shepp?" I whisper, wiggling my wrists together and loosening the rope even more. "Please don't be hurt," I mutter to myself as my head falls back. My eyes squeeze shut, and I take a deep breath.

You can do this. You've survived much worse.

Thank God for my sister. I never would have gotten out of these ropes without her. God, I hope she's okay. I don't even know where she is or where she's going. He could be severely hurting her right now, and I'm the only one to blame for it.

Finally, I'm free from my chair after a few seconds of cursing the rough ropes, and I climb to my shaky feet, threatening to send me to the ground. Without hesitation, I reach Shepp and gently lay a hand on his cheek.

"Shepp?" I whisper, leaning down to put my ear against his rising chest.

The room seems to still, quieting to almost nothing as I attune myself to the heady beat of his heart. *Thump. Thump.*

Thump. Relief soars through me the more I listen. It's music to my ears. Better than fucking *Whispered Words* lulling me to sleep. There. His life force. The organ beating triumphantly to keep him alive. My beacon of fucking hope that Shepp will wake up stronger than ever. "We're going to be okay," I murmur, resting there for a split second and soaking in his body heat.

We'll make it through this. I hope, at least. It's the only thing I can do at this point. We're trapped in a room that only has one way out. No windows. Only one door. And the room keeps getting darker and darker.

But Shepp needs me. While the light is barely there, I lift my head and check Shepp over. I can barely make out the light droplets of blood staining his white dress shirt under his wrinkled suit. Blood. A breath whooshes from my lungs and my thoughts run rampant.

My hands wander over his chest, lifting the shirt and exposing his flesh to search for wounds.

Memories of the initiation ball ring in my mind, reminding me of when Gabriel had me cornered and got the information from me so damn easily.

"Tell me now, Little Snake," he hisses directly in my face.

"It's under Josie Wells, in a Swedish bank account," I *cough out, desperate to bring oxygen back into my lungs. "Please don't hurt her. She's been through enough."* I shake *my head as tears roll down my cheeks from the lack of air.*

"What a good girl," he says, roughly tapping my cheek. *"I knew I could count on you again."*

Shame rears up inside me. I did just what Jericho said I would. I gave up information. All to save my sister. Again. And look where it got us—separated at the hands of another evil man.

Only this time, I barely know what he's capable of. I've only been given glimpses of what Shepp has told me about his father.

But it's enough to know we're in dangerous territory. Wherever it is. Possibly the island Jenni told me about. Shit. If we're on the island, then we're in the middle of nowhere. How far away did she say it was? Fuck, I can't even remember.

"I'm sorry," I murmur, caressing Shepp's cheek softly, examining every inch of his handsome features.

My finger runs down the deep scar on his face, tracing it— another reminder that the man holding us here is unstable. Every muscle in Shepp's body relaxes as I trace down his nose, over his lips, and around his jaw, memorizing his features in the dark.

My fingers run behind his neck, gently checking for injuries. When I bring my fingers back, warm blood paints my fingertips, and my panic rises.

"You're bleeding, Big Guy," I whisper, turning his face to the side, trying to get a better look at his injury.

Panic claws at my throat when the darkness moves around me, cradling me in

My fingers retrace the small wound, and relief drags my shoulders down.

But it's no use—the darkness of the room seeps in, coating every nook and cranny with its presence.

"They must have gotten you good." I shake my head, leaning in further to get a better look at the small wound on the back of his skull. "God. What did they do to you? How did they get you?" I rest my forehead on his chest, squeezing my eyes shut again. "Are the others okay, too? Please tell me they didn't get shot or hurt."

Tears burn at the backs of my eyes, and I squeeze them shut. I'm so tired of crying tonight. So tired of begging and pleading. The warmth of Shepp's body pours through the tiny scrap of material I'm wearing. The dress they picked out for me barely covers anything. It was nice for dinner, but shivers run through me in the darkness of this cave.

Everything aches as I curl up at his side, wishing I could do more to wake him.

If he wakes up.

Fuck.

I suck in a breath, burying my face in his chest, taking in the hints of his cologne. I breathe him in, relishing the feel of him beside me before the darkness of my mind takes over.

And sleep pulls me under for once in my life.

CHAPTER THREE

Shepp

A SOOTHING WARMTH PRESSES ON MY CHEST, ROUSING ME from unconsciousness. A fog settles over my brain, aching to fall back into the land of darkness and peace.

Something nags at me, though. It's a faint sound poking at my brain and keeping me in the present instead of falling back to sleep like I want.

A biting chill seems to sear through the bones at my back, rattling them inside me and sending sharp shivers down my spine. My toes curl when the incessant chill takes me hostage. The only thing pulling my mind from the blistering cold is the faint sound tickling at my senses again, calling me far away from the peaceful darkness that had engulfed me for....

Well, I don't know how long. Or why? Why was I asleep anyway? Or was I?

Confusion spikes through my veins, sending my heart rate into a frenzy, pounding against my chest. Something flickers in the back of my mind, reminding me of an old movie sputtering to life without sound and cracked photos. Images of Journey in a revealing dress, displaying her smooth back and the tattoo on her chest. She was gorgeous, smiling up at us despite the circumstances of the event and who was mingling in the crowd.

My fingers twitch with the urge to grab my canvas and

paint. Aching to etch her essence onto my canvas forever, never forgetting the night we spent together. I could paint a thousand images of only her and hang them in a gallery dedicated to her name.

Journey West. All for her. Always.

Jericho's smug grin comes next, flashing by as quickly as it came. Arrow's voice comes through next, boasting about his rocket launcher in the coatroom. Hints of disappointment, fear, and utter betrayal all pass through me, hitting me hard.

But why? Through the massive fog of my brain, I couldn't figure out why I was so panicked and fearful.

Did something happen?

I swallow thickly over the lump in my throat, noting the desert on the stump of my tongue and inside my mouth like cotton stuffing my cheeks. Dryness has my lips smacking together, aching to quench my thirst with cold water.

On instinct, my fingers reach out toward the nightstand next to our bed, searching for the water bottle I always keep at our side.

My brows furrow when my fingers find nothing but a rough floor made of what feels like ice at my fingertips. I groan, wiggling my body against my mattress. Why is my bed so damn lumpy against my aching bones? And where are my blankets?

But more importantly. How the fuck did I get to bed? We were at the party and then…

Nothing.

When I pull my hand back, resting it on the body draped over me. Soft skin greets my fingertips as I gently trace the curve of their back up to their shoulders and back again. Tiny goosebumps form under my touch, and I sigh with contentedness. I love it when Journey falls asleep beside me. Or on top of me. The warmth of her body always placates me, sending me into a heavenly rest filled with pleasant dreams. Something that doesn't happen often. More often than not, I find myself in my art room, painting her beautiful face.

Tonight, though, we must have fallen asleep quickly after coming home—at least, I think. It's the only explanation I can think of because my mind is blank and filled to the brim with fog.

"He took her," she mumbles emotionlessly against my chest several times.

I attempt to shake off the fog in my brain again, begging it to lift so I can fully understand what the hell is happening. Or maybe be able to open my eyes, which is a feat in itself. It's almost as if Arrow shot me with one of his needles and dosed me into unconsciousness. I've seen it plenty of times with his victims. If he did, I'm going to slam my aching fists into his face until his nose hangs sideways. He'll only laugh through the pain, but he'll never see it coming. I'm not one to exert violence to get what I want. One look at me usually has our prisoners shitting their pants. I'm tall, scarred, and exude danger.

But I'm far from it.

"He took her," she mutters again, sucking in a desperate breath as her aching voice quivers when she says it over and over again.

It must be a nightmare, like the few I've witnessed before. Even before I knew about her monster and who he had taken from her, I understood what she was saying. Her sister is missing because Gabriel Viotto is holding her hostage and using it to control Journey, so she'll spy on us, among other things. One day, I'll be Journey's knight in shining armor and get her back.

I gently run my fingers through her curls, softly massaging her scalp to wake her from her fitful dreams. It's a scene I've witnessed too many times with her. It'll escalate from here if I'm not able to wake her up from the nightmare holding her hostage. In the time before, I was able to coax her back to sleep with the use of my voice.

A sound I've only been able to use around her.

My lips pop open to speak softly to soothe her worries. Like before. A sweat breaks out across my flesh. A thick barrier rests around my vocal cords, freezing and constricting them into nonuse. I push and push. Trying to force my voice through the wall constructed around it. But it doesn't seem to work.

Nothing seems to fucking work. It's like the day my tongue was removed. I couldn't speak. Think. Nothing. It was only pain. For days and days, I endured it, unable to speak. He took it from me.

My voice. My innocence. My everything.

With her, though. I could regain that piece of me. The woman who holds my heart with hers as they beat in sync together—we're one.

She helped bring my voice back to me. Whether it was the panic or the fear of seeing her wide-eyed and terrified. She did that for me. In turn, I talked her through her nightmares and then spoke to her normally.

Journey West reset my life. Now, I need to reset hers.

I test the waters again, flopping my lips and sucking in air, begging for my voice to return to me so I can soothe the girl who has stolen my heart.

But I come up short.

It's like someone's fingers are wrapping tighter and tighter around my throat and blocking my voice from emerging. It's annoying.

"He took her." This time, her voice echoes through the space with a haunting tinge.

Her distress has the hairs on the nape of my neck standing on end. But that's not the only thing that pierces through the fog. When she says the phrase again on repeat, I hone in on the echoes bouncing back to us. Why the hell is her voice echoing in our room? I know it's big, but it almost sounds like we're in a cave.

I gently rub her scalp, moving my hand down her bare back, attempting to pull the memories from the back of my mind. They're slightly out of reach, so I push harder, attempting to remember the night's events.

Every sense in my body wakes when she mumbles the words again. The hairs on my arms stand on end when it all hits me. Raging floodgates open inside my skull, releasing a multitude of emotions that threaten to drown me in the tumultuous waters of the storm.

Stark images of the events that led to me lying here with Journey flash before my eyes, vivid and unrelenting, each a piece of the puzzle, reconstructing the night my mind let slip through its fingers.

The initiation ball.

The four of us dressed to the nines in our expensive outfits, standing around in the crowded room filled with the Viotto Crime Family, awaiting our ceremony of manhood. Then, the moment we stepped on stage–all hell broke loose.

Standing tall in front of the crowd with our shirts wide open, exposing the wounds inflicted on us during our initiation. It was the night we fell to our knees and pledged ourselves to the family.

Only we pledged for ourselves and the future we were going to bring to the town of Briar Cove and the Viotto Crime Family.

As we stood proudly in front of the entire Viotto family, they cheered us on. Men and women politely clapped as the man at the microphone called us by name, smiling politely in our direction. His grin set my nerves on edge, and suspicion arose inside me.

Our conversation from earlier nags at me. Who is this guy, and why don't I recognize him? Sure, there are a lot of men and women in the family I don't know by name, but this man doesn't seem to fit in.

I click my rings beside Jericho's ear, discreetly signing to him when he looks my way. 'Who is this guy?'

Jericho shrugs, turning slightly so the crowd can't see his hands. 'No idea. I thought he was a cousin.'

'That ain't no cousin,' Arrow signs with a frown. 'Think I can peel his skin off and get some answers?' His face practically lights up at the prospect.

Jericho shakes his head. 'Not yet,' he signs as we turn our attention back to the ceremony.

'Every party has a pooper, and the pooper is you, Jer,' Arrow signs behind his back with a pout.

For once, I grin at his antics. 'Later,' I sign with a snort.

Arrow vibrates with excitement, rubbing his hands together. There's no doubt in my mind that he'll reward himself with some debauchery tonight when we go home.

Then, we'll celebrate with Journey.

My eyes catch on several servers in red vests making their way toward the stage with their trays held high. Several members of the family reach for the full drinks, but they walk right by them without batting an eye.

My stomach drops—an eerie feeling gnawing at my mind in warning.

'Something isn't right,' I sign, swallowing hard when a man in a server's uniform walks on stage and pushes the announcer out of the way.

"What on earth?" the man on the ground growls, attempting to get to his feet. "That was not a part of it!" he hisses, lifting his nose in the air.

The server in front of the microphone grins. "Who said I agreed to it? Hmm?"

Jer and I exchange looks when he silently reaches into his jacket, touching his hidden weapon. For whatever reason, he doesn't pull it out and start shooting our enemies. He leaves it there, hovering above it like he's taking note of what's going down.

It's a good thing we came prepared and ready for a turn of events like this.

The man in front of the microphone nods to another server on stage. I stiffen when, out of nowhere, one of the female servers whacks our announcer over the head with a heavy tray, and he collapses into unconsciousness.

"Secure them," the short, balding man in front of the microphone says to the other servers on stage with us.

"Attention!" he shouts into the microphone with a manic grin. "My name is Ernie, and I'd like to thank the Viotto Family for coming together in one place. This makes it much easier to do this," the man says in a low voice, ripping his shirt open and revealing a large bomb strapped to his chest. He turns slightly, nodding to the three on stage with us as they pull their weapons.

Jericho's eyes discreetly drift toward the stairwell. Determination settles on his features, and I know exactly who he's looking at because I ache to look, too.

Journey.

But Arrow and I refuse to look. The last thing we need to do is draw attention to our girl waiting backstage when gun-toting imbeciles glare at us with murder in their eyes. It'll give her time to get to safety.

I swallow hard when guns are pressed into our temples by the three people who had worked the room handing out drinks and snacks. I eye their tight expressions. Not recognizing them from anywhere. Ernie blabbers into the microphone, pledging his allegiance to Shadow and his organization.

How the hell did these fuckers get past security? How was this even allowed to happen?

The crowd watches without emotions hiding behind their eyes, staying neutral as Ernie talks a big game. He never once reaches for the bomb to activate it.

There's something fishy going on here.

My eyes catch on Jericho's hand, slightly moving at his side as he spells out each letter of every word he's trying to say.

Discreetly at my side, I give him the thumbs up, acknowledging his plan, and Arrow does the same, letting a manic grin spread across his lips. He's no doubt ready to take these fuckers down with his weapon in the coatroom.

'Three, two....' Jericho doesn't have to get to one when we're moving in sync and knocking the guns out of their hands and onto the ground.

Each server's eyes widen in horror as they look up at us and then attempt to scramble for their weapons, like clueless soldiers taken by surprise.

Why are they not more prepared if they're working for Shadow? Something isn't adding up.

"Looking for these?" Arrow coos, kicking the gun into his hands as Jericho and I grab them.

"Wait," the server in front of me whispers frantically. "Please don't..." she trails off, shaking her head.

"Who exactly sent you?" Jericho demands, stepping until the gun pushes into the man's forehead before him.

"Don't," the man hisses at the other two. "Tell them nothing. They'll figure it out soon enough."

"You know, if you were Shadow's heathens, then you'd proudly say so," Arrow says with a grin. "Tell me. Tell me!" he says, practically bouncing on his toes. Arrow's eyes darken, and his true form peeks from beneath the surface—mayhem.

"So, you're not?" Jericho asks, raising a brow.

The three servers don't say another word, staring into our eyes with no emotions.

"Fine, then." Jericho shrugs, enacting the plan. "Go find Journey! Now! We've been had." *Jericho's words from the night before swim in my mind, and the worry coating his tough exterior.* "Now, Shepp!" he hisses urgently, shooing me away.

Indecision gnaws at my insides. Leaving them here to defend themselves seems dangerous. We've always prided ourselves on staying together and fighting the battles as three. Not two.

But Journey needs me. It's our plan. I don't know what's happening or why. But she's no longer by the steps watching us. She's vanished backstage.

Jericho's beady eyes turn to the gunman that he's knocked to the ground with one punch. I don't hear the words he utters to the three prisoners at his feet before gunshots ring through the air. And life is lost. Hopefully.

I groan inwardly, attempting to move my body off the cold, hard surface beneath me. But it's no use. Sludge moves through my veins and mind, making my thoughts foggy and moving a difficult task. Even opening my eyes to witness Journey's nightmare seems impossible.

"Go find Journey!" Jericho's words pierce through the fog again.

Journey.

Fuck!

I suck in a breath when my eyes finally fly open. Nothing but darkness greets me. My gaze darts around, aching to latch onto anything familiar. My bed or canvas. Anything at all. But it's as if I've been locked in the basement of my nightmares in my father's home without light to guide me away from it. I squeeze my eyes shut when my father's demented voice echoes through my skull. It's always there in my lowest moments to pull me under and drown me.

My heart pounds uncontrollably, thumping against my aching lungs. It's then I notice the pounding in the back of my head, thumping in tune with the beat of my erratic heart, sending pain down my neck and arms. Every muscle tenses when the pressure on my chest shifts, and a small voice pulls me from the panic creeping through me.

Journey. By the sound of her haunted voice, she's in the midst of her nightmare.

"Shepp, he took her," she whispers with such defeat, moving up my body until her forehead rests against mine. It's not too out of the ordinary for her to move, speak, and have her eyes open while dreaming. But this is new. "He took my sister. I'm so sorry. I thought..." Her breath shutters in the darkness, blowing across my chin when she leans in more. "I thought... he was dead. I thought..." she trails off, sucking in more breaths, like she's trying to pull herself back from the cliff of despair.

But she's not making any sense.

I open my mouth several times, aching to reassure her that everything will be okay. But my words fail me once again. It's like the last few months of progress have vanished. Nothing seems to slip through, and I'm left unable to speak again.

"I thought he was dead," she mutters repeatedly, burying her face in my chest and whimpering uncontrollably. "He was dead. He was dead," she chants again, digging her nails into my shirt and gripping hard. "He was fucking dead!" Her angered shouts echo through the dark, trembling in my grip.

She's so lost in the fog again and torn from whatever happened that she can't make it back. Only this time, she's not in a nightmare.

My fingers gingerly run through her curls, petting her until she softens.

"You're awake," she says, jolting beneath my fingertips. "Thank fuck you're finally awake." Her voice screams exhaustion and pain.

Shivers run through me when her touch ghosts over my jawline, tracing the smooth skin with precision like she's attempting to memorize my features in the dim darkness. My hand finds her, steadying her there as we sit in the silence of the dark. Only our breaths echo through the room wherever that is.

"Shepp, do you feel okay?" she murmurs with concern.

I'm sure her beautiful face twists with anxiety and fear, but I can't see through the shadows plaguing the room. Only the outline of her face comes into view.

I grip her hand against my face, nodding slightly. I attempt to open my mouth again, begging my anxiety to fall away and let me speak to her. Then, I could tell her about the pain in the back of my head and the fog in my brain.

What the fuck happened to me?

"Do you remember what happened to you?" she murmurs, as if reading my mind.

I shake my head, letting her feel the movement.

"You were on stage," she chokes out. "At the-the cere-mony. I was backstage, and... Gabriel came out of nowhere. This is all my fault. I know it is. If I hadn't spoken to him. If I had just gone on stage with you. We'd all be fine. We'd..." she rambles more, but my brain doesn't tune in to what she's saying now. It's falling into the deep abyss of my memories formed only a little while ago.

'I'll find her!" I urgently sign, taking off down the stairs and exiting the stage.

A weird calm sits in the backstage area. There's no sign of her anywhere. Small whispers leading toward the emergency exit grab my ears and drag me toward it.

"No! I will kill you!" Her shouts have the hairs on my arms standing on end when I finally reach her.

Or would have.

The emergency exit door slams shut, muffling the sounds of her screams. The moment they stop. My body stiffens, and panic engulfs me, but I'm stopped by the presence to my right, watching with a smirk.

"Good things are coming my way, Sheppard," Gabriel Viotto confidently says, adjusting his suit jacket. "And there's nothing that can be done. Soon enough, I'll have the world in

the palm of my hand. Beyond Briar Cove. The entire country will eat out of my hand."

A fiery rage burns through my body, eager to tear into him and rip out his heart.

"What did you do?" I shout in a raspy voice, causing him to falter a step, and his eyes widen.

It's not very often that Gabriel Viotto stumbles. But today was the day for that.

"What I had to do," he says with a shrug. "That's the thing about business, Shepp. Sometimes, it hurts, especially if it betters you. Like what your father did to you. It furthered his business to keep you quiet." He grins, watching my stance morph into nothing but rage.

My fists ball at my sides when he steps up to me. Or tries. Standing at six foot six has its advantages, especially right now when he only reaches my chest. But his arrogance will also knock him down a peg.

Or my fist.

Without a second thought, my knuckles slam into the side of his head, and he cries out, huffing and puffing about my actions. He shouts and screams when I take him to the ground, mercilessly beating his face without thinking about the repercussions. Fuck the consequences. Fuck Gabriel Viotto. He doesn't deserve to hold power over anyone.

Especially Journey.

Abruptly, I stand with a heaving chest, taking in the carnage I've laid out on the ground. He's barely alive, hopefully, on his way to meet the devil himself and burn for eternity. My stomach turns at the blood on my knuckles and coating my white shirt. Normally, I'd stay out of it, but this was unavoidable. Violence is all Gabriel knows, and now violence has taken him out, too. I check his breaths. They're barely there. His skin turns ashy gray, morphing him into a dying man. I can only hope my efforts sent him to his grave.

He's as good as dead in my eyes.

I run through the emergency exit door, trailing quickly behind three figures with Journey drooped over their shoulders. I'm ten seconds behind when I grunt as pain envelops the back of my skull, causing me to stumble over my feet and tumble down the stairs until I'm soaring. I heave a breath, begging for oxygen as the metal stairs dig into every inch of my body. When I finally land, tears distort my vision as a face pops up above me and sighs.

"It looks like it's a two-for-one kind of deal. He won't be too disappointed to see you..." the voice trails off, and my brows furrow. "He's always eager to get his hands on the Viotto's inner circle."

"You," I garble out, immediately recognizing him as one of our own—someone we trusted with every fiber of our being.

His eyes widen slightly, and his jaw pops open. "Time to meet Shadow," he says, shoving his hand into his pocket and pulling out a familiar-looking syringe with a capped needle. "You were one of the good ones," he murmurs, uncapping the top.

Pain takes me over as I try to move and roll away from the strike he's trying to land. But it's useless. A sting pokes through my neck, and I swallow hard, feeling the effects immediately taking over.

"Shadow?" I grunt, attempting to get my limbs to work with me, but it's futile. Everything locks up as if concrete now makes up the blood in my veins and the bones in my body. "Journey?" I slur, attempting to move again, but the figure above me hovers, and he shakes his head.

"You'll see her again, I'm sure of it. He'll have plans for the both of you." His grim expression is the last thing I see before I surrender to the darkness, with his last promise echoing in my mind: I'd see her again, even if we were in Shadow's clutches. We'd be together again.

Everything comes back to me simultaneously, albeit slightly fuzzy around the edges.

My hand tightens on Journey's, and renewed strength takes me over. I grunt, forcing my aching body to sit up.

"Shepp..." she murmurs with vulnerability in her voice. "I'm so sorry you're in this mess."

I clutch her face, slowly bringing her lips to mine. The moment our flesh meets and my lips overtake hers, a multitude of emotions rush through me. Relief that she's in my arms. Heat, because I'm finally touching her again. Only she can bring this amazing sense of stability and strength to my soul. Until I pull back, desperate to utter soothing words.

My mouth flops open, and I grunt in frustration when nothing comes out. My voice hides itself deep in my throat, refusing to cooperate with me. If I had my voice, I'd tell her there's nowhere I'd rather be than with her. At least I'm here to join her in whatever hell we're about to enter. But I can't. Gently, I take her hand in mine, leaving her palm up.

'We'll be okay,' I write slowly on her palm.

"What?" Her tone is gentle but wracked with grief as she speaks to me. I can practically feel the heat of her eyes spearing through my skull, even when I can't see them through the cave's darkness.

I lick my lips and trace her palm again, spelling word after word. For every word I write, she says them back to me until she's completed a sentence. "There's nowhere you'd rather be," she murmurs, bringing her other hand to my head when I nod in agreement. "Oh, Shepp." Her worried-filled sigh fills the room as she continues to stroke my face.

She shudders against me, nodding until her forehead lies against mine. The silence engulfs us as she trembles, and the shadows play tricks on her mind.

"Gabriel sold me to Shadow," she whispers, clutching my shirt. "He... He's going to take the money, Shepp. He forced me to tell him where it was hidden. I couldn't..." her head shakes. "I can't seem to do anything right," she mumbles so low that I almost don't hear it. "I'm so fucking stupid. God, I couldn't even protect my sister. I couldn't protect anyone. Not even myself."

She was abused, left alone, manipulated, and forced to do things she didn't want to do.

"He tortured me. He left me in the darkness..." she trails off, lurching forward to bury her face in my neck.

I cling to her tightly, holding her against me so she feels the warmth radiating off me. I'll be whatever she wants me to be—her knight, her pillow, whatever comfort I can bring her. I'll do it.

"All because I killed him, Shepp. I... I stabbed him over and over. He touched my sister. He touched me. And now he has her again because Gabriel sold us to him for... God! I don't even know why." She sucks in several breaths, clinging tightly to my body. "He took my sister," she whispers over and over. "My sister. Fuck. My sister." Her entire being trembles in my grip.

I shake my head violently, attempting to bring her gaze to mine. Through the darkness, I can barely see the tears glistening in her eyes and the panic twisting her faint expression.

I take her hand in mine again, leaving her in my lap. 'We'll find her. We'll get her back.'

"He has her, Shepp," she murmurs in a quivering voice, giving me a glimpse of the emotions she's wrapped up in. "Shadow has Sunny, and we're stuck in his prison."

My muscles stiffen. *'Shadow has Sunny?'* I spell out on her palm.

The only thing I hear is the sound of her deep breaths. "Yes," she croaks with devastation.

I swallow hard. An eerie feeling envelops me as the reality of our situation pushes on my chest. 'Do you know where we are?' I spell out on her palm.

"No," she whispers as my fingers trail through her hair, and she whimpers when I roam over a small wound with what feels like warm blood oozing from it.

'What happened?' I spell out.

Journey flinches as the lights in the room grow brighter. We watch, eyes glued to the door, as the locks disengage and a grinning man walks through.

Everything inside me completely stops, turning cold when his gaze looks me up and down with satisfaction. He's dressed in jeans and a T-shirt. Unlike my childhood, he spent his days in black scrubs for work or a suit for the family.

"I've decided what I want to do with you two," he says with an unsettling grin. My hackles immediately rise when he squats, looking us over. "You haven't changed a bit, son." He tilts his head, examining me.

I shake my head in disbelief. Every inch of me shakes in his presence as much as I don't want it to. The man from my nightmares. The man who took my tongue without remorse. He's supposed to be dead.

Why is he here before me? Why isn't he in the ground? Whose body did we burn to get the ashes and place them at the cemetery? So many questions simmer in my throat, but I can't voice them when he tsks, standing tall again.

"You're going to prove your loyalties to me," he says like we ever would. "I know what you did for Gabriel, and he was dumb enough to just hand the both of you over like it was nothing. There will be trials, though. I have to make sure you aren't going to bullshit me."

"What?" Journey croaks, looking up at him finally. Her head shakes. Fingers curl. Something unfurls inside her, erasing her turmoil. Her chest puffs out with determination, taking over her features. "Why would we ever be loyal to you?" she snarls, climbing from my lap and regaining her strength.

Shadow. Or my sperm donor. Or whatever he wants to be called, wrinkles his nose at her. "You show me your loyalties, or you die. He dies. Sunny dies. And oh, boy. That would be the worst death of them all. You know why, Journey West?"

He steps up to her in that intimidating way, getting in her face until they're only a millimeter apart.

She swallows hard but remains rooted in the spot, refusing to give him authority over her. Even though my brain screams at me to hide in the corner, I climb to my feet, too. Coming close to her, I circle my hands around her waist, pulling her back into me.

"I see," he hums, grinning wider. "I'll leave you two to think about it. You either show yourselves as useful to me and my cause against Gabriel Viotto, or I'll murder you all. Starting with him, then your sister, and then you." He raises a brow when we don't respond to his words like he's trying to get a rise out of us. "So, tell me all your secrets, Journey," he whispers, coming in closer again.

My fingers tighten on her waist, holding her steady. "What do you want to know?" she growls, standing tall against him.

"Everything," he growls. "I want to know where he sleeps at night, who is in his bed, and, most importantly, I want to know every facet of his operations."

"Weren't you privy to that?" she huffs.

"My, my. I'm curious. Did you mention to Shepp how you got yourself taken by Gabriel?"

She stiffens.

"I'll take that as a no," he chuckles. "How about I tell you a story about a girl?"

"I murdered your father when he tried to rape not only me but my sister, too," she says without looking back at me. "I stabbed him over twenty times until he was a bloody mess on the ground. How pathetic," she spits out, looking him up and down. "He deserved every fucking stab."

Anger washes over Shadow. He thought he had her where he wanted her, but she's played this game for too long against Gabriel. He gets in her face again, sneering at her. I've been born and bred into violence. Not that it was ever my favorite activity. But I'd stab this man for her. Hurt him until he cries if he lays a hand on her.

"I can't wait to watch them tear you apart. The loyalty games begin soon. I hope you enjoy knives." He doesn't spare a glance in my direction when he races out the door, slamming it behind him. I listen carefully as the locks engage, shutting us in here. The lights dim again as soon as he's gone, leaving us in the faint darkness from before.

Journey turns herself into my arms. "I'm sorry," she whispers, full of regret. "But he..."

My lips slam into hers with a heat I never expected. I nibble on her bottom lip, holding her close as I continue to assault her with gratitude.

'Never apologize for taking out the trash.' I sign on her palm.

"But I didn't complete the job," she murmurs, resting her forehead on my chest with a huff.

'Idea,' I spell out, gaining her attention again.

"Yeah?"

'We play the games.'

"You... want to?" she questions.

'Fuck him. Fuck Gabriel,' I write out, hoping she understands. *'We play the games. Tell him everything he wants to know about Gabriel. We win. We survive. Then we take them both down together. Once and for all.'*

If Gabriel is still alive. I didn't take the time to examine him when I took him down. My primary concern was getting to Journey and extracting her from the enemy's arms. Good that did because we're here now. Together, at least.

Journey's silence fills my ears with static as she ponders my words for what feels like several hours straight.

"Okay," she whispers.

'Together.'

"Together," she murmurs.

Her entire body stiffens against mine when all the lights in the room click off, plunging us into complete darkness.

"Let the games begin," an ominous voice echoes through our prison, laughing through a speaker placed somewhere.

Journey clings to me, practically climbing into my lap. I hold her there, consoling her through the darkness.

"I hope you enjoy the darkness." is all they say before the speaker clicks off and something else clicks on.

"Cameras," she says, slightly shivering against me. "The red blinking light."

My eyes roam through the room, finding the blinking lights from the upper right corner repeatedly.

They're watching us.

"How long will they leave us like this?" she murmurs in a low voice.

I can only feel the heat of her flesh against mine. The darkness completely swallows us whole.

'I don't know, but you've got me.' I write in her palm. *'No matter what happens.'*

She nods in response several times, digging her nails into my flesh. I soothe her with my hands, roaming them through her hair and down her back again. Her muscles strain. Whimpers echo through the room until she's silent and pliant against me.

"Shepp?"

I swallow hard at the sound of her hollow voice. My need to stomp out our enemies rises. This is what they do to her. They take an amazing woman and grind her into nothing but a husk.

I will kill them for stomping her out.

'Yeah?'

"What happened to Jericho and Arrow?"

My heart skips a beat.

'Hopefully they got away.' Hopefully, they're holed up in our cabin in the mountains, plotting to bring us home.

CHAPTER FOUR

Jericho

SOMETHING IS WRONG—OFF. ONLY I CAN'T QUITE PUT A finger on it.

Or anything, really. A darkness like a thick fog clinging to every fold of my brain—has me under its tortuous spell. I'm barely conscious enough to remember who the hell I am.

Jericho Viotto. Mafia heir. Owner of Rave. Residing in the Viotto mansion.

Or that is what I like to think. My brain is too muddled to have any coherent thoughts.

A yawn rips from my lips, attempting to pull oxygen in and refuel my mind. My fingers curl at my sides, gathering the plush comforter in my hands. I revel in its softness and coolness under my touch, sinking further into the comforter that reminds me I'm home. Even the savory smells filling my nose hint at home and—wait. I sniff harder, pulling the scent into my lungs. Soot. Ashes.

What?

I could nod off and fall back into the darkness of my mind and slip into the dreams that beckon me again. I shouldn't, though. Whatever has happened needs me awake and alert. I feel it deep in my bones.

An omen of what is coming when I can finally peel my

eyes open. Not now, though. I'll stare into the darkness of my eyelids until someone needs me.

Silence cocoons me. Static fills my ears, soothing the edge of panic roaring up inside me, like a fire simmering deep in my gut, growing bigger and bigger until I can't ignore it anymore. Something has happened. Bad? Good? I haven't a fucking clue. By the frantic pounding in my skull pulsating with the beating of my heart, I'd say I'm in for a world of hurt. Now, if I could only remember how I got this way. Pain reverberates through each of my limbs. But mostly through my right shoulder, which protests with every move. My fingers twitch at my sides again, releasing the comforter from my shaky grasp.

This feeling reminds me of the time Arrow shoved a needle in my neck, and I awoke to quite the scene. Right here in this bedroom. Fuck. I can practically smell the massive amounts of sex and cum with hints of smoke. Again. What the hell is that smell?

Bright sunlight beams through the open windows of the room, piercing through my eyelids, which I have yet to open. I'm going to kill Shepp for opening the damn blackout curtains. Again. Just go into the kitchen and make your damn breakfast like you do every morning, and let me rest more. Since Journey came into my life, sleep has come to me quicker and better. Once my arms wrap around her warm body, I'm done for. She's the shutoff button to my overactive mind, calming me in seconds.

Sandpaper rests behind my eyes. Every attempt to open them has me squeezing them shut.

Fuck. More pain splinters through me.

Water forms in my eyes the moment I pop them open, and I blink rapidly to push the uncomfortable feeling away. Lazily, my eyes roam over our bedroom, checking it over. But it all looks the same. Sans the people, that is.

My fingers brush over my bare chest toward the boxers I've been left in. Confusion swarms through me. What the hell? Did I undress before getting into bed? Wait. When the Hell did I come to bed in the first place? I shake my head, which is a mistake on its own. My mind swims again, swirling the room in a multitude of colors, forcing my eyes shut.

I sit up, groaning and holding my head. The deep ache in my skull pulsates more the moment I'm sitting on the edge of the bed. Fuck. I feel like I rolled in front of a bus and let it hit me repeatedly. Every damn molecule screams in protest when I attempt to stretch again.

"Fuck," I hoarsely cry when my right shoulder shifts into an awkward position, and I tense.

Bravely, I inspect the wound, grazing over what feels like gauze packed and taped on my flesh, and probe the area. The regret is immediate. Pain grips me hard as I try to regain my breath, and my mind swirls into darkness.

What the absolute fuck is happening?

Panic wars inside me more, tearing at my insides. I have a fucking wound on my shoulder. It's bandaged to perfection like a doctor came by and fixed me up. No matter how much my shoulder protests, I peel the gauze from my skin and peer at the small wound. My muscles shake with protest, but I blow out a breath, slumping forward.

"It's merely a flesh wound," I mutter to myself sarcastically, putting the gauze back over the injury. Whoever fixed me up, for God knows why, cleaned it. Later, after I've gotten in the shower to wash this gunk off my skin, I will look at it further and get a better idea of what I'm working with.

Now my next problem is. How the fuck did I get this wound in the first place?

I dig my palms into my eyes, trying to swipe away the fog, holding tight to my mind and refusing to give me any sort of insight. This feels exactly like I did with Arrow's drugs, but more intense. Worse, even. It feels like I stepped in front of Will Smith's character in Men in Black and let him take my memories from me.

"Remember," I murmur, squeezing my tired eyes closed and attempting to pull through the memories.

The initiation ball. The attack on the Family. The servers drawing guns and pointing them at us. A fight.

Journey…My muscles tighten with realization. Journey. Arrow. Shepp. Where in the absolute fuck are they?

I stumble off the bed, searching the bathroom and our walk-in closet. Bile rises in my throat when I look back at the bed. The only part of the comforter wrinkled is my side, as if no one had come to bed with me after my injury.

So, if they are not here or anywhere in this room. Are they in the rest of the house?

I listen again over the beating of my heart. It falls into my stomach when no noises greet my ears. Sure, this is a big place to get lost in. But I can always hear something from far away. The sound of Shepp occasionally listening to music as he paints. Arrow's loud talking. Scraping of plates and the sizzle of bacon.

But there's nothing. At all. Which means they might not be here. Perhaps they're out gathering food. Or maybe not.

My brain is still feeling empty as footsteps approach from outside my bedroom. A lock clicks, meaning I am locked inside here like a prisoner, and my bedroom door opens. Shallow breaths fill my lungs. When his sneering face enters my room, I retract all my feelings into a black hole before I see red and explode. Calmly, I suck in a breath and use Shepp's method he taught me years before to calm my nerves and count backward from ten, easing my tension.

My shoulders loosen, and I stand near the doorway to our closet, watching him as closely as he watches me. There is a predatory gleam in his eyes—a spider who has caught the fly in his web and is eager to suck out his insides. He's trapped me.

Now, what will he do?

Something big has happened. A broken time in my

memory that I can't quite remember right now. I will, though, in time. For now, I must pretend I'm as compliant as possible. I don't want to ruffle feathers. Or make them think I'm a threat. I am, but they can look at me like Aiden is looking at me right now.

"Good, you're awake."

My eyes roam over his body, fitted with a familiar black security uniform and a gun at his waist—something my father gives to all his employees who guard him and his properties. A piece of clothing I have never had my employees wear.

Aiden.

The lead security at Rave. The man who aided us in searching for listening bugs at the club my father signed over to me before my initiation. A man I thought I had complete trust in with everything.

How did I not see this coming? There's no question who his loyalties lie with now. Gabriel Viotto. A man who has never known what loyalty truly is. He uses and abuses, discarding his men like pieces of torn paper. He doesn't care about them like I tried to do with my most trusted.

Funny how that worked out.

"Aiden?" I question in a smooth voice. "What are you doing here? Is there a problem at the club?" Obviously, there's not. Or he would not be wearing that attire.

So, I play dumb.

Aiden eyes me stoically. "It's shut down for now." Well, that's news to me. Unless something drastically changed, it shouldn't have shut its doors for good at all.

"Shut down?" I ask, coming forward to stand near the bed and match his tense posture. "Why exactly?"

He walks to the middle of the room and stands a few feet from me. His chest puffs out. Pride emanating from him.

Aiden. My former employee has betrayed us. I bet if he sank to his knees, he'd suck my father's cock with enthusiasm.

Disgusting.

"Your father will explain." It's all he says when he eyes my shoulder and then jerks his gaze away.

Interesting.

"My father?" I play coy.

"Yes," he says stiffly, shifting his weight from foot to foot. "He's expecting you." Well, double interesting. He's expecting me. Yet, he hasn't summoned me with a text or phone call. Or perhaps he has. I woke up with fewer clothes than I suspect I went to bed with.

Mission one: find my fucking phone. Mission two: find my fucking family.

"In how long?" I cock my head, ignoring my screaming muscles, begging me to go easy on myself. But there is no time.

"Whenever you're dressed," he says, lifting his chin. "He's downstairs waiting for you."

Now, that admittance makes me pause. Downstairs? In the very house he has refused to come back to since he built his impregnable tower after my mother left us without a word. I sniff, immediately catching a whiff of something fishy.

The hairs on my arms stand on end, with Aiden sending me a downright evil grin that could wake the devil from a nap. He braces himself, eyeing me up and down with contempt.

"Downstairs? In this residence?" I ask, pointing toward the floor. I need to hear him confirm to believe it. Even though in the back of my mind, I know it's true.

This must be the omen my body was trying to warn me about. Gabriel Viotto has changed direction. Houses. That's something he never does. He's a man of habit. Formed from his paranoia that began plaguing him years before.

When Grace Viotto existed on this property, she made it beautiful—spending hours outside watering the gardens and bringing the flowers to life. Whether it was to get away from Gabriel's overbearing ass or to teach me in the sunshine, I'm not too sure. I have the faintest memories of her. My mother.

Resting somewhere deep in the back of my mind that's been inaccessible for some time now. Visually, I can see her smiling face. But holes plague the only five years I had with her. We spent some time outside. She read to me every night before my father would pull her away.

What good of a son am I if I can't remember what my mother looked like? Spoke like? I can barely remember her.

Grace Viotto is more of a myth to me—a ghost who sits in every corner of this mansion.

Even now, with the toxic fog stealing my thoughts and memories, I wouldn't be able to recollect her.

I shake my aching skull, returning to the present, where Aiden watches me closely. He was never the most observant man, but he made a damn good security guard standing outside our VIP room and guarding us.

"Yes. He's downstairs waiting for you," Aiden says smugly, lifting his chin. "Lunch will be prepared and served soon. Shall we?" He gestures toward the door with impatience.

After all these years, Gabriel has finally come back to the mansion. My only question is. Why? Nothing has brought him back in the past. Even a bomb getting set off or death threats with my name on them. He stayed as far away as he could.

Until now.

More now than ever, I wonder where the fuck Arrow and Shepp are. If my father is waiting for me for lunch. Are they down there, too? He's always considered them a part of my inner circle. Doting on them and raising them. Especially Shepp when his father died. And when he took Arrow under his wing after the priest couldn't control him.

So, my question stands. Where are my brothers? And if they're not on the property, where has my father stashed them?

All in due time, I suppose.

So, I swallow the panic clawing at my throat, begging to come out and play, and put on my mask of indifference. If my father even sniffs a hint of emotions on me, he'll toss me in the dark closet in the basement and throw away the key. Permanently, this time.

"Will we be alone?" I inquire, slowly moving toward my walk-in closet to gather some clean clothes before I step into the shower to collect myself, holding in a wince—every step I take jostles my newest wound.

Aiden's gaze stays on me no matter where I wander in the room. Later, I'll check for the weapons Arrow has stashed around here. Do I know their exact location? No. But I'm sure he has a plethora of weaponry ready for me to steal. He's Arrow, after all. Filled with chaos, but he always seems to have a backup plan.

"No," Aiden confirms.

"Then tell my father I'll be down when I'm well and ready." I raise a brow when Aiden swallows hard again, not moving from the middle of the room.

Scurry along, you little fucking traitor. I've got weapons to find and a phone to uncover.

"Then I'll wait," he says without emotion, blinking rapidly when I stand before him with my clothes draped over my good shoulder.

Of fucking course he will. He's probably been instructed not to take his eyeballs off me.

"I see," I say in a low voice, stepping forward.

"You see?" he rushes out, almost tripping over his tongue.

Scaredy fucking cat in a position of power. How ironic, huh? This one needs his heart clawed from his chest.

"Indeed. I see what lies you hide," I whisper, staring directly into his devious eyes. "Traitor," I hiss, making him flinch back.

He's been lying to me from day one. It's a good thing I've never fully trusted my employees at the club. Shepp, Arrow, and I turned Rave completely around at just eighteen, even adding high-stakes poker games and other means to line our pockets. Other important aspects were implemented long ago at the urging of Arrow. He may always carry a small vial of knockout drugs in his pocket, but he cares for the community —just like his father, the priest.

Aiden's face hardens when he steps back. "You say a lot of shit for someone who is unarmed." He gestures to the gun at his hip with confidence.

Not for long, asshole.

"And you say a lot for a man who is a traitor. You know what happens to traitors in the Viotto family?"

He licks his lips. Of course, he isn't aware. He's an employee. A no one in the eyes of Viotto. He hasn't fallen to his knees and pledged an oath while his chest bled for them. Not yet, at least. I'm wondering now if my father has promised something he can't give to Aiden—a piece of our paradise.

"In the night, they sneak into your room and tear you apart inch by inch. You can't move to defend yourself. But the pain..." I grin when he pales, reveling in his realization of what type of organization he is fully committing to.

It's not a threat for what's to come. It's a promise. Besides, I could reach for Aiden's weapon, have it in hand, and silently jam it into his throat, all before he could beg for his life before I blew the bullet through the back of his skull. If Arrow were here, he'd protest at my simple kill, begging to do it his way. And his way always involves his two pet lions—Max and Nova. And Shepp? Well, he'd stand stoically beside us with a grim expression, making sure we didn't go too far. Ever the hero to our villainous ways.

My father has always underestimated me. Never seeing the true potential inside me. He morphed me into the person I am, taking me by the hand and ruining every innocent part of me.

He's never thought I'd amount to anything special. Hoped, of course. But never truly saw what I was capable of.

Well, here I am, Father.

"I'm here to take you to lunch. Do what you need to do. I'll radio your father and let him know you're getting cleaned up.

And wear something nice; it'll be formal," he grits out, turning on his heel and marching toward the door to stand guard so I don't run away.

"I'm curious," I say, startling him to a stop. "What did Gabriel offer you to turn your back on me? Or were you.."

"He didn't offer me anything. I was never on your side to begin with. I can be a good actor, Jericho." The venom in his voice has my teeth grinding more than his admission. "But I will be a part of this family. I'll graduate from security to his second-in-command." Oh, so that's his goal. Interesting. I wonder if the great Gabriel whispered those little lies in his ears to get his way.

"Big goals, Traitor," I taunt with a laugh. "You think he'd ever trust you in a place of authority within the Viotto Crime Family?" My father wouldn't. He's seen how easily swayed Aiden is. No way in Hell will Aiden ever advance. He'll be another cog in my father's well-oiled mafia machine.

Aiden pledged himself to me and my club. My cause. But it was never mine to begin with. It was all an elaborate ruse, so my father had eyes and ears on me at all times. It makes me wonder how Aiden's security partner, Brandon, is fairing now. They were always together in the club, watching the patrons and protecting us. Was he in on it? Probably. I'll find him, though, and ask him the same questions before putting a bullet through his brain for ever stepping out on Arrow, Shepp, and me.

Aiden huffs, facing me in the doorway before marching back into my room and plopping on my bed. My marital fucking bed. The space my wife and I share with Arrow and Shepp. That simple action has red hazing my vision. My fingers curl at my sides. Murder is on the fucking horizon.

I have to play the game, though. Wait until the right moment.

Aiden doesn't seem to notice as he sniffs, wiggling onto the mattress. "Don't worry. I'll wait right here for you. You probably shouldn't be alone anyway with all that." He points to the bandage on my arm with annoyance. I'm five seconds from asking him what happened, but I bite my tongue. "Get your shower or whatever. He won't wait too long for you." He digs out his phone and plays a loud arcade-sounding game.

Wonderful. He's staying. On my fucking bed. I swear the next time he and I are alone, I'm carving out his heart and presenting it to my missing wife.

My teeth clench when I turn on my heel, heading toward the large bathroom. Memories of Journey and I, after she was released from jail, soar through my mind, which is inconvenient. My dick springs up at the memories of her naked body beneath her jail outfit. Something that should be the farthest from my mind right now, considering my psycho father is waiting for me downstairs, and my family seems to have disappeared.

I had plans to search for weapons and my phone while Aiden stepped out so I could shower. But now, those are up in smoke. I have no choice but to wash the grime off me and then go to lunch with my father.

It gives me quality thinking time to go over the situation as best I can.

I flip the lights on, illuminating the bathroom, and turn to lock the door behind me. It's a semblance of peace and security for now. A moment for me to look in the mirror, reach into my fucking memories, and figure out what the fuck is happening.

Now, I need my foggy brain to get on board.

A black hole sits in the back of my mind, swallowing all the information I'm seeking. Nothing floods through, though. It's gone. Disappeared. And I'm left here trying to deal with the fallout of… what? Whoever fucking drugged me mustn't have had a clue as to what they were doing. It was too much. I feel it in my dry mouth and aching skull. Not like Arrow. The fucking psycho. He carries around those vials of knock-out meds with precise measurements to knock out even the biggest man. Or perhaps whoever administered these meds gave me more than necessary to knock my ass out longer. Per my father's orders, I can only assume.

It is his M.O. I've seen it before.

I squeeze my eyes shut, attempting to force it out of my damn skull. In my gut, I know for sure something went down.

But where? When? And most importantly… why?

Peeling my eyes open, I take stock of my body, counting the bruises marring my skin. Dark. Purple. Blue. Red puffy skin. It paints me like Shepp and his visions on canvas. I'm a piece of art for some sort of violent attack that occurred. Meaning, I've only been out for a short period of time since the initiation ball. If more time had passed since that night where my last memories reside, they'd have faded into yellow by now, and the swelling would have gone down.

As my eyes wander up my body, I stop at the white bandage on my right shoulder. Gritting my teeth, I peel it off again, revealing a small wound with a shiny glaze over it.

"A graze," I mutter, scrunching my brows.

So, I was shot at. They missed, of course, barely grazing my skin.

I remember the fight once we got on stage—the yelling and the gunshots ringing out. Obviously, something happened at that initiation ball. Things went south—and fast.

Fuck!

My fingers turn white, gripping the edge of the countertop. If I was injured in this fight, then what about the others? Are they lying in a goddamn morgue while I'm here? Fuck this. Fuck all this! A monster wells up inside me, taking the reins of my chaotic emotions. Without thinking, I grip a soap dish and toss it across the room. My chest heaves, and momentary satisfaction roars through my system at the sound of it breaking across the tile. It shatters into a million pieces, lining the ground.

Much like me.

I grunt, pulling at my hair until nothing but pain takes me over. Why can't I remember? Why can't the past come back? I slam my palm into my temple several times, hoping to jostle them from my memories.

"My name is Ernie, and I would like to thank the Viotto Family for coming together in one place. This makes it much easier to do this," the man says in a deep voice.

I stand tall, giving the person holding a gun to my temple a blank look. They think they've frightened me into submission. But I will never submit to Shadow's men.

A shuddering breath works through me. The imagery is so crisp and clear, playing in my mind.

Fuck. I shake my head. It's one of the last things I remember from the event. Those assholes storming the stage and taking over our celebration. After that, it's fuzzy around the edges. I know I aided in gunning down the enemies. We made quick work. But the ending? How I got here? No idea.

I'm shattering myself, dissolving at the edges when I'm supposed to remain calm and keep my cool. It's impossible now. The panic has set in. The memories play on repeat. A war ensuing during our fucking celebration. I grip my hair.

They're gone. My brothers. My fucking wife.

I'll rip this mansion apart to find them again.

"Jericho?" Aiden's rough voice breaks through the bathroom door with urgency. "You aren't dead, are you?"

No. You'd like that too much, dickface. I am very much alive. Feeling way too many emotions to stay on my fucking feet. I slide down the wall, avoiding the rogue pieces of the soap dish, and catch my breath. It's sobering to hear his voice. To realize only a door separates us. He could peek inside and see me sitting on the ground with my fingers wrapped in my hair in the midst of a full-blown panic attack.

Aiden has been working for my father even after he had pledged his allegiance to me at Rave.

I put a sliver of trust in him to guard my business. Me. My brothers. Fuck, even my wife, if it came down to it. Maybe that was my first mistake, thinking I could rely on any man my father had previously employed to be loyal to me. No matter how much respect I gave him. Call me naïve for my hope. My leadership would naturally form mutual respect and loyalty.

I was wrong. So very fucking wrong.

Has my blind trust put the ones I love the most in harm's way? Fuck. I stare at the ceiling, counting backward in my mind, attempting to release the emotions choking the life out of me.

And when I leave this house, I'll right those wrongs. But first, I must play this ridiculous part and greet my father for lunch. Perhaps he'll have some insight as to why my wife and brothers are absent to tamp down the racing of my heart.

I say nothing when Aiden knocks on the door again, asking what the hell is happening. He doesn't deserve an answer. Or my attention. Eventually, he sighs and gives up, probably wishing I had met my maker.

Under the warm spray, I shake off the agitation that caused me to lose my shit.

There are a few things I know for sure.

One, my father did something. There's no doubt about that. Two, someone shot me. When, where, and how—I haven't the foggiest idea. It's as if someone reached in and stole the event from my memories. Three, wherever my wife and brothers are, I'll stop at nothing to get them back.

If my father has hidden them away, I'll incapacitate him and drag him to the basement, where I can torture the answers from him.

Now, I need to face the beast.

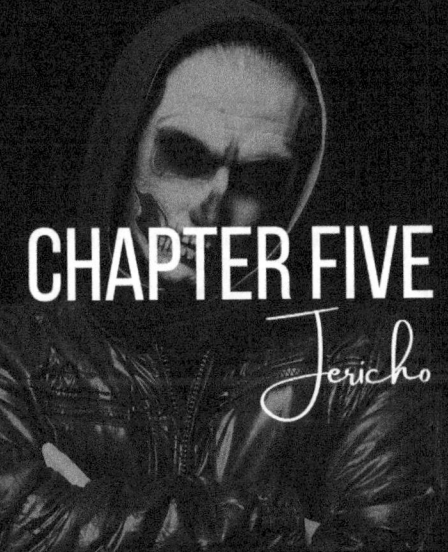

CHAPTER FIVE
Jericho

"So, you and my father, hmm?" I ask, tilting my head to examine Aiden's fallen face as I button up my dress shirt after taking my time in the shower. Before putting on my clothes, I even reapplied and secured my bandage. I refuse to let an infection take me down now. There is too much work to be done.

Aiden says nothing as he watches me slip on my shiny black dress shoes and buckle my belt. In fact, he puts his nose in the air like he's better than this conversation. So strange how I missed his double-crossing ways. Was he always this way, and I missed it? Or does my father hold something over his head to keep him in line to be his spy? That would make sense. Considering that's what happened to my wife. My father held her sister over her head for years, using her to do his bidding.

Nothing surprises me about my father anymore.

No matter. One way or another, I'll get the answers I need from his lips. Bloody or not. It's his choice, really.

He's stoking the fire, adding accelerant to the flames with every word he doesn't speak. Soon, I'll explode. And I'm not quite sure I'll be able to reel myself back in after I've lost it.

"Fine then, keep your secrets." I'll extract them later.

My father may have built and lived in this house, but this

place is my home, my domain. I know every nook and cranny, creak in the floor, and where Arrow likes to hide his knives and needles for fast retrieval.

Aiden rolls his eyes—such confidence for a dead man walking.

"Your father is waiting rather impatiently," Aiden grits out, grabbing my good arm and urgently dragging me forward.

I allow it—for now. I'm giving Aiden all the power here, after all. I'm allowing him to believe I'm submissive in this situation when I'm just the predator in sheep's clothing. Aiden doesn't know what's coming yet.

"How wonderful of him to wait," I mutter when he drags me down the short hall, past several closed doors.

My ears perk when the sound of a shower running catches my attention from Shepp's art studio. My brows furrow. No one in this house uses that shower or sink, only Shepp when he needs to wash his brushes or hands.

"And who else will join us? Sheppard?" I inquire, returning my attention to the matter at hand—Aiden's grubby fingers on me. "Arrow? Journey?" It's on the tip of my tongue to call her my wife, but I'd rather not have them know she means so much to me. No doubt Gabriel would use every ounce of ammunition to force me to heel at his side.

I'm no fucking dog.

Aiden's gaze eats away at me when we stop at the top of the stairs. His fingers tighten around my arm. Thankfully, it's the good one, or we'd have a problem. Despite the shot being a graze, it still hurts like hell with every step I take.

"As far as I know. It's just you and your daddy." He grins, pulling me toward him. "No one else survived." His beady eyes take in my unmoving expression. I stare back, noting every lying twitch of his face.

He knows something and isn't telling me, but he's also lying about their survival. It's written in the twitch of his lips and the demented twinkle in his eyes.

"Did they now?" I hum, tilting my head. "Tell me, what exactly happened at the initiation ball?" It's not very subtle on my end, but I'm desperate for answers about my family.

Aiden huffs, yanking me down a few steps. "You mean last night?" He peers back at me. Anger written all over his face. "We were ambushed."

Colors swirl in my vision, making it difficult to see my surroundings. Ambushed. Of course. I remember them storming the stage. The words they spoke. The guns in my face. My ears ring as he yanks me down the rest of the stairs and shoves my unsteady feet into the dining room.

My vision clears in time to witness my father's gleaming eyes and wicked smile. His fingers move along the dining room table, swirling over the pattern of the wood. My father's dark eyes lazily run over Aiden's hand placement, and he raises a brow until Aiden forcefully drops my arm. Pain throbs through my shoulder from the jostling movements. But the outside world wouldn't have a clue.

Never show your enemies what weakens you. Including the mysterious bullet wound.

"Father," I say, stepping forward.

My gaze lingers on my father's face, filled with a multitude of black and blue bruises. Interesting. Someone beat him to a pulp. Whoever they are, I'd like to shake their hand and give them a prize. Instead, I hold my composure, not showing the glee simmering within me that he felt a pinch of pain.

"Son," he says, clearing his throat. "You're dismissed, Aiden." Gabriel stands from his seat expectantly.

"Yes, sir," the obedient little puppy says, respectfully bowing. "I'll retire to my room for the night. Radio if you need anything." He smirks at me like he's won the golden goose.

Fat chance.

"Come, have a seat," my father says with joy seeping into his voice and gesturing to the seat across from him.

He can't hold back the grin ripping across his lips when

he embraces me tightly, slapping my back several times affectionately. I startle at the affections he's showing. It's odd. This isn't Gabriel Viotto. Not one bit. He never hugs or shows an ounce of physical affection. Maybe a few praises here and there. But this? Has someone body-snatched him and replaced him with a gentler alien? I eye him skeptically as I slowly pull back from the hug and move to settle in my chair. He rounds the table, sitting opposite me with a contented sigh.

Well, no antenna or green skin. Perhaps a shapeshifter has replaced this joyful man, sipping his whiskey. Maybe he'll be more apt to answer my questions instead of brushing them off.

"Afternoon, Father. You seem pleased today," I say, leaning back in the chair as a few workers burst into the dining room with salad plates and set them in front of us before they scurry off into the kitchen again, disappearing.

Interesting. He's integrated his staff into my home.

"War is afoot, son. And new developments are unraveling."

"War?" I question, eyeing the pristine lettuce topped with parmesan and croutons. Just then, my stomach makes itself known to the room, gurgling loudly.

My father raises a brow. "Yes, war. Last night, Shadow infiltrated my tower. Do you not remember?" He eyes me critically, taking in my expression as I ponder his question.

"And we're certain it was Shadow?" I question without answering his own.

He tilts his head. "Hmm. Of course. They announced themselves, son. They spoke to the entire family about what they were there to do." He pauses briefly, eyeing my shoulder. "And how's the shoulder this morning? Dr. Weaver administered extra pain meds to make you more comfortable. Your screaming was filling the house."

The look he sends me has irritation spiking in my veins. Me? Not able to handle the pain of a graze? I'd understand if it was a full bullet wound. But this? Sure, it hurts. But screaming and crying so much he had to sedate me? I think not. His motivations for doing so are incredibly suspicious.

"It's fine." Not completely. He doesn't need to know every time I shift, my pain flares up. "I'm assuming Shadow's forces shot at me," I state, gauging his oddly favorable mood.

If I can get answers from him and patch the holes in my memory, I'll be better off. Knowledge is power, after all, even with him acting so strangely. He reminds me of a kid excited for Christmas, barely able to contain himself.

"Unfortunately. A lot of the family is feeling the effects of his attack. Many were wounded. Most survived. In the end, we shot each and every one of his people, taking them down before they could get to anyone else. You were the last of their victims." He shakes his head in disappointment. "How about a whiskey to celebrate your speedy recovery?" my father says, clapping his hands until another server emerges from the kitchen and they quickly pour us each a fresh glass of whiskey.

There seems to be no rage resting in his words. He is giddy with delight, smiling at the workers moving around us again, heading back to their stations. Where is the outrage over Shadow attacking us? Or that I got shot? Gabriel from a month ago would have tossed me in a cell until I recovered. Not giving me pain meds to knock me out.

Something stinks. Badly. But I must pretend everything is okie dokie, or I will tip my father off and face his wrath.

"It's five o'clock somewhere," I quip, tossing the burning whiskey down my throat. In the back of my mind, I secretly hope there were no drugs at the bottom of the glass. It would be quite unfortunate if I lost my wits around my father when he's obviously scheming.

"Refill," my father demands with gritted teeth to the server, who hovers in the corner of the room now, waiting for Gabriel's demands.

Ah. There he is. The man beneath his jovial mask peeking out to rear his ugly head. I knew he'd return.

My glass is refilled, and I nod my thanks to the server, who slowly backs away. But I have no intention of consuming more alcohol when my father is being unpredictable.

Gabriel fixes me with a stern look, erasing the warmth from his expression. "To dismantling Shadow's organization piece by piece," my father says, shoving his whiskey glass into the air. "Someday soon, everything we've put into play will fall in line."

I'd love nothing more than to reach over and gut my father where he sits, so his kingdom is mine. I'd right his wrongs. Take back what is ours and heal our fucking community. Like most days, I resent being the dutiful heir, putting on the show of a lifetime to appease my psycho father, who would rather slit my throat than be a parent.

"Here, here," I say, clinking my glass against his, attempting to keep my questions to myself.

Do I want to know where my wife is? Yes, desperately. With Gabriel Viotto, I have to ease into this conversation to not alarm him of any intentions. I've learned this from watching him from afar for so long and being in his presence.

I pretend to sip my whiskey and set it down. "Will Shepp and Arrow be joining us this afternoon? It's odd to see you back home after so long." I add the last part quickly, eyeing my father's stiffening shoulders.

Interesting.

My father carefully sets his glass on the table, wrapping his fingers around it, and I mimic his movements.

"It is unfortunate they both won't be joining us tonight. Arrow, of course, has been in a coma since the explosion. And Shepp? I'm afraid the search is about to be called off."

My grip tightens on my glass as the words register. It's the only thing grounding and keeping me from jumping from my chair. Coma? Search? I swallow the bile burning in the back of my throat, remembering the wretched stench of smoke coming from me when I woke up from my drug-induced sleep.

"No!" I hiss, breaching through the curtain just in time to face Arrow, who grins at me. A fucking rocket launcher sits on his shoulder.

Safety off. Finger on the trigger. Arrow shifts his feet shoulder-length apart. He leans slightly back and then pulls the trigger. Smoke plums out behind him before the rocket launches out of the tube, sending more smoke in front of him.

"And Viotto tower?" If Arrow truly set off the rocket launcher inside the ballroom, the explosion undoubtedly decimated the entire building. Perhaps that's why he's here in my domain. He has nowhere else to go.

"A total loss. I will move all my operations here for the next six months until I rebuild my headquarters better than ever," he says, picking up his fork.

Like absolute fuck will that happen long term. This is my home now. A place I made for my brothers and I. Fuck, even my wife.

"And no word on Journey?" I have no clue how I utter those words without revealing my internal freakout. It's wound tight inside me, ready to spring forth at the drop of a hat. If Journey is hurt, dead, or fucking missing, I don't know what I'll do. Kill my father? That's a possibility. If I could only remember the last time I laid eyes on her.

"We're still searching for remains in the rubble. Such a shame what happened." He clicks his tongue several times before daintily taking a bite of his salad.

"Yes. A shame," I say, swallowing another mouthful of whiskey to hide the vomit I'm threatening to expel.

I'm decidedly not staying on task with staying sober and instead falling victim to alcohol to numb my soul.

Journey and Shepp are unaccounted for. Arrow is in a coma. I was down with a bullet graze and heavily drugged at the hands of my father's doctor. I've lost time. Precious fucking time. I don't know how to reclaim it all when we're all spread out in the wind.

I suck in a breath, counting backward from ten. Again and again. Just like Shepp taught me to do. It's calming. Mind clearing. Sweeping away the worries drowning me.

I watch my father again. Watching the slight tic of his jawline and how he gobbles down his drinks. My father can tell a lie with a smile on his face and the proof in his hands.

So, what's stopping him from lying straight to my face about where they are? It'd be a little too convenient for everyone to be dead, missing, or in a coma. Wouldn't it?

Gabriel swallows hard, signaling for another drink. Agitation boils to the surface of his skin when he snaps his fingers hurriedly at the poor server. My gaze wanders over their movements. All the pain and panic ease inside me like a record screeching to a halt.

Gabriel is bluffing through this, hoping I won't ask questions. And if I do? He has perfectly tailored responses up his sleeve.

"And efforts are being made to find them?" And there it is —the twitch under his right eye, alluding to his lies.

Gabriel Viotto is hiding something, too.

If my family is under the rubble of the tower—if it fell at all—then I'd march down there and dig them out myself. But I have a funny feeling they are not there. The question is— where?

My father chews the remnants of his salad slowly, eyes roaming over my tight facial features. "Indeed, son. They won't rest until your wife and Sheppard are found alive." His words ring in my ears as static fills them. My wife? He knows Journey and I were married? Well, this can't be a good fucking sign. He'll use this against me every step of the way. "As for Arrow, they've assured me he'll be fine. Now, how about we enjoy our lunch?" He gestures toward the food, uncharacteristically giving me the answers I need.

But of course, he didn't, really. He's skirted the entire Q and A, giving me minuscule crumbs but no solid answers.

With that information, I know he's manipulating me into doing whatever he wants. If Journey, Shepp, and Arrow are out of the picture. Where does that leave me? Alone. Vulnerable. Perfect for the fucking taking.

Or so he thinks.

Not only do I have to worry about where my family is, but now, I have to worry about what Gabriel has up his sleeves. Aiden has been on top of me since I woke up, escorting me from my bedroom to here, and I'm sure the same will happen once I'm done.

I have a feeling I'm about to become my father's unwilling prisoner, trapped within the walls of this mansion.

"Then I can help," I say, tapping my foot. "I'll march down there after lunch and offer my assistance. They're my concern." The sooner I get out from under my father's nose. The fucking better. And what better way than to poke and prod at his thin story?

"If you must." My father shrugs. "We have a very important guest joining us soon." A creepy smile lights up the dark features of his face, something I haven't seen since I was a child and my mom was by his side.

"Who?" I ask without holding my tongue.

"Jericho?" a feminine voice whispers from behind me, forcing the hairs on my neck to stand on end. "Darling?" she whispers again, her emotion cracking her tone.

My father immediately jumps to his feet, moving around the table at warp speed until he's out of sight. Odd. The man never moves for anyone like that—not me or the boys. He's only ever concerned with himself.

The only person he ever moved quickly for was my mother. Or, from what I can remember of her.

My heart pounds against my ribs, threatening to shatter them into pieces. Her voice rings through my mind, bringing the memories of her existence back to life.

My breaths shudder when I finally stand on wobbly legs and lean against the table.

"Oh, Jericho," she whispers remorsefully. "You've gotten so tall."

A warm hand rests on my good shoulder, gently squeezing. French-tipped nails come into view, leading down my arm. My mind goes to the clouds, floating there until I turn on my heels and meet her gaze.

The woman who disappeared off the face of the planet, leaving me to fend for myself. Deep, soul-splitting agony spears right through me at the sight of her. She hasn't changed from my memories. She is dainty, meek, and always holds a smile for me.

Grace Viotto.

"Mother?" I rasp, squeezing my fingers into fists as her crisp blue eyes take me in.

This can't be real. After so long.

"I'm finally home, baby," she murmurs, with tears glistening in her eyes. "I've finally made it back after so long."

Age hasn't done anything to her outer appearance. Seeming as beautiful and graceful as she was when I was younger. Her skin is flawless, free from wrinkles and blemishes. She shines under the sun, streaming in from the windows, giving her a heavenly glow.

It's like she's walked out of a picture from the past without changing her outer appearance. But I'm familiar with the pain in her gaze.

She's hiding something deep in the depths of her soul. Something so heinous it'll take months to unravel. Maybe the reason she disappeared so long ago without reason.

"Come and sit, Grace," my father all but demands, placing his arm around her delicate shoulders and guiding her to the head of the table.

His seat. He pulls it out and helps her sit with the biggest smile on his face. His gaze never leaves her.

"Can you believe it, son?" he marvels, brushing the hair from her face and putting it over her shoulders.

"No," I rasp, shaking my head as I move on autopilot and take my seat.

As soon as our asses hit the seats, servers burst into the dining room carrying trays of delicious-smelling meals. The aroma fills the room, and my stomach rumbles loudly from the effects.

It's on the tip of my tongue as I watch my father hand my mother a fork to ask if I've fallen into another universe. She's here. My father is acting uncharacteristically engaged and showing his genuine emotions like he did before when she was around near the beginning of my life.

What the absolute fuck happened? To me? To this fucking house?

"I'm sure you have questions," my mother says timidly, grasping my wrists softly.

That's a goddamn understatement.

"Eat," my father insists impatiently, gesturing for her to take another bite. "You'll need your strength."

My ears ring when I look her over with a skeptical eye. This was the woman my father loved so damn much that he built her this home without a second thought. Then, he bought her a zoo so she'd have the animals she loved dearly right in her backyard. Something he has not maintained since she disappeared when I was little. So young, I barely remember her existence outside of her disappearance and my father leaving me all alone in this mansion with the ghost of every-thing. I swallow hard as she bites into her salad.

"Your mother has returned from the depths of Shadow's dungeon." My father lifts his chin, staring at my mother with a protective gaze. It is like he has been transported back in time to the moment she left or was kidnapped. Where he is madly, deeply, head over heels in love with her, but that's not the spark in his eyes I see right now. It is possession. Control. "I should have known it was that rat bastard's first point of attack! Taking what was mine from the very beginning."

I tilt my head. Math has never been my strong suit. Right now, though? It's racing through my mind and calculating the lies. My mother disappeared when I was young. If Shadow stole her from us, then that would mean he's been around plotting for almost twenty years. My father could have had an enemy for that long, but Shadow didn't start coming onto our radar until three years ago.

How fucking suspicious this story is turning out to be.

"Were you able to leave after Shadow bombed us yesterday?" I casually ask, despite my heart threatening to burst through my chest. To distract myself, I cut into my food and take another bite.

She offers me a tight smile. "Yes," she whispers. "It was the only time in all these years I could get out of the dungeon he locked me in."

I do not know what happened to her. My father never elaborated on the subject, refusing to speak her name before he left here, wiping her existence from this home. Before abandoning me here, he could barely look at the palace he built for her.

"Shadow's dungeon?" My eyes float between the two of them, waiting for their answer.

"Indeed. Hence why war is about to begin. Not only did that heathen attack us in our domain, but he also had my fucking wife this entire time," he growls, tightening his grip on his whiskey tumbler. "I will take them down piece by piece when I get my hands on them," he snarls now, filling the room with rage.

The entire time? All twenty-some years of her being missing? Has Shadow been hiding out for that long, waiting for the right moments to strike?

Something isn't adding up.

"Yes," my mother whispers in a small voice, giving me a sad smile. "Many years ago, I was taken right off the street."

She shakes her head, tears glistening in her eyes. "Throughout my torture and imprisonment, you and your father were all I thought about. I ached to get back here."

"He took you?" I ask, tilting my head.

She moves slightly, repositioning herself in the chair before giving me a slight nod. "Yes," she murmurs. "Shadow has been around for years, plotting against your father and his empire," she says, reaching over to take my hand in hers. "I can't believe I'm finally able to touch your hand. You've grown so much," she whispers as tears fall down her cheeks and cascade off her chin to the table.

Warning bells ring in my mind when I look into her eyes and see nothing—no love, life, or emotions.

"Then you know who he is? Have you seen his face? Where is his headquarters? We need to get ahead of this now before he discovers you've gone away," I say, retracting my hand from her touch and abruptly standing. "If we can attack first, then we can be on top."

My mother's lips pop open. Her emotionless eyes track my movements as I pace a few steps.

"Sit the fuck down and shut up," my father growls, coming to her defense. "No more questions. Let's have a nice lunch together like it should have been. You're upsetting your mother," my father hisses, his angry mask slipping through the facade he's putting on. "We'll discuss this more over dessert. She's told me everything I need to know."

"I'll expect answers later," I demand, easing myself into the chair.

My father glares at me. "Do you now, boy? Do you think you deserve answers?"

"Gabe," my mom murmurs, pulling his hand into hers. It's incredible to witness how he melts for her. Odd, too. Gabriel doesn't bow to anyone. Or listen to words of advice. But for Grace? She seems to be the key to it all.

My brain aches the more I sit here, listening to my parents

speak to each other in hushed tones. My mother placates him, patting his hand and talking him down from the angry ledge. It's like they've slipped into their roles again, even though they've been apart for years.

After we've finished our appetizer of salad, our main course of salmon, asparagus, and a side of rice to complete the meal, my stomach revolts from so much food inside of it, nearly sending me to the bathroom.

My eyes drift over my parents from across the table. She looks at him, sending him a blinding smile, dazzling him instantly. He leans forward like a love-sick fool, captivated by everything she whispers to him. He's in her web of whatever bullshit she's peddling, and I'll be the first to figure it out.

"So, how did you make it home?" I ask, eyeing her when her crystal blue eyes land on me.

"Oh, Jericho," she murmurs, clasping my hand tightly and avoiding my questions altogether. If I were trapped in a dungeon, I'd be eager to spill all of Shadow's secrets, including how I escaped.

"How did you escape?" I rasp, eyeing her French-tipped nails as they rest against my flesh. I raise my brow at her pristine nails. It is too surreal to have her back here. The woman I prayed and begged to come home every night after she disappeared. Now, she's here in the flesh, but I'm not sure she's the same woman she once was.

I know for a fact she's not.

My mother takes a deep breath, squeezing again. "Oh, baby," she murmurs. "It's a long story of how I finally got away. But I'm here now. And I'm going to help your father take him down." She sniffles slightly, leaning into my father as he dabs her cheeks with a napkin. "I'm here to stay," she says with a sad smile.

"Here to stay?" I repeat her words, staring at the smile on her face that doesn't reach her lifeless eyes.

Something in my gut sends warning bells to my mind

again. Isn't this just a little too convenient? My mother is back here after so long. And she's avoiding answering my questions. She's just another person to add to my ever-growing list of suspects.

I'll keep my eye on her. No matter how demure and weak she pretends to be. There's something nefarious brewing behind her eyes. And my father is too fucking stupid to see it. How fitting, though. Right? My father. The man who thinks he's too smart for the fucking world will get taken down by his wife, who sleeps in his sheets.

"Excuse me," my father mumbles, holding up a finger as he reaches into his pocket. His brows raise as he gets up and walks out of the room, aggressively bringing his phone to his ear.

I watch as he goes, narrowing my eyes when his hushed words reach my ears, but I'm unable to tell what he's saying.

"So, your father brought me up to speed while you were out on what you've done for the family so far. You're a man now," my mother's soft voice breaks through the rampant thoughts going through my mind. "You've gone through your initiation and the ball. How are you feeling?" she politely asks.

"How wonderful it is for him to keep you up to date on my life," I say with a gleaming smile. "I feel complete now after bending my knees and pledging myself to this organization. I was raised that way, you know? I'm a man now. A true Viotto for the family."

If I hadn't been observing her so carefully, I never would have seen the stiffening of her shoulders. "Oh, I know. Your father is so proud of you." Yeah, that's bullshit, too. I'm doubtful he used those exact words to describe how he feels about me.

"Who is he, Mother?" I ask, point blank. "Shadow has been gunning for us for years, sending bombs and death threats and attacking our celebration. Surely, after all those years of captivity, you know who he is."

My mother offers me another smile, this one with malice hiding behind it like a sneaky shadow showing her true colors, just as I suspected.

"I never saw his face, Love. You can ask your father, who'll tell you the same thing. They kept me prisoner in the dark dungeons beneath the ocean. He operates off the coast."

"You never saw his face?" I raise my drink to my lips, sipping it. "You were gone for twenty years. Surely, you caught sight of him at some point. That is a long time to be locked up."

"Yes, well. In that time, I did not see his face," she says faintly. "You do not understand what I've been through, Jericho. It was awful." Her shoulders shake, and she puts her face into her hands, sniffling several times.

That's what putting pressure on people does. It makes all their emotions bleed through. Whether they like it or fucking not.

And my mother? Oh, she deserves a round of applause for her performance.

"I'm sorry, Mother," I say with a false sense of calm and sincerity.

She's hiding something—way too many things for my liking. I'll unravel them string by string. For now, there are a million things I need to do. I need to find Journey. And I, one hundred percent, don't trust my father in what he's saying. If Shepp and Journey are buried under the tower's rubble, I need to be there, not playing happy family with my father and mother. Not to mention, I'm in disbelief that Shepp and Journey are under there in the first place. I would have done anything to protect Journey. We all would have.

My father moves back into the room, slowly pocketing his phone. A perplexed look crosses his face when he sits down in his spot and folds his hands on the table.

"What's wrong, Gabe?" my mother whispers, reaching out

to lay a hand on his wrist and stroking her thumb along it. Under normal circumstances, my father would have shooed her touch away, but I'm guessing these aren't normal circumstances.

"It appears they've found Shepp and your wife," my father says, not mincing his words. "Dead." His expression never changes, except for a twinkle in his eyes as he delivers the devastating news. "Such a shame," he says with false sadness, taking a sip of his whiskey which has yet to empty.

I blink several times, throwing back the remnants of my drink to give myself a moment to think. Many thoughts rush through my mind. Is it real? Are they truly dead? Surely, they can't be. I'd feel it shatter my soul the moment they left this world. Right? Fuck. My disbelief leans toward no. They're alive somewhere. Captive, maybe? My father has told me too many lies over the years, and this? This is the fucking cherry on top of his house of falling cards.

I don't believe a fucking word he says. But I have to play the part, right?

"No," I rasp, shaking my head as my glass tumbles from my fingers. "How?" My word trails off as I cover my mouth, keeping my gaze on my father.

"Gabe," my mother chastises in horror. "How can you say it like that?" she asks, bringing a fist to her painted lips as they quiver. "His wife." Her eyes squeeze shut dramatically, holding back the tears in her eyes.

"How certain are you?" I ask, masking my feelings as my brain scrambles together a plan.

What my father does not know about Journey's ass, the better. There's one way I will know if she is truly under that building. The fucking tracker Arrow's crazy ass put in her beneath the UV tattoo of our initials she's never discovered. Sure, she had a wicked bruise Arrow monitored, putting oint-ments—among other fluids he had no business using—on her flesh to soothe the pain away, so she didn't irritate it further.

We couldn't exactly come out and tell her we'd marked her as ours in all possible ways.

She would have slaughtered us one by one. And that wasn't a risk I was willing to take. She was already too stubborn for her own good. Finding out we put a tracker in her would have thrown her over the edge.

"It's unfortunate what happened, son," he says with false sympathy, lacing his tone as his head shakes in disgust. "We'll avenge them," he growls. "We'll march into Shadow's territories and destroy what is precious to him." His teeth gnash together when he sucks in a breath, calming himself down.

And the Oscar goes to… Gabriel Viotto, for his leading role in fake sympathy. An emotion he's never quite mastered. He should keep trying, though. Maybe one day, he'll fool us all with false tears.

"And I'll help," my mother whispers. "I'll tell you everything you need to know about Shadow and his headquarters. I know it like the back of my hand."

If she was imprisoned for years and tortured in a cave-like dungeon, how would she know it like the back of her hand? Nothing is adding up, but my father seems to lick it up like milk.

"That's right," Gabe says as a deadly look crosses his expression. "Your mother has insider knowledge."

"So, you don't know who he is?" I rasp out, swallowing the lump in my throat.

See, if anyone deserves an Oscar—it's fucking me.

She offers me a soft smile. "I don't know who he is, love. He never showed his face, hiding behind masks and his recruits. But I know where he hides. I was there for years, darling. Trapped within the walls of his prison underneath the ocean."

A hint of sadness clouds over her features. My mother's pain overtakes everything about her, twisting her meek features and displaying it all over her face. But her words make little sense. Trapped within the walls of a prison. So, how does she have insight? It's something I'll have to discuss with her at great length.

"Under the ocean?" I question, raising a brow. "How is that possible?"

"Enough of this chatter at the lunch table," my father chastises gruffly. "Your mother and I are heading out for a meeting at the church with the other members of the family. You're not invited just yet. You're to go to your room until dinner. We're having special guests tonight." Reaching into his back pocket, he pulls out a walky-talky. "Aiden, come," he grunts, placing it back in his pocket.

I shake off the anger crawling beneath my flesh. I need to regroup. Find my fucking phone. Then, I can see if Journey is truly dead, which I have my doubts about. Shepp, on the other hand? I have no clue. I only hope in my heart he's with her. Wherever she may be, maybe I should have taken Arrow up on the offer to put trackers in each of us for cases like this.

"Has he always been your errand boy?" I question, standing tall at the table when my father takes my mother's hand.

He smirks at me. "Keeping you close and safe is of the utmost importance right now. Many of the families were injured in the battle at the tower. Arrow is in the hospital. Sheppard is gone. How would I survive if you weren't here?" he asks, shaking his head. "You're my heir. I need to protect you from the wrath of Shadow and anyone else who may have a vendetta against the Viotto name."

Answer—he wouldn't.

I'm his bargaining chip and tool to use when he pleases. He thinks he's a very smart man, but I'm beginning to believe his delusions are setting in deeper. How can he trust my mother, who stands beside him with a smile like no time has passed? She may be a doe-eyed-looking woman standing demurely next to him. But there's something more there behind the facade she's erected.

"Oh, I think you'd carry on, Father," I say, curling my fingers on the table.

"You're my heir, Jericho. You're the one who is going to carry on after all this. So, we'll see you this evening for dinner. Then, we can talk about the future more. Now, your mother and I have a lot to catch up on." He grins again, gently nudging her until they leave the dining room and head toward the attached garage door.

"Come on," Aiden grumbles, nodding toward the stairs.

"Such a good dog, aren't you?" I ask, raising a brow when he smirks.

"I've got more freedom than you," he snorts. "Now that the other two are out of the picture, you've got nothing and no one to back you up."

Oh, wonderful. He's taunting the sleeping wolf. He doesn't realize what I've got in store for him, does he? As everyone sleeps soundly in their beds tonight, Aiden and I will have a very serious loyalty conversation.

For now, I'm on the hunt for my phone, wherever it may be, because it's the most secure piece of technology I have.

"So, you're going to play puppy dog to a man who doesn't give a shit about you?" I question as we climb the stairs.

Aiden's fist flinches at his side, showing his aggravation. "I'm not a goddamn puppy dog, asshole," he growls, turning on his toes to face me on the top step. His finger pokes into my chest. "Every goddamn thing you've done at that club. Every word you've said behind your father's back has been relayed to him." He grins at that. "I was the perfect Trojan horse, wasn't I? The perfect spy to stand beyond the VIP door, waiting for you to fuck up."

"Hmmm. And what exactly did you catch for Daddy Dearest?" I raise a brow, shoving my hands into my pockets.

The boys and I were always conscientious about what was

said within the walls of the club, considering it still belonged to my father. He had plenty of security cameras mounted on the walls—guards who continued to do his bidding. There were enough opportunities for him to spy. Then, out of the blue, he signed it over to me as a present for becoming a part of the family. We worked our asses off to make that club what it is today with no help from the man slowly bankrupting the family to death with his careless spending. My father has dipped his fingers into every business he owns—which is a lot all over town and even beyond.

Our best security measure was ensuring that we'd use sign language if we discussed anything related to my father. Only the three of us seemed to know the language, and no one else had a clue.

Aiden's smile slips a millimeter. So, he's been feeding the old man little slivers of conversations he can understand when we're not signing to one another.

'What exactly did you tell him, Aiden?' I sign in his face, watching the movement in his eyes.

"Come on," he grunts. "Let's lock you in your room for the night so I can get on with my life. I have a job to do."

Interesting. He cannot understand sign language. So, what did he have to say to my father? Sure, he knows what we do for the public since he has escorted needy patrons into our office at Rave. But that is the extent of what he knows. Besides, my father would not mind the loans and safe havens we have given to people. It gives a good name to the Viotto family.

"You do what you have to do," I say once I walk through the threshold of our large bedroom. "And I'll do what I have to do," I say, sending Aiden a scathing smile when he closes the double doors behind me, and a lock from the outside clicks into place.

Interestingly, they locked me in here, not knowing what I may have hidden on the inside. My eyes scan the room in search of cameras or other devices that may spy on me while my father is away. I place my ear to the door, listening to Aiden as he mutters to himself while leaning heavily against it.

I purse my lips, satisfied with being alone, to gather myself and find my phone. If I can find the tracking information, I can get my eyes on Journey to know she is safe. Knowing my father like I do, though. I know he's taken every piece of technology out of this room and hidden it from me for the foreseeable future.

CHAPTER SIX

Journey

WATER DRIPS FROM THE CORNER OF THE PRISON WE'VE BEEN trapped in for God knows how long.

The ever-present darkness surrounds us, pushing heavily on our shoulders.

Mine especially.

In the dark, I see the demons of my past. The screams of my victims that were forced upon me. The begging uttered when I held a knife to their necks or stabbed through their ribs. No matter the harm I caused, it haunts my every waking moment. Intensified by the complete darkness we were plunged into after the person muttered, "Let the loyalty games begin."

Here, I don't have music to drown out the haunting night-mares. Or the sleeping pills to pull the dreams away.

It's just Shepp and me. The prison and us. Locked away and forgotten.

Despite the warmth Shepp has offered me through this ordeal, the bitter cold seeps through the evening dress barely covering my skin.

Shepp's presence cocoons me, keeping me safe from the realities of our situation. The warmth of his body keeps me close. The brush of his breath against my cheek when I lay my head on his chest lets me know I'm alive. His presence drowns out the darkness building inside me, begging to burst and hurt everyone who has taken our freedom from us.

But I prevail, not drowning in the inky existence churning inside me.

Shepp is the only one keeping me grounded.

Arrow and Jericho, too. Where are they? Are they looking for us? Was that explosion from them? God. It's driving me up the wall not knowing if they are safe. Sunny sits in the back of my mind, as always. Is she okay? Are they treating her better than my monster did? Or is she suffering, too? How is her heart holding up?

God, I want to hold her again. She was there for a split second in my sights. Then, yanked out of my hold once again.

My head leans against Shepp's chest, listening to the beating of his heart. Thump. Thump. Slow and methodical, sending relief through my system.

We are alive. Barely.

My chapped lips nearly stick together from lack of water and food. We're slowly starving to death and barely surviving on the drips of water collecting in the corner of the room. At least we have that. I'm sure it's only been a day or two. To me, it feels like a damn eternity here in the dark.

If we have to spend one more day in this dark room without the means to survive—we'll die in each other's arms. Internally, I shake that dismal thought away, refusing for it to take root.

We won't die here. I won't allow it.

Shepp and I deserve a happy life. Away from here. With the ones we love.

But how will we make it out of here?

We have yanked on the door, tried to pry it open, and attempted to remove the hinges, all while stumbling through the dark. I'm sure whoever oversees watching us is eating popcorn and enjoying our misery.

"You okay?" I murmur groggily into his chest.

My energy reserve sits at zero. The thought of moving from this spot sends my head into a dizzy spell.

'Yes,' he writes on my palm with shaky movements. *'I'm fine.'*

"How about some more water?" With as much as I can muster, I lift my head from his chest. My fingers reach out, clasping his cheeks.

Whenever we wake up from falling asleep, I check him over. His face. His drooping shoulders.

Since seeing his father, he's internalized a lot.

My breath shudders when he interlocks our fingers, dragging them away from his face. He squeezes three times.

God, I miss the desperate sound of his voice right now. The assurance it always gave me when he spoke only for me.

But in these circumstances, I understand. His father returned from the land of the dead and stood before us with menacing instructions.

We're fucked.

My heart skips a beat when Shepp tightens his hold on me. The lights around us flicker to life. I squeeze my eyes shut. After being in the dark for so damn long, I've gotten used to the nothingness around us.

"How's everyone feeling today?" a voice asks through the speaker, echoing through the vast room.

My eyes blink open, and I glare toward the speaker, focusing on it. With shaky limbs, I remove myself from Shepp's lap and get to my wobbly feet. With my arms wide, I turn in a circle.

"What do you want from us?" I growl.

Or attempt to. It comes out weaker than I would have liked.

"Want from you?" he chuckles. "I think it's you who needs something from me."

I stop dead, standing still beside the spinning in my head. "And what is that?"

"You want to survive, Journey?" the voice asks, dipping low with venom spouting from his voice. "You want to protect your sister? Keep Sheppard alive?"

My heart drops into my stomach. What is with all these villains using my sister against me? Oh, right. They know they can control everything I do to ensure her safety, and I've shown them repeatedly what she means to me.

"What are you offering?" I ask, lifting my chin.

Warm hands squeeze my shoulders, holding me steady.

"Food. Water. Whatever you may need. In exchange for your loyalty."

"Why're you so desperate for it?" I ask, shaking my head.

I don't understand why he wants us to be loyal to him. What the hell does it even matter? We're his prisoners now, and there is no escape from this place.

Nothing more has come from the speakers for some time. Shepp and I stand in the middle of our prison, blankly staring at our surroundings. It's been so long since I've seen it. So, I need to memorize it again before the lights go out. I have no doubt that if I don't give him an answer, he will continue to break us down until we give in.

Eventually, we will.

All humans do. We're not immune to the torture. If we're not careful, we'll die.

"I'll tell you anything you need to know," I say, licking my dry lips. "Anything about Gabriel."

I swallow hard when nothing comes from the speakers still. I know this tactic. He's holding out and expecting me to keep going and spilling my guts.

"He's after you," I say. "Especially after what you pulled at the initiation ball." My breaths come in heavy pants as my head spins. My stomach aches from the lack of food.

God, this is so taxing—even to speak, move, or breathe. I want to survive, but at what cost? How much weaker can I get?

"The initiation ball?" Shadow's voice crackles through the speakers.

Shepp tightens his hold on me, clinging to me as I nod. "Yeah. You attacked them."

Shadow scoffs. "Why the fuck would I do that?"

I blink several times. "Because you hate him and want his territory?"

Isn't it obvious? Shadow is the villain of Gabriel's story, causing havoc and mayhem.

"Is that what he has to say about me behind my back? That I'm the bad guy?"

'Tell him about the man who bombed our mansion,' Shepp writes on my palm.

Wait, what?

"You sent a bomb to the mansion."

"Interesting. So, I attacked your stupid initiation ball and sent a bomb? I've been up to a lot these days, haven't I?" he chuckles through the speaker. "I have more creative ways to fuck with Gabriel."

'It wasn't him?' Shepp writes on my palm. *'That doesn't make sense.'*

He's right. It doesn't make sense—at all. The people who attacked at the initiation ball said Shadow's name, bellowing about him setting it up. So why would he lie?

My breath stalls in my chest when I turn to look into Shepp's eyes. He's pale. Too fucking pale. His eyes practically sink into his skull, and life is no longer present in his vibrant eyes.

This cave has killed him.

And me.

"So you're saying it wasn't you?" I ask, furrowing my brows.

Shadow says nothing else through the speaker for some time, leaving us in the light of the room.

I sigh, sitting down on the ground, and Shepp follows suit. At this point, for our survival, the smartest thing to do is go to Shadow's side and tell him everything he wants to hear. It's a good strategy to consider. We have nothing else.

My ears perk up when I hear a screeching sound near the door. The sound reveals two bottles of water and packaged food being pushed in through a small hatch in the door on a metal tray.

Shepp eyes it wearily as he walks toward it and picks up the metal tray.

His eyes implore mine as he sets it in front of us.

Silently, I check the seals on everything and shrug. It seems sealed tight. I'm so desperate for the minuscule snack and drink that I will take anything at this point.

'It seems clean,' he writes on my palm.

I nod in response, trying to keep our conversation private.

Shepp opens the bottle of water for me, passing it to me. I gulp it down. I rip into the two granola bars for me and urge Shepp with my eyes to drink and eat his. He nods, gulps half his water, and then eats his two granola bars.

"I want to play a game," Shadow says through the speaker, drawing our attention to it.

I stiffen. What is this? Are we on the set of *Saw*?

"What kind of game?" I ask carefully, setting my water bottle down.

Fear crawls beneath my skin when the silence wafts through our prison.

"I know what you'll do for your sister. You've done it over and over again, haven't you?"

My back stiffens at the ominous sound of his voice.

"You already know that," I say, attempting to hold my fear at bay. Slowly, I get to my feet, raising my chin. I will face my enemy like a woman. "She had better be okay." My darkness shifts inside me, ready to protect my emotions at any second.

"Oh, she's more than fine," he says confidently. "But she won't be. And neither will one of you."

My eyes widen, darting back to Sheppard, who comes to stand beside me.

"What do you mean?"

"We're going to play a game. One of those waters has poison in it..." his chuckles fill the room.

My stomach drops. My eyes fall to the two water bottles half empty. I swallow hard. Poison? Does he want to kill us or use us?

There has to be a reason for this. It is a game, after all.

"What would you gain? Don't you want information?" I rasp, curling my fingers at my side.

"Everything. I want to take down that fucking psychopath. Own his empire. But I'd like to have a little fun in the process. What better way than having Gabe's little puppet and his son's guard?"

Shepp grunts behind me, falling to his knees.

"No!" I cry out, holding his face in my palms. "What's happening?" I ask.

At the first hint of his discomfort, panic consumes me. He clutches his stomach, his light eyes gazing into mine.

"What's happening is, within the next three hours, the poison will eat away at his insides. Unless you win."

"Win what? What do you want?" I shout, climbing to my feet and marching toward the speaker.

"Gabe never beat you hard enough, did he? He may have locked you in a pretty little prison and taught you his ways, but you still show your weaknesses every chance you get," he tsks at me. "Tell me, Journey. Have you ever killed a man?"

I swallow the bile in my throat burning through my damn esophagus. I'm still weak and half-delirious.

"Yes," I croak, sucking in a breath.

"How many?" Shadow asks with curiosity.

How many men and women have I killed in the name of

protecting my sister? There are too many to count. Yet I know the exact number because I can never forget them.

"Fifty-five." I blink several times, letting a slight haze take over my vision.

"Well, he used you and abused you, didn't he?"

I nod in response, recoiling in on myself. I resent the number of people he blackmailed me into killing. I hate that I've taken lives at all. I like to pretend that every time I do it; I don't lose a piece of my humanity with the blood that flows from their veins. In some ways, I justify it. The men and women I'm forced to take down are all bad people. Lawyers with twisted values. Doctors who don't follow Gabe's rules. Some are innocent. Wrong place-wrong time, kind of situation. They saw something they shouldn't have, and it all fell on my shoulders to correct it for him.

"Interesting…" he hums.

I turn and look over my shoulder at Shepp, kneeling on the ground. Red takes over his once-pale face, and his eyes roam over my body.

"What do you need me to do to save Shepp?" I question, blowing out a big breath.

"What would you be willing to do? Show me your tits? Get naked? Kill whoever I say?"

Sweat breaks out across my flesh. Not that, anything but that. How can I refuse, though? Shepp deserves happiness— not poison in his water, not dying in a small cave prison with no food or water.

"Anything." I nod with false confidence.

Am I willing to lay down my life for them? Yes. If it means Shepp gets the help he needs. If it means Sunshine will live a long life. Yes. I'm willing to do it all in the name of my family. Because that's what they all are—mine.

Shepp claps his hands, getting my attention. He shakes his head, reddening by the second. Gasps spill from his lips, and he looks like he's on the brink of collapsing and passing out.

Whatever I have to do.

"Then let the games begin," Shadow chuckles again, grating on my damn nerves.

I cannot wait to fucking stab him in the throat for all the terrible things he has done.

"I'm sorry," I choke out, tears forming in my eyes.

How I have any, I don't have a clue. The water we received barely quenched my thirst. Not to mention the granola bars. They didn't touch the hunger pains eating away at me.

I'm weak and vulnerable, heading into the unknown of Shadow's depravity.

Shepp shakes his head again when the door squeaks open ominously.

I move, falling before Shepp and taking his face in my hands. Maybe for the last time. Those light eyes cloud over with fear, begging me to reconsider. But how can I? I can't sit here and watch him die right before my eyes when I can do something about it.

"I promise you; we'll get out of here. I'll be fucked if I let you die from poisoned water." My voice quivers with every word. The darkness within me swirls to life when all my emotions drown in the blackness crawling beneath my skin.

Shepp shakes his head, grabbing for me before another hint of pain takes him over. His body folds forward, and he groans, shivering.

"Give him the antidote!" I shout, jumping to my feet. Tears stream down my cheeks. "Stop hurting him!" I promised myself years before that I wouldn't beg monsters for results. Here, though? I have no fucking choice. He's about to kill his son. And for what? Why? I don't have a fucking clue. He took me. Big fucking deal. I've been through this before. He took Shepp and my goddamn sister. That makes it personal.

I'll live my entire life in this cave if Shepp and Sunshine are safe.

"Walk out the door," Shadow growls.

"Not before you make him better!" I hiss, crossing my arms with stubbornness.

I peek at Shepp, withering away before my fucking eyes. I can't let him die. He's taken care of me for years now. Between the food he left in my fridge, the donuts, and the nurturing at the mansion.

He's been my rock.

And he shared the biggest piece of himself with me. Something he couldn't share with the others. His voice. His being.

"Shepp," I breathe with apologies on the tip of my tongue.

But he's fading and fast.

"I'm sorry," I choke out.

I try to keep all my emotions inside, but I fail miserably. My tears drip faster down my cheeks when I walk outside the door into the darkened hallway, lit by tiny lights on the cave-like walls.

My soul nearly leaps out of my body when the door slams behind me, and I turn to look at the only exit from my prison, locking the man I love inside.

I swallow hard, searching the length of the hall. From my viewpoint, it seems to go on forever.

"Walk," Shadow says from behind me, causing me to whirl around.

He grins down at me, eyeing me with his lone eye. It lights up at the sight of my discomfort and pain. Fueling Shadow's madness.

"Not until you help him," I growl, clenching my teeth. "He's your son!" Not that he ever thought about him like that.

Shadow smirks. "Is he, though?" He shrugs a shoulder with nonchalance. "He won't be helped until you're in The Pit."

"What's The Pit?" I question.

"The sooner you walk, the sooner you'll find out. Then, I'll let dear old Shepp get the antidote," he barks, pushing me backward with force.

I swallow all the words on the tip of my tongue and turn on

my heels. Despite the nagging inside my head, begging me to stab Shadow in the throat. I can't.

I have to blindly trust him to heal his son while I'm doing god knows what. The Pit? The sinking in my stomach continues the further away we walk from Shepp. I'm abandoning him. Or that's what it feels like.

For what seems like ten minutes, we travel down the long hall and up a set of stairs until we're in an above-ground room. The pressure physically changes around me, and my ears clear out.

Shadow clutches my upper arm tight, pulling me toward another door. The faint hint of a roaring crowd is my only warning when Shadow shoves me through it, and we enter a dank locker room.

"Now, the real fun begins," he says with a smirk, staring me down. "You're our entertainment for the night."

"Entertainment?" I ask, lifting my chin.

I can do this. For my sister. For Shepp's safety.

No matter what it is. No matter how much my fear sits in the pit of my stomach, telling me to run away and go back to check on Shepp.

"And I do this…" I trail off.

"Then Sheppard will be revived, yes." Pulling out his phone, he shrugs again like it's no big deal. He clicks a few times and grins more, turning it toward me.

My breath stalls at the image of Shepp lying on the ground, barely moving. His chest moves. Barely. Like he's clinging to life.

It has not been that long. Have they weakened him enough with the lack of food and water that his body will fail?

"So, you see. You are running out of time. If you do not get out there, he's as good as dead."

His words ring in my mind when he drags me through another door to the edge of an area.

The stench of old blood tinges the air.

"Show me what Gabriel taught you," he says with a slight smirk. "Prove to me you are worthy of proving your loyalty. Survive this, and you can survive anything.

Ugh. Again, with the loyalty crap. Does this monster 2.0 think I want to be loyal to him? Why would I? He is just like Gabriel. Hellbent on taking over the fucking world, for God knows what reason. And he might be worse. He has no boundaries. At least with the monster I am familiar with, I know what he is capable of. Did he smack me around when I fucked up? Yes. Did he ever touch me inappropriately or threaten me? No.

But with Shadow? We have history. He touched my sister with his hands. Held her the fuck down and tried to take something that did not belong to him and touched me in places I didn't consent to. Now, he's here begging for our loyalty and throwing me into an arena filled with bloodthirsty people.

"H-how?" My eyes move through the enormous crowd seated in the stands, rising toward the ceiling.

They're everywhere. Watching the blood-stained dirt floor with glee in their eyes. They cheer. Hoot and holler as a man appears in the arena, waving his arms around. My heart beats so fast in my chest, I swear it's about to punch through and run away, much like I want to.

But I can't.

Shepp's pain sweeps through my mind. The furrow of his brows. The twisting of his face. His hands on his stomach, cradling it as the poison took hold of him.

This is all I can do to protect him. I don't have a choice.

"Consider this your penance."

"What is this exactly?" My gaze flickers between Shadow and the man doing cartwheels in the bloodstains with a grin. He's playing into the crowds' chants of his name.

Brian! Brian!

"Pick your weapon. Kill the man. Or you will be killed. Simple as that," Shadow sneers, eyeing me with malice.

Oh, so it's a fight to the death to prove my worth and loyalty and to save Shepp and Sunny.

Wonderful.

"And if I win?"

Shadow has the audacity to snort. "If you win, Sheppard will get the antidote and survive. And your sister? I'll give her a new heart. And you'll live, of course. But if you lose, everyone loses."

"Of course," I say, swallowing all the emotions bubbling in my throat.

Now is not the time to swim in the feelings roaring inside me. Now is the time to dive deep into the darkness. It is begging me to surrender to it after all this time of just dipping my toes into it.

Everything seems to shift inside me. Like the torture I endured comes to the surface of my flesh, clawing its way out and running free. In its place is the darkness shifting inside me. Starting at my toes, it works its way up until I'm drowning in the numbness and nothingness.

My eyes scan the arena again. Everything falls away. The excitement and shouts. Even Brian's dancing ass fades into nothing. I examine the exits, the grounds, and everything that might be to my advantage.

"If it's a fight you want. Then, it's a fight you'll get," I hum, curling my fingers into fists.

Shadow stares down at me and shrugs. "Good luck. Hopefully, he doesn't throw a knife through your throat. But if he does, I might feel a little happy. One life down, one to go." He hums as he retreats, going through the door behind us.

Before anything else can happen, I tear the beautiful thin dress Jericho gave me for the event at the legs. It may have cost ten thousand dollars and makes my heart hurt doing it, but I have to move to fight. It's been my only source of clothing these past few days. If you could even call it that. It's barely a scrap of fabric. Perfect for an evening of dancing and drinking.

Terrible for a night of kidnapping in a dank, dark cave. I rip it until it only reaches my thighs, giving me enough space to move my legs fully.

And then the lights dim. The crowd roars, and a spotlight blinds me.

I guess it's my time to shine.

CHAPTER SEVEN

Jericho

My eyes roam the scenery through my bedroom window with a bored sigh. It's only been a few hours since Aiden locked me away and threw out the key. Leaving me bored and eager to get this show on the road. I have an escape to manage. The trees sway in the evening summer air, blowing in the wild winds coming from the west. I tilt my head, my annoyance rising.

Iron bars now partially obscure my once beautiful view of the property, blocking the window and preventing me from sneaking through.

My fingers curl at my side. This has my father's name written all over it.

Controlling cunt.

He moved quickly. I'll give him that. In one night, he took complete control of my living space and made it a prison—no doubt, ordering his men around and forcing them to put these bars on the windows.

I blow out a calming breath. It's no matter. I'm on the second floor. I'd rather not roll an ankle in an attempt to run from this place. He's undoubtedly got guards patrolling the land, with orders to shoot me on sight. Or maim me. Not enough to kill. Just enough to subdue me into compliance and bring me back to rot in this hellhole.

He can plot and keep me captive all he likes. I have a solid plan. Once the moon sits high in the sky, I'll walk out the front door with my head held high and grab my getaway car, getting to Arrow and then East Point Bluff as fast as possible.

No matter who I must murder. There is no doubt in my mind that blood will paint the pristine white walls if I can't get my hands on my fucking wife.

I tilt my head, going over the plan in my mind repeatedly. One misstep and my father will have me chained in the basement to get whatever it is he wants.

I'm the heir of this goddamn town, and soon, I'll be in charge. He has overstayed his welcome as head of the Viotto Crime Family for long enough. Changes are on the horizon. Something that should have happened the moment my brothers and I began planning his demise. But you can't take down an empire in a single night. It takes years of building up allies and getting your ducks in a row.

For now, I'll patiently wait until the sun goes down and everyone is asleep.

Then, Aiden and I will have some words. Fists. Stabs. You name it, we're going to have it. Then, he'll expire, and I'll be a little happier.

My feet carry me across the room as anxiety itches beneath my skin. Get to Journey. My mind screams. She needs you. Arrow needs you. Shepp needs you. Everyone needs you. Now. Not later.

Fuck. I pull at my hair.

My fingers itch to play my violin, the object that brings me back from the brink of darkness and grounds me here, like Journey. Without her or my melodies, I'm bound to lose myself in the violence building like poison in my veins.

The only positive of being locked in my bedroom—I was able to find my phone in the chaos of my discarded suit stained with blood on the ground. Thankfully, they didn't think to take it away. I was too foggy-headed before to even think about looking for it in my old pants pocket.

Fucking morons.

It's possible they thought nothing would be on it, anyway. With AntiEyes installed, deleting messages, emails, and everything in between from prying eyes. They probably figured it was a lost cause. It also helps that Olivia has made my phone practically impenetrable and untraceable, as well.

Win-win for me. It's like a damn fort without my fingerprint to enter.

It works to my advantage. Because the moment I opened my phone, I went straight to the tracking app to check Journey's location.

On the plus side, she isn't buried under a tower in the middle of Briar Cove. On the downside, her tracker is currently blinking in the middle of the fucking ocean near a large island fifty miles off the coast of California. But I have a few ideas about why she might be there. However odd, my mother's words about her confinement come to mind.

Shadow's dungeon beneath the ocean.

After witnessing my father's bold lies straight to my face, I can only assume Shepp is with her. Hopefully comforting her through whatever they're facing. They have each other, at least.

Fuck. I hope.

Red takes over my vision, darkening the world around me. Rage boils in my blood. Desperation claws at my flesh. If I can't get to my goddamn wife and best friend in the next twenty-four hours, I'm going on a murder spree.

They have to be alive.

Or I'll burn the goddamn world to ashes without an ounce of remorse and finally give into my violent tendencies.

Fuck. I pull at my hair again, reveling in the pain developing in my scalp. I need the physical ache to cope with the gaping black hole attacking my beating heart.

They're all gone, and I'm a sitting duck, forced to interact with a monster in waiting. Who somehow brought my mother back from whatever wasteland she crawled out of.

Did she get kidnapped by Shadow, as she claims?

I'll get to the bottom of everything. One step at a time.

They can bury all their truths as deeply as they want to. But I'll dig them up—all of them.

First, I must focus on my plans and stop hyper-focusing on what I can't fix.

Don't think about things you can't fucking touch right now.

Useless. Fucking. Sitting. Duck.

Fuck!

I yank my hands from my hair before I remove every strand or irritate my right shoulder. I must keep my wits and stop focusing on the things I cannot change.

I'm losing it.

I blow out a breath, attempting to concentrate on the room. A tune I've been working on for Journey plays through my mind. The echo of my violin and the whine of the strings.

Anything to calm myself down from spiraling into the abyss of my mind.

I turn my back toward the door and inspect the barred window as I pull my phone out of my pocket. I'm sure once my jailers get wind that I have my phone, they'll take it from me— if they care.

And that can't happen.

Bringing up maps for the millionth time, I study the uncharted island where Journey's tracker taunts me. Shadow's Island, no doubt. He has done well in hiding what is on it.

Blink. Again. Blink. The red dot does not move an inch. I blow out a breath, regaining my ever-slipping composure. One false move—I'll snap. Usually, that is not my department. That's Arrow's.

According to the Internet, nothing is on the island but vast tropical land featuring waterfalls and volcanic rocks. Oh, and island goats. According to the Internet, anyway. But nothing more about other inhabitants. People? More animals? Buildings?

No matter. I'll find out soon enough when I charter a boat with Veritas. I must play this smart, or I'll die. If I die, she dies. Arrow dies. Shepp dies–if he is where I think he is, anyway.

Their lives depend on me. And me alone.

I sigh, hiding my phone in my closet and locking my obsessive thoughts into a cage in my mind. Moving toward our bed, I plant myself on the edge, staring mindlessly ahead at the door, separating me from the rest of the house.

I'll give it to my father. He covered all his bases in keeping me compliant and secure here—isolated, trapped.

"Of course, Mr. Viotto." Aiden's muffled voice comes through the door, and his walky-talky buzzes to life with the sound of my father's muffled voice, demanding my presence.

Wonderful. He is such a dutiful, pathetic excuse for a human being. But he played me, now, didn't he? Slightly. I trust no one fully—only Arrow, Shepp, and even Journey, despite her spying ways.

My bedroom door flies open with more force than necessary. I eye the tiny nick in the wall, narrowing my eyes as the drywall sprinkles on the floor like snow. Slowly, I get up from the edge of the bed, glaring in his direction.

"Was that necessary?" I ask, shoving my hands into my slack pockets.

Aiden's jaw tics with agitation.

Good. Get angry.

"I'm curious. How did you hide your disdain for me so well?" I question, stepping forward.

Hook. Line. Sinker.

He snarls at me, eyeing me up and down. Loathing seeps from his pours like an acid working through the air.

"Wasn't easy," he hisses. "But a job is a job." Ah, that's all I was.

"So, another spy for the great Gabriel Viotto? What did he promise you? A pay raise? Promotion? Look at you now, babysitting the man you want to rip apart." I grin manically when he steps up to me. "How about your coworkers? Any rats in the mix with you?"

Hit me. Give me a goddamn reason to remove your liver in one punch.

Nose to nose. I feel his putrid breath against my flesh, and darkness flashes in his eyes.

"Only me. I'm just that fucking good," he growls in my face. So, that answers that. He acted alone. But that doesn't put me at ease. My father could have had a million more spies on our ass that Aiden was unaware of. "I'd betray you again and again while watching you and your little friends play mafia boss."

"Playing?" My head tilts when his face tightens more, if that's even possible. "I don't recall playing. If my memory serves me correctly, my boys and I had a good thing going for the community." I raise a brow when the veins in his forehead rise off his flesh, looking as if they'll pop.

I grin more, the angrier he gets. A thrill rushes through me, sparking me back to life.

"You'll never be the king of this kingdom, asshole," he hisses in a low tone, barely speaking.

"Oh? And who will? You?"

He tenses more, letting every letter of my words puncture through his skin and hit him right in the gut.

"You don't have what it takes, Aiden," I whisper, pressing my nose into his. His eyes dart back and forth between mine, inspecting me like I do him. "You'll never be the king of this town or family. You don't have the guts."

Perhaps it's a dare I have flung at him. Judging by the redness creeping up his neck, he knows I'm telling the truth.

There is no way Aiden will ever survive this family with a

trigger finger and temper. He has not been trained like I have. I know how to weather Gabriel Viotto.

"You're in for a rude awakening," he hisses, pushing me back a step.

For the record, I let him. I could stand my ground and pummel his face until he's unrecognizable. But I'm curious what secrets Aiden will let slip when his anger has him by the balls.

"Oh? Please elaborate," I taunt.

Get a man emotional, and they'll tell you all the secrets written into their souls.

He grins, stepping back. "They're all gone. You don't have anyone left. Shepp is with Shadow." Pride puffs out his chest. "Journey is with Shadow. Your father traded them for your mother. Oh, and the money. Also, Arrow is braindead."

Thanks for confirming my suspicions, asshole.

"Your doing?" I ask, raising an unbothered brow when I'm anything but calm.

I am vengeful. Full of fucking violence, begging to come to the surface and rip his heart out.

All this confirming information will help when I make it to East Point Bluff and invade my cousin's house to regroup. Olivia Viotto. Secret government agent with Veritas. A higher up, too. In a pinch, she dedicates herself to helping the boys and me solve problems. I try not to bring too much fucked up shit to her doorstep. But this is unavoidable.

"Of course it was," he growls, gnashing his teeth together before straightening his spine and washing away his visible emotions. "Now, you are being paged for dinner. Wear a jacket." Aiden scowls at me when I shrug and grab a nice suit jacket to throw over my white dress shirt.

"What a good lap dog you are," I quip, shouldering past him through the door. "Next, he'll pull out the peanut butter, slather it on his dick, and you'll lick it off without a fight."

Aiden is more than a loyal little doggy. He's quite the informant. No wonder my father brought him on board to work for him and spy on our endeavors. Not that it matters. I still held Aiden at arm's length. Was there an ounce of trust there? Yes. Did I suspect he was a traitor? No.

That just makes me naïve and pisses me off all in one go.

"I'm not a fucking dog," he hisses, catching up to me as I march down the stairs, jumping headfirst into whatever bullshit my father is about to pull.

I smirk, remembering those words from a vastly different mouth. A delicious mouth with plump lips and attitude for days —my strong Little Chaos. I can only hope she is fighting tooth and nail against Shadow and whatever he is having her do. If Aiden is correct, then Shepp is also by her side, keeping strong.

"Are you sure about that?" I whisper, eyeing him when his eyes flare in anger.

He says nothing when he grabs my arm again and drags me forward. Again, I let him. I could rip out his heart with my bare hands—which will happen later—but right now, I'm playing a part for my father: dutiful son, fully embracing his prison sentence.

Aiden grunts as he drags me into the beautifully decorated dining room. He says something to my father, who sits at the head of the table with a cocky smirk. Formal suit. Red tie. Dark hair styled to perfection. Even his face looks more healed than the last time I saw him at lunch. The bruises have faded beneath what looks like makeup. It's such a shame. Those bruises deserve to shine and show that someone got the best of him.

Whoever got the jump on my father got him fucking good. I wonder how long it took him to recover. Surely, he got knocked out and laid on the ground for an extended period of time. Oh, to be a fly on the wall for that. In my heart, I hope it was Shepp. Visions of him leaping off stage to protect Journey run through my mind. The frantic tone of my voice and the worry lines creasing his forehead. Sheppard Mondelli reacts when pushed too far. Violently.

My timid mother sits to his left, leaving her eyes on the table and her hands resting in her lap. Nothing like the vibrant woman I remember from my childhood. She never let my father boss her around too much when I was a kid. Ever more the reason to wipe Shadow's existence off the map.

Her tight black dress hugs her small frame. Diamonds drip from my mother's neck and ears. He's painted her up as the perfect mafia wife, sitting beside him without saying a word.

So meek and fragile.

It's odd to me, leaving me more than curious about where she came from and why she's back now. What's her game? There has to be one. You don't just mysteriously escape a prison you've been stuck in for twenty years without a plan. Or ulterior motives.

There's always a reason for everything. Despite her claims of being stuck in Shadow's prison, I can tell she's hiding skeletons in her closet. Loads of them. And they're bound to spill out at some point.

I'm so focused on the snake sitting at the table that I almost miss the rest of the company slithering up to my father. Snakes, the lot of them, sit there with their smug grins and polite conversations.

Mr. and Mrs. Satin. Owner and operators of Satin Firearms.

Immediately, my eyes fall on the petite blonde sitting across from her parents. She daintily sips her wine, eyeing me with a familiar sparkle lighting up her eyes.

Chloe. Fucking. Satin.

I school my features, but dread fills my gut. If they're here, then that means only one thing. My father is moving quickly to secure a better future for himself. Fuck what I think about anything.

"So nice of you to join us, son. We've got a lot of planning to do," my father says, gesturing toward the seat between my mother and Chloe.

"Planning, you say?" I question, not bothering to argue when I take the seat.

I bite my tongue when Chloe Satin grins at me, seductively fluttering her fake eyelashes. If by seductive, I mean she looks like she's blinking cum out of her eyelashes while sucking on a lemon—then, yeah—seductively.

Fuck me. This meal is going to be painful—like pulling teeth.

"Wedding planning," she coos, resting a hand on my arm. "It's been decided!" She squeaks with excitement, slightly jostling me in my seat. My teeth grit from the pain of my flesh wound, and I gently remove her from my arm.

"Hmmm," I hum, not reacting to her words. "A wedding, you say?" My eyes dart to my father, who raises a brow for my compliance.

His expression screams—play your part or pay the price. There's the father I know and hate.

Right. He'd probably chop my fingers off to get me to comply with his demands. Whatever. I'll pretend this will come to fruition.

"Three weeks from now, on Saturday," my father says in a deep voice, "At the church. Father Amour will marry you. We've got the entire family coming in to witness the union." He raises a glass as a toast: "To the coming together of our family."

"Here, here," Mr. Satin proudly says, lifting his glass and slightly swaying.

My father could probably ask him for his kidney, and he'd comply. He's a blind follower. Offering his daughter and money whenever needed. He'd probably throw in his company, too. I'm unsure what connection the two have, but I know something is there.

"Indeed," I say, lifting my glass without hesitation.

Despite wanting to light this entire house on fire with each of them tied to a chair, screaming as their flesh boils off, I'm playing a part. No amount of joy fills my being. Chloe insists on touching me, making me want to throw her to the lions. Hmmm. Not a bad idea. I bet they're hungry by now. I'm sure the zoo keeper Arrow keeps on staff has maintained their cage and gone about their duties. But what's one more piece of meat for them to enjoy?

One thing I will never let my father catch onto is that I would rather claw my eyes out than show up to a wedding that would not even be valid.

If Journey is out there somewhere in the middle of the ocean with her tracker still intact, then I will find her. If she is floating, then I will float, too. I gave my life to that woman, and I will never let her out of my sight again. If it means never coming back here and marrying this conniving girl, then I am down.

"I can't wait," Chloe coos, leaning her head on my shoulder. "This was fate. You and me, Jericho. We have been destined for years. I have always had a crush on you." Her breaths pick up as her hand drops to my leg under the table, stroking my thigh. Reaching below, I grab her hand and hold it hostage in my rough grip.

Her brows pucker, and a frown pulls at her lips.

Fate, my ass.

This is precisely why my father is locking me in this prison. And he will for the next few weeks until I walk down the aisle and cement whatever he's promised Mr. Satin.

A partnership? Obviously, this is something that was planned even before our initiation ball, regardless of my marriage to Journey.

How long? No clue.

My Journey was always the one promised to me. Not Chloe. Maybe that's why my father is pretending Journey has died so he can fulfill this plan he's been concocting.

My gaze discreetly finds my mother sitting silently next to my father. Her eyes scan his face, filled with love and devotion. My mind wanders to Shepp's mom, who has been by my father's side since her husband met his end.

"And where is your wife tonight?" I ask my father, raising a brow when he sips his drink.

"Beside me," he says, setting his crystal glass down.

"The other one," I say, tilting my head. "The one you married the moment her husband was placed in an urn."

My father's jaw stiffens with anger. "She didn't make it either. It's a shame the tower fell in on her and the others." He wants to say more but holds back, biting his tongue for whatever reason.

Interesting.

There's something in his eye, giving every single thought he has away. She's not gone. But he made her gone. Where did he stash the former Mrs. Mondelli? Surely, the woman deserves a break after suffering through Thomas and now, my father.

"There's no need to dwell on the past, darling," my mother says softly. "We're only looking to the future now." She reaches over and clasps his arm, gently squeezing him. Her head tilts as she continues to look at him with love sparkling in her light eyes.

"Yes, to the future. No more dwelling in the past, son. You've got a lot ahead of you."

"Like a wedding," I say stiffly, trying to shake Chloe off my shoulder, but she is relentless. She acts as if we have been in a relationship for years and do not have animosity toward one another. Besides, I am not the one she has eyes for. "And what about Leighton LeMaster?"

Chloe completely stills. "What about him?" she asks, raising her head to look into my eyes, giving me the fuel to my fire.

"You two were looking quite cozy at the initiation ball," I say with a smirk, sitting back in my seat.

That much I remember about that night. I remember our evening climbing on stage. But the rest? It's fucking fuzzy memory that I'm desperate to remember.

"He's a family friend, boy. No need to worry about him. She's all yours," Mr. Satin says gruffly, raising his brows at his daughter expectantly.

"Yes. All yours," she reaffirms with a shaky grin.

I will be out of here before she can cry over her missed opportunity with Leighton, with whom she is obviously in love. I will leave tonight to rescue Arrow from whatever hell he has been put under, and then I will go straight to Olivia. Only Veritas can help me find Journey now. I must trust that my wife is alive and well, even if it says she is in the ocean.

"Oh, darling, let me get you some more," my mother says softly, smiling at my father as she rises from the chair.

"Grace," he grumbles. "That's what the staff is for. They'll get me more."

"Nonsense. I'm eager to help," she argues, grabbing his crystal glass. "Does anyone else need a refill?" her brows raise when Mr. Satin agrees, and she takes both to the mini-bar with her back toward us.

My father rubs his temple, anger simmering under the surface of his skin. "She was always an independent woman," he quips through clenched teeth.

"They all start like that," Mr. Satin chuckles, throwing an arm over his wife's chair, who flinches at the action, eyeing her husband with fear.

Wonderful.

My mother gracefully sits their glasses in front of them with a soft smile, watching eagerly when they each take a sip of their drinks, and she sits down with her glass of wine.

"So, the wedding," my mother offers softly, with no apprehension. "Do you have a dress yet?"

Chloe's cheeks redden, causing my fists to clench. "Oh, yes."

"I bet it's simply gorgeous, like you, darling. Jericho is a lucky man," she says, sipping her drink.

"Lucky, indeed," I hum, keeping the sarcasm out of my voice. Or try to, at least. This has to be a dream, right? I've woken up in some alternate universe and need to find the wormhole to take me back.

Anxiety rises inside me like never before, clawing to be set free. The faster we get this dinner done and over with, the faster I can put my plan into motion. But if I give myself away too quickly, my father will know what I am planning. And for such a smart man, he's too smug to realize that my escape is imminent.

The evening continues with several courses of a celebratory meal, including dessert. Conversation flows easily the drunker my father and Mr. Satin get. My mother sits stoically by my father's side, smiling at every word he says.

"It was wonderful to have you all over. I look forward to strengthening our relationship," my father says, putting an arm around my mother's shoulders.

How they've fallen into such a groove with their relationship already, I don't have a clue. I always knew he loved her more than life itself, but it's odd to see after witnessing such a cold man all these years.

"I look forward to it, Gabe," Mr. Satin rumbles, shaking my father's hand before they all walk out the door with full bellies and the promise to unite our families under marriage.

"Aiden!" my father says, slightly coughing.

"Yes, sir?" Aiden asks stiffly, walking into the foyer with a grim expression.

"Escort Jericho to his room and stand guard for the night." My father's eyes cut to me, down to the bone like a laser. "Make sure he doesn't step out of there until morning when he's needed again. We have a golf outing with Mr. Satin and his daughter."

Golf. What a joy.

"And why is that, Father?" I question, shoving my hands into my pockets. "Do you think I'm going to run for the hills?" I raise a brow when he slightly coughs again, shaking his head.

"I know you better than you think I do, son. But I've got my eyes on you. You don't have your little friends to control. You're under my thumb now. I made sure of it." He grins like he's won already.

"How ironic you don't trust me," I quip, stepping up to him slightly. "What are you afraid of?" That I'll slit your throat? I'll ensure you're in the ground when I take over this business and weed out the bad people.

He's taken the Viotto family off track, and it's snowballing into bigger mistakes.

My father clears his throat. "Of course, I don't trust you," he grunts, heaving a breath. "You've been undermining me since the moment you were semi-initiated at sixteen. I am nipping you in the bud before you can even fucking sprout," he growls, squaring his shoulders.

"Of course," I say with a straight face.

"Here's the deal, you ungrateful shit," he breathes heavily, grabbing me by the collar of my shirt. "You will walk down the aisle and say I do with Chloe fucking Satin. You'll take her to your swanky little home and create heirs. You will do as you're fucking told. I have the doctors at the hospital on standby. The moment you walk out of this house without marrying her, I'll have them inject Arrow with a toxic cocktail of medications that will stop his heart within a matter of seconds." He grins at that, loving what he holds over my head. "Now, go to your fucking room while your mother and I reconnect some more." He shoves me away, knocking me slightly back, but I catch myself.

"Have a wonderful evening, Mother," I say, bowing slightly as her eyes widen at my father's words.

"Have a wonderful night, dear," she says softly, watching me head toward the stairs with Aiden on my tail.

"I'll be outside your room all night. You fucking leave, and he'll gut me."

No, I want to say. I'll be the one to gut you. But I don't. I keep my lips sealed as he escorts me into my bedroom.

"Don't worry, Aiden. I'll be here all night." I smile, tilting my head when he nods.

"Better be, asshole. Don't mess up my job here."

Ah, of course. It's the job he seems to love.

It only takes a few hours for the house to quiet down. Doors slam. People settle in.

And Aiden stands guard right outside my bedroom door, standing tall.

A sitting duck waiting for me to strike.

CHAPTER EIGHT

Journey

HEAVY SMOKE PERMEATES THE AIR. THE LINGERING SCENT OF tobacco washes over me, slightly mixed with weed and other substances floating in the dust particles.

Heat pours down on me as I overlook the vicious crowd, hurling obscenities at me from where they sit. Food flies onto the ring, landing in the old blood with a splat but never hitting me.

I blink at the red stains, retreating further into my darkness. Swallow me whole. Make me not feel the next hour of my life. Take it all away from me before I drown in the emotions of everything consuming me.

Shepp is dying on the cold ground of a prison, barely clinging to life. My sister. She's in the damn wind. And Arrow and Jericho? I don't even know.

If I survive this, I'll fight tooth and nail to reclaim my life.

Flickering lights illuminate the faces staring back at me with sneers decorating their lips. Chants egging on my demise ring through the air.

Kill the bitch! Down with the whore! Bring her to her knees!

Jesus. It's like *The Hunger Games*, in here.

Their deep voices puncture through my skin, straight to my aching bones, as my eyes take in everything that might be to my advantage. Hidden weapons. Escape routes. Anything to aid me in killing this man who will be after me as soon as this starts.

Women make their way through the stands holding beers and popcorn, hollering their prices in skimpy outfits. I tilt my head. Are they here by their own choice? Or are they like me —a prisoner held captive by Shadow?

Whatever it is, it seems we're all trying to survive this assault of loud voices.

From where I stand, Shadow tossed me in here, hoping to kill two birds with one stone—literally. He doesn't want me to win this. He doesn't want my loyalty. Hell, maybe he got all he wanted from me when I spilled about Gabe. Or, like he said, perhaps this is his revenge for me stabbing him so many times.

Whatever it is, it's not fucking cool, and I want to speak to his manager. Right the fuck now.

I thought my life couldn't get any worse when I was under my monster's thumb. If only I had glimpsed the future, I would have seen how great I had it. I lived at home. Granted, my mom was a druggy who didn't care about me. But I had my own room with sunshine streaming through it and brightening my day. All I had to do was go on missions for a man who wanted revenge on me for killing his second-in-command.

What a waste of time on his part.

I wish I could go back in time, kidnap my sister, and run away before any of this could be set into motion. But alas, I don't know how to time travel. So, I'm stuck fighting a lunatic who looks like he wants to tear the flesh from my bones. Not to mention Shepp, Arrow, and Jericho. I never would have met them if I hadn't been on this trajectory.

Everything happens for a reason, right?

So, what's the reasoning for this? This torture? The starvation? Fuck. I wish I knew his endgame.

I blow out a breath, centering myself. My darkness twirls inside me, blocking out all the commotion trying to penetrate through my iron facade. Numbness takes me over, fogging my brain and fueling my focus.

Finally, my darkness has entered the equation, ready to take down anyone who comes near me.

Before Shadow waltzed out of the ring to do God knows what, he presented several weapons to me on a silver platter. Knives of every size. Swords. Large, heavy weapons that I haven't seen or used before. But to me, there was no contest as to what I would choose.

My fingers tighten around the two small knives nestled in my grip, no longer than six inches from base to tip. Gabriel may not have prepared me for much.

Murder? Sure, I can do that with my eyes closed. I don't want to. I hate taking lives. But I can do it if it comes down to it. Sneaking around? Yup. One of my specialties. Need someone to sneak around in the shadows and gather information? I'm your gal.

But fighting? Hand-to-hand combat?

Yeah, I missed those classes. Thanks a lot, Monster. Good for nothing asshole.

The spotlight follows me as I walk across the arena to the man standing tall in the middle of the blood-soaked dirt. He grins at me, showing off his missing teeth. Despite the muscles bulging on every inch of his being, he looks ragged. Yet, I can tell from the lift of his shoulders that he's a soldier for Shadow. Loyal, too.

"So, you're the little girl fighting me tonight?" He grins, looking me up and down, scoffing at the knives in my hands.

"I suppose so," I say in an even tone, relishing in the point of his brow.

He doesn't expect me to be able to fight him. He thinks he's going to take me down easily and that I'm a quivering little girl who can't bring him to his knees. Well, the jokes on him. I may not be a fighter, but I have people to fight for. My family. My boys. My fucking sister. I don't give a shit if I live or die right now for myself. It's all for them.

Besides, I have my wit.

"I'm guessing five," he says, circling me with predatory intent.

I could reach him now and stab his eyeball out. But I don't think the game has begun. He's sizing me up, feeling me out. And I'm doing the same.

"Why five?" I ask in a monotone voice again, watching him at every turn.

Never leave your back to your enemies. If you're on my time, you'll watch every move they make. Besides, you don't know when a snake will strike, Little Snake.

He grins. "Five seconds until your guts are on the ground. Just last night, I gutted a man right there." He points to where the bloodstains still smear across the dirt.

"Sure," I say, shrugging my shoulders.

Pay attention to the small details of your enemies. Their bodies give away their intentions before their words ever do.

I watch him again, taking in how he walks and carries himself. A slight limp forces him to hobble on his left leg, letting me know he's losing strength on one side. I wonder how long he's been at this.

He laughs more, waving his arms around for the crowd, riling them up. His greasy blond hair flops into his eyes, but he quickly swipes it away before it gets stuck in his eyes.

Noted.

"This is going to be so much fun, little girl," he chuckles. "I'm the reigning champion."

"How many weeks in a row?" I indulge his words, letting him think he's getting to me.

He tilts his head. "You think you have a chance against me?"

He thinks I don't.

My eyes look him up and down, taking in the angle of his toes, pointing outward. "Maybe," I say, shrugging again.

"Tell you what, baby doll." *Oh, gag.* "I'll give you an out. You can drop to your knees, open your mouth, and suck my dick like a good girl. Then, I'll spare you." He grabs himself, showing it off to the crowd, who roar with laughter.

This is a goddamn comedy show.

I raise a brow. Drop to my knees? Typical fucking man who thinks he's in a position of power. But while he exerts all his energy on the crowd falling for his whims, I'm storing mine for when the time is right.

"Sure," I say with a small smile.

He stops dead. "Sure?" he questions, turning to face me now. Sweat glistens on his overly tanned-skin.

"Isn't that what you want?" I question again as the crowd settles in and suddenly quiets down.

He observes me again, taking in my torn dress and barely covered tits. His eyes focus on the tattoo concealing the scar between my breasts, getting lost in the hypnotic pattern.

"Gentlemen!" a loud voice roars, echoing through the room.

For a moment, I take my eyes off the enemy standing in front of me and focus on my other enemy, standing on a lifted stage above the entire arena, looking down on his subjects.

My heart aches in my chest when my sister comes into view. She smiles softly beside him, looking at the crowd with a spark in her eyes. Confidence takes over her entire demeanor, as if she belongs by his side and in front of all these people. Health radiates off her, something I haven't seen in years.

She looks good.

"Welcome to your entertainment for the night!" he shouts with glee. Those beady eyes that haunted my nightmares are glued to me. "Our champion, Brian Bell, returns to face off against a new opponent!"

The crowd goes fucking ballistic, causing my ears to ring. Shadow says more, introducing me as the traitor.

Then, something strange happens. My sister pulls on his shirt, forcing him to stop. He looks down. An odd sense of pride shines in his eyes when she whispers something in his ear. He nods, taking in her words. I blink several times as he yammers on more, riling up the crowd. Even Brian jumps from foot to foot, exerting his energy.

"Let the games begin!" Shadow shouts, stepping back from his ledge with my sister, who doesn't spare me a glance.

Interesting. She's up to something.

The lights drop from the crowd. Only leaving Brian and me illuminated. He grins. I don't move. I watch his staggering movements. His chest heaves, and exhaustion pulls at his loose limbs. Interesting. He exerted himself with the crowd earlier.

Maybe this will be easier than I thought. Outwit the dimwit with what he wants most. And I, too, will save my energy. Or lack thereof. After what feels like days of no meals or water, I'm running on thin fumes. My sense of time has flown out the window. Among other things, I am willing to stay safe.

"So, how about you drop to those pretty knees and show me what you got," he says, grinning with ease.

But his fingers tighten on the end of his sword, repositioning them at his side.

Noted.

"What would you like to do with me on my knees?" I rasp, putting a raw edge to my tone.

He follows my movements with his eyes—the curve of my neck. The deep breaths, pushing my tits out. He stares. Enamored with my presence.

"I'm going to fuck your face, and then I will own you. All for your life, of course. I won't kill you. Yet. Deal?" Confidence tinges his tone. He ignores the knives in my hands, as if he doesn't believe I'll use them. Jokes on him, though.

"Of course," I say simply, tilting my chin with false bravado.

"The crowd will love it," he says with a grin, loosening his grip on his sword.

Again, noted. He's getting comfortable with my presence, telling me everything through slight movements.

I bat my eyelashes as I lower myself, presenting myself as a trophy for him. Harmless. Demure. On my knees without protest.

"Like this?" I question, looking at him from the ground. My teeth sink into my bottom lip.

I have to sell it and all.

"Holy fuck," he grunts with haste, thinking with his dick over the fight we were supposed to have. "Oh, God, yeah. No one has ever taken the deal."

It's good to know he's tried this on every breathing person who has been presented before him.

"And how many was that?"

He smirks. "Forty-six. And you're the only one who sold herself to me."

"I want to live." It's not a lie. Not completely. I won't be sucking his schlong to prolong my life.

But it's all about my act. Make him believe. Besides, I haven't said it was a deal, anyhow.

His hard dick springs free from his pants. Nearly poking my eye out. Jesus. But I hold myself still, looking at him in his twinkling eyes. The crowd roars. But I tune them out.

"You're a big, strong fighter, aren't you?" I coo, not making a move to touch him yet. I could lower his defenses by brushing my fingers along his thighs. But that might make him remember the weapons in my hands.

Idiot.

His eyes shine. Boost a man's over-inflated ego, and he'll present like a damn peacock.

"Open your fucking mouth," he demands, tapping my cheek with the tip of his sword, nicking my flesh.

A threat. He's presenting me with the bigger picture—he's in charge and has a weapon to back it up.

"And then you'll save me?" I question softly, infusing emotions into my voice.

This is my stage, my weapon. I may not be able to fight him physically, but I can talk and act my way out of this situation without breaking a sweat.

He strokes himself with his free hand. Disgust rolls through me, even when I pop open my lips. The tip of his sword sits against my throat, threatening to cut me more if I so much as flinch.

Good thing I won't flinch.

"Now, are you ready to become my little bitch for the rest of your life?" He inches his dick closer to me.

The looser and more vulnerable he gets, the more confident I feel with my plan.

"I am no one's bitch," I say, jamming my knife right through his dick and the other through his wrist, forcing him to drop his sword as he wails.

I don't give him a second to retaliate. Or move. Or breathe. While he's focused on his dick in the dirt and the blood rushing from his wrist, I slit his throat. His flesh parts like butter beneath the knife he wasn't worried about me having.

Rookie ass mistake, Brian.

Red runs down my flesh. Over my dress. Onto the ground. It surrounds me like in my nightmares.

Only this time, my darkness cuts out the emotions. The guilt. Everything from forming inside me. There is no reasoning with myself as to why this man had to die.

I belong to no one. That's the only reason I need.

No monsters can hold me down and use me for their purposes. I will do what it takes to get my sister, Shepp, and me out of this prison and back to my other two men.

But I will no longer be anyone's person to use.
I'm in charge now.

CHAPTER NINE

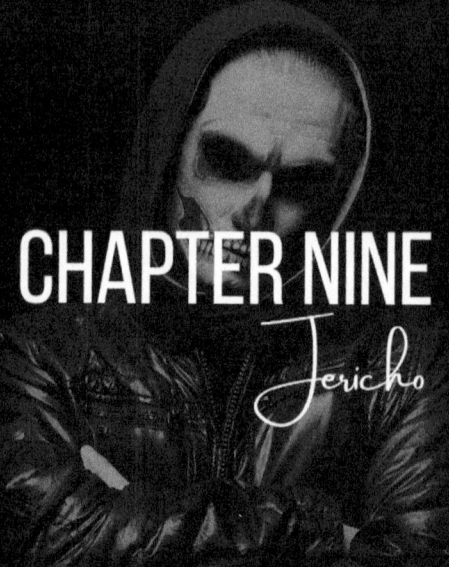

Jericho

A SENSE OF SATISFACTION SOARS THROUGH ME WHEN I PICK the lock to my bedroom door, successfully disengaging the deadbolt that keeps me locked inside. Pins and needles rise inside my body as I wait, prickling my skin with excitement. For what I'm about to do. For leaving this wretched fucking mansion as a free man. Then, a new mission will start.

I've been stuck here for hours now after that horrendous dinner where my father informed me I was to marry Chloe Satin. I nearly gag at the thought. No way in Hell is that happening on my watch. I'll claw my eyes out before I ever walk down the aisle with that snake who only wants me for the money or family loyalty. Fuck the allies of the Viotto's. Gabriel has gone too far this time.

During my time of solitude, I've been meticulously plotting. My leave. My father's demise. Searching for where my mother truly went all these years. You name it. I've been plotting against it. My number one priority now is taking out my frustrations on a certain traitorous guard who rests just outside my bedroom door.

He won't live to tell the tale of his demise. They'll only remember him for his unrecognizable face and bloodless body.

I'm going to fucking gut him.

The loud game Aiden insists on playing on his phone

vibrates through the wood of my door. Loud and obnoxious—which is fitting for him. Giving me the perfect opportunity to break his fucking neck and exact my revenge while he's too absorbed to notice.

First, Aiden will die at my hands with the weapons Arrow so generously left lying around. His blood will smear the walls of our shower until he gives me all the information I need, like where Arrow is exactly and what my father has planned for the next few weeks. There has to be more to it than shoving me in this room between mealtimes and hoping I don't escape.

Slowly, I move the bedroom door open a crack and peek out. A grin stretches my lips as the darkness I've held tightly to comes out from its hiding space inside me and roars with excitement.

This is what I needed to round out the end of my day. Excitement. Murder. Finally, I'll be moving forward and taking a step further toward my family, who is lost in the wind.

Thankfully, the door doesn't squeak or give me away when I open it further. Aiden sits on the opposite wall, nose in his phone. His fingers tap tirelessly on the screen, advancing him in the game. It's a shame his back isn't to me. I could easily pull him into the room, shut the door, and lock it again.

It's like putting our enemies in the pen with the lions and watching them scrambling to escape the massive cats eager to eat them. Except this time, I'm the fucking cat eager to kill the rat.

Opening the door further, I let it hit the wall. Aiden jumps, nearly dropping his phone with surprise.

"Is this what you do on the job?" I smirk when his face completely folds, twisting to a snarl as he yanks his phone off the ground.

His body expands, seeming bigger than usual when he marches up to me. "How the fuck," he grunts, pushing me back into my room with one shove. A shove, I let him get in. There is nothing more thrilling than riling him up.

"I should ask the same," I say, righting myself a few feet from the door jamb. "Is that what my father pays you to do on the job? Such a waste of space. Maybe I should discuss your shortcomings with him. He would not take too kindly to–" I grunt when Aiden's fist connects with my face repeatedly.

I stagger back several steps. My heart fucking explodes in my chest. Adrenaline pours through my veins, making every hair on my body stand on end like electricity zapping through my system.

This is it. This is my fucking moment. The bloodbath I've been craving to sate my demon has begun.

I heave a breath, staring at Aiden. He glares back with a gloss forming over his eyes. Frantic breaths pour through his nostrils, flaring them. My blood drips from his knuckles.

"You won't say shit," he growls. "You will stay in this goddamn room and shut the fuck up."

I smirk, wiping the blood from my lip and nose. Oh, how deliciously it burns when my skin tears in two from the force of his blows.

"Won't I?" I question, putting my bloodied hands into my pockets. See? I'm no threat to him right now. "I'd gladly tell him what you've been up to when you were supposed to be watching over me. Your captive."

Aiden steps back toward the door, and for a second, I think I've misread everything. He isn't supposed to flee from this fight. He's supposed to lock himself inside with me and pummel my face in. He's out for blood. Needing someone to take his aggression out on when he can't with my father. Gabriel has too much control over him. Most likely dangling something over his head to get him to comply—the title, of course. Or maybe something more. A sibling in custody? A parent in peril? Whatever it is, Aiden jumps when Gabriel says to.

"You think he'd let someone like you, who can't keep his

son in line, be his second-in-command?" I snort, wincing at the pain from my face.

But the pain helps me to remember I'm alive. Breathing. Fucking walking around. And I'm about to remove Aiden from the equation. All he has to do is…

Aiden slams my bedroom door shut, locking it from the inside with a smirk. Perfect. He thinks he's got me as he rolls up his sleeves, exposing the tattoos on his forearms.

"Shut the fuck up, Jericho. Your father said I could punish you any way I saw fit. He knew you'd try to escape. He has measures in place." Measures, he says. Interesting. I wonder what precautions my father has taken to ensure I stay put.

Guards at every exit? Most likely. Gun? Oh, yes. He isn't above shooting me in the legs and then breaking them to keep me here and compliant.

"Oh? So, beating my ass is your solution?" I taunt him, standing in my relaxed pose. He could hit me again, and I'd laugh in his face.

He has no idea what sort of monster he's up against. Underestimate me, dickbag. Let's see how much you like fire and brimstone, because that's where I'm sending your ass tonight.

"Every day until you fucking stop pushing my buttons."

"My father will see how dedicated you are if you do that. Desperate times call for desperate measures, right?" I lift a brow when he advances on me again.

It's a good thing this room is far away from my father's old bedroom. In fact, it's an entire floor away from the main bedroom.

No one will hear Aiden's screams.

Aiden punches me again four times in a row. Admittedly, the last one to my temple rocks me a little. I sway on my feet, keeping my hands in my pockets.

"Fight back!" he grunts, heaving more breaths as sweat glistens on his forehead.

He's getting quite the workout, isn't he?

"You'd enjoy that, wouldn't you?" I question, removing my hands from my pockets and securing one of Arrow's extra needles in my hand. Bless his crazy soul for leaving his knockout drugs in convenient places around this room. He's like a squirrel keeping his stash hidden in small areas. "You want me to fight back, Aiden? You want me to hit you in the jaw until your teeth are bleeding?"

Aiden squares his shoulders, standing confidently and ready to strike. His arm moves. Fist flies. Until it is not. I smirk when I catch it, squeezing with all my might to stop his movements. He grunts, fighting against me.

"I thought you wanted to hit me," I taunt again, holding his fist in the air. "It's too bad," I tsk, jamming the needle into his arm and quickly administering the sedative inside.

"What the fuck?" he slurs. "What did you…" Aiden falls to his knees, unable to keep himself upright any longer. His hand falls away from me as he tries to catch himself but ends with his back on the floor. Those beady eyes filled with hate stare up at me. "You drugged me," he slurs again as drool dribbles from the edge of his lips. "You cheating bastard."

All is fair in love and war—I think to myself as I hover above him. And this is war, after all. He'll pay for his sins, and I'll dole out the punishment for his crimes.

It's a win-win. For me, at least.

"Not really my move. You can thank Arrow for the inspiration. Only this time, I won't knock you out for hours. I need you compliant." I grin, capping the used needle, and toss it in the trash. Aiden won't be going anywhere on his own for some time. "You see, I did some research on his favorite drug. Given in full doses, it's meant to knock the victim out for two to five hours, depending on their size. But this dose?" I say, pointing to him. "It'll disable you for about thirty minutes max, which gives me enough time to ensure I have you where I want you.

You can't move your muscles, but you'll still feel everything I do to you."

"I'll tell him everything, you shit bag. It may give you a thirty-minute head start, but he'll know everything. Even when you leave," he slurs again, sucking in breaths frantically.

"Oh." Leaning my head to one side, I roll up the sleeves of my white shirt. "You think I'm leaving you here so you can snitch more?" I chuckle at that, grabbing both of his arms and dragging him. "Can't leave a mess for when my wife gets home. She would be upset to see the blood on the furniture. I can't upset her or Shepp. Now, Arrow? He'd be more than thrilled to see what I did to you. I should film this for him."

Aiden attempts to struggle. And I do say attempts. He's unable to move as the drug takes hold, and the only thing he can do is whine his protests. Of course, his voice still works. I need it to. I only want to incapacitate him for a brief time until I can get all the answers I need.

"What are you doing?" he garbles when I pull his shoes off and neatly put them together under the sink.

"You won't need clothing for the fun we're about to have."

If Aiden could stiffen his muscles, I think he would. Instead, he gives me another glare filled with so much hate I should be on fire. Too bad he can't do anything about it. He's vulnerable and at my fucking mercy.

I remove most of his clothing besides his boxers. He can keep those on to protect his virtue and my eyes. I'd rather not glimpse the sniveling worm in his pants. Once I'm satisfied he can't make any moves, I drag him into our shower and haphazardly toss him inside. He lands with an oomph on his back, wheezing.

"You see these?" I ask, jostling a few rings in the large shower of our bathroom. "There's eight of them. Four in the ceiling and four attached here, here, here, and here," I say, pointing to the corners. "Arrow installed them. I always wondered why, but now I think I have my answers."

Honestly, I should have snooped in our room ages ago. But it wasn't my domain. My office is my life where the things I hold precious reside—like my violin and business notes.

Arrow, on the other hand, stashed away so many goodies inside this bedroom—his domain. Like these ropes, for instance. Sure, he used them on me when he drugged me, tied me to the chair, and fucked my wife in front of me as punishment. I knew they were somewhere special. Imagine my surprise when I opened his bedside table and found a plethora of Arrow's toys for the taking. Ropes, dildos—which were everywhere— needles filled with his favorite drugs. Hell, he stashed more around in hidey holes. I think he has hoarding issues.

"Let the fun begin." I grin, getting to work and tying each of his limbs with the pieces of rope and hanging him from rings on the ceiling until his feet dangle above the drain and his wrists turn red. "I bet you can't even feel that yet, can you?" I ask, heaving a breath.

Who knew deadweight could be so taxing on the body? I've buried the dead before—a plethora of them in our back garden. But never by myself, with little help.

"No," he gurgles out, chin hanging near his chest, unable to raise it to look at me.

"Then we'll wait. In the meantime, would you like to talk about my father's plans, maybe?" I tap a foot, stepping back from his dangling form.

"Gabriel!" Aiden shouts with panic rising in his voice when he does it repeatedly.

I sigh. "I see. Still up for snitching, are we?" I shake my head, remove the ball gag from my pocket, and hold it up. Aiden can't see it, of course. He's too weak to move his neck, but I examine it. Remembering the feeling of it in my mouth that night Arrow tied me to the chair.

Who knew getting so kinky could be such a turn-on? It seems every day I'm discovering fun things about myself I never would have before. Voyeurism, for one. To say I enjoyed watching them fuck Journey while I was indisposed is an understatement. Add in the heightened effects of being tied down.

God damn.

It was filthy. Filthy fucking good.

When I get my hands on my wife, I'm going to fuck her into oblivion.

I stop my musings and lift Aiden's chin, letting his head fall back completely. The only part of his face he can move is his eyes. They widen comically large, like two saucers sitting on his face—poor guy. I don't think he's ever seen a gag before.

"Jericho," he slurs. "Don't. I'll tell you what I know..." he trails off, gagging when I shove the red ball between his teeth, leaving him unable to move his jaw.

"Hold still now, Aiden. This won't take very long," I quip, chuckling as I fasten the straps together and tighten them too tight. "Comfortable?"

He gurgles something I don't care about when I step out of the shower, leaving him suspended by the ropes. Normally, when an act like this occurs between lovers, it's against etiquette to leave your partner in such a position—tied to a chair with a gag. Don't leave them unattended. It's unsafe and could cause disastrous consequences. With Aiden, though? I don't give a rat's ass if he swallows his tongue, chokes to death, and shits his pants.

Please take him.

But not until after he tells me what I need to know.

"Be a good boy, Aiden, and stay right there. I'll be back after I check over my injuries. It was rude of you to put your hands on me. While I'm away, I'd love for you to think over what my father has said and what he has in store for me, this city, and where Arrow might be located." He gurgles more, still unable to move. "Perfect." I grin, shut the glass door behind me, and walk to the mirror.

Blood seeps from my nose and the cut on my lip. Little bastard. These will leave bruises for days to come. Memories, I guess. A survival scar I can look back on and remember the time I pulled one over on my father and his little monkey, Aiden.

With a sigh, I clean the blood from my face and hands. I wonder what Journey and Shepp are doing? If they're being harmed or taken care of? Is Shadow torturing them? Fuck. I squeeze my eyes shut, attempting to bat the thoughts away. Desperation claws at my chest once again, aching to get to them. To her. To Arrow. To Shepp.

They all need me right now. To save them from whatever fates loom over their heads like a guillotine. I can only hope I'm taking all the proper steps to get to them.

One stepping stone at a time, Jericho. First, extract information from Aiden. Find Arrow. Go to East Point for Olivia and Carter's help.

Then, save your family.

I suck in a breath, counting down from ten to ease the worry gnawing at my brain. Once I hit the number one in my brain, I open my eyes and stare at my reflection. He's battered and bruised up. The life in his eyes is dull and hazy.

But it's me.

I'm alive.

And Aiden won't be for long.

The scuffing of Aiden's tippy toes on the shower floor drags my attention back to my prisoner. Good, the sedative is slowly wearing off. There's no escape for him. It's almost comical he thought he would be drugged and left behind. He has vital information for me. I know he does.

"You awake in there, Aiden?" I question, tossing the clear shower door open. I grin when his eyes find mine. His head rests on his arm, extending toward the ceiling, and his fingers wiggle, aching to get free. A redness forms around his wrists, whitening his hands. "Ah, looks like the blood flow has stopped pumping to your fingers. A shame. So, shall we get started?" I question, tapping the gag. "You won't scream, will you?"

He shakes his head at me.

"Wonderful," I say, grinning as I undo the gag. I am not stupid enough to think Aiden will be quiet. Not that they will hear him, anyway.

"Gab…" He doesn't get the scream out fast enough before my fist flies into his teeth, knocking a few loose. Ah, I love the sound of teeth hitting the ground to get the blood flowing.

"I thought we had an agreement," I say, holding his chin between my fingers, forcing him to look at me. Those rage-filled eyes glare holes through my face. Too bad he's not going anywhere. "You were to stop calling him. The only reason you need to open your mouth is to tell me what hospital room Arrow is in."

There is only one hospital in Briar Cove. Unless my father shipped him far away, so I would not be able to get there in time. That is a possibility. But he does not control anyone outside of Briar Cove. My uncles, on the other hand? They police their territories and do not interfere elsewhere. So, calling them for aid is out of the question.

Aiden's harsh breaths reverberate through the room as he tries to move again. His feet kick out, barely missing my kneecap. I step back, casually watching him struggle more until tears wet his cheeks.

"You're a son of a bitch," he chokes out.

"I won't argue with you there." My head tilts, taking in the acceptance on his face. "So, what shall it be?" Without further prompting, I pull out a knife I conveniently found on Arrow's side of the room. Mentally, I send him a thank you for being so prepared. It's like he knew we'd be torturing someone in our shower one day.

"We can come to an agreement," he says, gritting his teeth as I run the knife over his cheek, soaking up his tears.

"We could," I say noncommittally.

I could agree to let him go if he gives me everything I need. I could let him walk back to his little girlfriend in the apartment they share with their poodle across town. I could do a lot of things. Give him a way out from under Gabriel. Money. Death. Anything I wanted. The thing about cockroaches like Aiden is they'll always come back. If I don't snuff the life from his eyes and make sure his snitch ass isn't breathing anymore, then he'll haunt me for the rest of my life.

And I can't have that.

So, false hope is the only thing I can offer him now.

"I'll tell you everything you want to know," Aiden begs when I push the knife in a little further, splitting his skin easily and creating a beautiful division of his flesh.

One deep cut down. More to go.

"Go on," I demand, tracing the freckles on his cheeks with the sharp edge of the knife, cutting into his flesh more as I go. Small streaks of blood pour from the wounds, painting him red. "Are you going to speak?"

"Please, Jericho!" he gasps, attempting to move back. His face turns left and right, trying to avoid the knife. But he fails.

"Open your mouth and spill your words before I spill more blood." An eerie calm takes hold of my insides. The sight of his blood seeping from the wounds, falling down his neck like a beautiful river of red, has excitement streaking through me.

This is what I live for. What I was made for. Blood. Destruction. Devastation. Bringing me closer to getting what I want.

My family. No matter the cost.

"Arrow's at the Briar Cove Hospital. Second floor. Room twenty-two," he gasps out, cringing when I pull the knife away. Relief spills onto his slack face as he watches me. "He's in a medically-induced coma. That's all I know. Your father didn't tell me much. Only that."

Only that? He knew where Journey and Shepp were. Maybe he's keeping more secrets than I thought.

I raise a brow. "That's not much of a reward for your loyalties, is it?" I question with a hum, continuing to watch his blood flow and slowly drip onto the shower floor. His life force is leaving him and dripping and dripping as I wait for more.

"No, it isn't," he agrees solemnly.

"And that's all you know, Aiden? Beyond what you've told me before?"

"That's all I know. Shadow has Journey and Shepp. I overheard your dad discussing the deal with Shadow to get your mom back here. Said she'd been locked up for years. Shadow wanted Journey for some reason." He watches me with hope in his eyes. Long gone is the cocky attitude of a guard ready to advance through the family ranks. Not that he would. My father would have disposed of him as he saw fit whenever Aiden completed his task here.

"Now, why would Shadow—the mysterious villain never showing his face—want my wife and Shepp? And to make such a deal with Gabriel?" I eye Aiden expectantly, hoping he has all the answers I seek.

It is an odd confession, something I have been unable to wrap my head around. And if my father made such a deal. Did he not see the very man who was behind the mask? Why not eradicate him and end the turf war that has been happening and building for three years?

Aiden swallows hard, eyeing me as I lift the blood-stained knife in the air. My gaze wanders over it, filling me with glee as more blood drips from the edges.

"I... I heard Gabriel mention something about Journey owing Shadow, but he did not elaborate."

"So, in theory, he must know who Shadow is." I raise a

brow. "Any guesses?" I'm more than curious to come face to face with the being that's lived in the shadows of our town, infiltrating every inch of the city with his drugs and killings.

"No," Aiden murmurs. "I don't have a clue. I don't think your dad does either. I get the impression that it was not a direct meeting. He mentioned a speaker in a room filled with guards in masks." He swallows hard again, wincing when I put the knife at his throat.

"You've been a good sport, Aiden," I hum.

But now it's time for him to die.

Before he can open his mouth and scream for help, I cut through his windpipe. Blood pours from the large slash in his throat as he gurgles and tries to speak more words. I got what I needed from him.

Now, may he rest in Hell, where all the other dirty traitors go in the afterlife. But first, I'll leave my father a note he won't be able to burn after reading.

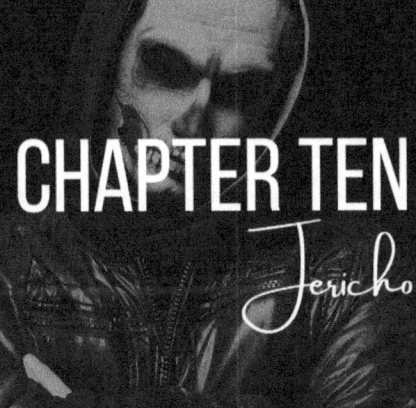

CHAPTER TEN

Jericho

THAT FAMILIAR ITCH CRAWLS UNDER MY SKIN. MY FINGERS twitch. Aiden's lifeless body now hangs inside my shower. His head back and throat open. Blood seeping everywhere. It splatters the walls. My clothes. My face and hands.

With all the help Aiden's given me, I know what I'm up against. Slightly. My father is a madman. Something I was aware of before tonight. He's made a deal with the fucking devil. His enemy and taken people he'll soon live to regret as soon as I've raised my army.

That familiar ache, tugging at my chest comes back full force. Get to Journey. Get to Arrow and Shepp. Find them. Save them.

If I have to, I'll swim fifty miles through the damn ocean just to get a glimpse of her. Touch her. Fucking breathe her in.

My need is growing higher and higher.

But I have to be reasonable. Swimming that far would be a death sentence on my own. Besides, I need backup so I can obliterate anyone in my way.

Next stop is Arrow's hospital room. At least Aiden had the sense to reveal what floor and room Arrow was being held in.

My eyes gaze over the words etched into Aiden's abdomen. *Your move.* A short and sweet message for my father when he discovers his golden goose has flown the coop.

Now, to actually fly.

My steps are slow and methodical as I go to the bathroom mirror. My eyes roam over the blood splatters on my face, clothes, and hands.

My eyes darken. My beast completely takes over when I smash my fist into the fucking mirror and revel in the pain. I huff. My breaths come in heavy pants. I squeeze my eyes shut. I only have a few hours to sneak through the guarded halls, get to the garage, start my car, and get the fuck out of here for good.

No one matters except Arrow, Shepp, and Journey.

I fucking got this.

After washing the blood off my skin and scrubbing myself down in the separate bathtub, I calm myself as the red stains the water. Erasing the life of Aiden and his traitorous ways. Cross me once, and it's the last thing you do. Then, I get dressed in Aiden's security outfit, attempting to disguise myself from my usual clothing. If they think I'm part of the guards, they won't even look twice when I walk through the halls.

I sigh when the pants do not button, and the black shirt clings to my biceps, nearly ripping with every move I make. Looking back at Aiden, I spit on the ground. What a wannabe, playing make-believe with the family.

"It'll do," I grumble, running a hand down my face.

Anticipation swarms through my veins. I can't make any mistakes when I sneak out of here. This has to go without a hitch, or I'm fucking screwed.

I grit my teeth. Stop the whining and get this shit done.

Your family is depending on you.

And not the asshole downstairs playing marriage with my mother.

Journey. Shepp. Arrow.

They're the only family I need.

I grab my phone stashed in my closet, shoving it into my

pocket. I also collect the multitude of small weapons Arrow has hidden around the room. Taped to the bottom of night-stands, under the mattress, and even in the bathroom cabinets. Anywhere, really. Who knew my psycho brother had prepared us for this moment so well? Not me. I'll have to thank him later, a million times over.

With one last look around the room, I grab a small black bag and shove extra clothes and my phone charger. I'm sure once I leave the estate, all my funds and everything else will be cut off. Well, what my father knows about, anyway.

I still have my resources.

I place my ear against the wood of my bedroom door, listening. Silence greets me. Nothing but the house creaking from the light winds outside. I blow out a breath, dispersing the tension from my body.

This is my moment. My escape. The one opportunity I have to run from the destiny my father has thrust upon me.

It's time to do what I should have done all along.

Walk the fuck away.

Screw the consequences.

I square my shoulders, unlock the door, and slowly open it. I peek out, eyeing the empty hallway. My one advantage to this situation is I've lived here for years. Every squeak and creak has been memorized in my mind.

I walk on silent feet toward the steps. My breaths slow when I peek downstairs, noting the silence.

Even the shadows stand still as I move through them.

Then I hear him. A deep, dry cough echoes through the darkened foyer, echoing off the tall ceilings. I flatten my back against the wall, slowly moving along it while focusing on the brightly lit kitchen.

My lips curl. My fingers work toward the weapons stored in my pocket in a sheath. If he comes any closer, I'll slit his throat, ending his existence for good.

I should.

I wish I could see his face when he finds Aiden carved to pieces in my shower. It's my war cry, after all. The bell ringing in the new enemy. It's my fucking vengeance for controlling my life. I want him to spiral into the abyss.

Like he's made me do so many times before.

Gabriel Viotto will be taken down. In blood. With weapons. Torture. You name it, he'll meet the end of it. It'll be slow and methodical—what he deserves.

Another horrible-sounding cough comes from the kitchen again. Water pours. And then, the coughing stops, followed by heavy breaths. I continue to watch for his presence until I get around the corner to the attached garage. A wall hides my presence, giving me ample time to spy. Once I'm in the garage, my car is my getaway. For now, at least. I have plans on how to get away without detection.

"I want the goddamn money!" he hoarsely shouts. The sound of his fist slamming into the countertop fills the air. "That twenty million dollars is mine. If you can't get it done, then I'll find someone else who can! It shouldn't be that fucking difficult."

Money, huh? I smirk. Of course, that's what this is all about. The money Journey's mom promised him when she sold Journey for marriage and torture. Her father, who had never been in her life, left her a twenty-million-dollar inheritance.

I wonder how Journey's mother, Sable, is doing in her treatment center. I have not called to see how sober living is treating her lately. The last call I made, she was desperate to talk to Journey. I am sure to get her wrongdoings off her guilty conscience.

"You gotta let me speak to her. It is important. I want to tell her how sorry I am." There's urgency in her tone, but something else as well. Whatever it is, she can wait. Like she made Journey wait for food and comfort while living under her roof.

Fuck Sable.

"You'll talk to her when I allow you to." There is no getting

around my rules. Sable will learn that soon enough. After all the torture she put Journey through, she does not deserve a second of her daughter's attention. "Goodbye, Sable."

"No! Wait, it is..." Click. I do not have time for her.

My father clears his throat, bringing me out of the memory. How odd. The great Gabriel never caves to his illnesses or weakness, which sounds ridiculous even to my ears. How can a man never bow to the flu or a cold? He always has. Either powering through it or meticulously taking his Vitamin C and other health concoctions my mother invented years before. He's always kept her recipes around; despite her absence, he's lived by them.

He says more meaningless words into the phone and saunters through the kitchen. Determination squares his shoulders as his voice carries through the phone. He wants the money and won't stop demanding it until it's in his pockets.

Boy, does he have another thing coming to him.

"Here, darling," my mother softly says with an edge.

I peek around the corner, watching her hand him a glass filled with an orange substance. I can practically smell it from here. Citrusy and fizzy. Tickling my nose. Like the same drink she gave me when I was a child. I shiver, squeezing my eyes shut as the memory assaults me. An occurrence that hasn't happened in years.

"Here, my Jericho. Drink up. This will help give your body all the extra vitamins and get you all better." She pets my dark locks when I sip, wrinkling my nose.

"Mommy," I groan through a hoarse rasp. My throat aches, and the cough comes back with a vengeance.

"I know, love. It tastes yucky. But you must drink it all. It's the only way you'll feel like Superman tomorrow." She smiles down at me affectionately, gently patting my head. "I'll take you to the zoo."

"Yours?" I perk up.

"Indeed. They're all so eager to meet you. I've told them about my boy Jericho as they've settled in."

I grin, chugging the weird-tasting orange drink, and hand the glass back.

"Now, baby. It's time for you to close your eyes and get your rest. Tomorrow, we have big plans."

My heart aches at the memory that's been locked in my mind for years. If I hadn't seen the drink clutched in my father's grip, I never would have recalled it. The moment my mother's presence left this mansion all those years ago, she was wiped from my brain. Gabriel made sure of that. Dark closets. Harsh words and even harsher punishments. He didn't spare me. I may have only been five, but I knew I had to forget her existence to survive. Looking at her now brings all the ghosts to the forefront of my mind, torturing me with vivid memories of our time together.

My father takes the drink without question, guzzling it while listening to whoever is on the phone. I cock my head with interest.

Despite the distance. Despite the paranoia Gabriel suffers from daily, he trusts her to fix him drinks. First the drink at dinner, which was suspicious at best. Now this. It's something he doesn't do very often. Maybe his mind is reminiscent of the past when she was his dutiful wife, doing anything to please him. Or perhaps he doesn't think she'd ever betray him.

Then it happens.

My breath fucking stalls. Her crystal blue eyes connect with mine from across the house, staring deep into my soul.

She blinks.

I blink.

I've been made. Any second now, she'll tap him on the shoulder, eager to show him he was right to lock me away.

My breath slowly pours from my nostrils. I don't react. Move. Fucking twitch a muscle. Hoping she merely sees an unmoving shadow against the wall. My eyes narrow when something strange happens.

Something odd.

She waves me on with a small smirk on her lips. Triumph glistens in her eyes.

I stand up straighter, eyeing her again. I cannot be seeing what I am seeing, right? Under normal circumstances, I would take that as my first sign to get the fuck out without a second thought or hesitation. But I am spellbound by her. My mother. The woman I did not know was alive or dead in a ditch.

I blow out a breath when she waves again with a stern look. I see it, then. Her meek mask falls off, and her face hardens. But why? My father's back remains to her when she waves one last time before I listen, mouthing *'Go.'*

So be it.

I sign my thanks, darting through the shadows to my car in the garage, praying the silent door will keep my exit hidden until the sun comes up and my father realizes I have gone missing.

Then all hell will break loose.

CHAPTER ELEVEN

Jericho

W<small>ELL</small>, <small>MY QUIET ESCAPE WAS FOILED BEFORE</small> I <small>EVEN HAD A</small> chance to press on the accelerator of my precious car. Turning my escape from the estate into an eventful affair.

More guards than necessary stood outside the mansion at every fucking corner with guns drawn, firing in my direction. Several shots hit my car, pinging through the aluminum and by my feet. I swear, if it were an inch over, my leg would be obliterated, and my father would get his wish. My death.

Fucking Gabriel. It is like they had a sixth sense I would take my leave.

Or someone who saw my escape tipped him off.

Maybe I should have gone with a bulletproof fucking car like Shepp suggested. Instead, I chose the fast, fun car. Bulletproof cars are too heavy for the fun I like to have. My car is the only splurge to bring me joy. Every other decision I've made has been out of necessity and duty. This baby, though? All for a good time.

"My goddamn car!" I shout, gunning the accelerator until my car makes it to the automatic gate, where it easily opens for me.

If my father hadn't noticed I was gone before. Well, now he knows. His threats from earlier ring in my mind.

"If you even attempt to escape, I have someone on standby at Arrow's bedside."

Arrow. That motherfucker seems unkillable. Indestructible, at best. He is always getting fucked up and smiles about it. If he bleeds, he laughs. Nothing can take him down. At least, that is what I am telling myself, rushing to be by his side.

My tires screech as I veer onto the main stretch of road, accelerating toward the hospital ten minutes away. The needle climbs higher and higher, matching the anxiety skyrocketing inside me. My family's safety is at the forefront of my damn mind.

Hospital. Arrow. Olivia.

In that goddamn order.

"Fuck, I'm sorry," I grunt at my car, driving as quickly and safely as I can. I am no use to them if I die in a fiery crash on the side of the road.

My heart pounds harder than before. Pummeling through my damn ribs the further I get away from the mansion. Breathe. Live. Fucking make it there safely.

Five minutes down. Five minutes to go to make it to Arrow's side. The clock is fucking ticking, and it is not on my damn side.

If Arrow, the indestructible, fucking dies. My sanity will slip like sand through my fingers, getting lost in the winds.

Ring.

My muscles lock up when his name flashes on the large screen of my car, displaying who's calling at such an ungodly hour.

Gabriel Viotto.

No surprise there. Undoubtedly, his guards were the first ones to run inside and snitch about my escape.

Against my better judgment, I answer the damn call.

"Gabriel," I reply smoothly, maneuvering around a slow-going car and slamming back into the right lane.

"Jericho." His stern, anger-filled voice rings throughout my car.

I would bow my head in submission if I were a weaker man. But I am not. He is. I have been stronger, bigger, and better than him for years.

It's time he realizes it.

"You left."

"Indeed," I hum nonchalantly, nearly running over the curb as I pull into the hospital parking lot. That's one way to stay discreet. Not. "Did you expect any less?"

I push the car into park, heaving a breath when everything slows down around me. I focus on my surroundings, noting the dark parking lot and lack of people. I'm far enough away that no one has noticed me.

"No." I raise a brow at his words. "But now I understand where your loyalties lie. You've signed your death warrant, son."

I roll my eyes as I reach and grab my bag from the passenger's seat.

"My loyalties lie with the family and their best interest," I retort, grabbing my phone from my pocket and bringing it to my ear after switching the call from my car to my phone and shutting off the engine. "Something you're failing."

"Failing?" he seethes.

I smirk. Poking the bear will become my favorite pastime. After I save Arrow from his coma, of course.

"You're forgetting who raised you. Who molded you into the man you are now," he growls again, slamming his fist down. I hear it thump against a wooden surface. Then he does it again, roaring through the phone with disdain.

My hackles immediately rise at the thump of his fist. The way the wood creaks and moans with every hit. I know exactly where he is.

He's in my domain—my office.

My sacred place of dwelling, filled with my books and a

secured safe with essential documents. But more importantly, my violin. I suck in a quiet breath, attempting to calm my nerves. That's my precious baby that soothes all the wrongs in the world, bringing me back from the brink of terrible things. When I need a second to breathe, my violin brings me that peace.

Now, she's in danger at the hands of my sadistic father.

The squeak of a hinge has my brows tightening. *He's opening the case.* My breath slows to a fucking halt. Blood echoes in my ears, pounding with the beat of my desperate heart.

They say to hit a man where it hurts the most. For the most part, that's his balls. But my father has an eye for detail. Take my girl and friends and put them in a terrible situation, so I'll follow his rules. I will follow, but escape will always be on my mind.

But this? This has my muscles frozen, locking in place and leaving me vulnerable when I should not be.

"You hear it, son?" he says in an even tone, breathing harshly through the phone. "I know how much this means to you. This chunk of wood you have dedicated your life to." Yeah, because he made me play it for entertainment purposes, forcing me to practice for hours on end until my fingers bled.

The tunes are my escape now. It's what takes me away when the world becomes too dim and my demons are nipping at my heels. It leaves me breathless. In the best way, of course. And now, he's gone and tainted my happiness.

Again.

My tongue locks between my teeth. Unable to speak or move when the first impact echoes through the phone.

It cries out, begging me to come and save it.

The second hard impact is deafening. Static fills my ears. Despair roars through my lifeless veins, lighting a fire of rage beneath my flesh. A sharp, explosive crack has my entire body shaking. With rage? Sadness? I am not quite sure.

The finale of his audio show explodes through the phone, landing the mark he so desperately wanted. The sound of splintering wood being pounded into my desk happens repeatedly. The strings whine, protesting the destruction. One by one, they snap from the force, giving one last high-pitched note of agony before falling silent and dying under his hand. The hollow body of my precious violin is no match for my father's brute strength and destructive behaviors.

He'll kill anything and anyone I love to get me to bend to his rules.

Even an inanimate object.

I sit silently, completely thrown off when he gets back on the phone, panting in my ear and awaiting my response.

He will get none.

"Are you done?" I say as bored as I can. Not giving him any hint of the distress sending my heart into a frenzy. Instead, I reroute the conversation. He will never get the satisfaction of knowing he's hit me where it hurts. Again. "I'm not forgetting who raised me, Father," I say, quietly climbing from my vehicle and gently closing the door behind me.

Forget about it. Don't think about what brought you joy. There are more important people to focus on. So, that's what I do. He destroyed my one-of-a-kind violin. So be it. I will buy another. Something better. More beautiful.

My eyes move through the surroundings again, taking in the empty parking lot with a few cars scattered in spots here and there. But it's lifeless without a person in sight, seeming deader than what I expected.

Suspicious.

So, if my father expected me to be here, he probably would have security stationed randomly throughout the property, ready to attack.

He's got deep pockets, but mine are deeper.

I move through the shadows with my father's frantic breathing in my ear. He should take up cardio to soothe that wheeze in his voice. Or maybe he's getting sick like I witnessed earlier and it's bringing him down.

"Your efforts were not enough. You're too late to save Arrow. You think I'd keep him alive?" He snarls rabidly into the phone. So much so I can practically feel the spittle on my face.

It's a threat. That's all. My father wants me to believe his words when I haven't believed him for years. Every word he spews is garbage wrapped in more fucking manipulations.

I'm done.

"And kill one of your greatest assets?" I question coolly, eyeing the outside of the hospital, searching for my point of entry.

I spy two men attempting to appear discreet, standing near the emergency room entrance. They linger on the outside, reading newspapers.

How discreet and not suspicious of them. Considering their guns bulge in their pants. Their beady eyes take in the surroundings. Obviously, my father gave his guards the heads up that I was on my way.

"Greatest assets?" my father chuckles at me. "You're all disposable. Everyone is. You've gotten me things I wanted. Maybe I have no use for you now." Liar, liar. Pants on fire.

"Yeah? And what about the wedding, then? Weren't you going to keep me locked tight so you could fulfill an alliance?"

Fuck. I roam the shadows, checking every door around the perimeter, and come up empty. Every door has guards with guns. I'm not equipped to get past them without causing a scene.

My knives will get me nowhere with guns.

My father chuckles. "You think you know what I'm capable of and what my intentions are? But you don't know, son. I'm a million steps ahead of you. Always. You may be the son who rebelled, but I have another one in my back pocket."

"You what?" I freeze.

"You truly think you're the only Viotto child I've kept alive?" He's got to be fucking kidding me, right?

"Keeping me alive is a severe understatement when you were barely around growing up."

Finally, I spot a first-story window that slides open—an answer to my unspoken prayers and no guards in sight. Thankfully, someone forgot to lock it. I kick the screen into the darkened room and carefully crawl through, landing in a small administrative office.

"My plans will move forward, with or without you."

Click.

My nose wrinkles when I pull my phone back and check the screen. Of course, Gabriel got the last damn word. No matter.

Arrow is my number one priority right now. The faster I get to him now that Gabriel isn't preoccupied, the better off we will be.

Because I cannot lose my best friend.

Using my phone as a flashlight, I make my way through the small office and find the door. Thankfully, there's a deadbolt on my side, and I unlock it with a soft click. Once the door opens a crack, I peek down the empty halls.

Administrative Wing.

Perfect. It is common knowledge that no one works these floors at night, except the janitors. And tonight, it seems completely desolate. Silent. With no humans around.

Unfortunately, the cameras in the corners of the halls will catch my every move, following my every step. If I had more time, I would have studied their blind spots to circumvent them seeing me. Fuck. But it's a move I have to make. A mistake that needs to happen.

Arrow needs me to stop whatever my father is up to. And I need my best friend alive and well.

I make a quick exit and follow the hall with my head down,

eyeing the signs guiding me toward the stairwell. Every step I take toward the second floor has my teeth on edge. There's no doubt there will be more guards outside Arrow's room. My father has everyone in his arsenal out to correct my escape. With another heir, whoever that may be, in my father's back pocket, they'll shoot me on sight. What use am I now if he can't force me to marry Chloe?

But also, who is this mysterious man that's his heir? Or is he bluffing?

My heart pounds when I slowly open the door and peek out onto the second floor, eyeing every nook and cranny for my father's guards. I'm not sure what side Arrow will be on, but I'm guessing not this side. The halls are empty. No guards are present.

Tiptoeing through the hospital with a knife in my hands was not on my to-do list for today. But here I am, listening to every beep, whisper, and footstep with suspicion.

I slip into a room, hiding in the doorway's shadows as a frantic nurse rushes past. With a gulp, I palm my knife, regaining control. I was bred for this and brought up with the concept of taking people's lives without remorse and hiding without anxiety. I am my father's best weapon. Only, I don't think he realizes what he's created over the years.

Once the coast is clear, I follow the numbers until I'm near Arrow's.

My brows furrow when no one stands outside, guarding his room. That's unusual. Not Gabriel's style. Unless.... A drumbeat erupts beneath my ribs, echoing in my ears as the realization dawns on me. They are inside. With Arrow. Snuffing the life out of his body and leaving him for me to discover.

My grip tightens on the knife again, ready to strike if necessary. If they are in there following the orders my father put in place, then I'll kill them.

Images of the men hovering above Arrow's lifeless body run through my mind. My skin tightens and tingles. My hair stands on end when I make my silent steps forward, standing outside his darkened room.

Slowly, I enter with my heart in my throat, eyeing the semi-empty room.

Despite wanting to rage and fucking throw things, I keep my composure. Arrow. My best friend, since we were kids, lies on the hospital bed with his eyes shut.

Pale. Lifeless.

So unlike Arrow.

All I can picture is the end of my friend's life.

Then there is her. None the wiser of my presence.

One nurse, standing with a needle in one hand and his IV bag in her other. Her hand shakes as she gently squeezes whatever is into the syringe into his line.

"Remove the needle," I bark, raising the knife. "Or bleed." I won't hesitate to end her fucking life for threatening Arrow's. We normally do not harm women or children. But this? This is necessary for his safety.

She yelps, dropping everything in her hands. Stepping back, she shakes her head repeatedly.

"Stop!"

I march toward her, cornering her against the wall. A red mist tinges my vision at the prospect of what she is about to do.

"Will he live?" I growl, holding the knife against her throat.

One slice is all it would take to end her before she kills my friend.

She shakes in my grasp. "Yes," she quivers out. "I was…I-I was waking him up." Her lower lip trembles under my glare, and tears shine in her eyes.

"Waking him up?" I ask coolly, keeping my weapon where it is.

"Y-yes," she whispers again.

"On whose orders?"

"M-my own," she says as tears stream down her cheeks.

"And why would you do that? You know who he is?" My eyes drift to her name badge.

Lori R.N.

Something odd sparks in the back of my mind. A familiarity hitting me hard. I have seen her before.

"I-I checked his charts. Someone purposely put him into a coma," she trails off when I slowly lift the knife. She gestures to an iPad beside his bed, and I let her get it. "S-see? Right here. It is in his orders. But no other injuries called for this concoction of meds."

"And you decided this all on your own?"

"Mr. Viotto," she murmurs, swallowing hard. "Arrow saved me not too long ago. You all did."

I tilt my head. "Lori…"

"I came to you not too long ago, begging for a loan. My husband was a drunk. Abusive to my kids and me. I came to you for safety. You gave me a home, money, and a car. I was able to protect my kids, get back into nursing, and form a new life. Without your help, I never would have achieved this. I owe you."

I stare at her. Every word she says pierced through my armor, and my muscles relax a little. Considering the circumstances, I will not fully let go until Arrow is awake and we are at Olivia's.

"Lori Heins."

"Yes," she whispers.

I take her in. She is in much better condition than the last time I saw her. More meat on her bones. Fewer bruises. She looks healthy after leaving her husband behind. Of course, after that visit Arrow managed to find the time to stop by Mr. Hein's home and give him a message from the Viotto's.

Do not fuck with women.

"You say they purposely put him into a coma?" I raise a

brow. Aiden told me as much in his distressed state, but I'm eager to confirm my father's psychopathic plans.

"Y-yes," she stutters again, heaving a breath. "He was brought in yesterday after the tower collapsed. He was subdued after a small injury to his hands. The doctor on call pumped him full of these drugs to make him sleep. All because of your father. He was here, ordering them to do it." I wonder if that's the same treatment I got. Except my confinement was to my bed. Not here.

"No other injuries?" I question with curiosity, praying that he wasn't harmed in the fight.

"No. It seems he was fine. Other than the hurt shoulder and hands." She shakes her head.

"And you can wake him?"

"It might take up to twenty-four hours for the drug to kick in and rouse him," she says softly, staring down at him.

With irritation, I rub my temples. I don't have a day to wait around and wake him up. I need him with me. But I need to get to Olivia as quickly as I can. It's of utmost importance for Journey and Shepp's survival. The sooner I get them away from Shadow's Island. The better off they'll be. Who knows what they're up against there?

I'm torn in two. My family is spread too thin and far away. Journey and Shepp reside with Shadow. A mysterious ruler of his people, attacking us left and right to gain land through disputes. And Arrow. He's here. Right in front of me, and his life depends on me getting him to safety. He's vulnerable. Unable to take care of himself and fight, the guards are eager to kill him. I need to move him. Take him with me—anything to bring him to safety.

But I can't.

Arrow will be a giant flag on my shoulder, begging them to come and find us. Same with wheeling him out in a wheel-chair. I checked. Every entrance and exit has guards surrounding it, waiting for me to come out so they can open fire. I'll be dead. No use to Arrow that way. Or the others. There is no solution in which I can get him out of this hospital undetected. And sooner rather than later, they'll be in this room with guns at the ready, trying to take our lives.

So, what do I do? How do I fix this giant mess my father and Shadow created in their mixed plans of domination?

"Fuck," I grunt, thrusting my fist into the wall. My breaths come in heavy pants, and I lean my forehead against the cool tile, calming myself down.

"Mr. Viotto," she whispers, startling me out of my funk. She gently takes my hand, her bony fingers examining the blood coating my knuckles.

"You say it'll take a day?" I ask in a deep voice, yanking my hand back.

I ignore the searing pain and opt to pretend it doesn't exist. What is pain, anyway? Nothing but a weakness that drags me down when I need to be strong for them.

She nods shakily, observing my reaction.

"He can't stay here. But I can't fucking carry him out of here," I growl. "They'll kill him if they find him. I'm not even supposed to be here."

Everything is spinning out of control and slipping between my fingers and blowing in the damn wind. I don't have the extra time.

"I can hide him."

Facing her, I note the determination in her sparkling eyes. "Hide him?"

She nods, marching toward her iPad. She clicks a few times and nods.

"The West Wing is no longer in use because of renovations. I can wheel him over there until he wakes up. I can watch him until then."

I tilt my head. "You'd go out of your way to ensure he lives? If my father gets wind of this..." I raise a brow at the implications.

He'll murder her, for sure. Lori won't have a family to go back to because they'll be dead. Gabriel will take no mercy on her for aiding our escape.

She swallows hard but nods. "I understand."

"Why?" I ask, stepping forward.

It's not every day someone puts their life on the line for us, especially a civilian who isn't under our control. She has no allegiance to us. Sure, we helped her get her life together, but it was not a charity. It was a loan.

"I already told you. You saved me. If I weren't back in this hospital, then I would be dead, anyway." She wipes the tears from her eyes.

Suspicious. But I have no other choice. I must leave him here.

But the thought of leaving him alone has my stomach twisting in knots. Maybe I could toss his ass through the window I came through and get him back to my car.

No. It would not work.

My father probably dispatched his guards to find me here and take me out, along with Arrow. Discretion is my best bet. But fuck. Leaving him here was never a part of the damn equation.

"We will wipe your debt clean. If you are successful in keeping my brother safe from the guards that will come to kill us, then we'll owe you. More than just erasing your debt, Lori." I raise a brow, hoping she understands where I'm going with this.

Lori will never have to worry about money again. She's living proof of why we help the citizens of this town with their problems. We're needed. She was helpless.

Her eyes widen. "But you... you gave me..."

"Thirty thousand. I'm aware. You got your new life and away from that man. Now, if you do this, the Viotto family will wipe away what is owed to us. If he survives," I say with ease, trying to keep my teeth from clenching at the prospect of my brother succumbing to my father's nefarious plans. "You understand? You'll be owed a great debt from the Family. Arrow must wake up and leave this hospital intact, though."

"Yes," she says shakily. "I will do everything I can. But you have to help me move him. I will administer the drug. But we need to wheel his bed to the other side of the hospital."

"Consider it done," I say with a nod. "Now, begin the wake-up process."

Lori gets to work as quickly as possible, injecting Arrow with the wake-up serum straight into his IV.

I watch closely, noting the shake of her hands and the paleness of her face.

"Where are the guards?" It is something that has bothered me since the moment I stepped foot into this room.

If my father was so adamant about killing Arrow to keep my obedience, then he had to have men standing outside waiting for me to arrive.

Unless he was bluffing.

But that's not Gabriel Viotto's modus operandi. He never bluffs. Always acts. It is how he has gotten himself to the top for so many years. Never caring about who he has hurt to get what he wants. Including the boy he essentially adopted from the priest so he could hone his psychopathic tendencies and use them for his gain.

Lori's eyes flick to me. "They usually stand outside, watching like statues. They were waiting for you." Were. So, they have gone somewhere.

"But there was no one there," I state it as fact as my shoulders tighten. "Did you, by chance, distract them?"

She discreetly nods.

"How?"

"I may have mentioned seeing someone suspicious. Like you in the ER waiting room. They wouldn't let me in here, so I had to get creative. I knew if Arrow was here and in this state, then he needed help."

"So, all along, you were going to wake him up without being told to?"

"I was trying to show my appreciation," she says with a small voice, stepping back from Arrow's IV. "Okay, it's in."

My muscles stiffen when squeaking footsteps come from outside the door. Murmured voices float through the air, sounding disgruntled and rage-filled. It's either the door guards returning to their post, or the rest of the goons outside have decided to join the party in their search for me.

"They're back," Lori squeaks, bringing her hands over her heart. She pales more, staring wide-eyed at me like I have all the answers. Something I'm not confident I have right now.

I heave a calming breath, counting inside my mind. All I need is a simple solution to save Arrow, Lori, and myself. My fingers clench at my sides the moment the beast inside my chest awakens, clawing to break free, sensing the bloodshed about to happen.

I shake out the tension in my body, taking a centering breath. Everything falls away from me.

"In order to get him to safety, I'm going to have to get rid of the guards standing outside." I raise a brow when she shakily nods at me.

I am accustomed to violence and blood. It lives in my soul. Just like my father wanted. Only I am not as cold and calculating as he would have liked. Calculated? Yes. Cold? Without Journey, yes.

But Lori?

She is shaking like a leaf, eyeing me with a wariness that has my teeth aching from clenching them so hard.

"Wh-what do…"

I put a hand up to stop her trembling voice from escalating. In a matter of seconds, they will be here, sweeping the room. They abandoned their post, finding nothing. So, they will be extra pissed that they defied orders and did not let the other guards stationed outside take care of the sighting.

"You're officially protected by me at this moment. And that's why I need you to climb into that cabinet and shut the door. Cover your ears. What you hear and see won't be pretty."

Her entire body locks up when the door handle jiggles slightly, and the voices of what sounds like two guards get closer than ever.

Marching forward, I grab Lori by the shoulders and gently help her into the cabinet.

"It's of utmost importance that you do not make a peep. If they hear you because I'm guessing you aren't assigned to his care, they'll dispose of you. Cover your ears tight."

She nods in compliance, slowly covering her ears with her hands. Her entire body contorts in the small cabinet, but it'll do. It has to.

A coldness hits me out of nowhere as all my emotions flee for their lives as my beast slams down on me. My humanity barely clings on, whimpering as I give into the darkness clouding my eyes.

I shut the cabinet softly and lean against it, staring at the door. My body rests in the shadows of the dim room. For the briefest second, I look Arrow's unmoving body over with a sharp eye. He's deadly still and breathing normally. How I thought this would go off without a hitch has me mentally chastising myself. I knew anything Gabriel put into place would be almost impossible to defeat. Almost being the keyword.

I palm two knives hidden away in my security get-up and slowly walk toward the door, aiming to hide behind it.

"We tell no one that fucking happened." Ah, I recognize that voice. Gerard. My father's number one bodyguard, who always stands by his side at public events. Conveniently, he wasn't at the initiation ball. How fucking curious that is.

"Boss will fucking kill us," another voice hisses.

No. Your boss won't murder you. I will.

"Not a word that we left our post. We were here the whole time. I'll take care of the security tapes."

I smirk. It's funny how one determined nurse had the power to get them to move away from their assigned post. Gabriel will not be too happy when he hears about this.

"I swear I saw him on the surveillance video," the other voice I do not recognize says with rage. "He was here, sneaking around."

"Boss says to pull the plug," Gerard rumbles with a sigh. "Let's check the room. We need to get this done ASAP."

Good luck with that.

I ready myself as the door opens and closes, permitting them entry. I do not bother with pleasantries. *Hi. How unfortunate to see you again. Now, goodbye.*

Instead, I take Arrow's approach. Stab first and ask questions later.

My knives plunge through their backs and into their chests, hopefully nicking their hearts all in one go. But I am not that lucky. The unknown guard falls face first, his body jerking violently until he stops altogether.

Pathetic.

One down. One to go.

Gerard pivots on his heel with a familiar scowl. But then he wobbles, staring down at the wound on his chest. His meaty fingers swipe at the blood staining his shirt. Then, like a good boy, he drops to his knees before me.

"No one will touch Arrow."

And I mean that. He may be able to protect himself. But I'm his goddamn keeper. Today. Tomorrow. For fucking ever.

"Jericho," Gerard bubbles out, blood seeping between his lips, staining them red. It appears I hit his lung instead of his heart—such a shame. An inch over, I'd have hit my mark.

"Any last words? I ask, quickly disarming him and pocketing the two handguns that were tucked in his pants. A fun treat I'll use later. I palm the bloodied knife again, waiting for his words.

"You'll never win," he rasps out, laughing maniacally. "Ever. There are so many plans in place. You cannot even fathom."

I click my tongue at him, noting his lack of fight. They are supposed to protect their jobs at all costs. But some men think dying on duty is the ultimate honor. That Gabriel will walk their bodies through the streets in a hero's parade for protecting their asset.

Gag me.

"You're not going to beg for your life? No tears or pleas?" I raise a brow when I rest the knife against his throat.

He swallows a lump. "I never beg. You'll never see my tears. Boss taught me better than that," he hisses with venom.

"Indeed. He taught us all better than that, didn't he? Even his five-year-old son, who he flung into a closet." I shake my head at the memory of my cries and pleas as my father walked away, leaving this asshole in his place.

Gerard smirks, obviously remembering where my mind went. "Poor little Jericho locked in a closet crying for his mommy." My eyes glaze over with red, tinting my vision.

"You enjoyed the show, though. Didn't you?" I dig the edge of the knife into his neck. "The sufferings of a little boy who lost his mother."

Gerard grins at that, exposing his yellowing teeth tinged with blood and putrid breath. "Best entertainment I had in years." He spits blood on the ground lazily, unable to move well with my knife threatening his life.

"I'm curious," I say, leaning in closer. He will die whether or not I slit his throat. The wound on his chest guarantees that, not to mention the blood coating his trachea.

He smirks. "Curious? What could you be curious about? Hmm?" He lifts his chin further, practically begging me to end his suffering.

All in due time, Gerard.

"About my brother," I say, tilting my head. I am going on an assumption, of course. The Viotto Crime Family does not put women in charge. They are second-class citizens within the organization. Sexist? Yes. Women can be powerful leaders. Like my fucking queen. She will rule this land.

If we live to see it.

So, in theory. I have a mysterious brother out there. Someone my father has kept hidden from the masses—a secret weapon. But I have my doubts. Gabriel is not known for his truths. Only lies.

Gerald's eyes widen slightly, muscles stiffening. "What fucking brother? You are the only Viotto fuck from Daddy Dearest," he snarls.

I smirk. "And thank fuck for that," I say, digging the teeth of my knife deeper into his flesh until more blood seeps out. "So, no other heirs to my throne, hmm?

"Fuck no," Gerard wheezes out, gagging loudly and sending more blood spewing from his lips and onto my clothes, distracting me from his movements. In that split second, I miss the knife he grabs from somewhere on his person and thrusts through the calf of my left leg.

Pain fucking explodes through my calf, and I bite my tongue when he slightly twists it in his weakening state. It burns, sending fire through my nerves. It's worse than anything I have experienced in a long time. But you know what they say about pain? It proves you are still alive. Feeling.

"You motherfucker," I grit out, thrusting my knife through his throat and out through his neck.

Life drains from his eyes and, much to my disappointment, he falls to the side without divulging information. Such a pity.

My teeth grit to dust when I stupidly kick his body and regret it immediately. I stumble back, gasping for breath. A sharp pain radiates from the fresh knife wound, seeping small amounts of blood through my fucking pants.

Fuck. God damn it. That hurts. Burns. Fucking throbs beneath my flesh like a spider crawling beneath and biting every nerve ending along the way. Standing straight, I close my eyes. That is two guards down and probably a million to go. I cannot linger here any longer. Or keep Arrow unarmed. I need to get him settled then and get on my way to East Point. Until then, I must survive this fucking stab wound and not bleed out.

Stiffly, I bend down, checking the two guards for a pulse. Dead. Worthless, motherfuckers. Good fucking riddance. Moving as quickly as I can on an injured leg, I drag the bodies of both guards into the bathroom and set them in the shower. Although whoever enters this room will see the blood on the floor, they will have to investigate further to find them. This leaves me with a smidge of guilt for whichever innocent person walks through those doors to check on Arrow and gets the surprise of their lives.

I quickly wash the blood from my skin with a heavy sigh. Once Arrow settles in his new room, I will change out of these blood-stained clothes and have Lori check over my wound.

After cleaning up, I head to the cabinet and open it slowly, pleasantly surprised that Lori listened to my instructions. She presses her hands against her ears and squeezes her eyes shut.

"Lori," I say gently, tapping her hand.

Her eyes pop open, and she jumps when she sees me looking down at her. Slowly, she removes her hands from her ears, staring wide-eyed at my bloody clothes.

"It's done. The guards stationed at this door will no longer be an issue. But I can't say the same about the others lingering on the property." I step back, giving her shaky body enough room to crawl out.

Her eyes dart around the hospital room, stopping on the large puddle of blood pooling on the floor. She swallows hard and shakes her head.

"Okay," she breathes. "Let's get him out of here."

Lori and I get to work, maneuvering his bed out the door and down the hallway. We take several turns, avoiding the other nurses and doctors. Finally, after sneaking past several people in the halls, we make our way into the abandoned part of the hospital.

Quiet descends on us the moment we push through the double doors. My only worry now is the cameras that followed our every move. Something I'll take care of with a quick text.

ME

Suppose I need someone to erase a hospital's security feed.

CARTER

... It's 3 A.M. And why the fuck would I help you?

He's always so pleasant to speak with and eager to be in my company. Or anyone's, really. The only person I've ever seen calm him down is his wife.

ME

Because you're my cousin's partner.

CARTER

Text her. Not me, asshole.

ME

Well, if my cousin was a computer genius, I would. But she can barely log into her emails...

I can practically feel his rage from here.

CARTER

What hospital? Timestamp? Do I even want the reason?

ME

Briar Cove Memorial. Erase the last twenty-four hours of events. Especially the second floor.

CARTER

You owe me.

ME

thumbs up emoji

CARTER

You fucking contact me at three in the morning for this shit and then give me the thumbs-up emoji?

I smirk. We're not on the best of terms. We only know each other through my cousin, Olivia. He disapproves of my business. And I raise a brow at his being a government agent. But there are a few things we've agreed on in the past.

He does something for me. I take out someone for him.

I put my phone into my pocket, watching Lori with a sharp stare.

"He should be safe here. No one will bother him." Lori gently sets up his IV bag above him and wipes her hands down her scrubs. "I'll keep an eye out. But I have to go back to my station. I wasn't even supposed to be in his room. I'm technically on break."

"Thank you for your assistance." I nod in her direction.

She offers me a soft smile. "I'll take care of Arrow. I promise. I—oh my God. You're bleeding!" Her face pales when she looks down at the floor.

Indeed. I am bleeding and apparently leaving a small trail in my wake. I eye the red in the darkness of the room, barely able to make out the small trail from the door to here. Great. The stab wound will be my damn downfall.

"Gerard stabbed me," I say, staring down at the blood soaking through.

My body slightly wavers. A cold prickling crawls up my spine as a sheen of sweat appears on my flesh. Well, then. I am a little worse off than I thought. Perhaps I should sit and let Lori tend to my wounds. There is no way I'd make it to Olivia's on half a tank of fucking blood.

"I can look at it. Give me just a second to grab some gloves, and I can patch you up as best I can," Lori whispers, giving me a reassuring smile before leaving the room. In seconds, she's back with gloves and a suturing kit. "Come here," she says, waving me over to a chair and pointing for me to sit. I follow her instructions, and I'm thankful I'm somewhere that can aid with my wound.

"Thank you, Lori," I say, leaning my head back with a sigh. A dull ache begins in the back of my skull as the stress of everything pushes down on me. Arrow's safe. For the time being. Shepp and Journey, on the other hand? In God's hands, I suppose.

Lori gets to work, gently raising my pant leg. Whatever she sees, she doesn't make a face. "It doesn't look too bad," Lori says, looking at me from the floor. "Is your leg functioning, okay?" she asks as she opens the sterile suturing kit and sets it up.

I nod. "Surprisingly, yes." Perhaps it's the adrenaline keeping me going. Or my own sheer will. Whatever it is, it needs to last me a few more hours until I can get properly checked out in East Point Bluff.

I grit my teeth a few times as she sews me up and then puts two large bandages over the wound.

"This was a quick sew-up job. Mr. Viotto. From what I could tell, it does not seem like you have any damage to the bones or ligaments. But I'd have a doctor check it out, just in case. You could have nerve damage..." she trails off when her iPad beeps. "Damn it," she mutters, clicking a few times. "I need to go back to my station." Her brows furrow as she collects the trash and throws it away in a nearby garbage can.

"No need to worry about me. I will have someone do an in-depth checkup at my next destination." I offer her a thankful nod for everything she is doing: helping Arrow, hiding him, and patching me up. She has gone beyond what any regular citizen would.

"I will check on him in an hour to ensure his vitals are fine. I promise I will get him out of here." Her chin raises when she looks me in the eye like a dutiful soldier pledging her life to the Viotto Family.

At least we have allies in the people we have helped.

"Thank you for your sacrifice, Lori. I deeply appreciate you helping me. We will be in contact later." I offer her a sharp nod.

Lori nods, heading out the door with more promises of helping him escape. Once the door closes, I sigh, staring at him. For such a Devil when his eyes are open, he sure sleeps like an angel.

Shaking my head, I remove my backpack and remove Aiden's too-small clothes. I hiss when my pants and socks come off, sticking to my flesh from the blood. I grunt, tossing them aside, and stare at the bandaged area free of blood. For now. I am sure she did the best she could, but I know I'll need something more. Pain meds would be mighty handy. But I am sure driving on them would only complicate things further. So, I push ahead with my quickly formed plan.

Once, I'm dressed in loose-fitting sweatpants and a T-shirt, disguising myself from my usual attire. I turn to Arrow and lean against the railing of his hospital bed.

"Things are well and truly fucked," I say to his sleeping form. "And my father is at the center of this fuckery. I am sure when you wake, you will leave a trail of bodies behind." I smirk at the imagery.

Once Arrow wakes, he will be on a damn warpath to get Journey back. He only has three things he genuinely cares about. Torture. The Devils. Journey. And she is always number one.

"I'm counting on you, Arrow," I murmur, pinching the bridge of my nose. "It's you and me until we get them back."

You and me against the fucking world we have to burn down to get our girl and best friend away from Shadow.

Fuck.

Urgency hits me as I look through the cabinets, finally coming across a notepad and a worn-down pencil. How lucky?

Arrow-

Time is not on our side. The milk is bad. You know the drill. Find me where the pines touch snow.

-J

"It's up to us." The world crashes down on my shoulders when I tuck the note into his hand. Hopefully, when he opens his eyes, he will understand the code.

Get to the cabin, our rendezvous point. I will meet you there. Then, we will get our girl and brother back.

I take one last look over my shoulder at him. One last look before I leave him behind in the hands of strangers.

Strangers I have to trust will take care of him while I'm gone.

CHAPTER TWELVE

Arrow

"SAY HELLO TO MY LITTLE FRIEND!"

At least, that's what I think I said. It was kind of a miscalculation on my part. No one ever explicitly said, "Arrow, don't fire the rocket launcher inside." If they had… Well, I probably wouldn't have listened, anyway.

It's Arrow's way or the highway.

It was my desperation. Yeah, I'll blame it on that. Desperation. An ache to get my Kitten in front of my eyes after she slipped backstage, and we were ambushed.

Was she safe? Did Shepp take her away like he said he would?

I knew taking the handcuffs off Journey was a huge mistake. We should have kept her glued to us at all times. Instead, we got caught on stage with our pants down. Not literally. Our shirts were open. Then, guns were to our heads with the intent on killing us.

Pfft. Bunch of amateurs, if you ask me. No. Seriously. They weren't prepared in the slightest. It's like someone trained them over a weekend and then set them free. Like a "pretend to be a killer seminar" put on by some stupid teachers.

Odd, ain't it?

Anywho.

Time to get this IV out of my arm. Oh, and find my phone.

Nothing says good morning like waking up alone in a dark hospital room. Fucking alone! Well, I found the helpful note Jericho left behind clutched in my fingers. Such a man of words. A poet, and he didn't know it.

And silly as hell.

If that oaf thinks I will meet him at the cabin we secured years ago as a rendezvous point if our world goes sideways, he's got another thing coming.

Because I have my ways.

I grunt when I rip the IV out of my flesh. My eyes fall on the blood trickling from my arm, and I smile. Ah, the satisfying sight of seeing red on my skin. It makes my dick throb, and excitement rushes through me. Down, boy. Save that for later when you're reunited with Journey's holes—all three of them.

I sit on the edge of the bed, swinging my legs. I haven't felt this rested and put together in… Well, ever. Sure, I sleep like the dead. But this? I felt like I took a week-long nap. Actually, I might have. Who knows how long I've been in dreamland.

Also, why the fuck I was.

The last thing I remember… My brows furrow. It was me, the boys, and our lady at the initiation ball. Everything went sideways when we were attacked. The entire family was in a fit. But I saved them with my rocket launcher.

Then…. well, there's nothing. Just a blank hole.

Weird.

Maybe I passed out? Is that why I'm here? I peer around the room and purse my lips. Odd that it's so damn empty here. No noises come from outside. I'm sure my Daddy Jer made sure I was safe and secure when he left me here. Bastard. I can't believe he just walked away without me. It could give a guy a complex. Or abandonment issues. Well, if I had any.

No matter. I can make my own way and…

"Oh! You're awake!" My head jerks up at the gasp coming

from the nurse standing in the doorway. She shakes off her shock and closes the door behind her, locking it.

When she turns to face me again, coming into the dim lights. Her identity hits me like a train. Memories of her sunken face and lifeless eyes as she waltzed into our club, begging us for a loan.

"I never forget a face," I say, snapping my fingers. "Lori." I grin, remembering the visit I paid to her husband.

"No, please don't chop off my hand! I need it to work."

Wahh. He was really attached to those things. Don't worry, I severed them without a problem. It'll help him not to hit his wife and kids. Or pick up another drink. I did the world a solid by getting rid of his hands and tossing them away. I even helped him not bleed out.

I'm an outstanding guy like that.

"Yes," she says, hurrying toward me. Her eyes widen when she looks at the discarded IV on the ground. "I can't believe you're awake. You were in a coma."

I tilt my head. "I was." A coma, huh? That's interesting. That explains a lot, too. I wonder how long it took them to dose me and knock me out. Or how many days I was gone. "I was in a coma?"

She nods, standing in front of me and checking me over. After she's satisfied, she checks her smartwatch.

"It's only been thirty minutes since I gave you the medication."

"And what exactly did you give me?" I raise a brow.

What Lori doesn't know is that I've been slowly dosing myself with poison over the years. Weird? Probably. But it's given me a hell of a tolerance toward any medication. Or poison. Just a tiny drop here and there, and my body fights it like a champ. Nothing can kill me or take me down. Or so I thought.

She swallows hard. "You were in a medically-induced

coma for almost two days. I woke you up with the proper medication."

She says it so casually. Well, that's a lie. There's a tiny tremble in her voice. And in her fingers. In fact, I think her entire body is shaking.

Poor Lori.

Am I that terrifying to her? She's not someone I want to fear me unless she's threatening my Kitten or brothers. Then, down with the bad nurse. My gut tells me she's a good egg who doesn't need to be cracked.

"Are you afraid of me?" I watch her as she rounds the bed and inspects the wound left by the IV.

"Not you," she says, giving me a tight smile.

"The family?" I inquire, pushing more.

I'm mainly curious why she's even here or checking me over. Also, I need to know why she's trembling like a little leaf.

Her eyes flick to my face, and she swallows hard. Oh. It's the family she fears. We do have quite the reputation to live up to. Murders. Heists. Gun runs. You name it, we've got our paws in it.

"Jericho made sure you were in a safe place. I helped him bring you here." She gives me a sharp nod, avoiding eye contact.

So. The heir. My bestie. My boner brother. Left me. In a damn coma. Alone. In a dark hospital room.

Ain't he a peach?

I'll show him my appreciation later when I track his ass down. All I need now is my phone.

"Did I happen to come in with clothes and my phone?"

My phone. I need it like I need air. It'll give me all the answers I'm seeking.

Her spine stiffens, and she nods. "I think so. I... I think they're in your old room. Shoot. I'll go get them for you!" I watch as she scurries out of the room, slamming the door behind her.

Interesting. Old room? So, this isn't where I was before. She did say Jer hid me away. What a good boy.

I take the time to climb to my feet. Fuck. I grunt, nearly falling over. The room spins. My knees give out, but I catch myself on the bed, huffing for breath.

Phew. That was close.

My toes wiggle against the cold floor as I gain strength and finally stand tall. My legs wobble slightly beneath me, but I regain my balance. While waiting for the nurse to return my belongings, I search through the drawers and cabinets. You never know what you'll find.

Weapons? Maybe. Anything can be a weapon if you have imagination. Take this tongue depressor I found in the back of a drawer, for instance. I could shove this through an eyeball and make a kabob.

Easy peasy.

Although, my knives would have been a much better gift from Jericho than a piece of paper with instructions. Wasn't he prepared? Actually, I don't know what the fuck is happening right now.

I lay the tongue depressor on the countertop with furrowed brows. Now that my brain is finally kicking back after its two-day nap, more holes are forming.

Why did he leave me a note and not stay to help? Why wasn't he prepared? That maniac is ready for everything. Secret weddings. Ambushes. You name it, he always has a plan up his sleeve.

But this? He came in half-cocked. I smirk to myself. Who am I kidding? The poor fella is always half-cocked compared to me. And he'll be even more so when I punch him in the nads for not taking me on his field trip.

I know, I know. Jer probably had good reasons. And I can

totally fight my way out of this hospital. Damn it. I hate it when nothing makes sense.

"Here are your belongings," Lori says urgently, barging in through the door. She's pale and trembling when she hands me a hospital bag filled with my suit.

Ugh.

The suit. Which suspiciously smells like fire.

Whatever. Maybe I'll steal some doctor's scrubs on my way out. I refuse to wear this stupid shit again. Not only is it my least favorite outfit, but it also stinks. It probably carries some bad juju or something, anyway. Not that I can't handle anything thrown my way, but I'd rather walk out of here without getting caught.

"There are guards everywhere, looking for you." Her eyes dart over her shoulder, and she shudders violently.

Poor thing. She's not meant for this depraved life. She'd probably have a heart attack if she knew how her husband was doing. Or what I did to him. And his friends.

My anger got the better of me that night. It's like tunnel vision gripping me by the shoulders and whispering for me to kill, kill, kill.

"Everywhere? So, blocking exists, I presume?" I shuffle the things in my bag, digging for my phone at the bottom. Luckily, it's there.

Unluckily, it's dead.

Next stop, find a charger. And from the tone of Jericho's note, there's no way I can go home. Having to meet at the cabin means our home base is compromised. My guess? Gabriel fucking Viotto. I can't wait to make a necklace out of his ears.

"Y-yes," she shudders. "I think so."

"Do you happen to know what happened in Briar Cove that brought me here?" I eye the hospital room, thankful it's semi-dark, as I slip my boxer briefs on while wearing the god-awful hospital gown.

Although there's a pleasant breeze on my cheeks, I need to get dressed to figure out what's going on.

"Oh. Um. Viotto Tower was damaged pretty badly. I-they said there was a party or something and that there was an attack. It... um... collapsed."

My spine stiffens. Well, shit.

"Collapsed? Completely?" That's not good at all. That would mean Gabriel moved his operations somewhere. Probably the damn mansion. Shit. No wonder Jericho wanted to tuck tail and go to the cabin.

"No. Not entirely. It crumbled on one side into the street, and it's unusable."

Huh. Interesting. Gabe can't use his precious tower. I wonder if it's my fault. Ah. A sense of pride fills my chest when I discard the hospital gown, letting it drop to the floor.

"I... um... shoot!" she hisses, looking down at the iPad in her hand. "I need to get back to work. You'll be okay?"

Pfft. Define okay. I'm never okay. But in this instance, I have a feeling I'm about to rock some people's worlds. If Gabe has multiple guards around the hospital, I'm in for a treat. Although going on a murder spree throughout a hospital is probably frowned upon.

Party poopers.

"Thanks for all the help," I say with sincerity. Because she could have left me to rot but didn't. She aided Jericho and me.

"Anything for you guys. Like I told Mr. Viotto. You helped me at my lowest, and I can't repay you enough." She nods once before slipping out the door and not allowing me to retort.

We'll have to think of a way to stop her repayments and let her off the hook.

First things first, though. I need to get out of here without being detected.

CHAPTER THIRTEEN

Arrow

WHENEVER I FIND JOURNEY AGAIN, WE'RE GOING TO PLAY A rousing game of doctor and patient. The medicine? My dick and cum. Then, she'll be all better. No more ailments for my girl.

I grin, looking at myself in the mirror. Green scrubs cling to my body. Which still feels weak after being under. My legs wobble with every step. Hence, my new disguise. I'll cover my face and hair with this fun get-up, steal a car, find a charger, and then track down Jericho. He's earned a sharp punch to the jaw.

Although, I think I could still take down a grown-ass man if need be. I'll poke him with a tongue depressor. Oh! And the scalpel I found in the closet filled with doctor's things. All I need now is my white coat, and my outfit will be complete.

Doctor role-play, here I come.

My eyes roam over the small closet I found in the deserted wing Lori left me in. There's absolutely no sign of life here. All the hallways are dark and gloomy. Perfect for washing away wanted men.

Show time.

I step out of the closet with my scrubs, face mask, and surgical hat to hide my hair. I look quite official if I do say so myself.

Humming softly, I walked toward the stairs. Thankfully, I'm on the second floor. I descend the stairs with my head held high. Fake it till you make it, I always say. I've had to pretend to fit in for most of my life. Well, *fit in* is a loose phrase. I've always been on my own plane or existence—in Arrow land. I've never quite conformed to my father's expectations. I got so bad that he basically sold me to the mafia. With good intentions, I guess. He wanted the best for his son.

And boy, did Gabriel take advantage of that.

I hate the man with every fiber of my being. He used, abused, and fucking annihilated our childhoods. Jericho got locked in dark rooms. At nine, he trained me to kill, and at fifteen, I went on a mission with him, taking my first life. Ever. And Shepp. He had his own hell to live through with his own shade of nightmare.

But Gabriel taught me everything I know. That's the only thing I'm thankful for right now.

The bright lights of the Briar Cove Hospital lobby come into view as I step out of the stairwell. My eyes dart around the place, looking for the telltale signs of Gabriel's guards. They never seem to be too inconspicuous, always standing out among the civilians.

Take the guy reading a paper by the large windows. Every so often, his eyes dart around, looking for someone. Or something. Maybe me. He never turns the page. And besides Jericho's old man ass, who has time to read the paper?

Stupid spies. That's who.

He's dumb, anyway. I walk right past him as he takes another look around the room. I wonder if they expected me to waltz out of this hospital in my suit with a grin. Probably. If I had weapons—real ones—I would have. What better place to kill bad guys than at the hospital?

Without incident, I walk through the automatic sliding doors and stop outside the hospital. Two men lean against poles, holding up the overhang above us. Their eyes scan the parking lot.

Idiots.

I'm right here.

I could saunter right by them without saying a word. But where's the fun in that? Besides, Gabriel needs to recognize his mistakes—which is a lot—starting with the whole coma ordeal.

"Excuse me, sirs," I say in a deeper voice than usual. "Do either of you have an Android phone?"

They both whip their gazes at me, eyeing me up and down. All they find is the icy color of my eyes, which cloud over when their brows furrow. Discreetly, I reach into my pocket, palming the scalpel I stole. If surgeons can use them to slice through flesh. Why can't I? They look fun. In another life, maybe I would have been a surgeon.

"Yeah. Why do you ask?" The one on the right confirms, eyeing me up and down with suspicion, pulling out his phone.

He should be suspicious.

Because he has the same phone as me. Meaning his charger will work with mine. Man, I love it when everything comes together so easily.

"Got a charger?" I ask again in my deep voice.

He nods slowly, jerking his thumb over his shoulder and indicating his charger is in his car. Perfect. I've officially found my getaway car.

What a nice fella.

My brows furrow as I stare at the man's side. "You're bleeding!" I point at his side, causing him to lose focus when he peers down.

"No, I'm…"

But he doesn't get to finish his sentence when I jam the scalpel into his side over and over. He cries out. *Boo hoo.* Screaming at me to stop. But I can't at the sight of red dripping onto the concrete, pulling my focus to it.

"Whoops," I say with a manic laugh. "Yeah, now you're bleeding." I shift my other hand into his pockets, stealing and pocketing his keys.

Oh, and his phone, too.

"You're a dumber motherfucker than I thought you'd be. Almost had me fooled," the one behind me snarls, pushing the tip of a gun into the back of my skull.

Oh, I'm so scared.

Not.

"I want you to do me a favor," I hum, releasing the man I stabbed and reveling in his pain when he falls to his knees, holding his side.

Didn't Gabriel teach these wannabes anything? Obviously not. He needs a new training camp for these pussies to go through. Like the ones we had to go through. They were tough and rigid, teaching us how to fight through the pain and all that.

"I don't give favors to dead men," he snarls, pushing the muzzle further into my scalp. "I was given instructions to shoot on sight."

Ah, then he's defying a direct order. Also, how rude of Gabriel to murder me on sight. The coward had me in a coma. The fucking audacity of that man.

"Didn't they ever teach you executions 101? Or did you skip that class, too?" I huff with disappointment. "The worst mistake you could ever make is this…" I grin when I swivel on my feet, nearly going deaf when the asshole pulls the trigger. Thankfully, the round shoots to the side of my head before I can knock the gun out of his hand. It clatters to the ground. "Never put the muzzle of a gun directly against someone. It's amateur shit, my dude."

I grin when my fist connects with his face over and over, rendering him useless on the ground. They both moan and groan, wallowing in their pain.

"And you see that? That is how you incapacitate people.

Losers," I grunt, spitting on the ground after lowering my mask.

I had no intention of murdering people on the hospital grounds. Meh, whatever.

I peek over my shoulder when approaching footsteps catch my attention. The cocking of a gun makes me all giddy inside. I turn around and face my death in the face—or would-be death.

The man with the newspaper.

But I don't have time for him.

"I should have known it was you," he says calmly, eyeing me up and down. "You almost had us, huh?"

I snort. "Almost?"

I throw the scalpel right into his open eyeball without hesitation. He shoots! He scores! He drops the gun, crying out when the scalpel finds its mark. I need to get out of here before they call the cops. I can already see the security personnel making their way over here from inside the building.

"Ah! You fucking fuck." Well, so much for the eerie calm he tried to portray.

"I've been called worse," I chuckle. "Give Gabriel a message for me," I hum, stepping back. "Let him know we'll be back for war. This shit isn't fucking over."

With that, I turn on my heels and sprint with the keys in my hand. I click the unlock button several times, finding the car. Quickly, I get in, start the engine, and then I'm off. Once I'm on the road out of Briar Cove, I pull over and plug my phone in.

I have no idea right now where anyone is, but I'll find them once my tracking app loads. Because what my brothers don't know is, I put trackers in their ass cheeks, too. Journey wasn't the only one to get special treatment.

I grin when my phone starts up again and reveals where Jericho took off to.

"Don't worry, Jer. I'm right behind you. I'll meet you in

East Point Bluff." I should have known he'd run straight for his cousin's house for help. We don't rely on her often—because hello, government agents—but she's always had our backs. And if he's scurrying there and leaving everything behind.

Our world must be truly fucked. I get confirmation when I find Shepp and Journey's dots sitting beside each other.

"In the middle of the ocean?" I ask myself, putting the car into drive. A car I'm most definitely going to dump before I make it to East Point.

Whatever. I'll find everyone, even if I leave a trail of bodies behind.

CHAPTER FOURTEEN

Jericho

BLOOD DRIPS FROM MY STAB WOUND STRAIGHT INTO MY SHOE, pooling there in my sock. No one likes wet socks in shoes. Particularly shoes filled with blood.

It's fucking annoying.

Even more annoying is that the suture didn't seem to take. It's not Lori's fault. It's probably all mine. I've been on the damn run, getting places quickly without taking special care of what Gerard did to me.

Now, I'm paying for it.

My fucking eyes droop when the car I stole three hours ago sinks to the bottom of the ocean after I forced it off one of the tall bluffs.

Now, no one will ever find it. Me. Or my blood that stains the carpets. My only regret is having to leave my precious car on the side of the road as it roasted under the flames, incinerating it for good.

My goddamn car didn't deserve that.

But neither did Journey.

Oh, the things I do for love.

I'd sacrifice the world. Burn it to pieces—just to have her back in my arms. Even if it means losing my fucking car. My blood. My goddamn sanity.

Anything for my wife.

I suck in a breath, marching my way back toward my cousin's house. Conveniently, she lives near the bluffs on an extensive property a mile from where I stand. But in the same breath, it is inconvenient because she lives in a gated community with excellent security.

Just one more obstacle to climb over.

My muscles weaken the more I walk. My brain swims in a fog, producing hallucinations of my wife standing at my side. Her voice rings in my ears, begging me to find her. Save her. Hold her and fuck her again.

Everything aches when I climb over the tall black iron fence, which keeps people out and scares them away, but it does nothing to deter my determination.

Get to Olivia's. She's my only hope of getting Journey out of the hell she is undoubtedly enduring.

With caution, I move through the shadows toward their massive estate. Their three-story mansion looms in front of me. Dark. Foreboding. And secured by the best security in the land.

"Well, well, well," a familiar voice echoes in my ear just as the sharp end of a knife pushes into my throat.

Case in point—the best security is the resident psycho, who is alive and well.

"Malic," I say through a breath. "Wonderful to see you again." It's sarcasm, of course.

Malic, or Maniac, as he seems to be called, is anything but rational, living up to his nickname. He makes Arrow look tame as fuck. He's unpredictable. Obsessive. And somehow got my level-headed cousin to fall in love with him. Now that I think about it, it was probably the stalking he did.

"I'm hoping you at least have clothes on while you're outside," I quip.

The amount of times that man has shown me his dick because he refuses to wear clothes is astronomical.

"I'm not torturing anyone…" he chuckles softly. "Yet."

Oh, goody.

"No need to torture family."

"Family are the ones who deserve torture the most," he tuts, clicking his tongue.

Facts.

"Can't deny that. But I'd like to plead my case, at least." I side-eye him, and he grins. Shirtless, of course. His buff, Viking-like body towers over me—a beast of a man I'd never want to piss off. Covered in tattoos and piercings. Probably in places I don't want to imagine.

"Beg me," he says in a low voice. "Or My Liv will be down a cousin." He grins again, showing off all his teeth. "No matter how much I like you."

Like me? For fuck's sake. If this is how he shows affection, I'd be terrified to see how he treats someone he hates.

"I need to speak with her. It's urgent. My wife was taken from me, and I need Liv to help me," I grit out.

Just like that, Malic removes the knife from my throat and hums. Sometimes, it pays to know which buttons to press on someone. If there's something I know about Malic, it's that he's obsessed with my cousin, and if he lost her—he'd kill everyone in his way.

"A missing wife? The one you married without her consent?"

Fucking Olivia. She'll punish me for the rest of my life for taking what I needed.

"That would be the one. My father has done something with her. My tracker…"

"Ohhh, the good old tracker trick! Where'd you put it?" He grins at that, slapping me on the back with force. "I put mine in Olivia's clothes. Oh, her phone. Then, buried in the back of her neck. You can never be too careful. Especially when she was trying to run from me." He shakes his head like memories are floating through his mind.

I grunt, gritting my teeth. "In her ass cheek beneath our

claim." My head swims, and the world slightly tilts from the loss of blood currently seeping onto his porch.

"You're bleeding," he states, leaning down to lift my pant leg. "Oh, you were shot? Or stabbed? How fun!"

Fun. He says it like being shot or stabbed is a dream come true. Maybe for him, but I'd rather not have a bullet or knife go through my flesh.

"Unfortunately," I grumble when he stands tall in front of me.

"Care to explain the wound?" he asks with a grin, grabbing my upper arm. "Anyone on your tail? Follow you here? Because I'd like a fun game of manhunt." Of course he would. He's like a dog with a bone. Give him a bad person to chase down, and he'll eliminate them in two point five seconds.

"My father stole my mansion and my freedom. So, I stole my car. His guards attempted to shoot me, and then I was stabbed. Don't worry, though. I ended his pathetic life. No one followed me here."

I know for a fact that I may have my phone, but it's untraceable. Thanks to Olivia. I knew this would be useful for all three of us one day. Gabriel can attempt to track us down all he wants, but it won't matter. He'll never find us. Not to mention the AntiEyes on our phones from the moment we semi-initiated.

I'm nothing more than a rag doll behind Malic as he drags me through the house and toward the kitchen, where he stops abruptly, picks me up, and sets me on the countertop like a child.

"Need an assassin?" Malic asks, rifling through the lower cabinets, humming a tune. "I'm an excellent shot. I can get him right through the eyeball."

"Maybe," I say through a sigh, rubbing at the bridge of my nose. "Except he's surrounded by extra security. And up to something." That's an understatement. He's planning something major, and I've yet to unearth it.

"You underestimate my skills." He grins, holding up a first aid kit.

"That's where you're wrong," I grunt when he rips open the fabric of my jeans, tearing it at the ankle to my knee. "Fuck," I hiss when he puts the tip of his finger into the bloodied wound through the bandage Lori administered, rifling around until more blood pours out. I grit my teeth, focusing through the pain like the family trained to do.

"Hurt?" he asks with that crazy grin of his, watching as my fingers flex around the edge of the countertop.

"Like a kitten scratch," I wheeze.

It hurts like a bitch. My wound throbs. At least, I thought it was hurting until he poured straight vodka on it. Where he pulled it from, I do not know.

But fuck did that burn. I'm ready to jack him in the jaw for all the extra pain he's caused, but he steps back, clapping his hands.

I fucking hate this man. Where the fuck is his keeper, Wilder? I swear to God…

"Well, you're in luck, Old Chap. It looks like the wound is clean and went straight through the other side."

Yeah, no shit, Sherlock. That is what I want to say. But I'm almost positive he'd injure me further. He's a goddamn sadist like that. Pain is the only thing he knows and enjoys. Inflicting. Receiving. Whichever, he's down for it. His childhood… I internally shake my head, dispelling the thoughts.

"Wonderful." It's all I can say as he gets to work fixing my leg again by taking off the bloodied bandage and examining the wound.

"What…" My head snaps toward Olivia, stopping at the threshold in nothing more than a robe tied tightly around her body. Confusion warps her expression at the sight of blood lining Malic's hands and me sitting in her kitchen. "The fuck?" she murmurs, shaking her long brown locks from side to side.

"Your cousin had a minor mishap. Got himself stabbed," Malic informs her with way too much glee.

"You're way too happy about that, Mal," she grumbles, marching forward.

I can tell the moment she puts on her Veritas persona. Her face hardens. Arms fold over her chest.

"What happened?"

Determination twitches through her as she leans down and examines my wound, too. Or what's left of it. I grunt again when Malic stabs me with a needle and begins sewing up my cut his way.

"Fuck," I huff, sucking in a breath.

My training be damned. It hurts like a motherfucker because the motherfucker doing it doesn't give a damn about injuring me.

"Uncle?" she breathes, searching my eyes.

"Off the fucking rails," I hiss through clenched teeth.

"That's why he's here, Crumpet," Malic hums to Olivia with hearts in his eyes. "Took his wife…"

"Everyone," I say, sucking in a breath. "My father removed everyone from my life with the flick of his wrist. Locked me in a room to ensure a marriage. He's fucking insane."

"Journey?" she asks, furrowing her brows. "She's…"

I swallow hard, pulling out my phone. "This is why I'm here, Liv, as much as I enjoy your company. Journey is missing, and this is the only clue I have."

Journey's dot blinks on the screen as I stare intently at it. Wishing I could reach through the fucking phone and pull her to me.

My desperation reaches new heights when Liv lifts the phone from my hand, staring at the tiny dot representing the only woman who holds my heart in her palm.

No one will ever replace her. Or be her. She is my one and only. I have nothing left to burn for if I don't have her.

"She's…" Olivia's brows furrow when her gaze whips to me. "She's on an island…"

"Tropical?" Mal asks, stepping back when I glare at him. "Oh, maybe she's sipping margaritas."

"Shut up," Liv murmurs. "Have some decency in a situation like this. Imagine if I was on some unknown island." She raises a brow.

Malic frowns. "Well, when you put it like that. I'd get stabbed, too."

Unfeeling bastard.

"Research suggests it's an uncharted island. But before that, she was here," I say, pointing to the ocean beside the island. "It belongs to Shadow."

"The ocean?" Liv asks with furrowed brows until her eyes snap to mine. "Shadow?" she breathes out.

"The ocean beside Shadow's island. Along with Shepp, at least according to Aiden," I confirm. "Arrow is in a coma, hopefully waking soon. And my father is on a power trip. Took over the mansion." And life is shit and dismal without them. A literal black hole opens inside me, consuming every ounce of my feelings until they disappear. If I'm not careful, I'll become more of a monster than I already am.

The sooner my family is back as one, the sooner Gabriel Viotto will go down to the depths of hell.

Olivia sighs, rubbing her temple. "I heard some major rumblings through the grapevine about your father's tower and an attack by Shadow. My agents were sent to investigate the aftermath and keep it quiet from national and local news."

"Shadow?" Mal perks up. "Like…?"

"No. He's dead, remember?" Liv says, giving him a firm look.

"Shadow is a mystery in Briar Cove. They sprung up a few years ago. And, Liv…" Her eyes return to mine. "My mother returned in all the chaos." Because in my gut, I know she is the fucking chaos. Why? I'm not fucking sure. Or how she fits into it all. She's done something to my father. I know that much.

But her current motivations make my head pound against my skull.

"Grace? How? What? She was…" Liv's voice quivers at the mention of my mother's name.

She knew her better than I did, having been around longer than I had.

"Dead? Missing? Apparently not. There's something odd about her, too. I just can't put my finger on it." It's beyond odd. Someone doesn't just wander out of Shadow's grip without repercussions.

"Don't worry, Jer. We'll sort this out, okay? I'll call Carter. He'll know exactly how to track this and look into the island."

CHAPTER FIFTEEN
Jericho

"OH, FUCK. JER, HIDE," LIV SAYS, MARCHING INTO THE LARGE family room as I rest on the couch, clutching a bottle of water.

"I don't hide," I quip, peeling open my weary eyes.

"Well, in this instance, you might want to because Journey's brothers came with Carter."

Wonderful. Not only have I had the pleasure of dealing with Olivia's Veritas partner, Carter—the grumpy dick. Now, my wife's brothers are on the prowl after I promised them she'd be safe and so would her money.

I swallow my thick saliva. After losing blood, my entire body feels worn and falling apart. I can barely lift my damn head off the couch without wincing like a pussy.

"You lost my sister?" the big one with tattoos howls, marching into the living room with the calm one on his tail.

Seger, I remember. Tall. Tattooed. He has an attitude and loves to eat. His twin, Zeppelin, walks stoically behind him, eyeing the situation—the serious, composed one. And they both have matching murderous expressions.

Great.

If getting stabbed didn't send me to my grave. Seger and Zeppelin West will gladly do it.

"After all that fucking talk about keeping her safe, you

went and fucking lost her!" he shouts again, cracking his knuckles.

"Don't," Liv grunts, stepping in front of him. "He was stabbed. Barely survived, okay? This is a mess, but not his fault."

Pfft. Barely survived? It was merely a flesh wound. I smirk at my joke.

The thing I said about family and wanting to torture them 100% does not include my loyal cousin. She's been nothing but accommodating my entire life, considering my line of work and hers do not mesh well. Me, the criminal, and her, the government agent. She should arrest me and my friends for everything we've done. Throw us in the infamous Veritas jail on an island so secluded that no one ever escapes.

But she doesn't. I guess she loves me, her younger cousin. And I love her in return. In my own way, of course. Besides, we grew up side-by-side in the trenches of our fathers' iron fists.

Liv's worse than mine.

"She was kidnapped." Helpful, I know.

Seger narrows his eyes, ready to retort. Or hit me. He looks like the punch first, talk later kind of guy.

"Shut the fuck up, West," Carter barks, walking into the room with a laptop tucked under his arm and a coffee in hand. That authoritative attitude fills the room, snapping our spines straight. "Sit the fuck down, and shut the fuck up."

His scowl could melt the flesh off any mere mortal. Thankfully, I'm immune to his gruffness. Or any gruffness, for that matter.

"You're such an asshole," Seger grunts, but obeys like a good little boy sitting opposite of me. His moss-green eyes, similar to Journey's, focus on me with a warning infused in them. He's going to murder me. Or he can try.

"Viotto. We meet again." Carter finds the recliner across from me and sits.

"A pleasure, as always." Exhaustion weighs me down, but for the sake of everyone else counting on me, I stay awake and conscious. "Now, my wife and second-in-command are missing."

"I've heard your fucking sob story. You fucking mafia assholes always get yourselves into shit. Like losing your wife and bestie. I, for one, wouldn't let that fucking stand." He raises a brow, challenging me.

"Shut it, Grumpy." A petite blonde woman, eyeing me, enters the room with pursed lips.

There's no caution in her gaze, fear, or any sort of feeling I'd expect to see from someone I've never met before. But I like her already. Seeing a grown man with as massive balls as Carter Cunningham shrivel under her glare is funny.

It must be his wife.

His face softens when he looks her up and down.

"Vixen," he murmurs, shaking his head.

"Well, be nice. Seger is just looking out for his sister." Her blue eyes find mine, and she softly smiles. "I'm Kaycee. They belong to me."

"Damn right we do, Angel," Seger says, pumping a fist.

"Jericho," I say in greeting, nodding my head. Then I turn my attention back to Carter when Seger scoops his wife onto his lap. "Well, I wasn't exactly the person to lose my goddamn wife. She was taken. Kidnapped. And thrown into the ocean or whatever and taken to Shadow's island…"

"It's a former island that housed a massive elite resort," Carter so nicely cuts me off. "Formerly owned by the Apocalypse Society."

"An elite resort?" I question. "And it still stands?" How strange. From my research, no such building was depicted to be there. Wildlife and bushes. No resort. It's no wonder Shadow claimed the island as their own and took it over. If there's a resort there, then they never have to leave.

"Intact, yes. It fucking takes up the entire back part of the island. Plus, a multitude of other buildings are still standing. It's out of fucking business, but it seems a corporation scooped it up fifteen years ago when it was sold."

"A corporation, you say?"

Oddly, Google didn't provide any of that information. Unless said corporation is so powerful, it wiped its old existence from the map. In that case, Shadow must have someone powerful backing his ventures.

"A corporation named *Contelli* purchased the entire island and its contents for four million. Ring any bells?" He raises a bushy brow in my direction, expecting me to know all the answers.

"Unfortunately, no," I hum, rubbing my temples with my tired fingers. If only I could catch a quick nap, but I refuse to close my eyes while the ones I love suffer.

"Don't worry," he says, offering me a creepy grin that sends shivers down my spine. "I'll know all about them in thirty minutes or less."

"Reassuring," I mumble.

"You don't have to worry, Jer. He's an asshole, but he knows what he's doing." Liv gives me a small pat on the shoulder as she sits next to me on the couch.

"I'll take what I can get. Asshole and all," I quip.

"You have no fucking choice," Carter grunts, typing like a madman on his computer.

Liv yelps when Malic reappears, scooping her into his lap, too.

"No touchy." He glares at me, holding her hands down possessively.

"He's my cousin, for fuck's sake," she grumbles, attempting to push off him. But it's no use. He's too strong. Too big. And way too controlling to escape from. I'll never understand how he allowed her to be with four other guys, especially when three of them had been associated with his rivals for years.

"No touchy," he grumbles again, snuggling his face into her neck. "Cousin, no cousin, doesn't fucking matter."

Gross. Like I'd ever think about my cousin in that way.

I look at the ceiling, letting my tired mind wander. "How have your other husbands slept through all this?"

"Um, they sleep like the dead. They won't wake up. Only this one doesn't sleep," Liv snorts, gesturing to Malic.

"Sleep is for the weak. Besides, I caught an intruder, didn't I?" He smirks in my direction, dragging his finger along his throat.

"But you didn't catch me, motherfucker."

My heart stops. I drag my eyes away from Mal's threats and stare at Arrow in green scrubs, standing in the living room like he belongs there. Tiny specks of blood decorate his outfit.

Everyone turns their attention to him. Some are more alarmed than others. Me, though? Relief soars through my veins, taking the slight pressure off my chest that's been suffocating me since I left Briar Cove alone.

I should never be alone.

"Arrow," I breathe. "How'd you get here so fast? And why are you here? We were supposed to meet at our rendezvous point."

It's only been a few hours at best.

He grins, cracking his knuckles with malice. Fuck. Vengeance lives in his light eyes, devoid of life. I've only seen this look when he's about to take extremities for sport. Or if someone wronged him.

"Journey isn't the only one who has a tracker in her ass cheek. You should thank me, too." As Arrow speaks, Malic nods in agreement, grinning like it's the most apparent thing on the planet to put trackers into unsuspecting people.

"When?" I groan, wishing I had the energy to get up. I'd hug him if I were the type. Or smack him for planting a damn tracker in me. Of course he did, though. That's Arrow. Always invasive. Well, until it comes in handy, like now.

My entire plan of meeting him at the cabin falls by the wayside.

"Don't worry your pretty little head about that, Daddy Jer." Stepping up to me, his shadow looms right above my body. "This is for leaving me behind, asshole."

I don't have time to see the fist coming toward my face until I'm knocked back with a groan, warm blood leaking out of my nose.

"Arrow," I growl, holding my face and glaring at his smug reaction. "I couldn't drag you out of the hospital without drawing attention. I already killed two of my father's guards to keep you safe and got stabbed."

"How the fuck did you get in my house?" Malic barks, narrowing his beady eyes at Arrow.

"I have my ways," Arrow says with an easy-going grin, transforming him in a matter of seconds from the man ready to murder me to this. "Now, how the fuck are we going to get my Kitten and Shepp back?" he growls, turning to Carter, who smirks knowingly.

"Don't fucking worry. I'm already planning."

Wonderful.

CHAPTER SIXTEEN
Journey

"THIS WAY." MY BROWS FURROW WHEN AN UNFAMILIAR MAN forces me from the fighting ring and hauls me behind him.

No, *hi, hello, how ya doing? I'm assbag extraordinaire. Just follow me.*

If it smells like a trap and walks like a trap, then it's probably a goddamn trap.

I peek over my shoulder, staring at the remnants of the man who was alive and confident five minutes ago. As soon as his blood hit the dirt—or, more accurately, his dick—he took his last breath before my eyes, staring at me like I had betrayed him in the worst way.

I never agreed to his deal. I may have dropped to my knees, but I never said, yes, sir, our deal is solid. It's his fault for believing I would.

Then came this soldier with dark hair and mean eyes, glaring holes through my flesh. He barely acknowledged me when he grabbed me from my kneeling position and forced me to walk on shaky legs.

This all feels like a terrible nightmare. Can I wake up yet?

I can only wonder if he's leading me to my death. Probably. Nothing went as planned for Shadow. Or, I can only assume. He wanted me dead, right? Was that the plan? Fuck. I don't even know anymore. What does he want from me? Or Shepp.

God, Shepp.

A sweat breaks out along my flesh like ants crawling all over my skin. Swallowing becomes more challenging, as does breathing. My worry intensifies with every step through the maze of darkened corridors, heading to God knows where. It feels like we're going up instead of down to the prison.

I can't stop thinking about Shepp and I's last few days together. And beyond. I miss watching Shepp paint and cook. God, I miss his food so much—the donuts especially. I need to get back to him. Touch him. Hug him. Make sure he's still living.

Exhaustion pulls heavily at every ounce of my being, begging for food, water, and a nap. At this point in my captivity, I'd do a lot of shady shit to ensure my freedom. Or a steak. God, a big juicy steak sounds like heaven right about now.

Blood drips from every inch of me—his blood. The man walked into the ring with a cruel chip on his shoulder and left without light in his eyes. My darkness clings to the edges of my being, holding my feelings at bay, erasing them.

But there's one nagging feeling I can't seem to ignore.

Everything about that fight seemed too simple. Right? Who the hell offers to spare a girl's life if she sucks his dick? A fucking pervert, that's who. That's beside the point, though. It's like he was set up, as if Shadow told him to say that to get me to fold. Whatever the reasoning was, Brian didn't expect me to use my knives. So, there's something extra going on here.

The man leading me tightens his hold on my upper arm when we push through the double swinging doors and walk through an unoccupied kitchen. My brows furrow, taking in the expensive appliances and ample space with metal countertops. Pots and skillets hang from a rack on the ceiling, looking brand new without dust on their surfaces. The entire room looks like a cleaning crew came through and left no crumbs behind.

"What the hell is this place?" I mutter to myself, looking around in awe.

"Was a hotel," the soldier replies without looking over his shoulder. "Now, it's Shadow's."

Okay, cool. He can tell me about the history of this place. But he can't even introduce himself? This place sucks.

"A hotel? Where the fuck are we?" I grumble, shaking my head.

I remember nothing about coming here except waking up in a dank cave. I'd love to know a little more about this place so we can plot our escape without getting caught. Or killed.

"Nowhere you need to worry about," he grunts without looking at me again, pulling me around like a rag doll.

I guess this is my life now.

"Fabulous. You're splendid company, by the way..." I trail off when he grunts again, pushing us through another large door. Then we stop.

I want to say more sarcastic things to ward off the feelings festering inside me as my darkness wanes, evaporating back into the depths of my mind.

I just killed a man. Slashed his throat and cut off his dick. Sure, he wasn't innocent. Definitely deserved it. But still. It's the fact I was forced to do it. Again. It was him or me, and I chose myself and the loved ones depending on me to be okay.

I had to. There was no way around it.

"You're free to go, Darrell." I raise a brow at the sound of Shadow's deep voice coming from a large dining room table in the center of the massive dining hall.

Darrell unwinds his fingers from my upper arm and drops his hand with a frown, stepping out from in front of me.

"Thank you, Sir." is all the soldier says before sauntering out the double doors and out of sight. Probably hanging outside of them to guard Shadow. That's how these mafia men work.

"Sit," Shadow says, shoving a roll into his mouth and gesturing toward the empty table. "Our other guest will join us once we've had a little chat."

"A chat?" I question cautiously as I take a seat directly across from him.

"Eat," he says, pushing a basket of rolls toward me.

Fuck. My mouth waters at the sight of them. The smell that wafts from them has my stomach performing a happy jig, ready to get a bite. But I stop myself, watching as he reaches for another one and shoves it in his mouth.

"Last time I accepted food from you, it was poisoned." I narrow my eyes when he chuckles at me, licking the butter from his fingers.

"You're a smart little fighter, aren't you? Did Gabriel teach you all you need to know?"

Haven't we already gone over this?

"Yes." That's all I'll reply until I figure out what game he's playing. Because he has to be, right?

"Your performance was impressive. You use your mind over your physical ability." Shadow continues to lick his fingers, watching me with his one beady eye.

"You did it on purpose," I say with a nod.

"I knew you were smart." He grins at that, shoving the basket of rolls in front of me again. "Now, eat a fucking roll."

God, why does he want me to eat them so badly? Of course, there wouldn't be any drugs in these, considering he's eating them, too. Maybe just one bite won't hurt. Okay, more than one bite. Once I start, I can't stop devouring four rolls with a satisfied groan with each bite I take.

"Did you make a deal with Brian?" I question, wiping my buttered fingers on a napkin beside me.

"Tired of him winning," Shadow says with a shrug. "I was losing money. I needed fresh blood. Besides, it came in handy."

I nod in response, sitting back and letting my food digest, when he pulls out his phone from underneath the table. Setting it in front of my face, he replays the video of me cutting the man's junk off and slitting his throat. Acid rises in my esophagus, the bread turning stale inside me.

So, this is why.

"Blackmail," I croak with understanding.

Of course. Why wouldn't he blackmail me? Because holding my sister hostage wasn't enough. Poisoning Shepp wasn't enough.

Thomas Mondelli is a fucking monster. I can't decide if he's worse than Gabriel or not.

"Brian's wife will wonder why he hasn't come home from his trucking job soon." Shadow smacks his lips and puts his phone away. "He was only here for funsies."

Brian and I have two very different ideas on what funsies are.

"He wasn't one of your men?" I ask, eyeing a glass of water and then taking a drink.

Fuck it if it's poisoned. My life is completely fucked now.

"The Pit boasts a lot of things, and anonymity is one of them. People from the main lands come, fight for their fucking lives, and if they win, they get money and favors. And they give me loyalty in return. It's a win-win."

"And that's all you want?" I ask, reaching for another roll. It's interesting when the villains give me all the information so easily. "Loyalty?"

"You're going to go do a few jobs for me." He's not asking. He's telling me. Maybe this is the key to my freedom? It's nothing I haven't done before.

"What jobs?" I ask, slowly chewing the roll with caution.

Alarm bells ring in my head when he locks his cold eyes with me and smirks.

"Bring him in!" Shadow shouts, rolling his wrist. "You'll see."

It's ominous at best, turning my stomach.

I lick my lips in anticipation of the scene. Elias White—my former target—strolls in with his hands in his pockets and a tight expression. My spine stiffens, forcing me to sit up straighter when he sits beside Shadow, and then his eyes find me.

"Journey," Elias says, cocking his head.

His expression gives nothing away. It's indifferent. Even as his eyes take in the blood soaking my flesh, he doesn't react or move.

"Elias." I nod in greeting.

"I was under the impression I was here to discuss business," Elias says, side-eyeing Shadow with raised brows.

"You are." Shadow claps his hands. "But we have a guest."

"I can see that."

"So, down to business," Shadow says, snapping his fingers three times.

A burst of motion happens around us. Steaming food emerges as more men pile into the room carrying trays. The aroma hits me immediately, making my stomach knot with anticipation. My mouth practically waters when a plate filled with a heaping scoop of spaghetti and meatballs with garlic bread on the side slides in front of me. Fuck. I'm so hungry, and I want to devour every bite.

But Shepp's face rolls through my mind. The memory of him in distress on the ground is so fresh, clinging to life. It's on the tip of my tongue to ask about him. Is he okay? Did you kill your son?

Because that would be it for me. I'd lose myself in the darkness inside me and drive a sword through his fucking skull.

No Shepp. No Journey.

I eye Shadow as he digs in without waiting for Elias to receive his plate. Spaghetti sauce flies everywhere around him, staining his clothes and face.

"How well did the last shipment distribute?" Shadow asks Elias with a mouth full of food.

Elias pokes at his spaghetti politely with his fork and nods. "Well." His eyes flash to me with curiosity.

"Pay her no mind," Shadow says, slurping a noodle loudly into his mouth.

"This is our business," Elias says smoothly, wrapping a few noodles around his fork and taking a tentative bite before setting his utensils down again.

With Shadow glaring in his direction, he takes out his phone and swipes up. His facial features don't change when he types and then puts his phone away like he's not in a semi-dangerous situation.

"My business," Shadow says, setting down his fork. "You just fucking work for me."

I swallow a bite of food, watching Shadow's changing posture. Every muscle I see turns rigid with rage, although his facial features don't let on. His one visible eye collects shadows, darkening with Elias' words.

"I want to discuss Briar Cove and the distribution of my products." Shadow's fingers drum on the table, thumping in beat with my heart.

"Hmm. And what about your products?" Elias asks with a calm demeanor. "Our deal is still intact. Business is going as usual." He takes a bite of his spaghetti, humming at the taste. Like he doesn't even fucking care that Shadow is grinding his teeth.

"Good. That settles it," Shadow says, taking another sloppy bite of his meal, slurping the noodles, and chewing loudly. "Then, let's enjoy our meal."

No mannered asshole.

"How's the wedding planning going?" Shadow asks, keeping his eyes on his food.

I stiffen at the thought of Jenni, my best friend. Former best friend? The girl I had to sell out to keep my sister alive. She told me once Elias would be the man she married despite her arranged marriage to Leighton, another man in the Viotto Crime Family.

And it looks like it's finally happening.

Good for her. Seriously, joy fills me at the thought. Jenni deserves happiness more than anyone I know. She never judged me or talked down to me. She looked after me, and I did the same—until I couldn't. It's a guilt that will never go away.

"You're marrying Jenni?" My throat feels tight when Elias' eyes connect with mine.

"In a week," he says, taking another bite without emotions.

I nod solemnly. "She always talked about how excited she was to marry you."

Elias inspects me again. "And she always told me what an amazing friend she found in you."

I blink several times at his words. Does he know the truth about what I've done? Who I've worked for?

"And what a joyous occasion it is," Shadow says with a creepy grin. "I've got my own daughter now, and the day she marries…," he trails off, sending me waves of anxiety.

"She's only fourteen," I say, letting my fork fall to the table. "You can't marry my sister off."

Besides, how am I supposed to believe he's her father? Despite my mother spreading her legs for anyone to get the drugs she needs, it's impossible to know which man is the father of Sunshine.

Shadow smirks, shaking his head. "Indeed. She only has four more years until I can marry her off. Maybe to the Russians. Or the Italians. Or whoever I fucking please. She's my daughter. My property. And she agreed to it."

You have no fucking say anymore—are the words weaved between his threat.

My heart drops into my stomach. "No." I shake my head at the thought of my sister, dressed in all white, being forced to marry a dangerous man.

I want to argue that she's my goddamn sister, and that I raised her. Not him. Not my goddamn mom. Me. But I keep that to myself. Because I'm the most unlucky bitch on the planet, my sister keeps getting used as a damn pawn against me. I can't let any of this happen.

Not again.

"Well, this has been quite the meeting. Are we done?" Elias asks, setting his utensils down softly.

"As long as business is still intact and being managed." Shadow sits back in his chair, pushing his plate away. "I expect my next shipment to hit your docks in one week. The night after your wedding."

"As it always is under my watchful eye," Elias retorts, standing from his chair. "My men and I will be there to get the products. Then, I'll go on my honeymoon."

"Then our business is complete for today," Shadow says smugly. "I'll send a few guards to assist, per our agreement."

Elias fixes his shirt as he strides away and then abruptly stops. "I'll see both of you at the wedding, then. Plus one for each of you. At the Grand Cove Hotel. Don't miss it." He fixes me with a stare before sauntering through the doors and disappearing.

His words register in my mind. It's a way out—a way to take Shepp and my sister and run under the guise of going to his wedding.

Silence stretches between Shadow and me. He finishes his meal, and I slowly finish mine. The spaghetti tastes like ash on my tongue, sinking into my churning stomach and threatening to come back up.

"You'll go to the wedding." Shadow doesn't look at me when he shoves another roll in his mouth.

"Why?"

What's his angle?

"He's your job." Shadow folds his arms over his chest with a smug smirk.

Internally, I groan, wanting to throw my hands in the air. Or possibly in his face. What's so interesting about Elias White that both these monsters want to use me to spy on him? He's not that damn interesting. Is he? They act like he's building a secret army behind their backs, ready to take over their empires. Hell, maybe he is.

"Don't you think that's suspicious?" I question bravely, taking a small bite of spaghetti.

"I don't give a fuck if it's suspicious. You'll be my little spy. Or I marry your sister off to the first fucking man I see." A cruel smirk pulls at his lips.

First, it was my sister's health held over my head. Now, it's her goddamn virtue and innocence.

"Gabriel had me spy on him."

"I'm aware," Shadow answers without emotion. "That's why you're perfect. So now you'll spy more. Find out what that asshole is doing with my goddamn product."

"Is he stealing it?" Sometimes, I'm too nosey for my own good, but I have to know what I'm getting myself into. There's a reason he's sending me to do this and not one of his soldiers.

"You be the spy and tell me what he's up to."

This again? Fuck my life. I can't catch a damn break with these monsters. They use me until they're done with me.

"Just at the wedding?" I raise a brow at his flawed plan.

"That'll be the start of it. After the wedding, you'll continue to worm your way into their good graces. Be a fucking friend, fuck buddy, or a whore for his men. Whatever you have to do, do it. I want information."

My nose wrinkles. I'll pass on the whore part, thanks. I already have three men I'm mildly in love with. Besides, Arrow would skin them alive if they touched me.

"Why me?" I ask, raising my eyes. "Gabriel did the same thing to me. He held my sister's life over my head if I did this and that for him. Don't you have other people to do this for you?"

Shadow leans his elbows on the table, eyeing me critically. "Gabriel may have held your sister over your head, but did he ever give you freedom? He stole you. Tortured you…"

"Yeah, for killing you. But you're still here." My teeth clench together when he smiles, nodding.

"I am. But that's what I'm offering. Hell, I'll even give you Shepp, alive and well. Do my bidding, and I'll give you freedom."

"What about my sister?" I ask, mulling over his words.

"She'll have a choice…"

"But why? Why do you even care about her or Shepp now? You… you cut out his fucking tongue and then tried to take advantage of my fucking sister!" I shout, jumping up from the chair on wobbly legs, trying to control my breath.

This is all so confusing to me. Why bother now?

"Take it or fucking leave it," he growls, clenching his fists on the table. "Or waste away in the fucking caves." He nods once to someone behind me, and I'm seized. "I'll give you a day or two to think about it." He snaps his stupid fingers again.

The doors slam open, revealing the broody guard, Darrell, with a frown still on his face. Without another hi or hello, he grips my upper arm and drags me behind him, forcing me to walk.

Images of the darkness lingering in the cave haunt me with every step. Shepp's pained expression before I had to leave him for the pit has my eyes squeezing shut.

I can't do this. Not again. I have to protect him. My sister. Me. Everyone. Who knows? Next time, he'll go after Jericho and Arrow. I don't know how much power Shadow holds in Briar Cove.

"Wait!" I say, halting our movements and yanking my arm out of his hold.

Like fuck will I go back to that prison and starve in the darkness. I have to get stronger. Eat. Sleep. So I can plan Shadow's demise with a logical mind.

"Yes?" Shadow asks with a smirk, rising from his seat at the table. He throws down a napkin and comes to stand in front of me.

"I want to negotiate." I swallow hard when his eyebrows raise. Good. Keep him on his toes. "I'll do whatever you want. But my sister has to be safe."

Shadow rocks on his toes and nods. "Make you a deal. Your sister is safe here. She's my legacy, after all. Her health is being taken care of. You do your end of the deal, and I'll do mine."

"So I do your job with Shepp and my sister will be safe?"

"Safer than she was with that bastard," he says smugly. "Now. Take her to the room."

CHAPTER SEVENTEEN

Journey

"This way," Darrell says, grabbing my arm.

Rude.

I'm so fucking exhausted. Between the standoff with Shadow. The death match. And all the other bullshit mixed up together. I'm ready to sleep for a year. Oh, and shower, too. Not to mention the indigestion brewing in my stomach. Maybe that asshole poisoned me, after all.

Figures that's how I'd go out. It wasn't the sword in the death ring. It was the poison in the dining room by the mafia leader. Wait. Gang leader? What the hell is Shadow? He's not affiliated with the Viotto family. Or the Blue Spider Gang.

Shit. He's in a league of his own making.

"Seems I'll be here awhile. What exactly is this place?" Crickets. "Nothing? You're going to drag me through this…"

"Hotel," he grunts, pulling me along. "But I already told you that."

He did. It was right before he pulled me into the meeting with Shadow. I need more information. I wonder what magic I could pull to make him spill his secrets. My monster would claim seduction would be the key to unraveling men. But I'd rather not.

Maybe I can torture him with words and kindness to make him a little more talkative.

"Yeah, that. This hotel."

My eyes wander again as he drags me through the dining hall, a large lobby filled with fancy chandeliers, marble floors, countertops, and finally to a working elevator. Everything about this hotel screams clean, fully functional, and lots and lots of money.

"Where exactly are you taking me?" I ask when the door pops open and cheesy elevator music hits my ears. "My room is…" I attempt to point down toward the stupid prison caves, but I'm yanked toward him again.

Someone needs to teach Darrell some manners. And that someone might be me.

"On the eighth floor now." He doesn't look at me when he drags me into the elevator. And I say drag because I'm digging my heels in with all my might, which isn't much now.

"No. Wait. I need to get back to Shepp." My worry for the man I left behind has my stomach in knots. He has to be okay. I fought. I won. Shepp should be alive. But Shadow is unpredictable and has something major up his sleeves.

I again attempt to pull out of his grasp, but he clings tighter.

Strong bastard, unhand me! Ugh. I'm about to claw his eyes out and track Shepp down.

"If you hang on any tighter to me, I'll start to think you like me," I quip, grunting when he pulls me closer to his body. So close I feel the heat of his body against mine.

Yeah, he needs to be stabbed for invading my personal space. Especially in this bloodied dress I'm still wearing that barely covers my goods. I need a shower, a drink, and Shepp to soothe this anxiety warring inside me.

"Not my type," he says monotonously, not bothering to meet my eyes.

"Seriously. That's fine and all. But I need to get back to him. Is he okay? Is he…" but I'm cut off when the door opens on the eighth floor, and he drags me down the carpeted hallway, kicking and screaming. "For shit's sake! You don't have to do this…" I yank and grunt with all my might, trying to peel his fingers off my arm. I even whack him with my fists, hoping to loosen his damn fingers.

Notta. Nothing. Zilch. It doesn't fucking work.

He's a brute, forcing me into another prison I don't want to entertain. I inspect his unmoving face when he glares at me. What did he expect? For me to go quietly like a good girl. For too many years, I've fought too many monsters. I'm fucking done pandering to these douche canoes, damn it. I want to go home.

"Go in the room," he demands with a tight expression.

Would it kill the guy to make different facial expressions besides brooding and rude?

Probably.

I sigh. Well, then. I apparently have no choice. If I had those knives from the fight, I'd stab this asshole in the throat and make a run for it. It'd give me a good head start until I found Shepp in the basement.

All I have to do is go downstairs and retrace our steps. Spying 101: Always remember your exits and where you came from. I could do it, but… No. I can't do that.

I deflate and mentally groan, remembering why I'm going along with this ridiculous venture.

Sunshine.

There's no way I'd be able to get my hands on her. She's locked up tight with Shadow and is unreachable for now. I'll get to talk to her soon. Hopefully before the wedding. One week. That's all I have to wait before we can exit and hide from Shadow's cruel hand.

"Fine." But I'm not happy about this, and I will make that loud and clear.

He nods, pulls out a key from his pocket, unlocks the door, and licks his lips with a huff.

"He's inside." Darrell motions for me to go inside the room with the flick of his wrist.

My heart practically leaps from my chest with anxiety. What state will I find Shepp in? Is he alive? Okay? Fucking breathing? Hurt?

My stomach turns.

"Now, go."

I swear he mutters, *so you shut the fuck up* underneath his breath, and I decide to ignore that minor detail, putting it on ice until I can enact my damn revenge on him.

Darrell is officially on my shit list, which seems to be growing a mile every day. Who is at the top, you ask? Fucking Gabriel Viotto. The bastard who sold me out to the other bastard. Coming in at number two on my list: Shadow, AKA Thomas Mondelli. And Darrell makes three.

"Thanks," I say, watching Darrell with a skeptical eye.

He rolls his eyes. "Tonight, I will lock you in from the outside. Tomorrow, Shadow will give you free rein to walk around the hotel and island. You should know that you can't escape. It's impossible. There are guards and cameras everywhere. I wouldn't advise the window, either. You'd meet a grisly end." He gives me a look, basically saying without words, there's no way to escape this hellhole. Period.

We're stuck here until Shadow decides what to do with us. Or that's what they want us to think. *Don't escape.* I call bullshit. There has to be some way for us to leave undetected. Whether by boat or swimming our asses to the next shore. We're leaving this island with Sunny. That's that.

"Don't escape. Got it." I nod, stepping into the room and spotting Shepp on the bed, all sprawled out and sleeping peacefully through even breaths.

Good for him. The last thing that man needs is more trauma inflicted by his father. His tattered suit slightly hangs open at the chest, revealing his dirty, muscular flesh riddled with old battle scars.

He's breathing.

He's okay.

At least from here.

I don't even worry about the asshole locking me in the room. Fuck Shadow. Fuck Darrell. The only person who matters right now is the man on the bed. In a flash, my feet carry me to him. The urgency to hold and touch him rides me hard.

"Shepp," I whisper with tears burning my eyes and cascading down my cheeks, carving a river of my pain into my flesh. "Shepp," I weep again, completely losing myself in the feeling of his skin beneath my fingertips as I cup his cheeks. Leaning down, I put my forehead against his.

His warmth radiates off him. He's warm. Alive! Fucking breathing against me.

Shadow didn't win. We did.

Inside the pit, I didn't know what I'd come back to. Did his father truly poison him? Or was it all a ruse to force me into the situation? No matter what it was, it still felt real to me. It still does. The fear eats at me. Any second now, they could take Shepp away from me.

Tears drip from my eyes onto his flesh, trailing down his pale cheeks. His stricken face, the one he gave me as I left the cave, remains forever etched in my mind as a work of art. Never forgotten. The despair. His head shaking no. His hand reaching out to stop me from going. I squeeze my eyes shut, forcing my tears to slow down.

He's okay.

He's fucking okay.

Alive!

Breathing.

And he almost wasn't. They nearly took him from me.

My fingers trail over the scar on his cheek, tracing it up and down. An old wound. A long-lasting memento. All from the demented man who took us captive.

I'll help Shepp dismantle him piece by piece one day. That's his trophy. His right. Shadow has taken so much from so many people. Shepp the most.

"Why is everything so messed up?" I mumble through my sobs. "Why are we here?"

Every moment I shut my eyes and fall into a fitful sleep, I pray I wake up and this is all a dream. That I'm still nestled between Arrow, Jericho, and Shepp in our gigantic bed made for us. I pray it's my sleep medication taking me for a ride and the man I murdered didn't rise from the dead to take my monster's empire while using me and his son.

But then I pinch myself, knowing I'm still lucid in the land of the living. This is no dream.

It's a continuous nightmare.

I push myself off Shepp, checking him over again—the rise and fall of his chest. The flutter of his eyes beneath his lids, scurrying around like he's in a dream. Hopefully, it's a good one.

I don't know at this point. About anything.

I stand from the bed, holding my aching stomach. The food from dinner rumbles through my digestive tract unhappily, making a sour taste burst on my tongue. Our new prison is more luxurious and lit up than our last. Gone are the dim, dank walls of the cave. Now, we're greeted by shitty paintings, one queen-sized bed, and, oh my God, it's an actual bathroom; how I've missed toilets and showers.

There has to be a way for us to escape this damn nightmare. If we're in a hotel, we have to be somewhere close, right? There can't be a hotel out in the middle of the ocean? Right? I shake my head. No matter the answer, Shepp and I will explore tomorrow and find out. Darrell says the island is inescapable.

I don't believe him.

Every prison has a secret way of getting out of it. So, we'll remove ourselves from this place and return to Jericho and Arrow. No matter what.

My breath completely leaves my body when I open the drapes, revealing the outside world for the first time in days, and dimming sunlight streams through the window. I wince at the brightness until my eyes adjust, and I see it.

The ocean. Blue waves. Jagged rocks. And nothing for miles over the horizon from my vantage point. We're fucked. Stuck. My eyes trail down, down, down to the pit of jagged rocks near the turbulent sandy shore.

All hope evaporates.

There's no escaping through the window. We'd die. Miserably. Our bodies would break against the rocks, and we'd have nowhere to go. No boats. Or a sense of direction toward Briar Cove.

"He's some mysterious man living in the shadows or something. He has an island fifty minutes off the coast. Elias told me all about it. It's tropical. People are everywhere. It's wild."

The realization snacks into me. Hard. I nearly fall off my feet when Jenni's voice filters through my mind.

She told me all about this place. The night we went to Rave, we danced and drank together. Scratch that. It was more than drinking and dancing.

It was a whole damn experience.

Jenni showed off her vagina, puked in the bathroom, and then I experienced the hottest night of my life—enter Jericho, Shepp, and Arrow finger-fucking me on the dance floor.

My body aches for them again. Their comfort. Even though they're goddamn psychopaths who trapped me, married me, stole my damn IUD, and so much more.

But damn. I miss them—my psychos. They're my giant red flags waving in the wind.

My stomach rolls again, clenching and churning until acid drifts up my esophagus. Oh, fuck. I blow out a breath when the spaghetti does a damn dance inside me, aching to be free.

Grimacing, I rub my hand along my stomach, begging it to chill out. I just ate, damn it. After so many days without sustenance, I really need this food.

But it's a losing battle.

My feet move faster than my brain as I run into the bathroom, throw open the toilet, and relieve myself of all the delicious spaghetti and rolls I consumed. And let me tell you, it's not as delicious the second time around.

"Ugh," I groan into the toilet, squeezing my eyes shut.

Maybe it was the spaghetti that didn't agree with me. Or the stress. I'm leaning toward the stress of everything. Fight pit. Kidnapping. Starving in a cave. And the list goes on. Not to mention, I'm still in my murder dress, drenched in old blood.

Whatever it is, my body does not agree with it. And it's too damn bad because I needed the nutrients to regain my strength.

I nearly combust with relief when strong hands grip my hair, gently pulling it back as the last heave works its way out of me. Pain engulfs my empty stomach when I suck in a breath, reaching blindly to flush the toilet. I rest my forehead on the cool rim of the seat, reveling in the momentary relief. As the pain slowly wanes and the nausea subsides, Shepp rubs my back with his free hand, silently telling me he's worried about me.

"You're okay?" I rasp, forcing my eyes open and head off the toilet. "Are you hurt? Poisoned?" Every fear I've held back runs through me. I'm almost afraid to look back at him, but I force myself to.

He lifts my hand into his, despite how bloodied and dirty it is—never showing an ounce of disgust or recoiling from me. The warmth of his palm sends shivers down my spine.

He's real, right in front of me.

'Now that you're here, I am,' he writes on the palm of my hand. *'Are you?'* Torrid emotions reflect in his big ocean eyes, flashing as they wait for my answer. I can almost hear his

voice distantly in my head. The one he used when he painted my flesh. So free. So full of life.

But how do I answer that? Am I okay? Fuck no. Not by a long shot. Shadow has more blackmail on me than Gabriel ever did. Murder. Shepp. My fucking sister and her future. Her health. We're puppets on a string for him to play with—chess pieces to move around as he pleases. Everything Shadow wants is at his fingertips. All he has to do is say jump, and I'll have to say how high.

He'll spare no one to get what he wants.

"I need a shower," I murmur, peeling my gaze away from his. He's too perceptive, looking behind the wall in my soul. I feel him burning through me, staring at the thick red blood coating my flesh. What feels like spiders crawling across my skin has my muscles tightening and desperation to get clean, clawing at me. "I need..." I trail off, staring at the wall.

A black hole opens inside me. I'm hollow. Numb. Unsure of what I need. A shower. More food. Water. All of the above.

Shepp gently wipes away the vomit from my lips with a piece of toilet paper and tosses it into the trash. He waits me out, sitting beside me patiently as I regain myself.

'Is it...' he mouths, trailing off with a twisted expression filled with anguish.

He gestures at me. My dress. The blood on my skin. He runs his hands over every inch of me. Most likely looking for external wounds that aren't there. Only internal ones fester with pain, rotting me from the inside out.

"It's not mine," I say hurriedly, clutching his wrist. "It's not mine..." I trail off again with a hitch in my voice.

My skin crawls again, tightening the more he looks at me. Every inch goes untouched, slithering across my flesh, inspecting me more and more until he's satisfied I'm not the one bleeding out.

No. It's not me. It's the man I was forced to kill like so many times before. I'm a goddamn murderer. No matter the circumstances. No matter the—I had to do it to stay alive and keep my family alive—situation. Bile rises again, rumbling my upset stomach. My mind flip-flops, torturing me with my past and guilt.

"Fuck," I heave, leaning over the toilet again and emptying the remaining chunks of food from my guts.

So much for dinner, I guess I was only renting it.

I shudder a breath when he gently wipes my mouth again with more concern than before. Then he flushes the toilet, holding me tightly in his arms.

'Are you hurt?' he writes on my palm. *'What happened to you?'*

"No. Not hurt."

Not physically, maybe. But mentally, I'm sinking into my darkness more by the day, letting it consume the light I've clung to for years, keeping me afloat. To soothe the chaos inside and calm my nerves, I need my music and my sleeping pills to push through the nightmares sneaking past my defenses. I crave a normal life. I've felt like a pawn for so long. I don't know what it's like to just be Journey West.

Who would she be?

Shepp gently peels me off the ground, holding my head to his massive chest. The sound of his beating heart has my muscles loosening, and my stomach settles as his fingers work through my hair. Then, he picks up the small bottle of mouth-wash on the counter and hands me a cup to rinse my mouth. I take it gratefully, rinsing out the taste of vomit and spitting it into the sink.

Much better.

"Thank you," I mutter with a sigh.

'Let's get you in the shower.' He nods toward the tub, pulling me to my shaky feet.

"Okay," I whisper brokenly, trying to keep all the emotions festering inside at bay.

My tears want to spill over. Heartache wants to take me.

But I don't let it. I have to be aware, especially with Shadow and his nefarious plans eating away at my mind. So, I suck them down and don't let them to the surface. Yet.

'Want to talk about it?' he mouths, checking me over again.

No. I don't. Ever again. But I know it'll all come out. I can't stay silent forever. Not with him. Or Jericho. Or Arrow. They'll pull it out of me in creative ways.

I shake my head. "Later..." my voice trails off when he unzips my days-old dress, now soaked in blood, sweat, and tears. It peels from my body like a second skin, dropping to the floor in a rumpled mess, leaving me in nothing but my panties. Shepp gently peels those off, too, dropping them with my dress.

My eyes stray to the mess. How I wish we could burn the material. What started as a good night of dressing up and celebrating their initiation took a turn for the worst. It was something we didn't anticipate.

He hugs me from behind, squeezing me softly without saying a word, knocking me out of my thoughts. I'm desperate to stop thinking about it. All of it.

When he lets go, his warmth leaves with him. A hollow part of me opens without his touch, spreading dark tendrils throughout my veins and into my mind. It beckons me. Calling me to surrender to it and dive headfirst into the blackness that can take my feelings away.

But I refuse.

Shepp moves, opening the shower curtain. I force myself to watch his movements. Grounding myself in the moment. I'm alive. He's alive. Sunshine is alive. We'll make it out to safety by tomorrow—not staying here any longer than necessary.

We'll find a way.

Family always finds each other.

Reaching in, Shepp turns the hot water knob on full blast, and the first bit of happiness breaks through the darkness in me like sunshine breaking through the bleak clouds on a shitty day.

Hot fucking water.

"It works," I breathe with relief, my body physically relaxing at the sound of the water hitting the tub with force.

After being made to sit in a torn dress drenched in another man's blood, I'm ready to wash myself clean. Scrub his essence off me and never think about this night again. Or what I had to do to protect the people who mean the most to me.

Our next steps remain undetermined. But this shower? Fuck. It'll be a small bandage on our time here.

Shepp smiles softly at me, nodding as he undresses completely and then holds out his hand. We enter the shower together, reminding me of when he painted my body. He showed me a side of him no one else gets to see. Not even Jericho and Arrow.

"This brings back memories," I mumble as his big hands scrub at my flesh, working the blood off my skin and letting it float away with the water. "Only this time it's not paint..." I suck in a breath when he stalls his movements, and his eyes find mine.

There's reassurance there, staring back at me—words he cannot speak and emotions he refuses to show. He's staying strong. Holding on so he can comfort me through the hell I just walked through. Even though I want to remain strong and not let my tears or quivering lips out, it's hard to hang on when I want to let it all go. I feel like kicking and screaming and crying my fucking eyes out until the pain no longer tears me apart. Before, in the past, I have ended someone's life. I tell myself that repeatedly. But it never gets easier. I'm not that person. Not really.

He nods a few times before returning to rubbing my skin raw for me with a clean washcloth. My muscles relax under his touch, and the warmth from the shower washes away the last few days. Taking it down the drain and erasing the evidence of my fucked up night.

Only for a second does his fingers leave my flesh. Then he's cradling my chin and forcing me to look deep into his eyes. Oh, those ocean eyes full of wonder and concern peeking into my blackened soul and begging me to bear it all.

And so I do, with no more hesitation.

What's the point?

"He made me fight for my life," I choke out, rolling my lips together. Who knows what kinds of listening devices he has here? "All I could think about was you. He said he poisoned you, and if I didn't... If I didn't fight, he'd kill you." Shepp's thumb brushes along my bottom lip, gently silencing my thoughts. Silence fills the air as we stare into each other's eyes. "Are you okay? What happened after I left?"

He shakes his head. *'No poison.'*

"No?" Relief slams through me. "But... What was it? I don't understand."

But I do. Somewhat. Shadow wanted me out of that cave. Alone. Vulnerable. He could only get me to do what he wanted by threatening the man I cared about within grasp. He manipulated me into the ring. Just like he manipulated the entire fight so I would win and that asshole would lose. But how did he know I'd use those weapons to defend myself? I could have been a scared little girl crying the entire time.

Does Shadow know more about what I went through with Gabriel?

It's a possibility.

'I'm fine,' he mouths forcefully, aching for me to believe his words. Not likely. I could tell him I'm fine, too, until I'm blue in the face, but that would be a damn lie.

"What happened after I left? How'd you get here?" I search his eyes as they soften.

'Woke up here,' he mouths. *'Not sure if I passed out. Was*

waiting for you.' I nod. *'Then I heard you in here...'* he trails off, not adding the last part where I weakly puked my guts out.

I rest my forehead against his shoulder, sucking in breaths. Forget everything you went through tonight. Forget the life force that left that terrible man. He deserved everything that came to him. It's too bad I was the one to deliver it. Every soul I take weighs heavily on my mind, deepening my darkness. One day soon, if I'm not careful, I'll turn into the unstoppable machine my monster wanted me to be—a silent killer.

The water cascades down our bodies, continuously washing the blood from my flesh. Not that there's a lot more. But blood has a funny way of getting into the nooks and crannies. Believe me, I know. So many times, I've found blood where it shouldn't be, much to my monster's dismay. *Never leave a mess, Little Snake.* He'd say after slamming me back into my cage and locking the door with a sneer. I still remember how his beady eyes looked at me through the bars. Yeah, yeah. That's easier said than done.

"This entire thing is so fucked," I whisper brokenly, attempting to keep all my emotions bottled inside. I never fathomed I'd be in a position like this—stuck on an island and responsible for keeping my loved ones alive.

It's a new kind of Hell I want to run away from.

'It is,' he mouths, forcing me to watch his lips move. *'Let me wash your hair.'*

I nod in response, slowly lifting my head off his shoulder. Being in his arms and feeling his warmth surrounding me almost takes away all the morbid thoughts running through my mind. He's grounding me and keeping me sane.

Shepp eases my neck back, forcing my hair under the hot spray. Soft hums emanate from his throat as his fingers massage my scalp and work toward the ends of my hair. Meticulously making sure every strand gets worked over and cleaned.

A thick lump forms in my throat at his voice peeking through the simple melody. It's a hint of what he can do but only has for me. Goosebumps spread across my flesh when he gently massages my scalp under the heat of the water. With Shepp, I don't feel vulnerable or fragile. I feel pampered and taken care of. With the food, the touches, his voice, and the paintings, he'll forever be by my side.

That's why I vow to do everything I can for him.

Starting by admitting everything that happened tonight. Beyond the fucking pit of terrors.

"I fought in a pit tonight. It was him or me: him or you and Sunshine. I chose you and my sister," I whisper when his fingers stall their gentle touches. "Sunny was there, too. Right by your father's side. After the fight, he took me to dinner."

As I tell him everything about the dinner, that Sunshine is his sister, and who was there, I keep my voice low enough that the guards outside our room won't hear a thing. The last thing I need is someone listening in on my confessions and thoughts. I know Shadow will use them to his advantage.

Shepp's lips gently land on mine when I'm done whispering my secrets. He holds me impossibly close, molding my front to his, working his fingers through the wet strands of my hair and keeping me there.

'You did what you had to do. Okay?' he mouths with pain twisting his facial features. *'No one will judge you for it. Not me. Not Jericho. Fuck, Arrow will probably hump you for forty hours straight.'* He huffs slightly when my lips twist up into a smile.

"Hump me?" I murmur through a little laugh. "Probably more than that."

The echo of his words bounces around in my brain. No matter the pain I inflicted on the man who deserved it, I did what I had to do. It's a vicious fucking life to live. But that's just it. I had to keep going. If I didn't kill that man, someone else would have. And then, where would I be? In the caves? Slowly dying a miserable death without food, Shepp and my sister.

I did what I had to do. It's time I own it.

Shepp levels me with a playful glare, not easing up on his grip. *'You know Arrow would do so many things to you if he got wind of you covered in blood.'*

My fingers trail down his jaw, tracing up over the scar etched into his face. A scar he'll have to live with for the rest of his life because of the man who brought us here.

"We all have scars, don't we?" I murmur, furrowing my brows. "You. Me. Jericho. Arrow. This life..." I shake my head. I may not have been born and bred into the Mafia life as a child. But a new Journey was born in a pool of blood on the trailer floor of her mother's home after she murdered a man in a frenzy.

All to save her sister and save herself.

The new Journey West was taken from blood, put into the dark, starved, thrown around, and forced to complete tasks filled with death. The old me never could have fathomed it. And the new me? Well, she's going to take life by the balls and stop dwelling about the blood on her hands.

'We do,' Shepp mouths with a huff, resting his forehead against mine. *'So many scars. Like this one.'* He takes my hand, forcing it to trace the large scar lining the right side of his face as he shudders and closes his eyes.

Leaning in, I take him against me, softly running my tongue over the seam of his lips, noting the hesitation within him. Desperately, he clings to me harder, pressing frantically against me before letting my tongue in to explore his mouth. A soft moan escapes through his throat, vibrating through his chest and finally puncturing through me. It sets me on edge. Making me want to forget everything about myself.

A new Journey is on the horizon.

"Fuck me," I whisper when his lips travel down my neck, lightly sucking my skin between his teeth and leaving his mark. "Help me forget about everything, Shepp. Your touch is the only touch I want to think about for now."

Not Shadow's. Not the man who made me drop to my knees.

Just Shepp's.

I swallow a moan at the look in Shepp's eyes, glazing over without thought. His hardness pokes into my belly, jumping when my hand runs over the velvety tip. Gently, I run my thumb over his weeping slit, spreading the sticky pre-cum.

'If that's what you want,' he mouths, as slight groans seep between his lips.

"That's music to my ears, Shepp," I whisper, nipping his bottom lip. "Keep groaning. Keep making noise," I breathe, jerking him in my hand several times, reveling in the sounds coming from him.

He nods slowly, getting lost in the sensations of my hand on his cock.

"It's what I want," I moan softly, pecking his lips again. Desperate to feel every bit of him against me.

Without warning, he lifts me into his arms and slams my back against the cold shower wall. All the oxygen leaves my lungs as I cling to him, digging my nails into his shoulders, leaving crescent moon indentations on his flesh.

My mark.

'My Little Tempest,' he mouths, running his fingers over my lips as I watch his movements. *'You're a fucking storm.'*

"A storm?" I breathe when the tip of his cock slides through my slit, mercilessly teasing me until I'm aching for him to slam into me and fucking take me over. Possess me. Fucking use me until my mind can't form coherent thoughts.

'A storm,' he confirms, pushing inside me with a soft groan. Our chests heave when he slowly trails himself in and out. *'I watched you for so long. Taking care of you. Feeding you*

because your mom...' He shakes his head. I pulse around him at his confession, earning a slight, cocky smirk I never expected to see from him.

"No one has ever cared that much," I breathe as chills roll down my spine, and I want to scream in pleasure at the top of my lungs. Shepp must sense I'm about to slip up when he slams inside me again and covers my mouth with his lips. We're a frenzy of thrusts, soft moans, and nails digging into flesh. He shudders after a few more seconds, spilling himself deep inside me.

'You'll never have to worry again. We'll always provide for you,' he mouths earnestly, forcing me to stare into his eyes as his cock twitches inside me. *'Never again, Little Tempest.'*

"Even if you all are a little psycho," I quip, leaning my forehead against his.

'That, too,' he mouths, gently pulling out of me with a sigh. *'Let's get you cleaned up again and get out of here.'*

"Then we can sleep," I mutter, attempting to stand on my jelly legs. The warmth of the water soothes our skin again, washing away the evidence of our tryst. "I've missed a bed so much," I groan when he massages my shoulders, truly pampering me before the water turns cold and he shuts it off.

Shepp smiles at me softly when he offers me his hand, and we step out of the shower together onto the mat, catching the water dripping from our skin. He lifts a fluffy white towel from a rack above the toilet and holds it open until I step into it. With gentle hands, he dries every inch of me before drying himself off with a separate towel. Once completely dried, we wrap them around us, covering our bodies.

I've missed a bed, a shower, and all the other things I've taken for granted. Food. Shelter. Fuck. Who would have thought I'd miss my trailer with the creaking floors, suspect ceilings, and minimal food supplies?

But I've missed this the most—the intimacy and closeness I had with the three of them and the stability of a home. But not just any home. You see, my home doesn't have four walls. My home has three psychos who will do anything and everything for me.

They're my light in the darkness. My home.

"How exactly did you get into my house back then?" I ask, tilting my head.

He grins, drying the short strands of his hair, and then wraps the towel around his waist. *'I made a key,'* he mouths with a shrug, like it's no big deal that he broke into my home and fed me when I couldn't do it myself.

"That's not weird at all." I quip with a smile. "Thank you, Shepp. You took care of me when I couldn't do it myself." Emotions clog my throat at his dedication through the years. He's always looked after me, and I didn't have a damn clue.

He's my literal hero in a red cape, saving the day. Even now. He's the rock I lean on while processing all my bullshit.

And I'm his.

The soft click of the lock and swoosh of our hotel room door opening and closing has the hairs on my neck standing on end. My gaze whips to Shepp, who stiffly stares through the bathroom door with narrowed eyes.

"You hear that?" I whisper, attempting to keep my voice low.

Shepp nods in confirmation and cradles my cheeks in his palms. *'Whoever is out there. They won't get through me, okay?'* he mouths.

I nod. "Don't be a hero," I whisper, taking a deep breath.

'I'm not a hero, Little Tempest. I'm the villain.'

"You'll never be the villain in my story," I whisper, shaking my head in his grasp. "You are my hero. Today. Tomorrow. Forever." His face completely softens when he kisses me, sealing his lips over mine one last time.

'Then, let's face the monster waiting for us,' he mouths, gripping me tightly. *'No matter what....'* He leaves those words suspended in the air for me to understand that he'd do anything

for me right now. *'You've sacrificed yourself enough.'* Before I can respond, he grabs my hand and forces me behind him as he opens the door.

Silence fills the space as we stand before the man I never wanted to see again. I force myself not to blush when his eyes take in our towel-covered bodies. But he seems satisfied with whatever he sees and sneers at us.

"Well, well." Shadow grins, standing by our window. "How was it? Good?"

Shepp's hand squeezes mine at the sight of his father. Three times. It's his reassurance that he's here with me, despite the fear taking him over.

"Why are you here now?" I ask, stepping slightly in front of Shepp.

Because fuck this guy. I can only imagine how rough it is to see your abusive father after so many years of being dead and buried.

"Just wanted to let you know that I have some insight. Someone is attempting to stake out the island on a boat."

"Someone?" I ask, swallowing hard as my hopes get raised further. Could it be them? Finally, coming to save me from this hellhole. "Hmm, yes. Come look," Shadow says cockily, pulling back the curtains.

The sun lingers on the horizon, painting the blue sky pink and orange as it descends, but that's not what catches my eye. In the distance, a fireball explodes on the water, lighting up the surrounding area.

"What did you do?" I whisper, staring with furrowed brows.

Was it Arrow and Jericho? Or was it a random ship he's burning away to prove a point to us?

"Anyone who comes for you. Anyone who thinks they can save you will have a nice surprise. There's no way off this island. I have weapons that can destroy them before they can even step foot on my land. Because that's what this island is—

Shadows. They'd be trespassing, and I can use deadly force."
With a grin, he watches the burning boat as the fire completely
consumes it near the rocks. "I'm curious, though. How'd they
even know where to look?"

"No clue. Maybe they know more about you than you
think," I quip, swallowing the lump in my throat when his
hardened eyes glare through me.

"Do they? Because no one knows who the fuck I am," he
growls, balling his fingers into fists.

"Except Elias. Why does he get special privileges?" I raise
a brow, unable to hold my tongue against him.

"And you. And him." Shadow points a finger to the two of
us with a malicious grin, making an uneasy feeling bubble in
my stomach.

Why is us knowing who he is setting off alarm bells in my
mind?

"Elias is loyal to a fault. You two have no choice. Besides,
soon enough, everyone will know who Shadow is." He grins at
that, losing the anger written on his face. "The reveal is
coming." He straightens his shirt with pride, sending my
stomach into knots again.

Something fucky is afoot, and I can't figure out what it is.
Well, besides being on this fucking island and stuck in some
fancy hotel.

No choice. Right. He thinks he has us over a barrel, which
is fine. He can keep thinking that. I learned not to antagonize
the monster standing before me a long time ago. Well, mostly.
I still have my moments of defiance. Like right now. I can't
seem to hold my tongue, and I'm way too curious to find out
his intentions.

"Right," I agree with a nod.

"And when I send you out next weekend for your mission,
you'll be good little spies." He tilts his head, examining us.
"Or your sister gets married off to the first man I see." There it

is. There's the threat I've been waiting for. Do this, or your sister gets it.

I try not to let his words affect me as much as they do—my poor sister. I can't believe she agreed to that. But what better motivation to keep me in line? Sure, my sister couldn't have lived without her medications before. But the thought of her marrying an older man on this monster's orders has my stomach twisting into knots.

"Shepp, too," Shadow offers with a smirk when I turn rigid. "You think there aren't any women out there I could offer him up to? A Russian socialite with connections to the Bratva and an Italian princess is currently on the market. Maybe I could strengthen my ties to the Bratva and the Italians by offering my children on a silver platter. You'd love that, wouldn't you?" He narrows his eyes at me.

Is that why he allowed Shepp to be here when he wasn't supposed to be? Because he's useful to him for alliance reasons now? I can't wrap my head around this arranged marriage stuff, and then I remember I was in one, too.

My mother signed my life away to Gabriel Viotto, and it was all because of money. Money that Gabriel has undoubtedly gotten his fingers on already. Everything I had hoped for —for Sunny and me—is gone. That was going to be our ticket out.

"Is that why he's here, then? So, you can use him?"

Shadow scoffs, turning from the window as the fiery remnants of the boat in the distance sink to the bottom of the ocean. I'm barely holding myself above water right now at the thought of Jericho and Arrow somewhere else. They wouldn't be stupid enough to come here without looking at the island first, right? They wouldn't come here half-cocked and ready to storm the shores? No. That's not Jericho's M.O. He seems to have everything under control and is always two steps ahead of the game.

That's the tiny life jacket I'm hanging onto, anyway, clinging to it for dear life before I'm drowning.

"He wasn't supposed to be here at all. But then my insider found him sniffing around, and you became a two-for-one deal." Shadow smirks. "But it all works out. I can find something useful for him and you. You've already proved yourself to me in the pits."

I want to say because he rigged it. I wouldn't have survived if a certain someone hadn't put that bug in Brian's ear. But I hold my tongue. He could have me back in there before I can catch my breath.

"So, you're going to marry him off, too?" I ask, gripping Shepp's hand tighter.

"He has no say in it," Shadow quips, stepping up to me with a sneer. "Do as I say. You all live. Sunny gets to live. Fight me, and I will fight back. Kill everyone you love. You thought the pit was rough? Wait until you get an opponent who wants to fight you, little girl! You think you can walk through this life without receiving the consequences of your actions. Well, I've got another thing coming for you." His grin is so cruel that I want to shrivel up and die.

But I don't. If there's anything the pits taught me, it was to raise my chin and fight the fucking battle head-on. No matter the consequences.

I lift my chin. Despite the terror shaking my bones, I stare him in the eye. If he wants me to play the girl who will follow all his rules, I'll let him think I am. That's the best I can do for now. I can't fight him. Not physically. He's bigger than me. And so are the assholes in the rings. The only thing I can do is pretend. Pretend I'm following his word to keep Shepp and Sunny safe. And myself, too. Until the time comes we can all run away.

"Whatever you say." I give him a sharp nod. "Whatever you need me to do."

Shadow's eyes peer up and down Shepp's bare chest,

lingering on the long wound over his heart. The one that matches mine. The symbol of our loyalties to the Viotto family.

"There are clothes on the way for both of you. I can't have my heir wandering the halls naked. Or my prized fighter. Next weekend we will attend the wedding. I expect you all to be on your best behavior and hope you enjoy your stay at Shadow Island."

There's a threat there, lingering in his unsaid words. *I could throw you back into the pits and send Shepp away. So, be good.*

He grins widely and then saunters out of the room, slamming the door closed and leaving my heart pumping wildly in my chest.

I deflate immediately, blowing out a breath. Well, for only a second. Why the hell would Shepp and I get any peace on this godforsaken island?

The door of our hotel room bursts open again, revealing Darrell, the lovely guard from before. His dark brows furrow when he takes us in, standing around in our towels. Shepp steps in front of me, folding his arms over his chest and blocking Darrell's view of me.

Darrell huffs, "Your clothes." He sets them on the bed indifferently, immediately turning his back to us.

"So kind of you," I quip, keeping my distance from him.

He grunts in response, muscles tensing when he takes a step away. "I will lock the doors again until morning." Yeah, we know. Thanks for the reminder, Grumpy Pants. You've proven yourself to be so informative.

"No escaping. We know," I say through gritted teeth.

There's just something about Darrell that sets my teeth on edge and makes my hand twitchy. If I had those knives from the fight, I'd have him on the ground, gagged, and stabbed before he could cry to his mommy. Not that he looks like the crying type with his large muscles and broad body. But still.

He gets on my damn nerves, mainly when he sticks his nose in the air and saunters out the door with nothing else to say. Sure enough, the lock clicking into place reverberates through our fancy new prison.

"What kind of hotel do you think this used to be?" I ask, staring at the pile of clothes with a wrinkled nose. "Can you poison fabric?" I wouldn't put it past Darrell to drop poison into our clothes and watch as we slowly die on the floor of this place. Silent jerkbag.

Shepp's eyes scan the room, and he shrugs. *'Seems like a typical hotel room to me.'*

My back stiffens. "You don't think there are cameras in here, do you?" I murmur as his eyes scan the area again.

'Could be,' he mouths. *'Let's dress in the bathroom.'* With that, he takes the pile of clothes, and we go into the bathroom to get dressed in the sweatpants and sweatshirts provided for us.

"At least it's comfortable," I sigh, when we finally fall into bed, lying face to face.

'We'll get out of here,' he mouths as his warm breaths hit my flesh.

"How?" My breath hitches. "We're trapped here."

His fingers glide over my jaw again, tracing circles over my flesh. *'Tomorrow. The door will be unlocked. Right?'* I nod in response because that's what Darrell said before. We're locked in for the night and have a curfew, but we'll be able to get out of here in the morning. *'Then tomorrow, we look around. See the sights and make a plan.'*

A plan. God. Stress lifts off my heavy chest for the first time in what feels like forever. Finally, we won't be flailing in the abyss of being stuck. We have something to look forward to—a light at the end of our shitty tunnel.

"It's a plan."

With that, I snuggle into Shepp's side, pressing myself into him. It's like the nights we suffered in the cold cave, barely able to sleep comfortably. Only this time, we have the luxury of a bed and a toilet a few steps away. We're not in the clear, but we seem to be moving up in the world—one step at a damn time.

I wish this would be over already and I was back with Sunshine, keeping her safe at the mansion filled with Shepp's cooking, Jericho's violin, and Arrow's laughter. With that pleasant thought, I fall into a deep sleep.

CHAPTER EIGHTEEN

Shepp

JOURNEY WOULD NEVER KNOW THE TURMOIL FESTERING DEEP inside me, gnawing at my thoughts. Everything she had to do in that pit of bullshit was because I couldn't protect her.

Me. Sheppard Mondelli. Second-in-command to Jericho. Member of the Viotto Crime Family. Fucking useless.

I couldn't save her from my father years ago. Hell, I couldn't even save myself from his wrath. Even now. He's like an unbeatable boss at the end of a game, continuously coming back to life.

My fingers brush over her soft cheeks. Her skin is smooth beneath my touch, and I revel in it. Fucking possess me completely. Here in this room. This is our little slice of paradise in the Hellscape we've been dragged into.

Our room. Our time. Just us. We'll pretend we're fine, but we're anything but. Not until we can figure out a way to contact the others and pray they weren't on that fucking boat. Knowing Arrow's reckless ass, he was probably the captain of the stupid thing, guiding them directly into fucking harm's way. Good thing Jericho wouldn't have let him out of his sight —Arrow's reckless. Jericho's meticulous. Get the two together; it's a deadly combination of knocking heads. As for me? I'm the calm in the storm. The grounding force keeping us functioning.

Or at least, I try to be for them.

I blow out a breath, attempting to fight off all the pain and worry living deep inside my fucking soul. I want to rip my father's heart out and fucking watch as he suffers under my hands. My brain concocts so many scenarios where I'm the one to watch the light bleed from his eyes as he chokes on his blood and tongue while I laugh at his misery.

Instead of letting my anger fuel me as the sun passes through our window, I dedicate myself to counting the freckles dotting Journey's cheeks to calm myself. Years before, I'd count backward in my head. Even teaching it to Jericho to soothe his ferocious anger. But right now, I'm beyond visualizing the numbers in my mind. I need the visual of the woman I love finally sleeping peacefully in my arms after a night of whimpering and thrashing around.

I knew that's how this would end. That my girl would be fighting the demons of her past like so many times before. This time, I couldn't comfort her with my voice when she screamed out in pain, begging for her past torment to end. Only the touch of my fingers brings her back to me, and it helps soothe her. Only slightly.

Exhaustion weighs heavily on my aching eyes as I watch her. She wasn't the only one worried about my father sneaking in here at night and taking what he wanted. Fuck.

I clench my fist at my side. I'd lose myself in the colors and shapes if I had my paints and canvases. Forget about my worries and just be. But here? It's fucking impossible to think through the rage bellowing beneath the surface.

I have to be careful here. I can't let my guard down, not around my father. He has something up his sleeves. More than what he's said.

With a kiss on her forehead, I lift myself away from her embrace and get out of bed with a sigh. I spot a coffee machine with pods near the table and window, making a beeline toward it. The sweet scent of coffee fills the room, slightly calming my nerves. Journey doesn't stir, sleeping eerily still under the covers. Lowering myself into a chair across the bed, I sip the hot coffee and squeeze my eyes shut. The sweet burn of the liquid travels down my throat, warming my empty stomach.

My eyes stray out the window, peeking through the slit of the curtain. The sun highlights the rugged terrain again, giving way to the large island we're trapped on, with a dramatic drop to the rocks meeting the shoreline.

No escape.

That phrase rings repeatedly in my brain.

We're trapped birds in a cage. Only able to stand by and watch as the world moves around us while we're standing still. I sip my coffee, trying to knock the morbid thoughts out of my mind. We will escape here. No matter if we have to climb over the sharp rocks and swim our way back to Briar Cove.

I'll protect Journey and Sunshine with my damn life.

The soft click of the lock disengaging, followed by the gentle creak of the door swinging open, fills the silent room. I hold my breath, my coffee mug pausing midway to my lips. I eye Darrell, standing stoically in the doorframe, barely fitting through with a pile of clothes in his arms.

He frowns. I fucking frown. Tension rises. Then, I set my coffee cup on the table and stand, crossing my arms over my chest to prepare for a showdown. I'll fight if I have to. Even if my stomach turns and blood makes me slightly queasy.

I've done it before, and I'll do it again to keep the woman I'm obsessed with safe.

"Your father wants a word with you," he grumbles, tossing the stack of clothes at my chest, forcing me to catch them. I huff, looking at Journey. "Alone."

His words ring through the room like a fucking bullet. Alone? Fuck no. Over my dead body. My chest puffs up. A sense of protectiveness hits me hard.

I'll never leave her again. Ever.

Darrell holds up a finger with a sigh, stopping me from coming toward him. I'm going to tear his fucking head off, and then... I have no clue.

I look him up and down. He's huge. Muscular. Intimidating as hell. Could I take him? He's shorter than me. Yet, stockier. I could easily surprise him. But how far could I get?

Could I escape with him dead? Lock him in this room, steal his keys, and carry Journey and Sunny to safety? Possibly. Or not.

Darrell ignores my murderous glare and opens the door further, allowing another presence into the room.

A glow hangs around her frame. She smiles. Seeming so light and carefree, bouncing into the room on her toes. Despite where we are and who has her. And us.

It's so strange looking at her. Sunshine. It's fitting for her. She's someone I barely knew existed. Even after those years of caring for Journey, feeding her, and sneaking into her home, I had no clue she had a sister.

Our sister.

A child my lunatic of a father gave to the world.

It's something Journey and I share now. A sister. Something I've never had before. A sibling. It was always just me under my father's thumb. No one to share the burden. Not that I wanted that or needed it. I took it as best I could.

But now I have a sister. Someone who shares my blood with the man who ruined my life. Fuck. Will he ruin hers?

All the more reason to get us all the fuck away from this island.

A tightness forms in my chest when I look her over. She's small. Weak looking. Slightly pale. But oh-so confident. It oozes out of her in waves as she grins at Journey and me, like this situation doesn't bother her.

Walking into the room, she has a skip in her step, stopping right before me. Turning, she glares at Darrell, who immediately rolls his eyes, turns on his heel, and walks out the door before hesitating.

"I'll be waiting for you," he grunts, shutting the door behind him.

"She'll be okay. I'm going to take her downstairs with me." Her cheeks pinken slightly before she clears her throat, staring up at me. "We're going to make breakfast for all of us." She grins.

That smile—it's warm and inviting. It reminds me of Journey and what genuine joy would look like on my girl. But also him—my father. I see him inside her—the look in her eyes and the small expressions on her face.

Sunshine is a true mix of the two. It's odd to witness.

I sigh, spotting a notebook and pen on the nightstand beside the bed. Like most functioning hotels, this one has all the amenities—coffee, paper pads, thin sheets, and toilet paper.

The works.

I'm not sure what to say to Sunny. We've never spoken. Hell, I didn't know she existed for most of my time knowing Journey.

To say this is awkward is an understatement. What the hell do I say to her? Sorry, our dad is a fucking psycho, and you've been thrust into this bullshit?

'And you're okay?' I write quickly, showing her the piece of paper as I stand in front of her again.

She blinks a few times at my question and nods shakily. Something sparks in her eyes—a truth she's withholding. I've watched people for years. Observing their habits and tics. People slip up around a man who can't speak. Thinking he won't tell a soul.

But they're wrong.

Journey has been terrified for her sister. Day in and day out, worrying about what she's doing and if she's safe. Especially in the caves. Drenched in the unknown. It's all that's been on her mind. Well, besides the fight and me and all the other bullshit Journey holds on her shoulders.

I need to end that.

I couldn't stop my father's fuckery before. But it ends now. I'll protect Journey and her—my—sister, with my entire fucking soul.

'She worries about you constantly.' I write, clearing the sludge in my throat.

Sunny's gaze strays to the woman unmoving under the sheets. A soft snore rips from her lips, filling the room. Sunny giggles, covering her mouth with her delicate fingers.

"She really shouldn't anymore," she says breezily, shrugging.

Easier said than done. I level Sunny with a glare. She grins at me, exposing all her teeth.

"I can tell by your face exactly what you're thinking. J is the most hard-headed woman on the planet. Believe me. She constantly kept my candy away from me." She pouts with a huff. "It was torture."

"You weren't supposed to eat it," Journey croaks, not opening her eyes or moving. "Bad for your heart, Brat."

Sunny giggles again, raising her chin. "Good! You're awake! I've got lots of plans for us today," Sunny chirps with pep, jumping in place while clapping her hands.

"Ugh," Journey whines, waving a dismissive hand and mumbling into the pillows. "You're way too perky this morning," she practically gags out, pulling her finger to her lips.

"You can go," Sunny says, putting a hand on her hip, eyeing me. She makes a shooing motion again, basically kicking me out.

I blink several times. Seriously? This tiny person can't be serious. Right?

"Sunny," Journey chastises. "You can't just boss him around."

Sunny raises her brows, looking between us with a huff.

She may seem like an adult, but I have to remind myself that despite the circumstances. She's a child. Fourteen. Fuck.

She was born into such a fucked up situation. Lucky for her, though. She didn't have to endure living under our father's roof. Unlucky for her, though. She had to spend her youth under Sable West's. At least she had Journey growing up. A grounding source that protected her from the worst of the worst, taking the brunt of it herself.

My girl is a goddamn hero.

From the corner of my eye, Darrell loudly opens the door and hovers in the doorway with an impatient expression. He checks his wrist and taps his watch. Fuck. I guess that's my cue. Sunny will get her wish. I'm out. I have to be. My father apparently needs to have a discussion with me. Oh, the joy. To see his face every day is going to be a living hell. I erased him from my mind so long ago. The echoes of his abuses live on. In my heart. In my mouth where my tongue should be and in my fucking memories.

I shut it down, leaving all that shit in the back of my mind. Fuck it all.

I kiss Journey's forehead, lingering for longer than necessary. Do I want to let her out of my sight? No. Do I feel safe leaving her here with Sunny? Possibly. If they're going to make breakfast, maybe Sunny knows something we don't. She's been out here longer than us, free to do whatever she wants. I can only hope.

Hope is all we have right now.

'I have to meet my father.' I gently nudge Journey, forcing her to open her eyes and read the note.

"The fuck," Journey murmurs, sitting up quickly. Her hair stands on end, and her beautiful face twists with disgust until it pales. "Why? Let me come with you." She wavers a bit, shaking her head when her eyes squeeze shut.

"You can't," Darrell interrupts with a huff.

"No one asked you, Darrell," she grits out, curling her fists on the comforter.

'I have to. I'll be fine.' I write again, shoving it in her face to remove the tension between her and Darrell. Whatever happened between the two of them needs to be explained. Because the way she seethes whenever he enters the room has my hackles rising.

Darrell rolls his eyes in response, discreetly tapping his watch again—impatient bastard. Give me a goddamn minute.

"Shepp," Journey whispers, eyeing Darrell with apprehension. There's a lot she's not saying with her words. What if this asshole kills me and then comes back for her or Sunny?

'I know.' I write out as cryptically as I can. I don't want the other two to catch wind of our thoughts. Especially the man tapping his foot now. *'Have fun with your sister.'* I quickly peck Journey on the lips and back away before she can stop me again.

"Don't worry. We're going to have fun today," Sunny says as I pass before her. "You'll be okay, too," she whispers, gently squeezing my arm. There's a promise in her words. Like she knows something I don't know. It's odd, staring at her—our sister.

I nod, letting her know I've heard her words, and she drops my arm.

Before Darrell can grunt anymore instructions, I quickly get dressed in the clothes he tossed at me in the bathroom and reemerge. A feeling of apprehension settles on my shoulders, but I have no choice to follow when he takes a step away and nods for me to follow.

"Follow me. Quickly. Before he has a goddamn aneurysm," Darrell grits out quietly, ushering me out the door and toward the elevators.

Once inside, I stand beside him, eyeing the metal walls, our reflections staring back at me. Darrell grunts, hits two buttons and forces a keypad out.

"I'm taking you to the basement. It's where your father's office is." His eyes cut to me, and he raises his brows. "It's only accessible through this." The last half of his sentence is soft and telling, urging me to watch as he hits the code. 1.2.2.4. My brows furrow at the numbers before the keypad automatically disappears into the box it came from, and the elevator returns to normal. Odd. There seems to be a secret floor of this hotel that my father doesn't want anyone to know about. Well, except Darrell. And now me.

The elevator moves, and we stand in silence, letting the shitty music overtake the space between us.

'Any clue what he wants?' I write and shove it under Darrell's nose.

He reads the words carefully. "The request came this morning straight to me." His gaze eats away at my face when I take the notepad back and tuck it into my pocket with the pen. I'm sure my father will be irate when he sees I'm still writing messages instead of using my voice.

But fuck him.

He doesn't deserve to hear an ounce of my words. Only Journey does. For now. Soon, my brothers will, too. Everyone will know that I'm still inside, just locked away.

Darrell grumbles, holding his ear and shaking his head. "For fuck's sake," he grits out and taps his ear again. "I'll fucking be there. Just chill. Don't let them shoot anyone. Fucking Russians," he hisses the last part to himself, blowing out a breath. The elevator stops after a lengthy descent, and the doors open to a dimly lit hallway looking nothing like the hotel from above. None of the expensive touches to impress whoever he brings to the hotel lie here. It's plain and simple, like this is his little slice of paradise, which he brings no one else to.

So, the question still stands. Why am I here, then? Does he want me to see this? It's an odd flex for him.

"Your father has two offices. One in the penthouse suite where he lives and breathes, and this..." he trails off.

Two offices? Wouldn't he want me to peek at the expensive one to show me how well he's done and how much power he has? My brows furrow. So, he hides in an office far from his men and island?

'Secret?' I write out quickly, putting my foot in front of the closing door. Darrell grunts. Neither confirming nor denying my thoughts. Well, not until he rips the piece of paper off the notebook and tucks it into his pocket with a frown.

"Step out, go to the left. Follow it for twenty feet. It'll be the only door open to your right." He doesn't look at me; he simply shoos me away. "When you're done, all you have to do is hit the up button twice. The elevator will come to you empty and take you wherever you want. Now, I have to go take care of our goddamn unruly guests." He licks his lips, disappearing behind the closing metal doors that slam shut, and the elevator once again springs to life, taking him up.

In his absence, my chest tightens under my rampant thoughts of what will happen during this surprise meeting. The dimly lit hallway goes for what seems like miles—only lit by tiny lights on the walls. The flooring beneath my feet sticks to my shoes with every move I make, proving that this is a secret part of the hotel.

I wonder if there's an exit door here? Probably not. My sperm donor loves to trap his victims in basements with no way out.

Doing as Darrell said, I make my way down the hall toward the only light source coming from an open door, with his words ringing in my mind. Unruly guests? The Russians? Does my sperm donor have more people staying at this hotel besides his men? He must if Darrell had to rush off to deal with them.

But what does that mean?

With each step I take, I lose a piece of myself. Leaving

behind Sheppard Mondelli and becoming a shell. Numbness tingles in my mind, erasing every ounce of emotion running through me. If he hurts me, mentally or physically—I won't feel it. Every time I have to face this man—which hasn't been much since we got here—I die a little on the inside.

All the things that happened in the past slam back into me the closer I get. Papers ruffle. Feet shuffle. He's moving around his secret office with purpose. Either gearing up to hunt me down, or something else is happening.

"And everything is going according to plan?" My father's voice fills the hallway I'm standing in, hitting me square in the chest. His tone is different—loving and attentive, something he's never used with me or my mother.

"Oh, Thomas," the woman's voice says with a sigh over the speakerphone. "Better than ever, Love. You wouldn't believe how easy this was." She giggles.

"You haven't fucked him, have you?" he growls with possession. "If you..."

"God, you're insufferable sometimes. Did I fuck him? I have to play the part, Tommy. I always have..." she trails off with a sigh. "This is my goddamn operation. You best remember that."

Her operation? My brows furrow at the implications as they murmur something else to one another—something like loving words and heated whispers. I wish I could block it from my memories forever.

I force myself to tune back in, listening to every word they say. It could be important—something for our cause.

There's something about her voice that has my heart rate spiking. It's so familiar. But not my mother's. Not that he ever cared about her. He treated my mom like a rag doll and a sex toy, using her as he pleased. Hitting her where it hurt more. Sometimes, I'm surprised they had me together. The disdain he showed for my mother knew no bounds. And for me? He hated me. Used me. Fucked me up beyond measure.

My father hand-crafted me into the person I am. The fucked up version, that is.

"I fucking don't want to hear about that..." Pain slices through my father's tone the exact moment something goes flying and slams into the wall, shattering to pieces. Small particles fly into the hallway, and I hold my breath. I can only hide for so long before he comes to find me. "You knew how I felt about this entire operation," he hisses. The loud sounds of his footsteps going back and forth across the room echo in my ears. He's pacing. "You knew how I felt about it back then, too! You fucking him when you were mine..."

"It was a necessary evil, Tommy. You knew it. I knew it. Revenge has always been our plan. And this? God." She laughs loudly, taking me back to when I was a child, and my heart stops. I listen more carefully to the cadence of her voice. A voice I haven't heard since I was a child, playing with Jer in the backyard.

"Jericho! Sheppard!" she shouts, holding a tray with a smile etched into her face. She stares between the two of us with love in her eyes. "Oh, boys. I've got snacks for you while your fathers work." She carries the tray to a small picnic table near the zoo, taking up real estate on their property.

"Mommy," Jericho says with a grin, coming to hug her legs. She sighs, rubbing his back lovingly. "You're here." He grins at her.

"I wouldn't want to be anywhere else, baby," she says, tapping his nose. "Now, why don't you two take a second and snack? You've been playing really hard." She grins at us again, taking in my face. "You're okay, Sheppard?" she whispers, leaning in to swipe the hair from my eyes.

I nod. "Yes, Mrs. Viotto." I grin widely, exposing the missing tooth I dropped under my pillow last night.

"Oh, you lost your tooth." She giggles. "Did the tooth fairy come for a visit?"

I nod, but two imposing presences come from the house, walking directly toward us with scowls.

"It'll be okay," she whispers, standing tall. "Good afternoon, Gentleman." Her eyes bounce between Gabriel and my father, taking in their angry moods. I bite into my sandwich, breathing slowly as they converse. "Of course, darling," she says to Gabe, touching his chest with a sigh.

But that's not what stops me in my tracks. It's my father. His eyes bore into Mrs. Viotto and Jer's daddy. His jaw tightens, and his eyes harden.

What's wrong with him?

I swallow down the memory that was long forgotten. Maybe I had locked it away. Or perhaps I didn't realize what was happening at the time. How could I have? I was only four or five; I'm not entirely sure.

Her voice titters again with laughter as my father chuckles. Grace Viotto. A woman who disappeared years before, leaving Jericho in a dire situation without her. All of Gabe's rage landed on him. And only him. Not that she took the brunt of anything. He worshiped the ground Grace walked on. Giving her everything under the sun to please her. We all saw it. The way he loved her. Even now, his search was merciless. And now she's alive? Talking to my father on the phone?

I guess the amazing case of reappearing parents has begun for both of us.

"I have to go, Tommy. Just know things are progressing on my end. Everything we worked hard for these past three years is coming to fruition. Briar Cove will be all ours in a matter of a month. Nothing and no one will stop us. This is our time to shine." Her words ring out long after my father has hung up the phone.

Grace Viotto is alive and well. And working with my father, who is Shadow? What exactly is she doing, though?

I have so many questions I know I won't get the answers to. Thomas Mondelli wouldn't let go of that easily, especially if it meant telling me about his plans with Jericho's mom. He'd kill me before he told me his secrets.

Quietly, I suck in a breath and take a few silent steps back. If he knows I know something, he'll use it to torture me more. This entire situation has to be stealthy and just right.

The shrill sound of his phone ringing fills the air again, followed by a sharp hello. Now is as good a time as any. With as much noise as I can muster with my feet, I plant myself in the light of his office glimmering in the hallway. Nerves roll through me at the sight of him standing behind a small wooden desk in a desolate office. There are no paintings. No designs. Just old wallpaper peeling from the drywall. A musty odor wafts from almost every inch of the hallways and office. I wonder what the other doors on this floor hide from my probing eyes. Something to explore later, I suppose.

"God fucking damn it," he hisses, pacing again behind the small desk, stroking his chin. "Get them the fuck in line. Give them all the booze they can swallow. Order more from the ports and have our men bring as much back as possible on our next shipment." He stops dead when he sees me. He takes me in from head to toe with a frown. "Sit the fuck down!" he bellows, pointing to the chair in front of his rickety desk.

I do as I'm told. Playing it smart is way more important than showing him I'm stronger than him. I could easily throw him across the room and make a run for my life. He holds up a finger as he listens to whoever is on the other end of the phone. Then, with a sigh, he hangs up.

"Darrell is such a good little delivery boy, isn't he?" He huffs, tucking his phone into his pocket and sitting across from me. His hands fold on the desk, and a smirk lifts his lips. "You weren't supposed to be a part of the deal. You know that, right?" He raises a brow. "You weren't supposed to come here. Back in my fucking life." He shakes his head in disgust. "But it is what it is. You'll become useful. If anything."

I nod, remembering the whispered words of whoever

knocked me out with a needle to the neck. *I wasn't a part of the package deal.* Half of me feels like I recognized that person, but it's so fuzzy that I don't exactly remember what happened. Before I ended up on the emergency staircase, my fists met Gabriel's face in a glorious fight, knocking him to the ground. If I had stayed for three seconds longer, I could have ended one monster. Once and for all. But Journey. I remember her cries and shouts echoing from behind the exit, pulling me in her direction.

And then, nothing. Why can't I remember who knocked me out?

"But it all worked out, didn't it? You got to stay with your fucked up little girlfriend, and I got what I wanted."

But what exactly did he want with all this? What the fuck was the point? To hold something over Journey's head? Gain information? I'm not comprehending what went through his mind when he bartered for Journey.

'What did you want?' I bravely write on the slip of paper and hold it up for him to see. It's a gamble on my end. Despite wanting to silence me for eternity, he hates it when I don't use my voice.

He scowls. "Shadow needs alliances—friends in the world. We've already scalped Gabe's men. His brother's men. Anyone we could get our hands on. They come here. Get a better life and fight for us. We need stronger alliances. Better trades. More of an empire."

Not exactly the information I wanted. I need more on why Journey and Sunshine are here. It doesn't make sense.

'And us being here?' I write out again.

"Leverage. Revenge. Do you want full details, boy? Then use your goddamn voice. I didn't take that, did I?" Long ago, my father's words would have pierced me through the chest like arrows finding their mark and obliterating me. But not now. It easily rolls off my shoulders. "That's what I thought," he scoffs, waving a hand at me like he wants to dismiss me.

Fuck that.

He brought me down to his secret office for a reason. And I need to figure it out. So, I'll keep poking and prodding the monster. And if I have to worm my way onto his good side? Then so fucking be it. For Journey and Sunshine. For my own goddamn self. Our safety is the most important.

'Russians?' I write out again, lifting the paper for him to see.

This time, I'm met with no resistance—just a smirk.

"Unruly fucking pricks," he hisses with disdain and then checks his watch. "I've got a meeting with the head of the Bratva in thirty minutes. I want you there with me." He raises a brow when I swallow hard.

'Why me?'

He narrows his eyes. "You're my son. They're all about family ties strengthening their outfit. So, we are stronger together. That girl is fucking useless in this instance, but not for long." He stands abruptly, and I follow suit, eyeing him cautiously as he rounds the desk. He smirks. "Be a good fucking sport and behave during the meeting. Maybe I'll spare you in the marriage department. But fuck this up? I'll fuck you up. Now, keep up." He takes off down the long hallway with me in tow, eyeing his movements. "You want to know a secret, son?" he asks, hitting the up button twice on the elevator with a smirk. I nod. "There's going to be a new crowned king of the Bratva here shortly. Today, you'll meet Naum. Naum Antonov. And tomorrow? He won't exist."

Fuck. My heart drops. I've heard the horror stories about him. He's a goddamn nightmare. Psycho. Worse of the worse. And he's here? This can't be fucking good. And to top it all off, my sperm donor has confided in me. He's testing me—my loyalties. Everything rides on this moment between us.

So, if he's the leader of it all and a new king will be crowned soon, what does that mean? Death? Destruction? There's no way my sperm donor could take down the entire

Bratva. They're too powerful. More than him. More than fucking Gabriel's family. They're worldwide, with connections on every continent.

My father grins when the empty elevator opens, and he forces me inside. "Keep your eyes on him. That's what you're here for. Observe the fucking room. I want you by my side, looking for anything off." He straightens his shirt with a huff. "I know you won't say a goddamn word or write a note, will you? Naum is going down. That's what's going to happen."

Well, fuck.

CHAPTER NINETEEN

Shepp

"And then, the little shit thought he could sneak into my room and stab me through the heart. Joke's on the little bastard." Naum practically falls out of his seat with laughter, sloshing the whiskey mix in his glass.

Five men surround him. Four grown adults, chuckling at his words with broad smiles and sipping their drinks—his most loyal men within the Bratva. Tall. Foreboding. With a cold detachment in their eyes. They're the ones in charge of everything else. Finances. Takeovers. They're like a modern-day business with Naum at the head of it all. The CEO. The Mafia King. With every decision they make and every vote they take, it's all up to Naum to have the final say. He's the leader by default, like his father before him and so on. The position fell into his lap.

He was born to rule the Bratva. Jericho was born to rule the Viotto Crime Family of Briar Cove like Naum's teenage son—Mikhail—will do after he's gone.

Same hierarchy—different rules.

Mikhail sits rigidly beside the leader with a blank expression. Much like his father, Naum's, an amber drink rests tightly in his grip. Untouched. Not a sip taken. He seems to soak in every word spoken between the two parties. Nodding when necessary and laughing when needed. Uninterested when not engaged, possibly lost in thought.

I've heard rumors about him in passing. Vicious. Ruthless. Fitting in with the men of the Bratva. Born and bred for the lifestyle.

Like me. Jericho. Arrow.

In a way, he reminds me of Jericho with the weight of the world on his shoulders. Ruled by a crazed father obsessed with power and money. It's all there, right in front of me. A picture from the past where I witnessed my best friend sink further into the abyss of his father's rule, wishing he could escape him. Or overthrow him.

Is this the reason Naum won't exist tomorrow? Will Mikhail take him out?

For over an hour, we hang out in the Presidential Suite, shooting the shit while the guests drink excessive amounts of liquor, getting drunker by the minute. I eye my father, knocking back drinks with them but never losing himself to the effects of the alcohol.

"And your guards? Where were they when the enemy breached your room?" my sperm donor asks with a raised brow, smirking at Naum's antics.

"Guards? Pfft." He scans his men, giving them a *'Would you look at this guy'* kind of look. "You think I need fucking guards standing over me while I sleep? Pussy shit! I take care of what enters my domain with swift justice," he snarks with a huff, forming guns with his fingers while pointing at my father. "With a gun beneath my pillows and my finger on the trigger."

There's a weird tension in the room. Something is brewing behind my father's smile and Naum's raucous laughter. Unsaid words. Untold actions.

Naum is here for a reason. A reason I don't think he understands. Me, either. Shadow is up to some shit, and I need to find out what before it all goes down. An alliance? Doubtful. Shadow wouldn't have dragged me here if it was just that.

He wants me to witness his genius work.

"You're a better man than me," Shadow says, raising a glass. "But of course, I don't have to worry about anything while protected on this." He holds out his hands, slightly laughing as he gestures to the hotel and island. "My land. My men. Impenetrable."

"Explain to me how you procured such a piece of property for your operations," Naum asks, finishing his drink and setting the glass on an end table. A server quickly walks by and picks it up, but before she can move on, she's halted by Naum grabbing her wrist. "Another. Just the same," he says with a flirty wink, sending her on her way into the closed-off kitchen. "Is she available?" he asks, leaning his elbows on his knees, listening intently.

"They all are for a price," Shadow says coldly, shrugging.

Disgust has my stomach in knots at his words. For a price. Would he do the same to me? Journey? Sunny? Probably. He wouldn't hesitate to give us to the most willing person who wants to use us for nefarious things. If Naum asked, I bet my father would serve me on a silver platter with a smile and no shame in his actions.

Naum gives a lop-sided grin, humming a tune under his breath. "Well, then." He quickly takes out his wallet and slams a wad of bills onto the table, looking to total at least four grand. "Have someone for everyone. Except him, of course." He waves a hand at his son, who sets his drink on the table with a tight-lipped expression. He narrows his similar-looking eyes on Naum but doesn't say a word. "Too young to be corrupted, eh, boy? Eh, Mikhail?" he chants, reaching over to shake him by the shoulders with a grin.

Mikhail grunts, gently shoving his father's hands off him. "Of course," he says with a nod.

Naum smirks. "Well, why don't we get down to business, then? The boy has a meeting with his intended and would like to get the ball rolling, as the kids say." He rolls a wrist.

"Down to business already?" Shadow chuckles. "You must be eager to sign your name on the dotted line."

The boy's deep blue eyes shift to Shadow, eating him alive without saying a word. Or he would. His face doesn't change, remaining neutral in all the right areas. But his eyes. I've seen it a million times before in Jericho. The subtle shift of his mood shining bright. And this man? Well, he's transparent to me.

"No need for all the pleasantries. We concocted a deal for an alliance through marriage, and I am here to fulfill that. For my father." For himself, more than likely.

But wait. Marriage? I stiffen.

"Sunshine is yours." Shadow shrugs, setting his drink down. I stiffen at his words, attempting to relax my posture. Weakness is not an option in front of Naum's men. Or my sperm donor's. I swallow a mouthful of whiskey, relishing it as it burns down my throat and fills my stomach with warmth. "We've hammered out the details verbally over the phone, but how about in writing?" He takes out a simple stack of papers, no more than five, and sets it down in front of Naum. Before he can snatch it up and look over it, Mikhail takes it, looking it over meticulously.

Holy fuck. He's handing Sunshine off to the highest bidder like a piece of meat. Figures. Why else would he collect his long-lost daughter after so many years? He's not a father. He's a user.

"Such a little businessman," Naum quips, grabbing the fresh drink from the server as she sets it down. "You and me later, sweetheart." He winks, and she shrinks in on herself, swallowing hard.

"You can't hurt my property, Naum," Shadow says with a light chuckle that sounds anything but light. He's plotting a fucking murder. I can confirm that from his words earlier, but it's all in how he holds himself against Naum. His shoulders tense. No matter how hard he tries to smile in Naum's direction. All I can see is the ire he holds for him—the distaste when he smacks his lips after a drink. "Fuck her. I don't care. Use her up. But if you harm her, she can't do her job or return to her family..." his words trail off sternly, letting the threat hang in the air.

Naum is going down. My father is going to do it. But what about the boy sitting there? Is he next? Or an alliance opportunity?

"You speak like my dick will make her explode. Good explode, not bad explode," Naum laughs loudly. "I will not harm your server. Simply show her a good time and what a real man is like. One for each of my men, yes?" He raises a dark brow, waiting for my father's answer.

"The boundary remains the same. No injuries. They must work off their debts." Their debts. I look at the woman cowering in the corner, looking Naum over with genuine fear hanging in her gaze.

She has no choice in this—no words she can say to deter the man from putting his hands on her. I should stand up. Take her away from here and to safety. But I'm stuck, too.

"It's a deal, my friend," Naum proclaims, clapping his hands.

Shadow salutes them all with an enormous smile. "Darrell, radio down and have all the available women line up for viewing. They have guests to entertain for the evening before we kick off the festivities."

Darrell nods and steps out of the room, presumably to make the call.

"Everything seems in order," Mikhail says in a low voice, putting the pages back together into a neat stack. "Everything we discussed." He raises a brow.

"Of course. Everything, Mikhail," my father says, saluting him with his glass again. "You get to leave the island with my precious daughter, marry her, and then..."

"Our allegiance is yours. We will help you continue your decimation of the Viotto family."

Shadow grins. "Parts of our plans are already in place."

Grace. He means her. She's already knee-deep in whatever they've concocted, which is something I need to get to the bottom of. Maybe there's something in his secret office. Darrell showed it to me for a reason. Perhaps he thinks I wouldn't dare to sneak in there and find whatever he's hiding. Well, he's wrong. The perfect opportunity will come. And when it does? I'm grabbing fate by the balls and squeezing them until I get answers.

"Then, let's celebrate," Naum says with a clap. "To the fall of the great Viotto Family of California. Each of their parcels will become ours." Shadow grunts under his breath, sending him a glare and earning a smile in return. "Ours." He gestures with his glass between Shadow and him. "All the resources. All the businesses. Everything we could have imagined. The seaports."

The seaports. Of course. The Viotto brothers run most parts of California, including guns, drugs, and whatever gets distributed among the gangs and family. That's what they want. They don't just want the successful side of everything. They want it all.

I keep my rampant thoughts at bay, refusing to let them show in my expression. Or, I'd hoped. Mikhail eyes me critically, examining my face. His head tilts, and he smirks knowingly. Quickly, Mikhail signs the contract without a second thought.

"Then, it's settled. Why don't we celebrate?" Shadow says, standing tall, and I follow suit. "Let's say, tomorrow night, all of us have a lovely dinner and then view the fights we have slotted for the evening."

"To the death?" Naum asks, leaning in with a grin. "I do love a good bloody battle."

"To the death," Shadow says with a smirk. "It's the way of The Pits."

"Fucking good," Naum says, rubbing his hands together. "My boys and I will be there to watch the bloodshed."

Shadow holds up a hand. "Why don't we make dinner just a family event, yeah? Your son. My children. A nice dinner and drinking." That's not fucking suspicious at all.

"I like the way you think," Naum agrees, clapping his hands together. "Family is, of course, the utmost importance to us."

"Now, enjoy the suite; it is all yours. Darrell will escort the women to your room for viewing and picking."

"Why not leave them all here?" Naum chuckles darkly. "I've got quite an appetite." He turns quickly, gesturing for the server to come closer to him before taking hold of her neck and forcing her against the wall. "Dark, dark needs."

"I've got a date," Mikhail says with a sigh, shaking his head at his father with disgust. "As much as I'd love to see you dishonor my mother..." he trails off with disgust.

"That old hag?" Naum growls. "She's off in the city apartment, living her best life with the pool boy. Fuck off, son," he grunts, forcing the server into a large bedroom and shutting the door with a slam.

Mikhail schools his features, placing his hands in his pockets. "Since my Sunshine will be present, I assume your woman will also be. Care to accompany me?" He gestures to me, tilting his head toward the door.

"Go on, son. I've got plenty to keep me occupied," Shadow grumbles, staring at the door Naum disappeared behind. "But remember what we discussed?" How the hell could I forget? Don't fuck this up. Keep your mouth shut and pen down.

I nod. Not daring to argue when I'm weaponless and defenseless.

I follow Mikhail out the suite's door, slowly traipsing toward the elevators. Everything around me screams rich and over the top, with expensive paintings adorning the walls and soft lighting. Down to the small marble-topped table with a vase of fresh flowers right outside the elevator doors. Two small chairs rest on either side of it for decoration. It's so inviting. Soothing, even. The complete opposite of the dingy hallway in the basement that I can't take my mind off of.

How does a dead man with nothing to his old name create such an empire on nothing in only three years? Did Grace help him establish this? She'd been gone for such a long time. I don't know how she'd have the resources, either. Considering she wouldn't have access to Gabriel's funds. Maybe her family provided her with something. She is a mafia princess, after all.

It's something else I need to investigate while I'm on this island.

Without a word between us, I follow Mikhail onto the empty elevator, slinking to the back wall and leaning against it with so much on my damn mind. I sigh, rubbing my temples as my mind digests every damn word that was said in the meeting.

"Were you shocked to see your father again after so many years of being deceased?" Mikhail asks when the elevator doors shut.

My gaze whips to him, and he only looks me over with a straight face, awaiting my answer.

I frown. *'Of course, I was shocked, you fucking prick,'* I sign quickly with a huff and then dig out my notebook, knowing he wouldn't have understood a word I said. Just as I'm about to write out a more appropriate response, I stop dead.

'Interesting,' he signs back with a satisfied smirk. *'And when he died, did you feel...'* his fingers hang in the air as he trails off with a slightly changed expression, showing the vulnerability sparkling in his eyes.

I swallow hard in disbelief, but quickly shake it off. *'With a*

*father like mine and what he did, I danced on his grave. Well...
Until a few days ago.'*

"How interesting," Mikhail mutters, rubbing at his chin until the elevator door opens, revealing the hotel's fifth floor. "This way. Sunshine is waiting for me to assist her in making brunch. And from what I've heard, she's invited Journey along. Or..." He stops, turning to look at me as I reluctantly follow. "It's an odd arrangement you have, isn't it? The three of you and her? How does that work?"

My face heats at the judgment in his tone. A subject that is none of his business, especially with how young he seems.

'How old are you?' I sign, sizing him up. He speaks like he's a goddamn adult, but in the body of a middle schooler.

"Fourteen," he says, folding his hands together. "Why? Want to punch me? I wouldn't suggest it. Spies everywhere and all that. Besides, I'm sure you could pack a punch, eh?"

Infuriating little bastard. He's so smug. I want to punch him. But I have to remain on my best behavior—words courtesy of my father. The one thing I'd never want to do while trapped in this hellhole is piss off the person who granted us freedom after locking us up.

'Fourteen? And you're in a marriage contract already?' In our society, it doesn't happen until we're at our initiation ball. Sure, alliances are made, but they wait until we're men able to handle the life and a wife simultaneously.

Apparently not in the Bratva.

"Why wait?" he asks, scrunching his brows. "That's contrary to the Viotto's, correct? You're to wait until you're adults. Going through bootcamps and such. I've studied your ways of life for years now." God, years now? He's fourteen going on forty. "It's quite interesting what the head of your organization did to make you all into powerful men fit for his approval."

'Journey will not appreciate this arrangement. In fact, I'd guard yourself well tonight.' I offer him my best sadistic grin.

It's not me he needs to be afraid of. Sure, I could punch his face in until he's unrecognizable. Give him to Arrow for a little torture session. But Journey? Yeah, she's the one he needs to be fearful of. She'll have this boy by the damn balls and string him up like a piñata. Ah, what a sight to see.

Mikhail only grins, knocking lightly at the door. "Bring it on. I enjoy fighting. But don't worry. My Sunshine does not appreciate a fight between me and her sister, whom I've heard much about. In fact, If I could, I'd pledge my loyalty to someone like her. Someone who cares for the ones she loves so dearly that she risks her life daily." He raises a brow, smirking at me.

The door swings open before I can respond, revealing a smiling Sunshine. Her cheeks pinken. "Hi," she offers shyly.

Huh. I guess all she needed was a love interest to make her not so perky.

"Hello, my Sunshine," he offers, taking her hand and kissing the back of it.

She fucking giggles, staring at him with stars in her eyes. Then, there's Journey frowning right behind her, watching the entire interaction like a hawk zoning in on her prey. That's right, my Little Tempest.

"What is this?" she asks, gesturing between them with her finger.

"Ah, hello. You must be Journey," Mikhail says, grasping Sunshine's hand and pulling her into his side possessively. Although he seems to respect Journey and her relationship with her sister, he has no qualms about staking his claim.

Wrong move, Prick.

Journey frowns more. "Sunshine..." she trails off with a warning in her voice.

"This is Mikhail, he's my..."

"Fiancé," Mikhail supplies with pride. "I am Sunshine's intended."

Great. Another bomb to defuse.

CHAPTER TWENTY

Jericho

"WHAT DO YOU MEAN HE BLEW UP THE BOAT?"

Arrow's entire face reddens with every word he speaks. A grunt falls from his lips when his leg bounces in place. Destruction rests in the back of his eyes. If he doesn't get his eyes on Journey soon, he'll completely lose his shit.

"I could have gone there, and no one would have known I was there. I'm a mother fuckin' ghost! Give me a boat, my weapons, and bam! They'll all be dead." His hands move as he speaks, getting more erratic with his mood.

He's liable to murder someone at this point.

My head pounds in tune with my heart. And my goddamn leg. Who knew a stab wound could be so inconvenient? Not me. Of course, I've been shot and stabbed before. It's a hazard of the job. But this? This is tearing through me like an infection I can't take my mind off of.

Or maybe it's the loss of my wife, not by my side. The withdrawals are kicking in with a vengeance. I itch to hold her again. Touch her. Kiss her. And most importantly, protect her from anyone for eternity.

When I get my hands on her again, I'm locking her in a gilded cage. No matter how many times she tells me no. She has no fucking choice.

"Then I'll fucking send you next time and watch as you

fucking burn to death!" Carter yells, throwing his hand around with a scowl.

"That's the thing, though," Arrow says with a slight lift of his lips. "I wouldn't have died. I would have been invisible. By myself, I could have made it through that hotel, found my girl and my guy, and fucking left no crumbs behind."

Cocky fucking idiot.

"Shut the fuck up," Carter growls, inching closer to Arrow with a snarl. "Those were my men."

"Shut up, Arrow," I grumble, massaging my temples.

"Well, I'm just saying, Daddy Jer. He let boys do the job I could have done better." He crosses his arms like a child, throwing himself back into the oversized chair he's sitting in.

Carter grinds his teeth. Again. I'm almost positive that's his general state of being. My cousin told me he's always been an angry person, hurling insults and throwing punches at the drop of a hat. Maybe if he punches Arrow, it'll knock a few more screws loose.

"Fuck!" Carter shouts, punching the wall beside him.

"So, obviously Shadow has quite the weaponry and has no issue with using them on people," I say, raising a brow when Carter turns on his heel to face me.

"State the fucking obvious, Mafia Douche," he grunts, rubbing a hand down his face. "I'm waiting to hear from my contacts."

"Contacts?" Arrow asks, re-engaging in the conversation.

"Do tell," I say, waving a hand.

"I have intel on the island." He holds my gaze.

I raise a brow. "As in, you had it before I brought the island up. Is this perhaps how you knew about it?" And why Google had shit all to tell me.

"Shadow has been on our radar for three years since he popped up. He's started turf wars with smaller gangs, basically absorbing them into his organization to build his forces. Along with your fucking father."

I cringe at the fact his blood runs through my veins. "The same could be said for Shadow and my sperm donor. Shadow has been sending men into Briar Cove for almost three years, trying to take our father down."

"He sent a guy with a bomb. It was fucking amazing," Arrow chuckles. "Remember, Jer? How he told us all his secrets, and then BAM! He exploded, decorating us with his guts. Good times."

Carter blinks several times, looking Arrow up and down. "He's fucking serious?" he asks me point blank.

"Over time, you get used to his antics. He's just a murdery teddy bear," I quip.

"I resent that, Daddy Jer. Murdery teddy bear? I'm much more intimidating than that. I made a man piss himself once without doing anything."

"You were literally holding a flamethrower to his face," I say, shaking my head. "I'm not sure that's the definition of not doing anything."

"Meh. Semantics. I may have melted his face off, but he was a traitor," he grunts.

"Right. Melted his face off," Carter says in a daze, blinking several times.

"Careful, Arrow. He could be making a list to indict you," I snort when Arrow sits up taller, narrowing his eyes.

"He wouldn't dare," he says suddenly, deadly serious.

Carter rolls his eyes. "As if my ball-buster partner would let me," he huffs. "Besides, you're not the only assholes who have tortured people." That familiar, cruel smile crosses his lips as he rounds his desk and plops down. "Now, shut the fuck up so I can get some work done. I'm waiting on my contact to fucking text me with information again."

"Again?" I question.

"Yes. He delightfully fucking informed me that my men were at the bottom of the goddamn ocean thanks to that fucking bastard's firepower. He also mentioned a few newcomers."

"You couldn't have led with that?" I sit up straighter when he smirks.

"That got you to fucking shut up."

"Spill the beans, Agent Man! Tell me how my Kitten and bestie are." Arrow puts his face in his hands, looking as innocent as possible. "I'm desperate here, dude."

"He confirmed they were on the island, along with a third person. A teenage girl. Says Shadow is doting on her and claims it's his fucking kid. Claims to be Sunshine West." He shrugs. "No confirmed ID on the kid. Through the pictures I've sent, he has positively IDed a one Sheppard Mondelli and a Journey West." His expression grows grim, and I see a flicker of emotions pass over his face for the first time. And considering he's not in the presence of his wife, it's odd to see. "Shadow has a lot of fucked up things on that island."

"Fucked up? Like, fucked up I would like? Or fucked up I would want to murder over?" Arrow asks, leaning in slightly.

"Murder over," Carter says, shaking his head. "He has a fucking fighting pit. People from all over can sign up and take the challenge, and if they're the winner, Shadow grants them money and favors. The more they win, the more important they become. My source confirmed your girl was in the fucking pit..." he trails off when I shoot daggers in his direction.

"Don't play with me," Arrow growls, gritting his teeth.

"She won."

"She..." I trail off, my heart beating a million miles a minute. "You're fucking telling me that my wife was forced into a fight, and she fucking won?"

Carter grimaces. "It appears that way."

"What other secrets are you hiding in your colossal head?" Arrow asks, slowly getting up from his seat. His fingers twitch at his sides, aching to wrap around Carter's throat—and possibly more.

I sigh, getting to my feet. I come to a halt in front of Arrow, blocking his view. "You can't murder the fucking agent," I hiss, shaking my head.

"Come on. You never let me have any fun. Wouldn't his skin look good peeled off?" Arrow asks, peeking around me and sizing Carter up.

"Not him," I say, gripping his shoulder tight. "Save that for Shadow."

"You're no fun," he gripes, tossing my hand off his shoulder. "And I'm still mad at you." He pouts like a damn child. Again.

"Mad at me?" I sigh, pinching the bridge of my nose. "Still?"

"You left me," he says through clenched teeth. "I could have died."

"I made sure that nurse was prepared to fucking escort you to safety. In fact, I helped her do that. I killed my father's fucking guards for you, Arrow. I got stabbed! It would have aroused suspicion if I had left with your body draped over my shoulder. Don't you think so?"

Something flares in Arrow's eyes when he steps back from me. He's being an irrational child, holding something against me that I couldn't help.

"Don't be a child, Arrow. If I could have dragged you out of there myself, I would have..."

"Never leave a man behind," he huffs, lifting his chin. "I would have slaughtered the world to bring you out of that hospital had it been you." Then, he turns on his heel and marches out of Carter's lush office, slamming the door behind him.

"Wonderful," I mutter, staring at the door in his wake. "Fucking great." He's never going to forgive me. Arrow's the type to hold a grudge for as long as he's breathing.

"Would he really fucking skin me alive? Do I need to lock doors and protect what's fucking mine?" Carter's deep voice penetrates through the worry fogging my brain.

"Harmless as a puppy until provoked," I grumble, sitting on the couch. This room seems to be the quietest in his home. A place he invited us to stay at to discuss more business.

"I've got a bazillion fucking kids in this house, asshole. If he..." I put up a hand to stop him from continuing.

"He wouldn't harm a child. It may be hard to believe, but that psychopath is the leader of our Help the Community movement. He's set up shop in his father's church, going to the confessionals to aid abused women and children and help them escape their circumstances. He wouldn't harm your family. Perhaps I need to find him an outlet for his anger." Someone who would deserve to die, that is.

Carter rubs his chin. "I know a guy who knows a guy who has a fighting ring. It's here in town."

"If they don't mind dying," I quip. "Arrow doesn't stop once the violence takes over. But it might be a good outlet if I can control him." My heart aches at the thought of Shepp. Our silent giant doesn't utter words, but Arrow always listens to him. It keeps his demons at bay.

"I'll text Ruthless to see if he needs new fighters tonight. He'll want Arrow to promise not to kill anyone," he says, raising a brow.

"That I can do." At least, I hope I can.

Arrow and I have been at odds since I left him at the hospital. He can't comprehend why I left him in the abandoned wing with a nurse who swore her allegiance. I had no choice. He doesn't seem to understand my reasoning.

"Now, any word on my wife? Or what the plan might entail? I want to be a part of this entire operation." I raise a brow when he rolls his eyes, sitting back in his chair.

"These kinds of situations take fucking patience. Do we know she's fucking there? Yes. But an exact location? We don't fucking know. If we do that too prematurely, we chance fucking killing her. And dear God, if I have to hear the fucking West assholes gripe I got their sister killed. I'll never hear the end of it."

I blow out a breath. "Patience is not my virtue. But I suppose I waited years to claim what's mine. What's a few more days before we can rescue?"

"Yeah, well. If it makes you feel any fucking better. My source says they're both being cared for like a king and queen. Now, at least. Once she fucking proved herself to him, something changed. I just don't know what the fuck did."

"Well, then. I'll be waiting," I say, getting to my feet. "And I should probably track down my murderous brother before he finds someone else to take his rage out on." As I turn to leave, a beep from Carter's phone stops me in my tracks. I glance back at him, waiting expectantly for a solution to my Arrow problem.

"Ruthless says that you're in luck. There's an opening tonight after someone dropped out. I'll send you a text with all the details." He quickly types on his phone and then sets it down just as my phone vibrates in my pocket.

"Ruthless, hmm?" I hum, rubbing my chin. "Now, why does that sound so goddamn familiar?"

"No fucking clue. Now, leave me the fuck alone. I got work to do. Unless you want your wife and bestie to fucking stay on the island." He raises a brow, scowling at me.

Asshole.

"And that's my cue," I murmur, waving as I exit the room and wander around the first floor of their home. The same home Olivia escorted us to this morning before the fucking sun had risen so we could get right to work with Carter.

Olivia's voice echoes through the ample space, mixed with the squeal of kid's laughter. I follow the noise, hoping to glimpse my best friend and talk some sense into him. Or hell, maybe let him beat my ass for what he thinks I did.

"This is LuLu," a little girl's voice fills the air when I stop outside a gigantic playroom filled with a massive amount of toys lining the walls.

"LuLu," Arrow chortles with a grin, spinning the Barbie doll around. "Does LuLu like purses?" He places the doll's feet on the ground, making her dance in front of the little girl, who giggles at his antics.

Maybe he would make a good father one day.

"LuLu likes puppies and kitties," she retorts, holding up a small dog and cat. "See!" She giggles again when Arrow does something funny with the doll and chuckles.

"You play with dolls?" a little boy asks, eyeing Arrow with a frown.

"Why not?" Arrow asks, putting shoes on the barbie while poking his tongue out in concentration.

"Cuz it's for girls," the little boy huffs with annoyance.

"Go away, Roman," the little girl hisses, waving her hand. "I play with dolls. He likes dolls. Go play with your boogers."

Roman huffs, rolling his eyes. "I don't need dolls, Maggie. I have my iPad." He says it like his iPad is more superior than her toys, looking down on her like an older brother would. "I'm only here because Mom said I had to supervise you, anyway. So you don't eat another Barbie shoe." He levels her with a glare, and she scoffs at him.

I never had toys to keep me company as a kid. Once my mother was out of the picture, my father forbade them. The only toys I was allowed to touch were sharp and pointy. I'm surprised I never cut off a finger—or his.

My phone vibrates in my pocket again, indicating a text has come through. I bring it out, eyeing Arrow before dropping my gaze to the screen. My heart drops completely into my ass when the name Blue Spider Fucker, aka Elias White, pops onto the screen. He and I have never had any sort of civil relationship. He's been a thorn in my side, distributing drugs into my community and killing innocent people.

BLUE SPIDER FUCKER

It seems you've misplaced something
important to you

Then, the picture comes through.

My wife. At a table, all alone, covered in blood from head
to toe.

Sweat collects on my palms, and I nearly drop the phone.
But I don't miss the fact that fucker was near her and I wasn't. I
take several breaths, turning my back on the playroom, getting
away from the many children and Arrow occupying the space.
The last thing innocent kids need to see is me reaching through
the phone and strangling that bastard once and for all.

Tension encapsulates every inch of my muscles, tightening
them like rubber bands ready to spring free. But I shake it all
off. Anger will get me nowhere when it comes to situations
like this. I need to use the training my father drilled into my
head and face this with a level head and clear mind.

And that's how I find myself outside, on the back patio of
Carter's home, lounging on a chair and taking in the scenery.
Olivia once mentioned that the Wests—or Cole family—as
they took their wife's last name—built this house with the
utmost security measures. I don't blame them. After what they
each went through at the old prep school here in town and had
to endure, I'd doubly make sure that the secret society behind
the murders never made an emergence again.

"Jericho Viotto," Elias's deep voice comes through the
phone smoothly.

"Elias White," I say in a clear, unbothered voice when I'm
anything but unbothered. "Care to explain why you were near
my wife while she was covered in blood?" I can only surmise
it's from the fight pits Carter mentioned earlier. It's the only
logical explanation I can think of as to why her appearance
was bloodied.

"I could," he says easily. "But maybe I don't want to."

"Is there anything I could entice you with to encourage loose lips?" I pinch the bridge of my nose in annoyance. This is what it's going to come down to. If I have something he wants, he'll aid us in whatever Veritas can't.

"There are many things in life, Jericho. Maybe I'll give this one for free if you offer to meet with me later to discuss business."

My spine snaps straight. "Business?" I question. "I didn't think you did business with the likes of me." Only my father, if I recall correctly. The last time we spoke business was when I had to threaten his balls for distributing lethally spiked drugs into Briar Cove. The bodies were piling up, and the coroner was finding a singular cause in every case—laced drugs. Fentanyl, to be exact.

"Times change," he snaps, momentarily losing his cool. "They change when leaders slip and threaten what shouldn't be touched."

I raise a brow. "Agreed, then. Did you happen to see my second-in-command? Tall. Scar on his face. Doesn't speak?" My heart thumps loudly at the prospect of getting information about him.

"No." Fuck. How was Shepp not there by her damn side? "A little birdy told me you've escaped Briar Cove?"

"It's a possibility," I confirm.

"I want to set up a meeting for this evening. Say 9 p.m. at the old East Point Prep gym?"

"East Point, huh?" I hum. "Did your little birdy give you those clues?" Because according to the text Carter sent me, that's the exact location of our fight tonight.

"No. My brother did. He mentioned someone named Arrow needs to let off some steam in his fighting ring. I told him he was being fucking daft for letting a person like him fight and to have the coroner paid off for the evening. But he laughed at me instead." I can practically hear the roll of his eyes from behind the phone.

Well, then. What a small world, after all.

"Then it's settled. I'll meet you there where we can have a nice long talk about my wife and friend."

"He won't harm her," he says lazily, with a hint of emotion. "His son and your wife are too important to him right now. They're a good bargaining chip for whatever he's got cooking. But that's what we'll discuss tonight."

"And his son is?"

Elias chuckles to himself, sounding proud. "Few men have met the man called Shadow face to face. I've had the displeasure several times. He's a real piece of work. Unpredictable at best. But he's a good businessman because he learned from the best." Cryptic fucking bastard. Why does everyone around me insist on speaking in riddles? If we spoke directly and got to the damn point, everyone would stop wasting my time.

"Explain," I say, losing my patience.

"Shadow learned everything he knows from your father. Because once upon a time, before he died and became reborn, he was Thomas Mondelli. So, no. He won't harm them. He can still use them. But you had better believe that when they prove no longer useful, he'll eliminate them. But not before he tries to marry his children off."

I rarely blanch. Ever. Or lose my cool. But at the moment, I swear everything stops inside me. My heart. Blood. Thinking. Everything ceases as his words play on repeat.

Thomas Mondelli is alive?

How is that possible? I remember the day we celebrated the death of Thomas Mondelli, dancing on his grave with smiles on our faces. That rat bastard was supposed to be rotting in Hell for an eternity. Not walking around and kidnapping his son and my fucking wife.

This is not good. Not good at all. Thomas is unstable at best. Always has been, especially if alcohol has been swimming in his veins. And if Shepp is locked on an island with his father—well, nothing good can come of that.

"Children?" I question, shaking my head in confusion. From my knowledge, he only has Shepp. Of course, he could have been like my father and been hoarding heirs. Something I'm still not sure my father did. Only time will tell, though. Whoever the poor bastard is, they're in for a rude awakening when my father takes them.

My entire skull aches from all the secrets slipping out in the past few days. I need a day's sleep to heal my mind and leg. Time is not on our side, though. The more these things keep piling on, the more desperate I am to retrieve my friend and wife.

"Indeed. Speaking of weddings, Jericho. You're invited to mine if you don't mind returning to your old stomping grounds. Briar Cove Grand Hotel. I'll tell you the details tonight."

Click.

I blink several times, staring at the phone in disbelief.

Fuck.

A headache immediately forms in my mind. A-fucking-gain. Aching when I close my eyes. The information processes at a slow rate. Anxiety boils under my skin.

"I hear I have a fight. Can I skin one of them alive?" Arrow's dark voice comes from beside me, sitting on the patio furniture. "I'm desperate, Jer. It's… bad." He pounds his skull a few times, closing his eyes with sweet relief.

I know that look. I've seen it many times in the past when the demon inside him gets to be too much. It's riding him hard, aching for bloodshed and mayhem. Well, he's about to get his wish, minus the murder part.

I peek one eye open. "Apparently, they've been warned about your tendencies. No murder, though."

"Boo, you whore. You're no fun. What's a fight without the loss of life?" His eyes darken immediately when he checks me over. "Who was on the phone, Jericho? It sounds like you were making plans without me again." He narrows his eyes, and the hurt is evident in them.

"While you fight, I have a meeting with Elias White." I dig my phone out and show him the message and picture of Journey covered in blood.

His head tilts curiously, taking in our girl. "Uh, instant boner-alert. Warn a guy before you present him porn." His tongue pokes out, and he taps a few times on my phone and then grins. "I sent it to myself. You think she'd be mad if I blew the picture up and put it on my wall?"

"You're not even the least bit concerned that she's covered in blood and sitting at an unknown table?"

Arrow's face doesn't move an inch, but his fingers tighten on my phone. "Well, when you put it like that. Yeah, it makes me a little angry." More than a little. His features darken further as his demon takes him over. The Devil is truly shining through him right now.

"Elias saw her. This is from what I assume is the fighting pit Carter spoke about. Remember, she won. Elias had a meeting with Shadow. Apparently, he's seen his face and knows exactly who he is. Shadow is Thomas Mondelli."

A pin could drop between us and be heard for miles. Arrow doesn't react immediately; simply soaks in the information like I did. No doubt remembering the funeral where we surrounded Shepp in support and laughed when Thomas' ashes were put to rest.

It makes me wonder if my father has known this whole time and has said nothing. But if he knew Shadow was his former second-in-command, would he have done anything? Surely, he would have tried to get Shadow in his pocket or eliminated him for good.

"So, my Kitten and our bestie are with his father," he snarls. Ah, there's the reaction I was waiting for. "You know what that bastard did to him!" He jumps to his feet, throwing my phone back at me. "We need to swim to that island right now. I want to slaughter every fucking inch of that place and make it rain blood." He cracks his knuckles in preparation.

"Patience," I say, holding up a hand, attempting to reel him back in. "I know it's not your strong suit. Mine, either. We can't think with our rage and desperation right now. We know exactly what he is capable of. He'll rip our fucking heads off before we can even enter the building. We have to plan this carefully and rely on Veritas to help."

Arrow roars toward the sky, letting all his agitation go. Momentarily, at least. He'll be back to his disturbed self in a second or two. For now, he's draining the rage from his system.

"I'm trusting you with this, Jer," he growls, huffing a breath. "I need her so goddamn bad. And Shepp. I feel like a piece of our quad is gone."

"Our quad?" I quip, chuckling at his words.

"We're a fucking quad. We can't live without Shepp and my Kitten." With a huff, he plops down in the chair again, running his fingers through his blond hair. "I'm..." He shakes his head, wincing when he rubs his chest.

"I feel it, too," I murmur. "But we're not giving up until they're back with us, okay? Trust the process, even if it takes another week to get the manpower to get there. And if Veritas doesn't come up with a plan, I will. We'll gather our own damn soldiers and invade that island."

Arrow tilts his head. "We should do that, anyway." He grins. A diabolical plan obviously springs to life inside him. Once again, granting him life in his darkened eyes. "That's what we'll do. We'll build an army and take on Shadow and your father. Fuck. We can take them both down."

"You're absolutely right. But that would mean returning to Briar Cove."

"Yeah. We can take up the apartment at the club and start recruiting our soldiers. We can erase your dad off the damn maps, and we'll hide with the citizens we've vowed to protect."

"And you don't think Gabe the Great would see that coming?" I quip, rubbing my temple again. I need a damn nap before we venture to our meeting spot tonight.

"He wouldn't," Olivia murmurs, sitting beside me as she cradles a hot cup of coffee.

"He knows everything, Liv. Hell, I'm pretty sure he knew you were in town." He's like a damn wizard with eyes living in the walls of every establishment in his territory. The worst fucking Viotto to ever live, and there are six brothers to compete for that title. Even over Liv's piece of shit father, who never amounted to anything but became her biggest nightmare. Maybe they're tied.

Our fathers could win a prize for the shittiest humans in the entire universe.

Liv licks her lips and nods. "Veritas has agents in almost every crime organization in the world. You name the family. We've got people undercover." Huh. Why didn't I think of that?

I side-eye her. Of course, she'd have agents infiltrating the family she grew up in. She knows the ins and outs of what it takes to be a Viotto. "Really?" I grunt, shaking my head. "Of course you do."

"Who is it, Livy? Let me at 'em," Arrow says with a grin. "I just want to talk to him. Just a little."

"That's a negative," she says, raising her middle finger to Arrow, who pouts back into his chair.

"No one in the Viotto family will let me have any fun. What's a little murder? Come onnnnnn," he whines again, playfully stomping his feet.

"Call me the fun-ruiner," she quips, sipping her coffee and sighing, staring off into the distance. "I just got word this morning that Gabriel is sick. He's still functioning as the head of the family, but he's visibly pale in public and slurring his words." She raises a brow to emphasize the catastrophe brewing over Briar Cove. "He's holding secret meetings. Meetings your mother is attending with him."

"Ill?" I say with an even tone, sitting up in the chair. My muscles turn rigid. Before sneaking out, my father was coughing, and my dear mother was handling it. "Gabriel Viotto doesn't fall ill. He..." Fights through it. He doesn't get sick. Never has. Never will. But apparently... "And my mother is helping?" Well, that's very suspicious, isn't it? Considering she was following him around with drinks in her hands, offering him her help.

"That's the word on the street. So, it seems we have bigger problems than him retaliating against you. We have an ailing mafia leader who is experiencing unrest within the organization. No word on what's got him down." My mother is the one who has him down. She's done something. "If it's a permanent thing or not. There's talk about overthrowing him, anyway." She side-eyes me with a knowing look. "From people who aren't you."

Yeah. That was us. We were the ones who were going to overthrow his tyrant ass.

I shake my head. "He won't die until I put a bullet in his skull."

It's a promise. After all the hell he's reigned down on me, Journey, Arrow, Shepp, and anyone in between. It's the least I could do to make him suffer. Hell, I'll let Arrow drill holes through his flesh in retribution for it all.

"And I'll help," Arrow chimes in, laughing maniacally in his seat.

Olivia raises a brow in his direction, worry tinting her eyes. I know that look. It's the same look she gave us as kids when she thought we were headed over the edge—which we are. We're teetering on the edge of a tall mountain, about to plummet head-first into the abyss below. The valley. The darkness. If we don't reclaim what is ours soon, we'll be gone for good. Arrow has held onto his humanity by a thread for years, and I have a funny feeling that it's about to be snipped.

"Arrow and I have a meeting tonight at the old East Point Prep gymnasium."

"Oh?" she questions, sipping her coffee again like she already knows.

"Indeed," I hum, counting down the hours until I could talk to Elias face to face.

"Need backup?"

"No. I can handle Elias White while Arrow pummels whoever dares to enter the ring with him."

Olivia snorts. "Oh, bless their hearts for even trying to fight him."

CHAPTER TWENTY-ONE

Jericho

NERVES I RARELY FEEL EAT AWAY AT ME THE MOMENT WE saunter into the venue. Tension hangs in the air. People mull around, whispering to each other and pointing at the empty octagon. A line starts at a small booth where two people take money, write names, and take bets placed for the fighters of the night.

It's a crowded place—an old gymnasium of an abandoned prep school that once functioned and housed the country's most influential people until a deadly society that got their rocks off on murdering people for money ruined it.

What a fucking world we live in.

I take a deep breath, centering myself the best way I know how. The faint sound of a violin beautifully playing classical music springs into my mind. Ah, how I miss the feel of my baby beneath my fingers, easing whatever tension I might have. I ache to touch it, play it, and do anything to have it back in my hands. But my father has commandeered that, too. Erasing it from existence by smashing it to pieces.

No matter. I'll find a new one. A better one.

Arrow's eyes light up at the prospect of fighting someone. He practically vibrates with excitement—something I haven't seen since we reunited. The only feelings we've experienced are rage, hate, and desperation as we search for our wife.

What's worse is that we know exactly where she is, but there's no way of safely retrieving her.

It's a new kind of Hell.

"This is going to be good, Jer." A grin lights up his face as he soaks in the atmosphere almost built for him. "Now, I won't have to punch you so much."

Yeah, about that. I've felt his fury through his fist. No matter how much I tell him it was impossible to carry him out of the hospital without arousing suspicion, he won't listen. Or maybe it goes deeper than that. I can feel the resentment wafting off him when he thinks I'm not looking.

Maybe he blames me as much as I blame myself for not bringing Journey on stage with us. I didn't protect her as I should have. We didn't protect her from my father when we should have. I should have known he would pull something like that when he tried to get her alone. I underestimated him. But that will never happen again. I'll never underestimate that man again.

"Just don't murder whoever they put you up against," I say, walking further into the large room and taking it in.

"I can't promise that." Arrow grins at me. "Someone needs to die." He shrugs before I can protest.

"You must be the replacement," a gruff voice says from over my shoulder.

I turn quickly, watching a tall man with a scar down his cheek standing before us with a straight face. He's an older version of Elias in stature and looks—it has to be Ruthless, the leader of this fight ring. He inspects us with a glowering expression, taking in the bloodlust shining in Arrow's eyes.

"I'm Ruthless. This is my establishment. I feel like we should go over some rules." He darts his hand out and shakes both of our hands, squeezing to display his superiority.

"I'm Jericho Viotto," I say in return.

"Arrow Amour."

"So, I've heard. The great heir of Briar Cove and his lackey."

Well, that isn't polite. I see the moment Arrow takes offense to the word lackey. He visibly recoils, staring at the man and wondering where he got the audacity. Then, the evil grin comes. Yay. He's concocting a plan for revenge.

"You can't kill the person I pit you against," Ruthless says, straightening his spine. "I've seen that look plenty of times before. You murder someone here, and I murder you. Got it? I don't give a fuck who you are or where you came from. This is my domain. No fucking murders." He eyes the two of us suspiciously, narrowing in on Arrow, who grins more.

I stiffen at his threat.

"You think you could?" Arrow taunts with a grin, cracking his knuckles playfully.

"I possess skills and talents that might surprise you." Although Ruthless spoke deceptively calmly, the underlying threat didn't escape my notice.

Yeah, he could murder us and dispose of our bodies with no problem. Not to mention, his men linger everywhere, watching our every move. This is his territory, after all.

"Arrow won't murder anyone," I say confidently, turning to the man in question. "Not our territory."

Arrow scoffs at me. "Fine. No death. But they'll wish for it." His grin would send chills down anyone's spine—except Ruthless. Amusement flickers across his face, and he grins, eyeing Arrow differently now.

"I think I might enjoy your company. Maybe one day, our two families can come to an agreement," Ruthless says, nodding his head.

"And do you have the same setup as your brother, Elias?" I question.

Ruthless grins. "Welcome to the Blue Spider compound. My brother and I have several territories throughout California. Much like the notorious Viotto family. Although we offer more than just casinos and nightclubs for profit." He taps the side of his nose.

"So, you've done your homework," I say with a respectable nod.

"When my brother invites the mafia heir of Briar Cove to my establishment, I tend to look into who is stepping foot on my territory. Not that we didn't know who you were. I'm hoping there will be no bad blood between us."

"I'll consider this a neutral zone," I say out of respect for his hospitality.

If I had known this was another sect of Elias' gang, I might have thought twice about bringing Arrow here. He's unstable at best without the other two members of our quad. God, now I'm starting to sound like Arrow. *Our quad.* Fucking hell.

"Good talk," Ruthless says, clapping his hands several times. "Now, you're up first." He nods toward the ring, and Arrow practically sprints off with an excited bounce in his step. "And my brother has reserved a private viewing room to give your conversation privacy."

"Much appreciated," I say with gratitude, stepping toward the side, but he stops me.

"I've heard of your misfortunes. Keep it peaceful. I don't mind cleaning brain matter off the wall," he threatens nonchalantly, then lets me go.

Well, then. That was dramatic. I have no intention of harming his brother. Or him. In fact, I don't have a weapon, which leaves me vulnerable and left for dead. But what can I do? Everything I had access to lies in the hands of my parents. And Carter was less than accommodating with weaponry, expressing how much he did not trust us not to shoot him in the face. Such faith he has in us.

"Elias," I say respectfully, finding him resting on a couch in a small room off the central hub of people.

"Jericho Viotto," he says smoothly, sipping his beer. "Can I offer you a drink?" He gestures to a small bucket of ice filled with bottles of beer.

I nod, grabbing a beer and popping the cap off. I take a sip, settling on the opposite side of the couch, my gaze following Arrow as he enters the ring shirtless through the large window overlooking the show.

"I'm assuming my brother had the no-murder talk with you," Elias quips, taking another drink.

"Yes. We even had a nice discussion about brain matter on walls and all that jazz," I say, sipping my beer.

Elias leans back, leisurely looking out at the crowd as they chant the other opponent's name with vigor, tossing their fists in the air.

"Good," Elias comments.

"How long have you known Shadow was Thomas Mondelli?" I question, getting right into the thick of the conversation. It's been bothering me since he mentioned the mind-blowing news.

"Shadow and I have had an ongoing business relationship for two years."

"What kind of business do you two share?" My eyes glue on Arrow, who dances around the cage, flipping off the crowd and cackling at their boos.

They won't be booing soon when he wins because that's the thing about Arrow Amour. He never loses. If you hit him, it's because he let you. He wants the pain, absorbing it like a drug into his veins and using it to fuel his violence.

"I want to offer you a deal," Elias says, dancing around my damn question.

"Yeah? What kind of deal?" Finally, I peel my eyes off Arrow's dance and stare into the eyes of Elias as he tilts his head expectantly.

"We're two men in similar situations. I've got roots in Briar Cove, as do you. I think an alliance of our families will stop the animosity between us. At least between you and me."

"I'm curious what we could bring to the table for one another?" I question.

"Well, I'd have much more to offer in this negotiation, wouldn't I? It seems to me you're on the run while your father completely decimates the city that I've grown my budding business in." He raises a brow.

"I'll be going back eventually," I say. "We just need time to..."

"Recuperate, and then what, Viotto? Are you going to storm the castle and take him by surprise?" He chuckles. "He's leveled you to the ground. Taken your friends, your wife, and set you up to marry another woman. Believe me, you cannot single-handedly reclaim what he took from you."

"Not exactly," I say coolly, taking another drink. Despite my teeth grinding together and my fists tightening, I have to remain calm and not pummel his face in.

"Here," he says, pulling out a white envelope and slipping it into my hands. "An invitation to my wedding. The date, place, and time are stamped on it so you won't forget. And I don't think you want to forget."

For fuck's sake. I'm getting whiplash with this conversation.

"Yeah, and why is that?" I don't mind making an appearance at the wedding. Jenni was a classmate. Although, I murdered her father for his ties to Shadow and traitorous ways. I suppose that's how these two got married.

"Because I invited Shadow and his bloodied-up guest the night I had dinner with them," he says nonchalantly, but my fucking heart stops. "And he wouldn't shy away from showing his face in town now that your father seems to have lost his edge. Shadow is no longer a shadow on the fringes of society. Shadow is coming out for all to know who the fuck he is. His days of hiding are over."

"Journey is going to be there? What about..."

"He'll be her plus one, I can only assume. I'm giving you

an opportunity to speak to them and get close to them. It's the only time you'll be able to. Shadow has them on his island. There's no way of getting close to it without getting yourself killed." He takes a sip, taking in my straight-faced expression. "Unless you enter The Pit." He raises a brow. "Of course, Shadow would have you slaughtered on sight for even stepping into his palace. He rules there."

I won't mention to him that the men of Veritas are already attempting to break onto the island and have gone up in flames. Then, he'd be aware I have connections to the government and be less apt to help me. But The Pit? The same pit my wife fought in? I'd slaughter everyone who dared to fight me. But Arrow? Yeah, he'd have the time of his life.

"And you're one hundred percent sure that Shadow will come through?" My heart aches with desperation for this entire situation to be true. It could be a setup. One to bring us all to a location and then end our lives.

Elias shrugs. "No one can be one hundred percent about anything in this world. But a wedding is a wedding. It brings out everyone. It's much like a celebration. Shadow will make an appearance."

"So, what kind of deal were you thinking?" I ask, studying the invitation with a skeptical eye. It could all be a trap, but if I can shake his hand by the end of the night and verbally come to whatever agreement he has in mind, then maybe I can get my place back at my home.

"I want the Blue Spiders to help run Briar Cove." He takes a drink, eyeing me as the words sink in. "In return, I want your loyalty. And with that loyalty, I'll help you take down Shadow from the inside, get your girl back and your friend, and then take down your father. This benefits both of us. I have the arsenal at my disposal. The men who are willing to fight."

Briar Cove is my birthright. The achievement I've been preparing for since I was five, and my father locked me away to toughen me up. His words. Not mine. Sitting on the throne of the Viotto Crime Family has always been my destiny. My knee-jerk reaction is to tell Elias to get fucked. Veritas can easily help me get back Journey and Shepp. And they have inside help, too.

But do I want a broken legacy handed down from Viotto to Viotto? Only time will tell.

"I can see you're thinking it over. Maybe I should give you some time to consider my deal. Let's say until my wedding. I'll be holding meetings there, anyway."

It's not too far off to hold meetings during a time of celebration when the leader is more charitable and giving. Many attend weddings hoping to create alliances and earn forgiveness for past transgressions. Mafia or gang, it doesn't seem to matter.

"And what would my role be in all this? Briar Cove is mine." In the future, at least.

I was born for this role. Tortured for it. Given complexes for it. It's a hard piece of myself to let go of and let someone else step up to the plate, especially when it's Elias White, rival gang member.

"You can still have your cake and eat it." He shrugs. "I want out of the shadows, Viotto. My family has a role there, too. Something your father has pushed to the outskirts and banished. Sure, we had a deal. But it only benefited him."

"The drugs you bring into my city?" I raise a brow, attempting to release my teeth grinding together. "There are more deaths attributed to those laced drugs than from anything else."

"You should check who the distributor is of those drugs you're accusing me of possessing," he says cooly, not letting on to the nerve I just hit. "Everyone likes to point a finger and blame my family. I provide the purest form of our products. They're tested and not tampered with. No lacing is going on from my end or Shadow's. Your father is the one attempting to keep everyone out of his territory. Even though he and I made a deal."

I digest his words. "If you're not the one doing the lacing, who is?" I question, not fully believing in what he's saying. He could be giving me one lie after another. We've never been friends, after all. We exist in the same town, attempting to run our businesses harmoniously.

"I think that's something you should ask your father," he says, taking one last drink of his beer.

"Him?" I raise a brow.

"And I'd hurry for a visit if I were you. Your entire empire is hanging by a thread. Word is, your father is sick and lacking in his duties. If he's not careful, someone will swoop in and take what should be yours."

I lick my lips, looking out into the silent crowd. Arrow struts through the octagon with blood coating his face and chest. He raises his hands, laughing as two other guys take the other guy out of the cage. He doesn't move and barely looks like he's breathing. I guess Arrow was right when he said the other man would wish for death.

"Come to my wedding and see for yourself. Your father is no threat to you right now. Others, though? Maybe. I suggest hiding out in the shadows. It'll give you a taste of your own medicine."

"The family would be there to back his every move," I say, taking several gulps of my beer.

"That's the thing about family, though, isn't it? Are they truly there to help the town of Briar Cove? Or are they after the throne for themselves? Where money and power are involved, others will trample the rest of you to gain it."

"How exactly do you know all this information?" I question, tilting my head.

It seems odd for a man who lives on the edge of town to know all our business. He's hiding something vital, but I'm not sure what.

"I have sources, Viotto. Viable sources within the family have come to me with concerns about our town and your father." With that, Elias gets up from the couch and nods for me to follow. "You might want to carry your friend out of here before my brother makes him disappear."

Without another word, I follow Elias out of the small viewing room and make my way to Arrow, pushing through the crowd.

"Arrow," I say, standing beside him, marveling at the blood coating his flesh. "We may want to take our leave."

Arrow snorts. "But I want to stay and watch the rest of the fights. Did you see me, Daddy Jer? I fucked that guy up!" he howls, throwing his head back with excitement.

"I did, indeed."

"It was a good fight. If you ever think about leaving your organization and coming here, I'd offer you a permanent spot," Ruthless says, standing beside his brother with a smirk. Well, at least he doesn't seem too upset. "Like that one." He nods toward the next fighter beside the ring. "Found him outside a bar. He's a rock star. Former junky. This was his opportunity. Smart kid."

I watch the tall, blond-haired fighter stare off into space. Earbuds rest in his ears as he bounces from side to side, preparing himself. Tattoos etch into his flesh, bringing my eyes to the neon stars above his heart. I've always been told tattoos represent something of importance if they're above the thumping organ pumping blood throughout your body.

Maybe it's true.

"Is he any good?" I ask, my eyes sliding to his large opponent, eyeing him up and down. He's larger. Larger than the man he's about to throw fists with. In fact, it looks like he could kill the other one with one punch.

"You could stay and watch if you'd like. Everyone underestimates him. But he's got a hell of a gift."

"Oh, yeah? And what's that?"

Ruthless grins when the bell rings and the two enter the ring. "He's got a photographic memory. Every move the person opposite of him makes, he stores it inside his brain."

"A photographic memory?" I mumble, staring at the tatted man with raised brows.

What a horrible thing for a brain to do. Worthy for a fight like this, being able to determine the others' move. My mind has blocked out a lot from my past. The feelings I held when my father took his anger out on me or locked me in the closet for crying—like a child should. It would all be there in reach. Every emotion. Every movement. It would be a damn burden.

"So, not a junky anymore?" I ask, watching him enter the ring. Long gone are the earbuds in his ears. His light eyes dart around the ring, taking us all in and landing on his opponent. He sizes him up without emotion, taking in the large muscles bulging on his arms.

"Wouldn't let him fight if he was. Just watch him." Ruthless nods to the kid in the octagon as the bell rings, indicating their fight is starting.

The kid doesn't waste a moment. He watches his competitor, and no shit, predicts his moves. One punch. Two punches. A kick to the kidneys. Then, one last blow to the jaw, forcing the bigger man to the ground.

Arrow grins, watching him with a challenge in his eyes. "Can I fight him next?" he quips, cracking his bloodied knuckles.

"Not a chance in hell," Ruthless grunts. "That's my crowd favorite." AKA, he brings in a lot of money, and Arrow would decimate the competition with his fury fists.

"Boo, you're no fun," Arrow pouts, crossing his arms.

"That's our cue, then," I say, standing beside Arrow.

He seems lighter now that he's pounded someone's face in and has blood on his skin.

"The offer still stands," Ruthless says, holding his hand for me to shake. "And consider what my brother has to offer. You'll need allies in your fight against two evils."

"And adding in a third evil is good?" I ask, raising a brow.

Ruthless smirks. "I am neither good nor evil. I'm a third party with six brothers at my beck and call. Elias runs his own, taking himself to the top after working from the bottom."

"I'm curious why your family would willingly insert themselves into my family's battle?"

Ruthless finally lets go of my hand and raises his chin. "Everyone needs an ally, Viotto. You should consider it."

"Ally, indeed. But it still makes me question why you'd willingly do that. We've had zero business together." Not to mention the beef I've had with Elias and the drugs he's given to people of Briar Cove, poisoning some. Or maybe it wasn't him. I need time to reflect on what the past has shown me. Has my father been manipulating things from behind the scenes? To what? Create a false narrative against outsiders?

Possibly.

"But we could," Ruthless says, pursing his lips. "Consider the offer. Then, we can have another meeting and discuss further details. It would be in everyone's best interest to wipe out Gabriel Viotto and the cruel empire he's erected and take Shadow down with him."

With that, Ruthless tips his chin at us and then saunters through the crowd toward the stage. He slaps the kid who won on the shoulder, leaning in to talk to him discreetly.

"Well, they seem trustworthy," Arrow quips, whooping with unexpelled energy.

"I'm not convinced," I say, tipping my head for him to follow so we can talk in the vehicle Olivia let me borrow.

We stay silent until we jump into the SUV, closing the doors and cutting off the chaotic world around us.

"Do we trust them?" I ask, looking forward as a crowd surges into the space through one tiny door. "They want an alliance and loyalty. In return, they're offering their men as soldiers in our fight. We'd be one. They'd rule half of Briar Cove. And us the other." It's truly something to consider, but I'm failing to see why. Why put their people on the line? Would they double-cross us and attempt to take the entire town for their own?

"I want to fight again. So, yes," Arrow quips with a grin.

"Elias wants to work with us to take down Gabriel." I want to make sure he understands the severity of our situation. He's got the gory fight on his brain and blood on his flesh. He's eager to please whoever can help tamp down his demon.

"Why? What's the deal he wants?" Arrow asks with furrowed brows.

"He wants to help rule Briar Cove when it's all said and done."

"Pfft. Like the family would ever agree to that, we've held Briar Cove for years. Why the hell would we give it up to a gang?" He rolls his eyes for dramatic effect.

I sigh, rubbing my temple. "My thoughts exactly. But Elias's words make me think something more is happening back at home that we need to be present for." I raise a brow when Arrow grins. "Like we need to head back and hide out so we can observe what's happening."

"Go home, you say? I'm down for that. Besides, I miss my babies, Shepp, and my girl," he pouts.

"Then it's settled. We'll discuss this with Liv and Carter first. But no matter what, we're returning to Briar Cove, come hell or high waters. Besides, we have a wedding to attend," I say, starting the vehicle.

"A wedding?" Arrow groans. "I hate weddings—unless it's my own." He smirks. "But you know allllll about getting married, don't you?"

Asshole.

"Well, no matter your hatred for weddings, you'll want to attend this one."

"Yeah, and why is that?"

"Because Journey and Shepp will be in attendance. It may be our only chance to grab them and run." Run straight to the cabin to make up for lost time and get our bearings before going back to conquer my father.

"Fuck yes. A fight and a kidnapping at a wedding? Count me the fuck in," he hoots, punching the ceiling.

"We can't go in half-cocked, Arrow. We need to plan this to a T so there are no mistakes. This may be our only chance to get them away from Shadow's grasp."

Arrow's grin sends shivers down my spine when he nods. "No half-cocked here. We'll go in fully cocked. With guns and a plan to get my Kitten back into my arms."

"That begs the question of what we do next?"

"Go back home." Arrow smirks. "We need to get back into Briar Cove and scope out what's happening there. Maybe take down a few assholes along the way. My dad will have insight. And he's not a traitor. Also, I need to break out my babies. They're probably dying without me." And where does Arrow think he will stash two lions once he breaks them out? I know he's been in contact with the zookeeper, who feeds and tends to them daily. They're probably safer in their cage than on the outside.

"We'll take care of it all," I say with finality, pulling into Olivia's driveway. "The real work begins now. We escaped from the fates Gabriel insisted we needed." I cringe.

"Yeah. Me with death and you with... other death," he snickers at that.

"The marriage between Chloe and I wouldn't have been legal, anyway. No matter what my father said. She didn't want me." I shake my head. "Once we return to Briar Cove, we'll contact Brandon." The man who helped Aiden run our club as head of security. "We need to test his loyalties because Aiden proved to be a double-crossing pussy. We also need to visit your father and talk with the police chief."

"I love testing loyalties," Arrow quips, jumping out of the

car, still covered in blood. "I'll text Dad and make sure he's good for a meeting. If one of those assholes touched him or hurt him because of me..." he trails off, the gleam of the fight falling from his face.

"Don't worry, Arrow. If someone has messed with the priest, it'll be the last thing that they do."

"Fuck yeah," he says with a smirk. "I'm this close to forgiving you." He holds his fingers together, holding them an inch apart. It's something, but not total forgiveness. I will do whatever I have to do to get my best friend on the right track.

"Then it's settled. We need someone on our side," I grumble. "It seems like everyone we knew in the family was in on my father's plans to take us down and eliminate us."

Well, not me, of course. He wanted to marry me off and use Arrow as the motivation. It's not the first time my father has used the people around me to get what he wants. Not the last time, either.

Gabriel Viotto will continue to control my life until he falls on his knees with blood surrounding him.

It's time that ends.

"Let's go home." I grin as I step outside the vehicle with Arrow.

"And fuck some shit up!" he shouts into the night sky. No doubt disrupting the few neighbors Olivia has in her gated community.

CHAPTER TWENTY-TWO

Arrow

EXCITEMENT ROARS THROUGH MY VEINS THE CLOSER WE GET to our home base. Briar Cove. The land I grew up in. My dick practically rises in my jeans the moment we drive through the city limits and all the familiar sights come into view.

"What a lovely day to be home," I sing, much to the dismay of Jericho, who grips the steering wheel of our shitty stolen vehicle.

Sure, we could have taken the car Olivia was offering, but it was too shiny and too new. It would have drawn every eye in our direction, and that's the last thing we need at a time like this. Be discreet and all that good stuff.

"And you've sent word?" Jericho questions, huffing under his breath.

"Oh, yes," I sing-song with a grin.

"And he's willing to meet?"

I side-eye Jericho. "You should know that he never did like what Gabriel did with me."

And that's a fact. My father, the priest, felt heavily manipulated when he signed over his rights to Gabriel, making him my new guardian. He thought Gabe would take away the blood lust, not intensify it. I'm not upset that my blood lust is sated, and I've learned how to hone it in on the bad guys. Being a young kid and having that darkness in me nagging to kill and feel the blood on my fingertips was a wild ride. My dad never could have come to terms with that or helped me with it. Unless he put me in an asylum or something. But nah, that wouldn't have worked.

The one thing I know is that my father has always been on my side. He may help the family out and give them a spot for initiation, but they also donate a shit ton of money to his church, giving him protection and the means to live. Hopefully, that doesn't sway him.

"To the church, driver!" I shout, pointing the way toward the church in the distance.

The dark sky conceals us when we pull into the parking lot and park.

"His doing? Or the family's?" Jericho mutters, staring at the darkened lights that once lit the space, illuminating everyone from danger. Not that anyone would touch this church with a ten-foot pole. Everyone and their mother knows it's protected by the Viotto's—even my dad.

"If it were the family's, they would have lit us up with bullets already." I grin, jumping out of the car without a second thought. I'm goddamn Arrow Amour. No one can take me down.

"Arrow! For fuck's sake," Jericho hisses, coming beside me. His eyes dart around, looking for the mysterious gunmen hiding in the shadows, ready to take us out. "You're going to get yourself killed one of these days."

Doesn't he know I'm fucking invisible? Amateur.

"Eh. They can't take us down, Daddy Jer." I grin, take a few steps away from him, and enter the back of the church.

"I don't know how you've kept yourself alive all these years," he growls, gently shutting the open door behind us. "I swear to God."

"In the house of the Lord, that's not a nice thing to do, Daddy Jer," I quip, taking in my old home.

I grew up here. Well, kind of. My father hid me here after

my junky mom said bye. Not only was he never supposed to have sex, but he wasn't supposed to have a kid or raise him, either. Throw in my murdery ways, and he was truly fucked over. Maybe I am the reflection of his sins. His words. Not mine.

I have many fond memories of hiding from other church members or sitting in the back of the pews on Sunday morning as my father led the congregation in songs, prayers, and smiles —something he rarely offered me. Our relationship has strengthened since I left his nest and lived with Gabriel. He sees the humanity living inside me now, begging to take care of the people who were like my mother. The downtrodden and drug addicted, hoping to emerge from the patterns that brought them there. They come to me to get healthy, to leave their abusive husbands or wives or relatives, and I give them a brand new start.

Me.

The boy who aches to make people bleed.

But I also have a heart. A heart not many people find in me. But Jericho did. Shepp did. And now, my Kitten does. They see the true man beneath the layers of jokes and blood lust.

Even if they want to murder me sometimes. For, let's say —taking out Journey's birth control without her knowing and then hanging said birth control in my lair. Meh, she'll get over it, right? The other two seemed to move on without spilling the beans. I just had to open my big mouth at the initiation ball.

Oh, well. If it gets her pregnant, then so be it. I want her stuck with us, carrying all our spawns and shit... I should not be getting a boner in church. What would God think of me, then?

"This way," I mutter, grabbing his arm and taking him down a set of stairs toward another basement area. It houses the Sunday school classrooms, rec room, basketball court, and my father's offices. A place he often hides, sleeps, and hell—even lives here sometimes.

Jericho and I make it through the darkened space I memorized as a kid. I don't dare turn on any lights or make a noise as we make our way down the hall toward my father's office, where one singular light shines. I've been here many times. And in many instances, it's after I've tortured someone for information and am covered in blood. I come to ask my father about my actions or simply talk to him about my ideas. He listens with an open heart and no judgment. It's something he adopted after he handed me to Gabriel.

Before we reach my father's office, I pull Jericho into a room next to it—another office for his secretary. I gently knock on the wall five times, and then I wait. My ears perk up when the same knock greets my ears, giving me the all-clear.

"It means he's alone," I say without moving a muscle. "But I'm listening just in case." We stick our ears against the wall, listening for any other movement, but hear none.

I grab Jericho and pull him into my father's well-lit office. I grin at him.

"Daddy-O," I say, moving forward and wrapping him in my arms.

"Arrow," he whispers into my ear, clinging harder than expected. "You're here. Alive." He pulls back, gently gripping my cheek in his palm. "You're both alive."

"Is there something we should know?" Jericho asks, raising a brow with suspicion.

"A lot of rumors floating in the air, consisting of your deaths. Although I know your father doesn't believe that."

"Have you been in contact with him?" I ask, tilting my head. "Word on the street is this is all hanging by an itty bitty thread."

"I've gotten a few texts here and there confirming initiation dates. He has something on the schedule two Sundays from now in the basement."

"Are you in the know of what it is?" Jericho asks, folding his hands in front of him.

"A meeting is all the text said when he reached out to let me know it would be needed. He never really elaborates unless it's an initiation for the family."

My face twists. "On a Sunday? The most holy days of the family?" I question, tapping my chin several times.

"It is strange," Jericho chimes in. "My father only schedules these types of things in the evenings on weekdays. And if it's in the basement, it's only used for initiations or annihilation."

"Has someone been bad?" I ask, lighting up at the thought of taking a traitor down. Then, I realize. I might be considered a traitor in the family's eyes. I went against Gabriel's orders and fell out of my coma. But, pfft. Why would I stay down when everyone I considered mine was in danger? Nah, fuck that. I needed to be up and alert so I could take down everyone who put me there, including Gabriel himself.

"I am unaware of what is happening on Sunday during their meeting. But he has been here a few times to discuss situations with the ones closest to him with a woman at his side."

Jericho blanches. Only slightly, though. You rarely see Jericho react.

"Seems my mother has inserted herself into business matters," he says, tapping his fingers on his worn jeans several times.

"Your mother?" my dad asks, tilting his head. " I thought..."

"She was. But now, she's suddenly back from her captivity and has freed herself." He shakes his head in confusion. Something only I can read on his face, when my dad's lips pop open.

"We need to know everything that's been happening here since Gabe's headquarters took a tumble," I say, garnering my father's attention.

My father swallows hard, nodding his head. "There seems

to be upset from outside forces. Shadow attacked the night headquarters fell. And no one has seen you two, Shepp, or the girl you had with you since then. There's been whispers of your demise." Tears fill his eyes when he looks at me. "I thought for sure something had happened to you, son. In my heart, though. I felt your soul, and God brought me back from the brink of it all. When I finally got your text, it brought me to my knees. You're alive."

His words pierce through the thick armor I usually don't feel. Seeing the tears in his eyes and the joy shining through— that he's excited I'm still alive—makes my heart flip-flop in my chest.

"Well, I'm alive and kicking," I say with a grin, spreading my arms out.

"With all due respect, Priest. We've come for information. It has come to my attention that being in Briar Cove is a mistake. My father was after all of us." Jericho gets straight down to business. Mr. Business all the time, fucker.

"Yes." My dad clears his throat. "Of course. Why don't you boys have a seat?"

"And we're safe here?" Jericho asks, reluctantly standing behind the chair with a sour expression.

Fuck. It was like pulling teeth to get him here in the first place. He kept insisting Daddy Dearest would turn us over to the family. But I told him he wouldn't. I told Daddy Jer we'd be safe and sound inside the walls of this church. My dad may be in the pockets of the family, but he's loyal to me, too. He keeps my humanitarian adventures under his belt and is safe from the men who want to take it over and credit themselves for it. But it's mine. Fuckers.

"You're safe behind the walls of this church and with me. No one will get to you here. Not on my watch," he says with a sharp nod, gesturing for us to sit again.

Jericho side-eyes me when I sit down with ease. I've been in this chair—this office—so many times before. My father hid me behind these walls, away from the public's prying eyes. I was simply an orphan my father took in. Or that's what he told people so he could keep me here. They never noticed the similarities because there weren't any. Our eyes are the same shade of blue. But everything else must come from my mother.

Reluctantly, Jericho sits beside me. Every muscle in his body remains rigid. We need Journey back to make him loosen up a bit. The fucker is too wound tight and needs a good lay to bring him back to earth. Ugh. I miss my Kitten so damn bad I can barely contain the rage living inside me. Granted, that fight helped to curb my blood lust in the other direction. But I'm aching for a fight again. Half of me hopes the family is lurking in the shadows so I can steal their guns and send them straight to Hell. Just to help me feel better.

I snap back into the rigid conversation, focusing on my father's tightening face.

"Yes. They boarded up your club. Any business your father has his fingers in has been closed momentarily." He folds his hands on the desk and sighs. "They're all changing owners and in the process of reopening."

Jericho's eyes darken. "And how did you hear about the changing of ownership?"

My dad swallows hard. "You think I'll let the mafia in the basement of my church without secretly listening to what is going on in this city? After what your father promised me would happen with Arrow and breaking those promises the moment I signed my rights over." He shakes his head, disgust rolling through him. "I occupy this building. I am the church. Therefore, your business is my business."

I always wondered what my father thought about my upbringing. He tried his best with me. But I was a little shit. My activities included killing bunnies and looking at their insides. Oh, I also brought them home for Dad to look at. I was so damn proud. Then, I started fighting in school—which was fun, by the way. It caught Jericho's attention, at least. I think my impulsiveness was the straw that broke my father's back. I couldn't control myself. If I wanted it. I took it.

"So, every meeting that's happened in the basement?" Jericho questions, sitting back in the chair.

"I was there to witness them all." No fear rests in my father's eyes. "When they were held here, anyway. The more I've gotten to know your father, the more paranoid he's become. Over the years, he's gone from the basement to his tower for meetings with others. If you were in my position. What would you do?"

"I'd listen in on every grizzly detail," I say with a grin, rubbing my hands together.

"As would I," Jericho agrees. "So, you have information on the new owners?"

"No. I don't have names. I only have that. No names were said in the meetings, but the men of the family are absolutely pissed that it's happening. Those clubs seem to be a major revenue for the entire Viotto family."

"They are," Jericho says with a nod.

It's an understatement, really. The family has many businesses—legit and not so legit. Those clubs are fronts to wash and distribute our laundered money under the radar. We've had our hands in gun runs and gambling ventures. In fact, we have casinos in many regions of California that put money in our pockets, giving us the leeway to do whatever the fuck we want.

"Whoever is doing it wants to take everything from us," I say with a frown. "Who the fuck would want to do that? And why now?"

I have one guess, but I don't know if Jericho will like it. It's too much of a coincidence that his mom would waltz back into his life after being gone for so long.

"I have some ideas," Jericho says cryptically, meaning we'll discuss them later because he still doesn't trust my dad.

"Oh, me, too," I say with a grin. And I can't wait to say it. Maybe that fucker will punch me in the nose again. God. A rush goes through my damn veins. I want to feel alive and fucking bleed.

I need Journey back.

"You say our club has been boarded up for good?" Jericho asks, tilting his head.

"Yes."

Ah, that makes sense. That club no longer belongs to Gabriel. It's Jericho's. I wonder if they boarded it up because it didn't belong to them, but they probably still had the keys. We never knew the true intentions of Gabriel signing over Rave to Jericho all willy-nilly. It was Gabe's one day and then Jericho's the next, without rhyme or reason. I swore he was going to fuck Jericho over the second he could.

Something works in Jericho's mind when he nods, standing from the chair. "I'm hoping that this relationship can be mutually beneficial. I scratch your back, and you scratch mine."

My dad stands, extending his hand to Jericho and gently shaking it. "I will relay as much information as possible before I'm found out. I hope that you boys stay safe while visiting Briar Cove." His eyes look into each of ours with a warning ringing in them.

"Lay low, got it," I say, pulling my dad in for a bear hug. "Thanks, Dad," I murmur, squeezing him tight until he's wheezing in my arms.

Maybe after this entire fiasco ends, my dad and I can get back on track. We've slightly fallen apart since he gave me up and can't be seen with me in public. It's dumb. I wish he could acknowledge me in front of everyone, but it's not possible to keep his position at the church if he does.

"We should go," Jericho says, eyeing the time.

"Fine," I sigh, pulling back from my father and standing beside Jericho. "You'll keep safe, too?"

"Don't worry about me. I have all the protection I need," he says, rubbing the cross dangling around his neck.

Sometimes, I wonder how a man as honorable as my father got himself entangled with my mom.

"Why don't I have a mom?" I ask, looking up at my dad.

He grins and hands me a plate from the sink. I wipe the towel across it, removing the water.

"Your mom was a godly woman, Arrow. But she was very sad." He's a liar. She wasn't sad. He doesn't know. I've overheard him mumbling to himself about this Darla person leaving me behind for drugs. *"So sad that she knew she couldn't care for you, and she gave you to me."*

I nod a few times, drying the plate and setting it on the counter. "Can you tell me the story?" My heart aches when he looks down at me with the brightest grin I've ever seen. My dad has always been so loving toward me in private. But he said my existence could take away his role as the priest. He said he felt he owed it to the people of Briar Cove because their souls also needed him.

Even though I'm four, I understand what he's saying. Even though he gets mad at me sometimes, that's okay. I still love my dad.

"Once upon a time, there was a woman who loved her son so much, but she knew she couldn't love him the way he needed. So, she gave him to the next best person she could think of. The man she had fallen in love with. A priest. A man she knew could take their son into the godly light and give him the world she had dreamed of." He smiles down at me, ruffling my hair. "I will love you no matter what, Arrow. You're the sunshine in my life now. I will gladly share anything with you." Leaning down, my father squats before me, taking my face in his palms. "So, I want to ask you something."

"What is it?" I ask, furrowing my brows.

"What goes through your mind when you're climbing that big tree?" I inspect his calming face and grin. "You terrified me today, Arrow. I thought you were going to fall."

My brows furrow when I think about the tree right outside

on the playground. It's huge. Also, it's my favorite thing to climb. The thrill that runs through me when I'm so high up I can see above the church is unmatched. Daddy doesn't like it, though. He says I'll fall out like I've done before and broke my arm. I don't remember that either.

"When I hung from the tall branch?" It was amazing. My feet dangled in the wind. If I would have let go, I could have flown. Daddy said I'd go splat on the ground, but I don't think so.

"Yes. I felt scared today, Arrow. You have to remember that you could die or get hurt. I know in your brain it doesn't feel like it." He's holding back on something, but I can't tell what.

I purse my lips, irrational thoughts going through my mind. He hates what I do. I can tell that from the softening of his eyes.

"There's a man who wants to help you." And that's when I recognize the sadness in my father's voice for the first time. It's not disappointment or anger. He's sad that I make him sad. That I do these things that go against him.

"A man?" I breathe. 'What do you mean? You don't want me?"

"No. It's not that. I want you. With all my heart, Arrow. You know you're so important to me. But if you give this man a chance, he could help you with those urges..."

"Urges?" I question. "You mean when I take risks you don't like?" Dad says I'm too impulsive and don't seem to grasp the consequences of what's happening. Maybe he's right.

"Yes," he says with glistening eyes. "He can help you become something great and help you pinpoint those urges into something productive. Would you want to meet him?" He swallows hard, hope glistening in the crest of his eyes.

I furrow my brows, looking at the dishes that still need to be done.

"You'd be free, Arrow. I wouldn't have to hide you at the back of the church anymore." Right. I'm his biggest, most

special secret. He loves me so much that he has to keep me
hidden from the big bosses of the church. Even being so young,
I understand that. Kind of. I don't want to be hidden anymore.
I don't want him to lose his job or...

"*Okay.*" *I nod a few times.* "*I'll meet him.*"

"We'll be in touch," Jericho says stiffly, knocking me out of
my head and motioning for me to follow his lead.

"Until next time, Dad." I salute him with a smirk before
following Jericho out into the darkened hallway of the church
with the memory on my mind.

CHAPTER TWENTY-THREE

Arrow

MY HAIR STANDS ON END WHEN WE WEAVE OUR WAY THROUGH the long corridor, coming to a halt near the back door we entered through.

"Whattya say, Daddy Jer? We in the clear?" I murmur, looking through the small window. The parking lot is the only thing that greets my eyes—nothing but shadows and trees blowing in the wind.

"I'm not exactly sure anymore," he sighs, with an odd sense of vulnerability. "But I think we should be in the clear to get to the car. There doesn't appear to be anyone out there."

"If there is, I'll gut them with my bare hands." I grin.

Anticipation runs through me at the thought of blood dripping down my flesh. Hell, maybe I can hold a beating heart in my palm. That's the dream, am I right? Even though the fight helped satisfy my bloodlust, it fades with every second I spend back in my hometown. An ache to track down my Kitten and murder everyone around her has me by the damn balls, riding me hard. She should be doing that, thank you very much. My girl needs my cock ASAP. So I can continue the process of knocking her up.

"Are you seriously getting a boner right now?" Jericho murmurs, slowly opening the back door. He stops momentarily, eyeing the shadows for the people possibly after our heads.

"Just thinking about my Kitten," I pout, looking in the opposite direction and taking it all in. "You think she's knocked up by now?"

I feel Jericho's stare burning through me. "Possibly," he grunts, standing tall as we walk to our stolen car.

"Well, if she's not. Once we get her back, I'm tying her to our bed and fucking her until she's knocked up. You can join if you want," I say, grinning when he glares at me.

"We're in danger even being here, and all you can think with is your dick?" He raises a haughty brow at me, thinking he's so much better.

I know for a fact he's thinking about her sprawled out naked on the bed, begging for his cock.

"Well, it's better than thinking about the family coming after us and hoping to end our lives. So, my cock wins." I shrug when we get into the car, each of us taking a calming breath. "So, you thinking what I'm thinking?"

"It depends. If you're still thinking with your cock, then no. But if you're thinking that Rave will become our new head-quarters while it's shut down, then yes." He taps his fingers on the steering wheel several times before starting the car. "I know my father and his plans well, but if my mother is in charge or pulling strings, I don't know what anyone is capable of."

"We're on our own," I hum with displeasure. It'd be nice to have the fam in our back pockets, but I have an awful feeling brewing that the family we've come to know and barely tolerate will be after our heads. "You're the heir, and I'm the spare..." I grin when he huffs at my words. "They'll be awfully trigger-happy in our company."

"If my father has fallen, I'm the next in line of the throne. If they can eliminate me, then... Someone else is the new king." He shakes his head when he pulls onto the road, and we begin our journey across town toward Rave.

"And who would it be?" I hum, tapping my chin.

"It could be anyone that stood behind my father and had an ounce of power. The bosses who studied beneath him watched his rule. Anyone could do it."

"Civil war is a foot in the house of Viotto," I chuckle, rubbing my hands together. "And I'm going to be the new general in charge."

Jericho side-eyes me again as he takes back streets through Briar Cove, attempting to conceal our presence here. "Then we need to build up an army," he says, pulling into the darkened parking lot across the street from Rave.

"An army, you say? I like the sound of that. So, what's the plan? Anything specific?"

Jericho cracks his knuckles, staring out the windshield. "First things first, we get our girl and best friend back from Shadow before he can do anything drastic to them. From what Elias said, they seem to be okay. For now."

"Oh, fun. So, we're going to a wedding?" I ask, throwing the passenger side door open without a care in the world. War is on the way. Blood is about to be spilled. And my dick is harder than it's been in weeks at the prospect of it all. I wonder if my Kitten would let me fuck her in a pool of blood from our enemies? I'll add that to my bucket list right after fucking her ass. Which, sadly, I never got to do. What a shame. But I can make it up to her. All I need are some new buttplugs, lube, and her. Then we're all set.

"Indeed." Jericho nods and comes beside me as we stare at the building we've called our home base for years. Boards hang over every window and door, giving it an abandoned feel, despite it being in operation before our lives got fucked. "I've got a few ideas and calls to make. But I know we won't be able to do this alone. We need reinforcements." Then, he takes off, walking across the parking lot toward the backside of Rave.

"Wait, whoa! Reinforcements? Are you thinking about taking Elias up on his offer?" I hiss when he stops at the back door, covered by a large piece of wood. A sign stating the property was repossessed hangs from the wood, forbidding anyone from stepping inside. Except for us, of course. There's no way this building was taken back. His fingers brush against the hard surface as his brows furrow with hesitation.

"At this point, Arrow. All I want is my fucking home back. My girl. My best fucking friend. You. And nothing else. I'd give up my goddamn empire to make sure that all happened." His jaw works back and forth as he peels the piece of plywood off one edge of the door.

"You'd give it all up, Daddy Jer? Everything for..."

"Yes," he grits out, cutting me off. "If I don't have my family, then I have nothing. I'd be the king of an empty town with a cold heart and nothing more. I'm not my fucking father. He wanted nothing more than power. He sacrificed my child-hood, possibly my mother, and so much more to bring us this." He shakes his head with a huff. "I won't lose the only people who mean something to me."

My grin grows when he cracks open the back door and squeezes through the wood to enter. It's like music to my ears when we enter the darkened club that usually never sleeps. It's always lit up and full of life and dancing fuckers eager to spend their money on our booze. Now, it's just the two of us maneuvering through the table setup and liquor bottles on display. Jericho grabs his phone and lights up the space with his flashlight. As we pass one bar, he grabs a top-shelf bottle of scotch before making his way up the stairs with me on his heels.

"Fucking Aiden," he grunts, pushing through the door. Probably recounting the betrayal that we didn't see coming.

"Have we heard from Brandon?" I hum, turning on a small lamp in our VIP area, illuminating our sitting area. How convenient that we still have power.

"I'm almost afraid to reach out," Jericho says, pinching the bridge of his nose. "Everything I've ever fucking known has been covered in shit." With that statement, he opens the bottle of sipping scotch and takes several long pulls, not even wincing when he cradles the bottle between his legs with a groan.

In all the time I've known Jericho, he's never been one to break down. He's always got an idea. A plan. Anything to get us out of whatever hole we've dug ourselves into. Now, though? He seems to be holding on by a damn string. I get it, bro. I do. Our girl. Our silent giant. Our everything is lost in the wind somewhere we can't get to. No matter how hard we try. We're trapped. Stuck. Fucking sitting ducks. If anyone finds us.

Well, not sitting ducks. It's more like they'll be the sitting ducks if anyone comes here to find us or attempts to attack us. I have several tricks up my sleeves, like weapons. Knock out drugs. Anything I could conjure up, it's at the tip of my fingers.

"Give him a jingle, Jer," I say with a grin, marching over to a spot on the wall and tapping it twice. "If Brandon even thinks about fucking us over, I'll put a bullet in his head." I grin when I grab a handgun from my gun case hidden in the wall and check the bullets.

I wouldn't hesitate for a moment. Anyone who fucks with my family will meet the end of my gun. Or fists. Or a torture chamber. Oh, I like that idea better. Maybe I could drag Brandon down to the basement and show him a thing or two. Like my saw collection. Oh! Even better—my knife collection. I bet he'd get a big kick out of my big stabber, especially when it goes through flesh and hearts. I look down at my dick, bouncing at the possibilities. Calm down, Big A. It's not happening yet. Yet—being the keyword. Do I want Brandon to be a backstabber? Not really. Do I want to torture some fellas and swim in their blood? Yes, yes, I do.

My eyes catch on Jer after peeling my gaze from my dick, which instantly deflates at the sight of his distress. He leans back, eyes squeezed shut. I see the wheels turning in his brain as he counts to ten silently in his mind. Good old Sheppy Boy, teaching our uptight friend how to chill the fuck out. If he didn't, he'd probably develop some ulcers in his stomach and puke up blood.

I'm a blood guy and all that, but seeing my bestie down and out makes feelings stir inside me. Weird feelings. Like butterflies in my stomach and concern in the back of my mind. I'm not an unfeeling psycho like some would describe me. I have them. Well, somewhere inside me. Probably hiding. But this is how God made me—my dad's words, not mine. He loved to tell me that as a kid.

"This is just how God made you, Arrow." He smiles down at me, scrubbing my hands with warm water and dish soap. *"But playing with dead animals is gross."*

"I just wanted to see their guts," I say with a grin, earning a chuckle from him.

"Then we'll find safe ways for that, okay?"

I was four when that conversation happened. I remember it like yesterday. My dad may have given me up because he could no longer control my urges, but I know he loves me. He also worries a lot, like now. I know he's pacing his office, trying to figure out how to help us more.

Jer gets up from his spot on the couch, meandering over to the large window that looks over our club with his hands clasped behind his back. It's his thinking pose. Or overthinking pose. Obviously, something brilliant is brewing in his devious mind. Like always. He's our leader for a reason. He makes all the decisions. Well, Shepp helps to even it out. I'm just the muscle, stabbing people and shit, so no one gets in our way.

And I'm happy to do it.

"What's up, Daddy Jer? Got something cooking?" I ask, shoving the gun into my waistband. Ah, nothing beats the cool metal of the firearm touching your flesh.

"Possibly," he mutters.

I move closer until I stand beside him, looking down at the darkened club. It's odd seeing it so empty. It's usually full of life, laughter, sex, and booze. Damn, I should make that into a bathroom sign. Fuck live, laugh, love. We got booze, sex, and dancing.

"Share with the class," I quip, grinning.

"There are a lot of moving pieces in our lives right now. Shadow stole from us. My father is with my mother now, doing God knows what. Someone is stealing his property right under his nose. We need to see whose name is going on those deeds and why my father is so oblivious." He shakes his head.

"It's strange. Daddy Gabe was always so damn paranoid. Why is he letting his guard down now?" I rub my chin.

"The only factor that has changed in my father's life is my mother's presence." His brows furrow. "Is he so blinded by his love and fascination for her that he's allowing her to make these changes?" He sighs, pinching the bridge of his nose. "We have a wedding to attend, as well, amid all this bullshit."

"But she'll be there, right? With Sheppy Boy?" I ask with hope, tilting my head when he nods.

"According to Elias, he invited them and Shadow."

"You think we could get the jump on that flighty bastard and take him down?" I grin, rubbing my hands together at the prospect.

"I don't think that's our call to make," Jer says, shaking his head. "Imagine taking that kill away from the people it belongs to."

"Then we vow. Shadow is Shepp's. Maybe Journey's, too." I agree with a nod. "But I can totally assist. Need me to knock him out? Drag him out? Tie him to a chair? I am your guy. It gives me no greater pleasure than taking out the trash."

"Our problem is we've amassed more trash than we know what to do with," Jericho grumbles with indecision.

"Then we focus on the worst of the two. I say we start with Shadow, kidnap him, lock him in our basement, and then feed him to Max and Nova when the time is right. Sprinkle a little torture in there, where Sheppy lays out all his revenge.

Then, BAM! Grab Gabe, too. It's easy peasy," I hum as the images of their screams, blood, and guts run through my mind. Chills race through me at the thought of it all happening.

"And if we focus on one and not the other, then how do we play that? Shadow is bad, but my father is evil..."

"Evil to a crumbling city," I say, pursing my lips. "We need insight. We need a delicious little spy to give us all the information on him and Shadow..." I tap my chin again and then grin. "We need to call Brandon if he's still alive. He was there that night. We'll meet in public, with lots of weapons strapped to us. Oh! Maybe we can do some recon. You know how I love recon! I want to find him and follow him. Can I drug him? Can I..." I frown when Jericho puts his hand over my mouth, silencing my rambling thoughts.

See what happens when murder is on the mind?

"Yes, to all of it." He raises a brow with a silent demand, begging me to shut up before he takes his hand away.

"Yes, to it all? So, you want me to get a disguise and follow him around? Drug him a little? Say less."

"You're way too giddy at the prospect of following someone. We need to locate him first and follow him around to see if he's on anyone's payroll. If not, we bring him to the basement to see what he knows." I open my mouth to ask about my drugs, but Jericho nods with a sigh. "And yes, you can drug him."

"Oh, goody! I have so many vials stashed around here," I whoop, tossing a fist in the air.

It's the first positive note since we left Olivia's house, saw my father, and came here. Everything else has been utter shit. It's time we get on the up and up. We need a win. Something to celebrate while we wait for our long-lost lover to return to us with our bestie in tow.

"How many do you keep handy?" I feel his eyes on me when I go to the couch and dig into the cushions. My tongue pokes out as I feel around in the secret compartment and pull out three vials full of my favorite drug.

"Enough," I say with a shrug, putting the three things in my pocket and then turning to him. "So, shall we go hunting?"

"Arrow, it's late," he grumbles. "We need rest if we're going to be at our best." He shakes his head again, grabs the discarded bottle of booze from the end table, and then sits down again, guzzling a few more drinks.

Oh, goody. If he keeps that up, he'll be out like a light in ten seconds. Even though the bastard barely sleeps. I know for a fact he hasn't slowed down for days now. Between his injuries and worry, he should pass out lickity split.

"Who can sleep at a time like this?" I pout, throwing myself into the chair across from him. "I'm too amped up."

I want to track down Brandon sooner rather than later and drag the answers from him. By any means possible, of course. He was there the night of the ball, manning the bar as our spy. We needed someone there as backup. Well, that didn't go as planned. Apparently, he wasn't aware of that little invasion of the servers. I still can't wrap my mind around the fact they made it past extensive security. Every Viotto in a hundred-mile radius was in attendance with weapons. Oh, and incompetence. Watching them run through the ballroom once shots started ringing was an embarrassment to everyone, especially Gabe. Actually, now that I think about it, I didn't see that rat anywhere after the fighting started, not even when I pulled out my rocket launcher and set Viotto Tower on fire. Oops. My bad. I think it might be my fault it half-way collapsed.

Oh, well. Fuck the tower. Fuck Gabe. And everything in between. My rocket launcher was definitely necessary, anyway. It'll be a cold day in hell before I give my baby up.

I grin when soft snores spill from Jericho. Aw, isn't he adorable when he finally sleeps? I swear, I haven't witnessed him close his eyes lately. He's been through a lot. Poor guy. I'll take this time to be a good Arrow and not do anything stupid.

Nope. Not me. I definitely won't steal the keys from his pocket, take our stolen car across town, and find Brandon at his apartment.

Because the thing about me is I always keep track of our employees. Did I miss the signs with Aiden? Yes. But he was always here. He never spoke to Gabe on his phone—which I totally have access to—and always seemed to be working for us. I think he was. Until Gabe got in his ear when we were out of the picture, maybe he paid him more.

No matter.

Once I'm successfully out of Rave with weapons tucked into my jeans, I get into the car and start driving.

Will Jer wake up angry? Oh, yes.

Do I care?

Not a chance in hell.

CHAPTER TWENTY-FOUR

Arrow

"DING-DONG. IS THERE ANYBODY HOME?" I SING TO MYSELF AS I stick to the shadows of Brandon's apartment building. How convenient of them to offer balconies for every resident. And how nice of them to make them climbable.

I peek in the sliding glass door of Brandon's apartment. According to his tracker—yes, everyone has one, if I can get my hands on them—he's home. Probably sound asleep in his bed, dreaming of whatever he dreams about. You know, now that I think about it, I don't know him that well. He's worked for us since we started at the club a few years ago—a gift from Gabe. We practically inherited the man. But he's always been elusive and private. Well, I guess that changes now.

I wiggle the knife I brought along through the crack of the sliding glass door and pop the lock—easy, peasy, lemon squeezy. I slide the door open as quietly as possible, stepping inside the small, dark kitchen, barely able to see a thing. Oh, well. I'll find his bedroom and then be on my way. People act like breaking into someone's house is hard. It's as easy as pie. It's as easy as...

"You've been lurking for some time," Brandon grumbles, turning on the kitchen light with a frown. He makes his way to the small kitchen table with chairs and plops down. Damn. I must be out of practice. I didn't hear him coming. A small handgun rests on the table near his hand, and he shakes his head. "Couldn't have waited until morning?"

"Ah, well. You're awake! So, what's all the fuss about?" I grin at him, pull out a chair at the small kitchen table he's at, and relax. "We needed to have a word, anyway."

"You're lucky I didn't shoot you," he says, flipping the safety back on.

Interesting. He must trust me if he's not keeping his weapon all cocked and ready. Maybe I won't earn an extra hole today. It's my lucky day.

"You wouldn't have shot me," I say confidently, waving a hand. "Besides, you act like I'm not used to it." I raise my chin when he scoffs.

"What do you want?"

I tilt my head, finally taking in poor Brandon. Dark circles rest under his eyes, and tiredness weighs his face down. Day-old stubble lines his usually perfect jawline. And holy shit. He's exhausted.

"What's been keeping you up at night, Brandon? Enemies? Pussy?" He rolls his eyes. "Dick? I don't judge."

"Keeping me up?" he growls, gritting his teeth. "My life is in goddamn danger, and then you just waltz in here..."

I hold up a hand, stopping his tirade. I've heard too many angry rants to last a lifetime these past few days.

"Fine. Fine. Last time I saw you, you were working the bar at the tower. I see you made it out." I make it a point to look his ragged body over. Damn, my dude needs to get some more sleep. Might make him feel better.

His face completely falls, and he throws his hands in the air. "Yeah. I barely escaped after my psycho boss let off a damn rocket launcher. What a goddamn disaster," he grumbles with a huff.

"Refresh my memory. What happened after the rocket launcher went off? Was it epic? A fireball? Was it as amazing as tits?" I lean forward, eager to hear his words, but the fucker just glares at me.

"Epic is one fucking way to put it," he grunts, standing from the chair and throwing it across the kitchen. Man, he's crankier than I remember. Where's the respectable guy that said yes sir, no sir, and didn't throw chairs in my presence? Shit, maybe I broke him. Damn it. "After the rocket launcher blew the room to smithereens, everyone ran and finally started fighting fire with fire. But your dumbass was missing. I don't even know what the fuck happened in there. All three of you went poof, and I couldn't protect you."

My dumbass. I resent that. I am not a dumbass. I frown. Sweat drips from his forehead as he looks at me, and then it dawns on me. A light bulb goes off in my overactive mind.

"Oh! Oh! You thought I was here to kill you," I chuckle, slapping my knee.

"I failed," he says, clenching his jaw. "You. The family. I work for you three, and you're all gone..." he trails off, shaking his head with shame. "I couldn't fight off Shadow's men in the ballroom. All I could do was escape unnoticed and try to find the three of you. But I failed. Miserably. I couldn't save anyone." But himself. I keep my lips sealed, though. I get the feeling he's swimming in some sort of guilt over the fact we all went missing.

Poor Brandon. My guy thinks he fucked up. The only fuck up would be him switching sides and whispering in Gabriel's ear.

"Nah, Brandon. You're not a failure. Not to us, anyway. I'm here to make sure you're not a traitor." I twirl my knife in my hands, humming when the scrape of a chair is righted and set back down, which brings my eyes back to him. "I'll stab ya if you are." It's not my best threat, but it seems to hit the mark.

More sweat beads are on his brow, and he looks white, like a ghost. Bam! I got him. Now, all I need him to do is talk the talk. Then, he'll be coming with me. For his protection, of course. If Gabriel gets wind that our soldier is on the loose, he might, well—cut him loose by ending his life.

I can't stand for that.

"After everything you've done for me?" His voice lowers, and he barks out an unhinged laugh. "Like fuck would I ever think about betraying you all. Working for you three and helping you build something... The greatest thing I've done to date."

Man, maybe I can keep him on board with us forever. He's turning into me. God, I'm so damn proud. Before I can stop myself, I pat his head like he's a dog. He's never, ever leaving us again. He can't. I have a tracker inside of him.

"Well, that's a relief, Brandon. So, let's go!" I say, nodding toward the front door after jumping up from the chair.

He stares at me like I'm crazy. "Go?" he questions with a frown, following my movements.

"Uh, yeah. Go. We've got a home base set up, and you're coming with me." I flash him my best smile, but all it does is make him shudder a little. So, I pull back.

Maybe my smile is a little scary. Or unhinged. Or, yeah, I should probably stop myself.

Brandon stands, shaking his head. "I'd ask if you were fucking nuts, but I know you are!" he grunts, pacing in front of me.

Weird. I am nuts. Have some, too. But it isn't polite to point that out. My dad always said it wasn't nice to voice what's on our minds. Well, fine.

"Why exactly am I nuts?" I hum, twirling the knife again. Maybe if he sees it, he'll slow his roll and stop slinging hurtful words at me. Who am I kidding? They aren't all that hurtful. It's the principle of it, though. Only my Kitten can tell me I've got a screw loose inside my skull. For her, yeah, I do. Damn it, now I miss her more than life itself. I want to hold her. Fuck her. Get her pregnant so she can never leave us again.

Normal things.

"Because the family has lost their damn mind," Brandon grunts, running a hand down his face.

"Please elaborate, or I'll start poking holes." I flash him my grin again, not bothering to hide the manic feeling bubbling inside me.

His gaze whips to mine. Then, the knife twirling in my fingers. Oh, and then they drop to his stomach, and he shudders again.

"Can we agree not to stab me?"

"Only if you agree you'll tell me everything cooking inside that brain of yours. Tell Arrow everything you know about the state of Briar Cove." Otherwise, it's stab-o'clock until his blood paints the kitchen, and his wails fill the air.

A man can dream. Wait, no. I like Brandon. Good soldier. Fuck. Bloodlust is absolutely fogging over my damn mind. I need to fight again. Or fuck. Or get my Kitten back. So many things could tamp down this incessant feeling boiling inside me.

His entire body slumps when he leans against his kitchen counter. "Word on the street is Gabriel is down with some mysterious illness. I haven't seen him since his Viotto Tower fell to the ground."

"And who are your sources?"

Brandon's brows furrow. "Other guards who have been hired on. Our men. We've been waiting for you guys to resurface before we do anything."

Right. Brandon and Aiden were the head of security at Rave together. They searched for bugs almost every week for us. Knowing old Gabe, he would have listened to us any chance he got. Hence, we used sign language in front of everyone to hide our discussions. Honestly, everyone should learn ASL.

"Right. The others..." I trail off, tapping my chin with the edge of the knife. The burn of the cut in my flesh has my mind finally slowing down, and I nod. "Yeah, of course. The others."

We've been slowly recruiting the other soldiers to our side through the years. It started with Brandon and Aiden when they became our head of security. We showed them respect and valued their contributions to us. And in return, they valued us, too. At the time, at least. Aiden proved to be Gabriel's double agent. What makes Brandon any different? "Have you spoken to Aiden lately? Weren't you two best buddies?"

Brandon recoils. "Respectfully, sir. We worked together, but that was it."

Hmmm. I tilt my head. Okay, that reaction was pretty sincere. I guess Aiden was always a little sneaky.

"Well, that's good news. Aiden was a dirty little traitor. A good actor, too. That's not in your skill set, is it?"

He swallows hard at my accusation. "Not in a million years. I pledged myself to the family years ago. But it wasn't until Jericho, you, and Shepp came into the club to take it over that I felt valued as a member. You guys gave me a purpose at Rave."

"Okie dokie then, Brandon. Let's go now."

I can detect evil and lies all day long, but getting into this sappy moment without understanding what he's saying throws me for a loop. Give me a body, blood, guts, and gore—I'm amazing at that. The guy. The legend, Arrow. Give me feelings and tears, like the big lug opposite of me is giving me. I'm utterly fucking confused.

He doesn't fight me when he pushes off the counter. "Let me put some clothes on, and then I'll go with you." He seems resigned to the fact we might hurt him.

But I have no intention of poking holes in him. Today, at least.

I drum my fingers along the table I'm resting at and tilt my head. Shadows move somewhere outside, drawing my eyes to the bushes. Interesting. I wonder what's going on out there? Hopefully, someone will follow me, and I can disembowel them ASAP. It'll help me in the long run. It's like a doctor giving me a prescription for mayhem and murder. It's necessary to my being.

With nonchalance, I turn the kitchen light off and crouch low. The entire apartment falls victim to the darkness as I watch the shadows move in the parking lot beyond the balcony.

"I'd crouch if I were you," I sing-song to the footsteps approaching me. "Oh, and maybe grab a gun or two."

"Fuck," Brandon hisses, dropping beside me on his stomach. "Why?" I can practically feel his eyes scanning the outside and squinting at the nothingness. "I see nothing."

"And they call you the head of security," I scoff, pointing a finger at the moving figures crouching between cars. "You see those little fuckers? There are at least five out there. Who they belong to, I don't know. Are they after you? Anything suspicious I should be aware of?" One little fucker who needs to die. Two little fuckers who need to roast. Three little fuckers who will meet my knife. And so on.

Brandon blows out a breath. "Fuck."

"Good fuck or bad fuck?" I question, reaching into my waistline, taking out a fully loaded gun, and taking the safety off.

"Bad fuck. What else?" he groans as the sound of his safety coming off clicks in the air. "You think the family would come after me?"

"You're a loose end loyal to the three heirs they tried to get rid of. So, maybe?" I shrug because I don't technically know what the fuck is happening right now. "How about your friends? Have any of them dropped dead lately?"

I feel his eyes burning a hole through my head when he should watch the enemy advancing through the parking lot toward his apartment building.

"Not that I'm aware."

"But you were scared for your own life?" I hum.

"Naturally. You're my fucking boss," he growls, probably through clenched teeth.

"Naturally," I agree with a chuckle. "New plan. We need to ambush the amateurs before they ambush us."

"I can take the living room. You stay here and position yourself to shoot them as they enter the front door," Brandon grunts, slowly crawling away from me toward the living room.

"Well, who said they're all coming in through the front door?" I grin.

Anticipation roars through me at the prospect of dropping some baddies like it's hot. I'm about to make it rain. Blood. Bodies. And anything in between.

"Got 'em," I murmur as the sliding glass door slowly opens without a fuss, and Mr. Intruder slowly walks into the kitchen, letting one of his pals follow him. At the same time, the front door slams open, causing a commotion.

Ah, they're the distraction.

Brandon lights up the intruders in the living room. One shot. Five shots. Ten shots. Then they fall silent. All while I keep my two right in my sights. I love the element of surprise.

"Aaron!" one in the kitchen hisses to the one that entered through the front door. At least, I assume he's speaking to them.

Maybe I should clarify.

"Who is Aaron?" I ask from my hiding spot, aiming my gun in his direction.

Through the darkness, I hear the breath hitch in his throat before bullets rain around me. But never in me. There are only a few things and people allowed inside me. I grin.

"That's rude," I mutter, firing a few shots. One hits shadow number two in the skull, killing him instantly. The other hits its mark with shadow number one, hitting him in the leg and taking him down with a yelp. "Ah, the yelp heard around the world. How many more of you are there?" I crawl toward shadow number one and hover above his face, shoving the end of my gun into his neck. I grin. "Oh, Trevor. You poor, poor soul."

"Arrow," he hisses, reaching for his bleeding leg. "You're not supposed to be here…" he trails off with confusion.

Oh. So, our infamous escape wasn't told around a camp-fire? That's very disappointing. Although, it might be good for Daddy Jer and me. We can walk through this town without someone trying to kill us—the element of surprise and all that good shit.

Anywho. Back to killing.

"Good to see you again, there, pal. But I have questions," I hum, shoving his hand away and putting my finger into his bloodied wound. The sound of his cries fills the room. I'd ask him again how many more gunmen are waiting outside this apartment, but I don't think he'd answer. He's from the family. Unless I give him some incentive, he won't give me anything if he's properly trained like I think he might be.

"Fuck you," he hisses.

Well, until I use the darkness to knock him out with my gun. Ah, I love the feeling of violence at my fingertips. It leaves me craving more, though. But that's okay. Trevor and I will have a nice long discussion about what he's doing here and who sent him.

I get giddy at the prospect.

"I think that was all of them," Brandon murmurs, cautiously crawling toward me.

"Could be. Or not. But what I do know is we need to get this asshole back to headquarters." And torture the shit out of him before he dies of this leg wound. Daddy Jer will not be happy to see I brought baggage back into our hiding spot. But If I hadn't, then Brandon would have been toast. "Go grab a belt for Trevor's leg. We want to make sure he arrives alive." Brandon nods, getting to his feet and coming back with a belt. We quickly secure the bleeding wound.

"Okay," he says, lifting the guy into his arms and leading the way out the front door.

I scan the parking lot, holding my weapons, but don't find any more assholes out and about. They probably heard the fall of their comrades and ran the other way. Bummer. I was looking for a fight with multiple casualties. It's like an orgy but with death. A de-orgy? Nah, that doesn't sound right. An org-ath? Nope. Even worse. Ah, well. Whatever.

"Throw asshole in the trunk," I say with a hum, keeping an eye out in the shadows. Since Brandon can't seem to see the danger he is in.

Brandon shuts the trunk and climbs into the passenger's seat while I climb into the driver's.

"Now, let's go home." I grin, starting the car and peeling out of the parking lot with my eyes peeled. If there are more people, they're probably wondering where Jer and I are hiding in town. Or maybe they don't know we're back yet. Thankfully, the only witness alive is in my trunk, bleeding out with loud groans and knocking on the inside. "He's going to be a feisty one," I hum, making a few extra left turns and then a few right, trying to throw off anyone who might be following.

"I think we're in the clear," Brandon says, looking in all directions.

"Oh, good. But just to be safe," I say, pulling into an empty tree line and sigh. "We'll walk to Rave from here. I'll knock out Mr. Loud-Pants."

Brandon's head whips to me. "Are you fucking insane? No, wait. You are. You're fucking... You can't carry a half-conscious man who has blood spewing from him..." Blah. Blah. Blah. I block out his words when I jump out of the car and open the trunk.

"Night, night," I sing-song before punching him square in the nose. His head bounces back, and he gasps, ready to tear into me. But I was just getting started. I viciously pound my fist into his face and jaw until he stops moving.

"Stop," Brandon grunts, gripping my wrist. The audacity of this motherfucker. "You kill him here, and we'll never know whose orders he was on to kill me and why."

I purse my lips and step back. Momentarily, the demon inside me simmers down, giving me the relaxation I need and want. So I can think clearly as we weave through the darkened areas and finally return to Rave just as the sun peaks over the horizon.

"Honey, I'm home!" I shout into the empty club, carrying the bloodied man on my shoulder.

And wouldn't you know it? Jericho stands at the top of the stairs with a frown carved so deep on his face he looks constipated. He should take care of that. Or get the stick out of his ass for once. Either way. That look needs to go. He should throw me a parade or something. Oh, confetti!

"You know, if you leave your face like that, people will think you have RBF or that you need to poop," I say with a grin, wiggling the guy on my shoulder. "I brought back visitors. Break out the mimosas. We've got quite the morning ahead of us."

Jericho shakes his head with disappointment, coming down the stairs rigidly.

Oops. I think I made Daddy Jer mad. My bad. But not really. I saved Brandon's life.

"You left without me? You left me sleeping to..." Jericho's eyes scan Brandon as he stands at attention. "To retrieve him! I thought we had an agreement. I didn't think I had to worry about you sneaking off in the middle of the fucking night," Jericho grits out, waving a hand.

"Sorry, Daddy Jer. But you know, I saved his life. If I hadn't been there, he'd be dead. Courtesy of this guy and his cool gang of dead gunmen."

"Who the fuck is that?" Jericho grits out, walking up to the guy on my shoulder and lifting his face up with a sigh. "He's unrecognizable. Do you think he'll actually wake up now?

You've beat him into oblivion because you couldn't stop yourself."

He's getting on my nerves lately. We usually breathe and move as one. Like a centipede or... Wait, no. That brings back images of that disgusting movie I forced them to watch. It was interesting, though. I wonder if it's possible? Hmmm... Anyway, ever since he abandoned me in Briar Cove—hello, abandonment issues—he's left a bitter taste in my mouth. I know he's worried. And I know he had no choice but to leave me behind without getting himself killed. I recognize what he had to do. Would I have done the same? Absolutely not. Jer would have been tied to my back while I scaled the hospital to escape. So, sure. I get his reasons. Even though they were stupid as fuck.

I'm just a Petty Betty Bitch, and he'll suffer for leaving me behind.

"Trevor. He works with your dad. Or did," Brandon answers with a head shake. "He and five other guards broke into my apartment with weapons and fired at me. If Arrow hadn't snuck in, I wouldn't have known what was about to hit me. But I've been paranoid since that night of the initiation ball."

"Paranoid?" Jericho asks, dropping the fool's head. "Why?"

"Because I failed you. I was there to be insight for you, and I went and fucked it all up."

"Explain yourself," Jericho barks impatiently.

Damn. Daddy Jer needs another nap. He's awfully cranky right now. I bet he'll be a little nicer once Journey and Shepp are back. Maybe. Or I could punch him again. He seemed to like that.

Brandon straightens, and I roll my eyes, tossing the asshole on my shoulder into a wooden chair. I quickly find ropes and all that fun stuff from around the club while they have a little chit-chat. Brandon explains his failures and guilt. Jericho reassures him it is okay.

"As long as you're not a traitor," Jericho says at the end of their discussion, just in time for the asshole to rouse from his forced slumber.

"Wakey, wakey, eggs and bakey. We've got a lot to discuss, Trevor. Oh! And I brought a fun friend eager to speak with you." I grin, stepping back and letting Jericho come into Trevor's view.

CHAPTER TWENTY-FIVE

Jericho

THERE ARE MANY THINGS I HATE IN LIFE. ONE IS BEING LEFT behind. Ironic? Yes. Considering not too long ago, I left my best friend lying in a hospital bed. Helpless.

And it seems he's still holding a solid grudge against me for that.

Wonderful.

It is something he should work on getting over. It's unlike him to hold on to something for so long. Well, besides obsession. It's become insufferable and tedious when he rebels and runs away. Like tonight. Getting Brandon was supposed to be a joint effort.

Maybe he and I need to duke it out once and for all. A grudge match. He got his hit in at Olivia's.

Now, it's my turn to lay the idiot out. Knock some damn sense into him before he gets us killed.

Perhaps my actions are not the real issues, though. I don't have blinders on. I see why he's being a prick and running off to do missions himself.

Not only is he impatient. In his eyes, I'm the reason we lost Journey and Shepp in the first place. My father handed them over to Shadow. Scattering the four of us across the land and ocean.

A black hole opens inside my chest at the thought of my two missing pieces. And what they must be enduring. Torture? Forced fights? The images of Journey alone, covered in someone else's blood, play in my mind on repeat. Tormenting me and upping my desperation to retrieve them and shield them.

I will fucking find them.

I'm not a heavy sleeper by any means, but I've avoided closing my eyes since I met with Elias. Everything that's happened plays behind my eyes, projecting like a horror movie on repeat.

My jaw clenches. Elias White. Another dreadful human being that has rage boiling beneath my flesh. He wants a partnership. No. He wants joint ownership of Briar Cove. In exchange, he'll give me the soldiers I need to assist in the upheaval of the empire my father has built.

It will fall.

Implode.

And I'll be the one with the bomb at the heart of what my father loves most—his empire. He cares for no one. Only himself. Possibly not even my mother. She's a tool in his arsenal. Someone to parade around for looks. That's it. Like everyone else. They're for his image. For power.

But for now, Arrow and I need to settle our differences. Our efforts must go toward the enemies after us and those we love most.

"Good to see you again, Trevor. It's been a while. How's my father doing?" I pull up a chair across from him as he glares at me.

Trevor. A member of the family with deep roots. His father has been in the family since he was eighteen. And, in turn, he followed in his father's footsteps. Although poor Trevor didn't make it far. Fucking up left and right. He became a guard. Never anything higher up.

Trevor's swollen lip curls, and he grunts, attempting to free his hands. But if there's one thing I know about Arrow, he likes to bind them. There's no escape for him.

"Oh, you're a regular old Chatty Cathy," Arrow says tauntingly. "Maybe I should give him some incentive to talk?" He wiggles his brows as he digs in his pants.

For a split second, I think he's dragging out his dick—for what? I have no clue. But he proves my tired mind wrong when he produces a large knife that has no business being near his balls.

"You had that in your pants?" I ask, rubbing my aching temple.

"Desperate times call for desperate measures, Daddy Jer." That is all he says when he puts the edge of the knife near the man's crotch.

Well, when he's not interested in nearly chopping off his balls, he's interested in chopping off someone else's—his go-to. Right now, we don't have Max and Nova to assist us with questioning.

So, we have to resort to torture techniques.

Our favorite.

The thought of blood has my hair standing on end. Goosebumps prickle across my skin when Arrow leans into Trevor's face, giving him a sadistic grin. The tip of the knife sinks into Trevor's crotch like it's moving through butter. His cries fill the room as Arrow does it, despite the man's pleas for Arrow to stop poking holes in him.

I sit back with Brandon beside me, enjoying the bloody show Arrow puts on.

"We want some insight," Arrow says with an eerie calm that's anything but his normal voice. "We want to know why you were trying to kill Brandon over there."

Serenity and peace seem to sweep in and take his emotions hostage. His light eyes take in the pain he's inflicting, feeding off the shouts and screams of Trevor. It nourishes the darkening demon living in his soul and helps to fight off the agitation.

Arrow revels in the sobs and tears of our captive. Now, he grins when Trevor's head falls forward, and he gasps for breath.

It's his final bow before the curtain falls.

His death is imminent. I feel it in my bones. I sit up straighter. Giving Trevor my undivided attention.

"Okay, I'll tell you. Please, stop."

Ah, the music to my ears.

Arrow's fingers dig into Trevor's hair, forcefully pulling his head back with a grunt. Trevor's unrecognizable face swells more under the scrutiny of our eyes. He's barely breathing, living, and surviving this ordeal. But that's all right. We only need him to loosen his tongue a smidge.

"Go on then," Arrow chirps, shoving the tip of the knife into Trevor's chin. "Tell Arrow all your sins. Then you can repent for them." AKA he can die and drift slowly to Hell, where he'll burn for an eternity.

According to Father Amour, of course.

"Indulge us, Trevor." I fold my hands in front of me as I move forward, leaning down to stare into the slits of his eyes. "Why were you sent to kill Brandon? More importantly, who sent you?" I raise a brow when he heaves a few breaths, savoring the life he still has left until we snuff it out once and for all.

"Every miserable piece of you and your existence is being wiped out." His bloody teeth gnash together, spitting saliva and blood onto my face.

I don't move. Don't react. If I do, it'll only encourage him to continue. So, I grin, tilting my head when he wheezes to breathe. Sticky red blood slowly drips onto the dance floor. Something that would irritate me if we were open for business —that'll come soon enough—but for now, I want to swim in it. Lap it up and laugh as he slowly dies.

Fuck.

I shake my head, reeling myself in from the darkness that resides in me—begging for more, more, more. Blood. Violence. Everything in between until this town is under our thumbs, and we kill every enemy coming to stand before us.

"Hear that, Jer. Someone's looking to kill us and everyone associated with us."

"Hmm, I did," I hum, standing to my full height and turning to Brandon, who stares on with cold abandon. "I'd suggest getting into contact with the ones loyal to you and us."

"Yes, Sir," he responds, stiffening when he pulls his phone out.

"They're all dead," Trevor laughs, exposing his teeth again. "We made sure that no one survived who'd align with you," he spits as best as he can, cursing our names. "Including your precious allies in the police force."

Well, then. That puts quite the damper on things, doesn't it? If we don't have our alliance with the police chief. Then what do we have?

"Why?" Arrow pouts, digging the tip of the knife in deeper. More blood flows from his wound, making my toes curl at the sight.

Perhaps Arrow wasn't the only one who needed a little escapism through violence to relieve the pressure mounting inside him. I did, too.

I heave a breath, marching forward. I hold out my hand with a pleading in my eyes. Arrow doesn't fight me when he hands over the knife. He huffs with a knowing nod and steps back. His arms fold across his chest as he looks on.

"My turn," I smirk, gently brushing the tip of the knife down his upper arms. If we were in the cage, I'd tear his clothes off and feed him to the lions for his crimes. "I would like some names. For every second you defy me, I will poke a hole in your flesh. Starting with your neck, upper arms, and forearms, then each finger one by one until I've cut every single digit off. If you don't speak, then I'll sew up your wounds and give you a blood transfusion and meds. Then, we'll start the process again until your body can't take it anymore..."

Trevor stiffens beneath my weapon. He pants. Wiggles. Tries to run away from the inevitable, but it's no use. He's my new official pin cushion, and I can't wait to play.

"Who is giving you the orders?"

No answer. I nick his neck. Not enough to bleed, but enough for him to feel the burn for minutes to come as oxygen mixes with his wound.

"Who is giving you the orders to kill our men?"

No answer. So, I repeat the process an inch lower, nicking him but not making him bleed.

"Let me at him, Jer. Let me fuck him up so hard that he'll give us all the answers..." Arrow trails off when a tiny whisper comes from Trevor. "What was that, old boy? Can you repeat it?" Arrow grins, leaning in with his hand by his ear, listening intently as Trevor's lips move again.

"Your father," he hisses and pants again.

"My, my! The boss himself?" Arrow asks, holding a hand to his heart.

I still. Not daring to move a muscle as his confession sits in the air.

"My father, huh?" Word on the street is he's fallen ill.

"Yes," Trevor wheezes, coughing more blood.

"Oh, goody. Daddy Gabe is all kinds of mad, isn't he?" Arrow leans in, waiting for more answers from Trevor, who barely clings to life.

"More than that," he grunts.

"So, you're telling me that my own flesh and blood are attempting to eradicate Arrow, Shepp, and me?" I raise a brow when the man wheezes again.

Unfortunately, he seems on death's door—a shame. I need

more information from him before I step back out the door and try to reclaim what's mine.

If my father is genuinely setting out to get rid of us, then so be it. We won't go down without a fight.

"Yes," he gasps out, choking on his spit.

"I'm curious," I say, digging the knife into his skin, barely breaking through. He tenses, softly crying out from the pain. I never said I'd stop once he gave me names. "Is he attempting to start a war within the family?"

Trevor chuckles under his dying breath. "There is no attempt about it. The Viotto dynasty is coming to an end. Gabriel is sick, and you're on Death's list. You're done, Viotto." Or so he thinks.

I smile, getting eye level with him. "I'm never done, Trevor. Ever. The Viotto name will live on. Do you think the other members of our family will take kindly to a civil war? Plenty of men have come for our name and kingdoms. But they died the moment their heads got too big."

Trevor scoffs, spitting blood everywhere. "You'll go down, Viotto. You don't see it yet. Your father is going to take you down," he chuckles in a raspy voice.

For some reason, I'm not convinced. Sure, my father was adamant about locking me in the mansion, so I'd marry Chloe Satin in unholy bliss. But this is not his style. Sending out soldiers to kill anyone associated with us?

I guess I could see it.

But if Gabriel wants to take me down, he'd do it himself. Not send others to collect me. Not only that, my father would want to drive home how far we had fucked up. He'd capture us, lock us in the basement, and show the family what happens to disobedient little boys.

So, if he's attempting to kill us, he's out of his damn mind. Or someone else is in control.

"Come on, Jer. Let me at him. Let me cut his dick off, and

then we can see what else he knows," Arrow says in a deep voice, moving to undo Trevor's pants.

I have no doubt in my mind that he'll actually do it. If we were with the lions, he'd feed the appendage to them, displaying his power. But we're not. It will only result in Trevor dying quickly without giving us any more names.

"I don't know anything else," he gasps out when Arrow moves the knife down Trevor's abdomen, heading straight for his open zipper. "I'm just following orders!" His shouts bounce off the walls, echoing around us.

I tilt my head. Well, that worked faster than I thought it would. Threaten a man's manhood, and you threaten every-thing. I suppose that's why Arrow has always seemed so fond of cutting off men's jewels.

"Do you believe him, Jer?" Arrow says, narrowing his eyes on the man tied to the chair with blood dripping from almost every inch of him.

"I'm not quite sure," I hum, rubbing my chin. "Maybe we should entice him to continue speaking..." I trail off when Arrow grins more, working the knife closer and closer to his dick.

"I don't!" he shouts like a pussy.

How pathetic that a man from the family, trained and initi-ated as one of us, would spill secrets like they were nothing. We're told to die with the words on our tongues, not reveal anything. Besides, he knows death is imminent, anyway. There's no way we'd keep him breathing for longer than necessary.

"I don't know anything else! Only what our team was asked to do!"

"How were you handed these orders?" If my father gives out orders, it's direct. He either assembles his soldiers at the tower, hands out instructions, and then sets them free. Or he delivers them through private messages with his signature and the go word—a secret word meant to signify it's him. Everyone in the family knows it by heart.

"By the man himself." He glowers at me, watching as I pace in front of him, attempting to piece the puzzle together.

"Where does Gabriel have you meet for these types of meetings now? Since the tower is down."

And he would never bring someone to the mansion. It was once a place for business; he brought everyone there to enjoy some gin, and then they'd discuss a truce or whatever else they intended to speak about. But after a bomb went off and his life was put in danger, he no longer wanted to give people a blue-print of where he slept or how to get there. Hence, the tower being built. A fortress, really.

Trevor rolls his lips together with a pained expression, tightening his features.

"Make him speak," I say aloud, stopping in front of Trevor. "Make him tell me every filthy secret regarding the family stored in his walnut brain." I raise a brow to Arrow, who beams at me.

"That's one way to get back into my good graces, Daddy Jer," he chuckles, moving the knife lower until Trevor screams out in pain.

I don't even bother correcting the name he calls me anymore. I'm used to it. But I'd never tell him that. So, I give him this win.

"Speak or forever hold your secrets, dickbag. Gimme them all. Tell me where you have these meetings. And let's get extra, super-duper specific with them." Arrow's eyes darken the more he digs the tip of the knife into Trevor—blood spills. Arrow's demon celebrates beneath his flesh, dancing as more blood covers his fingers and splatters his face.

"Slow down," I instruct Arrow with a sharp eye.

"You are a party pooper sometimes," he hisses, pulling the knife back and heaving a breath.

"I am. But if you keep carving him up like a turkey, he

won't be able to speak or breathe any longer. I want where the meetings are being held, Trevor."

Wheezes fill the air, nearly sounding like gargles. My heart falls when Trevor gives out one last gurgle in his throat—the death gurgle—and slumps in his chair.

"Fuck," I shout, grabbing a chair and throwing it across the empty dance floor. My breaths pick up as I stare at the wall, imagining all the information we could have gotten from him but didn't. It's not Arrow's fault entirely. He did what he had to do to get him here and get him talking.

"Well, what a waste. I didn't even get to stab him fully." Arrow's faint pout floats through the thick air, almost as if I stand in water, losing myself to the madness growing inside me.

"He has a phone." A thud happens as Brandon speaks.

"A phone?" I say, pivoting on my heel.

My gaze meets Brandon's furrowed brows, and he nods softly. "Yeah, it's fingerprint access, too."

"Oh! I can sever his finger," Arrow says with too much glee as he gets to work and cuts Trevor's thumb off.

"How do you know it's the thumb?" Brandon asks with confusion, not blanching when Arrow proudly holds up the finger.

"Oh, good point," he says, nodding, tossing the thumb into Brandon's hand.

I smirk when Brandon swallows hard, staring down at the severed finger. A slight green tint takes him over until he huffs a breath, putting the thumb to the screen.

"That wasn't it," he says, discarding the thumb on the ground, shivering after touching it.

"Don't worry. I got them all!" Arrow says with pride, holding nine severed fingers.

"Perfect," I mutter, watching with glossy eyes as they get to work, checking to see which finger unlocks his phone.

Finally, after several attempts, they discover his right-hand pinky finger was the golden ticket.

"I can look through this if you want me to," Brandon says, sitting beside me.

I rub my temple. "If he has AntiEyes like all of us were equipped to have, then we won't be able to find anything. We'll need someone to hack into it and gather all the necessary information."

"Who the hell can hack AntiEyes?" Arrow asks, tossing the severed fingers around like he's juggling them. "It's impossible." He hums to himself as he dances around Trevor's body with victory. At least this murder will sate him until we can further plan to get Journey and Shepp back.

I sigh, rubbing my forehead as the day's events sit heavily on my chest. "I'm sure I know a few people."

In fact, I know I do. I just know they will not be too damn excited to see our faces again. Especially Carter. He's liable to chew my face off than ever step foot into the Mafia business again. But it's vital we get this information off Trevor's phone.

"A text just came through," Brandon says, swiping to view it. His brows furrow. "Whoever is sending the message wants an update on the mission." His dark eyes find mine, and I shrug.

"If it's my father, he'll expect exact words." Brandon nods, handing me the phone so I can view the message.

BOSS

Need updates! Did you eliminate the traitors?

I raise a brow, saying the message out loud to Arrow. He purses his lips when he catches what I caught.

BOSS

Are all you idiots dead?

"It's not him," I say, keeping the phone lit because the text messages will disappear forever when it darkens. It's how AntiEyes works and why we all have it installed on our devices.

"You're positive?" Brandon asks, leaning over to look at the messages again.

"Indeed," I say, staring at the messages again.

TREVOR

All targets have been eliminated. 466.

"You signed with the code," Brandon states, staring at me.

"I'm interested to see if the person on the other end will think to add it in. If it's my father, he wouldn't have forgotten." I've gotten plenty of lectures on how I should be more responsible and remember to end my messages to him with those numbers. AntiEyes might be impenetrable, but the government thinks it can access everything.

Not only is the wording funny from the other end, but the lack of numbers has my suspicions growing. I need someone to crack the AntiEyes and hack into phone locations. And there's only one person I know who does that besides Carter.

BOSS

Meet me in 20 so we can discuss your successes.

TREVOR

It's only me. The others didn't make it. 466.

"So not Daddy Gabe," Arrow chuckles.

"Is it even someone from the family?" I wonder aloud, staring at the screen as messages disappear, their time limit running out.

"Everyone who deals with him directly knows his ways and codes," Brandon says, furrowing his brows. "Even if orders come from the other bosses. The numbers are always there." He gives a firm nod just as another text pops up.

BOSS

Here are the coordinates. Be there.

"If it smells like a trap and looks like a trap..." Arrow trails off, stepping away from me. "It's definitely a trap!" he says, pointing the cut-off finger toward me.

"Would you stop pointing that thing everywhere?" I grumble, staring at the message. "Write this down?" I ask Brandon, who is already typing the coordinates into his phone with a nod.

"Looks like it's down by the docks..." he trails off, shaking his head. "It's in Blue Spider Gang territory."

"Blue Spider, huh?" I ask, blowing out a breath. "This just keeps getting better and better, doesn't it?"

"You think Elias is up to something?" Arrow asks, tilting his head. "I could take care of him, you know? I'm sure his little compound isn't too hard to break into. Cut some lights and then add in my rocket launcher! I can take them all out without blinking." He grins at that, rocking on his heels.

"Your excitement is disturbing," I quip, smirking when his eyes dart to me.

"You owe me," he says, crossing his arms.

"I do," I admit. "But we can't go into this situation…"

"Half-cocked, I know. That's why I'm fully cocked. With lots of weapons at my disposal," he sasses back, pointing the stupid finger at me again.

"First things first. We need to discard Trevor here."

"We should take him to the meeting spot," Arrow says with a grin, an obvious plan forming in his mind. "They say twenty minutes. How long would it take us to get there from here?"

Brandon's fingers fly over his screen. "Ten minutes."

"If we leave now, we can get there before anyone else shows up. Then we can glimpse whoever is behind this." I nod.

"Then, let's get a move on," Arrow says, throwing the

bloodied body over his shoulder. "We've got work to do. Oh, Daddy Jer! Go upstairs and grab my rocket launcher."

"Didn't it die at the tower?" I grumble, standing tall when he sends me a scathing look.

"Who said I only had one?" His grin sends shivers down my spine.

"Do I want to know how many you've acquired?"

"Don't ask stupid questions, Jer. You'll only get stupid answers."

Well, then. That means Arrow has more rocket launchers than he knows what to do with. Wonderful.

CHAPTER TWENTY-SIX

Journey

SUNSHINE'S INTENDED. FIANCÉ? MARRIAGE? AT FOURTEEN?

I think the fuck not.

I've protected her since I was sixteen. From everything. Including the bastards selling her off to....

Him.

Her so-called intended. Fiancé. Future husband. Whatever you want to call it, it's not happening.

Over my dead fucking body.

I squint, really taking him in. He's a child dressed in a suit, with shiny shoes and a damn smirk. Defiantly, he lifts his chin, staring straight into my eyes. He's issuing a challenge for me by saying he's not backing down.

Well, challenge accepted, motherfucker. I have an arsenal of crazy in my back pocket. Me. Arrow. Jericho. We'd be able to take him on.

All in due time.

Is it wrong to want to punch him? Wait! How is this even legal? Is he even of age?

He's tall. Maybe 5'7". So, not fully grown. No facial hair, either. But he did have a slight accent. Russian, maybe?

Fuck! Shadow's words from before filter through my mind about marrying Sunshine off to mafia heirs and whoever else he could get his hands on.

I'd do anything to protect my sister. If I have to banish her fiancé into a cement pit, then so be it. He'll float with the fishes. And Sunshine? She'll be none the wiser.

"I think I have something in my ears. Your what now?" I ask, looking the little intruder up and down again.

"Journey," Sunshine says, turning beet red. "Um, maybe we could talk. And..." I hold up a hand, stopping her immediately.

Sunshine has always been my responsibility. My sister. The girl I carried to and from doctor's appointments, trying to find a solution to our problems with our limited resources. I killed for her, protected her from all this. As best I could, I guess. And now she's gone, thrown all my work in the trash, and promised herself to this little Jericho clone.

"Who the hell are you? And why do you think you can marry my little sister? She's fourteen." My fingers curl into a fist, ready to rear back and smack him into next week.

"Perhaps we should take this into Sunshine's suite and discuss why I am marrying your sister." This boy raises his dark brows, demanding obedience with one glare.

I'm about to tell him to fuck right the hell off, but Shepp jumps in and stops me, putting his hands on my shoulder, cutting off my view of them.

His eyes soften. Those ocean eyes I could get lost in. Find comfort in. They pull me in, draining the rage pouring through me. With just one touch on my chin, he offers me a smile.

"Did you know about this?" I swallow hard, attempting to find the answers in his eyes that give nothing away.

He immediately shakes his head, somehow leading me into the room so Sunshine and the dead man walking can enter without dying.

Shepp digs in his pocket with a sigh, scribbling a note with determination.

I eye Sunshine and the prick, walking toward the sofa

across the way. His arm wraps around her tightly. Possessively. Like a precious jewel.

The room is massive. A suite fitted with a kitchen, living room, and separate bedrooms—two, if I'm seeing it right.

Well, I see who the favorite child is.

She got this massive room, and we got the regular one. Of course, we were defiant prisoners, and she was the compliant one. I guess she's given Shadow precisely what he wanted—a chess piece he can move on his board.

'I had no clue until five minutes ago when my father and that prick signed a contract for Sunshine's hand in marriage. He's only 14. And the heir to the Bratva.'

The paper hangs in front of me, taunting me with its words. Fourteen? Marriage? Contract? Bratva? Those words shouldn't exist together in a sentence—especially the fourteen part.

They're goddamn children being forced into adult roles.

I fucking hate it.

I jerk my gaze to Sunshine, who looks so fucking guilty, staring up at me with wide eyes from the loveseat across the room. She swallows hard. Her face shows all her emotions.

"J," she whispers with a plea, begging me to understand.

But I don't. Kind of. A little voice reminds me of what I've done for her. And what she said to me before she walked out of the caves with Shadow.

It was her turn to be the hero for me. But not like this. Not with a marriage to a stranger.

"Explain this, please," I say, trying to take deep breaths. I can't just fucking explode. Not on Sunshine. I'm sure she has good intentions. I hope. "A contract marriage, Sunshine..." I trail off, my words tinted with hurt—memories of my own float through my mind.

My mother sold me to Gabriel, giving me to Jericho like a prized pig. Granted, it didn't turn out horribly for me. Jericho could have been worse. His friends, too. I mean, he only married me without my permission and let his bestie take out my birth control. Now, I belong to them. Fit in with them.

Fuck. Remind me why I miss them so badly.

"And you knew about this?" I breathe to her, trying to bite my tongue.

"It just happened, J. I swear. It... I'll be okay." Sunshine nods, trying to reassure me with her sweet smile and bobbing head that she'll be okay.

And maybe I'll believe it in the future. Right now, I'm too lost. Too broken from everything that's happened.

The little punk sits tall beside her, holding her in his arms. His pinched expression takes in the hurt oozing from her and takes it on himself.

His deep blue eyes slice through me with a frown. "It's for her safety," Mikhail says, raising his chin with a challenge. "And I can assure her of that." He says nothing further when he unwraps from her and stands, offering her his hand. "Now, I heard we were making breakfast this morning, Princess."

Sunshine beams at him, erasing all the hurt from her expression. They peer into each other's eyes, holding contact longer than necessary. I've seen that look before. When he looks at her, the light in his eyes is tinged with a bout of crazy. He means what he says. He believes it with all his damn heart.

But how can I allow this to happen? How can I let her go with him to wherever he's from and get married? They're so young. So naïve.

I shake myself from my thoughts.

"Her safety? You don't know the first thing about her safety. Or what she's been through. Or..." I roll my lips together when my stomach sloshes. I swear, since we got on this island, I can't keep anything down. Mixing that with the crazy emotions roaring through me has me wanting to puke my brains out.

Maybe I need this brunch more than I thought. Oh, and a nap, too.

Mikhail runs a hand down Sunshine's back, gently soothing her as she cracks an egg and then another. She relaxes into his touch like they've known each other for years. He leans in and kisses her cheek, whispering something in her ear. She giggles. Fucking giggles at him, sounding freer than I've ever heard her before.

She went from a trailer prison to a hospital and now to this. Everywhere she's been, there have been four walls holding her hostage. Will he?

Shepp gently grabs my hand, pulling me to the loveseat. Something about his touch sends fireworks through my system —a rightness, a calmness. I squeeze my eyes shut.

Breathe, you idiot. Just calm down and think about the future.

"There's no stopping this, is there?" I murmur, swallowing my unease.

Shepp's lips roll together, and he shakes his head.

"Wonderful," I murmur, rubbing my temples.

The sound of bacon sizzles on the stovetop, filling the air with its aroma. My stomach turns, knots, and then freaking growls from the smells. I sigh, sealing my lips together, and lean on Shepp's shoulder. His arm wraps around me, holding me close. Watching my sister and the inevitable about to happen has tears prickling my eyes.

Fuck.

What is wrong with me? Can I stand by and let her get married for safety reasons?

"Join us?" Sunshine asks softly, gesturing toward the small round table fit for four people. "We've got eggs, bacon, and even some pancakes."

"With sprinkles," Mikhail chuckles, moving beside her.

"Even sprinkles," she sighs, taking in his softened expression.

"Shall we?" Mikhail eyes me as he speaks, setting four empty plates and forks on the table.

Reluctantly, Shepp and I sit at the table, taking it all in.

"So, you cook?" I ask Mikhail, gesturing to the food.

Mikhail cocks his head. "You ask that like it's strange for a man like me to do all this." He nods toward the food and fills Sunshine's plate, piling it high.

"Not strange," I say, clearing my throat. My eyes drift to Shepp, who eyes me with a smirk. "It's just unexpected. How long have you been cooking for?"

Internally, I cringe at my questions. I'm just so lost on what to say. Do I want to grill his ass for stepping in and taking my sister away? Yes, absolutely. I could convince him to back off and leave her alone. I could do a lot of things.

But I can't.

Sunshine lights up when he gently hands her a fork and gestures for her to eat the food he had plated, including the fruit bowl.

"Ever since I could remember. My parents have always been away on trips for business, leaving me at home to learn. Through our private cook, I've learned invaluable skills." He leans down, takes a bite of his eggs, and hums.

"It's so good, Mik," Sunshine says, batting her eyelashes like crazy.

Mikhail smiles, his entire body melting at her words.

"And you were born into the mafia?" I ask again, pushing my food with my fork.

Half of me is concerned about poison after what happened to Shepp and me in the caves. But the other half watches as Sunshine digs in and smiles, eating without worry.

"Born and raised," he smirks. "Just like Shepp, eh?"

Shepp stiffens beside me, quickly signing something. Mikhail nods, chuckling under his breath, and signs something back.

Son of a bitch. I need to learn ASL sooner rather than later. So I can be in on the special conversations.

A knock sounds at the door, halting all our movements.

Mikhail stands with a huff, answering it. He nods a few times, then shuts and locks it stiffly. Mikhail keeps his back to us for a few beats. Several deep breaths expand his back and move his shoulders with the movements before he turns toward us. There's nothing written on his face when he looks us over again.

"Well, it seems we're needed elsewhere," he hums, taking Sunshine's empty plate and putting it in the sink. "We've got a meeting with our fathers. Business to discuss." His face stays impassive, but the fire in his eyes has my brows furrowing. "It seems we'll have to discuss more at a later date. More private-ly," he adds the last part in a softer voice when he helps Sunshine from her chair.

"I'll see you at dinner tonight, J." Coming around the table, Sunshine wraps her arms around me in a tight hug. She sighs in my embrace before pulling back. "Try to... To think it over, okay? I'll be fine." She nods her head once, keeping her hands on my shoulders.

My eyes stray to Mikhail, who patiently waits behind us, watching her closely.

"I will." I gently kiss her cheek and then let her go out the door and into whatever type of meeting they have.

Shepp wraps an arm around my shoulders when we leave the room and head down the hall.

"Shall we explore?" I murmur.

Shepp nods eagerly, taking my hand.

CHAPTER TWENTY-SEVEN

Journey

"I THINK I'M FIGHTING A LOSING BATTLE, SHEPP." THE WORDS barely make it from my lips.

My toes dig into the cool sand of the beach, having kicked off my shoes the moment we found the ocean at the edge of the island. Chilly air engulfs us, swirling around our bodies in the constant wind whipping off the seawater. Sharp shivers roll down my spine, causing goosebumps on my flesh.

But I ignore it all. My mind is too focused on my sister's news, taking me deep into the depths of denial, rage, and finally, resignation.

My little sister is sacrificing herself for me. For Shepp. For our freedom from Shadow. Like I've done too many times before.

Shepp squeezes my hand three times, holding me tight and pulling me from my drowning thoughts. He's my rock right now. The light on the ocean when I'm amid darkness and bullshit.

"There's nothing I can do to stop her from marrying him, is there?" I swallow hard, staring at the endless ocean and taking in the waves crashing into the sand a few feet away.

Darrell wasn't joking when he said there was no escape. Sure, there are boats docked in a marina that we could steal in the middle of the night and ride out of here in a blaze of glory.

But there are guards everywhere. Even watching us as we freely walk around the island. They have mounted cameras on every corner of this property. Freedom? What a joke here. There's no ounce of that. Not with thousands of Shadow's men lurking around and using the island like their home.

We're truly stuck and fucked.

Shepp shakes his head. *'No,'* he mouths soundlessly.

"That's what I thought…" my words trail off, taken by the wind and the hopeless black hole opening in my chest.

If I can't protect her, then what good am I?

The sun slowly sinks in the distance. Another day gone. Another one will begin. How many days will we suffer here without a way out?

Shepp's massive hands cup my cheeks, forcing my gaze to his. His eyes remind me of the ocean before us. So full of depth and emotions. It eats away at me, digging deep into my brain. He chips away at me with one look, knowing precisely what has my eyes filling with tears and my fingers curling into fists.

What it's always been. Sunshine. Her safety. Her health. I've always been the one hanging on so tightly.

'She will be fine,' he mouths again.

Will she?

"How can you be so sure?" I whisper. "She's fourteen. He's… the mafia. I'm…" I squeeze my eyes shut. A pressure pushes heavily on my chest like a goddamn elephant rests there, breaking my ribs. My heart seems to rip in two. "I feel so helpless again, Shepp. I feel like her life is slipping from me again. Before, I didn't know where she was, but I knew she was being cared for. What about now?" I gasp out breathlessly, heaving. "What if he…"

Shepp covers my mouth with his hand, stopping my words. My eyes fly open, brows furrowing, when he gives me a stern look.

'She's not helpless. She's a warrior.' He gives me a pointed look. *'He may be mafia. But he seems okay.'*

"Seems okay?" I mutter behind his hand. "He's mafia. That means…" I stop when Shepp sighs, nearly flinching at my words.

Shepp is mafia. Jericho and Arrow, too. They've killed and hurt people and made plans about drugs and money.

'Are we bad?' he mouths, watching my fallen expression.

I shake my head immediately, on instinct. That's a loaded question my brain can't compute. Are they bad? Jericho. Arrow. Shepp. They're the absolute worst, but in the best way possible. Sure, they've some shitty things. Hell, they kidnapped me to force my hand.

But they saved me.

"You all saved me."

Shepp fed me before I knew they existed outside of school, stocking my fridge and ensuring I didn't go hungry because my mother didn't care.

Jericho. He took me, held me captive, and kept me safe as much as he could. He helped me hide my inheritance so my monster couldn't get his hands on it. Well, in his own Jericho way, I guess.

And Arrow. That man took Leighton's finger for me and knocked out his teeth. All because he touched me.

The three of them have given me so much more than I expected anyone to give me. Sacrificed for me.

'And he won't save her?' Shepp mouths.

I lean forward, embracing Shepp. I bury my face in his chest, taking in the scent of his clothes. It's all wrong. Smells nothing like him. Yet, it brings me peace to be surrounded by him.

"What if he's cruel? What if he makes her do things…" I peel my face away, shaking my head.

Shepp's face softens. *What if he's what she needs? It's an escape, Little Tempest. Freedom for her to get away from my father. Don't forget what he did to her.'*

How could I ever? I remember that night vividly; it haunts me during my darkest moments.

"In the unknown..." At least with my monster, I knew what to expect. But Mikhail? The Russian mafia? I have no clue. "You're so calm about this."

Shepp sighs. *'I read people. Well. He seems sincere. Truthful.'*

"More like a little shit," I grumble, earning a soft chuckle.

It's music to my ears, softening me more. I miss the sound of his raspy voice.

I scowl, though. It's not exactly the answer I was hoping for. I want... Well, I'm not exactly sure what I want. It's reassuring on one front that Mikhail seems trustworthy.

But on the other hand? I want Shepp to tell me we will escape before the inevitable happens. Before we're forced to go to Jenni's wedding. That'll split us all up. Sunshine will go her own way with Mikhail, while Shepp and I go our own way.

Shepp sighs, grabbing my hand as we walk in the sand again. My eyes stray to the horizon, thoughts running wild as the memories of our brunch rush through my mind. Mikhail's gaze on my sister, watching her every move with love shining in his eyes.

"Maybe he loves her," I mutter, stalling our feet in the sand. The cool waves lap at our bare feet, grounding me in the moment. "The way he held her like a precious jewel reminded me of..." I lick my lips. Jericho. The way he looked at me with fire in his eyes and promises on his tongue. It's the same between my sister and her little shit of a fiancé.

I can't believe that's even a thought in my head.

It's crazy to think that long ago, I thought I was going to rescue her from the hospital and ride off into the sunset. Running until we couldn't anymore and hole up in a cabin in the woods with new identities.

Now, we're here. In this shit hole of an island, getting married and taking off with a Russian mafia prince.

Shepp smirks and nods. Understanding exactly where my mind went.

Before their time here is up, I'll give him a chance. Sunny has proven herself to me. She can be the hero. For now, at least. But I'll get to the bottom of everything and discover Mikhail's intentions with her.

"For what this place is, it's beautiful," I sigh, shaking off all the negative thoughts. Stress permanently lives on my shoulders, weakening me.

One day, I'll have my happily ever after. I have to swim through this bullshit to get to the other side.

Shepp pulls me close, forcing my back to his front. He gently kisses my cheek, humming a soft tune. It eases my mind and helps me forget where we are and who we're here with.

"I love it when you hum," I murmur, turning in his arms. "Will you teach me to sign?" I search his eyes. I could read books and learn, but there's none here.

Shepp smiles big and nods. *'Yes.'*

Shepp and I sit in the sand as the sun goes down. The number of things on my mind has my shoulders in my ears, but I shake it off. Especially when Shepp gets down to business, teaching me the basics of sign language, starting with the alphabet.

We sit there together until Darrell comes to retrieve us for dinner with Shadow. Then we're escorted back into our room, and the door locks behind us.

"Tomorrow morning, you'll be free again," Darrell grumbles unhappily. "More clothes will be brought to you tomorrow night, where you'll have dinner and the fights." He scowls more, obviously hating playing errand boy.

And with a huff, Darrell shuts the door and locks us in.

CHAPTER TWENTY-EIGHT

Shepp

JOURNEY STARES AT HERSELF IN THE MIRROR WITH A FROWN, smoothing down the dress that clings perfectly to her body. A gift from my sperm donor a few hours before. Hand-delivered by Darrell and his unbreakable expression.

I can't take my eyes off her. My breath slips away with every swipe of her hands down her revealing dress. It draws me in. Hypnotizing me. It's long, black, nearly touching the ground, resembling the one she wore to our initiation ball. It dips in the front, exposing her tattoo and hidden scar.

My beautiful Little Tempest. My storm. She has no idea how powerful she is. Dressed like that or even in sweats, she could take Shadow down with the swish of her hips.

Add me to the damn list. Every second I stare, I fall deeper down the Journey rabbit hole, turning to steel in my pants.

"This is so creepy," she states, side-eyeing me with a frown, unaware of her effect on me. "He knows my perfect size. It's fucking weird." She turns slightly, checking out her ass in the mirror, her eyebrows furrowing. "Seriously? How the hell does he know?"

I'm wondering the same thing as I stare at the perfectly fitted black suit I was told to wear. Sure, we've had clothes delivered to us since, but it's odd how Shadow knows the exact sizes we need, even in suits and dresses. My expression falls in the mirror as my hand glides along the dark fabric over my chest toward the simple bow tie around my throat. More gifts from my sperm donor. Along with a pair of shiny shoes.

I take her hand in mine, bringing her into me. The frantic beating of her heart slams through her chest into mine. Even the tiny hitch of her breath has my toes curling.

What I wouldn't give for privacy on this island to do bad things to her. Fuck. My eyes sweep down her body, admiring the dress painted on her body. He spared no expense for us. Expensive clothes and shoes. Including the makeup on her face.

No matter how my girl looks, I will always think she's the most beautiful thing I've ever laid eyes on.

'You're gorgeous as always, Little Tempest,' I mouth as she reads my lips.

Yesterday, we sat by the ocean as I taught her the basics of sign language. It's not something she'll be able to learn overnight, but it's a start to breaking through our communication barrier.

For now. Until I can find my voice again. I will—one day.

She blushes up at me. The redness of her cheeks stirring the thick emotions bubbling inside me.

She could have suffered through this alone. The caves. The fight. Starvation. Dehydration. Every fucking thing. Alone. Without me here to wipe her tears or be her pillow.

If I hadn't gone after her kidnappers or beaten Gabriel to a bloody pulp. I wouldn't be here with her.

My Little Tempest has survived a lot in life. She's a warrior. A fucking fighter. But this? Fuck. It's taking its toll on her and weighing her down with every breath she takes.

It's visible on her face and in her actions. Her body sways more. Unsteady on her feet. Darkness swirls in her eyes more often than not. Her thoughts are holding her in a prison of her own making.

And there's nothing I can do to stop it.

Not to mention, she's having difficulty keeping food down. She always runs to the bathroom to vomit, and then she's better than ever.

"You're not too bad yourself," she murmurs, reaching up to adjust my bowtie. Getting on her tippy toes, she attempts to kiss my cheek, but I pull her in until my lips rest on hers in a gentle kiss. "Shepp," she whispers, clinging to my suit jacket.

My hand cradles the back of her skull, holding her tight against me. Her tongue sneaks into my mouth, swiping the emptiness with a soft moan. My cock stiffens more, eager to plunge deep inside her. Ready to take her again and again. To show her she matters and that the world would be bleaker without her.

Fuck. I feel so damn alive with my lips on hers, and her body pressed tightly against mine. I want to stay here forever. Hold her forever. And never let her go. There's something about her that sparks something deep inside, like a flame flickering to life and eager to explode.

I never want to let this go.

She riles me up. Winding me tighter and tighter. Until precum leaks from the tip of my cock, preparing for what won't come. Cameras are everywhere on the island, and guards patrol every inch of the hotel. So, who is to say they aren't watching our every move from behind a screen as we speak? I'd love nothing more than to lay her down and gently fuck her until we both reach completion to calm our nerves.

But I won't risk anyone else seeing her bare. That's only reserved for me. Right now, at least. Once we're free, she's Arrow's and Jericho's, too.

My grip loosens on her, gently pulling back. Breathless, seeking oxygen. Our eyes connect, and our souls rejoice from being near one another.

'I want you so badly,' I mouth, kissing her hand.

She blushes again, resembling the color I want to take and put on my canvas. She's my muse. My Little Tempest. My brushes call to me, and my fingers twitch in response. I want to lay her out again. Have a repeat of what we did in my room. Paint on her body. Paint on mine. Capture all her scars and imperfections again. Show her how truly beautiful she is. Inside and out.

"But we shouldn't." She swallows hard, her eyes dilating.

'Not in here,' I mouth in agreement, pulling her hand into mine and gently kissing it.

Worry pulls down her features again when I pull back, and her brows furrow. No doubt, going back to the dark places in her mind, worrying over Sunshine and her fate.

I softly clear my throat, bringing her focus back to me. *'We'll be okay.'*

"We have to be." She shrugs, attempting to shake off her thoughts. But she can't. "I just can't get over what Sunny said. I'm..."

Instinctively, she traces the scar hidden beneath her beautiful tattoo, which I've witnessed her do frequently as a comfort.

"I'm terrified, Shepp. I can't save her or help her. One wrong move..." There's something in her tone that sets my teeth on edge.

What I wouldn't give to remove all her fear and protect her from everything.

I've seen her scared before, sad, and concerned. Journey holds her emotions close—or as close as she can. I still remember the time in our kitchen when she hugged me. I held her tight, never wanting to let her go. She was so shocked by the hug—almost as if no one had held her like that for years. Or possibly in her entire existence.

Any time I can, I hold her in my arms. To show her she can have me. Us. Everything at her fingertips.

'I know. I'm scared, too,' I mouth, trying to reassure her. *'But Sunshine is a tough girl.'* Sometimes I think she's stronger than me and she's only fourteen. She went into this situation

with her head held high, having no idea what was in store for her. That takes bravery. *'She'll be okay.'*

Journey nods, swallowing a lump in her throat. She's still not convinced. Even after breaking down last night at the beach and admitting her defeat. It's futile; no matter what we do, Sunshine is determined to marry Mikhail.

Everything in the future depends on what happens at the dinner with Shadow, Naum, and Mikhail tonight. A dinner from fucking hell.

Will we survive it? I'm sure Naum won't. Shadow—because that's all he is to me, not a father any longer—has made it clear that Naum was about to meet his end.

If only I knew how and when.

Will this help to ease Journey's worry? Probably not. It'll only make it worse. Force her to backtrack and return to her thoughts on taking Sunshine with us.

A knock on the door before opening has us turning around to inspect Darrell. He raises a silent brow in our direction before nodding at us to follow him.

"Such a man of many words," Journey quips with a snort.

Darrell barely reacts to her dig, only rolling his eyes as he gestures for us to follow again. Grabbing Journey's hand, I gently squeeze three times.

We'll be okay. I love you—anything to soothe her worries.

We follow Darrell into the silent hall as our door shuts behind us.

"This way," he grunts, moving in front of us quickly until we walk to the elevators, climb in, and take it down.

This time, he doesn't hit extra buttons or type in the code to take us to the lower level. Sometime soon, I'll get on this elevator and do the same. I'll discover what my father has in his secret office—one way or another.

As we step out into the main lobby, I tightly grip Journey and hold her close. I can't risk losing her in the fray of the chaos. My muscles stiffen at the sight of everyone milling around, talking loudly, and laughing together in fancy attire.

It's a goddamn party.

People pack the lounge, sipping what I can only assume are alcoholic beverages and sampling appetizers in large groups. Several servers in blue vests carry trays around the room, greeting everyone with smiles and offering free samples.

"Guests," Darrell grunts, gesturing to them without emotion.

"Russian?" Journey murmurs, tightening her hold on me as her eyes scan the area.

She takes them in. One by one. Just like I do. At least fifty of them mill around, speaking to one another in Russian and dressed in their best outfits. Suits and ties. Women in long dresses clinging to their men with smiles.

The entire fucking Bratva followed Naum to this secret island.

Fuck. This isn't a good sign. If Shadow is inviting strangers to his secret hideout and exposing what he has, then there's no telling what he's liable to do in the future by exposing himself.

"Mhmm," Darrell barely confirms in his non-committal way.

Journey squeezes my hand as we walk through the thick crowds of people until we reach a quiet corridor devoid of guests. Darrell doesn't utter another word or grunt when he pauses and turns to look at us with an expectant stare.

"He's waiting." Darrell's features tighten like unsaid words rest on his tongue, and he's eager to warn us about something. But he keeps to himself and shakes his head, throwing the door open and ushering us into the dining hall.

A massive weight rests on my chest when we enter the mostly empty room, except for Shadow. Who grins the moment we walk into what feels like our execution. Standing from his chair, he fixes his suit jacket and straightens his crooked tie while chuckling at our bewildered expense. His eyes rove over our bodies, taking in our attire, and he grunts his approval.

"Welcome to the party," he says ominously with a grin, gesturing for us to sit across from him.

And what a fucking party it will become.

CHAPTER TWENTY-NINE

Journey

THE THICK AIR OF THE DINING ROOM DOES NOTHING TO EASE
the pressure on my chest. Heavy. Suffocating. Foreboding.
eye my captor from across the table, loudly chewing on a
Caesar salad presented to us all.

It's been nothing but silence since our asses hit the chairs
Nothing but staring at Shadow with twisted expressions as he
eats like a goddamn cow grazing in the pasture.

You think he'd notice if I picked up my fork and stabbed
him in the eyeballs?

Probably.

He'd scream and cause a commotion, luring his guards in
And I'd be dead meat. There's no way I can back out now
when my sister's life is on the line. I'm still reeling from the
news that she's shacking up with some fourteen-year-old mafia
prince and riding off into the sunset. Is it for the better'
Maybe. I'm still coming to terms with it. No matter how hard I
try to convince myself that she'll be safer with that demented
little twit, who I still want to drag into the ocean and drown fo
taking her away from me. Dramatic? Probably. Needed? Only
time will fucking tell. For now, I have to breathe through my
nose and trust the damn process. Whatever that is. Sunshine
knows what she's doing. Mikhail—even though I don't trus
him as far as I can throw him, which isn't far—has treated me

sister fairly. I have to remind myself that he looks at her the way Jericho looks at me.

On second thought, that's semi-scary.

The warmth of a hand gliding across my thigh knocks the murderous thought from my mind. Gently, Shepp squeezes three times, grounding me to the moment instead of drowning Mikhail while he sleeps. Silently, I say thanks to him with a soft smile, and he nods in understanding. It's like he's tapped into my mind and can read everything I'm worrying myself sick over.

Shadow clears his throat, tapping his fork against his salad bowl. "You're probably wondering why I brought you here."

Yeah. No shit, Sherlock.

"It crossed my mind," I snark, pushing around a piece of Romaine lettuce, fantasizing about eating it. But any thought of food has my stomach in knots and acid in my throat. My new norm, apparently. "But enlighten me."

He glares at me. "You're thinking about running away from me and my hospitality," Shadow says, taking another bite while watching me with a neutral expression.

"Whatever gave you that idea? Your hospitality has been unmatched," I quip, taking a small bite of the salad.

The combination of dressing, lettuce, cheese, and croutons tastes like ash on my tongue and heavy lead on my churning stomach. But I swallow it down, attempting to act normal. *Don't be suspicious. Don't be suspicious.* I need the nutrients to fuel me if I'm going to be strong enough to make it through this hellacious dinner filled with tension.

Tonight is supposed to be a celebration of the families coming together. But I smell something very fucking suspicious. It almost smells like pure bullshit. Actually, that's anything that comes out of Shadow's mouth. He could say the sky is blue, and I'd never believe him. He's up to something tonight—something big—like Naum's death. Yeah, Shepp told me all about Shadow's ominous warnings when he attended the meeting upstairs while I helped make breakfast with Sunshine. So, that's fun. We've been on our toes since Darrell dropped off our fancy attire and told us to be ready by seven.

So, here we are—front row and center to the destruction of a mafia king. What a time to be alive.

Shadow's smirk has my stomach turning more, and I barely hold the tiny bite I swallowed down, which is now threatening to come back up. Do not throw up chunks on the dining room floor. That's most certainly a one-way ticket to the damn caves.

"The truth is, Journey West. We need each other. At my word, your sister will be killed. Do you think her new keepers will keep her safe and secure? You're only sending her to a fancier prison."

That's what I'm afraid of. That's what I've been trying to keep her from. This life. The one I got myself in the middle of. Sunny doesn't deserve it. She's too innocent and bubbly to let the darkness touch her and dampen her brightness.

I'm already tainted.

"Don't lie to the poor girl!" A thick, accented voice comes from the other side of the room.

I startle, sitting straight up in my chair. My head whips toward the unfamiliar voice, and I nearly gasp at seeing him. Fitted in a tight suit with a tie, he sucks on an old pipe, puffing smoke around him with a mischievous grin.

But it's more than that.

Malice lives behind his dark, beady eyes, taking the scene in. He's calculating something. His next move? Ours? Who knows? His graying hair slicks back on his head, highlighting the receding hairline showcasing his massive forehead.

Something in my gut has me recoiling from him. A warning. That doesn't bode well for my damn sister and her well-being. Because if I had to hazard a guess, that's Mikhail's father, Naum.

The Bratva leader. Overseer of the damn Russian Mafia.

"I don't lie," Shadow scoffs. "Come and sit." He gestures to the chairs around us with a stern look.

"No introduction?" the mysterious man asks, raising a dark, bushy brow.

"Figured you'd want to do that yourself," Shadow quips, devoid of humor. There's a hint of tightness in his voice. But he's covering it up well. As well as one can, I guess.

One of my favorite lessons Gabriel taught me was observation, watching people's movements, and guessing their intentions. Oh, that man stuck his watch in his pocket and then glanced at it again? It means he's waiting for someone. Or he's impatient. Gabriel may have tortured me, made me kill people, and forced the darkness inside me. But he trained me well.

And what my training is saying right now is there's something off.

"Isn't it rude not to introduce your guests to your other guests?" The man chuckles, sauntering closer to us, puffing a few more clouds of smoke from his pipe as he rounds the table with a grin. "Well, since Shadow of Briar Cove Island is so rude. My name is Naum Antonov." He holds out his hand and shakes ours in a tight grip.

"I'm Journey, and this is Shepp." My words seem relaxed as they come out. Not hinting to him that every muscle in my body tightens as he sits down at the head of the table.

"Oh, the sister," he says with a mischievous grin. "Understandable." I stiffen at his words and even more when he looks me over. His head tilts, really taking me in.

"Yeah," Shadow gruffly grunts, shoving the rest of his salad in his mouth. "The annoying sister."

Well, that's just rude as fuck. I'm not annoying. Since my forced arrival on this island, I've been nothing but compliant. But I keep my mouth shut. Be a good girl and all that nonsense.

All for Sunny—I tell myself for the millionth time.

"They'll be here in a minute. I've never seen my boy so

smitten before," Naum says, cocking his head with a pensive look. "He is absolutely captivated by her. She lives up to her name."

I offer him a tight smile. "My sister is something else. You better believe she won't take your shit." I clutch my fork tighter, threatening to stab him in the damn eye.

"Hmmm. She's a queen in the making." he shrugs. "She'll overthrow us all." His grin widens when the door opens behind us.

Sunshine walks into the room on Mikhail's arm as he protectively holds her close to his body. His light eyes scan the table, narrowing on his father. His muscles bunch beneath his suit. A tic forms in his jaw as he clenches his teeth tight. But in a flash, it's all gone. He erases any feelings from his expression and becomes indifferent before anyone else can see the minute changes. I swallow hard when he politely nods at me, and I nod back.

My sister looks at him with a soft, warm smile, clinging to him with every step. The glow on her skin takes me aback again. It's like seeing her earlier when she was in his presence as they made breakfast together seamlessly like they had done it so many times before. True happiness wafts from her—joy I've never seen before in my damn life. She's always been my little sister—practically my daughter. The girl I carted to doctor's appointments and prayed to whoever was above to save her or give her a stronger heart. She's survived so much and has always had a sunny disposition.

I deflate in my chair, keeping my gaze on her. Who am I to stomp all over her feelings? I can't hold her back when she seems to have a way out.

Even if it's with that little punk.

"Wonderful! Mikhail," Naum says, standing up again and clapping his hands. "Come join us for dinner! Let's celebrate the future union of my heir."

"Father," he says in a low voice, pulling Sunshine closer.

Protective. Like a fourteen-year-old shouldn't be able to possess. Sunshine doesn't react. She smiles more, looking around the room with ease.

There's something in the stiffening of Mikhail's shoulders and the curling of his fists. It's how his father looks at him with clear control that has my nerves rising. She didn't seem to notice because Mikhail shields her away from it all.

But I do.

"Sunshine," Naum says slowly and raises his brows.

"Sit. So we can enjoy our fucking meal. Our entertainment awaits us," Shadow spits impatiently, forcing everyone to sit down.

Thankfully, Sunshine occupies the seat beside mine. Giving me access to her free hand, which I immediately clutch in mine.

"Sunny," I murmur, checking her over until I'm satisfied she's truly safe. It's only been a day since we spent time together, but so many things can change in that time.

"Journey," she says with a smile, gently squeezing back. "You remember Mikhail." She raises a brow as if to say, be nice to him.

I smile sweetly at her words. Mikhail observes me with darkening eyes and an unmoving face. Coldness wafts off him, but evil doesn't. Compassion lives within his soul, especially when he looks at Sunshine with the same devotion she offers him.

Maybe Sunshine has glimpsed the man underneath—like I have with Jericho. He's more than what he lets the world see. Caring. Giving. Protective. I suppose being raised by a monster can cause immeasurable damage.

And these mafia offspring are the prime examples.

I wasn't raised in the life. I merely existed and trained in it for six months before my cage was opened, and I was freed to do my monster's bidding. It nearly cut the soul from my body.

So, imagine being there from the get-go and undergoing the training from day one.

It must have been hell.

"It's nice to see you again," I offer with a respectful nod.

A genuine grin lights up his face, and he nods. "It's an honor to see you again, as well. Your sister has been talking about you non-stop." I blush, whipping my gaze to Sunshine, who grins and winks at me. What the hell? "About what a wonderful provider and protector you've been since she was younger, like a mother shielding her from everything and taking care of her health. I thank you for that. Thank you for keeping her safe until this point." He tilts his head to the side, not showing any more emotions than necessary. Looking into his eyes is unnerving, but I don't dare break our gaze. "But I can take it from here," he says possessively in my direction as he takes her hand, laying it on his lap.

I swallow down the instant retort on my tongue. Something like, over my dead body or get fucked, you little prick, before taking my sister and running to a boat. I have been her protector for so long. Years. Since the day she popped out of my mom, the woman handed her to me, saying she was my responsibility. After days of hospital tests, doctors deemed my sister broken.

Sunshine was not broken. She just needed a little extra love. And even at the young age I was when she was born, I did everything in my power to make life good for her.

Now, I'm expected to let her go. Just let her slip through my fingers like sand. But I have to, don't I? I can't protect my sister in this fancy-ass hotel. I can barely protect myself or Shepp.

So, I nod with a tight smile. "It seems to be that way."

Sunshine perks up, her entire body turning rigid. "You mean it?" she whispers, tears forming in her eyes when Mikhail kisses the back of her hand.

Do I mean it? Not really. But I'm going to release her from

my care and put all my faith into the little mafia prince. Just this once. Even if it's tearing me apart on the inside and breaking my heart in two, I have to let her go. She'll be safer with him.

I hope.

"You'd better take care of her," I warn, tilting my head when he smiles at me.

"Always," he mutters.

"Wonderful. Now, that is out of the way. Let's get this dinner started. More wine!" Shadow snarls, pounding his fist into the tabletop with impatience.

Shepp stiffens beside me and blows out a breath at Shadow's fist, echoing through the room as if memories of his time with his father pour through his mind. The abusive asshole who stole his tongue and did God knows what else. I never would have guessed it affected him if I hadn't caught the slight movement.

But his fear of his father is palpable.

Reaching over, I clasp Shepp's massive hand in mine. I gently squeeze three times to soothe the worry creasing his brows. I swallow hard when he returns three squeezes and his body relaxes. We don't look at each other. No matter how hard I want to gaze into his eyes and reassure him everything will be okay.

My lips roll together as servers bring steaming entrees out and set them in front of us, giving each person a glass of red wine. Well, everyone but me. I tilt my head, eyeing the lighter concoction sloshing in my glass. I sniff it. Apple juice? Shadow smirks at me when I look at him with furrowed brows, but he doesn't say a word. Neither do I, despite the confusion.

Alarm bells ring in my head when he stands, forcefully pushing his chair backward. "To health! To the union of two families," Shadow says, raising the glass in the air. His eyes sweep the room, glossing over us until they land on Naum.

"To health, alliances, and deals!" Naum shouts, tapping his

glass against Shadow's with a grin. "To new family." His eyes zero in on my sister again as she shifts in her seat, staring straight down at her glass. "Well, it's not hard liquor, but it'll do." Naum takes a large drink of his wine, downing it like a shot until it's all gone and the glass is empty.

"Here, here," I mutter, setting the glass down without taking a drink. My damn stomach turns more at the smell of the apple juice.

It's incredibly off-putting. For whatever reason.

I rub my stomach, trying to ease the rumbling happening inside. If I'm not careful, I'll spew the minuscule amount of salad I ate onto the ground. And that would be embarrassing, to say the least.

Naum sits smugly in his seat and raises his empty glass. Without a word or request, it's filled again by a server to the brim. He takes another large gulp, emptying it again.

"Father, your wine consumption is becoming alarming," Mikhail says, placing an arm over Sunshine's chair.

"Shut it, boy," he says, slurring slightly as a server repeatedly fills his glass.

"If that's what you request," Mikhail says, taking a tentative bite of his salad. "This salad is exemplary," he remarks, swallowing his bite with a hum.

What the fuck kind of fourteen-year-old says exemplary? Or speaks like a grown-ass adult? Of course, he doesn't seem fourteen to me. In looks, sure. But his aura screams maturity. Maybe the life he's been living has given him a reason to be an adult.

"Thank my chef. He's got an eye for it," Shadow grunts, taking the last bite of his salad. "Just wait for the main course. It'll knock your socks off."

Mikhail blinks several times at Shadow and nods. "Can't wait for the main bit. Will it be much longer?"

"No. It should be two minutes max," Shadow says with an unhinged grin, taking up the majority of his face.

Shivers roll down my spine when they continue to lock eyes and then go about eating and taking sips of wine. Mikhail doesn't seem to touch his drink, staring at it like it holds poison. Not that he should consume it, anyhow. He even stops Sunshine from touching hers, gently shaking his head and imploring her with his softened eyes.

My gut lurches. Something is about to happen. I can feel it in my gut, just like before we walked in here.

I stare at my glass and then at Shepp's. He hasn't touched it either, opting to eat his salad and scarf it down as best he can, avoiding his father's stare.

"What?" Naum pales, looking at the glass of wine and then at Shadow. Blood pours from his eyes and ears, trailing down his flesh like a faucet opening up.

"I hope you enjoyed my wine and hospitality, but I'm afraid it's the last thing you'll ever see or feel." Shadow sits back in his chair, watching as Naum slumps in his seat, gargling blood until it pools from between his lips, painting them red.

"My son..." he garbles out with accusation.

"I'm afraid you've overstayed your welcome in the Antonov family," Mikhail says in a smooth voice. "There's a new head now." He smiles sweetly at his father, taking in his final breaths with light in his eyes.

"Mik..." Sunshine whispers with quivering lips, attempting to pull away from him.

"The deal still stands," Shadow says in Mikhail's direction. "Sunshine is yours. Your father has met his end. We have sealed our deal.

Mikhail softens when he cradles Sunshine's face in his palms. I want to jump over and yank his hands away from her. Protect her from the big evil teenager who set his father up for murder. Was he swindled into doing it?

"What just happened, Mik?" Sunshine whispers with apparent distress bubbling in her tone. "I don't understand..."

"In time, Love. You'll understand everything. Just know, I

did it for you." His tone softens with her, begging her to understand his reasonings. "He would have harmed you. Like…" He rolls his lips together, shaking his head.

"I'd like to know the reason, too." I lick my lips, staring between my sister and Mikhail. How am I supposed to trust this kid with my sister when he just offed his father in front of our eyes?

Mikhail's gaze promises words later. It's written on his face that he can't tell me now.

"You're on a need-to-know fucking basis," Shadow spits with a growl. "This isn't your business. It's something Mikhail and I discussed when they stepped foot here. It's an alliance."

An alliance, of course, that's all that matters.

Two servers walk into the room and quietly remove Naum's body from the chair. I didn't even hear his death gurgle, but judging by the missing light in his eyes—he's dead. Gone. And he's never coming back. Leaving the fucking child clinging to my sister as the de facto leader of the Bratva.

How terrifying.

Once the body is out of sight, more servers enter the room, carrying sizzling plates of steak, potatoes, and delicious mac and cheese. Our main course. Who the fuck can eat after witnessing such a brutal murder? It's almost worse than if Shadow had pulled a gun and blew his brains out. I'm used to guts and blood. Well, somewhat. But Naum never saw it coming. I never saw it coming, either. It was hidden within his drink. Unsuspecting.

Who the fuck is next?

"Now, to the new head of the Antonov family," Shadow says, raising his glass of wine. His beady eyes take us in, slowly cataloging everyone in the room. "I have it on good authority you'll discuss this mishap with the rest of your counsel?" There's almost a hint of fear in his tone. It's a piece of Shadow I've never heard before.

Mikhail clears his throat as he gets to his feet near his

chair. Lifting his glass, he smirks. "Of course, I've already informed the council about the trash that needed taking out. They all agreed on this sacrifice and have given me their blessing." He confidently raises his glass in the air, pulling his shoulders back. "To new alliances and prosperity," Mikhail says, lifting his glass further.

But once again, he doesn't take a sip. He sets it on the table with a sigh as he retakes his seat. He reaches over, taking Sunshine's hand, gently lifting it to his mouth, and placing a gentlemanly kiss there. "This was for the good of our future," he says softly, kissing her flesh again.

The telltale signs of his affection shine through when Sunshine blushes and he chuckles.

Something in his eyes puts me at ease, which is weird. He honestly seems to be smitten with my sister even though they haven't known each other for a long time—a few days.

Mikhail's eyes move from her to me. He tilts his head, giving me silent words of reassurance, which doesn't help.

My stomach ties into knots. Again. Like, that's fucking new. But I force myself to settle down. No matter what happens, I'll keep my sister safe, even if I have to go off and murder people for Shadow and become his assassin.

"Now, let's eat our fucking dinner and go to the fight. I have a lot of fun entertainment for us to watch." He grins, stabbing his food like it's still alive, making noise, and chomping on it like he belongs in the pasture.

Fucking animal.

CHAPTER THIRTY

Journey

Dinner turns my stomach even more than the salad. But what's new lately?

Everything is so fucking exhausting at this point. My eyelids droop, desperate for sixteen hours of uninterrupted sleep. Hell, put me in a coma for a year so I can finally get some shut-eye and ignore the world and pretend I'm not stuck on an island with a psycho as the leader who poisons people.

Good times.

The only thing I can think of as I shove delicious steak and potatoes down my throat is—will I be next? Will he poison Shepp and me before we can even make it to the fight?

He didn't. For whatever reason, he seems to want us around. Whether it's to continue our torture and enact his revenge on us or to use us for whatever he sees fit. We're here. Alive. And very fucking annoyed.

Fuck. My head hurts.

Even worse when Shadow leads us to the top of The Pits into the stands and gives us a private viewing box to witness the murders of people with guards in tow.

Staring down, I note the same blood stains I walked across before murdering the man in cold blood. Well, not exactly cold blood. He seemed to deserve it, regardless of how he was set up to die at my hands.

"Any idea as to what's going on?" I murmur to Shepp, who sits beside me, watching the scene unfold with a blank expression.

The muted shouts of the men in the stand muffle through the glass box, and I see more and more of Shadow's soldiers lining the benches everywhere I look. Even his guards stand silently with narrowed eyes.

We're surrounded by the enemy.

Shepp shakes his head, taking my hand in his. 'No clue,' he mouths.

I nod in response, curling my fingers around his. The warmth of his palm in mine settles the aches roaring through my weary bones. If I have to watch a fight to the death, then I'll do it, holding onto the one person who has been able to ground me this entire time.

Shepp has been my lighthouse in the storm, guiding me back from the brink of drowning. Repeatedly. I wouldn't have survived this if he hadn't been taken, too. I would have succumbed to my darkness and become the unfeeling soldier my monster molded.

I owe Shepp everything. Including the support he deserves, too.

Looking at his solemn face, devoid of color and the spark that makes him–him, has shivers creeping up my spine. An aura of sadness and fear wafts from him. Crushing my fucking heart. Everything about this experience is shaping the two of us into different people. Vastly different individuals from who we were a mere week ago.

A larger-than-life presence invades my personal bubble to my left. Settling on the bench beside me like this is an everyday occurrence. I swear the hairs on my arms stand on end, prickling when his gaze finds mine.

Mikhail. The little devil himself.

He shifts in his seat, observing the crowd down below through the streak-free glass, giving us a perfect view of the fight about to begin. He folds his hands in his lap, patiently watching Shadow with a calculated stare.

The mask around Mikhail falls away, revealing the man beneath. He openly glares. With hatred. At the man holding Sunshine's arm in his tight grasp. Bruising will no doubt be left behind on her flesh.

Mikhail flexes his fist. Until his mask slips back into place, replacing his anger with indifference. I want to believe he's letting me see the real him and his displeasure at Shadow. The same as me.

Shadow moves around the private box with determination etched into his face with Sunshine in tow, muttering beneath his breath. Sunny doesn't say a word as he drags her along, appearing like a rag doll doing whatever he says.

"You're with me," he grunts, dragging a compliant Sunshine out the private box's glass door. It leads out to the stage I saw him on when I was in the ring, fighting for my life.

Sunshine smiles beside him like a dutiful daughter as Shadow speaks to the crowd through the microphone in front of him. Shadow's booming voice barely breaks through the glass we're surrounded by, giving the illusion of privacy. The crowd's noise dissipates, completely washing away when they fully take their seats. His people look at him with wide eyes, grins, and utter devotion.

I wonder how they have kept his identity secret all these years without anyone slipping up. He must have a tight hold on them. Something over their heads to keep their lips sealed. No one gives unquestioning loyalty like that. Do they?

"My father had terrible plans for your sister. Ones I disapproved of." Mikhail turns to look at me, taking in my neutral expression. "You don't trust me."

Not entirely. I'm trying so hard for my sister's sake. She pleaded with me to think it over, and I have. I conceded with the fact I wouldn't be able to break them up. It would only get worse from there. So, I'm helpless with this—a participant with no say in the matter.

I take a deep breath, trying to contain myself. But that's hard when Sunshine is involved in the matter. My sister is my primary worry—even over myself—and she always has been. I try to remember how Mikhail looks at my sister with love in his eyes and how she reciprocates.

They care for one another, and I can only hope that continues when he whisks her away, but I still have questions for him—questions I wasn't able to ask in our short time together.

"Why would I?" I ask, tilting my head. "You've known my sister for two days. I've known her forever. And I'm supposed to believe you have her best interest in mind? What game are you playing?"

I bite my tongue, sinking my teeth deep into the traitorous body part. Hard enough to taste the blood flowing from my new wounds. Okay, so that wasn't as smooth and collected as I intended it to be. I could have been a little less direct and to the point. You know, subtle. In an attempt to gain his trust and make him like me enough to tell me all his secrets. But my fuse is short. I'm exhausted. And I'm so over being on this stupid island.

Fuck it.

This little shit has my sister in some sort of spell, and I want to know how.

Also, why?

Mikhail breaks out in a smile, chuckling under his breath. "Understandable. I am nothing but a stranger to you. But to Sunshine, I am someone. And she is the most important thing to me."

"How?" I don't mention he's a literal child parading around like a man, and she's a child, too.

"Try three years," he says, raising a challenging brow.

"Three?" I scoff. "There's no way. They locked her away in

a hospital room without access to anyone. Besides, she would have contacted me first if she had that capability. I am her sister, after all.

"Three years ago, I met an exceptional person through online gaming. She was lonely. I was lonely. But she was also traumatized by the events she witnessed. She saw her sister murder for her."

I pale, stiffening at the memories sneaking through the darkness of my mind and trying to haunt me. Sunshine told a random person on the internet about my crimes? Wonderful. I'm sure the FBI knows all about it now. I'm doomed. Dead. About to go to fucking prison for eternity for the attempted murder of Thomas Mondelli.

"She also mentioned that a bad man took her sister. Oh, and that she was being held in a hospital against her will. But she didn't know the location or anything about it. They kept her under lock and key, watching her almost every hour of the day. Her only reprieve was the hour a day she was granted an iPad to play games online. Something she used to her advantage." He tilts his head, watching her through the glass of the small room. "Your sister will never be trapped again. I will make sure of that. She is mine to keep." He levels me with a soft expression, opening the windows to his soul to reveal a man with genuine intentions, meaning every word he says.

My chest constricts at the hint of betrayal—my sister, the girl I sacrificed everything for—had a way to communicate with the outside world? I was out there busting my ass to keep her safe, and she reached out to people online and didn't have the guts to contact me? I blow out a breath, tracing the line of the scar hidden beneath my tattoo. It's grounding, bringing me back to the scene unfolding before my eyes—death and destruction.

Mikhail's words bounce around in my brain, playing on repeat like an annoying ass record, reminding me of what I've done for the past three years for my sister to keep her safe.

And she wasn't able to contact me.

Logically, I know she wouldn't have been able to. If she had a tablet to play games, there's no way she could have gotten my number or messaged me. Her options were limited. And I'm sure her fear led her to other means of finding friendship and comfort. I couldn't be there for her physically. Through notes, sure. But those were so few and far between that she had to seek someone else out. So, why not? If she found solace in Mikhail—I'll never understand why, little bastard—but he brought her comfort in her dire days.

I wish she could have gotten the word out to me some way without putting herself in front of a loaded gun.

"But why not me?" I mumble more to myself than anyone, still reeling from the shock of his confession.

"Believe my words when I say she wanted to. Your life was also always in danger. She didn't want to risk your well-being because she attempted to reach out. Even through me, Journey. It was too dangerous. She was under the same scrutiny as you were. Not to mention, constantly monitored by Gabriel Viotto's men." How the hell does this little shit know more about my life than I probably do?

Jesus. My sister revealed all our secrets. Didn't she? She trusted this boy with everything about our lives, with no regrets.

I'm so boned.

If he's mafia, he'll hold this over our heads and bend us to his will. I can see it now. The past always repeats itself.

I side-eye the little shit, scrutinizing his thinned-out face. He could almost pass as an adult, but the lack of facial hair and pimples gives him away. He's still a child. But he's her only hope in getting to safety.

"Why did she tell you all of this? You were a damn stranger. You can't expect me to hand my sister to you because you've been internet pals with her, and now..." I trail off, biting my tongue again. As much as I wanted to think I was okay with this, the doubt creeps up on me. I want to question everything.

Stop showing your damn hand, Little Snake! My monster's words pound me over the head much like he did back then, too, whenever I disobeyed. Bam! A crack right to the skull. You'd think I would have learned by now to be a dutiful little snake and not show any of my emotions.

But I've consistently failed miserably. He couldn't pry my humanity out of my soul. Ever. He tried but never succeeded.

"She is my wife," he says, adjusting his posture to his full height. "And I will take her where I please. She'll be treated like a queen. My queen." He blows out a breath, still watching through the window. "I have every intention of providing for her. I have the means. The want. She will be safe with me. Safer than here with him. I promise you that, Journey. No harm will come to your sister. Ever again." He shakes his head, looking Shadow up and down. "She told me why you stabbed him, and it's going to happen again if you don't let me take her out of here."

A full-body shudder works through me. Those words pierce through my chest like a knife slicing through butter. Right to my damn heart. That shatters with the memories of what brought me here. Him—Shadow. Touching her where she shouldn't have been touched. She was a child, and he was a monster high on his horse with power, exuding it over an innocent girl.

Never again.

I protected her from it once in our trailer. Here, though? She's in the same vicinity as him. He could sneak into her room and traumatize her for good. I'm so fucking torn. He's a monster. Worse than Gabriel, that's for sure. He shouldn't be trusted around anyone, especially a child like Sunshine. I know she's been doing everything she can to manipulate him and wrap him around her finger. It's shown.

But that can only save her for so long. Eventually, he'll take what he wants.

"You're fourteen!" I hiss, squeezing Shepp's hand for reassurance. "You can't expect me to...to believe..." I shake my head, trying to wrap my mind around the situation.

"I may be young. In your eyes, I'm probably dumb and jumping the gun. Last night, we married with her father's permission. Legally speaking, Sunshine is mine. My wife. My prized jewel. I want to prove myself to you, Journey. I know what it's like to be protective of my siblings. We look out for each other. I can't thank you enough for doing what you did for her. You saved her from something terrible. Now, it's my turn. She wants this."

She wants me, is what he's not saying.

Does she want this, though? Is this truly the life my little sister wants? It's like a mother letting go of her daughter's hand and willingly handing her over to the shadows of the night. To the dangerous world I tried to shield her from for so many years.

I suck in a breath, pinching the bridge of my nose to distract myself from attempting to punch Mikhail in the face for taking her away. Or hug him for keeping her safe? I'm so torn and confused by how I feel.

He could be lying. Or he could be telling the truth. It's only a matter of time before his true form shows. When will that be, though? Today? Tomorrow? When they go back to his home, isolating my sister from everybody?

"I found a match for her in the system. I'm taking her back to Miami. She will have a new heart." He licks his lips, slowly looking at me with a softened face full of desperation for me to understand. "Isn't that all you've ever dreamed of? And why you sacrificed your freedom to provide for her and her health all those years ago?"

Everything I've dreamed of since her doctors told me she needed a transplant flashes before my eyes. I tried so hard to get her higher on the list. To find her matches that would be compatible with her. Anything to make her healthier. It seemed like I'd never see this day. Now, her new husband snaps his fingers and gets it done without blinking an eye.

I'm a goddamn failure of epic proportions. But grateful someone could do that for her.

Defeat settles in my soul. Maybe this move will be better for her. If he's telling the truth, that is. I'm so wishy-washy with my feelings regarding him and her. Ugh. I want her by my side. But I don't want her to stay in Shadow's vicinity. If I do that, Sunshine will attract even more attention from Shadow. If I let her go with Mikhail, she'll be safer. I can't be everywhere at once. I need to trust his words and trust in him. A fucking stranger to make sure my sister is safe and gets the healthcare she needs.

It's a lot of trust to put on someone so young. Oh, and someone I barely know.

"I would do anything for her," I whisper. "She's my sister. My responsibility. She..." I squeeze my eyes shut, clamping them tight.

She's my everything. The reason I fucking live and breathe. Always has been and always will be. I raised her. Well, until they took her away from me. I sacrificed my childhood to feed and provide clothing for her. Hell, I even stole for her so we could live and survive. Sunshine is my heart. The air. The everything.

Every step I take, life I break—it was for her.

And now, I need to loosen the reins. Drop them entirely and let her go. Into the arms of a man—no, he's still a boy—who is promising her the world. Mikhail can deliver what he's promising. I see it in his eyes when he looks at her with dedication ringing back.

They say the best things in life often break you.

Well, I'm about to break.

"Then you and I have similar interests with her. I assure

you, Sunshine will find nothing but happiness at my side. I will do nothing to put her in danger." Mikhail raises a brow when Shepp loudly scoffs, rolling his eyes, interjecting into our quiet conversation for the first time since we arrived.

Shepp takes out his notebook and writes, *'He's the head of the Russian mafia. Danger will always find them.'* Shepp tosses a hand, gesturing for me to show Mikhail what he said. He glares at the child mafia leader with disdain, gritting his teeth so hard, I'm afraid he'll break them.

A side I haven't really seen from Shepp.

I turn the notebook toward Mikhail and read the words out loud. "He says you're the head of the Russian Mafia now. Danger will always find you. How can I trust that you'll keep my sister safe?"

"And more danger would find her here. It's no coincidence my father struck a deal with Shadow." His lips almost curl in disgust when he spits out Shadow's name. "It's because I made it happen. I am the brains of the operation. Your sister is safe in my hands. I promise." Mikhail holds out his hand, leaving it suspended in the air.

I stare at it, waiting for me to take it. This is the moment I've been dreading. We're agreeing with too few words. My gut rolls with indecision.

Patience sparkles in his eyes when I lift my gaze to examine the softness of his boyish face. He's a boy playing a man's part. Will he change as they age? Will Sunshine be able to step away if Mikhail proves to be as ruthless as the rest of the mafia men? Only time will tell.

I could keep asking myself questions repeatedly until I'm blue in the face. But this is an out for Sunshine—an out she wants.

I swear an entire year passes. I count the lines on his palm, the calluses lining his flesh, until I finally grip his hand, shaking it with more force than necessary. I may look like a meek woman in his eyes, but I'm anything but.

These hands have had blood staining them; I'm not afraid to paint them with his.

Mikhail yanks me closer, staring dead into my eyes. "Sunshine will be safe. I pledge my allegiance to her. Like I'll pledge the backing of the Russian Bratva to you, Mrs. Viotto."

Mrs. Viotto.

Fuck.

Jericho.

I shakily nod, taking all his words in. Shepp's hands grab my shoulders, gently pulling me back from Mikhail's orbit with a possessive growl. He grounds me again, glaring daggers in Mikhail's direction, looking nothing like the docile Shepp I love.

Mikhail signs to Shepp.

I'm slowly learning with Shepp. He's teaching me a few things here and there, so I'm familiar with it. Once we're off the island, I'll crack open some books and hunker down to learn. It's only fair.

Shepp scowls, reluctantly signing back. The tension bleeds from his face, and he nods several times as they converse silently. Something drastic must have changed for Shepp to look so relaxed after they finally set their hands down and respectively shake hands. Mikhail must have proved himself.

Somehow.

"I've heard things about Briar Cove and Gabriel Viotto's rulings. I've also heard rumblings of his kingdom falling. Whatever you go back to in Briar Cove will be messy and chaotic," Mikhail says, straightening his spine again and following Sunshine with a new level of overbearing and protectiveness as she stands stock-still beside Shadow just outside the box.

Before I can hold my tongue, I spout, "Do you know if..."

"They ran. They're fine. I have friends in high places all over the world." He raises his chin with confidence.

Smug, little bastard.

"You're fucking fourteen," I grumble, earning a grin from him.

"No matter how young I am, it doesn't make a difference. I was brought up in this world as a weapon. That's what I was for my father—someone to be used for deals. I've seen a lot of things in my life. So, when I leave, I'll give you my contact information. My address. Whatever you need to feel secure with Sunshine's safety. I would never hold her hostage like The Viotto's." He side-eyes us just as Shadow and Sunshine step down from the ledge and approach the room. "That I can promise. Your sister is still your sister. But she's also my wife."

His words ping-pong inside my head. It could be worse, right? Sunshine could be stuck in this hellhole island for the rest of her life, with Shadow as her guide. Although Mikhail may now lead the Bratva, he seems to genuinely care about Sunshine. But then again, it's always better to go with the devil you know. Fuck. I may regret this, but I can't deny my little sister this opportunity to escape her father.

I have to have faith that Mikhail will take care of her, including her new heart.

But faith is the last thing I have in the fucking mafia.

"You have a deal," I blurt. "Keep her safe. I swear to God, if she gets hurt, I will fucking track you down. That's not a threat, either. My sister gets hurt or doesn't get the heart you're promising her. You're fucking dead." I level him with my best glare that promises a world of hurt if he fucks this up.

"I have no doubts about that, Mrs. Viotto," he says with a sly grin. "You have my word. And my word is my best attribute. With my word, I'll offer you backup when the time comes, and I know it will. This isn't the last time you'll see me or my army. Have Jericho contact me when you're all situated."

Without another word, Mikhail scoots away from me down the bench, leaving enough room for Sunshine to sit beside him as she makes her way into the glass box, none the wiser. His arm immediately goes around her shoulders, holding her close and whispering in her ear. I can only assume he's retelling the plans to her when she looks in my direction. Her brows furrow, but the biggest grin I've ever witnessed greets me.

"Thank you," she whispers, launching herself at me. Her arms wrap tightly around my body, squeezing me with all her might. "I promise I'll be safe," she says under her breath. "This will be for the best."

Seeing the happiness physically light up my sister's face brings joy to my heart. She's been sick for so long and stuck in bed her entire life, eating healthy foods and avoiding activities. Sunshine has been careful her whole life, living it to the dullest. Now, she can leave the norm and finally receive the care she needs.

I can't deny my sister the joy Mikhail brings her, even if it's an act. If it is an act, I'll save her whenever she needs me.

"I love you, Sunshine," I murmur, kissing the top of her head and hugging her back. "I only want what's best for you."

"I know," she chokes out. "But I promise, this is a good thing." She nods once, peeling herself away from me. Tears cloud her eyes as she scoots into Mikhail's waiting arms.

"You're a good sister, Journey," Mikhail says, possessively cuddling Sunshine.

Yeah, you better remember that. I'm a good fucking sister with the protective instinct of a mama bear.

CHAPTER THIRTY-ONE

Journey

SHADOW PUSHES THROUGH THE GLASS DOOR WITH A LOUD laugh, filling the space with his sadistic joy. I swear the atmosphere instantly changes, turning heavy and suppressive.

"Who is ready for the fight of the fucking century?" Shadow says with a grin, rubbing his hands together. He moves to stand at the window, looking down at the pit.

"Why? Did you set it up again?" I ask, getting up from the bench and standing at the window to view the tragedy. When in reality, I'd rather be anywhere else than here. I imagine myself tucked into my bed at the mansion with all the guys around me. Longing hits me, and my mood instantly sours.

God, I want to go home. But when did the mansion become my home? I was only there for a short time. And it wasn't of my volition. Bastards kidnapped me, and yet, here I am, simping for them again.

"Fair fight this time," Shadow says with annoyance, eyeing me through the corner of his eyes with disdain.

"And what would your patrons think if they knew you set that last one up?" Women walk through the stands again, holding popcorn, cotton candy, and alcoholic beverages. Mostly beer in cans. Not a bottle in sight.

"They wouldn't give a fuck. Besides, you lived, didn't you?"

Asshole.

Shaking my head, I focus on the women walking around the arena again. I tilt my head, focusing on a familiar-looking girl walking like a zombie through the various men, groping her ass and buying beer. She doesn't even bat them away. She just simply walks forward like it's her fucking job to endure their hands on her. Then, when her face turns, I see the blank expression on her features. Dead fucking eyes. No joy or life. No anything. The woman down there is a walking corpse doing the job they trained her for.

Every muscle in my body turns rigid when her fading blonde hair swishes at her back until she stops again, handing the next man his beer. He slaps her ass, but she doesn't respond. Again. Something about her has the hairs on my neck standing on end. A buzzing roars through my veins when she stops, like she feels my eyes burning through her. Her head lifts toward the box we're in. Her dead eyes look straight through me.

Despite having a lot on my mind that one morning after the guys chased me into the woods and fucked me into oblivion. I still remember the newspaper Jericho was reading and the article that he waved in front of my face. Fucking old man and his morning paper. The article was about the missing girl, Carolyn Crider, whose parents desperately sought info on her disappearance. They offered a reward for her return. Then, Arrow got a call from their security guard at Rave, saying they had found footage of a woman leading these girls out nearly half asleep.

It was her—that girl down there.

I inspect every woman walking through the crowds. Skimpy clothes. Dazed expressions. They're zombies walking the stands, not caring if men feel them up or take advantage of them. Exactly how he wants them, drugged beyond belief, so they don't realize what's happening until it's too late.

I'd recognize that stare from miles away. I've seen my

mom in those dazes, wandering around the house without a clue as to what she was doing, bumping into walls before toppling over and lying on the floor in defeat.

My goddamn blood boils in my veins. Rage almost consumes me at their expense. How dare he take these girls from the club and bring them to this isolated island to work them to death.

I watch them for another minute, absorbing the new information for later. I can't help them escape if I don't play Shadow's weird games. So, I blow out a breath and center myself.

I look back at Shepp, who remains seated with a pensive expression. His eyes glaze over as he stares through the glass walls, looking at nothing. Mentally, I don't think he's here. I know I wouldn't want to be. Not in the same room as my father, who cut out my fucking tongue. My heart aches for him. Splinters in fucking two at how difficult this must be, breathing the same air as the man who tormented him his entire life. It has to flash before his eyes.

Like his father's almost-murder does mine. That night lives in infamy in my mind. Never truly leaving me. So, for Shepp. Who endured so much at his hands.

This has to be a goddamn nightmare.

I brace myself, peeling my eyes away from the man I love, and stare at the man I loathe. Shadow stands tall, watching the fight begin below. Two women in barely-there clothing fight with long swords, barely able to handle them. They grunt and scream, thrashing the sharpened blades at one another. But they have yet to leave a mark.

It's only a matter of time.

"So it was you." I gaze forward, locking on the missing girls walking through the stands.

"A lot of things were me. Get specific." His voice dips low with agitation, nearly sneering at me.

"The women down there." I gesture to each of them as they work. "You've been taking them from Jericho's club..." I trail off, noting their innocent faces and committing them to memory.

He used a woman to lure them out. I remember that much. The Rave security camera caught her, but they've never been able to pinpoint her. Or find her.

The atmosphere in the glass viewing box plummets. Goosebumps prickle at my skin in warning when Shadow stiffens beside me. I swear the guards standing close take a step toward me, ready to fucking grab me and beat me for my words.

"Would you like to join them down there, Journey? I could make it happen. Instead of dressing you like a doll and ensuring you're kept safe."

He raises a brow, noting my unmoving face. Do not allow this man to know how fucking terrified you are right now. Do not let him know you could probably piss yourself from his darkened expression alone. But it's more than that for me—it's the imprisonment that has my muscles freezing and my breaths stalling in my lungs. Unable to break free.

It's the fact he could hold me here for the rest of my life, drug me up, and force me to work for him, like my monster. Only I wouldn't be murdering people. I'd be satisfying them with beer and ass grabs—probably more.

Shadow steps toward me, curling his fingers into fists. "I could put you in a cage every night, feed you drugs to make you compliant, and then dress you in barely-there clothes for men to ooooh and ahhh over. Let them touch you. Let them do whatever they pay for..." He smirks when my face falls—no doubt paling at his words. And as much as I don't want them to, my fingers tremble. But I quickly hide them behind my back, take a breath, and ground myself with happier memories.

Or, at least, I try.

Memories of my experience in the cage come to the front of my mind. Replaying repeatedly until I'm shivering where I stand. I can play it off as being cold. Considering this dress is barely-there and thin.

I swallow the lump in my throat, dreaming of the violin that once settled my aching bones in my prison. The melodies sang to me to sleep, eradicating my day's anxiety. And it was all Jericho. If I could watch him play again. See him in action. Maybe I'd feel more settled.

Seeing Arrow and Jericho together is more like it. Just having them all by my side, knowing they were safe, instead of the unknown. That's what kills me. I don't know if they're at their cabin. They briefly mentioned if things went sideways. If they have each other to fight, whatever the hell, we will have to fight. Then, that's all that matters.

But it still makes me sick to my damn stomach.

"I'm just trying to make sense of it all," I say with a shrug, returning to the conversation. My heart rate slows, and I force myself to stop the memories from flashing by. "I don't care." I do, though. And it's probably something he can sense. "Seems like a hell of an operation." That's an understatement.

"Even living in the shadows, I have to make a living. Why not steal spoiled brats and see if their parents will pay the ransom? Those girls down there are paying off the money their parents owe me." He's smug about it. Almost fucking proud he's ruined girl's lives.

Owe him? Seriously? What delusions does he live in? Oh, yeah. His own. Because he's delusional as hell and belongs six-feet-deep. I swear to God, one day, Shadow will be nothing more than a horrid memory. For now, though, we have to survive somehow.

"Interesting," I hum, gazing at the fight below. "And have they not paid, then?" If they're still here, that must mean their parents haven't given in to the demands for money.

Shadow smirks, puffing out his chest. "Oh, they paid. They eventually leave." Yeah, I bet in a body bag or floating in the ocean.

My fists curl. So, I focus on the other women battling it out with their swords. Blood pours from one's head while the other screams, throwing her heavy sword around until it hits her opponent again, slicing through her flesh and sending her to her knees. She cries out. The pain in her voice is evident as they both catch their breath.

The crowd goes fucking wild, calling for one of their deaths. They stand. Stomp. And fucking cheer so loudly my ears ring from the force of it.

"They stole from me," Shadow says smugly, gesturing to the two girls in the ring.

"Stole from you?" Mikhail asks, standing by Shadow and watching the show blankly.

Shadow grins. "I promised them freedom if they fought. Well, one of them. It's a fight to the death."

"And are you truly granting the other one freedom?" Mikhail asks, tilting his head as a woman falls to her knees, crying out when her arm flops beside her—severed from the elbow down.

I blink several times. Is this what I looked like in Shadow's eyes when I severed the man's dick to reclaim my life? Probably. It's gruesome and puke-inducing. It has my stomach turning and nightmares flaring to life. I have spent the past five years immersed in violence, blood, and death.

And it doesn't look like it will change any time soon. Considering I'm married to the damn heir of Briar Cove.

Shadow chuckles. "They'll never be free. She'll return to her prison, begging for another chance. But I don't give second chances." His eyes slide to me. I feel it burning into the back of my skull in warning.

We're distracted by the sound of a sword penetrating through the chest of the woman who was once on top. The blonde-haired girl rises from the ground with blood pouring from her missing arm as she twists the weapon in the other woman's chest, screaming her victory. She raises her intact arm, agony written all over her face as she faces the crowd with pleading eyes. She immediately looks up at Shadow, pleading with him to help her.

"Are you going to help her?" It's a miracle my voice doesn't come out shriller, but I remain neutral.

"Eh, she can wait." She really can't. She's already collapsed to her knees again, paler than usual. The pain is taking over and the blood loss, too. She doesn't have time to wait. But maybe death is better than having to go back to her prison.

The rest of us don't bother speaking when he takes out his phone and quickly types out a message. She passes out in the ring just in time for his guards to pull her and the dead body out.

"Will she live?" Mikhail asks with curiosity, watching the entire exchange with a spark in his eyes.

"Does it matter?" Shadow asks with a shrug. "It's just one more thing I don't have to worry about. They'll try to stop the bleeding. Then she'll go back to her cell."

"This is quite the entertainment you have set up. Who are all these men in the stands?" Mikhail gestures to the rowdy crowd, excitedly shouting as two more people enter the ring. Men this time. Without any weapons.

Shadow tucks his phone away and grins. "These are my people. Some stay with me. Some stay wherever they want and come back for their duties. I provide them with this, and they provide me with their loyalties." He holds his arms out wide like a king addressing his people.

"Interesting tactics," Mikhail says, rubbing his chin.

"You're the big man in charge now. You might take some notes." Shadow's smugness will get him nothing but payback from Mik, which I can see hanging in his eyes.

"I'll keep that in mind. Although, I have a few tricks up my sleeve."

"And you think grown men will listen to a kid?" Shadow chuckles. "You've got a lot to learn about this life." He slaps

Mikhail on the shoulder several times, which seems to be the biggest mistake of his life.

Mikhail's face darkens when he takes Shadow's hand, removing it from his shoulder with disdain. He pulls Shadow's pointer finger back, almost to the point of breaking it.

"My suggestion to you would be that you never touch me like that again," Mikhail says in a low voice, inching closer to Shadow, who hasn't moved a muscle. "I'm respecting you because I'm a guest, and your hospitality has been excellent, but don't mistake my respect and kindness toward you for weakness." He raises his brow, pulling the finger back a little more. "Are we in agreement?"

Shadow stares at Mik without emotion. "Of course," he says in a cheery tone. "There's no need for this." He gestures to his hand, still held captive.

Mikhail gently releases his hand and finger with a nod. "As long as I'm understood, our agreement still stands."

"It does," Shadow says, taking his hand back and putting it in his pocket. "Besides, what kind of guy would I be to separate a husband and wife?" He grins in Mik's direction, earning a smirk.

"It would be the gravest mistake you ever make," Mikhail says, taking a step back. "Now, if you don't mind, my wife and I want to retire to our room." He holds a hand to Sunny, who stares wide-eyed between the two. "And we'll see you in the morning when we embark into the city by boat."

Shadow doesn't say a word to them as they take their leave. A few guards follow Mikhail out, accompanying them through the door and out to the hotel.

"Tomorrow, we leave for Briar Cove for Elias' wedding. I want you to watch Mikhail and Elias while we're there." Shadow's eyes find mine, and I nod. "I'll give you a task. Don't fuck it up."

"That's what I'm here for, right?"

Shadow grinds his teeth, nodding. "That little shit would be dead, too, if it wasn't for the deal we made."

"And what kind of deal did you make with him?" I ask, desperate to know more about what my sister is getting into.

"I don't give second fucking chances. This is your only chance to stay on my good side. Or you'll be just like them down there, walking the stands. And him?" He smirks, turning on his heel to stare Shepp down. "I'll take every fucking body part, one at a time. You fuck up, Journey West, I'll fuck him up. And I know how much you love him." He gives me the coldest look possible, sending shivers down my spine. He doesn't even look human right now. No, he's a damn demon spitting his threats. "Now, get the fuck out of my sight. Maybe a night in the fucking caves will convince you two to be good little soldiers." He waves a hand as two guards enter the room. "Put them in separate rooms."

My heart rate spikes when one grabs me by the upper arm, dragging me away from Shepp, who remains seated on the bench, staring up at his father with a bitter expression. The Shepp I know and love retreated the moment we were stuck in a small room with the man who made his life hell.

My only reprieve is knowing that tomorrow, the two of us will accompany Shadow to Briar Cove.

And then, no matter how much it fucking hurts me, we'll leave the wedding and find a hiding place. Something we haven't truly discussed yet.

CHAPTER THIRTY-TWO

Shepp

EVERY INSTINCT INSIDE OF ME SCREAMS. MY MUSCLES TENSE, tightening with every step she takes away from me.

My Little Tempest.

A guard, who has a death wish, grabs tightly to her upper arm, dragging her from the small viewing box above the finished fight. Fresh blood soaks into the dirt of the pit, splattered everywhere from the carnage. The men in the audience cheer loudly, shaking the box with their noise.

My ears ring from the rage brewing inside me. My fingers curl into fists, ready to aim at Shadow's head and take back my girl.

My stomach twists into knots at the silent fear in Journey's eyes when she gazes at me with a blank expression.

"Maybe a night in the caves will teach you. Alone."

I want to reach out and grab her arms, hold her close, and kill anyone who dares to put their hands on her. I'll channel my inner Arrow, chop off the guard's fingers for bruising her skin, and offer them to her as gifts.

Even if the thought of blood makes my stomach turn more. What's worse, though?

There's nothing I can do.

I can't save her from her fate of going into the caves. Or jump and kill everyone in this room.

I can't. They'll stop me before I can even lift a finger.

I was born and bled into the Viotto Crime family, where I was taught that all my instincts must be fought against. Be different. Learn to smile politely when addressed, but never flinch if a gun is pointed at your head. Don't show your fears or weaknesses to the enemy. This is one of those moments where I'm helpless in the face of danger.

My limbs lock up, paralyzing every inch of me. Even if I wanted to, I couldn't move. Not with Shadow's eyes blazing a hole straight through me. He's testing me. Seeing if I'll go against his orders and chase after the girl who holds my heart so he can punish me, too.

I won't.

I can't.

He'll kill me before I move. Probably her, too.

We're not a necessity to him. We're expendable. Sunshine was. She was his pawn to move around on the board. We're simply the spares he has to put up with.

I lock my muscles in place, holding eye contact with her. Hoping my gaze says all the things my lips can't. *You'll be okay. I'll make sure we're safe. I'll do everything in my power to get back to you.*

Journey's gaze pleads with me not to put up a fight. Almost saying not to worry about her. Despite the fear swirling in her moss-green eyes, she remains composed. Emotionless. Well, as composed as she can. My upbringing taught me to read people. Watch their movements and tics. I've used it many times to help my brothers on missions. And right now? My girl is screaming on the inside. A slight tremor works through her jaw, tightening when all the emotions bleeding through her eyes cease to exist.

Her darkness. It comes over her, stealing away her emotions. An after-effect of her monster's teachings. A necessity for her to live. Something she and I, as well as the rest of us, have in common.

My expression stays impassive when I catch Journey's gaze one last time before the shadows swallow her whole, and she's out of my sight—slipped out the door with the guard practically dragging her by the arm toward the exit.

A little piece of me chips away. A feeling of separation hits me in the chest as I shatter internally.

"Get up, boy. You're with me," Shadow demands, grabbing me by the arm and pulling me to my feet.

I don't respond. I nod when I face him, staring deep into his unmerciful eyes. True evil lives there, deep within him. Always exposing his true nature. He's never tried to hide it from me. Or my mother. Letting alcohol fuel his rage every night during dinner.

Shadow smirks. "We've got business to attend to. Be a compliant little shit, and I'll let you stay in your comfy bed. Defy me? You'll get reacquainted with the caves just like your little girlfriend. Alone, this time." He levels me with a look. "Fuck with me, and I kill her." I know by the tone of his voice that he means it. He'll murder Journey in a heartbeat to fuck with me.

I nod in agreement, with my heart pounding in my ears, following my father through the raging crowd of the pit. Despite the fights having stopped and blood being shed, they continue to drink, shout, and fight. It's pure fucking chaos. As Shadow passes through, they move out of his way with shouts of joy and grins.

They fucking love it here.

"Keep up, boy," Shadow grunts, hurrying toward the elevators in the hotel's main lobby.

Once inside, he hits the button and exposes the secret pad. Unlike when Darrell brought me here, Shadow steps in front of the keypad, blocking my view of the code. Too bad I'll never forget what his guard inadvertently showed me. On purpose? Possibly. I'm still trying to figure Darrell out. There seems to be another side of him I haven't unraveled yet. The elevator sinks lower, taking us to the dingy lower level, and we step out into the dim hallway.

Shadow stops, running a hand over his jawline, deep in thought. "You're going to assist me in taking out the trash." He raises a brow, looking me over. "Someone attempted to pull one over on me." A grin spreads across his lips. "And now it's time for retribution."

I nod again in response, knowing I could write several questions on my pad of paper. But he wouldn't bother with an answer. Shadow has always kept me on a need-to-know basis, even as a young child. I either follow his commands without questions or get punched in the face for having the courage to speak out against him.

And he stole my voice the last time I spoke up against him.

"Are you with me, boy? Ready to make them bleed for what they've taken from me?" He eyes me up and down when I nod again, attempting to relax my muscles.

I am a product of what he wanted—a silent boy who can't speak up for himself or defend himself, a dummy doing his bidding without questioning his motives.

"Then let's get this show on the road." He doesn't peer back when we march down the long hall past his open office. He doesn't seem to lock. Something I'll remember for later when I get the chance to snoop.

Something about it calls to me, begging me to rifle through it and find out what he's hiding there. I'll get my opportunity soon. I know he's leaving tomorrow for the damn wedding and no doubt leaving me behind. I feel it in my damn bones. He made that clear when he separated us. Hopefully, Journey will take the chance to escape while in Briar Cove.

I shake my head, stopping my thoughts from wandering, and follow Shadow down the long, dim corridor. The further we get, the more the wallpaper peels away, and mold grows in certain areas. It's such a contrast to the beautiful oasis he's built on the upper floors. It makes me wonder why such care wasn't put into this part. I can only guess he never wants people to see the lower lever. So, he keeps it shabby and hidden like his office, which I'm sure is full of telling goodies I need to get my hands on.

At the end of the long hallway, it opens into a large ballroom with vaulted ceilings and columns. Weathered from the environment, a lone velvet chair sits near the wall, looking at the immense space.

"This used to be a fancy conference center for the elite. They held their live streams here," Shadow says, finally stopping in what seems like an old ballroom, fit with chandeliers and tall ceilings. It's a wonder it's down here and not on the main level.

Live streams? What the fuck kind of elite are these people?

"I can see it on your face. Live streams. You're wondering what they did in the darkness of this basement." He grins sadistically. "You see, the elite owners of this island used to take people for entertainment and live-stream their misery to paying customers. Polls would go up, and they'd auction off their torture." I swallow the bile rising in my throat. "It's just a shame the feds caught up to them. We could have all lived in harmony." He hums the last part, stroking his chin like he's thinking of starting it up again. It wouldn't surprise me in the least. If it brought this great elite society the big bucks, my father would be invested.

"All right, onto the good part." He grabs my upper arm again, forcefully leading me into a small room. "There he is." He gestures to one lone male strapped to the ceiling by ropes with his eyes covered. His half-nude body shivers, sagging against the restraints. His blond, shaggy hair sticks to his forehead as sweat encases his flesh.

"Hello again, Agent." My back stiffens when Shadow marches forward, ripping the blindfold off the man's malnourished face. His eyes squeeze shut, slowly blinking open to glare at my father with disdain. Same, buddy. Same. "I've brought back up this time." He gestures to me with a sadistic grin. "Care to have a chat?"

The agent blinks a few times, looking around the dimly lit room and taking it in. His brows furrow with confusion as they volley back and forth, committing the room to memory. Has he been subjected to the caves this entire time? Judging by the sickly pale skin and sunken eyes, I'd hazard a guess that the caves have been his home since the boat blew up and he was captured. His gaze burns through me as he takes me in. Questions sparkle in his dim eyes. Almost like recognition. But he doesn't speak to either of us, simply shutting down. His lips roll in, and he sighs heavily, relaxing every inch of his body.

"Would you like to share with Shepp your backstory since you won't share it with me?" Shadow smirks, folding his arms over his chest.

The agent doesn't budge, even when Shadow throws his fist into his gut. The only sound that leaves him is the air in his lungs, expelling out of his mouth as a gasp.

"Oh, I see. We're still the strong, silent type, huh? Never mind that," Shadow hums, waltzing toward a cart in the room's corner, lined with small torture devices. He picks a small knife up, holding it to the dim light, and nods. "He hasn't spoken a word, son. He seems to think he can suffer here in silence and die without telling me who he is and why he's at my home." Shadow pulls something else from the tray and throws it at me with a snarl. "But by looking at his badge, you can tell exactly who he is and where he came from. The only question is, who the fuck is Veritas?"

My heart drops into my ass when I focus on the badge, unable to peel my eyes away from the name stamped into the shiny metal. Veritas. Agent 10. I know what this means. All because of Olivia. I'll keep it that way if he doesn't know who Veritas is.

It's the organization Olivia is a part of. She's an agent. He's an agent. The question stands, though. Why is he here? Is he a damn spy sent by the organization to watch Shadow? Grab Journey and me? But how does my father not know about Veritas? They appear to be a super underground government agency that only emerges when our three-letter organizations can't catch the bad guys. I've heard the stories from Liv. How they swoop in and do whatever is necessary. Whatever it takes. Then, they take the people to some island prison that's almost impossible to escape from.

I shake myself from my stupor and pull my notebook from my pocket. Quickly, I write a note, holding it up to Shadow, who scoffs at me. He wants to tell me to use my voice again, but he doesn't. Maybe he's finally come to terms with what he did to me by taking my tongue in his drunken stupor.

'Where did he come from?'

"The boat," Shadow says through gritted teeth. "This Veritas person thought they could sneak up on my island and stake it out." I stiffen.

The agent in question watches Shadow pace back and forth with the knife in his hand, ready to stab him at any time.

"I want answers. And you're going to help me," Shadow growls, turning on his heels to eye me. "You're going to use this and cut when and how I say."

Another challenge. He's testing my loyalty to him and his gang.

"If you do this and do it well, I won't harm your precious Journey. She's in the caves, sitting in the dark and wondering what you're doing. So, what will it be? Some stranger over her? Or..." he trails off with a grin when I shove the badge of the Veritas agent into my pocket to keep for later. As much as I don't want to participate, I have to. And if this agent dies under my father's watch, then someone, somewhere, will look for him.

I told Journey before. I'm not a hero, but a villain. And today, for her, I will live up to that label. This agent has done nothing to me. Not directly. Shit, Liv could have sent him to retrieve us. I'm sure after whatever Jericho and Arrow went through, they met up at the cabin and then went to her for help.

Stepping up, I grip the small knife from my father tightly. I swallow the bile in my throat and settle my brain, which urges me to run in the opposite direction. I hate this. Having to slice into someone's flesh to get them to open their mouths has never been my intimidation tactic. I'm not Arrow or Jericho, who can handle this with ease.

I'm Sheppard Mondelli. A mafia man disgusted by the sight of blood.

"We've been through this before, Agent. Who sent you? Why? And where'd you come from?" My father paces, putting his hands behind his back.

The agent's tired eyes volley between us, finally landing on me. He blinks several times, showing off the deep blue of his eyes.

"I sent myself. You're a suspect in terrorist acts against humanity. And I came from your mom," the agent says sarcastically, smirking.

"You better start telling the truth," Shadow growls, gripping the man by the neck and squeezing. "Tell me everything I want, or I'll leave you here until you do. Cut his fucking cheek, son."

Cut his fucking cheek, son. Like I cut yours for defying me at every step. Cut him, son, like I cut out your tongue for speaking up against me and my ways. Cut him, son, like I used to when I snuck into your room after drinking myself sick and taking whatever I wanted.

Cut him.

Cut him!

My body tenses, stuck to the floor. Despite the look Shadow gives me when he finally stops pacing. Something shifts in his eyes—darkness swirling there, zoning in on me as I remain stuck in place with his words ping-ponging in my mind. Indecision takes me over. Do I? Don't I? I have no choice. To keep breathing for one more day so I can escape from this island with my life, I have to sacrifice my morals.

"Today, son! Fucking do it, or I'll call someone who can!" Angry spittle roars from his lips as he shouts at me, knocking me from my stupor. And I do it. I mark the agent with the small knife from the bottom of his left eye to the edge of his jaw. Instantly, it bleeds, sending waves of blood down his pale skin.

"Well, I didn't fucking think you had it in you, Sheppard." He almost sounds proud when he chuckles, clutching my shoulder tightly and squeezing. "Now, let's fucking start again. This time, I want a mark for every question that goes unanswered. Can you do that, boy? Can you make your father proud?"

I turn myself off at those words, muting everything around me until I'm a hollow husk of a man. It's something I learned to do as a kid under his assault. The beatings. The touching. I became anyone but myself, disappearing into the void.

We go round and round with the agent until he's completely passed out and bloodied with so many cuts, I don't know how he's still breathing. Luckily for him, I never went too deep. Only leaving superficial cuts that have bloodied his skin.

I stumble out of the room, covered in blood splatters. On my skin. On my clothes. It's everywhere, reminding me of what I was forced to do. Shadow continues to shout at the agent, who passed out. I press my fist to my lips, attempting to contain my sloshing stomach, and finally plopping onto the old velvet chair to regain myself. My lungs burn as I choke back breaths. My head falls back, clunking against the moldy wall. I wince, forcing myself to count the cracks in the ceiling. One. Two. Three. Repeatedly until my mind returns to a sense of calm. Or as calm as I can get after torturing someone for information.

But they're not here. I'm alone with the fucking devil, hell-bent on bending me to his vicious will. But I won't succumb.

My stomach twists and turns when I bring my hands to my face, gently wiping the wetness from it and coating my hands in blood. Red. It's everywhere on my flesh.

I almost killed him.

My stomach lurches.

After so many years of doing this, you'd think I would be accustomed to the blood and chaos. But I'm not. The hell my father put me through as a child has taken its toll on my mental health, constantly taking me back to those moments of abuse.

Soft footsteps approach from the space I vacated. Eager to leave the carnage I inflicted on an innocent man undeserving of my ire. As his steps get closer, I shut myself off. Turning all of my emotions into nothing but dust, leaving my feelings of rage, disgust, and desperation at the door.

"Well, color me impressed, son. You gave him a beating." Shadow emerges from the room, wiping his hands on a towel, looking pleased. For the first time in his life, he regards me with pride shining in his eyes. Like I've finally become the monster he was so eager to craft. "I knew you had it in you."

'But he didn't talk,' I write out with exasperation.

"Meh. You took the knife like a good boy and used it like I taught you. It was fun, besides if someone was so concerned about their little agent. Then they'd be here by now. They don't give two fucks about him." He's too cocky for his own good, which only means disaster is on the horizon.

Veritas is sneaky in its efforts against people.

'And you?' I write out, holding it up when I finally get to my shaky legs and stand tall. Almost eye to eye with him.

"I'm not fucking worried," he growls, throwing the bloodied towel on the ground. "What are they going to do? Storm my fucking island? They'll have a big goddamn surprise in store for them." A grin stretches his lips. "They won't make it past the barrier. Just like the last boat." He points to the room the agent is in with a shrug. "Now, let's leave this shitbag to stew in his fucking blood." He waltzes off, leaving me behind without a glance back, making his way to his office.

The light flicks on down the hall, lighting up the shitty carpet outside the room. My heart echoes in my ears when I peer back at the space we vacated. There's nothing more I can do without getting myself killed. Or Journey. Or Sunshine. Too many people I care about are in my father's crosshairs.

So, I drag my feet down the hall and stand in the light of his room, taking it all in. He sits in his chair, rifling through a million pieces of paper. I'm mesmerized by his movements, sucked into the past we shared.

The heinous, ugly fucking hell he put me through for years. And now, I have to look him in the eyes and pretend his hands never touched me or his fists never hit me or my mom. I have to pretend he didn't force his five-year-old to stand in the corner of the room as he tortured someone for hours on end. Only then he didn't offer me the knife to help. He forced me to watch and take notes to be just like him.

"Stick with me, son. You'll live your greatest life here." He leans back, closing his eyes with a satisfied smile. Blood coats his clothes and skin, splattering across him. But he doesn't seem to mind. He's satisfied with what he's done.

Get fucked, asshole—is what I want to say. Instead, I nod, walking further into his office until I stand opposite him. My eyes scan the room, taking in its contents and committing them to memory.

His desk. The paintings on the walls. The trash in the corners. I plan to search through everything Shadow owns. No matter how long it takes, I'll find the answers I need— anything to help me get out of here safely with Journey.

If he's only taking Journey to the wedding, I'll use the opportunity to dig.

A sharp knock on the door pulls our attention to Darrell standing tall in the doorway with another burly man standing slightly behind him. "The Russians are vacating the island," he says with a scowl.

Shadow stops his movements and sighs. "Let them. We've agreed on paper. If they go back on their word, well, I'll show the Bratva what Shadow is capable of," he snorts. "Shall we see them off, son? Let Mikhail and his little army of counselors know we've got our eyes on them?" He doesn't bother waiting for me to nod or respond; he gets up, and I reluctantly follow him into the hallway.

He stops before the burly man I've never seen and discreetly nods at him. The burly man nods back, and they have a whole discussion without saying a word.

Shadow pats him on the shoulder before walking toward the elevators, with Darrell trailing behind us. But I don't miss the way Darrell eyes the other man as he disappears down the hall, coming from the room Shadow and I left the agent in.

Weird.

We make it up the elevator in relative silence. Darrell sneaks looks at me, furrowing his brows. Reminding me I still have blood splattered on my clothes and skin. I shrug it off, mentally ignoring the fact I'm covered in some agent's blood as we follow Shadow out of the elevator and converge in the lobby.

"Mikhail!" my father shouts out sharply, walking up to him with purpose. "Are you leaving my hospitality so soon?"

Mikhail offers him a soft smile, folding his hands in front of him. "As much as we have appreciated your hospitality, I must get my wife back home and tended to."

"Tended to?" Shadow asks, shifting his feet slightly.

It almost seems as if he cares.

"Yes. Tended to. My wife will receive a new heart within the week." Fuck. He's leaving with Sunshine before Journey has time to see them off.

They say actions speak louder than words; I believe it with Mik. I know Journey has reservations about him. Even after coming to terms with this is the best course of action for Sunshine. She's still too weary to trust anyone with Sunshine's health. Understandable. But he's proving his point.

"Within the week," Shadow whistles. "You move quickly."

"Indeed. Now, if you don't mind, I'd love to settle her in her new home before next Friday." Mikhail raises a no-nonsense brow, begging Shadow to question his motives.

"Of course," Shadow says, gritting his teeth. "You're all free to leave as you please. I certainly hope our contract is still intact."

Mikhail smiles, displaying all his teeth. "Of course. I wouldn't turn my back on a new ally who helped eradicate the world of my father." I eye the other council members standing behind Mikhail and take in the way they look down at Shadow, ready to cut him down if he makes one wrong move.

I wish they would. They'd save me the trouble.

"Sheppard," Mikhail says, breaking away from Shadow's glare. "It was a pleasure to meet you and Journey." His eyes travel around me. "Please send her my regards. It's such a shame she won't be able to say goodbye to her sister. Tell her how truly sorry I am for that." Mikhail shoves his hand into mine, squeezing it tightly. I don't react when a rough texture sits between our two hands, and he slips it into my grip without detection. "Take care, Sheppard." He nods at me.

I nod in response, immediately tucking my hand into my pocket while waving with the other. Mikhail watches my actions with a critical eye, nodding one last time before he turns his back to me.

All Mikhail's associates file out of the hotel, quietly heading toward the docks down a set of brightly lit stairs outside. One by one, they file down, successfully making it to several boats docked on the island.

"That little prick is up to something," Shadow growls, thrashing his arms about. "He's going to betray us. I fucking know it."

I watch through the darkened windows as the lights of their boats fade, no doubt heading to Briar Cove to get on a plane and leave the area for good. Good riddance, Mik. You better take care of Sunshine before Shadow figures out how to get his hands back on her. Because he will, I can tell he's already plotting through his rage.

They weren't supposed to leave yet. They were supposed to go to the wedding with all of us and celebrate the alliance with Elias.

"I want all their rooms checked over. Fuck. I don't have time for this shit," Shadow grunts. "I have to leave in the fucking morning." He cuts a glare to Darrell. "Make sure everyone does their fucking part. I need to have a little chat with my most prized prisoner."

I bristle at his words, turning to eye him. "This is how it's going to play out. You're going to be a good little boy and go to your fucking room. Darrell, escort him back. Lock him up. Tomorrow, you will stay there while your girlfriend and I take an important field trip to Elias' wedding. If she completes the task I give her, we'll return safely. If she doesn't. Well…" he trails off menacingly. "She'll fucking die. Then I'll come back and make your life a living fucking hell." Like he already has? Every second in his presence is a second in hell.

Task? What the fuck is he talking about? Stay here?

I realize then.

He separated us for good. For a reason. Giving her something to do at Elias' wedding on land. He's going to take her. Use her. And there's nothing I can do about it. Again.

I step forward to ask him questions, but Darrell puts a hand on my bicep, stopping my movements. I look back at him with questioning eyes. Discreetly, he shakes his head.

If he doesn't bring Journey back alive and safe, he will have a whole new problem.

Me.

The entire way back to my room, Darrell side-eyes me with a frown of disapproval. "Bloody night?" he grunts, looking me up and down with a critical eye, taking in the stains all over my body.

I nod. *'Something like that.'* I write it on my notepad, holding it up for him to see.

The memories of our assault against the silent agent play on repeat in my mind. He didn't beg or plead with us to stop. He took it. The look in the agent's eyes as I dug the knife into his flesh and wreaked havoc on him was crushing. I didn't want to. Not really. I wanted to run. Show my fear. But I stood firm in my father's eyes to prove my loyalty to him. To Journey. So we were protected from his rage. For whatever he had in store for us.

Shame fills me. Guilt tears through me. But I stop it all before it can infect me like a disease. I can't think like that. He was just another job. Another life to fuck with as we please. With Jericho and Arrow, we spend our time going after the bad people, taking down the lowlifes for the people of our town. Not that we haven't cut down someone who didn't directly deserve it. We have. For the Family. Always doing what we're told. But we knew if they were associated with the mafia, then they had done evil in their life.

The agent is innocent in a sense. He's working to clean up the nation of the worst of the worst. Or at least, I like to pretend he has. Maybe he is terrible, and that's why he's here. But I don't honestly know.

Fuck.

I'm part of the Devils of Briar Cove. The muscle of the group. The person our enemy hates to see slowly coming at them because they know Jericho and Arrow aren't far behind. They're the blood of the group—the takers—removing the seedy monsters of the world.

Shit. I miss my brothers. I miss Journey.

Darrell eyes me suspiciously again. His gaze burns straight

through me. But he says nothing further after dropping me off at my room.

"Same rules apply," he says, leveling me with a look. A look I can't figure out like unsaid words. "Tomorrow, you'll be free to roam. Shadow won't be here. It'll be a skeleton crew on the island." He raises his brows, leaning forward as if to say—now is your fucking chance to scope out his office.

And I'll take it.

Tomorrow, come Hell or high water; I'm breaking into that fucking office and finding my unanswered questions.

Our lives depend on it.

CHAPTER THIRTY-THREE

Journey

THE DARKNESS SINKS ALL AROUND ME, PULLING ME FURTHER into its grasp. Like so many times before, my nightmares come out to play, taunting me with the mistakes of my past. The screams. Cries. My monster's voice. They're all there to coax me into the darkness and fall into their trap of bullshit.

I hug my knees, shivering in the tiny dress they left me in. It does nothing to ward off the cold ground or walls, constantly pouring in the chill. My mind wanders to Shepp, wondering where the fuck he is and if he's okay.

He had better be. Or Shadow will feel the full extent of my wrath.

Murderous plots take hold in my mind the longer I squeeze my eyes shut, listening to the incessant drips of water coming from the corner of the room. It's like a torture device set up to drive me to the brink of my sanity. And it's fucking working. I put my hands over my ears, trying to block this entire thing out, but it doesn't work. If I had my music. My sleeping pills. Then, I'd be okay. My life revolved around those to get me to finally shut my eyes. And turn off my mind.

I wonder if I could stab Shadow the next time I see him. Would I get away? Probably not. Fuck. Why can't he die? Maybe a heart attack in his sleep? A little poison in his wine?

It's all doable now if nature would take its course and rid the world of his evil self.

I lie my head against the rough terrain of the cave wall. Occasionally, a rogue moan of pain echoes through my prison from somewhere down the long, dark hallway. My thoughts return to the woman who lost her arm in the fight yet still won. Is it her? Is she the one suffering in the dark with a wound that will probably kill her?

I squeeze my eyes shut. Whispered Words lyrics roll through my mind. Their melodies and lyrics are stamped in my memories forever. Whenever I'm down or need sleep, I can practically hear Kieran Knight's deep voice singing my favorite songs.

My breaths even out on the uncomfortable floor, and my mind fades into nothing. The darkness consumes me, taking me into dreamland.

At least for a little while.

I jolt awake when the squeak of the door opening pulls me from my frantic dreams. My heart pounds so hard, I swear it's about to jump out of my chest and leave me altogether. I lick my lips, pulling myself into the sitting position, never taking my eyes off the man approaching me.

Shadow waltzes in with his hands shoved in his pockets. A slight smirk plays on his lips when he crouches in front of me as I sit against the wall.

"Good, you're awake." He tilts his head. "We have things to discuss."

"What things?" I rasp, rubbing my upper arms, attempting to warm them up. Shivers roll through me when he watches me closely, noting the goosebumps dimpling across my flesh.

"Expectations on how this trip is going to go."

"Okay," I say, raising my chin defiantly.

He smiles. "We're going to go to this wedding. Just you and I. Mikhail fled with your sister. It seems he has trust issues. Of course, he has a funeral to put on." He clicks his tongue several times before the news truly sets in.

My stomach drops into my stomach when he purses his lips. My sister is gone, whisked away by the child mafia leader. I didn't get to say goodbye. Again. And now, I don't have a fucking clue where they are. Except he's in Miami. So, that tells me a lot. Not.

But wait. He said just him and I. So that means…

"No Shepp?" I ask, swallowing hard.

"Sheppard has some lessons to learn here. By himself. Without you meddling in what he's going to do."

No.

Fuck.

No.

Fingers grip my fucking frantic heart, bleeding me dry. He's going to separate us once and for all. Why he hasn't before, I don't have a clue. Why keep us together? All so he could rip us apart in the end.

Panic swarms my insides, a relentless tide threatening to drown me beneath the waves pulling me under. I sputter for oxygen, drowning in the knowledge of my sister and Shepp. It's all too much. Way too fucking soon. No doubt showing my panic on the outside. So, not my finest moments. My protective nature bubbles to the surface, aching to shield Shepp from the misery of his father and take my sister away from danger.

It's all too fucking much for me to handle.

Blasts of images from dinner flash through my mind. The visceral fear in his eyes every time his father beat the table with his fists. The stiffening of his muscles. Every flinch. It was all there, as plain as day. There's no way he can survive in this hellhole by himself. Not for much longer, anyway.

I lick my lips. Desperate and trembling. My mind races. A whirlwind of thoughts and half-formed plans, screaming for a way to keep us together. To prevent the separation that looms like a death sentence. Because that's what it would be. If he takes me away from Shepp, then more suffering will happen.

For both of us.

"What are you going to do to him?" I growl, staring directly into his beady eyes. Evil darkens his pupils. Giving him a demon-like appearance with no humanity present. "You better not fucking touch him—" I yelp when my head whips to the side, taking my body down with it. I smack into the cave floor, groaning at the pounding immediately taking over my forehead.

His fingers wrap around my throat, cinching tighter and tighter until he cuts off my oxygen, leaving me gaping like a fish out of water, begging to breathe.

I claw at him. Digging my fingernails into his flesh until blood trickles from his wounds and carves a path down his arms. He doesn't seem to notice, continuing to press away.

"Here's the thing, Journey. I don't give a fuck. Shepp is staying here for insurance. You'd never run from me, would you? I can still pull the trigger on every operation. Sunshine? Dead. Mikhail? Obliterated. Then, I'll save Sheppard for last. I'll tie him to a chair in the basement and remove the rest of his tongue. I'll take finger by finger for every second you're gone. Do not run from me at the wedding. No matter who is there." With every word, he jostles me, knocking the back of my head against the rough cave—my vision blurs. Dots dance before my eyes, on the brink of falling into the darkness.

Until he releases his fingers around my windpipe, giving me back the oxygen I need.

I gasp, sucking in the air, desperately trying to control myself. Tears spill down my cheeks, showing the weakness I've always kept at bay. I can practically hear my monster's words in the back of my mind, berating me for failing.

Stupid, stupid little emotional snake. Can't keep it together? I'll give you something to fucking cry about.

"Why bring me?" I choke out, clinging to the throbbing spot on my throat, attempting to soothe the pain.

"Why wouldn't I?" he asks, tilting his head. "You're needed there."

"But why?" I croak, desperate for answers. I need to know what I'm going up against when he drags me away from Shepp.

"For appearances," he growls, clenching his fists. "Jenni was your friend. Was she not?"

My breath stalls. Of course, she was my friend. I have many fond memories of our time together. We laughed. Joked. We watched movies and danced together. Hell, she even got me drunk. Okay, there were more than just a few evenings of drinks and bullshitting. Jenni made it her mission to corrupt me with booze. It's too bad the entirety of our friendship was built on a complete and utter lie. I was the spy who watched her and her father's every move so I could report it back to my monster.

Then, her father disappeared.

Her mother, too.

And it's all my fault—I think. I mean, I'm not positive about what happened to them. But I know she was alone before Elias kidnapped her back to his fortress on the other side of town to keep her safe.

Now, they're getting married in an elaborate ceremony in Briar Cove.

God. My guilt gnaws at me for what I've done in the past. I couldn't help it, though. And I couldn't stop what I had to do because of my sister. I had to keep her protected from this cruel world. It's funny how that doesn't matter anymore.

"I mean, yeah. But it was all fake." I'd never allude to how real my friendship felt with Jenni. Was I sent to her to spy? Yes. But in the end, I enjoyed her company.

"Mhhmm," he says, rubbing his chin, losing himself deep in thought. When he snaps back to our conversation, something strange takes over his darkened eyes, like all humanity has disappeared. "Your duty to me is to keep your eyes on Elias. Then I want you to put a knife through his heart."

I blink several times. The words ring through my head. I repeat what he said in my mind—a knife through his heart. Did he say what I think he did?

"Why kill him? Isn't he an ally? Someone who runs your drugs?"

"From now on, when I say jump—you ask how high. That's it. No explanations. You will take Elias out. He is finished. He has betrayed my trust and is a traitor to my empire, and I want him gone. Got it?"

The familiar darkness I've become accustomed to whirls in, replacing my frantically beating heart with a steady one. My mind focuses on the task, taking in his orders, attempting to look like a good little soldier. He's taken everything from me again. My sister has shipped off. Shepp is locked somewhere else. Now, I've been assigned the task of murdering Elias White.

Why is my life like this? Why am I always the one to do these things?

This wedding is going to be one epic shit show of me trying to work the room.

CHAPTER THIRTY-FOUR
Journey

YEAH. THIS IS GOING TO BE A SLOW FUCKING DEATH. Humiliating, too.

I scoff internally at the ridiculous dress clinging to my body. It's thin. Barely fucking there. I practically had to wear damn floss between my cheeks and tape my tits into this monstrosity. I look down at them with a frown. They've been so damn tender lately, like I'm about to start my period but haven't. It's probably the stress of this adventure forcing Mother Nature into hiding. Good thing I'd rather not have to deal with tampons and pads with Shadow. It was bad enough with Arrow, Shepp, and Jericho, especially when Arrow took me to the damn store.

It was mortifying. Yet, romantic in a way.

Shadow hums an ominous tune under his breath beside me, reeking of aftershave. I swear my stomach turns more from his fragrance than the task.

The limo Shadow forced me into after we got off the miserable boat—which, yeah, made me sicker than hell— comes to a slow stop. Right outside the luxurious hotel I've only dreamed about entering.

Well, on my own, anyway. I've been here a few times under pretenses, spying on whoever the hell Gabriel wanted me to watch. Senators? Yup! Done that. Other members of the Viotto Family? Definitely. They all come here to dine at the fancy restaurant attached and then hold meetings as they eat. They never suspected the new server was someone to be concerned with. Or a front desk clerk. Or a bellhop. I'm honestly not sure how I pulled it off. Fake it till you make it.

Like now.

God. I have to pretend I'm fine. Pretending is my strong suit. It's something I've done for years now. I should be used to it. But I'll never be comfortable wearing a mask twenty-four-seven, playing a part. The only people I didn't have to wear a mask with were Jericho, Shepp, and Arrow.

They accept me for the hot mess I am.

Sometimes, at least.

My eyes wander, peering through the tinted window. Being here, watching the bright spotlight's beam through the sky, and eyeing the people meandering in—makes me want to hurl again. Seriously, I don't understand what's going on with my stomach. It won't settle, even with crackers and soup. Well, if I had any, that is.

"You better not fucking puke in my presence. I know that's all you've been doing, but hold it back," Shadow snarks, shifting on the leather seat. When he leans forward, a fresh scent smacks me in the face, knocking me back.

Alcohol.

I wrinkle my nose, attempting not to breathe in his unholy scent. His entire combination has saliva pooling in my mouth and bile shooting up my throat.

What do men say to women all the time? Puke on him; that'll slow him down from attacking you. Right? I size him up. He's wearing some fancy suit. It's wrinkled, giving him the *I don't give a fuck* attitude. Wait, he probably doesn't give a fuck about this. Or anyone else. So, a little vomit might spruce up his appearance. It'll make him smell better, too.

"I won't puke if you sit back," I gag out, holding a hand over my lips.

Jesus. What is wrong with me? I swear someone laced his food with poison that's slowly destroying my insides. I'm dying. That's the only answer I can think of.

"You remember the rules?" He grunts, shifting back and taking his gross scent with him. His finger taps on his knee several times with impatience.

I want to cut it off and shove it down his throat until he's a choking mess. But instead, I'm a good little girl and nod.

"Of course." How could I forget? He practically beat it into me. Shepp's not here because he's my goddamn insurance.

Shadow is so convinced I'm going to run. I mean, I would have if Shepp were here. But now? I'm stuck doing this stupid job, putting a knife through Elias' heart. Will I do it? I'm not fucking sure at this point. They're all wicked men in my fucking book.

He smirks. "What a good little spy you are."

Replace the word spy with snake, and you have Monster 2.0.

Now, I am going to throw up.

"I won't be stupid." Maybe not this time. But I'll figure out how to steal a boat eventually and make my escape once and for all. It might take a little time and patience. That's all I got right now.

A door opens and slams shut near the front of the limo, leaving my nerves buzzing.

This is it. My time to shine. Or kill. Or whatever.

"That's right, you fucking won't be," he huffs, throwing the door open and nearly knocking over his driver, who has climbed out to open his door.

The driver doesn't flinch when he shuts Shadow's door. Doesn't offer him a dirty look for practically taking his dick off with the door. Nothing. He goes back to his door and gets in.

Well, so much for helping me.

I sigh when the door slowly opens. The night air rushes into the comfortable air-conditioned cabin, making sweat glisten on every inch of my skin. Shadow's ugly mug peeks in with a smarmy grin, looking me up and down like he didn't dress me up like a living, breathing Barbie Doll.

For fuck's sake.

Shadow holds out his arm expectantly. I dream of chopping it off like his finger, but refrain. Why does the universe hate me so much? Huh? Oh, well. I sigh, shaking off the self-loathing. I have enough of that inside of me to drown in.

Reluctantly, I grab it. On the outside, I look like the happiest person on the planet. For the cameras, of course. But on the inside, I want to recoil and slap his arm away. It's too bad he hasn't given me the weapon to take down Elias yet. Oh, the things I could do with a sharp knife right about now.

He thinks I'm going to murder him.

And he wouldn't be fucking wrong.

"Big happy smiles, Journey. You're here with me. I'm debuting my face for the entire world to see." The smuggest grin I've ever seen crosses his lips, and his chest puffs out. He thinks he's so damn important. But I'm going to show him otherwise. Later.

Shadow yanks me down onto the red carpet in front of the hotel. The camera crew works behind velvet red ropes, capturing everyone who enters the high-profile wedding with curiosity. Shadow waves to them with his free hand, smiling and attempting to be charismatic.

Fuck. I think it's working.

The people behind the cameras eat it up, following his every move. Reporters bombard us with shouted questions. Who are you? Are you excited about the bride and groom? They keep coming until Shadow pulls us to a stop at the hotel's doors. He turns us, angling us toward the camera and forcing me to plaster on a clenched smile.

"We're thrilled for the bride and groom!" he bellows with fake joy. "I am Shadow, and this is my lovely date. We're here to help my business partner celebrate his union with her best friend. It's an eventful evening."

Then, all hell breaks loose with the reporters. More yelling. More questions. God, he gave them exactly what they wanted —a newsworthy story. It's the unveiling of a damn villain. And he implicated me in it all. Wonderful.

Why are there even reporters here, anyway? It seems weird that some gang members are getting married and the local news is interested.

Highly fucking suspect, if you ask me.

Shadow yanks me into the hotel with little regard to how I'm faring in these stupid heels he pushed on my feet. I swear to God, I will give him a taste of his own medicine soon.

As soon as we enter the hotel, my breath leaves my lungs. Sure, I've been here before, taking in the people. But I've never had the chance to stop and look around. Elegance meets the eyes. Everywhere. Even on the outside of the massive limestone building. Marbled floors and countertops. Chandeliers illuminate the tall ceilings. A baby grand piano with a player behind it sits in the corner, offering guests a beautiful, tranquil melody.

"Remember what I fucking said," Shadow hisses, slowing his pace as we make our way through the grand lobby.

"Of course," I hum, staring daggers in his direction.

If he sees my death stare, he doesn't comment. He drags me toward a set of wooden doors near the back of the lobby with a sign that reads: Presidential Conference Suite. I nearly snort at the sight of the two big, burly security guards watching us approach. They remind me of Secret Service members with their black suits and sunglasses. What douchebags wear sunglasses inside, anyway?

"Invitations?" the man demands, holding out his hand.

I take it back. He doesn't look like a Secret Service man.

He reminds me of those guards who sit on top of horses and aren't allowed to speak to you, smile, or show emotion.

Shadow smiles more. Giving me the damn ick. Then, he retrieves the invitation tucked into his suit jacket and presents it to the guard with smug satisfaction. The guard looks at him up and down, then scans his invitation with a wand and hums.

"Shadow," he says, never changing his emotions. Although, if his douchey inside sunglasses were off, I'm sure I'd see that spark of recognition in his eyes. "It's nice to meet you, sir."

Ew. Of course, this guard is going to try and suck up to Shadow. All these people think he's some God or something. But he's just a twat who should have died three years ago.

"Yeah, yeah. Can we go in now?" He waves a hand impatiently.

The guard gives him a sharp nod of approval. "Of course, sir. Enjoy the festivities." He gestures to a small checkpoint. "But first, we'll have to ask you both to walk through the metal detector."

"Of course," Shadow says. "Precautions and all."

"Can never be too careful, sir." There's a bite in his voice as he narrows his eyes. It's like his Spidey senses are tingly. Rightfully fucking so. Shadow's entire persona screams, I'm about to do something illegal!

I don't know how he will pull off getting a weapon here. But somehow, when we waltz through the machine, it doesn't beep. Shadow nods at the security guard manning the metal detector. He looks at Shadow with awe and wide eyes while bobbing his head with a smirk.

Oh, I see. That's how he's getting a weapon in here. He just needed a little help from his pal manning the metal detector. How many other assholes does he have on his tab?

The solid wood doors open automatically when we step up to them. Shadow forcefully puts my hand back into the crook of his arm, and then we waltz forward in sync. He looks everywhere, dragging his gaze along every person standing in what looks like another lobby. My brows furrow. It's a carbon copy of the hotel lobby, except there is no front desk. It's miles and miles of marble flooring with fancy decorations. People stand in tight circles, whispering with bubbly drinks in their flutes. Men wear black suits with ties, and women wear fancy dresses that cover everything. Fuck. I look down at my dress, nearly sneering at myself. He dressed me like some hooker looking for a good time.

Whatever. I can't change that now. So, on to the more important questions.

"So, he's under your thumb, huh?" I question, keeping the irritation out of my voice. Half of me wanted someone to stop him and take his weapons before we could even enter the wedding. But he's way too prepared for this. My nerves prickle at that realization. If he's this prepared, then what else does this fucking monster have up his sleeves?

"You're a mighty observant gnat, aren't you?" he spits, walking faster with me in tow.

"Well, I learned from the best." I shrug.

"Is that what Gabriel taught you?" He side-eyes me with his brows raised.

"Gabriel taught me many things, but people-watching was my number one skill." But that's why I'm here, isn't it? He wants to use my skills and everything to get what he wants.

"So a murderer and a good read on people, good to know," he says when we stop behind a small line of people waiting to enter the room.

Step by step, we slowly inch into the wedding hall. Excitement hums through me for an entirely different reason besides murder. It's for Jenni. I haven't seen her in weeks. I haven't seen her since I completed my mission, and Elias rescued Jenni and took her away.

People pack several rows of decorated chairs, fit for a wedding for a damn queen. My eyes scan all the faces, not seeing anyone familiar. Whoever they are, they're pumped to witness Elias and Jenni's union. Their smiles light up the damn room.

"Let's find our seat, shall we?"

CHAPTER THIRTY-FIVE

Journey

THE CHILLY AIR SENDS GOOSEBUMPS DOWN MY SPINE WHEN WE settle into the hard chairs of the large wedding venue. Shadow's presence looms over mine when he sits beside me, scanning the crowd with his beady eyes.

I swear to God, he's up to something. Besides murder, of course. It feels like whatever he's tasked me to do will be child's play compared to what he's got up his sleeve.

I blow out a breath, trying to center myself. Mentally, I'm spiraling down the drain in anticipation. What will he do? Will I have to end Elias tonight?

"We will post guards at every entrance to ensure the couple's safety." He smirks, toying with something inside his suit jacket. "That also means I'll know if you make a run for it. Elias may think he's in charge of a lot, but he's not really. I am the most important man in this room."

Jesus Christ. Can someone say narcissist? He thinks highly of himself. His empire will fall one day, and I can't wait to watch it burn.

I keep my eyes ahead at the people chatting with each other in their seats. True to his word, guards are posted at every emergency exit with guns holstered to their hips. Their beady eyes constantly scan the crowds, looking for anyone with ill intent.

Well, you're looking at her. Apparently.

"When the time is right," Shadow hums, leaning back like he doesn't have a care in the world. "Then you'll strike. What did Gabriel call you? His little snake?" he smirks at me, eyeing how my muscles tighten at the sound of that word. Snake. I fucking hate that term.

"And how would you know that if Gabriel doesn't have a clue you're still alive?" I hiss through gritted teeth, getting sick and tired of his attitude lately.

"Because that's what I do. I'm a fucking shadow. I collect information about everyone. Especially you. You were the one who propelled me into what I am. So have a little fucking gratitude because I could have killed you on sight. But I spared you. So, you owe me. A lot." He glares discreetly in my direction before smoothing out his face.

I open my mouth to defend myself but think better of it. He will use anything I say against me or store it in his mind. Whatever. Besides, the lights dim above the guests' seats when I lean in to tell him off.

Everyone around us hushes. People take their seats everywhere. The atmosphere seems to shift the moment the flower girl and ring bearer come toddling down the aisle, tossing the flowers, and gripping the pillow with rings.

An odd emotion takes me over at the sight of the two small children together. They look so happy. Free, even. Just by walking down the aisle in celebration of two people getting married. They probably don't understand what's happening and only do as they are told.

I swear my Grinch heart swells two sizes too big, threatening to jump out of my fucking chest. But I don't understand the feeling. Why am I getting slightly choked up? Or even jealous when the bridesmaids appear in dull pink dresses and sweep the floor as they walk beside the groomsmen.

Cheer. Utter fucking joy sweeps through the venue.

Everyone feels it in the seats as they swipe away the moisture from their eyes.

And then Jenni makes her grand appearance and takes my breath away again in her elegant gown.

I wish I could have helped her plan this, done her hair, or straightened up her makeup.

But I was a traitor instead.

If I could speak to her, I could explain that I only protected my little sister. I never intended to hurt her or her parents or whatever.

Jenni smiles so widely as Elias clings to her side protectively. Lovingly. Instead of standing at the altar waiting for her like normal grooms, he walks her down the aisle with pride puffing out his chest and happiness wafting off him. He probably would have done the honors if her father were still here.

But I killed him with my spying.

I've never seen two people so happy and in love with each other.

It makes me miss them more than anything.

Jericho. Arrow. And even Shepp, despite seeing him yesterday. My heart yearns to hold his hand again. To make sure he's okay after a night spent apart.

I desperately miss the boys so obsessed with me they forced me into their home, chased me through the woods in the pouring rain, and made promises I knew they couldn't keep.

Right now, my safety is at risk. I'm in the midst of bullshit with Shadow, who so cleverly left Shepp behind when we intended to run. Since Mikhail left with Sunny, disappearing into the sunset without an address or phone number, I'm at a loss.

Everything keeps falling apart, taking piece after piece from me. Soon, there won't be a Journey left behind. Just a mass of swirling darkness in my place. Cold and lifeless, devoid of anything but murder on the mind. The girl my monster wanted to shape me into being—his perfect weapon.

I don't want it to happen.

I want the light left in me to shine through and overtake the monstrous creation hiding deep in my soul. One day, I won't come back from the gnawing numbness it leaves behind.

Jenni's red hair curls down her back, bouncing with every small step she takes. The material of her dress swishes with every movement. Her smile grows wider when they finally stand hand in hand before the priest in front of the altar.

Love oozes off them.

I melt into my seat, wondering if Jericho could love me like Elias does Jenni.

Then I remember how he used to look at me when he thought no one was looking. Pure devotion and obsession flowed through his gaze, giving me the answer to my question. Given the opportunity, he could love me like that.

They exchange their vows, not bothering to draw out the ceremony any further than necessary. Watching the two of them join hands as the priest announces they're husband and wife has tears forming in my eyes, and I clap with everyone else.

Will I ever get that? Will I get the family I've always wanted with the boys? I've longed for something normal. Or what society deems as normal. A husband and wife living in harmony, navigating through life with one another. My story would never truly be like that. I'd never get the white picket fence or the actual wedding.

Because I'm already married. Legally, at least.

It's another thing a man took from me before I could give my consent.

Do I want to be married? Yes. In the future, of course. To Jericho? Well, the jury is still out. I know, in my gut, he did what he thought was necessary. It was to protect me and the inheritance I did not know about. So we could move the money to a secure bank out of Gabriel's hands. That didn't seem to work, though. I gave Gabriel every piece of ammunition he needed to take it all away from me. Just like Jericho said I would. He knew exactly what I would do when faced with danger against my Sunshine's life.

I could have done great things with the money in the future and donated to women's shelters—hell, I could have opened my own for women, children, and even men in need. I could have donated to drug rehab facilities, giving everyone a chance to get away from harmful drugs without the worry of the cost. My ultimate dream would be to help others who can't seem to help themselves.

Like my mother. Like me.

As Elias and Jenni walk down the aisle hand in hand again, I stiffen. Jenni's eyes bug out of her head when she sees me sitting in the crowd. The joy she feels doesn't slip off her face. In fact, her grin widens even further. Confusion hits me hard, but I offer her a smile as I wipe the tears from my cheeks. Is she not upset with me? Does she not hate me?

"If you would all join us across the way, we will start the reception. If you are here for favors, I will gladly receive you when the time is right and honor the tradition." Elias looks around the room with a foreboding presence. "Until then, please join me and my wife after our pictures have commenced." Elias waves a hand, leading Jenni away. Several guards surround them as they walk out of the ceremony room and on their way to have their professional pictures done.

Shadow's gaze inspects the area around us as people leave the room—no doubt following Elias' instructions. I sit patiently, taking in every face that passes, memorizing the tears in their eyes and smiles on their faces. Are they her family? His? Are they truly happy that they've come to witness this today?

I know I am.

"When the time comes, you're going to ask Elias for a favor," Shadow says, not bothering to look at me as he makes his unruly demands.

"And what kind of favor will I be asking?" I do the same, keeping my gaze on the now-empty room. All the applause and joy instantly evaporated when the others left the premises, taking it with them, leaving me to sit in the heaviness of the room beside Shadow.

"Such an archaic thing, isn't it? The head of an organization granting favors and forgiveness for wrongdoings," Shadow hums in his untrustworthy musings, digging into his suit jacket.

He's worse than my damn monster when it comes to his cryptic ways.

"I guess. Isn't this more of a mafia thing, though?" I eye the small pocket knife nestled in Shadow's grip. It's so tiny I wonder how he's expecting me to take someone down with it.

Shadow snorts, tossing the knife into my lap carelessly. Good thing it's folded down and not poking out. "Something like that. But remember. I have my eyes on you." Abruptly, he gets up from his chair and straightens out his suit. "Now, I have meetings of my own. People to see. Friends to make. Be a good girl and Shepp won't get hurt." A cruel smile passes over his lips. "If he hasn't been already," he hums, stepping away from me until the room is empty.

It's just me, my broken fucking heart, and the task he's given me.

Not that I'm going to do it. But I need time to come up with a plan. I can't kill Elias. He hasn't done anything to me. Besides, he's the one who got Jenni out of the arranged marriage and brought her here for a safer life.

Well, as safe as she can get with a gang leader.

I eye the tiny pocket knife cautiously before tucking it into my dress beneath my right boob. Thankfully, they're taped in and not moving, so the knife can snuggly stay there without being obvious. I hope at least.

I sigh softly, moving around the ceremony room easily, eyeing the decorations with envy. Beautiful flowers decorate almost every inch of the room. Jenni's touch, I can tell. She one hundred percent had a hand in making all this happen. It's her flare for expensive things, but it's done wonderfully.

I stand in the middle of the aisle, looking over my shoulder at the room. A stray voice here and there floats through the air from the party, cranking up to full volume across the way. People hoot and holler, chanting Jenni and Elias' names on repeat. Warmth spreads through me, envisioning their happiness on display like it was here. I can even feel the touches of love standing where they stood under the flower archway at the end of the aisle. Leaning back, I stare at the colorful flowers decorating the arch and gently run my fingers over the beautiful petals. I pluck a pink one, bringing it between my fingers and gently rubbing it.

I get lost in the feeling of it—the atmosphere. Everything ceases to exist around me. My mind tumbles through the trenches of darkness, trying to resurface from the depths of what I need to do, and killing Elias is not at the top of my list —speaking to him, yes. But killing? No. Maybe he and Jenni can help me get Shepp off the island. Fuck. Any way I look at it, there's no way I can leave him stranded there. Shadow said himself—there was no way to leave the island without dying, and the boat ride over here was a miserable hour-plus ride through the rough ocean waters. Who knew I could get so damn seasick? Not me.

Heat envelops my back, blanketing me with a familiar warmth. It's like diving into familiar sheets and snuggling down for a good night of sleep. It's home without the four walls. The smell you rejoice in the moment you walk in the door with a serene smile.

I sag into the embrace. Recognizing the pair of arms immediately. The same arms that have wrapped around me before in a loving embrace. Well, as loving as he can get. More like obsessive arms. I'd run away if I were a normal person. But I'm beyond that, even when his large, calloused hand wraps around my lips, stopping my complaints.

Because I have a lot of those, and if they're here, they'll listen to every word I say.

A hardened body presses into my trembling one from the front. Silence engulfs us like a bubble. We soak it up, embracing our small moment together before chaos ensues. It ticks by slowly—second by second, minute by minute.

I'm almost certain I'm hallucinating. Am I so desperate to have them back that my mind is cruelly tricking me?

Moisture pools in my eyes when Jericho stands before me with a pensive expression, taking every inch of me in with his calculated stare. I stare back, taking him in, waiting for him to speak. Dark bags droop beneath his weary eyes, aging him ten years. Exhaustion shines through his stare, but he relaxes in my presence.

What the hell have they been through since I was taken?

Jericho gazes around the room. "I promise I'll give you this one day. More extravagant than this. Whatever your heart desires, I'll provide. Always."

Always?

I shudder when his words slither through me. Promises fill his vision, and I'm helpless to look away. Stuck in his hypnotic gaze. Fire brews there. Determination grips him hard when he steps up to me, peeling—who I can only assume is—Arrow's hand from my lips. I suck in a rough breath, shuddering when his eyes fall to my lips. A deep hunger twists his face. With every breath I take, he watches me with an intensity that sets me on fire. Without another word, he dives in. Ruthlessly taking what he wants. With every swipe of his tongue against mine, he steals more pieces of me.

My breaths. Soul. Sanity.

Every fucking thing.

And I let him.

I lap it up and swallow it down.

A moan slips from between my lips as I leave everything behind. My fingers clutch his suit jacket, forcing him closer until I'm the meat in the sandwich. I forget it all. Losing myself in the sensations of Jericho and Arrow.

Jericho's lips journey down my jaw, nipping away at my flesh. My chest heaves as he marks me as his. And fuck. I want him to. I want him to fucking take me right here in the open, under the flowers and opulence. Anyone could walk in and see who owns me, mind, body, and soul.

The Devils.

My Devils.

Arrow's irritated voice filters through the fog permeating my consciousness. Rough hands work over me. My breasts. Squeezing them into oblivion until wetness coats my panties. Arrow grunts in my ear with possession.

"Mine. Mine. Mine. Kitten, don't you ever fucking leave me again." His lips suck on my neck. Opposite of Jericho. Marking me as his, too. "Never fucking leave me again. I'll handcuff you to me if I have to," he murmurs more, going on and on about keeping me close.

But I don't mind.

I melt into them, wishing we could continue this forever. But Arrow has other plans. Jericho's lips leave mine with a grunt. I peel my eyes open reluctantly, looking up at the towering man with swollen lips and vengeance in his gaze. His fingers curl at his sides, making fists. Ready to pounce on Arrow as he takes a step back with me in his arms, putting distance between the three of us.

"Arrow," Jericho says, raising a brow.

"You're being selfish. As always," Arrow snarks, poking a finger into Jericho's chest tauntingly. He takes another step back with me in his arms, holding my back to his front tightly.

Before I can protest or tell Arrow to chill—which never works—he spins me to face him, then abruptly dips me like in the movies. His face hovers above mine with a manic grin.

"I've always wanted to do this, Kitten. And in a wedding chapel, of all places. This is perfect. If I could fuck you right now, well, that'd be even better. I'd take you on the red carpet and leave my marks all over your porcelain skin. Fuck. I want to bruise you. Use you. Keep you. Now, I'm going to fuck you with my tongue." His lips are on mine in a feverish movement, taking whatever he can get. But I give right back, twirling my tongue with his. I lose myself again in the reunion of our bodies, letting the both of them take what they need.

Because I needed it, too.

They're my Devils. Mine to fuck and keep, as well. They can claim me over and over again, but I need to do the same.

Arrow's heavy breaths echo through the room when he detaches his lips and lays his forehead on mine. "On second thought, Kitten. I need you. Desperately. I can't let you walk out of this room without my cum dripping between your legs," he breathes with a desperate growl in his voice, pulling me impossibly closer. "Now, be a good girl and drop to your hands and knees. I'm going to live up to my promise."

I shudder at his words, wanting to tell him to get fucked. That I have business to attend to and can't stay here. Elias needs to help me get back to Shepp and keep him safe. The last thing I need to do is drop to my knees with pleading eyes and beg them to fuck me good.

I should walk away. Even though every fiber of my being calls to their souls, begging them to remind me who I belong to. Them. The Devils of Briar Cove.

Goosebumps sprout across my flesh when I investigate the depths of his light gray eyes. There are so many emotions shining back at me. Desire is the most potent, eating me alive. My pussy contracts around nothing when he silently begs without making a move.

I need to go. I need to save Shepp.

But my body has other ideas. Perking up at the feel of their bodies rubbing up against mine.

"Here?" I whisper with a slight quiver in my voice.

The venue is empty. The only noise comes from the crowd gathered at the reception across the way.

"Are you afraid, Kitten? Scared someone will walk in here and see me fucking you from behind while Jericho strokes his cock above your face?" Arrow whispers, leaning in with a smirk. "I dare you. I fucking dare you to take us both. Right here and now."

Jericho makes a noise in his throat but doesn't say a word when his teeth nip my neck with encouragement.

Am I afraid? Yes. It trembles down my limbs, shaking me to the core. If someone witnesses me on my knees with cock in my face and pussy—I'm dead. Shadow will take me out right here and now. If that's not his plan, anyway. I'm sure he's counting on me failing with my shitty knife. Elias will be my death. But this?

This will be my goddamn awakening from the darkness I've been in for so long. But Shepp... He's in the back of my mind. Images of him covered in bruises and bloodied after a torture session at the hand of Shadow's men.

What's happening to him while I'm here playing dress up and getting fucked by his two best friends?

"You're lost in thought," Jericho hums, pressing his lips against mine. The warmth of his tongue invades my mouth, taking me hostage and silencing the damaging thoughts roaring through me.

"It's Shepp," I gasp out when he bites my bottom lip, and the taste of copper hits my tastebuds. "He's not here." Before I realize it's happening, tears leak down my cheeks, carving their existence down my flesh. "He's back on Shadow's island and..." I trail off when Jericho's tongue laps at my tears, following the trail they made straight back to my eyes.

"We will deal with him after we deal with you." There's a hint of demand in his voice, dripping with so much lust—I know he's fallen into the depths of it. "We won't ask again, Little Chaos. Get on your knees and bend to our wills."

I want to say no. Get fucked, assholes. But my mind and body have detached. No longer working in sync.

My knees tremble at his words. I'm supposed to be a big bad bitch with a job to do. But I give up. Melt into them as if I'm their doll to prop up and fuck as they wish.

I shudder when Arrow's fingers curl in my hair, yanking my head back with force. His breaths echo in my ears, blowing down my exposed neck.

"Jericho, why don't you check our girl's pussy? Tell me how wet she is at the thought of getting caught." He chuckles lowly in my ear, locking me against him.

The hem of my skirt moves against my thighs, slowly working until the cool air of the room brushes against my slick pussy. Am I wet at the idea of getting caught? Absolutely not. Nope. Not me. Well, maybe. Or it could be their fingers working over me and consuming me. They don't hesitate to take what they want when they want.

And I'm fucking aching for it right now. It'll mend the tear in my heart where Shepp belongs.

A fog drifts through my mind. Their words and heated exchanges go right over my head. The heat of Jericho's fingers reaches my clit. A feather-light touch teases me, forcing my hips forward, seeking his touch.

I've missed him so goddamn much.

I gasp when his fingers tear through my barely there panties and straight into my pussy, only stopping until my pussy adjusts to the welcoming intrusion. He scissors his fingers, building an orgasm in my core. Fire consumes me. Moans spill from my lips. Not caring who sees us out in the open. It's so close to spilling over, and he's barely touched me. But I need him. Them.

Well, until he pulls his fingers out with a dark chuckle and holds them in front of our faces. His fingers drip with my arousal, glistening under the soft lights.

"I'd say my wife is very excited at the prospect of getting caught on her knees." I swallow hard at the dark look crossing over Jericho's face as he speaks. Wetness coats between my thighs, growing wetter by the second. Especially when he devours my desire, swirling his tongue over his fingers with a satisfied hum of approval.

I'm salivating to feel their cocks inside me. Daydreaming of the orgasm that's on the cusp of throwing me over the edge. One more touch and I'm fucking done for.

"Jericho," I whisper desperately, leaning against Arrow's shoulder.

A cloud of lust falls over us. Our chests heave.

"What shit, I didn't get a taste," Arrow grunts, grinding his dick against my ass. His fingers dig into my hip, no doubt leaving bruises behind. "But that's okay," he murmurs, nipping my ear lobe.

"Get on your knees, Little Chaos," Jericho says, freeing his cock from his pants and stroking it up and down. I lick my lips. "You're going to gag on my cock while Arrow fucks you from behind."

Arrow doesn't waste a moment guiding me to my knees until they're sinking into the plush red carpet.

"We have so much to talk about," I say, looking up at Jericho as he looms above me. Pre-cum glistens from the tip of his dick, practically rolling off.

"We do," he agrees, stroking himself a few times. "But first, we're going to fill you with our cum. Then we can discuss things."

"But…" I wish I could say I finished my thought. But I became so full of dick that the only thing I could do was squeak around Jericho's cock hitting the back of my throat.

"Fuckkk," Jericho growls, twirling his fingers in my hair. "I forgot what a good fucking girl you are, Little Chaos, always taking my cock. Just like that," he breathes, throwing his head back with his eyes squeezed shut.

"We won't last long, Kitten. Our dicks have missed you so much. Mine more than his," Arrow quips the last part, shoving my dress up further until my ass is completely exposed. "Arch your back, Kitten." Arrow's fingers work down my spine, tilting my hips until my back arches. "And say my goddamn name around your gag," he grunts in my ear, thrusting into me until I'm full.

I scream around Jericho's cock as they pound into me. Using me for all their pleasure and mine. My pussy convulses around Arrow's dick, building and building until I crash down with a muffled scream.

Fuck. Fuck. I shout in my mind as the salty taste of Jericho's cum spurts down my throat, and I swallow it without batting an eye.

Jericho breathes heavily above me. His chest tightening against his shirt with every inhale and exhale. Those dark eyes find mine as I jolt over and over from Arrow pounding me from behind, sparkling with unsaid words and affirmations. Warm fingers run through my hair, tucking it gently behind my ears as he leans down and presses his lips to my forehead.

"I've missed you, Little Chaos," he murmurs just loud enough for me to hear as he pulls his dick from my mouth. I gasp for breath, my lips forming a silent scream just as I was about to shout the same.

"Fuck, Kitten," Arrow says in a strangled moan, stopping all his movements as he fills me with his warmth, groaning against my neck, leaving hickeys with every nibble of his teeth. "You're my goddamn salvation," he murmurs in my ear. "Don't ever fucking leave us again."

I wish I could promise that. I wish I could say that I'll never get kidnapped again. But in this life? I'm sure I'm in for a hell of a ride.

I nearly groan when he pulls out of my pussy slowly, torturing me with his length.

"We'll celebrate rounds two and three later. For now..." Arrow trails off with a chuckle, tucking himself back in.

Jericho gently helps me to my wobbly feet, righting my dress until I'm completely covered. Arrow's cum mixes with my arousal on my thighs, making my flesh sticky with every step I take.

"Don't you dare wipe me away," Arrow says with a pointed look, wiggling his brows. "I want you smelling like me in front of all those people." His grin ends any worry I have within me. Well, for a moment.

"You said you have to tell us something?" Jericho asks, tucking his hands into his pockets. His dark eyes eat me alive, almost pulling me in for round two. If it weren't for the sounds of the people across the hall escalating, I'd happily do it again.

But this isn't the time. Or the place. I have a bigger fish to fry.

The bubble we've been in instantly pops. I pull my shoulders back, lifting my chin. I have a mission I need to go on, with or without them. Elias and I must have a conversation about getting me back to the island without Shadow knowing.

Shepp has saved me so much over the years, and it's my turn to step up and be his hero. My rock. My savior.

"So much stuff to catch you up on."

And so I do. I tell Jericho and Arrow everything that happened on the island. From the cave prison we were put into, to the fight pits, to Mikhail and Sunshine, to meeting with Elias, and finally to here. By the anger masking their expressions, I know it's wise that I left out the slight starvation and dehydration Shadow put Shepp and me through.

"So, your sister is with Mikhail Antonov?" Jericho asks with zero emotions in his tone. But by now, I've learned his emotions. The slightest twitch in his jaw and the widening of his pupils puts me on edge.

"Yes," I breathe with my heart squeezing in my chest. I trust him. He never gave me a reason to believe he'd put her in danger. Sunshine loves him. He loves her.

"And you're telling me that Shadow poisoned Naum? The head of the fucking Russian Mafia? Holy shit, this is worse than we thought." Arrow slightly chuckles, rubbing his hands together with a manic grin. Like this is the best Christmas present he's ever gotten.

"It means there's unrest within all organizations," Jericho muses with a frown, shaking his head.

"He said he'll get in touch with you. He said he'd vow his services to your cause here," I whisper.

"Seems we have more to think about then," Jericho hums.

"And this Darrell guy?" Arrow asks, leaning forward to look at me. "I'll kill him for ever putting his hands on you. Do you think he wants the tip of his nose? I can remove that for him and make a necklace." I nearly blanch and puke all at once, but I shake my head.

"Arrow, no." Bile rises in my throat at the imagery. It's so strange that my stomach has become so weakened by Arrow's violence.

Ugh. I should be used to this by now.

Never in my damn life did I think I'd be in a moment like this with men so obsessed. They made me theirs against my will, taking me and turning my world inside out. I thought they were the worst in the beginning. Fucking me with masks on, keeping their selves hidden when they knew exactly who I was.

I was set up from the get-go and bamboozled by their presence.

But they did so much for me. They took care of me at my lowest without me having a clue. Shepp with cooking. Jericho and Arrow with stalking.

But I'm not scared or wanting away.

I'm safe with them.

CHAPTER THIRTY-SIX

Journey

"Now, that's out of the way," Jericho murmurs at my back, gently kissing my bare shoulder. "We need to get you out of here. I can't stand another fucking minute without you beside me."

"Leave?" I murmur into Arrow's chest. "I can't leave yet," I rasp, shaking my head the best I can.

There's too much to do now. I have to speak with Elias and warn him of Shadow's plans. He may not be a good man, but I've seen how Jenni lights up around him. He's the sun in her universe; I can't let that die.

It's for the good of Briar Cove.

I turn in their embrace, struggling to look up at Jericho, who frowns. "No? You don't want to leave?" Anger weaves into his voice, but he doesn't show it on the outside. His face remains impassive except for the fire in his eyes.

"No," I whisper as tears form in my eyes. "I can't leave yet. I have to..."

"You don't have to do shit. The only reason I'm here is to retrieve you and Shepp." His eyes look past me, and his muscles tighten. "And I'm guessing he wasn't your plus one." His teeth grind to dust when he squeezes his eyes shut, taking several calming breaths—no doubt counting inside his head to bring his anger down. Jericho's mood sets me on edge, raising the hairs on my arms and plummeting my hopes into my stomach.

He's going to kidnap me again.

With or without Shepp.

I can't let that happen. Not tonight. Shepp's life depends on me going back to him. That's why I have to talk to Elias and Jenni. Make a damn plan to keep everyone safe from Shadow's wrath.

"He was supposed to be, but Shadow..."

"Speaking of that worm. Where is he?" Arrow asks with a menacing tone. "I'd like to have a fist or two with him."

"It's a word, not a fist," Jericho grunts with irritation.

"Oh, no. Not this time, Daddy Jer. It's fists. Because I'm going to put my fist so far down his throat, it'll come out of his asshole."

I blanch. Well, that's a visual I'll never unsee. Although, it wouldn't be the worst thing ever.

"No," I say, shaking my head. "You two need to lie low or something. I have something to take care of. I need to talk to Jenni and Elias. Shepp is still on that fucking island, and I can't leave here with you without him." I dig my heels in stupidly as they exchange looks, conversing silently with one another while I'm none the wiser.

I hate it when they do that. It's rude.

"A word with those two is fine. But I'm not leaving this fucking wedding without my goddamn wife." He levels me with a stare I don't understand, glaring daggers into my skull.

"And I'm not leaving this wedding without going back for Shepp," I challenge, raising my brows. Fight me, Jericho. I dare you. "I can't leave him to fend for himself. Shadow... He's..." I roll my lips together, trying to keep my emotions from bubbling over.

Jericho sighs, releasing all the pent-up anger inside him.

"We know," Jericho says, thumbing over my bottom lip. "Elias told us."

I blink several times. "You've had contact with Elias? What the..."

"He's the reason we're here, Kitten. He invited us to take you away from the big bad wolf. So, that's what we're going to do." I can hear the smile in Arrow's voice without having to look at him.

"He invited you for this?" I murmur, shuddering when Jericho gently shoves his thumb in my mouth. Possibly to arouse me into submission. Or to shut me up so he can get me out of here.

Not happening, Jerk-ico.

I will speak to Elias. Whether they like it or not.

"He said you'd be here, that he would make sure of it." Jericho's voice dips low, filled with emotions—heavy and unrelenting—like a wicked storm brewing in the distance and not showing its potential until it hits. "My Little Chaos," he whispers through a shuddering voice. "I've missed you dearly, my wife. The things I've done to get to this point. To get to you."

"The people he's killed. The flesh wounds. You should ask him about his shoulder and leg," Arrow quips. "All I had to do was slice some throats after my coma." My eyes widen. "Oh, right. You weren't there," Arrow hums, shaking his head.

"Shepp can fend for himself," Jericho says coldly, changing the subject with a frown.

"Not up against that!" I hiss, pushing him away with a grunt. "That's his sadistic father! And he's worse than yours."

Jericho blinks several times before his face softens with understanding. Something I think he only lets me see. Not the world. Not even Arrow. Warmth spreads across my cheeks when he cups my face affectionately, staring deep into my eyes.

"All the more reason to keep you away from him," he whispers, not elaborating further. Leaning in, he pecks my cheek and then steps back, straightening out his suit with a sigh. "You have to understand, Little Chaos. I'm doing this to keep you safe. Will I leave Shepp to do that alone without a backup plan? No. Believe me." He implores me with his eyes, taking in my fallen expression.

My heart aches at the thought of leaving Shepp behind. He wouldn't do the same to me. I can't leave him behind. Never.

"What kind of backup plan do you have?" I ask, furrowing my brows. "If that boat was your backup plan, it failed. I was so afraid..." I trail off, shaking my head.

"Aw, Kitten. Were you scared we were on the sinking ship?" Arrow asks playfully.

"Yes." My face tightens at his teasing. "Is it hard to believe I'd cry for you two?"

Jericho immediately takes my chin between his fingers and leans forward, gently kissing my lips. "It's not hard to believe. But I don't like to think of you shedding your tears."

I sigh, kissing him back slowly. I missed the way his lips felt against mine. The way their bodies pressed into mine. I missed their smells. Their demanding ways. How'd they work themselves under my skin so damn quickly without me realizing? Maybe it was how they cared for my needs long before I knew they existed. And then, beyond that.

"I need to speak with Elias while he's granting favors," I say as Jericho pulls back. I miss the way he kisses me immediately.

"Why?" he asks, leveling me with a jealous stare.

I offer him a tight smile as I slip from their grips. "Because I'm supposed to murder him when it comes time." I shrug, turning on my heels to leave them. I pat the spot beneath my right boob where the knife is supposed to be sitting and freeze.

"Looking for this, Kitten?"

Ugh. I spin on my heel, giving him my best sour expression. It makes him grin from ear to ear while holding the tiny knife. He flicks it open with one movement and stares at it.

"With this?" He hums, spinning the sharp end on the tip of his finger. "It doesn't even work," he says with a shrug, tossing it aside.

Jericho huffs behind him, leaning down to pick it up. "This isn't a very good knife, Little Chaos."

Well, no shit, Sherlocks, I want to shout. Of course, it's not. Because Shadow doesn't want me to fucking succeed. He wants me to try and get myself killed.

"Hold up, Kitten. I told you, if you're planning murder things you're supposed to include me. How should we do it, then? Gut him? Shoot him? I've got an arsenal in my pants." For fuck's sake, I don't want to know what the hell he's talking about. His dick? Maybe. Actual weapons. Probably. With a huff, I march forward as he continues babbling about weapons. "Oh, let's string him up and..." I slap a hand over his mouth, sending him a glare that would wither a grown man.

But Arrow doesn't budge.

In fact, he licks my hand with a grin.

"Supposed to is the key word, Arrow," I grumble, removing my hand from his lips and wiping it on my slinky dress. "I just need to talk to him. I need to make it seem like I'm doing the job for Shadow." Also, it'll give me a chance to talk to Elias. I need to devise a plan to get Shepp back to us and out of danger. He knows his way to the island and how to roam around without being killed.

The longer the four of us are apart, the longer Shadow and Gabriel will be in control.

"Damn. You know I enjoy being included in your murder plots," he grumbles, folding his arms.

"The question still stands, Little Chaos. What exactly do you need to speak to Elias about?" He raises a brow, inspecting my face.

I swear he's reading my mind. To get away from you two.

So, I can return to the island without putting Shepp in danger. I'm sure Shadow will know the moment I disappear from this hotel. He'll radio back to whoever has Shepp by the short and curlies to finish the job.

And I can't have that.

It's all for one or all for none. Because if I don't have my silent giant by my side, I'll level this town with Shadow and Gabriel at the bottom of the rubble.

"Can you trust me?" I ask, taking a step back.

"I'd give you my bleeding heart, lay it in your palm, and ask you to keep it safe. My trust in you is not the question. I want to know the plans running through your wicked little mind." He grins at me, stepping up to me to clasp my palm.

Well, when he puts it like that.

Fuck.

"Shepp is still on the island. Elias knows how to get there. I need his help to get him back." I stare into Jericho's dark eyes. He gives nothing away. No emotions. Or motives.

"Then, let's go have a discussion with Elias," he says in a low voice.

"Discreetly," I say, slowly taking my hand back. "I can't be seen with you two. Shadow will know. It'll put Shepp in danger," I murmur, swallowing hard. "I need to do this alone."

"Like fuck, Kitten," Arrow growls, stepping up to me and taking my chin between his fingers. "You'll never do anything alone again." He narrows his eyes. "Or leave my sight."

"No. She's right," Jericho says.

"What?!" Arrow's anger-filled shout fills the wedding venue with his rage. "She is not right. She can't go into that meeting room without us." He puffs out his bottom lip like a child.

"She's a big girl. We'll hang back. We can't tip off Shadow, especially when he has our friend, probably at gunpoint. I'm assuming one wrong move, and he's promised to harm him?"

I nod.

Arrow scoffs, turning on his heel to put his back to us. "I hate both of you." Then he peeks over his shoulder. "But not you, Kitten. But you." He glares at Jericho. "If this goes sideways, I'm taking your belly button as punishment."

"His belly button?" I sputter with wide eyes. "That's..."

"Go to your meeting, Little Chaos. My belly button is safe." However, Jericho doesn't seem so confident when he covers his stomach with his hand, grimacing at the thought.

Does the big, bad mafia man get queasy at the thought of his belly button being ripped open? Nope. On second thought, I'm nauseous thinking about it, too.

"For now," Arrow growls, the sound thick with menace, and his finger traces a slow, deliberate line across his throat.

"Should we meet back here afterward?" I ask, looking around the empty room.

"No. There's a small room at the back where wedding parties prepare for the events. Use the left door. But also take this," Jericho says, handing me a small phone from his pocket. "Tuck it into your dress and call us."

Without another word, Jericho kisses my cheek, lingering there longer than necessary. "We'll come after you if you aren't back in thirty minutes. No matter what happens, we'll drag you out of here kicking and screaming."

"And Shepp?" I bristle.

"I know it's hard to believe, but Shepp can fend for himself. With you away, he'll have extra motivation to remove himself from the situation. Shepp will swim fifty miles to have you back in his arms, if it comes to that. He's a strong man, Journey." His facial features soften when he pulls me closer, hovering his lips above mine. "If Shepp were here and I was there, he'd do the same." It's all he says before pressing his lips roughly into mine.

"Okay," I breathlessly say when he pulls back. Whatever he sees on my face must make him believe the lie I'm telling him.

It's not okay. Not really. I'm just pretending. I'll fight Heaven and Hell to get Shepp back. No matter if he can fend for himself. We went through something hellish together, and I don't plan on letting him rot in those caves without rescue, even if I have to run from Jericho and Arrow to forge ahead myself.

I will not leave Shepp behind.

"Be a good little Kitten," Arrow quips, gripping me by the back of the neck. "Do your job and then get back here. And if you need help murdering him, I've got weapons." He grins, shoving my hand against his pants.

I stiffen. "That's your…" He moves my hand to the left a little. "Oh." Well, that one's a gun. The first one? That was definitely his hard dick.

"The first thing you touched, we can reacquaint you with again later. Multiple times. He misses you already. Tell her, Big A. Tell her how much you want to fuck her and…" I lean up, putting my lips against his. Mainly to get him to shut up about his dick that he insists on calling Big A. I may feel a little off, but if he keeps it up, I will mount him again. I've missed them so damn much. My only regret is that I didn't fight hard enough for Shepp to come for a reunion. But there was no talking Shadow into allowing it. He had his heart set on me being his date and using Shepp as blackmail so I'd murder Elias.

God, I wonder what he's doing. Is he safe? I haven't seen Shepp since they tore me from the viewing box and threw me back into the caves. No doubt to break me even further so he could force me to do this.

"Shut up and go hide," I mumble, peeling his fingers off me.

Arrow grins again, adjusting himself. "You know how to make a bad boy want to fall to his knees and worship you like you're his goddess."

Fuck me.

I turn on my heels, quickly exiting the room with a sigh. Loud voices and music come from the wooden double doors across the hall, housing the wedding reception now in full swing.

I sigh, grounding myself in what I have to do.

CHAPTER THIRTY-SEVEN

Shepp

IT'S A PHONE NUMBER—NOTHING MORE. THERE ARE NO NAMES or indications of who it belongs to—just a phone number scribbled quickly. I stare at the piece of paper Mikhail slipped into my grip before he took off and committed the number to memory for later. For Journey, I know she'll want to speak to Sunshine as soon as she gets back and is able to.

God. My anxiety skyrockets at the thought of her. I don't know what the fuck to do. An hour ago, I watched from my window as Shadow and Journey boarded a boat together with my heart in my throat. It took every ounce of restraint inside me not to open the window and yell for her to come back. Beg for my father to not take her without me.

But I didn't.

Despite the desperation roaring through me, I held myself back even when her eyes connected with mine from below before she disappeared into the boat.

I ache to save her from her, but I know my Little Tempest is tough. She can survive anything. She already has. Multiple times over. She's a warrior—a goddamn queen. My queen.

I have no doubt she'll succeed with her mission. Whatever it may be.

When I had confirmation that Shadow, Journey, and his army of men were gone, I needed to scope out his secret office.

So, here I am, holding my breath when I step into the empty elevator with sweat prickling on my neck. Nerves buzz through my entire body with anticipation. If I'm caught, I'm fucking dead. All I have to do is get to the lower level without detection. Without stalling any longer, I perform Darrell's actions from before until the tiny keypad pops out, and I type in the code.

A breath whooshes from my lips when the doors close, and the elevator goes down, only stopping when it opens to the lower level. When the doors open, revealing the dank space, I immediately step out and let the doors shut behind me.

It's empty. Quiet. Perfect for concealing my presence here. No one else should be down here at any time. Shadow has made it known that only a few people can access this space. Thank Fuck. But I still have to keep an eye out for Darrell and his assessing eyes. I swear to fuck, he's hiding something. I just can't put my finger on what.

With a huff, I smoothed my palms down my jeans. There's one thing I have to do before I can think about going into Shadow's office. I need to check and see if the agent is still tied up in the room down the hall. I've been thinking about him all night since they locked me in my room. His metal badge has burned a hole in my jeans since I took it with me last night. In the moonlight of my room, I stared at it. Examining the number, symbols, and the Veritas name. I tossed and turned, unable to keep my thoughts from everything happening. Journey. Sunshine. The agent. Shadow's plans.

I stop dead in the doorway of the empty room, devoid of the one I hoped to see. Ropes hang from the ceiling where the agent once was. A blindfold rests on the bloodied floor. I'm not sure what I was expecting. Him here? Yeah, right. There's no doubt in my mind that the burly man who came with Darrell took him to the caves—or killed him.

I need to move on and get back to my mission before Darrell looks for me.

I hurry back to my father's office and walk into the unlocked space. Darkness spreads around me, sending chills down my spine. Something about this space sets my teeth on edge and puts my hackles up. I hit the switch, illuminating the space with the fluorescent lights that buzz overhead.

Nothing has changed in this room since the last time I was here. It is still messy, with a slight garbage stench. His desk remains in the middle of the room, with a chair behind it and two in front of it. Old beer cans and water bottles are toppled over and thrown on the ground. Trash lies in the corner of the room, overflowing from the small can onto the floor.

Memories from my childhood soar through my brain at the sight of his signature mess. For someone who went through medical school and became a surgeon, you'd think he'd be more organized and clean. But he never has been.

I guess some things never change.

Move, Shepp. Get this snooping done before someone notices you're gone.

I swallow hard when I gently shut the door behind me, concealing myself from anyone who might come down here. Taking a seat in his desk chair, I go through the piles of papers on his desk. I swear, it's like he hasn't thrown anything away. Ever. Instead, hoarding them here. Good for me, I guess.

My brows furrow as I read over the words: deeds, money, war—all written in Shadow's sloppy handwriting.

Deeds? Money? War? What the fuck does this even mean? His plans for the future? We already know he's been after Gabriel for three years now, sending bombs and attacking us.

I push that paper to the side, finding more hand scribbles. A phone number with crudely drawn hearts encasing the number. Hearts? Is he serious right now? The man who touched me, beat me, and cut out my tongue drew hearts on a piece of paper.

This has to be a sick fucking joke.

My stomach fucking churns again when I rifle through the

pages and uncover a stack of small photographs hidden beneath the mess.

A man and a woman stand happily outside Briar Cove High School. The same school I went to with Jer, Arrow, and even Journey.

His toned arm is around her shoulders, squeezing her into him affectionately. She grins up at him, lovingly looking at his smile while he stares at the camera.

By the look of the man, I can tell it's Shadow. Younger and more sane looking. There's something normal about him. Turning it over, my eyes widen at the inscription.

Tommy and Grace. Senior year.

Drawn hearts encase their names. My jaw falls open, and I flip the picture again, staring at their youthful faces.

My father is the man. And the woman? Jericho's mother, looking cozy and in love in each other's arms.

The next photo is a prom picture. The two of them dressed in their best in front of the Briar Cove Hotel. Hand in hand. Smiles on their faces. Pure joy radiates off them as they stare at the camera.

Tommy and Grace. Senior Prom. May 1st.

A figure lurks in the background behind them, staring in their direction with a scowl. Gabriel. His cold, dark eyes glare daggers into the two of them.

They look so damn happy in the pictures. So, unlike themselves from what I can remember. My father was volatile and a drunken mess. And Jer's mom? She never showed her emotions, constantly doing what Gabriel told her to do. She was meek and muted, almost cutting off herself from everyone except Jericho—her pride and joy.

There was never any indication that my father and her had

had a previous relationship—none at all. They barely looked at each other when he was around.

And then she disappeared.

I rub my temple. At least, that's how I remember it from the mind of my five-year-old self.

"Shut the fuck up, Aurora. Just fucking..." Glass shatters from somewhere downstairs.

My entire body stiffens at his outrage. His voice carries through the entire house. My mom cries out, begging him to stop his assault.

"It was never supposed to be you!" he shouts again, throwing something else against the wall and smashing it to smithereens.

I watch from between the rails from upstairs, trembling when he makes his way toward the front door. His chest heaves and sweat pours from his forehead. He rips the front door open, clinging to a nearly empty whiskey bottle.

"You were the worst fucking thing to ever happen to me, you fucking whore," he growls at my mother as she walks into the foyer, clasping her wrist. "You and that fucking..." His eyes connect with mine, and I reel back. They're darker. Evil. Like nothing lives in his soul. A side of him I had never truly seen before. "You were never supposed to be!" With that, he marches out the front door, slamming it in his wake.

The entire house falls into an eerie silence.

"Mommy?" I mutter from the top of the stairs, tears in my eyes as I descend.

"It's okay, Sheppy," she murmurs, embracing me when I toss my arms around her waist.

"Why is Daddy so mad?" I murmur, staring up at her.

"Because Grace Viotto has gone missing," she mutters bitterly under her breath, soothing a hand through my hair.

I blow out a breath, trying to forget that moment in our history. My mother never comforted me like that again, getting too drugged up and compliant to remember his abuses that only got worse the longer he was in the picture. Everything escalated from there.

Was Grace the catalyst of it all? Did she cause my father to go off the rails and lose himself in alcohol finally?

I shift in my chair, flipping to the next picture in the stack. My eyes widen. Oxygen stalls in my throat, nearly choking me. I check once. Twice. Finally, a third time until it all sinks in.

There are four people in the picture now.

Grace offers the camera a tight smile, smashed between Shadow and Gabriel. My mother rests on Shadow's other side with a demure expression I recognize. It's one I was familiar with as a child. She had checked out.

Diamond rings sit on the women's fingers, a long tradition upheld after the initiation presentation, where the men walk on stage and show off their wounds. They prove to the family that they're men now, no longer boys, able to take their brides and walk them down the aisle.

No one has a choice in who will be on their arms. It's a contract. An obligation we can't fight. Obviously, Shadow didn't win the bride he desperately wanted. How shitty it must have been to watch the woman he loved be with another man. Especially a psychopath like Gabriel Viotto, who no doubt had probably set the whole thing up. He had the power. His father, especially.

Hidden in the depths of the picture, I noticed the fire raging in Shadow's eyes, glaring at the camera like he wanted to burn the fucking world down and take Gabriel with him. Maybe he did, considering the woman he's been staring at lovingly was now in the arms of the Viotto Crime Family leader. Or future leader. At that point in time, he was like Jericho. A prince to the throne. One he got not long after fully initiating.

Turning the picture over, I read the inscription written in sloppy cursive and stained with small wet spots. Like tears dripped as they carved the letters of their destiny.

Thomas and Aurora. Grace and Gabriel. Initiation night. Engagements.

I run my fingers over their faces again.

They say a picture is worth a thousand words. They're right. I can see all their expressions as plain as day shining through the image. Shadow is seething. Grace is angry, too, but less obvious than Shadow. And Gabriel? Well, he's as smug as ever.

And that's when it all becomes clear, clicking into place like missing memories.

Shadow and Grace were in love with one another. Going on dates. To prom. Looking at each other like they were the only ones in the room. And because of the Viotto Crime Family, they were torn apart, ripped from each other's arms without a fight.

What a damn clusterfuck.

I set the picture in the pile, going to the next.

It's a celebration—a glimpse of a Viotto party in full swing at the mansion Gabriel built for Grace. A tall Christmas tree with lights sits in the corner of their living room, illuminating the ample space with greens and blues. People mingle in fine dresses and suits, looking at the man of the hour holding his glass in the air with a satisfied smile.

Grace looks like she's staring up at him from below, standing next to Shadow and Aurora like they did many times before. Gabriel was the head of it all, Shadow the second-in-command. They were always together, plotting their next moves for the family.

But what catches my attention are the side-eyes Grace and Shadow share. They catch each other's gazes with love still shining in their eyes. Turning it over, I look at the caption written in neat cursive.

Housewarming Christmas party.

Jericho used to say his father loved Grace so much that he built her a haven—a mansion on a hill, a zoo in the backyard with all her favorite animals to care for. But to her, it must have been a prison.

Fuck.

It was all a sham on Grace's end. She only stayed to survive. Then... Then she ran from him, leaving her only son behind in the crosshairs. My parents, too. They were never truly happy together and always fought and hurt each other.

They hated each other, but they were forced to remain married for obligations to the family. It was their duty to carry on, no matter what.

Even my existence was forced and necessary—an heir for the Mondelli's—a built-in second-in-command for Jericho when he grew up.

Thomas was never a good man. Too consumed with work, booze, and long nights out. When I was five, everything changed. Grace disappeared. Gabriel became unstable and reckless. And Shadow? He became my worst nightmare, spiraling down the drain with alcohol and drugs, losing himself in the family. Beating his wife and me. Torturing me, assaulting me. Whatever he could do to make me sorry for existing.

All these memories assault me, running through my mind like a vivid movie. Thoughts I had boxed up and put into the back of my mind so they couldn't haunt me any longer. After my father died, I moved forward and ignored what had happened to me. He was dead. Gone. I wouldn't have to worry about this shit any long. No one seemed to care what he did to us, anyway. So, why should I? Gabriel sold me out. I lost my tongue. It happened.

I stand abruptly, pulling at my hair. I want to scream into

the void. Punch a damn wall. Make Shadow bleed for all that I had to endure.

But I don't. I can't. He took so much from me, always taking, never giving, and never being a father to me when I needed one.

My mind swirls with the abuse. Resurfacing when I need to remain calm and collected and hidden without detection.

Stop!

I have to stop before the panic claws at me further, tearing me open and letting me bleed out.

I blow out a breath, softly pacing behind the desk, and count to ten, focusing on the room around me and grounding me.

Arranged marriages are barbaric. My father and Grace are the perfect examples.

When we walked across the stage, we knew that Gabriel only had Journey for Jericho and no one for Arrow and me. Perhaps he saw how it tore his second-in-command apart to lose the girl he loved. Or maybe he fucking hated us and didn't want to bring us happiness. Jokes on him, though.

I'm going with the latter. Even though he took me in the moment my father died and married my mother, he loathed us.

My fingers tremble when I get to the bottom of the pile of photographs. I shuffle through the papers, trying to find anything of importance, but find none. It's all scribbles about deeds and nonsense notes, listing off ideas I'm not clued into. I need to know his plans.

He's obviously in cahoots with Grace, but what is she doing? It sounds like she was with Gabriel, but I don't understand how he'd let her back in like that. He's paranoid as fuck. Barely letting anyone pass his security details. And she waltzes back in?

Nothing makes sense to me anymore. This motherfucker was supposed to be dead, and now he's back, haunting my every move again. I had finally found freedom from his cruel ways. But I'm stuck. Here. On a fucking island with his psycho ass.

I need to fucking escape.

Sitting back in the chair, I dig through the drawers stuffed with papers. If he has pictures of them just sitting here, imagine what he'll have buried in the drawers.

My brows furrow when I pull out a loose stack of envelopes filled with contents. Setting them on the messy desktop, I spread them out. Each envelope is addressed to My Dearest Tommy, and a P.O. box is listed as the address with no return address.

> My Dearest Tommy,
>
> Oh, how I miss you and our time together. I couldn't hold out any longer. I couldn't live under his thumb with what he demanded of me. He built me a zoo, Tommy. He tried to make me happy, but it wasn't going to happen. Not with what I carried.
>
> The guilt was too consuming, love. For my safety, I've fled. But you know that by now. I want you to know I'm safe in my little slice of paradise.
>
> We're safe.
>
> When the time is right... you'll know. I'll come and find you. For now... keep playing the part.
>
> Burn this after reading. No one can know.
>
> Your love,
>
> G.

I recheck the front, confirming there's no date stamped on it. This had to be when she left—a confirmation to my father that she was safe. But what was she carrying with her?

> My Dearest Tommy,

I miss you more than you could imagine ever since you left last night. I know it's silly to think we spent the night together in this hotel, but my heart aches to hold you. It's been over three years since I escaped my hell in Briar Cove, but you know exactly what to bring.

Blake was excited to spend time with you and cried when you left. He's getting better about our brief visits. I know you can only pretend for so long that you're on business trips to sneak away. One day soon, we'll have everything in place for you to be at my side.

We miss you.
With Love,
Your G.

I reread the letter several times. Who exactly is Blake, and why would he cry? It almost sounds like... My heart skips when I eagerly pull another letter out, trying to glimpse their love affair. They obviously never quit each other, even when they were forced to marry other people.

My Dearest Tommy,
You've missed meetings. Word through the grapevine has been rather disturbing. I've been hearing things. Add in you not meeting me, and I'm becoming concerned everything we've built will topple over. Is that what you want? Do you want me to fail before I've even begun?

This is your first and only warning. Don't fuck me over. The time is crawling toward a bright future. Here. On this island. You and me. My army will

become ours.
   Love,
   Your G.

   My Dearest Tommy,
   Everything is ready for you to join me. Our home is complete. Our army is solid. If the Devil wanted a war, we'll bring it to him. We've done all the work. Now, come to me.
   Love,
   Your G.

There are a few more notes in the pile of her telling him about the different renovations she had done to the hotel. Or details on how she was building this palace so that he could help her rule, too. But there was one note that had the blood in my veins turning to ice, sending shivers down my damn spine.

   My Dearest Tommy,
   And so our reign as Shadow begins. The time is right now. I will see you in a few days.
   Love,
   Your G.

All the papers fall from my trembling fingers onto the desk. I shake my head.

No fucking way.

I jump to my feet, staring at the pages with wide eyes. I had questions coming into this office, and now I have some answers I never expected. The chair rolls back, bumping into the wall behind me and shaking a painting half-hanging on the wall. I snarl, ripping it off the wall and tossing it against the damn wall opposite of me. Glass shatters. The painting falls apart at the fucking seams, crumbling the old frame.

My chest heaves. I squeeze my eyes shut, rubbing them with my palms.

So much for being inconspicuous and making it seem like I wasn't here. I wonder if he'd believe it naturally fell off the wall and threw itself across the room. Probably not. He'll fucking beat me senseless, but he'd have to catch me first. This is my goddamn opportunity to leave. No matter what he says. I have to go to Journey. Find Jericho and Arrow at the cabin. Anything but stay here and play helpless. Because I'm not.

Blowing out a breath, I kneel and remove the painting from its frame. I shake the glass off the painted image of a river bed flowing between mountains and wildlife drinking from the source. It's a beautiful, serene portrait. Turning it over, the same beautiful cursive spells out a message.

To my Tommy, may you remember me always. I will be back for you.

I check to see if a date was listed on it. It's dated one month before his death.

Fuck me. I sit on my ass, laying my head against the shitty wood-paneled walls, huffing in breaths. Why is this happening now? Couldn't this bastard stay dead? Now, he's back, ruining my life. Again and again. It's bullshit. And now, to find out he and Grace had this previous relationship? Did they continue it throughout their marriages? Or... I shake my head. I can't go down this fucking rabbit hole right now.

I need more information on what he's up to as Shadow.

I crawl on my hands and knees toward the desk. I rifle through all the contents, reading every piece of paper with an eagle eye. One catches my attention: fire, bombs, men in black with guns. Turning the paper, I see a blueprint detailing the space: a large venue with several attached rooms, a large ballroom, a dressing room, a bathroom, and elevators.

Briar Cove Grand Hotel.

My brows furrow at the name printed on the map. Why the hell?

My gaze bolts up, and I shake my head. No. No. Fuck! He's going to attack someone at Elias' wedding with Journey in tow. He's going to start a damn war on Gabriel's territory and fucking draw him out more. God fucking damn it.

I don't dare breathe when the door to his office creaks open, and Darrell stands there with an unreadable expression. Through all the noise of the glass shattering and my fucking mind spiraling, I didn't hear the elevators.

Darrell blinks several times, taking in the carnage of the room. His frown deepens.

"The fuck are you doing in here?" he grunts, eyeing me with narrowed eyes. "And what the fuck did you do?" He gestures stiffly to the painting on the ground.

CHAPTER THIRTY-EIGHT

Jericho

SHE'S GOING TO RUN. HARD AND FAST IN THE OPPOSITE direction. Far from me. Back to the island. To save the man she feels guilty for leaving behind.

Too bad I love the chase.

My entire being rattles with the prediction as I watch her leave, like an omen hanging over my head.

I know it's going to happen. The question is when.

My wife hides her emotions behind a thick mask. Most wouldn't be able to discern her moods. As for me? I watch her decisions swirl behind her expressive eyes. That's where she tells the world what she's up to. And there I saw the desperation and fear for Shepp's safety.

If I could have soothed her, I would have. Shepp is a big boy. A man who can take down an entire room with a toothpick if he wants to. So, I'm sure that with his father off to play mafia man and his girl missing, he's escaping.

Come hell or high water, Sheppard Mondelli will stand before us in a matter of hours.

"You think she's actually going to do what she says?" Arrow asks, pursing his lips. "Like walk in there and murder him?" He pouts, thinking more about it. "Without me?"

With what? Her bare hands. I think not. Although, she

seems to have tricks up her skirt. Besides, she mentioned speaking with him as opposed to murder.

I'd love to see her pull it off, though. Unfortunately, I can't let her. Considering he's my new ally and all.

Bummer.

Arrow's gray eyes roam around the vacant room, taking in the opulent decorations. Elias sure went all out for Jenni. I don't blame him, though. I've thought about it since the moment Journey chastised me for marrying her without her knowledge. But what else was I supposed to do to keep the money safe from my father's grubby hands? Not marry her? Let him take it? Absolutely fucking not.

When we're done warring with my father and Shadow and have successfully knocked them to their knees, I'll give Journey the wedding of her dreams.

Until then, she's my wife. I'm her husband. I will protect her with every fiber of my being.

Leading up to the night of our initiation ball, I knew something was amiss. My father was cagier than usual. Acting strange and benevolent. Wouldn't you know? He had something vindictive up his sleeves, a nefarious plan to take Journey's money and use it for himself. Considering that's the entire reason he held her hostage all those years.

Well, fuck him.

He'll get what's coming to him in due time.

That money will never get into his hands. Thanks to some friends in high places with untraceable accounts, I was able to keep it out of reach, even if he got the name associated with it or the account numbers. The only person who can access the funds is Journey herself. Now, Journey will do whatever she wants with it when the time comes.

"Not a chance in Hell," I say, shaking my head. "Journey is going to march in that room and demand Elias help her get back to the island to retrieve Shepp." She won't harm him because she needs him.

Arrow rolls his eyes and digs out his phone. Without a few touches of the screen, he grumbles under his breath. "Well, he's still there in the middle of the damn ocean."

"He's going to be so damn thrilled you installed that device without his knowledge."

Arrow grins. "That'll teach you to take drinks from me," he quips.

I rub the side of my neck with a frown. "Bastard."

Although, it's come in handy having tracking devices in each of our ass cheeks. He's been able to know where we've been. But also? Fucking invasive.

"You're just mad because the last time it was lights out, Jericho, I tied you to a chair and made you watch me fuck her repeatedly." He wiggles his brows and then stiffens. Realization lights up his face, and a knowing grin lifts his lips. "Her tits feel bigger to you? They do to me. Like plump watermelons. You think our little seedling is inside her yet?"

That perks me right up. All the more reason to whisk Journey away to our cabin on the mountain. Oh, she'll hate it. But it is what it is. That woman is never leaving my sight again.

"All the more reason she can't go back to the fucking island," I growl, cutting a hand through the air. Determination takes me over the longer we stand here, watching the empty room with frowns.

"Shouldn't we hide or something?" Arrow asks, scratching at his jaw.

I'm not convinced that's what we should truly do. If we hide and trust my wife to do as she says, she'll run for the first boat without a plan.

No.

"And miss the action? I'm sure he knows we're here by now and has some delightful words for us. Besides, we're the Devils of Briar Cove. We don't fucking hide." Ever. We're here for the fucking fight. I'll murder Shadow with my bare hands before I let him take my wife again.

Something clicks on the opposite side of the room, drawing my attention to the lone shadow looming in the darkness.

Wonderful. He's made this easy for us.

"Not even when a gun is pointed at us?" Arrow whispers dramatically, pointing toward the corner of the room with big movements.

So much for discretion on our end. Arrow has thrown that out the window. We could have gotten the jump on him and taken him down without all the dramatics he's about to display.

"Especially not that," I say with a tight smile, drifting my gaze again to the man I haven't seen since he died.

It's a shame he didn't stay that way.

It's quite a shock to the system to watch a man whose ashes were buried three years ago walking toward us with a smirk. Scars line his face and neck, and wrinkles tarnish his suit like he couldn't have been bothered to dress up and look presentable. He sure didn't spare any expense with how Journey was dolled up.

Well, this should be quite interesting.

"Thomas Mondelli," I say confidently, letting my voice travel through the large room. "After all these years. How wonderful to make your acquaintance again."

His lips quirk again into a half smile. "Wonderful isn't a fucking word I'd use to describe this meeting," he growls, stepping slowly out of the shadows to reveal himself completely.

It's almost as if he commands the surrounding darkness, forcing it to shroud his existence. From us. From the entirety of Briar Cove for so many years. Most importantly, my fucking father.

But no more.

If Shadow has come out of hiding and is uncovering his identity, then Briar Cove and my father's loose grasp on the family is coming to a head.

War is afoot.

Wonderful. Just what we need piling high on the multiple plates we're already balancing.

I need a vacation.

"No? Me either. I'm wondering, though. How does a dead man come back to life?" I ask when he finally settles directly in front of us, pointing his guns at our chests—one in each hand.

No doubt covering all his bases, but by the look in his sparkling eye, he's come for more than bloodshed. He would have shot us dead by now from his hiding spot.

So, what does he want, exactly?

"By not dying at all," he sneers, turning his nose up. "I gotta say, Viotto. You're the spitting image of your cunt of a father." He spits at the ground right beside my feet.

I've had many people spit verbal insults at me in the past. But this one has got to take the cake. A spitting image? That's downright disrespectful to me.

"Well, if you were trying to flatter me, it didn't work. Although, I do have to agree on the cunt part." I shrug.

"So, what do we owe the pleasure of your company?" Arrow asks, cocking his head. "Do you want to gossip about what you've been up to these past three years? Because I'd love a good tea-spilling session." He bats his eyelashes, unleashing a sadistic grin.

He's ready to pounce.

'Not yet.' I sign discreetly, attempting to shield my signed words from Shadow.

"I'm here to put bullets in your chests." So he says. If that were true, then he'd have done it by now. For whatever reason, he's stalling. "Then I will have dealt with two of my four problems."

Or perhaps he needs us for some asinine reason.

That brings me to plan A—a way to lure him into a false sense of security. Although, it wouldn't exactly be like him to do so. I'll play it by ear, and I hope Thomas doesn't unload his clips into our chests.

"How about we strike a deal?" I hum, crossing my arms.

"A deal? You think I'd make a deal with the spawn of my enemy?" he spits again, backhanding me with the gun closest to my face.

Well, then. Color me surprised. I should have seen that coming ten seconds ago. How dare I attempt to save my life with the deal of a lifetime? Or it would have been. It's too bad that I have no clue what I could offer Thomas in return for continuing to breathe.

Pain splinters through my cheek as a warmth drips from the impact. My fingers play in the blood, sending tingles down my spine and a renewed sense of justice. If this is how Thomas wants to play it, I shall unleash the demon beside me, begging to come out and play.

All is fair in love and war, after all.

"The spawn of your enemy, huh? If I recall, Thomas. You and my father were two peas in a pod. Compatible for so long. What changed?"

It's something I've been curious about since the moment Elias told me about his identity.

What happened between him and my father? Yes, Gabriel can be quite the cantankerous cunt. We all knew that. Even now, he hasn't changed his ways—only gotten worse.

Well, that is before he fell mysteriously ill.

I think I have my mother to thank for that. Which also reminds me about her and Shadow having some sort of connection—if she was telling the truth, that is. Who knows where she went all those years ago?

Shadow smirks again. "Your father knows exactly what he did to push me out of the way. It was his plan all along. He didn't like how close me and your mommy were."

I don't react at all, keeping my features smooth. "Oh? Were the two of you up to something? Hmm?"

"That's the past. This is now. I know what the Viotto name stands for. It's bullshit. Your sect of the family has taken this town far enough in the wrong direction. It's my time now." He grins, cocking the hammer of the gun. "In three, two..."

The floor shakes beneath our feet, rattling straight to my bones. Drywall rains from above us, covering us in a smattering of white dust. I quickly grab Arrow's shoulder to keep balance, and he does the same to me.

An explosion rocks through the large hotel, sending debris and fireballs in every direction. Sprinklers activate above us, sending jets of water everywhere. Frantic screams cry out in agony. Screams of death. Voices of the innocent.

My blood pressure spikes the moment the building stabilizes. The only thoughts I have running through my mind pertain to her. My wife. Our fucking girl. She walked through the reception room to speak with Elias—in the heart of the destruction.

I focus on Shadow, who grins at the damage and takes stock of what he just inflicted on the wedding party with glee.

His distracted state is his fatal flaw.

'Get ready,' I sign, righting myself beside Arrow, who salutes me with twinkling eyes.

But that slowly dies. Replaced by the demon that loves to come out to play, hiding any sign of light inside Arrow's soul. He knows the circumstances. The woman we love is in danger.

We need to go to her now. Not later.

"Your doing?" I ask in a cool tone, remaining as calm as possible.

Not that any of those family members aren't used to this sort of thing. They're all affiliated with Elias' gang. Or Jenni's family. Although, I didn't see many of them in the crowd.

Shadow smirks coldly, not showing any ounce of remorse or emotions. Not even when little children were in the crowd with their parents. To him, I'm sure it's just a way to eliminate his enemies in one swoop.

"Of course," he says with a shrug.

A glazed look takes over his eyes. A high blaring through him at the lives he's potentially taken with his bomb.

"But why?" Arrow asks, pursing his lips and calculating the right time to pounce. His demon is patient. But ruthless. "I thought you were butt buddies with Elias?"

Shadow's face darkens slightly. "This is my formal resignation from being associated with the Blue Spider Gang."

"That's one hell of a notice," I say, chuckling slightly at the circumstances.

I can't allude to the fact I'm aching to run and see if Journey is okay. He'll see through it all. He was my dad's associate, after all. I'm curious to understand what he and Elias had going on.

Why they were associated with each other in the first place, and how Elias knew his true identity and never said a word about it. I suppose he and I weren't on friendly terms a few months ago.

But now...

"Yes, it is. My new associates didn't like the competition. They thought eliminating them would help in our efforts."

"Your efforts, huh?" I shrug.

It's the flicker of movement. A moment Shadow lets his guard down. His eyes leave us for a split second, taking in the smoke billowing into the reception room and clinging to the ceilings with a look of pride. It burns my lungs.

But I know I won't have to wait much longer.

'Now,' I sign quickly to Arrow, who nods.

Arrow abruptly grins and punches Shadow straight in the fucking nose. It crunches under the blow, sending blood splatters onto the red carpet. He cries out, sending off a shot from both guns in the air.

My ears ring when one whizzes by my ears, nearly taking it off, but I shake my head, attempting to rid it of the sound blocking out the violence unfolding before me.

Arrow grunts, gasping for breath. But even a bullet doesn't stop him from jumping onto Shadow's back. He clings to him, digging his fingers into his eye.

Shadow lashes out. Crying in pain when Arrow sings him a song I don't recognize. Shouting it into the burning air until Shadow falls to his knees and loses his grip on the guns until they clatter to the floor, getting lost under a few chairs.

My ears ring with his shrill cries and pleas. But he doesn't give up. He wails and punches and attempts to dislodge Arrow. Nothing works. Arrow is stuck to him like glue. A scope fixed on his target, ready to kill. They wrestle more as I stand back. If I attempt to jump on, Arrow will likely hiss at me.

"For such a big bad Shadow, you fight like a pussy," Arrow spits, shoving his knee into Shadow's neck after forcing him to the ground.

I jump in, holding Shadow's flailing legs. Slowly but surely, his movements die off. Within a matter of seconds, he's out. Falling limp on the floor with blood pooling down his cheeks and his mouth stretched open.

Now, that was a dramatic takedown. Just not the one Shadow thought was going to happen.

Arrow grins at Shadow's knocked-out form on the ground. He chuckles, slamming the heel of his foot right on Shadow's dick. "If you would have just let me do this from the get-go. He was like a typical chatty villain." Arrow rolls his eyes with a huff, yanking his tie off.

"And what do you propose we do with him now?"

"Well, we aren't just going to let him lie here, Daddy Jer. He'll burn to a crisp while he slumbers. This motherfucker is going to pay. Severely. I'm tired of his fucking face," Arrow growls through gritted teeth, hog-tying Shadow with his tie. I cock my head, watching the nearly impossible feat he manages in under thirty seconds.

Sometimes, I underestimate what he's capable of.

"Okay. Now, let's go find my Kitten and make sure she's

okay," Arrow says, getting to his feet, holding tight to the bindings on Shadow's body.

"And him?"

Arrow smirks, picking Shadow up and letting his drooping head bounce off the floor. "Oh, I have ideas," he says before skipping away toward danger with Shadow in his hands. "There won't be a chance for him to get away from us."

"Interesting," I hum, following close behind him.

CHAPTER THIRTY-NINE

Jericho

SWEAT BEADS AT MY BROW WHEN WE'RE THRUST INTO THE LINE of fire. Several of Shadow's soldiers, dressed in black, meander through the crowds, randomly shooting at men firing in their direction.

War is here, and Shadow has declared it.

Screams echo all around us. Fires blaze hot in almost every direction, consuming the golden curtains and fanning across the decorated ceilings. If Shadow wanted to decimate this hotel with one attack, he is achieving his goals. In a matter of ten minutes, this place will be nothing more than ash. Another building obliterated in the heart of Briar Cove.

Desperation rears up inside me, aching to get to Journey as quickly as possible. My fingers itch to touch her again. Feel her. Consume her. Fully. Our brief tryst is not enough to quell the fire, begging to have her again.

To own every inch of her so she never forgets who she belongs to. Us. The Devils. Once we're all back together, we'll thoroughly remind her that her flesh is ours. Her soul belongs to us.

She can't run from us again.

If she does, I will chase her through the smoke and fire until my greedy fingers grab her.

Arrow and I swerve through the debris, holding our breaths

when we come to a stop. The smoke fills the space. My eyes burn as I try to look around and lock on our enemies surrounding the area. Elevators rest behind us, blocked off by falling supports and broken drywall. Large pillars still stand, offering us a brief reprieve from the carnage.

"Any ideas?" I ask, eyeing Arrow as he sits Shadow behind us. Not so gently knocking him around on the ground.

Arrow purses his lips, peeking around the pillar and rearing back with a huff. Several more shots fire our way, pinging off the marble floors and piercing through the burning drywall.

"Oh, I have a few." The grin he sends me has the hairs on the back of my neck standing on end. I've seen it many times before. It's his reckless look. The—I'm about to fuck shit up and probably get killed—look.

"Arrow—" But I don't get the words out in time before he's moving out from behind the pillar.

"Fuck this," Arrow says with a whistle, gaining their attention.

Well, this is either going to turn out well, or I'm going to be planning my best friend's funeral.

Fuck.

Why did I leave Shadow's guns behind? I could have picked them up and ravaged these assholes with the remaining bullets.

"What exactly is your fucking plan?" I hiss, ducking when bullets spray in our direction. Thankfully, the decorative pillar keeps me safe—this time. Since they know we're here, I'm sure we're about to be blown to bits.

"Uh, yeah. Let them shoot their shots. They can try to shoot me, but they'll never land one." Arrow proves his point by jogging in place. Or perhaps it's a dance. Whatever it is, Arrow dodges every small bullet that whizzes by, making it look easy. "Then, when they get close enough, I gut them. Imagine this place decorated in intestines! It'll be a bloody good time."

Oh, good. His demon is still in control, making his impulses flare to life.

"Arrow. What about Journey?" I need to remind him why we're fighting this battle and who we are trying to get to before she runs.

"To keep my Kitten safe and protected, I must murder all the assholes!" he grits out, moving just as another set of bullets comes our way.

Fuck this.

"Arrow, I have an idea. But I need you to continue to do this." I level him with a glare. He grins, holding his arms out wide. "Don't fucking die. I swear to God..." I trail off when he waves a hand at me.

"I would never die on your watch, Daddy Jer." And then, he's gone, rushing through the smoke without a backward glance.

Fuck.

"And you," I say to the passed-out Shadow. "Don't move an inch." I tilt my head when he sits there, unmoving. "Good fucking dick," I grunt, driving my shoe into his side. You know, for good measure and all that.

Carefully, I make it back into the ceremony room. Smoke fills the entire area, making it almost impossible to navigate. Fire bellows up the walls, crumbling them into ash. Windows break. Decorations burn. What a way to celebrate the union of two lives with fire. This will be a wedding they will never forget.

I drop to my knees, crawling along the ground to be able to breathe and see, finally making it to the two discarded guns. Luckily, they're still intact, although hot to the touch. Checking the clips, I count five left in each gun, giving me ten bullets in total.

It's enough to take down ten men.

"It'll do," I mumble, getting back to my feet.

I keep an eye out while moving through the smoke,

thankful for it hiding my existence as I navigate back to the smokey hallway. Arrow is nowhere in sight, but Shadow has awoken from his slumber.

He wiggles back and forth, trying to loosen the ties around his wrists and ankles. Knowing Arrow, though, there's no getting out of those knots. He's meticulously studied how to incapacitate someone for this very reason. Or, well—for Journey. But it all works the same in his mind. He'd never harm her. But Shadow? He'd cut off his blood flow in a heartbeat.

I press my foot into his neck, slowly bending down to look him in the eyes. "I think you've caused enough damage here."

He grins, snorting at my words. "This is only the beginning, Viotto. You kill me, and my legacy continues one way or another. I have so many plans in place, it'll make your fucking head spin."

I roll my eyes, knocking the gun into his temple. Repeatedly until his blood spills on the marble. He falls limp, gasping for breath before the darkness takes him again.

"Shut the fuck up," I growl, removing my foot from his neck and focusing on my surroundings.

I ready my guns, peeking around the pillars and stopping dead. "Arrow," I sigh.

Blood covers every inch of his body. The only facial feature visible beyond the red is the white of his teeth when he dances my way, hooting toward the burning ceiling.

"All right, Daddy Jer. Let's grab the trash and then our girl. Let's boogie the fuck out of here before this entire building blows." With that, he yanks up a bloodied Shadow, throwing him over his shoulder like he weighs nothing, and takes off through the smoke.

"What the fuck just happened?" I murmur to myself. Here I was prepared with weaponry, and Arrow single-handedly eradicated the enemy.

"Magic, Jer. It was magic! Look! I hung up the intestines with care," he sing-songs while pointing to the four intestines hanging from the fake bushes. "Shall we sing oh intestines tree? It would make a beautiful holiday song." The darkness in his eyes slowly dissipates the longer we speak and move toward the room Elias was last in.

If we're lucky, our girl is in there, too.

CHAPTER FORTY
Jericho

THE MOMENT WE CRASH THROUGH THE DOOR, GUNS POINT IN our direction. I hold up my hands, sighing with relief when they back down.

"Seems you've made some powerful enemies," I quip, shutting the door behind Arrow and securing it shut with the lock. Not that it would stop anyone from getting in and discovering our group meeting, but it would at least slow them down.

If Arrow left any of them alive, that is.

Speak of the devil. He waltzes in with nonchalance, tossing Shadow into the corner.

"Be a good sport," he quips, kicking Shadow's side several times. "And stay down." Turning on his heels, he doesn't waste a moment, pulling Journey into his arms. "Oh, my Kitten. I thought you were fire food."

"Fire food?" she questions, twisting herself to look me up and down. Her brows furrow more, and her lips pop open at the ash and blood lining my shirt.

Huh. I guess Shadow made a mess, after all.

"We're fine," I say, answering the question in her eyes. "But there's quite a blaze happening. We need to leave as soon as possible." There seems to be little to no damage in this room. I guess it makes sense. It's a little ways off the main hallway where we fought for our lives.

But if Elias was the target. Then why is he still barely standing?

"Was this your original meeting area?" I cock my head when Elias glares at me, clutching his chest. Blood oozes from between his fingers.

"No," Jenni says, answering for him in a small voice. "It was supposed to be…" She swallows hard, tears misting her eyes. "The room that the bomb went off in."

She trembles beside him, paling at the sight of his blood. Odd. She was the daughter of a prominent mafia man. He must have shielded her away from it all. Including bloodshed. A shame, really. If she had been around all along, she wouldn't look like such a frightened bird.

Seems they've been spared. But that won't last too long. The entire hotel is seconds from crumbling in an ashy grave.

"It wasn't you, was it, Kitten?" Arrow whispers, eyeing Elias' wound. I swear pride shines in his eyes at the thought of her inflicting pain on anyone.

"Me?" Journey asks, wrinkling her nose. "No!" she hisses, pushing away from him. "How could I have? Besides, you stole my knife."

"I thought maybe…" Arrow trails off with a grin. "Well, if you didn't shoot our bestie over there, then who did?"

"I am not your bestie," Elias growls through clenched teeth, hissing at the pain.

Understandable. It burns like hell when a bullet goes through flesh.

Elias glares in our direction. "Whoever Shadow has aligned himself with now." His eyes narrow, and I know exactly what he wants to do. "He so pleasantly let me know that our work together was done, and he needed a new fucking manufacturer and distributor." Every move he makes, he grunts painfully until he's standing and swaying on his feet.

"Then we moved in here. We could tell he was up to something," Jenni says, forcing Elias' arm around her shoulders to steady him.

"So, in the process of hiding yourself, you got yourself shot?" I raise a brow, trying to understand the events of the evening. I want them all to make sense before I jump into bed with Elias and his empire.

"What does it fucking look like?" Elias growls. "I was fucking shot, and then I fucking shot at them and missed. Not what I expected on my damn wedding day." He shakes his head, looking at Jenni apologetically.

"It's okay." She offers him a tight smile, gently leaning her head on his shoulder while he kisses her temple.

"So, Shadow broke ties with you and decided war was his best bet." I rub my chin.

"It's not only me he's breaking ties with, Viotto. He wants it all." He squeezes his eyes shut. "Fuck. We need to have a fucking discussion about our future. The future of this town. But right now…"

"We need to make haste with our exit," I say, sweeping a hand toward the door. "It's a little hairy out there." More like warm. The intense heat coming off through the walls, making sweat glisten on my brow.

"I'll fucking take him," Elias grits out, nodding to Shadow.

"That's a fuck no from me, Bestie," Arrow says, grinning when he yanks Shadow over his shoulder. "We've got beef with this asshole."

"And I don't?" Elias asks. "And we're not fucking besties. We're associates." The glare he levels at Arrow sets my teeth on edge.

I hold out a hand. "What if we give you some time alone in a dark room with him? At a later date, of course."

"And I can trust you to keep him alive that long?"

"It'll be the foundation of our new alliance," I say, holding out my hand. "I keep him kicking for your pleasure after the four of us go a few rounds with him. Then, you can get your kicks in, too."

Elias stares me up and down. "Fine. It's a deal. But I want the fucking death blow."

"That doesn't belong to you," Arrow says, stiffening at his words. "His death belongs to his son and only his son."

Something softens on Elias' face. Like through all his anger, he can clearly see. He nods.

"Then, it's settled. Let's get the fuck out of this death trap." He looks behind him, nodding at the men with guns. "You four go out first and clear a path. We'll be right behind you."

"Yes, sir," they say, marching toward the door.

"Careful, now. It's awfully smokey out there," I say, eyeing his guards.

When the door opens, smoke slowly drifts in, clouding our view of the hotel. Nothing seems to exist in the smoke except the crackling of the fire. In the distance, a fire alarm blares, and a faint strobe of light bounces through the thick smoke.

An eerie silence sits between us. Our eyes inspect one another before we finally follow Elias' guards out.

"Arrow, do you think you got them all?" I question, tossing him the extra gun I stole from Shadow.

"You bet your sweet ass I got every single one of them." He grins.

"There could be stragglers. I don't even know who these assholes are," Elias grunts, coming to stand beside me.

"Well, whoever they are, they're fucking dead. This is our city," I say, holding out my hand.

Elias doesn't hesitate to put his hand in mine. We might have had disagreements in the past over his drugs. But right now, I have no choice but to make amends and move forward.

"Our city," Elias says with a nod, shaking my hand.

"Now, shall we?"

Together, we march through the smoke and fire, making

our way through the hotel's main entrance until we're standing a block away, mostly unscathed.

Elias' facial features darken.

"I'll take your deal," I say, confirming our new alliance. "You want half of Briar Cove? Then, it's yours. We'll discuss the parameters of our arrangement later. For now, I'd like to take my wife away from here. And you probably need medical attention. Not to mention getting the fuck out of this town. Who knows what sort of backup plan Shadow has in his back pocket."

Elias eyes me and stiffly nods. "We'll reconvene at a later date and work out the logistics of everything."

"Then, we'll call it right here and now. We have a truce. Just between you and my small family. The other Viotto's aren't so innocent." More specifically, my fucking father and mother. Parents of the year, I say. "I'll text you the details of our secure location. I'm putting a lot of trust in you and our agreement." And that's a fact. But to show that I'm serious about sharing our city, I need to prove to him I trust him. If he betrays me, I have my fucking ways.

"I am not leaving!" Journey says with determination, coming to stand in front of me. Her lips curl back and she crosses her arms. Honestly, she's hot as sin when she attempts to tell me what to do. But I'm not the one in charge right now. "I will not leave Shepp out there all by himself. Elias said that..." she trails off when Arrow pops up behind her, sticking a needle into her neck. She fights him tooth and nail, kicking and flailing. "You fucking prick!" she slurs, heaving a breath. Her eyes stay open longer than anyone I've seen, burning with vengeance. "I'm going to chop your balls off."

Arrow's grin grows at the sound of her threat. "Sorry, Kitten. I can't leave you behind. You're ours to protect, and that's what we're going to do. You can't get Sheppy Boy off that island. Not by yourself or with Elias' help," Arrow murmurs, with a slight sadness creeping into his tone. He gently soothes her hair, cuddling her until she grows more limp.

"You'll pay," she slurs, fighting the serum in her veins with all her might. Her eyelids droop until she can't cling to consciousness any longer, and she slips into a deep sleep in Arrow's arms.

Arrow slumps, stroking her cheeks with affection. "I hate doing that to her," he says with a pout. "I like her awake and lively. Fighting me while I hunt her. Now, she can't even tell me I'm an asshole." Says the man who enjoyed sneaking through her window to glimpse her sleeping, not to mention the multiple pictures he took of her with his camera. Poor bastard. Maybe he's changing his ways for her. She seems to soothe the monster inside him.

Well, sometimes.

"It was the only way to get her to leave with us." I shake my head, a smidge of guilt eating away at me for what we had to do. "She would have snuck out before we could even think about getting her into the car."

"I could have retrieved him," Elias grunts. "I know that island now, like the back of my fucking hand."

Arrow grins, brings out his phone, and nods. "I don't think that'll be necessary, see?" He holds up the phone, and my heart fucking skips a beat.

"He's already on the way."

CHAPTER FORTY-ONE

Arrow

"YOU FUCKING PRICKS! I'M GOING TO MURDER EACH AND every one of you! My associates will drag you by the balls!" Shadow's pathetic wails echo within the soundproof basement walls.

It's music to my ears. Or it will be when he begs me to end his suffering. Which I won't. Shadow can suffer under our hands for years before Shepp puts an end to his fucking life.

For good this time.

"Sounds kinky, Shadow Daddy. Tell me more about what you want to do with my balls?" I grin, leaning forward. The death look he gives me with his one eye sends butterflies bursting in my stomach, making me all giddy and shit. "God, talk dirty to me. You're making me feel all kinds of things."

"You're a fucked-up boy, aren't you? But that's how the priest made you, isn't it? All fucked up and a goddamn psycho." Shadow spits on the ground, pulling at his restraints more.

Well, that's rude. How dare he speak of my father like that? He did none of those things. I was born this way. I walked out of the womb with a knife in my hand and murder on my mind.

Okay. That's an exaggeration.

I wasn't in control of myself like I am now. Younger me allowed his impulses to rule his life. If I wanted that candy bar? I stole it. If I wanted to see what blood looked like in my hands, I killed animals.

My father helped me contain my urges. Over and over again. He guided me. Well, until he couldn't hide me anymore. If the church found me, he'd lose everything he worked for.

So, he sacrificed me to a greater evil.

It was Gabriel who sucked me into mayhem and murder, letting me cut and maim anything and anyone I could get my hands on. He honed my skills. Refined my murderous impulses. All for his own gain, disguised as helping me.

Sad sack of shit.

Sometimes, I wonder how I would have turned out if my father had kept me hidden. Would I salivate at the prospect of maiming people like now? Or would I have been a good little altar boy in the church, helping my father with Sunday services? Perhaps I could have swallowed all my bloodlust and lived a normal life.

Only the other me in the alternate universe would know what living that life is like.

I sigh—stupid self-pity. I don't have it very often, but in times like these, it creeps up on me. Do I want this life? Sure. It's fun as fuck hearing them scream.

Shadow pulls at his binds like a maniac, rocking his chair back and forth with his movements.

It's great to watch. So, I grab the popcorn I brought down as a snack and shove the kernels into my mouth, humming with satisfaction. God, who knew buttery, salty goodness went so well with torture? This might replace orange juice and pickles. No, wait. No. My OJ and pickles are too precious to throw away completely. It's a delicious tradition.

"Ain't getting out of those binds. I tied them extra tight just for you." I wink, swallowing my mouth full of food.

Licking my lips, I sit back in the lone chair facing his execution spot because that's what's going to happen soon.

Once Elias gets our secret location and we all have a fun

talk about our futures, Shadow is fucking dead. Done. Finished.

For fucking good this time. There isn't any way he'll come back from this.

Then, I'll burn his body in the chimney, where he'll turn to ash. It's too bad we aren't around alligators; I'd toss him into the swamps without hesitation and watch as they chow on his bones.

Ah. The dream.

Sucks we're up in the mountains hundreds of miles away from Briar Cove. We could have at least picked a spot in Florida or something. Sunshine. The ocean. Instead, we get the high altitude, thin air, and snow.

I hate the snow.

I shake my head, coming back to the present. Shadow continues to pull at the ropes, grunting when it cuts into his flesh.

"Fancy a chat?" I grin at him when he glares at me.

"No. I don't fancy a fucking chat," he hisses, continuing to pull at his restraints.

"I took a class on how to tie good fucking knots. You know they have those?" I shrug when he glares at me again. "It was fun. I'm thinking... No, you know what. You don't deserve those words." I zip my lips, attempting not to imagine tying Journey up with those exact knots. Of course, she'd have a more comfortable and pleasurable time. But having her at my fucking mercy after so many weeks apart would be heavenly.

My dick picks that moment to thicken in my jeans. Not now, Big A. We've got some fun things to do, like inflicting lots and lots of pain on our beloved pal, Shadow.

So he gets harder. I guess inflicting pain and the prospect of bloodshed has that effect on me.

Maybe I am a fucked up guy. You know what, though? I'm comfortable with it. There's no masking what devil lives deep inside me and likes to play.

Speaking of…

"All right, Big Guy. Who are your new associates? They were awfully mean to us. They shot me!" I put a hand over my heart dramatically.

My chest still hurts from the impact of the bullets that rained down on me. Too bad for the masked bad boys, I had my handy-dandy armor on. I rub at the spot on my chest absentmindedly.

Shadow grins. "They missed the fucking mark. You're still kicking."

"Eh, well. It pays to have friends in high places." When his smile fades, I tilt my head. I send a silent thanks to Olivia and her genius move to protect us. I think she likes us. "Aw, you wanted to take us down, didn't you? You should have shot us the moment you were lurking in the shadows—poor guy. I'm flattered, though. You thought about me and Jer."

The question still stands—why didn't he? We were right there. Defenseless and none the wiser. He could have murdered us on sight. So why didn't he? I could be in a grave with Jer, haunting the rest of my friends for eternity.

"You think once I'm dead, this will all be over?" He raises his brow like he's up to something. But what? He's all tied up and busy. So, what kind of contingency plan does he have in place? "You don't know the army I have at my disposal."

Oh. So, that's what Shadow has cooking. An army, huh? I wonder how many minions follow him around spouting nonsense.

"Oh! I have so many questions. How many people we talking? A hundred? Five? A thousand?" My eyes widen dramatically when he scoffs at my eagerness. "Well, you may not want to tell me, but I have my ways."

I'm sure Journey knows a thing or two about his little island and his minions. Not to mention Shepp, too. Once he graces us with his presence, I'm sure he'll sing like a birdy.

Which reminds me! I pull out my phone and grin, watching

the little red dot move closer and closer to our location. It shouldn't be too long now before I can kiss his cheek. I missed the big fella.

"T-Minus, two hours before you have a fun family reunion." I clap a little, tucking my phone away. "Oh, how the tables have turned. You think he'll take mercy on you?" I raise my brow.

There's no way Shepp will grant his piece-of-shit father any mercy. Sheppy Boy may seem like a gentle giant, turning pale at the sight of blood, but he'd take Thomas Mondelli out in a heartbeat.

Shadow's face tightens. But his lips remained sealed about his son. It's almost as if he expected Shepp to stay imprisoned forever.

The bastard.

"Well, enlighten me. I love to learn new things!" I say, slapping my knees. "Tell me who you keep on your big, exclusive island and why there? How'd you have the funds for something so delicious? Huh?" I lean forward with interest, watching his every little twitch to sus out the information.

"You'll get nothing out of me. Ever. I trained under the best. You know how the family works," he says, relaxing in his seat. His expression turns blank, bleeding the life right out of him.

So unfortunate he thinks I won't be able to get the information. It's my happy place, after all.

"Ah, yes. The good old days of training, right? The torture sessions and teaching us all about keeping our mouths shut in front of the enemy. That was fun. We should reenact that." I stand from the chair abruptly. The chair's legs squeal in protest when I bump it back along the concrete floor and set my bowl of popcorn down.

Shadow's expression doesn't change an inch. He watches me with a cold, detached expression, like he's already disassociated from the situation. I can't have that.

Not yet.

"Have you met Rosa yet?" I ask, inching closer to him while fingering the large knife tucked into my pants. Jericho always wonders how I haven't chopped Big A off yet. Nosy fucker. I like my knives sharp and stabby. Just like my woman, Journey. The day she stabbed me in the chest was one of the best days of my life.

We should totally do that again. If I could fuck her in my blood and use it as lube to finally take her ass. Oh, yeah. Me likey. And so does Big A. Damn. He throbs in my pants, giving away all the ideas running through me.

Shadow rolls his lips in, eyeing me with disdain—party pooper. So, I march forward, whipping out my knife named Rosa, because she loves blood and guts. I place it right above his good eye, grinning when he stares at it without emotions.

"You think one big knife is going to scare me into talking about my business?" He raises a brow, nearly cutting himself on Rosa's sharpened edge. "That's amateur shit. I'm leagues above you, boy."

I pull back, frowning at my knife. "Well, you're right," I huff, tossing Rosa away. I'll have to bury her later in remembrance of her sacrifices.

He grins at that.

"I guess I need something new. Something fancier! Oh!" I turn around, heading to get my pliers from the tray. "Let's see how hard I have to yank to get your fingernails off." Usually, with enough force, they pop off easily. Sometimes, they don't. I'm hoping for the latter. Take a man's fingernails, and he'll wail like a pussy, giving me all the answers I need.

"Bring it on." His face doesn't twitch when he says those words, egging me on.

By the time I'm finished with him, he'll be wailing for mercy. If not? I'll come up with some creative ways to loosen his tongue.

Bummer. This didn't work out how I thought it would. He's a tough nut to crack. He didn't even cry. Rude. I put all my best work into him, and he didn't even blink. I'll have to up my game. But first, I need a breather.

Between the electric baton, taking his fingernails, putting a vice around his wrist, and squeezing. I'm exhausted. Food. Nap. Fucking. That's all in my future. But not in that order. Quite the opposite. I have plans for my Kitten. Dirty, dirty fucking plans.

For now, this prick can sit on ice and think about what he did like a good little villain all tied up.

"Well, then. I'll let you sit with all that. You're officially in timeout." I grin, patting his tense shoulder. "Also, how about we make this extra kinky and put this in?" I hold up a ball gag, letting it swing in front of his face.

His chest heaves. Blood drips from his fingertips, displaying the raw nerves exposed beneath. Sweat drips from every orifice.

Yet, he doesn't speak a word.

Little fucker.

I quickly fasten the gag over his mouth and secure the ties again, making sure he doesn't have a chance to escape the chair. And for extra measure to ensure my next fun torture takes hold, I tie his head to the back of the chair so he can't move an inch.

"Well, I had a lot of fun. Did you?" I grin when his brows furrow as he attempts to scowl at me. "Don't worry, we'll continue this at a later date after I've had some dinner."

And pussy, damn it. Big A needs to reunite with his cock pocket again and again.

I hum a tune as I set up my next torture device. A bright

lightbulb hangs directly in his face. Well, until I swing it slightly, so it's swaying around him like it's the sun and he's a planet.

"New little trick I picked up. I'll see you later today. Or maybe tomorrow." I grin, shutting down the rest of the lights in the room, leaving him with one bright bulb that will never stop moving around him.

CHAPTER FORTY-TWO

Jericho

My fingers run up Journey's bare leg, drawing circles around her scuffed-up knee. Wounds Shadow, without a doubt, inflicted on her. An infraction he'll pay for later when I get my fucking hands around his throat and block the air from his lungs.

My nostrils flare as my brain tortures me with images of Journey and Shepp being held against their will. Their screams. Cries of pain when Shadow inflicted his sadistic ways on them. No. I shake it away, refusing to think of the shit they went through.

They're tough. There's no doubt about that. They could walk through fire and come out the other side burned but ready to fight.

But I know they went through something awful.

The rage I feel bellowing inside me swarms through my veins. My muscles tighten, and I ache to bleed the anger from my system. Whether I fight Arrow to the brink of death or inflict pain on a thick tree trunk outside. I need an outlet before it consumes me and brings out the monster aching to reign free from inside me.

Only, I refuse to leave my wife's side. Ever the fuck again. The look on her face—so peaceful and serene—tamps down the feelings inside me. If I stare for long enough, I'll swallow it all. The Pain. Regret. Guilt. It all mixes in a deadly concoction.

I shake it off. For now. As best I can, at least. Journey is more important than the anger festering beneath my flesh. I have to remain strong for when she finally opens her eyes after Arrow drugged her to get her here. Half of me is thankful I didn't have to fight to get her into the stolen car we used to get to the mountains. And the other half? Pissed the fuck off Arrow had to drug her again.

No fucking more.

My black fucking heart aches dangerously in my chest, shattering for her. For Shepp. We've all lived through bullshit that would knock any normal man to his knees, begging for death.

Two medium-sized moles scatter over her right kneecap, peeking out from the red scrape. I know they've always been there like tiny dots on her flesh for me to trace. I work my fingertips up her leg, which rests over my lap. Arrow had been sitting, cradling her head. But his demon took over, and the need to torture answers out of Shadow's screaming throat became too much. Should I have unleashed him? Probably not. But there was no stopping him when he had finally had enough.

It was the bruises on her. The fresh wounds that once bled that tipped him over the edge.

The moment we got to our haven—the cabin in the woods that no one knows about—we stripped Journey of the god-awful dress Shadow dressed her up in. In its stead, we put her in an oversized long-sleeve pajama shirt with a fresh pair of panties and soft socks.

One of ours. With our scents on it.

Footsteps pull me from my thoughts, stomping up the wooden stairs from the basement—a door slams and locks engage.

Thick tension bleeds through the air when Arrow

reemerges. Bloodied and sweaty, looking demonic to anyone observing from the outside. But I see the tension slowly bleeding from his muscles and the demon retreating into his mind when his shoulders sag, and relief flows through him.

"Better?" I ask, leaning my tired head against the back of the couch.

"Mostly," he answers, gently raising Journey's head from the couch and placing her back on his lap. Between the two of us, her torso rests on the sofa.

"Any answers?" I turn to watch his slack face as his fingers run through her wild curls, getting stuck in their depths.

"Not a fucking word. But don't worry, Daddy Jer. He'll talk whether he wants to or not." He doesn't look away from her as he speaks. "He's gagged for now."

He can't. She's his magnet, drawing him in—especially when she sleeps. There's something that pulls him toward her the moment her eyes shut. It's why he's always sneaking out to watch her chest move as she rests.

"I know once we're truly done with him, he'll have a lot to say," I hum with a heavy sigh.

Exhaustion weighs heavily on my shoulders, drooping my eyes. If I could grasp sleep with my fingers and have it pull me under. I would. Too bad it continues to run from me. Every part of me begs for it. My mind—the main issue. Usually, I'd take out my frustrations on my violin, playing it until the dull ache ceased and my eyes hurt to keep open. Only then could I fall asleep without a problem.

My violin is gone. Therefore, sleep is out of the question until I can get another one, whenever that is.

"Any news from Brandon?" I ask.

Our loyal soldier stayed behind, watching Rave and ensuring our empire couldn't topple more. Through our secure lines, he's kept us updated on what's happening around town while he lies low from the people who were intent on killing him. AKA my fucking father. No matter what price is on his head, he's working his ass off and reconnecting the remnants of our army. Soon to be more prominent with Elias' help.

Arrow licks his lips, finally peeking up from Journey's face. "Yeah. He says Rave is still locked and secured. He's keeping it in tip-top shape until we can come back and reopen." He gives me a half-hearted grin. No doubt feeling the same thing I am.

Will there even be a Briar Cove to go back to? A legacy to continue? Only fucking time will tell.

"Fuck Gabriel," I grumble, pinching the bridge of my nose. "Have we discovered anything about the deeds to my father's businesses?"

"Dad has been working on it since we last spoke," Arrow throws in with a tight grin.

"Interesting," I mumble, stumbling over my heavy tongue.

"So, when Dad finds out something, he'll let us know," Arrow says, furrowing his brows. "You don't think…" he trails off, a hint of insecurity passing through his tone. His fingers brush over his lips, wiping back and forth several times, getting lost in his deprecating thoughts.

Strange. Arrow rarely shows any sort of vulnerability. Perhaps his father brings out that side of him.

"He seems very genuine in his love for you, Arrow. I don't think he'd ever sell us out to my father." And that's a fact. There's no way Father Amour would ever think about forsaking his only son.

Arrow doesn't outright acknowledge my words, but I know they've punctured through his skin when he awkwardly settles back into the couch, hauling Journey with him. He fidgets. Constantly moving his leg or fingers, tapping away on the couch.

He needs a distraction—something to take away the torturous thoughts consuming his mind.

"So, how long now?" I ask, peering down at her sleeping

form again with impatience. I'm eager to have her eyes open and get her anger out of the damn way.

I do not doubt that the moment Journey wakes up from her unintentional slumber, she'll have beautiful words for both of us. Not that I completely sanctioned what Arrow did to get her back to this cabin without a fuss.

Arrow pulls out his phone carefully from his pocket and hums, checking the time.

"Not too long now," he softly says, stroking her hair more.

I nod. "You know this can never happen again, Arrow. Not only will she take your balls this time, but I'm tired of seeing her like this." Like she's *Sleeping Beauty* waiting for Prince Charming to kiss her awake.

I hate that I can't see the storm raging in her eyes, the unshed tears threatening to spill, or the anger twisting her features. She's muted right now. Dead to the world. And I fucking hate it.

Arrow's face screws up, and he glares at me. "Well, you are a party pooper, Daddy Jer. What's the fun of friendship if we can't knock each other out every once in a while?"

I roll my eyes again at his antics.

"Shake on it, Arrow," I say, extending my hand. "No more drugging any of us. Reserve it for your enemies." I raise a brow when he stares at my hand with narrowed eyes until he thrusts his hand into mine, roughly shaking it.

"You'll never know if I have my fingers crossed," he grumbles, pulling away with a pout.

Well, it's nice to see the real Arrow peeking out from beneath the shadows. I only hope this experience doesn't affect us detrimentally.

CHAPTER FORTY-THREE

Jericho

My gaze drops to Journey's sleeping form again, laying with her legs across my lap and her head on Arrow's lap. My chest tightens like rubber bands, squeezing the breaths from my lungs. We could have lost her.

Permanently, this time. No coming back from it.

After so many weeks of planning and knowing exactly where she was, it was hard to stay put and not storm the fucking island to get back what was ours. Shepp and Journey. The pieces of our family.

We felt every second of them being away in the unknown. A hole formed. Deep inside my soul, consuming me and filling me with the need to run to them. Get them back. And Arrow? I don't know how he's stayed grounded. Maybe it was the fight to get here. Or the search that kept his mind occupied.

Whatever it was, it was slowly fraying at the ends, about to snap the remaining threads of humanity he has left in him.

It won't be until Journey wakes up and Shepp is back that he'll fully calm the fuck down.

Soon.

Very, very soon.

Speaking of.

I pull my phone from my pocket, bringing up my cousin's

conversation from the previous night when she informed me of her plan.

OLIVIA

Journey is confirmed to be at the wedding. We're moving in and securing the island while Shadow is away. He is showing his face, Jer.

JERICHO

Wonderful. And you'll keep me updated?

It's been nothing but crickets since. Not a—hey, we found Sheppard alive and well, unless he managed to remove himself from the island before Olivia showed up. Very unlikely. It seemed there was no way of escaping without someone seeing them. It was too dangerous.

ME

We've gotten Journey back... Any word on Sheppard? Or the raid?

OLIVIA

Good.

JERICHO

Only good? Are we playing the circle game again where I must guess whether or not you spoke with him?

OLIVIA

I can't discuss the dealings of an ongoing investigation, dear cousin.

I can almost hear the snark in her voice. That's her typical response when I'm eager to hear the information she has.

OLIVIA

Shepp looked good. We spoke. One of my
agents was with him and took him back to
land by boat... He was warned about where
to go when he got there.

JERICHO

Wonderful...

OLIVIA

What? That's it? Where's my thank you? I
saved your ass. Again. Like always...

JERICHO

You and I have two very different definitions
of saving.

I snicker when the dots jump on the screen like she's
typing and then disappear again. Only to reappear again before
her last message comes through.

OLIVIA

I wish my aunt never had you....

JERICHO

The feelings are mutual. Although, I do thank
you for your services. As always, Liv. You go
above and beyond.

See? That's growth. I can be polite when it's necessary.

OLIVIA

Huh. He can say thank you. Interesting...

JERICHO

Now, who is being the insulting one?

OLIVIA

For real. Stay low, Jer. Shit is hitting the fan
everywhere. Shadow cashed checks he
can't seem to fund. You feel me? No, stupid
shit. Stay at your little cabin with Journey...

JERICHO

No promises.

I smirk, putting my phone away despite it vibrating in my hand with new notifications. Liv always needs to get the last word in. Not this time.

Arrow gently brushes his fingers through Journey's hair, humming a low song to himself. I've always been curious as to what goes through his mind. Or what he's truly feeling.

"It won't be too long now," he hums into her ear, gently kissing her temple.

Such a contrast from the torture he put Shadow through. He's always gentle with Journey. Or as gentle as he can be. There will be times I'm sure he'll slip up and accidentally hurt her. But that's what Shepp and I are for. Right?

Speaking of...

"What's the status on Shepp?"

Arrow's head snaps in my direction when the words leave my lips.

He grins. "Last I checked, he was about two hours away from us. Somehow, the big lug got off the island, don't know how he managed that. And now..." His tongue pokes out when he retrieves his phone from his pocket and brings up the tracking screen. "I don't know how the big fella managed it, but he's an hour away now."

He's tougher than he looks. A man on a mission to get back to the woman he went to the ends of the earth to protect.

The world doesn't see Shepp like our unit does—the sensitive man put through unimaginable things by his own flesh and blood. The outside world sees a giant man with scars on his face. They shake in their boots at his silence. It's unnerving to the enemy. Having a man who stares deep into your soul without saying a word. He knows how to make them talk.

Some also see the non-confrontational man and think they can exploit his silence. He may be weary of blood and violence because of his upbringing, but he's as strong as a damn diamond. No matter the circumstances, if someone took Journey from him, he would devise a plan to find her, like the hopeless puppy dog he is.

We all are. Hopeless stalkers, begging for crumbs from her. We'll follow Journey into the fucking darkness with no armor. We'll fight to the ends of the earth for her. To be with her. Always for her.

Our entire existence is Journey.

Our veins bleed for her. Our souls yearn for her.

Everything about us beats for her. And only her.

She's safe now, closing the deep chasm splitting me from the inside out. She's safe. Warm. We will never again allow anyone to harm her.

This time, the person who hurt her is securely held in our soundproof basement. Oh, the plans I have for the monster writhing in the darkness. He won't know what hit him.

Me. It'll be me. I'll take all my fury out on his face, forcing him to bleed for repentance.

I contemplate for several minutes whether I should tell Olivia about Shadow in my basement but think better of it. If I bring him up and say he's in our custody, Veritas will stick their nose in our business and try to take him to their deadly prison so they can have all the fun. And I can't have that. Shepp can't have that. He deserves to kill that motherfucker repeatedly until he's nothing more than a distant memory.

This is Shepp's vengeance.

Not mine. Or Journey's, or Arrow's.

Shepp's.

And my father?

Well, he's all mine. But after learning what Journey has been through, she deserves some hits, too. We'll get these bastards if it's the last thing we do. They won't live to see another day and act on their evil plots.

My skin tingles with the thought of going after my father

and bringing him down. Once and for all. Gabriel Viotto needs to fall to his knees. Blood will drain from his body, rendering him useless under my torture. His demise will be my greatest accomplishment before I grasp my future by the balls and take what was always mine.

My father's position.

One thing at a time, though.

"What do you think Max and Nova are doing right now? Do you think they're being typical lions? Taken care of?" Arrow's face scrunches at the thought of his lions perishing under neglect.

"I'm sure Max and Nova are being attended to. My mother loves animals, after all." Or she did.

That was the whole point of my father building her a zoo on the property. To appease her and make her happy when she walked around with a frown, hopelessly peering out the windows and losing herself in her thoughts. I am startled by the thoughts racing through my mind. She left me when I was so young. The memories I have are fuzzy. But this one? It comes through so clearly; it's like I'm standing beside her forlorn figure from the past.

I swallow hard. The memory of her stricken face, riddled with mysterious doubts and sadness, flashes through my memories. How long had I locked that memory away in my mind? I was forced to stay there by the cruel hand of my father. Every night when I mentioned Mommy coming back, he threw me into the darkened closet with alcohol on his breath. He'd snarl at me, saying I needed to learn my lessons.

After my mother left, he loved me less than before. It was never much to begin with. Gabriel Viotto only wanted a son to fulfill his throne.

And here I am, about to overthrow it with my allies.

But what about my mother, who has been missing for close to twenty years? Her sudden reemergence has my head spinning with possibilities. Sure, she could have dragged herself from Shadow's prison once and for all, freeing herself and making it home. But Shadow didn't exist twenty years ago.

Or did he?

Another question on the mile-long sheet of paper in my mind to ask him when I visit him in the basement.

A sudden twitch of Journey's legs moving on my lap makes my mind return to the land of the living. I blink rapidly, taking in the scene I so quickly drifted away from. It doesn't happen often, only when I've deprived myself of the sleep I desperately need.

Right now, though, the only thing I can occupy my mind with is the woman whose eyelids flutter. Her dark lashes slowly peel from her bottom lids until they're completely open, revealing her beautiful moss-green eyes hazy with sleep.

"Oh, Kitten! You're finally awake," Arrow murmurs, leaning down to kiss her cheek several times.

Journey's brows furrow as she takes in the pinewood ceiling. She blinks several times—no doubt trying to get her mind back from the sedation pulling her into a fog. I know we'll lose our balls when she remembers what happened. Literally, she's going to squeeze them so hard and show us no mercy. Well, maybe just Arrow. I had nothing to do with the sedation.

I'm innocent.

"We've brought you to a secure location," I say, easing my hand up and down her calf with reassurance. "For your safety and ours." I don't dare mention the friend we have waiting for us to chat with.

That'll come later.

We're more than secure here. Our cabin is small but fucking mighty. It's just the way we built it. Intending to hide away here when things get to be too much in Briar Cove. Call us cowards all you want; it was survive here or die there.

We could get attacked by an army, and no one could penetrate through these walls. Even if they did, the secret tunnels we've dug over the years would give us the means to escape unharmed. No one will ever find out about this place, anyway. It's out in the middle of nowhere in the mountains, many miles away from civilization.

If it was up to me. We'd stay here for eternity, raising a family and being one under this roof. But as it stands, a war is brewing. Sooner rather than later, we'll have to jump in and toss our hats into the ring to fight this battle.

And we'll win.

"Secure location?" she rasps, clearing her throat multiple times.

"Perhaps you should get her some water?" I raise a brow at Arrow, who frowns at me, obviously not wanting to leave Journey's side. But this situation is his fault, and it's better for his well-being to remove himself before she remembers the needle he put in her neck. All in the name of keeping her safe. The moment that memory pops up, she'll have a few choice words for him. Hopefully, she'll leave some scratches as well.

"I'll get my Kitten whatever she needs," he hums, getting to his feet with hesitation.

"Water," she croaks with a nod, turning slightly pale at the movement.

"Little Chaos? Are you..." My heart drops when Journey's eyes widen. A small gag comes from the back of her throat, and she heaves where she sits. Her fingers curl around her lips as she jumps up from the couch on unsteady feet, swaying with every frantic step, looking for a place to empty her stomach. I quickly usher her to the garbage can in the corner of the kitchen ten steps away and hold back her hair, just in time for her to unleash into the trash can.

"Weird," Arrow says, cocking his head. "It's never had that effect."

No. Indeed, it hasn't. Sure, after waking up from his favorite drug of choice, the person should feel slightly groggy. The after-symptoms only last ten minutes before the rage of what Arrow has done takes over and holds you hostage. Then, it's murder plots. I can only speak for myself, though. He's done this so many times it's almost an invasion of our privacy. Including the damn tracker he put in my ass cheek without my permission, which came in handy. So, I can't quite reprimand him for that.

Not yet at least.

Journey gags again, heaving another time before her entire body slumps. She pants, barely able to stand when she straightens herself up. I take her in my arms, gently letting her get herself under control.

"All better?" I murmur in her ear.

"No," she grunts, touching her stomach again.

"Must be a side effect," Arrow hums, gently wiping Journey's mouth with a paper towel and then tossing it into the trash.

"A side effect?" Journey groans, leaning her head back against my shoulder.

Everything inside me settles at once. The turmoil. The time of being ripped apart from each other. Finally. I have her here against my chest. The feel of her skin against mine. She's home. In my arms. By my fucking side. And I'll never let her leave again. She's not allowed. I'll handcuff her to me like I did before. Only this time, my beautiful bride will never get free. Even if she needs to take a shower or use the restroom. I'm prepared to be a fucking parasite attached to her hip.

"Never mind." Arrow whistles to himself, trying to seem innocent.

The bastard never could, though.

"What the fuck are you talking about?" Journey grumbles, squeezing her eyes shut and licking her lips. All the color she attempted to regain escapes her flesh again, turning her gray. Sweat trickles on her brows that furrow. She sucks in a breath. One, two, and three times, attempting to ward off the sloshing of her stomach.

"How about some water, Kitten? It'll help," Arrow's voice dips low and soothing as he holds up a glass with a straw.

"Slowly. Your stomach won't be able to take too much," I hum in her ear as I soak in her essence. Being so close to her after knowing where she was for so long and not being able to act on my urges to swim to her, has me fucking rattled.

And Jericho fucking Viotto doesn't get rattled.

I guess when you take away his obsession, he does.

Journey sucks it down slowly, panting as the sedative slowly wears off. I can see the moment the lights click on in her brain. Anger roars to life in her eyes when she throws them open, glaring in Arrow's direction.

He gives her a blinding smile while plying her with enough water to sink a fucking boat.

"Knock it off," I grunt, pushing the glass of water away.

"One of these days, Arrow," she murmurs, squeezing her eyes shut again. "One of these goddamn days, I'm going to..." she trails off, putting her fist to her lips. The sounds escaping from her stomach have my own wanting to empty.

Sympathy vomits. I think that's what they might call it.

"Would you like to sit?" I question, gently running my hands over her body, almost in disbelief that she's finally back where she belongs. At my fucking side.

"You aren't the first person to say that to me," Arrow chuckles, pecking her cheek with a quick kiss. She swipes at him with a grunt but misses when he darts back.

"Next time," he quips with a wink.

"Let's get you on the couch, Little Chaos. Then we can plot Arrow's demise." I smirk at him when he flips me off.

"No. No sitting. I need..." she stalls again. Deep, guttural gurgles burst to life in her stomach like it's trying to process all the water Arrow gave her and is denying access. "What the hell did you do to me?" she whines, reeling forward until her face hovers over the same garbage can. I gently bring her hair back, holding tightly to it.

"I'm innocent," Arrow says, putting his hands up.

Worry seems to take him over when he nibbles his lip, watching as she gags again into the trash can.

"Are you truly ever that?" I quip, rubbing her back soothingly.

"I'm not wasting another second here," Journey declares into the garbage can, still holding the water down despite her gags. "Shepp is out there. He's on the island, and I need him back here."

"Ah, Kitten. He's on his way." Arrow confidently leans against the countertop with a knowing grin.

"On his way?" she asks skeptically, furrowing her brows. "What do you..." She stiffens completely, forgetting about the sickness holding her back when Arrow holds up his phone. Four dots show on the screen, blinking rapidly back at her with names assigned to each dot representing us. "What?" Her brows furrow more when she takes the phone and examines the screen. She pinches her fingers over it, zooming in and out on each dot. Finally, she settles on the dot farthest away. Shepp.

"That's us," Arrow says, puffing out his chest. "Each of us has a tracker. So, I know where we are at all times. It's kind of my thing." Besides stalking and entering Journey's room while taking pictures of her. Yeah, it's totally his thing.

Journey glares up at him. He smiles more. One day, Arrow will get what's coming to him.

"Don't look at me like that, Kitten. I might have to kidnap you to the bedroom and reacquaint myself with your body again. Can I eat you for lunch instead?" Arrow grunts when I slap him in the back of the head. Instantly, he loses his smile, huffing as he rubs the sore spot. "Spoil sport," he grumbles.

"Can someone explain where the hell I am?" Journey asks, looking down at the phone and shaking her head. "If this is me..." she trails off, pointing at the little red dot. "Then we're..."

"In the middle of nowhere," I confirm, smoothing her wild locks. Before discussing our next steps, she needs a nice hot shower, another set of clean clothes, and a large meal. "We're at our safe house."

Hell, even three days of non-stop fucking and cuddling sounds better than going to wage war against my father and his brainless minions.

"Safe house," she mutters, eyeing the cabin skeptically.

I don't blame her. She's been in an unknown location for a while now, trapped on an island with nowhere to go. Now, she's finally free from their rule and with us.

"No one will find us here, Little Chaos. This may look like a simple cabin, but we've put a lot of work into this place, making it the perfect safe house. If anyone tries to come here and fight us, we have escape routes through the basement."

"Oh, and a torture room!" Arrow says with glee, rubbing his hands together. "With a special guest," he stage-whispers.

"A special guest?" she asks, rubbing at her head. "Fuck. Why am I so woozy? I don't have time for this. So many things need to be done. Shepp..." Her eyes drift back to the phone, watching the little red dot with a hopeless expression. "He separated us on purpose so I wouldn't run. He locked us in the caves."

"That happened to be under the ocean?" I question, eager to learn about where she was kept and how. Not only because it's her, but also because my mother, too, said she was locked tight in some caves for so many years. Or was she? Who knows? I don't trust anyone besides the people in this room and Shepp.

That's it. No more. No less.

Journey shrugs. "I'm not sure. I woke up there with Sunshine and Shepp." She shakes her head, squeezing her eyes shut like the memories harm her. "And... They left us in a cave. The darkness. No food." She shudders in my arms, and her stomach sounds like it is turning again, grumbling out loud and protesting the water Arrow forced her to drink.

"Listen, we don't have to discuss it right now. We can wait." For her sake, at least. I don't want to overwhelm her too quickly and harm her more. I'm sure she's been through a lot. I've seen the bloodied picture of her at the dining table with Shadow. And whatever else he may have put her through. I'm far from being patient, but right now, the only thing that matters is my goddamn wife.

"We can't, though. Shadow..."

"That's our special guest, Kitten."

Journey's eyes fly open, assessing Arrow as he puffs out his chest with pride. "I hogtied him myself. He put up a nasty fight. Wanted to shoot me, too. Which is rude. But I got him all tucked away and tied to a chair. Just waiting for old Sheppy Boy to make it here, then we'll have a real welcoming party." Venom spews from his lips with every word he says, amping himself up more and more for a fight that won't happen for hours.

Not until Shepp returns and not before he's ready to face his monster.

"For now, let's get you cleaned up and fed," I murmur, trailing my fingers up and down her upper arms. "How about a nice hot bath?"

Journey sighs, nodding her head. "Yeah. I guess that sounds fine." There's a bite to her voice. I can tell she's not satisfied with my solutions to stay put and not go after anyone. "Do you really have Shadow in the basement?"

"Yes." Arrow grins, stepping up to her. He cups her cheeks, strumming his thumb along her bottom lip. "We'll take care of the trash later."

"But you recognize him, right?" she asks, swallowing hard.

"Shepp's sperm donor," I state without emotions because the things I want that man to endure are Hell on Earth.

She nods, licking her lips, nodding with hesitation. There's something there in the back of her eyes. Worry, maybe? For whom, though? I'm not quite sure. Perhaps it's for Shepp whenever he arrives. But she knows better than anyone that Shepp can face the monster head-on.

Arrow tilts his head, looking into her eyes. He must sense it, too.

"Let's get you into the tub," I say, holding her hand and guiding her toward the restroom. "We have a spectacular bathroom built just for this sort of occasion." More like with her in mind. When we built this place, she was the center of it all. Did we do it to keep us safe in case shit went sideways? Of course. But she was always on our minds, especially when we built the bathroom with a tub built for four.

Our destiny was always this. Her. Us. Our future together. Even war was on the horizon. Someone was bound to challenge my father for his position, taking what they wanted right out from under him.

Only, I thought it would be us.

"Oh, yes. We'll scrub your body clean, Kitten." Arrow winks with a deep chuckle. "With our dicks."

Have I smacked my best friend lately? Yes. Perhaps he needs another reminder that my dear wife has been under an unimaginable amount of stress after being kidnapped and drugged.

I narrow my eyes at him, catching his gaze. He grins more, humming the same tune under his breath. Bastard.

My grip tightens when we walk through the doorway of the only bedroom in the nine-hundred-square-foot cabin. Our bedroom at home in the mansion is large, sleek, and modern. But here? Here, we let all our comfort wants out and played with the designs until all three of us agreed. Comfort over looks. Warmth over modern.

We built our cabin to be the home we always wanted, filled with the love we all needed dearly.

Our cabin in the woods boasts a warm and inviting

bedroom, filled with a large king-sized bed and antique dressers we scrounged from the shops ten miles away in the nearest town. A heavenly warmth radiates from every inch of the room, from the bedside lamp brightly glowing and illuminating the dark shadows to the plush rug beneath our feet cushioning our footsteps. But the grandest thing we built is the stone fireplace, roaring with warmth from behind us. It has everything we need. Financially, we could live here forever on our secret bank accounts filled with money we've stashed away since we recognized the dangers my father posed.

Journey stops in a daze, taking in the ample space with a slack mouth. Her gaze eventually finds the dying flames dancing on the embers of the logs we added hours before.

"When did you guys get this?" she asks curiously, taking in the room again. "God, you even have a cabin-like quilt," she murmurs, stepping toward the bed and running her fingers over the patchwork quilt we purchased at the shop.

"And my skulls! Don't forget my trophies." Arrow's chest puffs out with pride when he brings her focus to the three human skulls on the mantle above the fire.

"Skulls…" Journey trails off, attempting to ward off the disgust begging to be seen.

I'll give it to her. She does well containing the twist of her lips when Arrow picks up one skull, moving its hinged jaw as if it were speaking directly to her.

"Have no fear, Kitten Dear," he mocks in a twisted voice, jostling the skull around.

"Erm. How about that bath?" Journey asks wearily, staring at Arrow before shaking her head.

"Aw, Kitten. Come on! He's fun! And you'll never believe the story of how he got here." Oh, I'm sure she'll believe every word that comes out of his mouth. Right down to the gritty details of how Arrow had fun hunting three humans in the woods surrounding our cabin for their treasonous crimes against the family.

More specifically, against his father.

Our cabin isn't just a safe house for us to unwind in. It's a place of interrogation when need be. Or a hunting lodge. All for our use only. No one in the family knows this place exists. They think we take them to a warehouse on the outskirts of town used by everyone.

"I'll take your word for it, Arrow," she says softly, patting him on the shoulder with a soft smile.

He instantly relaxes, leaning in to kiss her cheek gently. "Maybe later, Kitten," he murmurs uncharacteristically against her flesh.

"To answer your earlier question, this was Shepp's idea," I hum, eyeing the pine walls, remembering when we drew up a plan to escape our lives. Or have an escape when the time came. But it became more than that to the three of us.

This is ours. Only ours.

"There was a lot of talk for a few months about over-throwing my father and taking his throne..."

"It put us in danger. Jer is his only heir. And Shepp and I are the accessories he's trained to kill and protect our bestie."

"If things ever went sideways, we wanted a place to go where no one had a clue where we were. So, we can regroup and come up with a counterattack."

"Like now," Arrow grumbles with a frown.

"What is happening in Briar Cove?" Journey asks, furrowing her brows. "Did your dad..."

"Last I saw, he was in my mother's clutches," I say through clenched teeth, trying to shake the memory of my mother and father from my mind.

The last time I saw them, they were forcing me into a marriage with Chloe Satin. Who would have rather swallowed glass than marry me. No. She wasn't into me. Not at all. She was into Leighton. The way they were cuddled up at the initiation ball has my hackles rising once again. Their lovey-dovey smiles and touches. There's a spark between them—something hidden from the rest of the Family. Now, I'd investigate why if I could get closer to either of them.

But as it stands. I'm in the middle of nowhere, and they're still in Briar Cove, fighting the good fight. At least, I think they are.

"Your mother?" Journey asks with weary eyes when we enter the bathroom just a few steps from our bedroom.

The rustic and warm aura continues throughout the bathroom, creating an inviting room to unwind. I heave a breath, taking in the hints of lavender and vanilla spilling through the air. Instantly, my muscles relax, forgetting all the worries I once carried when I walked into this room.

I guess it's doing as intended. Relaxing our weary bodies.

Journey leans against the double vanity. Wide-eyed and slack-jawed again, eyeing the room in awe. The soft lights of the room beam off her porcelain and bruised skin, making my fingers slightly curl.

"This is the most beautiful bathroom I've ever fucking seen," she mumbles, more to herself than anyone.

My fingers caress the softness of her cheeks, bringing her gaze to mine. "I'll never let anyone harm you. Ever the fuck again," I whisper, swallowing the rage seething inside me.

"Promise?" A sheen glazes over her eyes, and she blinks rapidly, trying to dispel the tears she doesn't want me to see.

"Cross my heart and hope to die," I promise with a tight smile, trailing my fingers down her front. "Now, why don't we get into the tub and soak the afternoon away? Once Shepp returns, we'll regroup and figure out what we're going to do."

"I know what we're going to do," she says, raising her chin until I see the determination sparkling in her moss-green eyes.

"Oh, yeah?" Arrow asks, coming to her other side with his shirt off. "Turn." Journey doesn't even question it when she turns her back to him, and he gently pulls her shirt over her head. "Tell me in full detail, Kitten. I want to know what's going through your brain." I watch with envy as his fingers trail over her sides.

"We're going to fuck my monster up." Her nostril flares when Arrow gently caresses her breast, kneading it like dough in his hands.

"More," Arrow whispers in her ear, trailing kisses down her neck and onto her bare shoulder.

I swallow hard, removing my clothes until the three of us stand there completely naked, giving me a full view of her marred flesh.

"Why don't we get into the water?" I gesture to the tub filled with hot water.

"Party pooper," Arrow quips, kissing her cheek one last time before he steps back. "Let's snuggle in the water." With that, he takes her hand, leading her to the tub, where he gets in first and then pulls her in with him. She chuckles with a throaty laugh and nestles her back to his front, closing her eyes.

"You never answered my question about your mother," Journey hums as I enter the tub and sit opposite them. With a sigh, my back slides down the cool porcelain, balancing the heat of the water.

"It seems she's come back from wherever she fucked off to. Unfortunately, I don't think she returned because she was finally free." I shake my head. "She swore up and down Shadow had snatched her and held her captive this entire time."

"But you don't believe her?" she whispers.

I blow out a breath. "I don't know at this point." Her return has flipped my entire life upside down.

I don't know who or what to believe. The entire thing is one messed-up plot twist, and I'm not ready to wrap my mind around it.

"Would you like me to wash your hair?" I rasp, attempting to take my over-active mind away from the darkness it's trying to unravel. Between my wife's injuries, my best friend who is still MIA, and my parents' fucked-upness, I'm having a hard time staying in the present with a sound mind.

She nods her approval, sitting up to sit face-to-face with me. "Please." A vulnerability she rarely shows anyone sits on the edge of her voice, aching to be free. She swallows hard, moving her frizzy curls so they're at her back.

"Anything for you," I murmur, moving forward to cup her cheeks again. The warmth of the water rests between us when I lean in, placing a small kiss on her chapped lips. "Absolutely anything."

I've made several vows in my life. Pledging myself to the family twice over now with the pledge I'd fight until the end, spill blood, and die for the cause. But this vow is the most important one—besides my marriage vow.

I'd do anything for her to keep her safe and unharmed.

Arrow gently washes her back, scrubbing her skin in gentle circles. "Are you hungry, Kitten? We have plenty of goodies in the cabinets that will last us a month."

"Soup and crackers would be good," she sighs, leaning back as my fingers massage her scalp. I gently spray hot water over her hair, wetting it completely with the sprayer attached to the tub. "You said Shepp was on his way?" She peeks an eye open when I gently massage shampoo into her curly locks.

"He should be here shortly."

"Not too long now, Kitten," Arrow hums appreciatively.

She nods. "I wonder how he got away. It was..." She shakes her head, twisting her expression. "We would have left sooner, but my sister was there, too. And the rocks. We couldn't have…" Her raspy voice cracks with every word she speaks, emotions flaring deep inside her.

"Hmm. And where is she now?" I ask with curiosity.

She would not have gone to the wedding without Sunshine being in a secure location.

"Mikhail Antonov took my sister before I could say goodbye."

Fuck.

My movements stop. Did she say Mikhail Antonov? The prince of the fucking Bratva. Russian through and through. His father is the most ruthless mobster in Florida, practically owning the entire fucking state from his headquarters in Miami.

Fuck.

"The Bratva?" I question as levelly as I can muster.

Journey immediately tenses up, looking between the two of us for answers.

"Those crazy motherfuckers have your sister. God damn. How did,,," I shoot Arrow a pointed look, and he zips his lips and widens his eyes.

Way to be subtle, you fucking prick. If she thinks her sister is in any sort of goddamn danger, she'll run out of here and straight to Miami.

"What can you tell me about them?" she asks hurriedly, looking between us. "Please. He married her. He... He seemed genuine about it, though. I..."

My thoughts fall back to the little Antonov. The only time we greeted each other was long ago. He was stiff. Guarded. Even for a child way younger than me.

"I, unfortunately, know little about them. They did business with my father. Or attempted to. But it didn't work out. They left to go back to their territory on the ports of Miami, and we never heard from them again. Although the Bratva likes to make connections throughout the US, they never again asked my father for anything. Or any Viotto, for that matter." I rub my chin, thinking of the implications of Journey's confession.

"Shadow killed his father right before my eyes. Sunny and Mikhail were in a marriage contract, but before they left, they were married. They were supposed to be at the wedding, but he took her away before I could say goodbye."

"We'll find your sister. No matter what." My nostrils flare until Journey's gaze meets mine again. "What is it?"

She licks her lips. "Mikhail vowed to aid you in whatever fight that's coming. He said that, for her, he'd side with us and let us use his army."

For a price, I have no doubt. What could the Bratva possibly want with us? Something I'm sure I'll have to discuss with the leader of the Bratva now. So, what's one more associate in the fight to end my father's reign?

"So. If we have the Bratva and the Blue Spider Gang in our pocket. I suppose a meeting of sorts is in order." I rub my chin with a sigh.

That's a lot of powerful people to have in one room.

"I'll text Elias and attempt to set something up. But as for Mikhail, we'll find his contact information somehow. We have to..."

"I need to speak to Sunshine," Journey urges. "They left so quickly that I didn't get to speak to her or say goodbye." Again.

She didn't get to say goodbye again. It's something that's happened to her repeatedly throughout her life now. I'll make sure she never has to experience it again.

It's written on her saddened face. It's something I've rarely seen from her. Sure, I've wiped away her tears and consoled her. But she's always bounced back and made a full recovery. This time, though. This has shaken her to the core. Perhaps it's whatever she endured at Shadow's island. I have no doubt about that. I'll peel it out of her slowly and give her time to realize she's no longer in danger. Well, not as much danger with us. Despite being hunted for who we are and having my father after us.

"Little Chaos, I promise you this. We'll get you in contact with your sister, even if we have to track down the Miami address and go there ourselves. The Antonov family doesn't make promises easily." That is something I know for a fact from experience. "We'll get her back. I promise."

She nods. Not saying another word as we continue to wash her.

It's surreal to have her back in front of our eyes. Even though she was gone for a short time, having her away was the worst possible thing I could have experienced. Hell, having all my brothers away from me was torture.

"Let's get you dressed, Kitten. I have the perfect outfit." He smiles, helping her stand.

Water drips off their naked bodies, and although we're both hard as rocks, we don't push her buttons.

Arrow wraps a towel around her, drying every inch of her flesh. I take a towel to her hair, gently scrunching her curls until they're no longer dripping.

"Here ya go, Kitten." Arrow holds up a sleep tank top and a small pair of shorts with a grin. "It'll keep you nice and cool."

She narrows her eyes. "I want warmth. Not sexy," she grumbles, swiping the top and shorts from Arrow's hold and throwing them onto the bed. "Sweatpants? T-shirt?"

Arrow pouts at her choices but digs in the bottom dresser drawer while humming a tune. "You're lucky I love you, Kitten."

My eyes widen at his words when he gets to work on her unmoving body, putting a fresh pair of panties and a sports bra on her.

"You love me?" She takes the words right out of my mouth. "You…" Her brows scrunch.

Arrow is not the type of person who admits his love. If he can even feel it. He's the type of person to possess her. Stalk her. Take pictures of her. The genuine feeling of love, though? Not something I expected. He's vowed to her before and told her he'd kill for her. That's the type of love he gives out. Actions. Obsessions.

"Um, duh," he says with a shrug. "Why wouldn't I?" He steps back after putting his large t-shirt over her head and admires her outfit with a pleased grin.

"I didn't think..."

He waves a hand. "I love you, Kitten. My heart is your heart. I'll take down the enemy for you. Jump in front of a bullet for you. Anything to keep you breathing. My love may be slightly different, but it's all the same." He wiggles his eyebrows when he cups her cheeks, suddenly falling serious. "Don't doubt what I would do for you."

"I...." She licks her lips, staring him up and down.

"It's okay, Kitten. I know you have a hard time expressing those feelings. You don't have to say it. Besides, I need to feed and cuddle you, and then we can bathe in Shadow's blood together." He grins, tugging her hand for her to follow him, and walks out of the bedroom.

My obsession with Journey has become something greater than that. It's become love—an unfathomable feeling I never thought I'd get to experience, either. For so long, I've hidden myself from people, putting on a mask in front of the masses. My mother disappeared. My father hid behind alcohol and anger, never showing any affection.

The only people I've ever considered loving were the two men who became my brothers. My second-in-command and my protector. Sheppard and Arrow. Then, I was handed the picture of the girl I was obsessed with but forced away from.

Now, I'm almost positive I've fallen down the deep, dark rabbit hole of love.

I love Journey West.

A loud knock at the front door interrupts my musings, and Arrow grins brightly.

"I think that's for you, Kitten."

CHAPTER FORTY-FOUR

Shepp

I don't dare breathe when the door to Shadow's office creaks open, and Darrell stands there with an unreadable expression. Through all the noise of the glass shattering and my fucking mind spiraling, I didn't hear the elevators.

I heard nothing but my damn heart breaking.

Darrell blinks several times, taking in the carnage of the room. His frown deepens.

"The fuck are you doing in here?" he grunts, eyeing me with narrowed eyes. "And what the fuck did you do?" he gestures stiffly to the painting on the ground.

Darrell's sharp words hang in the air. What the fuck are you doing in here? It was a good question. I could lie my ass off and tell him I got lost and just wandered into this secret office.

Yeah, right.

He'd never believe that. But I was trying to save face. Save myself from the future of Shadow's wrath when he returns.

If he knew I was in here, then he'd hurt Journey. And me. Severely. Hell, even kill us. Us being here still doesn't make sense to me. He can tell me until I'm blue in the face that he wants to marry me off or have me prove my loyalties.

But why now? He didn't give a shit about me before. Still doesn't.

No matter the reason. I have to keep my guard up around Shadow, which means I have to keep myself guarded around Darrell, too. Considering Shadow trusts him so damn much.

Lifting my chin, I exhale all my worries, erasing the emotions from my expression. Facing Darrell, I stand tall, rolling my shoulders back. He stands slightly shorter than me, having to lift his chin to stare coldly into my eyes.

He takes a step back, closing us in the room together. Tension tightens my chest with anticipation. This motherfucker could take me down. Rat me out. One wrong move, and I'm toast, but I'm not the only one.

Not a peep comes from him again as he takes in the status of the room. He wrinkles his nose, almost huffing beneath his breath.

"The fuck you doing in here?" he grunts again, waltzing into the room, shaking his head. "Breaking shit?" He picks up the painting and nods once. "From Grace, huh?" My ears ring from the name he used. "Interesting," he mumbles. "So, you find anything useful?" His brows raise expectantly when he sets the painting on Shadow's desk.

'What about Grace?' I write out, holding it up for him to see.

He chuckles lowly. "I was hoping you'd get further than this. We've got a lot to discuss, Sheppard." His brows furrow when he looks at the pictures I left on top. "I only saw these a few times. But you get what happened, right?" He scowls, picking it up and reading the back of it. "Damn..." he mutters, trailing off.

'They were in love before Gabriel?'

Darrell snorts, handing the pictures to me. "Bingo. Thomas and Grace were an item throughout high school. They were made to be a match, too."

'A match? Like....'

"They were going to be married in June after high school

graduation. But never made it. Instead, Grace married Gabriel."

'They were forced to.' Even I know the answer to that.

Nodding to the pictures, he says, "Keep them. I'm sure you'll need them more than Shadow." I snatch them up and shove them into my pocket, pulling the piece of paper I found with the blueprints detailing instructions on the start of the war.

A massive explosion at the hotel where Elias and Jenni will get married.

'What's the meaning of this?' I write out, pointing to the blueprints. I'm almost positive I know what's going to happen. *'He's going to attack Elias at his wedding?'* I raise a brow when he reads the pages, rubbing his chin. I'm unsure why he's here and not dragging me back to my room. It makes no sense.

"Ah. It seems you've come across his plans for the day. Fucking wonderful." He shakes his head, reading over the page again until he turns to face me. His jaw tics and his fists curl. "What the fuck is that?" he hisses, snatching something from my pocket. I gape at him. Not remembering I had left the agent's badge from last night in my pocket. I don't even know what happened to him. "Where'd you get this?" he grits, stepping toward me with a menacing look. "Where the fuck is Agent 10?"

I blink several times at him as the badge hangs from a chain in front of my face, taunting me. *'Shadow had him tortured down the hall. Now, I don't know.'* I write out, earning a curse.

"I can't fucking take it anymore," he seethes, pulling out his phone while keeping his eyes on me. After a few rings, the phone clicks on, and a familiar female voice comes over the damn phone. "The time is right," Darrell grumbles into the phone. "Send everyone in. Shadow is gone. Secure the premises."

'What the fuck is happening?' I scribble quickly.

"This is where things are going to get so much fun, Shepp. Like I said, we have a lot to discuss. So, sit down and fucking listen." He gestures to the chairs with impatience, but I don't move.

I roll my wrist, insisting that he continue.

Darrell shoves his phone into his pocket and pinches the bridge of his nose. "I'm Agent Twelve with Veritas. Veritas sent me here a year and a half ago as an undercover agent. I received a call recently from my supervisor, Agent Seven. She was concerned about her cousin's friends, Shepp and Journey."

'Olivia.' I write out with realization. She's the only one who would have called it in. No doubt, Jericho and Arrow went to her first for help, knowing she had the manpower to get to us.

What I didn't expect was secret agents pretending to be in a gang.

"She wanted you two to have an ally of sorts. Although I don't think your wife likes me very much." An ally? Is that what he called dragging us around?

'You were rude.' I write out with a frown.

"Whatever," he grumbles, running a hand down his face.

'What's the plan?' If he's a Veritas agent, there must be an escape plan to get us both to safety.

But what about Journey?

"You're going to grab whatever you need from here, and then we're going to a boat and getting the fuck out of here. Veritas will fully control this place and take Shadow down if all goes well."

'Why not do it when he's here?'

Darrell levels me with a look. "We wouldn't have gotten close enough while he was here. There are too many warriors with weapons. We needed him away. Separated from the men here. It's the first part of our plan."

'And then you'll take him down?'

This is the most crucial part. I don't trust Shadow. He's a

roach, getting cut to bits and coming back to life more powerful than ever.

"We have eyes on him," Darrell says with a nod. "Now, get your shit together. We need to get out of here before shit hits the fan. Agents have been in place since the Russians took off."

'You've been planning this for a while.'

"Yeah. It was all coming to a head. Since Grace and Thomas split their plans, we've had eyes on both of them, trying to figure out what the hell is happening."

'So, she's been in on it from the beginning?'

Darrell reads my words repeatedly. "You don't truly understand what happened."

I shake my head. *'Enlighten me.'*

Darrell huffs, watching me stuff the letters and pictures into my pockets. I'd attempt to take the painting, too. But it won't fit anywhere.

"Grace was the beginning," Darrell says. "She's the original Shadow. The one who bought and revamped this island and hotel. It was all Grace. She brought Thomas here, and they ruled together. He helped her build their army of dumbasses." He throws an arm, pointing toward the wall. "So, you understand now? We're not dealing with one person named Shadow. They're an entity. A group. She's off doing..." He shakes his head. "No idea, actually. She never let me sit in on her meetings with Thomas. He kept tight-lipped about their true plans. But ever since she's been gone, he's gone off the fucking rails. Hence, why he's showing his face at a damn wedding."

Grace is fucking Shadow. No wonder he was talking to Grace on the phone. They're plotting together.

'Is this where she disappeared to?'

Darrell shrugs. "Grace became a person we kept our eye on the moment she purchased this island under a false company name a few years ago."

I scowl. *'Why the fuck hasn't anyone stepped in and arrested them already? You've been here for years?'*

"If there's one thing you'll learn about Veritas is that we're thorough in our investigations." He shrugs.

'Thorough or stupid?' I grunt, writing the word as rage burns through me. *'You could have taken them out by now and stopped them from threatening us. Bringing us here! What about Journey? Sunshine?'*

"Journey will be fine at the wedding. Do you think she'll be there with just him? We have Intel that suggests–" I growl when he says that. "Okay, more than suggests. Jericho and Arrow will be in attendance. They've been swayed to take her by any means possible to a safe location, where I will drop you off. My boss has been in constant contact with them." He shakes his head. "She's lucky she's the big boss," he mutters.

Something morphs on Darrell's face, twisting into an unreadable expression. The only gesture he makes is putting his finger over his lips.

I roll my eyes. *'Like I talk.'*

He quickly waves me off, moving to stand beside the door. Swallowing hard, he turns to me. "Someone is coming." I nod.

Great. *'Burly guy from yesterday?'*

Darrell nods when his brows furrow. "Brace yourself."

As soon as the door opens, Darrell lifts his gun, pointing it at the burly man's face.

"Fuck you doing here?" Darrell grunts out, not lowering his weapon.

"Boss asked me to check on some shit while he was gone. Looks like he was right." The burly man stands solidly in the doorframe with a frown, reaching for something in his jeans.

Darrell watches him closely, holding his weapon at the ready. "Was right about what?" he asks gruffly, stiffening at burly's man's movements.

"Right about you fuck–" burly man trails off when his eyes widen a second after two gunshots sound from the hall. He goes to turn but stops dead when he falls onto the ground with a thud and doesn't move again.

Darrell blows out a breath, moving forward with his gun pointed at a shadowy figure looming in the hallway. He almost blends in with the darkness surrounding him, standing tall and limping a few steps. Darrell hesitates with slow steps and shallow breaths, jerking the gun in his direction.

"Come out, motherfucker," Darrell hisses, trembling when the figure moves forward, revealing his face to the light of the office. "Before I..."

"Don't worry, he's fucking dead," his slightly familiar raspy voice says. "Should I light this asshole up next? I'd be glad to rid you of the extra weight." He gestures to me, not bothering to lift his gun.

"What..." Darrell breathes with disbelief. His eyes widen at the sight of the agent, paling like he's seen a ghost. The grip on his gun falls, and the small firearm falls to the ground without care. He doesn't seem to notice. His eyes never stray from the man in front of him. "Zane," Darrell chokes out, clasping his cheeks. "You..." Before I can blink, Darrell and Zane embrace, kissing for an embarrassingly long time.

"Wow, Big D. Glad to see you, too. Ready to admit your feelings for me?" Zane quips through a pained expression.

How is he even standing after what happened earlier?

"You know I would have. You know..." Darrell trails off.

"Not the time, okay? I'm assuming it was you who called in the brigade?"

Darrell nods. "Agent Seven is on her way with reinforcements. But we need to get out of here before the rest of the compound wakes up and grabs their weapons for the fight of the fucking century."

Zane hisses. "It's a little too late for that. Big guy here came down here to find you. Veritas is on the island. The fight has begun."

"Not for you," Darrell hisses. "You're too injured..."

"You can thank that fuck behind you and his father for all this. Fuck…." Zane trails off, heaving a breath.

Darrell's eyes glare through me. "The fuck you do?"

'Whatever I had to do to stay the fuck alive.' I turn the notepad so they can read.

Darrell takes a menacing step toward me, eyeing me with murder in his eyes. I don't blame him. Not at all. If his love for Zane is strong enough, he'd kill for him.

But I truly had no choice. I could have said no. And then? Well, I would have been tossed into the darkness.

Zane reached out, catching Darrell by the scruff of his shirt. "I'll be fine, Big D. Let's just argue about this later. Also, we'll discuss how you put me in the friend zone for three years, and now we're here. It was rude," Zane trails off, limping down the hall toward the elevators. "Also fucking unnecessary!" he shouts with a huff.

"I should punch you and leave you here," Darrell snarls, pointing a finger at my chest.

'But you won't. Because you've had to do shit you didn't want to, too. Do you think I wanted to do that? I had no choice.' I lift my chin when he reads it with narrowed eyes.

He knows I'm right. I can tell by the slight softening in his eyes. He nods, running a trembling hand down his face.

"We all have to do shit we don't want to do. Even if it's beyond our morals. Even if you're a part of the fucking mafia. After this, I'm asking for desk duty." He grabs my wrist and pulls me forward until we're all in the elevator, preparing ourselves for the unknown happening above us.

"It's a war zone up there. Be prepared to dodge bullets and shit," Zane grunts, digging guns out of ripped jeans.

"Where were you?" Darrell asks through a breath. "And how did you get those?"

"Asshole threw me in one of the rooms. He wanted to keep me alive, at least. He came to get me and asked me more questions, but a bomb went off outside. Saved by the bomb," he quips, wincing again. "Anywho, dumbass, forgot to lock me in, so I followed him down here and picked a few of these up along the way." He waves the gun a few times with a cocky smirk.

"How the fuck did you get to the lower level without the code?" Darrell asks wide-eyed.

"Oh, there's a code?" Zane grins, exposing his broken smile. "Here you go, asshole. Just don't use it on me. I was your fucking escape, by the way. So thanks for stabbing me a bunch." He frowns with a huff, wincing with pain.

I don't bother to write anything or acknowledge what I did. He's alive. I had to do it. It is what it is. I can't let the guilt eat me up.

"Big D, I suggest you march out first. They'll know your face and won't shoot. We'll be your backup." Zane assures him, squeezing his shoulder. "And, Dallas?" he murmurs, obviously using his real name. "When we're back on the mainland, I'm taking you out. No more hiding, you dickbag."

"No more hiding," Darrell or Dallas or whatever whispers with a nod.

"Now, don't die. Or I'll kill you myself." Zane gives him a crooked grin just as the elevator opens.

The sounds of bullets pinging off metal surfaces and the grunts of fighting hit my senses first. Angry shouts echo off the tall ceilings of the lobby. Weapons clink. Bullets fly. It's pure fucking chaos playing out.

Darrell stops me with a hand on the chest, glaring at me. "We're gonna join him in just a second. Your goal is to get out the fucking door and down to the docks. Olivia should be waiting for you."

I nod in response.

"That asshole really took your tongue?" I glare at him, and he grins like a psychopath when I nod again. "Interesting... I'm sure we'll torture him nice and slow when we get our hands on him."

Good. He deserves it, and I'm aching to pay my father back in spades. That motherfucker doesn't get to walk this earth any longer.

'Make it fucking hurt,' I write out messily with a snarl, and he nods, saying nothing further.

With that, we march out of the elevator with our guns raised, ready for action. Uniformed Veritas agents swarm the place, outnumbering Shadow's men by at least a dozen or more. Shadow's men fight against their hold as they bring them to their knees, handcuffing and hauling them away. Darrell keeps his gun raised, taking out a few of Shadow's men with direct hits to their chests. The utter shock of betrayal stays on their faces long after they've bled out on the ground. Clearly, they recognize Darrell as one of their own. Or so they thought.

"Put your weapons down now!" hollers a familiar female voice, shouting to the men attempting to fight for their lives against them. "Or die being dumbasses!" she shouts, popping off a few rounds and putting them into the legs of several of Shadow's men who hide in the room's darkness. They instantly fall, grunting and cursing her aim. She's always been good with a weapon—a sniper in the making for the family. Well, until that all fell apart, and she became an agent of the law. "Clear the room! One at a time! Make sure none of these motherfuckers are hanging around."

Olivia huffs, scanning the room again. An odd sense of silence filters through the air as Shadow's men drop their weapons and fall to their knees, giving in to her demands. Satisfaction shows on her face when she smiles widely and nods.

"Good choices!" She claps a few times as two lines of agents clear every room. More of them take the elevator and start going through the hotel above us, shouting for people to come out.

Zane wheezes, slowly returning to Olivia as they exchange

a few words. Her gaze checks over his wounds and nods at his words before gently clasping his shoulder.

"Go," she says, nodding toward the door. "You need medical." That he does; he's looking worse for the wear. And it's all because of me.

Zane snorts, passing me on his way out the door, and then stops. "Well, it looks like it's all under control now. No more dangerous toys for you. You might try to use this on me," he wheezes, nearly collapsing when he plucks the gun from my hands until Darrell grabs hold of him. "Ah, my savior!" he shouts joyously while flipping me the bird.

"Take him to the main boat for medical assistance," Olivia instructs, waving a finger at Darrell. "Then, we'll have a nice debriefing once we get back to headquarters!" she shouts at their backs before they disappear arm in arm out the hotel's front door.

"Sheppard Mondelli, you're a sight for sore eyes," she says, smiling at me sincerely. She gently nudges her shoulder into my arm. "Glad to see you made it out okay." Emotions glisten in her eyes. "Jer and Arrow came to me after the fallout in Briar Cove. They're fine. Or as fine as they can be." She rubs her temple. "After all of this is over, don't contact me again," she quips with a groan. "I'm so sick of this mafia and gang shit." She shakes her head playfully.

I snort, inspecting her more. There's a tension there in her jaw. Muscles rigid with fucking secrets she's not saying. I've known her since childhood, when her father worked with Gabe. They were brothers. Well, until hers fucked the family over, and he was outcasted to a mission far away to get them out of Gabriel's hair, taking her out of our sights for good. I guess that's why she landed in gang territory, forced to work with that douchebag that fucked her, her father, and her mother over. It wasn't until I had to attend her damn funeral did I understand the severity of it all.

'Did Jer and Arrow tell you where they were going?' I sign,

hoping she knows. She's always kept our secrets for some reason, looking out for us when we needed her most. Of course, we offer her assistance when we can.

"They said you'd know where to go?" she questions, raising a brow.

Ah, the cabin. The space we created as our own personal haven. Somewhere to hide out when everything fell to shit. Like now. I nod.

'And Journey?' My heart sinks at the thought of her. Shadow still has his claws in her. The wedding should be finished by now. He's either hiding out with her or something terrible has happened.

My heart pounds, overtaking my hearing as the blood rushes there.

Olivia cocks her head. "We had her pinpointed at the wedding earlier." Her face goes blank, raising my hackles.

She was at the wedding—the wedding that apparently everyone was supposed to die at if my father had his way.

'What aren't you saying?' I sign quickly as a boat pulls up to the docks with more agents inside them.

"Go to the mainland, Shepp. Go wherever they are. I promise it will all be okay," she says, squeezing my shoulder affectionately.

'You're holding back,' I sign with frustration. *'If something happened to her...'* I let her slip right between my fingers that night of the fight. She was dragged away from me with fear in her eyes. And I just... sat there. Now, she's somewhere in the wind. Possibly hurt from the plans I saw on Shadow's desk. But I need to hear her tell me about it.

"Remember this. Journey is so strong. She can make it through anything, okay?" She pinches the bridge of her nose and releases a heavy breath. "I have a feeling I'm going to regret this. But you're the most sensible one of my cousin's friends. She was at Elias' wedding. There was a disturbance there. Loud explosions. We got intel that Shadow was going to show his face. No clue that he was planning an act of terrorism. It's why we're here. Not only to rescue you, but to investigate here and see what we can find before he returns and we can take him down."

I nod, nausea taking over my stomach. *'Shadow succeeded? There's fire?'*

Olivia swallows hard at the mention of fire, slightly paling. "Yes. But we have tabs on what is happening there, okay? I'll give Darrell word with updates."

Utter desperation works its way through me. I swear to God, if anything happens to Journey, I'll slowly sink into the darkness that's always been inside me, staying there until death overtakes me.

'I'll hold you to it,' I sign quickly, my fingers shaking with the news. *'How long have you known that your Aunt Grace was Shadow, too?'* Jericho will lose his shit when he finds out Olivia knew this entire time where his mother was. He's wondered for years, yet his cousin knew it all.

Olivia's eyes fall to the ground, and she sighs. "Listen, this was an open investigation. I couldn't have said anything, even if I knew. Grace's involvement with Thomas was never crystal clear. She hid behind many false names, and her face never surfaced. Even this island is under a corporation. We've had our eyes on Thomas since he came onto the scene, watching what he does. But before that? Nada." Sometimes, I wonder how useful Veritas is. They've been watching Shadow for this long and haven't done anything to prevent him from hurting others. Like their own agent.

I could ask her why she hasn't intervened until now. But I hold my fingers still, watching the guilt play out on her face.

"We had to build a case, Shepp. Everything they've done as Shadow has been under the radar with no physical evidence."

'And now?'

"Now, we have enough evidence of their crimes—a trail of papers and eyewitnesses to put them away for eternity.

"Now, get going. We've got an island to take over." She grins at that. "Time to bring this piece of shit down, right? Darrell will accompany you across the waters. Okay?"

'If you find him...' I sign with a deep breath.

"He's all yours, Shepp. Believe me. Even if we cart his ass to Veritas prison, I'll give you all the glory. I fucking promise that." She nods.

'Thank you,' I sign, giving her a soft smile.

"Okay. Off you go. I'll keep Darrell updated with what we know. Go get your girl and your friends. I'm sure they're fucking tearing at the walls."

I'm only concerned about getting back to Journey, Jericho, and Arrow. They're my family. The real reason I do everything. My goddamn world.

Worry gnaws at my mind the entire time we cut through the ocean's waves. The night sky settles, giving way to the bright stars sparkling above us. The moon hangs high in the darkness, offering us little light with its crescent shape. It's so serene. So peaceful. I want to capture moments like this on my canvas in remembrance of the hell I overcame and the new hell I'm about to walk into without more answers.

But I have a few answers to our questions, but it's nothing Jericho will want to hear. Telling him that his mom is the final piece of the puzzle he's been trying to assemble since he was five will be brutal. More than fucking brutal.

We'll get through it, though. We'll fight until we secure Briar Cove and destroy our monsters. Because we're family, and no one can ever tear us apart again.

It takes hours to maneuver through the ocean and stop the boat at an abandoned marina on the outskirts of Briar Cove.

"You know where the fuck you're going?" Darrell asks with a frown as we sit side by side in the boat. Him at the wheel, and me beside him.

I nod, pulling out my notebook. *'Yes.'*

"Such a man of fucking words," he grumbles, fidgeting in his chair. I smile at that, chuckling softly. Darrell stiffens at the sound of my laugh. "Here," he says, pulling out a set of keys. "There's a jeep up there for us. I'm supposed to escort you back to your hiding place. No, I won't tell anyone. I don't really give a fuck. The big boss wants to make sure your buddies are still alive. Those are my orders. I have to abide by them." There's anguish in his tone when he sighs, pinching the bridge of his nose. There's a story between him and Zane, and he's eager to get back to him and ensure he's okay. Instead, he has to accompany me back to the cabin. A place I'm not necessarily positive his presence will be welcomed.

But it is what it is.

'Thanks for the help,' I write with a sigh.

"I don't understand why she helps you, but just know that when the time comes and we need something, you had better answer," Darrell grunts, waving a hand and standing.

'Family is family. No matter what agency they're in.' I write, standing from my seat with him as the water rocks us back and forth.

"Family..." he trails off with a nod. "Let's get this show on the road. The quicker I babysit you and take you back to mafia land, the quicker I can get back to..." he trails off, scoffing at himself.

To Zane. It makes me wonder how they're going to work out. He's obviously had repressed feelings for the man he hasn't seen in years.

Darrell and I leave the marina after securing the boat to the docks toward a jeep sitting in the empty parking lot.

"Hop in," he grunts, setting a bag in the backseat.

We both jump into the Jeep and take off toward the cabin in the mountains toward my family. My home. My people that I need to hold.

It takes several hours before we reach the remote cabin set

in the mountains, several hours away from Briar Cove. It's a breath of fresh air—a haven I've missed after being trapped on an island with a monster.

"This is it?" Darrell grumbles, slumping in the passenger's seat.

'You look like hell,' I write on my notepad with a snort.

"Let's get this over with. You should know that my boss has advised me on what I can and cannot say. But the most important information I can tell your friend is who his mom is and what she's done and will do." He raises a brow, inspecting my tightening face.

'He'll want to choke you.'

"Well, he better keep his fucking hands away from me. I'm an agent with Veritas. You best remember that." He doesn't give me a second to comprehend the shit storm that's brewing when he climbs out of the fucking Jeep and starts toward the front door.

I chase him, running in front of him with a sour expression. *'Let me,'* I write quickly, holding it up so he can see.

"Fine. You knock." He gestures for me to get to it.

So, I do.

I knock on the door, separating me from the only family that has ever cared for me. I knock until my heart hammers against my ribs, drowning out all other sounds, and the door opens to reveal the woman I have longed for since the night of the fights when she was taken from me.

CHAPTER FORTY-FIVE

Journey

My heart pounds against my ribs when another knock rocks through the cabin. Is it him? Has he truly escaped from the island? God, I fucking hope so. It's been hell without him by my side. The guilt I felt going to the wedding with that monster instead of Shepp nearly killed me. Maybe that's why my stomach is in such knots right now.

I lick my lips, swallowing down the bile attempting to shoot up my throat. All I need is food. Oh, and a nice long nap before things kick off in the basement. Arrow has promised Shadow's death when Shepp returned. There's no villain getting out of those restraints and sneaking away under our noses. I'm ready for it. They're ready for it. And I know for a fact, Shepp has been ready to end his father's life since the moment he magically came back to life.

Shadow deserves every ounce of torture for what he's done.

"Better answer it, Kitten. Your face is the only one he'll want to see." Arrow winks, shooing me away with the flick of his wrist.

My legs shake beneath me when I stand. God, I feel like a newborn deer stumbling over my feet. I catch myself on the arm of the couch with a huff. This has to be the effects of that damn drug Arrow gave me. Something I'll punish him for later because fuck him for doing that. Again. It wasn't like this before. Sure, I was groggy and had sand in my damn eyes, but this feels different. Like I need a full day's nap or a year's vacation. Yeah, that sounds better to me. Maybe once all this mafia shit is put to rest, we can go on a holiday and sit on the beach and do nothing at all.

But right now, I have a door to answer.

Jericho looms cautiously behind me, standing close when I peek out the window to confirm it's him. My heart nearly leaps from my chest at the sight of him standing outside. The sun beams down on him like he's a goddamn angel. He is my savior. The man who kept me sane in the darkness of the caves. The man who grounded me when I had to fight to stay alive.

Shepp.

I weep at the sight of him. My emotions go haywire before I finally step back from the window with a breath. He continues to knock, pounding so hard I swear the door will jump from its hinges and he'll march in.

"Open it, Little Chaos, before he beats it down," Jericho murmurs encouragingly. His warm breath blows across my flesh, sending goosebumps down my spine.

My fingers tremble when I open the door, revealing him. My neck cranes back as I take in every inch. Those ocean eyes I've lost myself in gleam with worry as he takes me in entirely from head to toe. We're frozen in the moment. Our feet grounded without movement. I can barely breathe. I'm barely able to process that he's finally in front of me, even if it's only been a few days.

Tension rises inside me before I launch myself at him, wrapping my legs around his waist. He hoists me up, resting his thick arms under my ass and keeping me close to him. The heat of his body feels surreal. He's here. He's okay. Shadow's men didn't hurt him while I was away.

His smell hits me first, settling my aching guts. It's like a piece of me has returned from the land of the dead and has found his way back into my arms. His large hands anchor me to him.

"You're okay," I choke out, nestling my face into his neck.

He hums something to me. Not really speaking, but it rumbles against my chest. Using the voice he has hidden within him, but only for me to hear. One day, he'll break through the anxiety of speaking. One day, Shepp will heal from the permanent damage his dad inflicted on him.

Pulling back, I hold his face in my hands. "How did you get out? I can't believe..." I trail off when his expression softens, and then a throat clearing makes me look to his left. I blink several times at the figure I've come to know on the island. The dick. "Darrell?" I ask, rearing back and looking at Shepp, who shrugs with a twisted expression. Basically telling me it's complicated.

All right, there's definitely a story there that I'm eager to hear.

"Not my name," he says, rubbing a hand down his face. "I can explain," he says, gesturing for us to enter the cabin for more privacy. But there's nothing for miles except a town I've been informed of that's small and trustworthy.

"Perhaps you can explain everything to me out here," Jericho says, stepping out with a menacing expression. "Who are you? And why have you come to my home?"

Darrel—or Not So Darrell—huffs a breath. "Does the name Olivia Viotto ring a bell?" Darrell raises a knowing brow. "She sent me along with Shepp to have a fun fucking discussion with you." God, he's such an idiot for giving Jericho lip. I wouldn't be surprised if Jericho tosses him out on his ass. Actually, I'd love to see that.

"What does she have to do with anything?" Jericho asks through clenched teeth, looking ten seconds away from ripping Not So Darrell's throat out.

"I am Agent Twelve with the Veritas agency. A certain

Agent Seven reached out in hopes her family could be extracted, with no one raising a brow. We tried several outside agents in boats to get to them without blowing my cover. But yet, here I am. Cover completely blown. You're welcome," he snarks back, folding his arms over his chest.

This idiot has a damn death wish.

Also, what the absolute fuck? He was an agent the entire time? Fooled me. He was a good actor. Asshole, too. I can't imagine the things he's seen or had to do in the name of Shadow. Hell, he had to haul us around for meetings. Probably had to kill people. In fact, he had to watch them die in the ring.

"Well, do come in, then," Jericho says, gesturing for us to come inside the cabin for a talk. I eye Jer's hands fisted at his sides, waiting for him to produce a weapon. There's no way in hell Jericho believed what he had to say.

"Kitten, I'm jelly. You didn't jump into my arms like that," Arrow pouts, shoving a cracker into his mouth as he advances on us. Without waiting for Shepp to put me down, Arrow wraps his arms around the two of us with a smile. "So happy to have you back, Sheppy Boy. It hasn't been the same since you disappeared." I frown at the crumbs spilling out of Arrow's mouth when he pulls away, and I wrinkle my nose. "Oh! These are for you." Arrow thrusts a sleeve of crackers into my hands.

"Uh, thanks," I murmur, looking between him and the crackers.

My stomach turns again at the prospect of eating. Or maybe it's my damn anxiety spiking. This whole situation is wearing me down. The quicker we can kill my monster and Shadow, the faster we can heal. But then what?

Shepp raises a brow, gently thumping Arrow's back with affection. I kiss Shepp's cheek before climbing down, preparing myself for what's about to come.

"Talk," Jericho growls at Darrell.

I swallow hard, ambling into the kitchen where they're

facing off. Jericho eyes Darrell like he's a bug invading his space.

"What do you mean, your name isn't Darrell?" I ask, taking a small bite of a Ritz cracker.

His shoulders tense. "I don't even know why I'm explaining this," he mutters. "Listen, I'm undercover. I told Shepp here all about it. I work with Olivia. They've had their eyes on Shadow's movements for a while now. It was at least a year and a half before we noticed he was becoming a threat. My assignment was to study his movements, but I did more than that."

Jericho puts a hand up. "And you've been relaying this information back to my cousin?"

"Yes. She oversees everything in the organization. Every step of the way, I've communicated with her while isolated on that stupid island."

Jericho nods a few times, taking it all in with a blank expression. Well, until he whips out his phone. His face hardens, shifting into something I've yet to witness before. Pure fucking fury. He pounds out a message with trembling fingers, barely containing the rage fueling him.

"So, you've been what? Playing in Shadow's gang for over a year?" I ask, watching Jericho carefully, hoping he doesn't reach over and strangle Not So Darrell with his bare hands. Thankfully, he puts his phone away in a huff and settles down.

"I worked hard to get into his inner circle. But it took more than a year to earn his trust. I was his main guard, transporting prisoners and having his back. I was in most of the meetings he held with other organizations as potential allies." Darrell raises a brow.

"Are you going to allude to what you know?" Jericho grits out impatiently.

"I bet he'd be happy to see you then," Arrow cuts in, chomping on another sleeve of crackers rustling in his hands.

Darrell narrows his eyes. "I'm only supposed to drop him

off and relay one piece of information, which Shepp has the evidence to show you. I don't want to know any fucking thing happening in this house." He raises his hands.

Arrow cocks his head. "Ah, Olivia, huh? Hmmm," he hums, stuffing his face again.

"Look, I have a message for you from Olivia. The one piece of evidence I can give you. She asked me to tell you not to do anything stupid with this, which includes murder." Darrel doesn't move, tensing when Jericho narrows his eyes.

Jericho straightens. "Okay," he says tonelessly. "Tell me."

Darrell looks up at the ceiling and then back to Jericho with pleading eyes. "Again. Don't fucking shoot me. I'm just an unwilling messenger, but they think you should know this intel."

"You're dragging this out, Agent. I suggest you..."

"I was in Shadow's meetings. The majority of them, at least. Especially when he started making headway with the new crew after he was completely in charge, he planned things. *They* planned things in secret."

"They?" Arrow asks, chomping on more food. "Like his merry band of sheepy psychos? Or partners? Please tell me partners, I'd love to have more throats to slash." He's way too giddy at the prospect of murdering people. But who am I kidding? He's Arrow. Of course, he loves slashing throats and drugging people.

Remind me to stomp his balls later.

Darrell sighs, probably regretting every single one of his life decisions. Also, he looks pale. Ghostly, even. For a super secret spy who held ranks within a gangster's army, he sure acts like he hasn't seen blood and death before.

Amateur.

Even I've witnessed murders. Oh, and taken lives, too. I wrinkle my nose. I'm not exactly proud of it. But being in a room full of people who have committed the same crimes as me has me loosening the reins.

"Thomas Mondelli wasn't the original Shadow. He was a sheep, following his leader's rules while she was away and holding down the fort. Until recently, that is." He grimaces. "He started making moves on his own. Telling the world who he was when the entire brains of the operation was away on a mission they plotted out together in secret. Shepp, the evidence," Darrell says, snapping a finger.

Shepp sighs, digging into his pockets and pulling out several small photos and pieces of paper.

"Elaborate," Jericho says stiffly, waving a hand with a pinched expression. Agitation roars through him when Shepp hands him everything, and he stares at the photos. "Is this..." Jericho blanches, moving through the pictures one after the other.

"You said he was a sheep? A follower?" I ask, trying to move this along.

"He may have acted like he built it all. But he has only been there for a few years since..."

"I killed him," I murmur, casting my gaze away.

"Right. Since you apparently killed him. I'm learning so much," Darrell mutters, pinching the bridge of his nose.

"Tell me this isn't who I think it is. Tell me you're not alluding to the fact that this woman right here. Is..." Jericho levels him with a demanding glare, pointing to the woman in the photo repeatedly. Vibrations seem to wrack his body. His fingers tremble with anticipation as Darrell squares his shoulders.

Oh fuck, this can't be good.

Darrell blows out a breath. "Fuck. Yes. Grace Viotto. Your mother. She's the one who started it all."

Jericho stands impossibly still, eyeing Darrell with a lethal glare. I swear if he stared any harder, Darrell would catch on fire and burn to death. Turn to ash right before our damn eyes.

Darrell must feel it, too. He swallows hard, instinctively taking a step back.

"I think I have something in my ears, Agent. You're saying that the woman who gave birth to me and who disappeared when I was five and miraculously made her return to my father's life is the spearhead of that entire operation?" The lethal edge to Jericho's voice has goosebumps erupting along my flesh.

Jericho doesn't move a damn muscle. Basically freezing in place. Is he breathing? I would be too if I just found out my mom was the person in charge of an underground gang trying to take down the Viotto's. But how? Shadow—Thomas—or whatever you want to call him, confessed to not attacking Gabriel at the tower. Or the bomb. Hell, he acted like he had never done a damn thing in his life.

So, what are they up to?

"This is better than daytime TV," Arrow whispers dramatically, watching the two of them with wide eyes while stuffing his damn face. "I need something better than crackers. Make the popcorn, Sheppy Boy." Shepp silently huffs when Arrow thumps him on the chest with puppy dog eyes. Shepp rolls his eyes and flips him off.

At least I know what that hand gesture means.

Jericho's jaw clenches tight, popping the veins of his neck and forehead. Still, he hasn't moved. His eyes glare holes through the photographs of a man and woman standing together.

"And you were there for some of the planning sessions?" I ask, nibbling my cracker, attempting to soothe my stomach.

"I've only been undercover for a year and a half or so. Sometimes. I witnessed meetings between alliances and Thomas. Thomas was the face of the operation to the masses. Those men wouldn't have followed her rule." Right. All those men. The masses in the crowds, cheering for death while smacking kidnapped girls on their asses.

"Did you get the girls out?" My brows furrow when Darrell nods.

"I'm sure they did," he says with reassurance. "I reported that, too."

"Good. They didn't deserve to be there."

"Girls?" Arrow asks, perking up. "What girls?"

"All those girls that went missing in Briar Cove were on the island. I recognized the one I read about in the paper that morning after..."

Arrow smirks. "After we chased you through the woods and fucked you. Oh! And then you stabbed me. Still gives me a boner, Kitten." He winks at me, shoving more food into his mouth. I blush at his words and clear my throat. Arrow dangles a piece of food over his lips like what was said suddenly hits him. "You're telling me that bastard stole women from our club for what?" His face immediately changes from lighthearted to deadly. I swear he can do that at the drop of a hat.

"Ransom," I answer quickly. "He told me all about it. He expects the parents to pay for their return. Even then, he doesn't return them. Just keeps using them. Drugs them." I shudder. Evil fucking prick. "They walked around his stupid fighting pit with drinks..." I trail off, not wanting to get into the groping hands of those poor girls.

"Tell me what Grace's end goal is?" Jericho rasps, flexing his fingers.

"Take everything from the man that took everything from her," he says, taking another step back. Maybe he's not dumb after all. He knows when someone dangerous is in the room, and he's about to escape before he's mauled to death.

"But that's all I've been permitted to say. Talk to Olivia. I'm sure she'll be cleared to recount more. Maybe." Darrell shrugs. Then he's gone as quickly as he came, hightailing it out of there like his ass is on fire.

I mean, it could be. Jericho looks more murderous than I've ever seen him.

I swallow hard. Jericho still hasn't moved. He's stuck in

one spot, staring aimlessly at the pictures shaking in his fingers.

"Should we... touch him?" I question, cocking my head to observe him. I lift a finger to poke his shoulder. Maybe it'll reset him like control, alt, delete, but a large hand stops my movement, gently squeezing. Shepp shakes his head, pulling me back to rest between him and Arrow. "I think he's broken," I whisper sadly.

"Give him just a sec to reboot, Kitten. He's brooding and plotting the demise of the people who gave him life," Arrow says, putting the empty sleeve of crackers on the counter and licking his fingers. "Yeah, yeah. I know, Sheppy Boy."

Shepp glares at him with a huff, moving his fingers rapidly and signing something to him again with determination. Arrow waves him off with a chuckle. Shepp shakes his head, running a hand down his face.

"I'm going to town," Jericho declares with rigid movements. "Alone."

We eye each other as he collects keys to a vehicle and slowly walks through the living room without looking back. Every muscle strains through his clothes, and his steps remain unhurried and staggered.

"You sure you're good, Daddy Jer? You look..." Arrow tilts his head, examining Jericho with inspecting eyes.

I have to agree. He looks.... Drunk. Upset. Completely tilted off his axis. Yeah, I don't think he should be driving right now. He's bound to kill a family of five because of his distracted state.

"I'm fucking fine," he snarls with jerky movements.

Yeah, okay. I'm not touching that with a ten-foot pole. He can drive to his heart's delight; hopefully, it'll help him come to terms with what we learned.

Arrow holds his hands up. "If you say so. I don't believe you right now." He narrows his eyes. "If you crash and die in a fiery blaze, I'll marry my Kitten to keep on the family name."

He grins, causing Jericho to storm out the front door, slamming it behind him. "If you're going to town, bring me back some more pickles! Oh! And some orange juice while you're at it! Murder is afoot, Daddy Jer!"

A second later, a vehicle comes to life, a garage door opens, and tires peel out of the driveway.

"I don't think he heard you," I say, shaking my head.

"Rude," Arrow huffs, pulling out his phone. "I'll just text him my demands. Anything for you, Kitten? Tampons? Chocolates?" He wiggles his brows after firing off a text and slips his phone back into his pocket.

"Uh, no. It's not time yet." I shake my head.

At least, I don't think it is. Shit. When was the last time I had my period? You know what? I'm blaming the stress of starving and fighting and everything else. Yup. That's it. It's not the fact they removed my IUD without my permission before I got kidnapped. Not that. It's time for a subject change before I castrate each of them.

"That's strange, though, right? He rarely walks away." Or backs down from something difficult, except right now. Not when he's faced with the fact his mom walked away from him and started her own gang for revenge.

Shepp signs to Arrow and drops his hands.

"Yeah. What he said," Arrow quips, earning a smack to the back of the head. "Ouch, dickbag. You'd think you'd be nice to me since we've been separated. I've missed you, Sheppy. Haven't you missed me?" Arrow bats his eyelashes playfully until Shepp flips him off. "Well, I feel the love now."

"You think he'll be okay?" I mutter, staring out the window.

"He'll be fine, Kitten. He's just going to blow off steam at the store. Fucker better not forget my snacks. No matter. I know how we can pass the time." Arrow moves so quickly that I squeak when he pulls me close. "Your tits bigger, Kitten?"

His fingers grope at my breasts, and he grins. "I gotta call Jer for this!"

I scrunch my nose when he skips away and out the door, pulling his phone out again and bringing it to his ear. He paces the porch, talking animatedly with his hands.

"What the hell?" I murmur. Shepp shrugs. "This is all so weird, right?" Shepp nods. "I need a goddamn nap.

Or a drink. Maybe all of it.

CHAPTER FORTY-SIX

Jericho

MY MOTHER. OF COURSE. IT ALL MAKES FUCKING SENSE.

Or does it?

I'm not entirely sure right now. My entire world has imploded. The future that has been mapped out for me since I was born has broken into a million pieces.

Not that I wanted it. Something I have come to realize over the past few months.

My father's legacy isn't mine.

If I had my way, my legacy would be my own. No one else's. I'd take my future by the damn horns and make it my bitch. For me. Not for my last name.

What future, though?

My mother ran from me as a child, leaving me with the man she must have known was a monster. I thought he loved her and cherished her. Worshiped the ground she walked on. He bought her a zoo. Built her a beautiful home full of the things she loved.

Perhaps I was wrong on all fronts.

My future is the people sitting in the cabin I walked out of several hours ago. But I had to. My mind is a relentless mess of fuckery and confusion, pulling me in every fucking direction.

If there's one thing I know for sure, it's that Gabriel Viotto needs to burn in hell for everything he's done and take my lying mother with him. I'm torn in two on what to believe. Veritas saw her at the island conducting work. And I can't wrap my mind around the imagery. My mother. Soft-spoken and demure, commanding hundreds of men and attacking Briar Cove. Whether by drugs or violence, it was apparently all at her hands.

Or was it?

Fuck.

My head pounds relentlessly, blurring my vision.

I sit back in the seat of my worn-out truck, something I specifically bought for the cabin and left in the attached garage. It's not fancy. Or made in the past ten years. No GPS. No electronics on the inside. Just me, the old tape player, and the open road. But it got me from point A to B when I needed it most—guiding me ten miles to the small-town grocery store to retrieve supplies for our stay. Short or long, I'm not sure how long we'll be holed up together. We'll survive through thick and thin.

We're a family, after all.

I had to walk off the utter betrayal from my mother. My father avoided mentioning her once she left. Never that she had walked away or been kidnapped, that would bring great shame to us.

I see that now.

The fog lifts. Their true actions come out.

My mother left me with a demon. Were her feelings of joy upon reuniting with me a facade? An act to hide the callousness of her actions.

Because that's what it is.

She left me. With a fucking monster. On purpose. There was no mistake about it. She walked out to raise a rebellion and left me there with him to suffer in silence. I had no choice. I was a fucking innocent child, depending on them to raise me.

The one who hid me in dark closets and controlled every inch of my fucking life.

Because of her actions.

My fingers curl around the steering wheel, knuckles turning white from the force. She's just another villain in a long line of bad people that I'm adding to my list.

Fuck.

I fall back into the seat, squeezing my eyes closed and attempting to shut out the rampant thoughts swirling in my mind. The moment I looked at those pictures and read the letters from my mother to Thomas. The reality of it all slammed into me. No matter how much I want to deny her hand in everything, I know I can't.

Digging in my pocket, I pull out the evidence handed over to us. God, she looked so bright in Thomas' arms, looking at him as if he held the moon in his palm. Just for her. The center of his universe. It's a similar look I throw Journey's way every time she walks into the room.

Love. Possession. Everything in between.

And my mother and Thomas had that.

Thinking back, I don't think she ever looked at Gabriel with hearts in her eyes. He did, though. Maybe not to a loving extent. It was more obsession on his end, trying to keep her near.

Whatever it was, it's over now. Everything is coming to an end.

But now…

I shove the letters and photographs away, yank out my phone with more force than necessary, and hit dial as I exit the parking lot of the bookstore I just came from. Something I never accounted for when we built the cabin was my wife's love of books.

So, I bought every book inside the quaint space so my wife won't get bored after getting the food supplies we'll need for the next week.

"He—"

"How long have you known that my mother is the real Shadow playing puppeteer in the background?" To my credit, I keep my voice level without letting my rage lead the conversation.

I'm a reasonable man for the most part. Olivia only has so much loyalty to me. We're blood. But her duties surpass our connection.

"Not very long, Jer," she says sadly.

"How long?" I ask tightly again.

"Not that long…"

"And what else have you discovered?"

"Promise me you won't do anything stupid."

"Stupid? I resent that," I say back with a huff.

I won't be stupid. I'll take everything from my mother and my father. No. I'll be smart about it all. Form my alliances and take my parents down.

"This is a complicated situation, Jer," she says through a heavy breath.

"Uncomplicate it then, Liv. Tell me what I need to know so I can fucking take them down. It's fucking time!" I shout, heaving a breath and trying to calm myself from exploding again.

Olivia's footsteps and a door closing penetrate through the anger. Killing the murderous haze clinging tightly to my being, nearly choking me. I want someone to bleed. I ache for it. Need it. Shadow will fucking pay when I get my hands on him tomorrow. He'll be the release we need to move forward and think clearly.

"Do I need to call you back in ten minutes when you've calmed down?" she asks softly with understanding. Oh, Liv. Always a good cousin with a big heart. A person to ground me when need be.

"No. I'm calm," I say, squaring my shoulders and attempting to ward off the tension.

"Right. Calm," she quips.

"Yeah, yeah. I'm fucking calm." It's a lie. I'm seething on the inside, unsure how to get rid of this incessant fire brewing beneath my flesh and putting pressure on every molecule of my body. I blow out a breath, putting my mask back in place. My anger will get me nowhere but jail—or worse, death. "Please, Liv," I say, licking my lips. "I need to defend everyone I care about. My parents have stabbed everyone in the back to get where they are…"

"Especially yours." There's a familiar pain in her voice that resonates with me. It's the reason I never wrote her off or shunned her like the rest of the family. We've always had a connection. A childhood we wanted to be erased from.

She was raised in the same life I was. My cousin. A mafia princess. Except more volatile and damning. Her family was shamed and exiled, forcing them away from Briar Cove straight into the arms of the most notorious gang in Southern California. Her father was always a fuck up. A man who wanted everything for himself without putting the work into it.

Well, until…

"Especially mine," I confirm. "She walked away, Olivia. And left me…" Anguish twists my blackened soul, forcing me to feel everything I've kept behind my carefully constructed mask of indifference. I'm Jericho Viotto. I'm not allowed to show my emotions. The days after my mother left and I was thrust into the darkness by my father's drunken antics, I grieved her.

She wasn't dead, but she was gone.

I grieved and grieved until I couldn't anymore. No more tears were shed. Perhaps from the punishments I endured to force away the feelings any normal person possesses. All because I missed my sweet mother, who read to me at night and shielded me from the man who became the devil of my story.

My villain.

To think, after all that grieving and wishing she'd come back to protect me, it was all a lie. A veil over my fucking eyes. The lack of a funeral and any extensive search for her should have alerted me to something being wrong. It was as if she had vanished into thin air.

Poof.

And now, after so many years, she's reemerged to do—what?—I haven't a clue.

"A large part of Shadow's men were present on the island. They confirmed they lived there in the hotel and followed the man you call Shadow's orders. They've been living by their own rules there with drugs and booze and girls. She was the true mastermind behind everything they've done, but lived in the shadows. We have confirmation that Thomas Mondelli and Grace Viotto worked side by side for three years until she recently disappeared…" she trails off.

So, that means my dear old mother is up to more than just reuniting with my father. She's out for some sort of revenge. Or else she'd never have shown back up. It seems only Thomas and my mother were privy to whatever they had planned that sent her back. It's good to know I have half of that equation in my basement, ready to answer his crimes before we bleed him dry.

"Did they talk willingly?" I quip, easing myself into the driveway of our cabin and park.

"Pfft. I have my ways. You wouldn't believe the amount of people living there. It seems like their most loyal stayed on the island." Olivia rambles, detailing her mundane encounters while detaining over fifty men and transporting them back to Veritas prison. "They'll be at home there with the other crimi-nals. Besides, it's an island, too," she huffs, yapping again.

More questions I'll get answers to from Shepp and Journey later. But also from our prisoner. My excitement ramps up the more we speak, and the anger fades into the background. It'll never leave. For now, though. I'm harboring it in the box in my mind to use as a weapon against the ones who have betrayed us most.

Once back at the cabin, I climb out of the truck with a clear mind. Rage and anger have left the building. Although, they're simmering in the background, ready to strike when the time is right and when I can unleash the monster trapped inside, aching for the blood on his hands.

I lean against the truck, staring off into the distance. The mountains around the cabin elevate us above the world, hiding our existence from any sort of enemy. The air is a little thinner. Cooler. And prickling my skin with goosebumps. It's our home away from home. A reprieve from normal routine, taking me from my role as the Briar Cove mafia heir. I'm the man who should have all the answers. A person the family looks up to. But I have a feeling my father has left me out of almost everything he had planned. I thought I had it all at one time in my life. Even a few months ago. An identity crisis in the damn making.

There's a new future in the making—brewing beneath the underbelly of Briar Cove and in the mountains miles away.

We're coming for Gabriel Viotto—an attack they'll see coming because they're probably expecting us. So, we'll be smart. Calculated. Ruthless as fuck. So when they see us, they won't know what got them.

No one on the wrong side will survive.

I hum and pull out my phone, intending to make moves. My chess pieces are gliding across the board, collecting my enemies until I'm on the other side with my much-needed allies.

I snort when the cabin's front door opens and shuts with a

slam, alerting me of Arrow approaching. Try as he might, he has no tact. He thinks he's a cat on the prowl, but his sneaking abilities are severely lacking this time. The only situation he seems to make no noise is when he's drugging people unexpectedly.

"Did you get it?" Arrow asks, bounding in front of me and bouncing on his toes.

"Do you think it'll turn out how we want?" A sliver of hope shines brightly inside me, elevating my mood.

Journey thick with our child flashes in my mind. Is it the ideal time? No. There's a raging war too close for comfort. She will stay far, far away from it all. Well, if I have my way.

I jerk my thumb toward the truck's backseat when he folds his hands, pleading with me.

"Daddy Jer, have no fear. Her tits are big. Her period is late. Her birth control is mounted in the basement. It's everything we talked about," he says, digging in the bags until he pulls out two boxes displaying pregnancy tests. He fucking whoops twice, almost banging his head off the car. "Now, to see the results!" he shouts, taking off toward the house, running at full speed.

Jesus. He's going to tackle her and force her to piss on the test right in front of him. Ugh. I pinch the bridge of my nose. I'll have to save her after I conduct my business. Shepp will protect her for now while I track down my allies.

Looking down at my phone, I dial one of the two people I need to speak with and let it ring.

"Jericho Viotto," Elias greets through the phone in a deep tone.

"Elias," I reply with a curt nod he can't see. "How're you feeling?" Since we parted ways after the explosion on his wedding day, we haven't exchanged more than a few words. Some here and there through text messages. So, I knew he was alive after being shot.

"Better than ever," he quips with a sigh.

"And married life?"

"As good as I hoped it would be. Now, what can I do for you today? I've got shit to do. A gang to run..." Elias trails off.

"I'd like to call a meeting of my newly formed allies and collect on our deal."

"Ah, yes. Our deal," Elias says smoothly. "Briar Cove could use the fighters." He tsks at me, clicking his tongue several times. "Seems there's a new sheriff in town." Yes. A woman claiming to be the new ruler.

"Any word on Gabriel? I've barely heard a peep since we last spoke," I say, kicking a rock with my shoe and watching as it falls down the sloped driveway and finally stops.

Is he still ill? Dead? Fuck, I hope so. The only issue I would have with that is he should die at my hand with Journey's help.

"Still head of the family and showing his face. There's a woman now with him, holding him afloat. He's looking sickly lately."

I raise my brow. "In the last three years that you were partnered with Shadow, did you happen to meet her?"

There's quiet on the other side of the line. "Her? As in who?" he inquires lazily.

"The woman parading around with my father. It seems she and Shadow had quite a partnership on the island. Making plans..." I trail off, watching the clouds move through the crisp sky.

"The only Shadow I knew was that fucker who attacked me at my goddamn wedding," he says with a tight voice. "We met here and there on the island. Dinner and planning, but no woman. Ever."

Interesting. So, if my mother was truly behind being Shadow, she never showed her face. She lived up to the name she had created for her alter ego and let Thomas take over the reins to build their army. My main question is how and why? She was away for twenty years. Why didn't she stay away?

"I'll give you my coordinates, and we'll meet up. We have many things to discuss in person."

Now, I have to track down the last half of my allies—Mikhail—someone who pledged themselves to Journey and our war.

"And that fucker you took?" Elias questions eagerly, knocking me from my thoughts.

"Awaiting his fucking execution," I grit out.

Elias and I say our goodbyes. A weight slightly lifts off my chest.

We have a plan, of sorts. But we'll figure it out. Elias is on my side. From what I can tell, at least. Could he double-cross me? Sure. But I'd be ready for him to do so.

I sigh, staring at my phone again, reading the number I programmed when Shepp handed Journey Sunshine's phone number. Now comes the hard part. Mikhail Antonov. The son of the head of the Bratva. Or, I guess he is the man in charge now after losing his father.

If there's one thing I know about the elusive Antonov family, they aren't ones to hand out their loyalties to anyone.

And so, the real work begins.

CHAPTER FORTY-SEVEN

Arrow

PEEING TOGETHER IS STAYING TOGETHER. RIGHT? IS THAT HOW the saying goes?

Eh, whatever.

I wave a hand and lean back on the couch in the corner of our living room. The sweet, comfy couch I insisted on when we bought this cabin as a hideout. Jericho only wanted a bed. Nothing else. Fucking weirdo.

We need lots of surfaces to fuck Journey on.

The bed. The couch. The kitchen cabinets. The shower. Every fucking surface will be tainted by my taint and bodily fluids.

I grin. I want to stay here forever. Fuck the wars and bloodshed. Fuck Gabriel and his weird shit. Just give me the mountains, my girl's pussy, and endless food—I'll be in Heaven.

Who needs death and murder, anyway?

Ah, well. I guess I do. It soothes my soul and makes me complete. I don't think I could ever completely toss away mayhem for domestic bliss. Could I?

I blow out a breath. There goes my plan to stay in this sex cabin, tie my Kitten up spread eagle until she's got so many cream pies she's dripping with our combined juices. Ah, yes. Now, that would be a sight to see.

Oh, there goes Big A trying to enter the chat. Down, boy.

We're only in fantasy mode. Besides, if she's knocked up, I'll have to be careful. How careful, though?

Wait a damn minute.

Will Big A poke the baby's head during sex? I recoil. I fucking hope not. My kid will lose an eye before he's even born. And there's no way I can deny my Kitten anything. I've read pregnant women are super horny all the time. Damn it. All my baby books are stashed at the mansion, filled with information I could use now.

All the more reason to leave this cabin and fuck Gabriel's life up. Fuck tranquility and endless sex. Okay, maybe not that last part. But still. That over-inflated fucker took our home. Now, I need to take back my pregnancy books if he hasn't destroyed them yet.

Shepp snaps his fingers in front of my face to gain my attention. Poor Sheppy Boy. His metal rings, the ones he kept on him for so long, are missing. I'm sure his daddy is to blame for stealing them away, so he's forced to use his voice. Not that he ever has. The gentle giant hasn't spoken a word since we were kids. How I miss the soft, soothing sound of his voice. I shake my head, coming back to myself. Damn, I need more sleep. Or my girl.

'What the hell are you grinning about?' Shepp signs with a scowl, watching my relaxed state.

"Oh, nothing." Nothing at all. I'm innocent. "Only about fucking my Kitten on every surface in this house. Over and over and…"

"Arrow," she groans, throwing her head back.

Yeah, Kitten. Just like that. Twenty-four-seven fuck fest.

"Yeah, exactly! You'll say my name just like that," I quip, pointing in her direction.

She's gotten mighty cozy in our cabin, wearing nothing but long shirts, panties, and fuzzy socks. No pants. My favorite outfit. Shepp made sure she was comfortable before he made us all lunch. He's like a little mother hen—but not so little—

taking care of us all. Our keeper. Sans Jericho, of course. He was on a mission to forget his mommy was a psycho with Shepp's dad and took off.

I wonder if their parents ever boned? Hmmm. Probably. I mean, if they're in cahoots, there has to be pussy involved. Right?

"You think your evil sperm donor and Jer's mommy ever fucked?" I ask, using my fingers to create the motion.

Shaking his head with a huff, Shepp signs, *'You're impossible.'*

His nose wrinkles. Oh, yeah. He's thinking about it now. In full fucking detail, by the paleness of his face. Sorry, fucker. If I have to see it. So do you. We're all scarred for life thinking about Thomas and Grace doing the nasty.

"Tell me something I don't know, Sheppy Boy." I grin when he runs a hand down his face in exasperation.

He missed me. I know he did. I missed him, too. Pushing his buttons and earning the finger from him are two of my favorite hobbies. Among other things, of course. He's so easy to rile up. But I love the big lug. Jericho, too. Apparently, I'm full of love for the people of my little family. Something I never thought I'd possess.

My brows scrunch. When did this feeling take over? It's like my heart is in overdrive, pounding against my ribs. Squeezing the breaths from my lungs every time I think about them getting hurt or taken. An entity has possessed my soul, lighting it with this lifting feeling. Love. I'm fucking in love. Infatuated. Obsessed. I could dance right here in the living room, but that might get me more stares.

Journey rolls her eyes and gets up from the seat across from us with a disgusted look. Why she didn't just sit on my lap to snuggle is beyond me. Rude, actually. I need to touch my Kitten every second of every day, especially after being away from her for so long.

She may be Jer's wife on paper. Reluctantly, might I add.

Because she didn't sign up for that voluntarily. He did it right under her nose. All our noses, actually. Bastard. I rub my chin with a frown. I need to up my game and tie his ass to a chair again. That familiar rage I felt before sizzles through me. I need to make him fucking suffer more. She's mine, too. I licked her first in the club. Oh, then at the party when my fingers found her pussy. Then, my dick. Speaking of. I look down at Big A standing at attention in my pants. If I think about fucking her anymore, I'll explode prematurely.

Down, boy. Don't embarrass me. Not yet.

Shepp watches Journey with soft eyes as she strolls across the living room, following her every move. Fucking stalker. Ah, who am I kidding? I'm watching her, too—the sway of her ass and the jiggle of her thighs. God, I want to bite her.

You know, I think the three of us balance this relationship out. Giving Journey different pieces of the Devil's cake. Shepp gives her all the affection she can swallow. Food? Safety? Getting Painted? He's got her covered. Jericho... Well, I'm still mad at him. Not only for leaving me behind but marrying her against her will. That's my job. I'm the one who forces her into things she doesn't approve of. So, Jericho? He doesn't deserve a long monologue on how he has her covered. Me, though? I deserve at least three paragraphs on how I let her stab me. Wound me. Over and over. She can do anything to me and Big A will always rise to the occasion—also, me. I'll always have her back. And front. Oh, and her side, too. Because I fucking love her. That organ inside me beating rapidly only does it for her. If she says jump off a cliff. I'll ask which rock she wants me to fall into.

I'm just that nice of a psycho. Anything for her.

And Journey?

My vicious Kitten is our ooey gooey center, like a cookie. And I like to eat cookies. A lot. I also like to eat her. A lot. God, I have so many plans to bring her to orgasm. It's too bad all my damn toys were left at the mansion under the mattress, in the closet, in the drawers, and in the basement. One day, I'll take her to my special room and show her all the fun things I do to bad people down there.

I smirk, stalking Journey with my eyes. "Oh! Where ya going, Kitten? Need a hand?" I wiggle my brows.

She thinks I'm implying sex. I so could be. Okay, I totally am. I wouldn't deny her a ride on Big A if she wanted. I'd tie her up and...

No. I have a very important mission to accomplish.

Unless she needs a pussy massage with my dick. I'm down. Only after I force her to pee on the magical stick in my pants—not my dick—so we can find out if she's preggers. Preggo. Swollen with our baby.

My Kitten would be so beautiful, thick, and engorged with the baby we planted there.

I waited for Jer to come home to set my plan in motion. AKA–force Journey to pee on a pregnancy test in front of my eyes. Creepy? Nah. She's used to my antics by now. So, as Jer talks on the phone outside, pacing back and forth while conducting business, I'll use the pregnancy tests I eagerly plucked from the backseat of his truck to initiate my plan.

And if she's not pregnant right now? I'm locking her ass down, and those cream pies are happening over and over until the test gives us a plus sign.

Journey twists her face. "Um. No? I'm going to pee. Why are you being so weird?"

Weird? I am not weird. I'm Arrow. Deadly. Unhinged. Powerful. Sexy. Never weird. Okay, that's a lie. My dad used to call me weird behind my back sometimes. My heart aches. I think that hurt more than anything. I tried so hard to be the perfect church-going boy for him and never seemed to be who he wanted me to be. Too many dead animal experiments and impulsive acts to be anything that Vincent Amour would ever want.

Bummer. I've made myself feel the sadness I've hidden

behind my mask. One day, my dad and I will patch things up completely. He's still my dad, after all. And I think after being apart for so many years, he loves me. I guess I love him, too. No matter the childhood he gave me. He's made up for it by learning to embrace me as I am.

Shepp smacks me again. *'Why the hell are you rubbing your nipple?'*

I look down with a frown. Huh. I was circling my right nipple while thinking about Journey. Definitely not my dad. It's all hard and wanting now. What I wouldn't give for a clamp or tongue. Oh! Or Journey's teeth on it.

'Journey?' I spell her name with a grin, earning an eye roll.

'You're being sus right now.' He glares at me hard, trying to figure out what I'm up to. That's not happening, big guy. I'm a psycho on a mission, and you can't stop me. *'Why are you sticking your tongue out at me?'* His face twists again when I put my tongue back in my mouth. How elementary of me. No matter. I got shits to do and a certain lady to force to pee. Easy peasy. Actually, I think she might chop me into pieces.

Whatever. Worth it!

"I'm not being weird." I offer her my best grin as she steps away from me toward the bathroom. *'Or sus,'* I sign back to him and promptly flip him off.

Shepp huffs. *'Yeah. You're being weird as fuck, dude. Weirder than normal,'* Shepp signs, leaning back on the couch. *'What exactly are you planning?'*

Jericho probably intended on Shepp keeping me guarded while he conducts business in the driveway. Blah. Blah. Blah. Jer's on the phone, and Shepp's not moving from this couch, It's not happening right now. I have one mission in mind.

Operation pee on a stick is underway.

I grin, shrugging, as I get up from the couch. "Just mind your business," I chuckle, moving behind Journey stealthily as she enters the bathroom and then shuts the door without locking it. Score! She's so clueless about the predator creeping up behind her.

Shepp won't mind his business. He's a goddamn busybody. He always puts his nose where it doesn't belong. It's good for us and the family business. He's always sussing out the bad guys and removing them from the club. But here? I can feel his eyes on me, stalking me through the living room as I disappear into the bedroom and stand outside the bathroom door, grinning more. If I don't lock my Kitten and me behind this door asap, Shepp is going to drag me away kicking and screaming. I'm not above biting him.

In my head, I count down as I stare at the wooden door. I'll give her five seconds to start and... I shove through the bathroom door, leaving it open. Silly goose forgot to lock it. It's such a shame. A tragedy. For her, anyway. My sitting duck is officially caught with her pants down and butt cheeks on the toilet.

Perfect.

"Do you fucking mind? Arrow!" she howls, covering up her lady bits in horror with a cute red blush covering her face.

She's so damn precious. My pretty Kitty, hiding herself from the big bad Devil. What? Like, I've never seen pee before. I've seen it plenty of times. From myself. My victims. Everyone pees. Poops. Cums. Bleeds. Screams. Humans are magical, like liquid piñatas ready for my knife.

"No need to hide yourself from me, Kitten. I've eaten, fucked, sucked, and so much more to that general area. It's my favorite." I grin more when she scowls. "In fact, I could take you into the bedroom after this, and we could play a game I call hide the sausage. The sausage being my dick. And your pussy being the bun." I bat my eyelashes in her direction, hoping she won't be mad.

But she's definitely mad.

Her face twists in horror now. Anger and outrage replace

the cute blush. Bummer. We could have had lots of fun. Not that this won't be the cherry on top.

"Arrow. Is there a fucking reason you're trying to watch me pee?" she growls, gritting her teeth together.

"Can't I watch?" I ask, puffing out my bottom lip.

This so isn't weird. Nope. Not at all. Perfectly normal in the realm of Arrow.

"No! That's fucking... fucking weird! Oh my God," she screeches as footsteps approach. Her eyes scan the horizon, practically begging me to shut the door. Or she wants Shepp to step in and sweep her off her feet. Sheppy Boy to the rescue with his cape to take our girl away from me.

Not happening. She's all mine right now. Bonding moment and all.

"Don't bother," I say, grinning at Shepp as he approaches with a frown. His steps get faster and his long legs bring him closer. "I've got this covered!" I shout, slamming the door in his face and locking it. He pounds several times, rattling the door and its frame. I'm sure he'd break through the wood if he tried hard enough. "You should learn to lock doors," I say, pointing at the doorknob. "Bad, bad, Kitten."

"Arrow," she says with a heavy sigh that expands her chest up and down. God. Her tits are enormous. Does she still fit in her bra? Maybe I should take her shopping downtown and force her to try some new ones on, and then I can peel them off with my teeth. "My eyes are up here," she quips with agitation, shifting slightly in her vulnerable position.

Right. Her eyes. She has those. Two of them, to be exact. I should totally look at those gorgeous moss-green orbs in her head and not her rising tits or exposed pussy covered by her hands. I'm slightly jealous of the toilet water getting to glimpse her right now when I haven't peeked since we fucked at the wedding. It's unfair. I want my turn with her. To comfort her after what she went through. To fuck her for so long, she forgets she was covered in blood and fought for her life at one point.

"Are you just going to stand there and watch me pee? Like, is this a new thing?" she asks, bringing me back to the conversation, waving a finger at me wearily. There's a slight intrigue in her eyes. She's desperate to know what I'm throwing down in here. Or weary. I can't be so sure. She's used to my antics by now, though.

"Nope," I say with a grin, reaching into my back pocket and producing the baby test. "I want to hold this while you pee."

I think that's the best sentence I've ever uttered. Her face tells me that, too. She's stunned into silence, blinking rapidly while looking between me and the test.

"That's the weirdest thing you've ever said to me. And you've said some pretty weird shit," she gripes, shaking her head when I step forward and kneel in front of her.

Ah, that's better. I can finally see the hairs above her pussy peeking out. Unkempt from her time in captivity. I wonder if she'd let me shave those for her?

"Seriously, Arrow."

"Seriously, Journey," I say, peering deep into her eyes, silently pleading with her to give me this. Just this once. Okay, there will be more times. She doesn't have to know that yet. "Will you let me?"

She sighs heavily, staring at me with a blank expression. Yes! It's a sign she's giving in to me and my crazy ways.

"I have a shy fucking bladder," she grits out, shaking her head before staring up at the ceiling. "But you won't leave until we do this, will you?" Nope. Not at all. I'll stay in this position until she can't hold it any longer.

I always get what I want.

I grin in response, uncapping the pregnancy test and holding it between her legs. Wait, is this where her urine comes out? Probably. I need to study the chart that the poor gynecologist gave me before I took his hands. That way, I can deliver our future children—all eighteen of them—safely, of course.

"Go ahead," I say, urging her to get on with it.

"I literally can't go with you staring at me like that," she hisses, grabbing my wrist and attempting to push me away.

Ah, ah, ah, Kitten. Not cool. You can't make me leave now. This has to happen! Staring at her like what? I shake my head and fix my expression. Maybe my smile is off-putting. So, I hide it with a pout.

"Ah, ah. I'm not leaving until you've peed on this stick, Kitten. I gotta know if I'm a daddy." Ah, that magical word. Daddy. I'd love it if Journey called me that in bed when I'm pounding her from behind. Well, fuck. Down, Big A. Now, is not the time to look turned on. She's already going to chop you to bits later. We have to watch our back.

"Why are you staring at your crotch? Arrow? Please don't tell me…"

"It's not your pee, it's the fucking I was imagining. Oh! And the word Daddy, too. Would you ever call me that while I slapped your ass?" I cock my head.

"Jesus Christ. This will never happen. Arrow, let me take it." Exhaustion leaks from her words. My poor Kitten needs a nice nap and snack. Later. After she does this, I'll give her everything she's ever dreamed of. Back rubs. Shoulder rubs. Pussy rubs. You name it, and my Kitten will get it.

I stare between her legs with a frown. "But I want to hold it." So, I can find out if she's pregnant before her, and then I can tell her the good news. She'd love that. Right?

"Arrow," Jericho's voice echoes from outside the door. Well, shit. It seems like Sheppy Boy went and told on me. Silent bastard. "Shepp says you're being more abnormal than usual."

My brows furrow when I look at Journey, and she snorts,

covering her face with her hands. "We're just working something out in here," she says calmly, sucking in a breath.

That's my girl. See? I knew there was a reason I loved my Kitten with my whole dick and heart. She sticks up for me. Some people have a problem with my unique attributes— mostly the men I murder. But, meh. Semantics. They're just upset because I took their lives. This is different. Better.

"You sure about that?" Jericho asks impatiently. He is most likely gritting his damn teeth. That's all he's done since we've been separated. Maybe I should punch him again so he knocks it off. That would help, right? Violence is always the answer. I can't believe I ever thought I could live without it. It's woven into my damn DNA. "I can get the goddamn key." Oh, so threatening. I'm shaking in my nonexistent boots.

"My Kitten said we're fine. Maybe we're doing some solo sexy time that doesn't require your assistance." That can be after this. I'll strip her down, bend her over the sink, and have my wicked way with her with my tongue. Then I'd fuck her into oblivion. She'd forget this entire interaction existed.

"That's it, asshole. I'm getting the key," Jericho grunts as his footsteps travel away from the door.

Good. That gets him out of the way momentarily. But then again. That means he'll be back and open the door. It's time to get this show on the road or pee out of the bladder. Whatever.

"I need you to turn on the faucet and stop looking directly into my eyes," she hisses, gesturing toward the sink behind me. I reach over and turn it on. The sound of running water fills the room.

"Better?" I ask, grinning.

"No. Close your eyes." She waggles her finger at me. "And don't move. I have to pretend like you're not even here," she mutters, more to herself with a huff.

My eyes squeeze shut, and I relax, kneeling in front of her as I should be. She's my queen, after all. Hopefully, this test will give us all the things we've talked about in the past. Knocking Journey up. Having eighteen babies. One after another. Or maybe the eighteen thing was something I thought up all on my own.

Journey pregnant. Journey pregnant again. And again. Hmmm. I count how many kids we can have from now until we're old and ripe. I'd take care of her every time. Feed her. Bathe her. Rub lotion on her back, stomach, and feet. God, I wouldn't be able to keep my hands off her. As soon as she popped one out, I'd put another one in there. I could get her a cum plug and force all our sperm to stay where it belongs—in her uterus.

"There," Journey sighs, pushing my hand away from between her legs. "You're supposed to cap it now and let it sit." She waves me away, and I do just that, making sure I don't get any pee on me, and then wash my hands. "Most ridiculous thing I've ever done. By the way, this is never happening again," she grumbles, wiping and then standing to pull up her pants. "And that better be negative, or your balls are going in the blender." She sends me a seething glare as the bathroom door swings open, letting my pissed-off Kitten out of her cage.

"Well, no Big A for you, Kitten. You can't just threaten him like that," I say, clicking my tongue at her with a grin.

She folds her arms over her chest as Jericho and Shepp lean into the large bathroom. I'm sure Shepp has learned the full extent of my antics by now. He doesn't seem too eager to save her. In fact, Jericho and Shepp look smug as fuck, watching her pout while tapping her foot. Mmmm. I love the sight of her like this.

I've missed her so damn much.

Now, I'm never letting her go. Ever.

"Can I get some water or something? Or are you two going to kidnap me into the bathroom, too, and force me to pee on a stick?" she grumbles with hostility.

Add mood swings to her ever-growing list of pregnancy symptoms. And check.

"Aren't you eager to see the positive sign, Kitten?" I ask, peering down at the stupid test that hasn't given me an answer yet. Work faster!

"It'll take about two minutes to show up, and I'm thirsty. Besides, I'm not pregnant. It was the stress of starving and being in the dark and shit."

That perks me up. Not in a good way, either. Journey has yet to discuss what happened to her and Shepp in Shadow's captivity. They've both been tight-lipped, avoiding the questions we've had for them. Granted, we haven't had all the time in the world to properly discuss this with each other.

But to drop a bomb like that? Fuck me. He's dead. There's no getting out of here for him. I'm going to make him suffer so hard that he won't be able to come back from it, even if he could. It's a good thing I turned out the lights and only left him with that annoying swinging bulb. I'll continue to starve him, too. And to think, I would be a good little captor and let him eat a sandwich. Fat chance that's happening now. Or any time soon. His body can eat itself for all I care.

"Did you say starving and the dark?" Jericho practically vibrates, turning his entire body toward her.

Even the hairs on my neck stand on end when he utters those dangerous words. Time to deflect and get back on track with what we're doing. There's no sense in getting pissed off now. Or that's what I tell myself, at least. We can harness that anger for later and direct it at the dickbag that deserves it. Besides, there are better things to do right now.

"It's okay, Jer. We've got him downstairs. Whatever he did to her, we can take it out on him repeatedly. Slowly, too. You think he'll want his toes?" I hum, looking down at the test again with a huff. "I could make them into a pretty necklace. A gift for you, Kitten. You liked Leighton's fingers and teeth, right?" That loathsome little bastard doesn't deserve to have fingers at all. It's too bad I couldn't permanently relieve him of those, like Lori's husband.

Speaking of. I wonder what old Leighton is up to right now. Jer let me in on the little secret one night about Chloe Satin and him in an arranged marriage set up by his father. Where does that leave ole' Leighton? They were in love, after all.

Journey turns a putrid green, gagging slightly. She sucks in a breath, shaking her head at me with narrowed eyes. "No. I don't want a necklace of toes," she grits out.

Oh, I made her angry and disgusted. Add morning sickness to the list of her symptoms. Check!

Shepp sidesteps and holds a hand for her to take, which she gladly does. They join hands and leave the bathroom together, side by side.

"I'll let you know how it goes!" I yell after them as they take off into the kitchen and grab some water. "I have a good feeling about this, Daddy Jer. It's like my balls know what's happening."

"Your balls?" he asks skeptically and checks his watch. "How long has it been?" See? Even he doesn't care I just forced his wife to pee on a stick. We're on the same page. In sync. Two brothers want their wife to be pregnant.

"Oh, probably two minutes…" I trail off, staring down at the test with a grin.

I hoist it into the air with a small whoop and do a little dance, much to the agitation of Jericho, who snatches it away with a huff. Staring down at the test, he looks up at me with what I can only assume is a pleased smile. I nod.

"Get ready to throw a funeral for your genitals," I quip. "We're gonna have one mad baby mama."

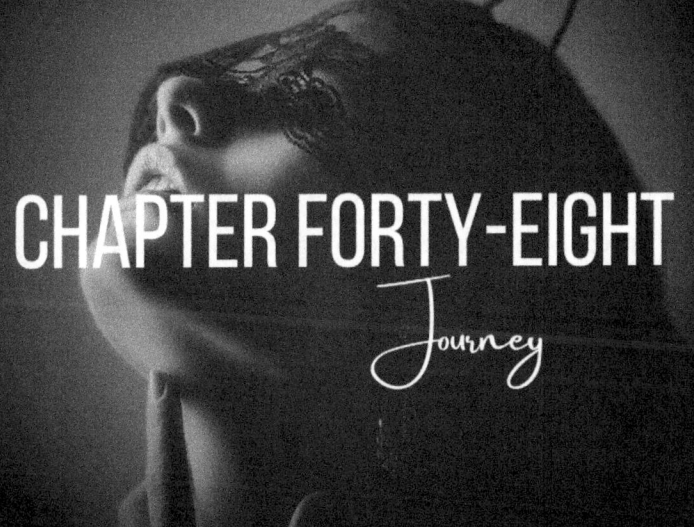

CHAPTER FORTY-EIGHT
Journey

WOULD ANYONE MISS THEM IF I SLAUGHTERED THEM TONIGHT? Because I'm contemplating murder, Blood. Guts. Screaming for me to stop until they're voiceless and strapped to tables naked. Not even the fun kind of naked, either. Just me in charge of punishing them for everything they've done.

Morbid? Yes. Absolutely. But it's the only thought I can think of as I stand beside Shepp in the kitchen, watching as he nonchalantly makes us sandwiches as a snack. So relaxed. No worries on his mind. He's thinking about turkey sandwiches. I'm thinking about hanging their guts up for decoration with Christmas lights.

We are not in the same headspace right now.

I'll start with Arrow, the grinning weirdo who forced me to pee on a pregnancy test in front of him. Never in my damn life did I think someone would want to do that. Even my monster gave me more privacy than that.

Well, sometimes, considering there weren't proper restrooms in the basement he left me in. But this? I thought the days of being humiliated by a man were behind me.

Internally, I roll my eyes. I should have expected it though. Maybe the distance fucked up my memories or something. He's Arrow Amour, after all. Resident psycho who loves to make people bleed and feed them to his lions. Among othe things. Like taking my IUD out without my permission or fucking knowledge. No. I had to find out at the initiation ball we attended.

Fucker.

I need to chop his balls to bits and not look back.

He never paid for that crime. So now, it's time to pay for them all. Arrow's demise is mine and mine alone.

I grit my teeth with annoyance. Is this my life now? Being paranoid about him following me into the bathroom? Nope. I won't allow that. I can't be paranoid every step I take that he's going to be behind me with some sort of fun surprise. And I use the word fun loosely. I'll put a bell around his neck before I let that happen again. Fuck. Maybe a collar.

I eye the bedroom door with narrowed eyes. My nerves explode more, turning my stomach into tight knots. They're in there still. Beyond the bed and in the bathroom, watching the test. Without me.

I swallow the bile in my throat. Reality crashes down on me again. The pregnancy test. One simple stick will tell us if I'm bringing an innocent soul into this world.

Fuck.

Nerves prickle beneath my flesh. What if? What happens if it's positive? Or negative? I've never thought about having kids. Convinced I'd be a terrible mother like my own. One who never showed me an ounce of love past the age of four.

But I practically raised Sunshine. The moment she was born, my mom waved her off. It was me getting up in the middle of the night to make sure she was fed. Me. Not her. I changed her diaper and kept her safe from harm. From my mom.

Right?

My breath stalls when a slight movement catches my eyes in the bedroom. I perk my ears, listening hard for any sort of conversation, but they're mumbling to each other. Not loud enough for me to catch their words.

The results of the pregnancy test he forced me to take rattles my mind on a constant loop of what-ifs. What if I am pregnant? Is it okay? After everything Shepp and I went through at the hands of Shadow. Will it survive? We were starved, dehydrated, and forced to stay in the dark. Surely a tiny little human can't survive that. Can they? Because I barely did.

My fingers rub the thick scar between my breasts as a comfort through the fabric of my oversized shirt. It's been a way to take my mind off the past, present, and future. It soothes me. For the moment, at least.

The loud shink of Shepp's knife cutting through Romaine lettuce brings my focus back to the present. He looks up at me expectantly with those ocean eyes cutting straight through my soul. It's funny. He seems to have this way with words without ever opening his mouth. I understand him in this instance, and he seems to get me.

Shepp gently sets down the large knife and grabs my wrist, stopping my movements. His head tilts with curiosity before gently kissing the back of my hand. Butterflies swarm in my belly, swooping left and right when his eyes meet my gaze again. All the words he needs to say sit there in his gaze.

"I'll be okay," I whisper, melting at his touch.

Oh, if past me could see me now. She thought she was in shit with her monster constantly on her ass. Now? Well, the current me melts at the sight of the three mafia men who forcefully kidnapped her. And despite wanting to murder them, current me wins the game.

'You sure?' he mouths easily, inspecting my face.

For what? I'm not sure. Maybe he's looking for the telltale signs of my lies, which he won't find. They're firmly placed behind the wall I've erected to hide my emotions.

Will it hold? Probably not. Especially if I'm carrying a baby.

Oh, how I long to hear the rasp of his voice reserved only

for me, like that time in his painting studio. He was carefree. One day, I know he'll open up completely. To Jer and Arrow. To the world. They'll know Sheppard Mondelli isn't silent any longer. But only when he's ready.

"Positive." Not really.

By the look in Shepp's sparkling eyes, he knows I'm lying because he's probably lying to himself, too.

We've both been through trauma in our childhoods. Fuck. Adulthoods, too. Spending time on Shadow's fucked up island is the cherry on top of our existence. I guess what we do with this trauma and how we proceed amid war will define us. Make us who we were meant to become. Hopefully for the greater good. We'll take down all the big bads and fucking win Briar Cove back from Gabriel and the family.

I sigh. That's the dream, at least.

Feet shuffle behind me. Not yet in the living room, lingering in the bedroom, whispering words I can't quite understand. I turn and look in that direction, catching the mischievous glint in Arrow's eyes.

Fucker.

I frown, turning back to Shepp, giving him all my attention.

"But I can't say the same for Arrow. You think he'd miss his nuts after I chop them off?" I say a little louder than necessary to get my point across.

Shepp winces at the thought. Right. Men and their precious balls. They're so protective of them.

Leaning in to kiss my cheek, Shepp lingers for longer than necessary. The scent of his body wash wraps me in a hug, cocooning me in the safety of his aura. I sigh, melting more. Shepp lovingly cups my cheeks and shakes his head before gently kissing my lips. Pulling back slightly, he examines my face again with that intense gaze that might bring me to my knees.

'I'll protect you.' he mouths, moving his eyes down my body before stopping at my stomach. *'And that, if it happens.'*

"I'm still mad at the three of you for knocking me out and stealing my IUD," I murmur, with no heat behind it.

I should be livid, I know. Make them kneel and beg for forgiveness for the next nine months. They did this to me. On purpose. Without my say so.

'We deserve it,' Shepp mouths, rubbing his neck and staring at the ground. Well, until two sets of footsteps finally make it into the kitchen.

"You'd really chop my balls off, Kitten?" Arrow asks with a pout, gaining my attention.

Yes. The answer is, fuck yes, I would. But I don't dignify it with words. Instead, I set my evil gaze on them, tracking their every movement as they get closer. I focus on their faces, trying to sus out their expressions. Do they give anything away? No. They're stoic. Emotionless. Not giving me any hints as to what the test says.

Now, the nerves set in. They wouldn't have left the bathroom without an answer.

"Yes," I hiss, crossing my arms. "I would chop your balls off." I give him my best stink eye, but it never works. He grins and bypasses me altogether. First, he makes me pee in front of him, and now he's ignoring me. Talk about whiplash. Before I can utter the words—what did it say—Arrow continues like I'm not on pins and needles.

"Whatcha making for a snack, Sheppy Boy? Anything good?" Arrow asks with a sneaky grin, shoving his hands into his pockets. Giddiness radiates off him in waves, making my stomach turn.

I'm fucking doomed. These are the emotions I was waiting for. He's either happy to have me pregnant or happy to fuck me some more so he can get me pregnant.

"What did it say?" I demand through a huff. "Am I pregnant?" My back stiffens when Arrow shrugs off my words, and

Jericho averts his eyes, moving away from us and to the small, round dining table. "Arrow," I hiss, gaining his attention. "Jericho?" I ask, looking his way.

"Kitten," he teases, taking a step back. "Please don't blend my Big A into mush." He bats his eyelashes at me, covering his nuts through his pants.

That's it. They're going in the blender ASAP. But wait...

I freeze. My stomach swoops. I swear I'm going to puke all over the kitchen floor.

"You..." Concrete encases my tongue, weighing it down. More words rest on the tip of it but refuse to come out. "I'm..." Pregnant.

I can't say it out loud. I refuse to. Then it would be real. And it would be all their fault. If I hadn't been so dickmatized by their alluring ways, maybe I wouldn't have ended up like this. IUD-less. Bun in the oven. Holy fucking shitballs. I'm pregnant. Really? This can't be happening. Is the big man in the sky looking down and laughing at me? Is this the karma I deserve after all these years of spying?

I swallow hard. My ears ring from the news. Even more when Arrow giddily thrusts the test under my gaze, I see for myself. The proof is in the pudding. Or, in this case, in my hand. On the test.

It's positive. A plus sign. Pregnant. Knocked up.

A confirmation I can't erase or shake away. The line—*this ain't no Etch A Sketch*—filters through my mind. Me and Juno have something in common. Except I didn't sleep with just one guy on a chair. I let these three fuck me everywhere. On the bed. In the woods. With gags and butt plugs. Hell, the night we tied Jericho up and made him watch, Shepp and Arrow fucked me at least five times each.

I'm going to kill them.

Oh, fuck me. Is it hot in here? I fan my face, feeling flush. Why am I sweating? I pull at the shirt on my body, moving it so air passes over my flesh.

"I think I'm going to pass out," I mumble, slurring my words until someone puts their hands on my shoulders, steadying me.

"See, Kitten? You're our baby mama now," he says proudly, puffing out his chest as he holds me steady. So not helping my mental freakout. "You're going to be the most gorgeous pregnant lady. I can't wait until your tits swell with milk." I blink several times at his words when he licks his lips.

"The fuck?" I grumble, pushing him away with protest, coming back to my damn senses. "That's…" He wants to drink my breast milk? I nearly recoil from the thought, but then again. No wait! This is no place to get all hot and bothered about his psycho ass and what he wants to do to me.

I'm fucking furious at him

Arrow shrugs again. "Then, once we have this baby, I'll knock you up again and again. You'll never get me off you. I'll just keep shoving that baby batter inside you until we have a whole gaggle of kids following us around." He sighs, lost in a damn daydream about knocking me up again. "Oh, and they'll help. I wasn't the only one on the—knock Journey up, so she's tied to us forever—plan. So, be mad at them, too." His grin widens when my mouth drops open.

Murder is on the menu, and I was right to start with Arrow first. No nookie for him. Ever again. For any of them! This vagina is closed for business until this child leaves the womb. And then? I'm tying my tubes so these bastards can never have another baby.

"If your dick comes anywhere near me in the next five minutes, I swear to God, Arrow," I grit out, stepping back from him. "I'm going to yank it off your body and make you gag on it."

Arrow shivers, holding tight to his dick while he still can. "Ouch, Kitten. First, the blender. Then, gagging me with it? I think you have a fetish for chopping off dicks." He pouts now, sticking out his bottom lip. "Big A loves you so much." My heart halts inside me. There's that word again. Love. Arrow's using it so freely, throwing it around like confetti at a parade.

Jericho snorts, shaking his head like he's innocent. "I'd hide that." Jericho points to Shepp, who holds a large knife over the cutting board again.

I could grab it. Stab Arrow through the heart. Then, I wouldn't have to worry about him and his raging hard-on to impregnate me every chance he got.

Shepp eyes the knife, gently putting it on the cutting board and pushing it out of reach. He offers me a soft smile, obviously trying to placate my erratic emotions. I want to cry, scream, and make them bleed, but I also need a nap and a bath. Ugh. My shoulders sag with exhaustion. I discreetly stash the test in my pocket, my heart pounding in my chest as I try to soothe my emotions.

I'll be okay. I always am.

"Kitten," Arrow says, holding up his hands. His voice dips low like he's talking to a wounded animal. "As much as I loved you stabbing me the last time. Maybe we should keep those stabbing motions for the villain in the basement." He nods like that'll convince me not to stab him in his sleep.

Arrow can wait, though. They did me more than dirty and deserve an ass-kicking. But he's right. Shadow is in the basement, awaiting what he deserves. And he gets much more than a stab to the damn heart. He'll get everything coming to him for all he's done to me, my sister, and Shepp.

"I wanted to discuss with you the phone call I had while outside," Jericho says, his demanding voice filling the kitchen. He deliberately steers the conversation away from me stabbing them and onto whatever he wants to say.

"Spill the beans, Daddy Jer," Arrow says with a grin, stepping back when Jericho stands abruptly, knocking his chair back with a loud squeak.

"Arrow, I swear to fuck," he grits out, leaning against the table like he's keeping himself back.

"You act like you hate it," Arrow quips with a snort.

"I do in fact hate it," Jericho seethes, plopping back into the chair with a grunt and righting himself.

"Could have fooled me," Arrow whispers in my direction, earning another glare. "You guys are no fun!" he huffs, planting himself in a chair opposite Jericho. "Go on, Jericho," he says, enunciating every syllable of his name.

Will that stop him from saying that ridiculous nickname? Absolutely not. I see it in his eyes when he looks in Jericho's direction. They sparkle with mischief.

Jericho looks around the room. His dark eyes assess us all as we turn to listen to him. His fingers steeple on the table. The official mafia heir is coming to the surface.

"I've contacted your sister."

I stiffen as his words echo in my mind. Well, then. That trumps baby in the belly, any day.

"What?" I rasp, moving forward a step. "Is she okay? Where is she? Is she…" He holds up a hand, stopping me mid-sentence.

Yeah. He's number two on the murder list tonight, right behind Arrow. I'm chopping his fingers to bits for cutting me off. And Shepp? Well, he's innocent-ish for now. He was my rock on the island. So he can survive. Maybe we'll walk hand in hand into the sunset after we bury the two bodies in the woods.

"She's just been through surgery. They were able to get her in earlier. Mikhail reached out, hoping we'd found each other by now. He wants me to assure you that she's getting stronger. His personal doctor has been watching over her since they arrived. He also assured me that the pact you made with him still stands."

"Still stands," I repeat, falling into a dining chair. Every emotion rocks through me. First, the baby. Now, my sister. What's next? Another fucking storm of bullshit knocking me down. Shadow breaking out and going on a murder spree? It wouldn't fucking surprise me.

"Mikhail has agreed to come here to meet with Elias and us. We're going to cook up a plan to take back Briar Cove and take down my father." He gives us all a pointed look, meaning this is not up for discussion. Everyone is coming here whether we like it or not.

"You're willing to depend on some kid to help?" Arrow asks, slowly moving to sit beside me. He acts like a wounded puppy, staring after me for affection while batting his eyelashes again.

Sorry, pal. That won't work on me right now.

"He wants to help," I murmur, shaking my head. "That's what he told me on the island. We talked." Cotton balls fill my brain with fog as I try to concentrate on the conversation happening now. It's pivotal. So important, but I can barely focus on anything but the pounding of my heart in my head.

I'm pregnant.

My fingers move over my abdomen, placing them on my flat stomach. There's something in there—living, breathing, with a heartbeat. We created it at the most inopportune time— there's a war on the horizon, and we're going to be smack dab in the middle of it.

We're going to have a baby.

"He said as much," Jericho says, sighing. "Little Chaos." His voice brokers no room for argument, forcing me to gaze deep into his dark eyes. "She'll be okay. Your sister got the heart she needed. It seems Mikhail and the rest of the Antonov have the best intentions." He raises his brow.

Mafia men and the best intentions? Yeah, right. However, Mikhail confessed why he wanted my sister so badly after having an online relationship with her for so long. It was hard to believe. A fourteen-year-old loving someone so much that he opted to marry her without knowing her further. Not only that, but he also promised me she'd go to the hospital and get the new heart she's needed for years. It was long past time for surgery. She was in dire need. The hospitalization my monster provided her with only extended her life, only by a little bit. She was hanging on the edge of demise with every beat of her broken heart.

I slump in my seat when Shepp sets a plate in front of me. My stomach curdles, making odd noises at the sight of it. A turkey sandwich with lettuce, tomatoes, and mayo. My mouth waters. Hunger pains eat me from the inside out, despite just having lunch a little while ago. I guess those days without food and water are catching up to me.

"Eat up, Kitten. You'll need your strength for later," Arrow quips, leaning his face on his palm, watching me as I take my first bite.

"Oh, yeah? Why do I need strength? To stab you again?" His grin only grows. Of course, that's what turns the psycho on.

"Fuck. I love it when you threaten me with violence. It does funny things to Big A. He likes it. Wants it." He bites his fist, groaning behind it.

"Arrow," Jericho grunts. "Knock it off, would you?"

Arrow pouts, crossing his arms. "But I've missed her, Daddy Jer! It was way too long without her. I've got blue balls," he stage-whispers, pointing down to his damn junk with down-turned lips.

"Arrow," Jericho sighs, pinching the bridge of his nose. "There's no such thing as blue balls." He shakes his head.

But I'm too in my head about everything and push my empty plate away. "I'm going to take a hot bath."

"I could join you! Rub your titties and back." Arrow grins at me, attempting to stand. "I do love a set of soapy titties to brighten up my day. And yours, of course." He winks with a heated stare.

Well, he can get bent. He's not touching my soapy titties with a ten-foot pole.

"Alone," I say with a frown, marching around the table to wallow in my self-pity.

Much to my relief, they let me go without a fight. Despite just taking a bath and getting cleaned up from the gunk of Shadow's dungeons, I need something to take my mind off everything. I haven't had a moment to myself in a while, but it's time to pull myself together. As I leave the room, the three of them mumble to one another, getting lost in a discussion.

CHAPTER FORTY-NINE

Shepp

I STARE AT HER WHEN SHE LEAVES THE TABLE. IT'S LIKE A piece of me has floated away, stuck in a dark headspace. Darker than on the island. We were in survival mode. Doing whatever we needed to make it until the next day. Now? She's obviously reliving our time in the dark. The fight she endured.

Now, the baby on top. And her sister?

She's crashing on a lonely highway and wants nothing to do with the three of us.

For now, at least. I don't think I can handle her being away for too long. When Shadow ripped us apart and took her to the wedding and left me behind, it did something to me. Broke me in two. I never want to take my eyes off her.

I'm over the moon that she's pregnant. It's everything we wanted. Selfishly, might I add. We were never ones to think these things through. Is this what Journey wanted? No. But hopefully, with time, she'll come to terms with the idea that she's having our baby. As Arrow would say, she literally has no choice.

'How long do we intend to hide out here?' I sign once I hear the door to the bathroom close and the water run.

"Forever," Arrow says with a grin. "Welcome to our new palace. Fuck Briar Cove," he scoffs, waving a hand. "They can blow it up more, and we'll be here making babies and raising 'em, too."

He doesn't mean it. Arrow would never walk away from a fight. Not this one, at least. He's been born and bred for this type of situation. The perfect weapon. He thinks in blood and mayhem. The last thing he'd ever do is walk away from this fight to protect the people he's always fought for—the citizens in need.

"I'd love to say I agree," Jericho mumbles, running a hand down his face. "Free from the life. Free for Journey to give her a more fulfilling life than what she's had under my father's thumb and her mother." He shakes his head, wearily looking between us. "But we can't abandon the people of our city. If war spills over, they're the ones in the crosshairs."

The news of his mother's betrayal has rocked him to the core. I see it in the bags under his eyes and wrinkles collecting across his face, pulling him down. His dark eyes haze over, getting lost in the fog of indecision—something my brother never has. Jericho is a leader—a man who always knows what to do and how to do it.

Right now, though? He's spiraling, too.

We all are.

We've been pushed out of our roles and thrust into the fringes of society. Cast out of Briar Cove like criminals while the real criminal holds power over the innocent and not-so-innocent. The list of things we need to get done in a short period of time continues to grow with every breath we take. Take down my sperm donor. Collect information from him and use it against Gabe. Take down Jericho's parents with what-ever they're doing and find out what Grace has up her sleeve. Once those are achieved, our next challenge is convincing the rest of the men in the Viotto Crime Family to follow our lead. That won't be an easy feat.

If protocol is followed, then they'll have no choice but to

bend their knees to us. But if their loyalties lie with Gabriel through thick and thin, they'll die for it.

Our childhoods formed us into what we are. Monsters to some. Villains to others. Saviors to the people of Briar Cove, depending on our services. And to Journey? I'm not entirely sure. She wears her feelings close and never lets people see her distress.

I did, though, throughout our captivity. I kept her afloat. She did the same for me. Like a life raft, I clung to her to keep my head above water. I tried to protect her and keep her out of my father's grasp the best I could.

He still got to her. Unsettled her. Rattled her fucking core.

And there was nothing I could do about it except watch helplessly as she left my sight to fight in a death match.

Never fucking again.

I didn't know what would come next besides the pain in my stomach. I had no idea I'd pass out and wake up in a hotel room, lying on a comfortable bed with confusion, waiting for her to return. If she didn't, I was going to riot against everyone. They'd all die at my hands for keeping her from me and harming her. He took her from me again a second time, splitting us up so he could parade her around a dangerous wedding he knew he'd blow up.

Journey West is my wife. Not legally. But in my heart. She will never be out of my sight again. I'll become Arrow, follow her through the shadows, and keep my eyes on her.

"And I can't call my uncles for aid. They'd never take their brother down. Or my mother. Or anyone else vying for the throne. Not their circus, as they love to say. They won't step in. Not since what happened with Olivia's nightmare of a father. This fight is ours. Regaining Briar Cove as ours," he says, interrupting my thoughts. "Our legacy." His brows furrow slightly. There's something in the depths of his expressive eyes that he's not saying. Is it possible that Jericho Viotto no longer wants the burden of the throne?

"So, the child and unstable Elias are our only damn allies? And we have to split up the territory? Pfft. The rest of the family isn't going to be pleased about these developments." Arrow frowns, slightly leaning back in his chair. "How do you think old Daddy Gabe's bosses will take this?" He raises a defiant brow, like he's uncertain we should even fight. "There's three of them and three of us." A malicious smile crawls across his lips. "Not that it's ever stopped us before."

"Where are they, then?" Jericho opens his arms wide, staring at the empty room. "The family is loyal to Gabriel and his laws. Not ours. They won't step in and help us or take Gabriel down. They're out for themselves and care nothing for the citizens. Only the money they gain and the power they hold. They won't fight against him even if he's failed them for the past five years. He's their leader. Even if they do fight against him, it wouldn't be for us. Everyone wants a piece of the pie. We must seize what is rightfully ours and claim our birthright as heirs. The throne belongs to the three of us. Together, we'll build Briar Cove into the city it should have been all along."

'And when we defeat him?' I sign hesitantly.

Gabriel Viotto isn't the only leader in charge we'll have to defeat. He has men around him. Bodyguards. Higher-up men in the family. His damn loyal bosses. They'll be the hardest to contain. They won't bow down easily. We're children in their eyes—no one of importance.

Jericho stares at me with a sigh. "We cross that road when we get there. Either they take him out, which they won't. Or I do. Reclaim what was rightfully mine." If he still wants it. Sometimes, I think Jericho would give it all to someone else if he could live a normal life with Journey. "Then everyone else will fall in line." We hope, at least. Or I do. "I am the heir to that kingdom. Or what's left of it."

Could we give up the perks of being mafia men? The

police in our pockets. The money flowing into our accounts. Everything that comes with it?

I eye Jericho when he huffs to himself. Seeing him so unsettled and unsure of our next moves is odd. We're stuck in limbo with short-term plans. Kill my father for information. Meet with Elias and Mikhail—who I'm not too eager to meet again. Although he treated Sunny with respect. Or so it seemed. Journey, too. He's still an unknown. Not an affiliate of our family. Of course, we can't call Jericho's uncles to aid us in this fight. It would be treason for them to fight against their own.

'You want to let the townspeople get slaughtered in a war?' My eyes volley between the two of them slumping in their chairs.

This is not the Arrow and Jericho I know. Of course, we've never been rocked like this before. Or hunted by the man we took orders from. This is a whole new level of Hell we've landed in, and navigating it without a map or resources has decimated us.

"We need more," Arrow says with furrowed brows. "What is even happening? Last I heard, your old dad was sick and keeling over. Maybe he's kicked the bucket." Too bad he hasn't already. Arrow pulls out his phone and sighs. "I'll call my dad. Maybe he can give us some insight on Gabe's happenings." Arrow doesn't wait for an answer. Or an argument from us. He gets up and walks out the front door and disappears with the phone pressed to his ear.

'You good?' I sign, watching Jericho closely.

"Define good?" His gaze lands on me, and worry is sitting in his eyes. *'I'm fucking terrified,'* he signs back, shaking his head. *'There's so much at stake. With us. With Journey. She's fucking pregnant. We did that to her in the middle of this bullshit.'* Guilt swarms him, pulling his face tight—a small tic forming in his jaw.

I grab his arm and gently squeeze. *'We'll fight through this. One thing at a time, Jer. Okay?'* I sign quickly, trying to calm his nerves.

Jericho sharply nods at me. "First things first. We need to have a nice long discussion with the man in the basement. I'm sure he's had enough time to think about what he's done."

That I'm sure of, too; he's been down there since I arrived. I haven't seen him since the fight I attended with Journey and Mikhail.

The front door slams, pulling us from the intense conversation. Arrow marches through the living room, pocketing his phone, and sits across from us again. An uneasy expression twists his lips together, and his eyes volley between Jericho and me. There's uncertainty there.

"Sunday," he says with a frown.

'What's Sunday?' I sign.

"The Family has the basement that night. My dad says he feels like something is going to happen. But I don't know what." Arrow looks perplexed, uncharacteristically rubbing his temples. He's a deadly golden retriever at best. So, seeing him and Jericho out of whack has my hackles rising.

'It could be a trap?' I question, looking between the two of them.

"Possibly," Jericho sighs. "But we need an inside look as to what is happening and why."

'So, we take the chance?'

"My dad is trustworthy, Sheppy Boy," Arrow chides with a scoff, shifting in his seat. "You think the great priest would lead us into a death trap?" He raises a brow at me. "Me? His child?" He shakes his head, glancing away from me.

Maybe. I've known the priest for as long as I've known Arrow. He's never seemed untrustworthy, giving all his loyalty to Arrow. Every chance Arrow had, he was there with his father for Sunday dinners and visiting. The thing about Arrow is he loves blood and guts, but spending time with his dad? That's a different story. His father loves him in his own special way. That's why he gave him to Gabriel —thinking that Gabe could turn Arrow's affinity for killing into something useful. It did. Gabe created the ultimate weapon of mass destruction—a weapon the priest didn't see coming.

"Given the priest's history, I say we approach with caution and follow our guts. He has done nothing to earn our suspicions," Jericho says with a firm nod.

Arrow shifts again with a blank stare without emotion. Something tells me he's not happy thinking about his father in any sort of negative light. He never has.

'Then we move out in three days,' I sign.

"Three more days," Arrow says with a grin.

"I was supposed to marry Chloe on Saturday," Jericho muses with a snort, finding humor in the fucked-up situation. "In that very church we're going to infiltrate."

"Fuck Chloe Satin," Arrow spits. "I can't believe the big guy did that."

"I can," Jericho scoffs. "Anything to gain new alliances. No matter who he hurts."

'You told us he knew you married Journey and that she was still alive. The marriage wouldn't have been valid,' I sign quickly, thinking deeply about Gabriel's motivations.

"As long as he convinced me she was dead, the marriage would have been real. I'm sure he would have forged death certificates or annulled the marriage completely." He shakes his head with a sigh. "You think my wife has drowned?" he asks, turning to look toward the bedroom with worry. I know he wants to hold her in his arms and suffocate her with his obsession. She's too angry. Too broken to let herself fall apart in front of him.

Right now, at least.

"I'll save you, Kitten," Arrow says with pride. He attempts to stand, but I pull him back by his shirt.

'She's stressed. Don't touch her,' I sign rapidly once he's seated again, glaring at me. *'You could hurt the baby.'*

Water splashes in the bathroom as Journey presumably settles further into the tub, catching our attention.

"We leave her be for now. She's been through enough for one day…" Jericho shakes his head, looking at me. "Is what she said about starvation true?" His fingers curl into fists on the table.

I swallow thickly, nodding once. *'Until we complied with his demands, he left us in the dark without food or water. We were weak by the time he came back. That's when he sent her to the Pit for the fight.'*

"Right," Jericho says, gritting his teeth. "The picture Elias showed me of her covered in blood at a fucking dinner with him and Shadow."

"What was his end game, Sheppy Boy?" Arrow asks, leaning in closer.

'No clue,' I sign with a shrug. *'We could always ask him.'*

"I like the way you think. Let's cut off some toes and get in the knows," Arrow quips, jumping from his chair with a whoop.

'Such a poet,' I sign sarcastically.

Jericho nods. "I'll inform my Chaos of where we're going. Hopefully, it'll give her time to think. Then she can join us." He saunters away with more uncertainty, disappearing into the bedroom.

"He seem different to you?" Arrow asks, sidling up to me when I stand as well.

'Yes and no,' I sign. Yes, because he's under stress, and no, because he's still the same Jericho. *'He just got his world turned upside down.'*

"True," Arrow says, turning and grabbing a drink from the fridge. "Better hydrate, Sheppy Boy. We've got loads of inter-rogations to do. And if my Spidey senses are on point, then your dear daddy is about to break." He grins, clapping me on the back before taking off into the basement and unlocking the door.

Thick rubber bands wrap tightly around my chest, squeezing tight at Arrow's optimism. Thomas Mondelli does not break. He never has. Even when Grace Viotto disappeared —the love of his life. A chasm sprouted in my father, severing his heart from his chest. But he didn't break. Not completely. He drowned his sorrows in booze, but he never revealed a goddamn thing. Maybe with his fists and touch he told us how much he hated us for existing.

But he never broke.

Now, I have to face the man who put me through all that hell. My stomach sloshes, shoving bile up my throat.

Can I do this? Can I face him head-on and not lose my shit? After everything on the island. My childhood.

I have no other choice. This moment is mine. Face Shadow and take him down. His life is mine to end.

"It'll be okay." Jericho's sharp voice echoes through my mind as a hand lands on my shoulder. "You do not have to face him. Arrow and I…"

I shake my head, cutting him off. *'He tortured me for too long not to see my face when he dies.'*

Jericho's dark eyes examine my face. "Fair enough. We need answers, though. What are his and my mother's plans for the future before we eviscerate him?"

My eyes strain toward the bedroom. My mind is on the brunette who walked away with ghosts in her eyes.

"She's processing it all. So rudely told me to fuck off before my balls were next." Jericho's lips pull into a smirk. "I'd love to see her try."

Yeah, me too.

I don't bother signing anything back. Journey is allowed to wallow in her feelings. Even though I want to bundle her in blankets, bake her donuts, and gently feed them to her.

All I want is for her to be safe. And happy.

Instead, I force myself down the steep stairs to face the man who made my childhood hell. Face the man who touched me while I slept and cut out my tongue so I couldn't speak of his crimes.

It's time to end his existence once and for all.

And I'll be the one to do it.

CHAPTER FIFTY
Shepp

My heart beats erratically in my ears, pounding away. It drowns out the sounds around me. Our footsteps. Arrow's cackles from below. The sound of water moving through the pipes.

I swallow the bile in my throat, pushing away the anxiety beating through me at the sight of him.

Thomas Mondelli. Bound. Gagged. Bloodied. Beaten.

His beady, swollen eyes glare through me. My world stops. My feet no longer move, and I'm stuck to the floor, staring at the man who stared in all my nightmares. Every time I shut my eyes, he was there with his wicked words and painful touch. A gloss forms over his eyes as he takes me in, no doubt snarling that I'm here and not on his shitty island. I want to tell him about Darrel's betrayal and rub it in his face.

But I stop myself and count to ten in my head.

"Welcome to the show, Sheppy Boy! Step right up and take a swing," Arrow says with a grin, maneuvering the large bat in his hands until it's suspended in the air, waiting for me to take it.

I swallow hard, shaking my head.

"Buzzkill," Arrow pouts. "Don't you want to fuck him up with this? Oh! Do you want something else?" He wiggles his brows as he digs through a damn pile of weapons and pulls something out.

"You good?" Jericho asks, sauntering beside me with furrowed brows. He tucks his hands deep in his pockets and trails his eyes over my tension-filled face, nodding once. He knows exactly what I'm feeling right now because he would be in the same position.

I'm not good. Not by a long shot. The concrete walls close in on me. Solid and cold. Much like the prison from my childhood. His cruel voice echoes in my ears. Taunting me and pushing my buttons.

The ghost of the leather straps he put me into wraps around my wrists and ankles.

I freeze, breathing through my mouth in heavy pants where my tongue is supposed to sit. A constant reminder of the punishment for speaking out against him and the sins he committed in the dark. Fuck.

"We won't think badly of you if you want to assist Journey in the tub. Walk away now before his blood spills." Jericho's brows raise when I whip my gaze to him.

"Yeah, Sheppy Boy. I'll spill all the blood in your name. You'll never have to see a drop. It'll be my fucking pleasure," Arrow quips, staring Shadow down with no emotions hiding in his eyes. They've evaporated into dust, giving us the Arrow who loves and aches for blood.

They can't take this away from me. I won't walk away just because my heart is beating through my fucking chest and my brain screams at me to run for the hills.

I plant my feet. *'No,'* I sign aggressively. *'I want to see blood spill and his life fall away. I need this.'* Sucking in several calming breaths, I never take my eyes off the man who deserves to die a slow and painful death at my hands. No one else. Arrow can torture him all he wants, but I call dibs when it comes to giving the death blow.

"If that's what you need, brother. That's what you get,"

Jericho murmurs in a low voice full of understanding. "But remember, we're your family." Jericho levels me with a look, staring deep into my eyes with understanding. "And family helps to take out the trash."

He doesn't have to utter the words—we're here for you. We're your brothers, and no one else can come between us. It's the way he's taking control and offering me his support.

Something inside me clicks into place. Yes. They're my family. My brothers. The men who have been here with me through everything my father has done to me. They picked me up and learned sign language for me so we could communicate.

The people in this house have my fucking heart.

And now, it's time to take the man who gave me life out. He took so much from me. Now, I'm about to take everything from him. His blood, soul, life, and fucking last breath.

Today is the day Thomas Mondelli says goodbye for good.

My fists curl at my sides when Arrow turns around, revealing the weapon of his choice. Of course. He's always been partial to fire and explosives. It almost makes me smile to see the happiness radiating off him.

"Are we ready?" Arrow asks, grinning as he lights a small torch and adjusts the height of the fire, which illuminates his face with an orange glow.

"We need answers," Jericho sighs, waving a finger for Arrow to turn it off.

"But fire, Daddy Jer," he pouts, slumping his body with disappointment.

"Later," Jericho says with a nod. "When we want to hear his screams for help. Not now. We need him to speak. So, shall you speak, Thomas?" He cocks his head in my father's direction.

Shadow doesn't move a muscle except for his eyes. They track everyone's movements like he's committing them to memory. But why? He won't make it out of this basement alive. The moment his heart stops beating, we'll incinerate his remains and make sure he never regenerates again.

"Later always means maybe, and we all know what maybe means—no," Arrow grumbles, turning off the flame and setting down the tiny torch. He sets it on his workbench with a loud clink.

"Let's start with removing the gag," Jericho says to Arrow, who enthusiastically nods, clapping his hands with glee.

He's way too perky in the torture room, bringing out another side of him completely. Sure, he's bubbly—on the psychotic side—but bringing him here, in his element, it's a whole new Arrow for the world to see. This torture wipes away all the worries he has weighing down his chest. Sometimes, I wish I was more like Jericho and Arrow. Their bloodlust has gotten us out of sticky situations and helped with our enemies.

My fingers curl into fists when the gag is removed from my sperm donor's mouth, and he smacks his swollen lips together with a groan. The sound of his voice grates on my nerves—more than before. I'm not in true survival mode in this cabin. I'm at peace. Home. Especially with our wife bathing upstairs without worrying about cameras following our moves. Having Shadow in this space is fucking with my mind, and I'm desperate to remove him.

"You boys finally come to your senses?" he rasps out in a terrible voice, sounding like he smoked an entire pack of cigarettes before sitting in the chair. "Oh, you've come to play." He grins at Arrow, who reaches for the torch again but stops when Jericho snaps his fingers and shakes his head.

"Our senses?" Jericho hums. "Enlighten me on what that would be?" He cocks his head, staring down at Shadow without an ounce of emotion. He's good at that. Shutting everything out and not letting the enemy know what he's feeling. I guess it's all the training his father gave him through his torturous childhood.

That's the thing about the three of us—The Devils. We've survived unimaginable childhoods riddled with abuse and power plays. Men who were supposed to protect us, abandoned us—used us like chess pieces on their boards.

And it's high time we take them down one by one and show them the monsters they've created.

Shadow grins, exposing his yellowing, missing teeth and cracked lips from lack of water. "That you know you've already been defeated."

"Defeated, huh?" Arrow quips, picking up a pair of pliers. "I could defeat you really fast. Tell me, how do you like your teeth?" Arrow leans in slightly, holding the tool in front of Shadow's face.

He laughs. Fucking laughs at Arrow's threat. "You think a set of tools and a small torch will break me open, boy?"

"I mean, I have more in my arsenal," Arrow quips. "Some fun devices they don't even make anymore. Like this finger splitter. All you have to do is set your finger in here, and bam! No more flesh. It's highly effective."

My sperm donor doesn't flinch when Arrow puts it on his finger and tightens the medieval-looking contraption so it's in the appropriate position and primed for use. I've only seen him use it once or twice before. Here and in the basement beneath the mansion. The man we held here for two days gave us everything we needed to know by removing the flesh of one finger. In the end, he died a coward. The woman, on the other hand? She lost all her fingers in two days and barely gave up the answers we were seeking.

So, it truly depends on the pain threshold of the person earning its ire.

"Hmmm. I think I've seen one of these before, boys. They're interesting, aren't they? Do you have the de-boner as well? It spices up torture nicely," Shadow says, sitting perfectly still.

The only instance of panic I can see is when his eyes shift

between us and then back to the device with unease. It's on the tip of his tongue to beg, but I know his tactics. He'll attempt to talk his way out of this situation. Manipulate those around him to set him free.

Funny, he can't manipulate us into doing anything like he's manipulated me so many times before.

All the memories of my childhood. What he did. How he did it. What he said. It all swirls there in my brain, echoing back to me.

My fingers curl harder, eager to hit Shadow in the nose and watch as he bleeds. Rage almost consumes me, firing through my veins. Eager to take over and make him pay. It's an all-consuming anger. Something I can't shake off.

"No, but tell me more," Arrow says, leaning in further. "I need more funsies." Funsies? How can he find this fun and liberating? He says it helps to cleanse the demon riding him hard. The one that begs for blood, broken bones, and death.

Me, though? I'm having a hard time keeping the burning bile out of my throat as it is. I know the moment my sperm donor's finger is skinned, I'm going to have to turn my back until I can control myself.

"Arrow," Jericho sing-songs, bringing Arrow back from the brink of his madness.

"Right. I'm being bad. Shadow, tell us your plans for Briar Cove and the Family. What's the endgame?" Arrow doesn't wait a second for him to answer when he presses on the device, and a loud sound comes from Shadow's finger before he wails in pain. "Fuck. I think I'm hard. Where's my Kitten? I want to fuck her in the blood of our enemy," Arrow whoops, staring down at his carnage with stars in his eyes. They practically sparkle with anticipation, eager to move on to the next form of torture.

My stomach turns—drool pools in my mouth. I'm ten seconds away from vomiting the snack I made. Hold it together, Shepp. Don't let the blood and broken bones stop you from witnessing the demise of a man who should have stayed dead. I stand tall, puffing out my damn chest despite the nausea swimming through me.

I will not fall at the sight of bodily fluids.

"Gonna lose your lunch, boy? You were always a terrible interrogator. Can't even handle the blood." His voice cuts through the fog in my brain, taunting me repeatedly from his chair. "Pathetic excuse for a fucking Mondelli. Always have been. I'm ashamed to give you the family name," he grunts through the pain of his finger, spitting on the ground near my feet.

"Oh, you want more?" Arrow quips, doing something else to make him howl in pain. "Ah, that's it. Give me something, Dead Man. I want to know all the plans you and Grace concocted together. Actually, did you fuck her?" Arrow stops suddenly, waiting for the answer of the hour. The answer only he fucking cares about.

"For God's sake, Arrow," Jericho hisses, thumping Arrow on the chest. "Don't discuss my mother's sex life." His face twists with disgust, and he shakes his head.

"What?" Arrow asks in defense, putting his bloodied hands in the air. "You act like you haven't thought about this guy and your mom boning over and over again. Those pictures! Come on, they were fucking in high school after prom. Weren't ya, Tommy Boy? I mean, how else did she lure him into her clutches and fake being Shadow? That was it, right? She pussy-whipped you into submission. So you were the face of the operation when the time came?" Arrow leans in, eagerly awaiting Shadow's words, but he's only met with a pale-face glare and silence. "Come on. Give me something here!" Arrow protests, stepping back and grabbing something else from his pile of tools.

Shadow laughs through the pain. "Plans? Do you want to know the plans? You mean everything that's already happened?" he cackles. "It's all done, boys. Why do you think

I'm here?" He laughs more. "I'm the goddamn sacrifice. My last fuck you to your father and the family. My last display of love for Grace. I do this for her."

I look between Jericho and Arrow with furrowed brows. There's a hidden meaning there. There's a reason my sperm donor gave himself over to us. Why would he?

"Elaborate more," Jericho hisses, slamming his fist into the side of Shadow's head. "I want more answers," he growls with impatience, hitting him repeatedly.

"Daddy Jer, you wanted him to keep speaking. Let him catch his breath," Arrow quips, grabbing Jericho's fist before he can sink it into Shadow's skull again.

Shadow groans under his breath as blood pours from the side of his head and ear.

Jericho's chest heaves when he throws Arrow off him, and he steps back, running his bloodied hands through his hair.

"We need something," Jericho hisses through clenched teeth.

'This was on purpose. He's a martyr. Something to keep us busy,' I quickly sign with agitation, shaking my head. *'They knew we'd come back after the dust settled. They're trying to keep us away.'* But what is that something? *'Maybe away from the church?'* I urgently sign.

Jericho stills, cocking his head. "Interesting," he says without giving himself away.

"What did the little shit say?" my sperm donor says through heavy breaths, eyeing me with narrowed eyes. "Use your voice, boy," he mocks in his old tone. His lips tilt up into a malicious smile. "Oh, right. You can't, can you? Someone snatched your voice from you, didn't they?" he laughs again. Sweat pours from his forehead and dampens his hairline. A ghostly paleness takes him over, but he refuses to back down, even when death is knocking at his door.

"I want to know about my mother, Grace," Jericho says, pivoting until he's standing right in Shadow's laughing form.

"What is your true history with her? We've seen the photos and read the letters. What's with you and my father? You were his loyal second-in-command for so long, and then..." He waves a hand, seeming to lose himself in the history of it all.

My sperm donor is *his* father's second-hand man, like me to Jericho. His mother is the ideal mafia wife, showing everyone else up in the Family. She was perfectly put together. Of course, she came from her own mafia background—a wealthy family from the East Coast that moved here for an alliance when she was a teenager.

"You'd love to know, wouldn't you? It's eating you up on the inside because you don't know why I'm so loyal to Grace and not her snake of a husband," he hisses, spitting on the floor again.

"Well, I'll give you the snake part. Gabriel Viotto is the epitome of a snake in the grass, waiting to strike at a moment's notice. He doesn't care who he hurts or ruins to get what he wants. Much like you." Jericho tucks his hands behind his back, pacing in front of Shadow now. A pensive expression takes over his features as he mulls over everything he's learned. "Is that what he did?" Jericho turns his indifferent stare to Shadow, who laughs in his face, exposing all his teeth. "He stole Grace right out from underneath you. You were to be married, and instead, she married him."

"Oh, boy. You're good at this. Did he give you special treatment when your mother took off to Oregon?" Shadow raises a brow.

"Oregon? What the fuck is in Oregon?" Arrow asks, falling right into the trap Shadow planted. He wants us to ask stupid questions until he bleeds out and gets nothing from us. All the while stalling us for what?

'He's stalling for some reason and baiting you into questions,' I sign, shaking my head.

'Why, though?' Jericho surmises, pursing his lips.

'Cuz he's crazy?' Arrow signs back with a shrug.

"I see. The three of you have your own special language going on, don't you?" Shadow teases, coughing slightly. "Is that how you plotted to take over the family?"

I clench my fists again at his mocking. He's always had something to say about the situation he forced upon me. I gave him what he wanted. I no longer talked to other people besides my friends through ASL. What the fuck more does he want from me? My life? Well, he already took my voice.

"Amongst other things," Jericho says, pacing again. "We've had plans in place long before you left."

Shadow smirks at Jericho. "How's that going for you, boys? Huh?" he mocks.

"Fine." Jericho brushes him off with another wave of his wrist. "How's it going for my mother?" He stops dead, turning toward Shadow blankly. "That's what this Shadow business is, isn't it?" Shadow smirks. "She took off and created her empire of running drugs and whatever else you may do..."

"Gambling. Kidnapping. Drugs. Guns. You name it, boy. We've done it. All for the mighty green," Shadow says with a grin.

'Not likely,' I sign with narrowed eyes. *'He's not telling us something. It's all too fishy.'* The agitation brewing inside me builds hotter and deeper than before. Talking with my sperm donor does nothing to quell the distaste I have for him. He's dancing around the questions like the pro he is. He was a higher-up in the family, after all.

"But why? Weren't you satisfied in the ranks of the family? Second-in-command isn't too bad. You were provided with so many opportunities to thrive. But you didn't get the woman you wanted. Is that it?"

"Being second-in-command was nothing but bitch work," Shadow snarls, wincing when he attempts to move his fingers into a fist. I don't have a clue how he's still coherent. It makes my stomach churn.

"Yeah, I wouldn't mess with those," Arrow hums, standing

back with a hammer. "You think he'd talk if I blew out his kneecaps? I can't take any more limbs, or he'll slip away and burn in Hell before we get to the conclusion." Arrow hums to himself, watching Shadow with keen eyes. He knows something is up. "And I really hate cliffhangers."

"By all means, maybe he'll sing," Jericho grumbles, stepping back and letting Arrow take a swing at Shadow's left knee. He howls again, filling the empty basement with his misery and pain.

The same pain he's made so many people before him feel. My mother. Me. Journey. Sunshine. That phrase runs through my mind on repeat. Over and over again, fueling my damn rage, ready to explode out of me.

"You wanna know all the dirty truths?" Shadow breathes heavily, focusing on me.

"I mean, that's why we're here, right? I'm just dying to know what you've been up to for the past three years and how you've stayed undetected," Arrow says, examining the hammer with his finger with a sigh.

"That's the beauty of the island your mother bought," Shadow says with a weak grin, slumping into his chair.

"I'm curious as to how she was able to obtain such an obscure island with no money?"

"No money?" Shadow scoffs. "Why the fuck do you think your father wanted her so badly and rigged the damn marriages?" He raises his brow and then laughs. "Right! You don't know about the history, do you?"

"Elaborate then and inform me," Jericho says with exhaustion. "Or perhaps Arrow should take your elbow this time."

"Oh, please! It'd hurt like a bitch, Shadow fucker. But goddamn, it would be so satisfying." He beams at the prospect, and finally, I see the moment my father slumps further, no longer having any reason to bite his tongue.

"It's true that Grace Contelli was my intended wife," Shadow frowns with an odd sadness. Fuck. I think he truly loved her, and the bitterness of losing her made him the man he is today. "My father told me when the deal was done. Her father agreed. He agreed. It was going to be a match made in heaven. Before the initiation, we knew we were destined for each other." His eyes gloss over more like he's stuck in memories.

"In Heaven, you say?" Jericho hums, attempting to bring Shadow back into the conversation. "Why exactly?"

"My father made the deal for me. Grace and I were in love." He smirks at that. "So yes. I have fucked your mother on so many occasions. Best pussy on this side of..." He doesn't get another word in before Jericho slams his fist into Shadow's lips, knocking the words from his lips.

"Don't speak of my fucking mother like that!" he growls, taking a step back with a heaving chest. A wild look crosses his eyes. Murder. He wants to take Shadow down right here and now.

Jericho stills but doesn't fall into the trap.

"I can hit his elbow for that, Daddy Jer. How rude," Arrow says, pulling the hammer back and beginning to aim for his elbow and slamming it down.

Shadow grunts, barely containing the shout threatening to spill from his lips. "That all you got, boy?" he wheezes as more sweat pours from his flesh.

"Oh, no. I've got more," Arrow growls between clenched teeth, throwing the hammer into the corner of the room. It lands with a thundering sound. "So many more toys to show you. Shit, I can stick down your dickhole and up your ass. I can break every fucking inch of you, and you'll be begging for me to end it."

"You won't end it, boy," Shadow wheezes again, throwing his head back into the chair to catch his breath. "You don't have it in you."

Blood pours from his lips onto his chin. Color leeches from his flesh when he tries to move his limbs but can't. His knee hangs to the side, proving he'll never walk again. Well, if he wasn't going to die right here.

For the first time in my fucking life, Shadow—my father—is nothing but a weakened man, wilting away beneath the hand of someone he helped to train for this very reason. A weak-ass man parading as a strong warrior. There's nothing strong about him. Never has been. I mean, who picks on a fucking kid and a weak woman.

Thomas Mondelli is a goddamn joke.

Always has been.

Always will be.

How have I been so scared of him? Letting him beat me down, steal my tongue, and make me into the man I am. There's no reason for me to be afraid of him anymore. He's a fucking joke. A love-sick fool so caught up in Grace Viotto he can't see straight.

"Oh, I have it in me, Shadow Fucker. I have it all in me. Death. Destruction. Every goddamn thing." Arrow grins, holding up a sharp, shiny knife in Shadow's face. He doesn't flinch. Instead, he grins at Arrow, saying without words that he should bring it on. He wants the pain to end and his suffering to cease.

"How's your wife, boys?" Shadow wheezes out, coughing more blood. "Have you found out about the baby yet?" He maniacally laughs when we all freeze, not daring to move at the news.

"How in the absolute fuck did you know about the baby?" Jericho asks, standing stock still.

"It was easy to see. She vomited every chance she got. It was apparent from the time she came in that she was—oh, what do they say? In the family way," he chuckles at his words. "She was pregnant. But is she still? Did I do damage?"

Before anyone else can make a move, I do. Something snaps inside me. Erupting like a volcano and seeping lava through my veins. I see red. My vision blurs when I march forward, grabbing the knife from Arrow's hand. He doesn't fight me. Only chuckles and gestures for me to step up to the plate and take my swing. Gladly.

Something fizzles in my throat, tossing off the cobwebs of my trauma. It happens slowly, coming out in small noises and waves, but once I get my bearings. I unleash.

Looking Shadow directly in the eye with clenched teeth, I stare into his soul.

"You starved us. Left us in the goddamn dark! You put her in harm's way every chance you got. You fucking piece of shit," I growl through a raspy voice, thrusting the knife directly into his throat without thought. His eyes widen, and he gurgles at me, choking on his own damn blood. "Speak up, Father. I can't fucking hear you through the knife in your throat!" My voice echoes off the basement walls, filling my ears with the rasp of my unused voice. Tears burn the backs of my eyes, spilling out onto my cheeks. "You took something from me repeatedly. You took my voice. But fuck you if you think I'm going to stay silent any longer," I hiss, pressing the knife straight through his cervical spine. Every inch of his body relaxes as his eyes plead with me. He gasps for air. His lips flap like a damn fish. "Goodbye, Shadow. The world won't miss you. Especially the second time." My chest heaves as I step back, watching the life drain from his eyes.

The blood doesn't bother me. Nothing does. Not right now. Because right now, I've been granted the freedom away from the man who took it all.

Now, he's dead.

"Shepp," Journey's sweet voice wraps around me, soothing the aches from my body.

I turn, facing her with a heavy breath. Eyeing the long sweatshirt and long socks covering her body after her bath. Gently, she gets on her tippy toes and wipes the tears from my cheeks with her warm fingers.

"Holy fucking shit, Kitten! Did you hear that?" Arrow

breathes with amazement. "Did you see that!" Excitement fills his voice, and he whoops, slapping me on the shoulder.

"I knew you had it in you," Journey whispers sincerely, cupping my cheek. "It's amazing to hear your voice again."

I smile at her. "It's over," I rasp, clinging to her hand. "It's all over. He's dead." I squeeze my eyes shut, losing myself in the feel of her hands on me. Her flesh on mine. Her warmth.

My home.

"Wait! She said again. What the fuck, Sheppy Boy?" Arrow quips, coming behind Journey and putting his hands on her hips. His hands run over her stomach, and he sighs. "Did he speak to you, Kitten? Did he tell you all the dirty things he wanted to do to you? But wait! What about your bros? Bros before hos, Sheppard. I'm aghast." Arrow holds a hand over his heart with feigned outrage.

I blush.

"You've spoken to her before?" Jericho asks curiously, tilting his head and watching me closely.

"Yes," I say, sighing at the sound of my voice. It's so odd, once again, to hear what I had lost for so long. A piece of me. My fucking identity.

And now, it's mine. I'm reclaiming it.

"Should we take him to bed, Kitten? Have him murmur all those naughty words in your ear as we run a train on you and make you airtight?" Arrow wiggles his brows, getting the reaction he needed from her.

Her pupils dilate.

"I think that's a yes. Don't you, Sheppy Boy?" Arrow grins, staring at me with pride in his eyes. "The last one up gets the last hole!" Arrow shouts, pulling Journey into his arms. She yelps, throwing her fists into his shoulders while cursing him out.

"You good?" Jericho asks, coming up beside me.

Turning over my shoulder, I look at the remnants of my

father with the knife sticking from his throat and blood coating his clothes.

"More than good now," I whisper, my throat tightening with every word, threatening to leave me again.

But I don't let it close this time. I don't let it stop my words from spilling out.

I killed the man who took everything from me.

This is my freedom.

CHAPTER FIFTY-ONE

Arrow

A LONG, LONG TIME AGO, I PROMISED MY KITTEN I'D SHOVE my dick so far up her ass that she'd see stars. Okay, well. I didn't use those words exactly. I want to be the first in that hole and put a flag with my name on it. Arrow was here first, suckers. Jericho got her damn pussy first. So, naturally, her asshole is mine. And she's agreed. Several times over, might I add. Sure, she may have been delirious from sexy times or half asleep or deep in her sleep, muttering yes to my questions.

The time is now. Big A is ready to enter uncharted territory and stake it as his. Mine. And the others don't get that privilege. Only me. Arrow. The man of the damn hour.

Shudders wrack my body as my imagination runs wild. All I can envision is her screaming my name until she comes hard on Jericho's dick in her pussy and mine in her ass. Fuckkkkk. I bite my fist.

I'm going to come within three minutes of stretching her out. Ah, well.

"Kitten," I murmur, laying her on the bed with care. My eyes roam to her flat stomach, mesmerized by the life we put inside her—all thanks to me and my quick thinking. I'm a damn genius for removing her IUD. Only, I wish I had done it at a later date. I'm afraid to put her in harm's way now. This war won't stop, and we need to intervene.

Journey frowns, staring up at me. "Did you have to manhandle me into bed?" she huffs, lightly hitting my chest again with no heat behind it.

My Kitten wants this so badly, she can't deny it. I see it in her blazing eyes and labored breaths. She needs my dick to help her out.

Anything for my girl.

"Yes," I say, grinning when I crawl over her body. Only stopping when my face hovers just above her belly button. "It won't hurt, will it?" I ask, pulling up her long shirt and exposing her panties and stomach completely.

I haven't thought this through. She is the vessel for our child. Its lifeline to live before it emerges.

"The baby?" she hums, staring at me with the same heat in her eyes.

I rub my nose in circles around her belly button and gently kiss it. "Yes. I'm not gonna poke their eyes out, will I? Or ruin their skull with my skills?" I recoil in horror. Will I have to tuck my dick away for the next nine months until that little booger emerges and gives me back my vagina? Fuck. I hope not. That's mine. I'm pretty sure I have my name tattooed inside her right now.

"Its skull?" she huffs. "Arrow, you won't hurt the baby. Pregnant women have sex all the time. Even though I shouldn't let you anywhere near me." She shouldn't.

This is my fault. Not that it will stop me. But there's a need in Journey's voice, begging me to eat her alive and make her come on my face. Sounds like a plan to me.

Your wish is my command. Anything my Kitten wants, I'll do. Humiliate me? Bring it on. Stab me some more? Fucking hell, use my blood as lube. Make me kneel for nine hours straight while singing the *Sound of Music* soundtrack? Count me the fuck in.

Journey is the absolute most important person in my life, even in front of my brothers. There, I said it.

"Like that could stop me," I chuckle, leaning down to press my lips against her stomach with a hum again. "Go to sleep, little swimmer. Daddy has some bad, bad things to do to your mommy." My eyes glide up her abdomen, over her covered tits, and up to her misty expression.

"Arrow," she murmurs, running her fingers through my hair. I expected a slap or a whack to the head, but she soothes me best. "Don't talk to the squish while promising to fuck me. It's weird." Her face twists, and she shivers.

"In that case, Kitten. I have an idea." I grin, rolling off her, and lie on my back, scooting closer to the headboard. "Okay, climb on," I say, slightly sticking my tongue out. "And hang on to your titties! I'm about to make you come so hard you forget your name." That's a promise I can get behind. All I want her to do is wrap her thighs around my head and let me wear her like a scarf. Well, a scarf that drenches me in pussy juice over and over again until she's so relaxed I can fuck her senseless.

God, I've missed her. Her body. Everything in between.

"Climb on?" she huffs, staring at me like I'm nuts. I mean, I am. Totally. Completely. And utterly fucking nuts. For her. She should be used to this by now. I'm her devoted king, ready to devour her before the other two idiots arrive. Shit, I should have locked the door and kept her to myself for an hour. That never goes over well, though. Jericho always finds a key to the rooms I lock her in. It's rude. And fucking invasive, too.

"My face," I say, nodding.

"You want me to ride your face?" she hums, twirling a finger up my leg against my skin.

I grin when Big A instantly stands at attention, pulsing and begging for his pussy to consume him. Pre-cum pushes out of my slit, wetting my boxers at the thought of her riding my face into oblivion.

"Come on, Kitten. I want to taste your pussy and cum. Give my tongue the best treat of all. I'll beg," I say, grinning when she shudders against me. That's right, you love the imagery of it all.

"Then beg," she says huskily.

Beg? I'll fucking get on my knees for hours, begging every minute of every day to get her to let me lick her cunt. Listen, I'd die a happy man between her legs as she smothered me.

I run my fingers through her curls, clutching them tight. A small moan leaks from between her lips when her eyes find mine again. There's nothing but desire looking back at me, dripping with absolute devotion and brattiness. Staring deep into her moss-green eyes, I get lost in the darkness swirling there. Similar to mine. We may have been born into different circumstances, but Journey and I are one and the same. I was born this way, and she was created into the being she is now.

Nothing but darkness.

"Journey, please spread your legs over my face and smother me with your pussy. I'll die a lucky man between your thighs. Please, please..." I'm breathless by the time the words leave my lips, and I heave a breath to steady myself. My fingers loosen from her curls when she grins, gently climbs off the bed, and removes her long sweatshirt, fuzzy socks, bra, and panties.

Fuck.

My eyes bulge out of my head, much like my damn dick does through my boxers. Fuck. Why am I still dressed when she's standing naked before me? Quickly, I discard my clothes, wiping the rogue blood drops from my skin, and stare at her.

Her heavy breasts sway as she moves toward me. The sight of her tiny hairs that are grown out over her cunt has my toes curling and my mouth watering. God, I want to fucking bite her so hard and leave my marks all over her pale skin. I want everyone to look at her and know she belongs to the Devils of Briar Cove. So, no fucking touchy, dickbags.

"Your tits are massive," I groan, reaching out to squeeze one in my palm. It's hot and heavy in my hands when I run my thumb over her budding nipple. A nipple that will soon feed our baby. Fuck.

What will they be like when they're full of milk and leaking as I fuck her. My tongue pokes out, wetting my lips as I imagine her milk brushing my tastebuds, and I groan.

She snorts, batting my hand away. "You're only here for orgasms."

She must be confused. Sure, I'm giving out orgasms because I love the taste of her. But after I give her at least five moan-worthy, body-melting spasms, I'm fucking her ass. I'm sure by then, the others will join in on the festivities, and this will become a cum fest.

"Fuck, Kitten. You're the most beautiful woman I've ever seen." My hands roam over her body, guiding her until her thighs are ear muffs and her other muff hangs above my lips, dripping with need and begging me to suckle it into my mouth. Well, Kitten, you don't have to wait much longer. I'm about to take a long drink I'll never return from. "Grip the fucking headboard. And hold on tight. I'm about to take you for a wild fucking ride you won't be able to get off of. Five orgasms minimum." She stiffens before she moans when I dive in, twirling my tongue in her cunt and swirling it around her clit. My hips buck, eager to sink inside her, but I don't. I'll wait until she comes and comes again before I bend her over the bed.

And that's exactly what I do in a matter of thirty fucking minutes without interruption. By the time I'm done giving her all the orgasms she can handle, I'm slathered in her juices, and my fingers are stretching out her ass with the help of lube. Preparing her for what's about to come while my other hand pumped at my dick, edging myself for when I fuck her.

Journey slumps breathlessly with my name on her damn tongue. "You really meant five," she breathes, removing her fingers from the headboard with a grimace.

Pleasure soars through my veins at the sight of her well-fucked face. Exhaustion weighs her down, and I know she's ten seconds from snoring on my shoulder. No can do right now. She's mine to fuck. I've warmed her up. Now, she needs more orgasms. Carefully, I remove my fingers from her ass, gently pulling out. She shudders again, groaning when she's bereft and left wanting.

"It had to be five, Kitten. We haven't had the proper time to stretch your ass again. We were supposed to use the plugs more and more, but you were kidnapped." At the thought of Gabriel selling her to that bastard Shadow, I pout. Fuckers. No one will ever touch her again. No one except the three of us. Speaking of.

I smirk, looking around her body to find Jericho and Shepp watching from the opposite side of the room with consuming desire written on their tense faces. It's like they sensed I needed this one on one time with her before we all went in on the fucking together. I don't mind sharing my Kitten. Sometimes. Other times, I'd rather have her impaled on my dick without another one trying to sneak into her other holes. Their dicks stand at attention through their pants, saluting me and letting me know I did fucking good and put on a fantastic show. A round of applause for Arrow Amour and his amazing tongue-fucking skills. Ahhh—and the crowd goes wild.

I smack her buttcheek two times, causing her to yelp with surprise. Her eyes were half-closed and ready to send her off into a slumber. Nu-huh. Not today, Kitten. Sleep time is later. She tries hard to get away from me, but I hold her in place, running my tongue over her sensitive clit again. God, I can't get over how delicious she tastes. She shivers, moaning when I suck her pussy lips into my mouth and let them go with a pop.

"Do you trust me, Kitten? To do this safely?" I hold my breath when her beautiful eyes connect with mine. They've glazed over and blissed the fuck out.

"I should say no," she practically slurs. "But I'm going to say yes." Beautiful idea, Kitten. Trust in the Arrow process.

I grin, working her down my body until we're sitting up face to face, and her pussy hovers above my hard dick. "Any time it hurts, Kitten. You tell me. I'm going to make this so fucking good for you. Then one of those two is going to take your pussy hard and fast. And then..." I run my fingers over her lips. "Someone is going to smear their cum on your lips while you swallow."

Air-fucking-tight!

My body relaxes the moment my dick stretches her pussy, soaking up her cum as lube. One pump. Two pumps. Shit, I'm about to lose it before I gently turn her around so her ass is facing me.

"I almost came in your pussy, Kitten," I murmur, reaching into the side drawer and pulling out the tiny bottle of lube. "I'm going to use my fingers to stretch you out again, but you should be relaxed enough from your orgasms."

"I'll distract her," Jericho rasps, moving closer to the bed sans clothes. Damn, when did he do that? "You'll be a good Little Chaos. Won't you? And take my cock so deep down your throat you'll gag and tear up."

Oh well, then.

That imagery has more pre-cum glistening on my tip again. Her crying out while he fucks her mouth and gagging as he hits the back of her throat. Spit dribbling down her chin, mixing with her tears as his cum spurts down her throat. God damn it. I bite my fist hard again, looking toward the ceiling with a groan. I'm so turned on I can barely fucking contain myself. If I'm not careful, I'll gush cum without touching my cock. Happened before. It'll happen again. And it all revolves around the woman bent over in front of me, showing me her pink and wet pussy.

Journey nods. "Yes," she moans when my lubed fingers prod at her tight hole, gently entering until she relaxes again. This time, it's easier to fit three fingers and then four in. In and out I go, stretching her wide so she'll be able to take me hard.

"Open wide, Little Chaos," Jericho grunts desperately, stroking his hard and red cock, aching for release.

Damn, bro. He's in the same boat as me. Probably from having to watch her come so many times in a row and not interrupting. Jer doesn't have to tell me; he likes to watch from afar with fire burning in his eyes, unable to touch himself.

"It's just like the plug, Kitten." If there's one thing I would never do, it's hurt my Kitten with unsafe practices. I want her to want this and enjoy every fucking thrust. Only when she's ready. "Good fucking girl. You're taking my fingers. Now open wide for Daddy Jer and let him fuck your throat." I grin when Jericho glares at me. Probably for the Daddy jest. Or maybe because I took control of the situation. He's the one with a stick up his ass at all times. Constantly barking orders at everyone and expecting them to fall in line.

Not today, Daddy Jer. I'm the sex king here, and you're my lowly peasant doing as I say.

I smirk. He scowls more. If he keeps that up, he'll get wrinkles. It's a fun tug-of-war of dominance. Well, until Journey moans and opens her mouth, rocking back into my fingers. His eyes heat more as he looks at her. More pre-cum glistens on his tip. He's going to break first.

"Please," she begs. Fucking begs! She's going to be the death of us all.

Jericho's fingers grip her wild curls, holding her head where he wants her. "You're going to be a good fucking girl, aren't you? You're going to gag on my cock while Arrow fucks your ass."

Hell, yes, she is! And hell, yes, I am so fucking ready for this. I have been since the moment I saw her dancing in the living room of the party house the night we fucked her until the sun came up. I swear, that was one of the best days of my life. The moment we got to claim her as ours.

"Yes," she practically whines.

Like lightning, Jer loses his damn cool and shoves his cock

so far down her throat, and she gags several times but never pulls away. Not that she could have done so with Jericho holding onto her hair so tightly, basically fucking her face with no restraint.

"Relax your throat, Little Chaos. Let me in. Breathe through your nose," he murmurs encouragingly, running a finger down her cheek.

And she must, because he fucking groans, pumping in and out of her mouth.

That's my cue! Time to spit-roast my Kitten.

Taking the lube, I spread it all over my damn cock and between her cheeks, making sure every inch of her I'm going to touch glistens.

Hmmm. I wonder if she knows about the invisible branding tattoo I put over her tracking device. Probably not, or I wouldn't have this dick to fuck her with. If she ever got an inkling of my stalking ways, she'd run for the hills. Not on my watch. Because I'd know exactly what hill she ran to, and I'd drag her back kicking and screaming.

Ah, true love.

"All right, Kitten. You're going to feel pressure. If you need me to tap out..."

"Hit my thigh if Arrow goes too deep and harms you," Jericho finishes for me with a nod.

My eyes fall to the globes of her ass as I slowly work my cock into her tight hole. She's so snug. I swear I'm going to come right here and now. Too fucking tight. Too fucking good.

"Fuck, Kitten. You feel so fucking good wrapped around my dick," I breathe, gripping her cheeks hard and pulling them apart so I can watch my cock disappear inside her.

"You're good?" Jericho asks breathlessly, stopping his movements and waiting for her to confirm. She does with a moan and nods at the same time I bottom out.

"Fuckkkkkkkkkkkk," I grit out, holding myself still, soaking up the feeling of her around me.

"Shepp, you doing good over there?" I chuckle at the dazed look adorning his face as he watches our epic spit-roast.

Yeah, buddy. You could be in on this, too. There's still one more hole to fill, and it's calling your name. All he has to do is walk over here and take what he wants.

He nods. "Yes." He's barely able to speak when his eyes flick to me, and I grin, slowly pumping in and out of Journey.

Fuck. Hearing his voice sends a thrill through me. My silent giant bestie has been quiet for so long; it's weird to hear it. But oh so liberating. One monster down, one to go. That's tomorrow's dragon to slay. Today? We fuck our girl until her legs are jello, and then we can feed her and do it all over again. Fuck, I've missed her ass. Literally. Just looking at it clenching around my cock has me wanting to stay here forever. I wonder if she'd be offended by that? There's cock warming, and then there's cock and ass warming. Oh, what a fun party that'd be.

"Sheppy Boy, someone needs to tend to our girl's pussy." My grin grows when he stiffens, flicking his gaze to me.

All for one and one for all. All the dicks and all that good stuff. Whatever.

No hole will go unscathed or remain empty. By the time we're done truly wrecking her, she'll be covered in our cum. Every goddamn inch.

Or, I hope, at least.

He stares at the three of us with steam practically boiling off his flesh. Reddened face. Sweat drips from his brow. Dilated eyes. All the damn signs are there. He's turned on as fuck. Barely holding back from marching over here and taking what he wants. Come on, big guy. Come pound her pussy and make her scream with me. Teamwork makes the dream work! Not to mention, his pulsating cock stiffens harder as he pumps his hand up and down. Only stopping to spread his pre-cum on his tip before stroking himself vigorously.

"Kitten, I'm going to live between your cheeks from now on. This spot is so..." Goddamn glorious. So glorious. My balls are about to betray my stamina by pulling up and nearly emptying their contents inside her. Fuck. Not now, boys. Big A, get your dangly friends under control. For fuck's sake. I blow out a breath, leaning over her and twirling my fingers around her already sensitive clit. She bucks, groaning around Jericho's dick. I can't help but chuckle, leaning close to her ear. "Oh, my Kitten. You're going to come again, aren't you?"

"Mmmphhh mmmphhh," she chokes out.

I'm sure she's moaning, "Yes, Arrow. I'm going to come a million times more." Even though she sent me an exhausted death glare. No matter. I continue my vigorous circles until she's screaming around his dick and coming so hard I think she might have forgotten how to breathe.

"The way your ass just tried to suck me in is a sign I should stay like this," I murmur in her ear, gently kissing her cheek.

"Mmmphh mmmmphhhh!" her muffled voice grumbles.

Jericho smirks above her, running his finger down her jaw. "Such a good Little Chaos. You're taking us so well. How about a position change, hmm?" He raises a brow when she sends him a look. Our balls would probably shrivel under that glare, but I think it just turns us on even more. Maybe just me. I can only speak for myself.

Whatever.

He pulls out so slowly I almost feel his tortious pain. But I don't. Because my dick is still ass deep. Sucker.

"All right, Kitten. You're coming with me," I grunt, grabbing her around the waist and forcing her back against my front. My fingers roam over her breasts, harshly pinching her nipples until they're red and hard. "We're all going to fuck you now. We're going to take what was taken from us when you were kidnapped. Wait... Did you fuck her on the island?" I narrow my eyes at Shepp, who turns beat red. "Ah-ha! You did! You had sexy time on the island without us! Rude! I should banish you from this room." I'm joking. Kind of. He had his fill of her, spending every day in Shadow's playland.

Now, it's our turn. But, honestly. Who could deny the big lug of anything? Certainly not me.

"We were kidnapped." Shepp glowers at me. "What was I supposed to do? Leave her unsatisfied in the shower?" Oh, this fucker. He's taunting me now. I grin, ready to retort, but he gets up and shakes his head. "You would have been even madder if I left her wanting all that time."

Well, facts. I guess. I don't want to admit he's right, but he's not wrong. Asshole. It's like he's known me my entire life and reads me so well.

"All right then, Sheppy Boy. Someone needs to tend to our girl's pussy." My grin grows when he stiffens, flicking his gaze to me and then to her. But whatever he sees on her beautiful face has him dropping his damn pants and shucking his shirt in two seconds flat. And there he is in all his damn glory. "Atta boy!" I quip.

"You're going to be a good girl and take us all, right?" Jericho asks, crawling onto the bed and meeting her in the middle. His fingers take her in, feeling everything he hadn't been able to from his position.

"Yes," she rasps, clenching around my cock.

"She's very excited about this," I chuckle, nibbling her neck and leaving marks as I go. Nothing says—you're mine—like red bite marks all over. I mean, I did it the first time I ever fucked her so she'd remember me—and them, I guess. For the weeks she'd have to live without us. I wanted her to look in the mirror and think—yeah, I did that.

Shepp hurries over, apparently coming out of his sex-watching stupor, and climbs onto the bed, putting Journey in the middle of us. Leaning in, he lays his lips on hers as Jericho and I, fulfill her other needs. He's moaning and panting by the time he comes up for air, leaving her breathless as well, which suits me. Her breasts heave up and down, playing right into Jericho's mouth as he nibbles and sucks.

"Okay, Sheppy Boy. You gotta lie down. She's going to

ride you until you're seeing stars while I do my thing from behind." I grin when Shepp glares at me but does what he's told. "Good Boy," I quip, earning another glare.

"I will hit you," Shepp grumbles, stroking himself slowly.

"Meh. I might like it," I chuckle, dragging Journey until her glistening pussy is right above his dick. "On three," I murmur into her ear. "You're going to drop down and gobble up his dick."

"Gobble up his dick?" she sours. "Arrow, that's not sexy at fucking all."

"Swallow it? Put it in its cock pocket? Slide his sword into your sheath? I could keep going, Kitten. Until you..."

Shepp stiffens, gasping when she clutches his cock and shoves it so deep inside her I can feel him rubbing against me. Well, that's certainly fucking new. Never thought I'd be rubbing dicks with my boy Shepp. But here we are. And damn, does it feel surprisingly fucking good and oh, so full.

"Okay," I wheeze, burying my face in her neck. "Now we have to move. Jer..."

"I'm fucking her mouth while you two get that," he says, grabbing the back of her head and seating himself to the side of Shepp. She squeals with delight when he leans in and kisses her. "Still good, baby?" he murmurs, clutching her face. Whatever he sees—because I certainly can't from her backside—lets him know she's good. "If it becomes too much, remember to tap my thighs."

"Okay," she moans when I slowly pull out and slam back in with a deep grunt of pleasure. Fuck. Once this commences, I won't be able to stop until I'm coming deep into her ass.

Jericho guides her face to his dick and groans when she practically swallows him again. "Fucking hell!" he shouts, looking up at the ceiling while her head bobs.

"That's our cue, Sheppy. Let's get this show on the road." I grin when he nods, and we work her up and down together quickly.

My eyes squeeze shut when goosebumps spread across my flesh. Right down to my damn balls. I don't notice what the other two are doing or if they've even left the party after emptying their balls. I only focus on the feel of her encasing me. Squeezing me. Fucking taking me over as I pound into her so hard, the sound of skin slapping together echoes through the room. Fireworks blossom behind my eyes. Fire rages through my veins until it falls down my spine and goes straight to my balls. Those fuckers squeeze, curling up toward my stomach, and finally, I blast what feels like a year's worth of cum into her ass.

"Yes, Kitten!" I shout, throwing my head back and holding her hips steady. I slump over her back, kissing her flesh and leaving more marks along her spine.

"Holy fuck!" Jericho grunts as his fingers curl into her hair. "Yes," he gasps, almost falling backward from the force of his orgasm. Well, hell. Our girl certainly has that quality about her.

And then, It's Sheppy's turn.

"Journey," he grunts softly, thrusting his hips toward hers in shuddered movements until they stop entirely, and he's panting.

Journey's body trembles by the time we all gently pull out, and she falls onto the bed with a sigh.

"I won't be fucking moving for two to three business days. Just leave me here," she groans, covering her face with her hands. The sweetest sheen of sweat covers her flesh, along with the cum dripping from every orifice.

"Now, Kitten," I chuckle, crawling behind her and spooning her. "Don't you want to bathe with us and then eat? Hmm? I'm sure Sheppy has a wonderful surprise he'd love to whip up for us."

Shepp snorts, shaking his head from where he's lying on the bed. "I could," he murmurs, turning to face her.

"Tacos and only tacos," she says, squeezing her eyes shut. "Like ten of them."

"Tacos it is, but first. Shall we shower and clean you up?"

"You want to clean this off her?" I quip, raising a brow.

Jericho shakes his head. "Not necessarily, but UTIs and all that. She should probably get cleaned up, and then we can cuddle in bed after eating tacos."

"Please," Journey says, lifting a hand in the air. Jericho takes it and helps her off the bed. He grunts, picks her up into his arms, and whispers words into her ears to soothe whatever she's saying.

Pure, unadulterated joy lives in my heart at the sight of her so well fucked. Not only that, though. It's like something lifts inside me—something monumental at the thought of my family finally being back together under one roof.

"Whaddya say, Sheppy Boy? Should we all go get soapy together?" I grin when he huffs at me, running a hand down his face. "It's not much different than feeling your cock against mine."

"Fucking hell, Arrow," he grunts, rolling away from me and climbing off the bed.

"Admit it! You loved playing sword fight!" I shout, getting to my feet and following them into the bathroom, where the shower runs hot and the steam fills the room.

Yeah. I fucking love my family. Love... I rub at my chest where my heart pounds against my ribs and echoes in my ears.

CHAPTER FIFTY-TWO

Journey

I'LL BE A MIRACLE IF I MAKE IT THROUGH THIS PREGNANCY alive, especially if they insist on fucking me like they did last night. I swear this demon child is slowly chipping away at my insides. Decide, little baby, if you want me to bring you nutrients or not. But I wish you would. I want to eat Shepp's food without immediately lying on the bathroom floor and spewing my soul from my mouth.

Only nine more months to go, or at least, I think. Fuck. I'm not sure how far along I am.

"I'm dying," I groan to myself on the bathroom floor.

It's so cool down here. The tile presses hard against my cheek, scrunching up my face. My entire body sags, finally relaxing after a morning of calling Ralph on the big white phone.

When will it end?

I groan again, trying to calm the storm in my stomach attempting to send me back to the toilet. Come on, little bean. Don't do this again. I'm desperate for food and no puking.

The toilet beckons me when I turn my head. Come to me, Journey. Puke up the nothingness in your stomach.

Fuck me.

I need to get off the floor. Who knows what germs are crawling all over my damn body. Not to mention, I'm currently living with three men. Three dicks. And their aim is disgustingly off.

First things first, I need to scrub this damn bathroom. But that would involve moving. And moving is not on my agenda right now. Sleep is. I squeeze my eyes shut, blowing out a breath.

There. My stomach settles.

Well, slightly.

"You better be a girl," I mumble to my flat stomach pressing against the floor.

Because if I have to live in a house full of little boys that have their DNA, I might run away. Ugh.

A whole new anxiety grips me right, shaking me with a realization I hadn't thought of before. I'm pregnant with a mafia heir—a very important fetus—VIF. Sure, there are three possible baby daddies, but they're all deep in the life of the crime family. An heir to the throne and his two bosses. Or whatever.

Does that make me the future queen of it all?

God fucking damn it. I will blend their balls into tiny pieces for putting me in this position.

Psychopaths.

My psychopaths.

They're unredeemable villains, taking what they want. But they've always shown me how much they care. No matter how absurd. The handcuffs. Contract. Putting my mom into rehab and stealing my home.

They care. In their own fucked up way.

So when it comes to our children, they'll no doubt move Heaven and earth to protect them from whatever the organization has in store for them.

I hope.

It's something that's festering deep inside me—the worry and fear for my unborn baby. They'll protect the baby.

And me.

They always have. Although, protected is way too strong of a word. *Possessed* is more like it.

They've possessed me since the moment they pulled their masks down, hiding their identities. They've been the blood in my veins since they fucked me that first night and in the woods.

They live in my bones, occupying every nook and cranny of my soul—mine. And I'm theirs. I'll put my trust in them to keep our future safe for all of us.

My eyes flutter shut as exhaustion sinks its deadly claws into me. Just leave me here to slowly rot until dinner's ready.

That's the true test of it all. Will I be able to keep it down? God, I hope so. If I have to lose another ounce of Shepp's cooking, I might lose my damn mind.

"Tonight, they'll come." Jericho's loud voice echoes through my mind. His eyes take on a coldness when his face hardens. "They'll be here by seven to discuss business." His eyes flash to me as I lay my head on Shepp's shoulder, wishing for a nap. "Jenni will accompany Elias."

I swallow hard, tensing beneath Shepp's hand on my leg.

And then I ran to the bathroom to puke up the breakfast I barely got to digest. Good fucking times.

Seven. It's only four now. Three more hours until the meeting begins. Three more hours until my former best friend waltzes through that door with no clue about the friendship I was forced to forge with her by my monster.

I was a fraud.

It's hung over my head for months now. Since my monster uttered the dreaded command to watch Jenni like a hawk and befriend her, all so I could spy on her father.

A goddamn fraud. That's what I am. Guilt churns in my throat, burning me from the inside out like a rapid explosion erupting.

At the time, I did what I had to. For Sunshine. My entire

existence has been for her. For her safety and health. Now she's safe with Mikhail and getting the help she needs.

When Jericho uttered Jenni's name, I knew what to do. I have no choice. Tell her everything. Clear the air between us. If we want to maintain any sort of friendship in the future, then we need to have a clean slate.

No matter how hard I want to bite my tongue and keep it to myself.

At the wedding, we barely had time to say hi. So, tonight is my chance. When the guys have their important meeting in the basement with Shadow's corpse, it'll be my time to fall, and I have no doubt she'll hate me for what I've done.

My phone buzzes in my pocket, drawing me from my own shitty self-pity. Ugh. Hormones can fuck off for life. I want to go back to letting my darkness take over instead of *feeling* this.

She's going to be an aunty.

SUNSHINE

I'm so sad I can't be there tonight. :(

JOURNEY

I want you here, too. But you need to rest, sis. Love you!

I type back with a soft smile. Being able to contact Sunshine any time of the day has me on a high. For so long, I ached for pieces of her. Now, I have all of her.

Thanks, Mikhail.

Mikhail, in all his coldness, left a number for me to text her with Shepp before he escaped Shadow's island.

You'll always be able to contact your sister. I will not keep her from you. And he meant it.

SUNSHINE

> Love you too! There are so many things I
> can't wait to show you when you visit soon. I
> wish I could have come with Mikhail, but I
> have company watching over me ;)

Company? That's the second time she's alluded to *company* with her. Someone is watching over her while Mikhail runs the damn mafia. But she's safe. I know that.

From the moment she and I started texting, she's shown me her new palace through video calls and photographs. It's elegant and massive, fit with a damn moat, and the beach is less than a mile away.

SUNSHINE

> It's huge, J. Like a mansion! Bigger than
> anything I've ever seen. It's got 12
> bathrooms. Can you believe that? 12!!!

Once the war has been fought and we are back in Briar Cove with everything under control, I'll visit my sister in her new life.

Then, everything will be right in the world.

Loud footsteps march through the bedroom, getting closer and closer until they stop at my bare feet near the open door. I'm surprised it took him this long to come and find me. It's only been forty minutes since I died on this bathroom floor. All three of them have been up my ass since we got back from the island. I can't even take a pee without Arrow wanting to be involved.

It's weird. But oddly enough, I'm used to it now.

I peek an eye open in time to watch Arrow cock his head with curiosity. "Aw, my little Kitten," Arrow coos in a slightly elevated voice.

"Arrow," I sigh, sucking in a breath when he drops beside me, positioning himself so we're face to face and lying on the bathroom floor.

We blink a few times, taking each other in. He's so damn close; I can count the freckles dotted on his cheeks and the wrinkles marring his forehead. Leaning down, Arrow roughly kisses my lips, humming with satisfaction.

"Arrow," I grumble, too weak to fight him off when he moves my hair from my face, still half squished on the tile floor.

"You're on the bathroom floor, Kitten. Wouldn't you be more comfy on the bed? With my cock sleeping inside you? I hear that's good for pregnant women. Cock soaking. You'd love it. It'd make you feel all kinds of good." He grins at that, rambling more about his cock and sleeping and whatever else he says.

I tune him out sometimes.

If I could lift my hand, I'd put it over his lips to shut him up. Can I punch the happiness out of him? If I'm miserable, he should be miserable. Maybe a fist to the gut will clue him in on my damn misery.

"You did this to me," I retort, finally batting him away until a low chuckle rumbles his bare chest. "This is all your fault."

His nose wrinkles when he leans down, setting his lips on my cheek. "And I'd do it again," he quips softly, kissing my cheek again. "And again. And again."

Great, now he's singing. He's still high from the torture he inflicted on Shadow a mere day ago, living off that rush.

"Then no one will be surprised when you go missing. Where's Arrow? No clue. In my backyard," I hiss.

He only grins in return. "You act like burying me in a coffin will keep me dead. I already told you, Kitten. I don't die. Not without you. Besides, you need this dick for at least eighteen more of those." He carefully pokes the side of my stomach he can reach.

He's so damn impossible to argue with when he says crazy-romantic words meant to make me swoon. And I do. The bastard. He's talking about death, and I'm sighing at him.

Wait. Did he say…

"Eighteen?" I sputter, nearly vomiting again. "No way in hell! Absolutely not. I am not going through this again. One and done." I shake my head, groaning when my stomach sloshes again.

Arrow whines like a dog, giving me his best puppy eyes.

"We'll see. I have my ways," he sing-songs. "You're so beautiful," he whispers, cupping my cheek and lovingly running his thumb over it.

What a damn suck-up.

Obviously, he's not threatened by my violence, despite knowing I can take a life. Not that I'm proud of it. But I've done it, damn it, even chopped off a man's schlong. Arrow should watch his dick.

"You're brave," Jericho huffs, stepping into the bathroom and shaking his head. Finally, a voice of reason. "She probably has a weapon stashed somewhere."

You know what? That's a good idea. A knife in my pocket won't hurt anyone. Well, unless that hurts me first.

I feel Jericho's heated stare travel over my body, inspecting me from the doorway. Earlier, when I first vomited, he was in here holding my hair back without gagging himself. Then I was in his arms, snuggling into his neck for comfort until he had to take a phone call.

Arrow's eyes widen with interest. "Do tell, Kitten. You know I love a good stabbing." Psycho-fucking-path.

I sigh when I feel his bulge growing against my thigh. "You know I hacked off a guy's dick, right? He screamed and begged for mercy. You better keep that thing away from me," I hiss, squeezing my eyes shut when Arrow makes an offending sound, sputtering at my threat.

His dick hardens further, pushing into my side. "Threats

only make me horny, Kitten. Even if you offended Big A with your promises of cutting him off. You love him, right?"

I don't fucking answer his ridiculous statement. No matter how hard my pussy throbs, aching for his dick. Make up your mind, would ya? We hate them right now! They purposefully knocked you up, and now you're the one suffering.

My eyes travel to Jericho standing tall at my feet. "You're on my shit list, too."

"You can't ignore me forever, Kitten," Arrow whispers, nibbling on my ear. "I lived without you for weeks. We missed you. Your pussy, your...."

"Arrow," Jericho grumbles, rubbing a hand down his face.

"What, Daddy Jer? You're telling me you don't feel that way, too?" Arrow narrows his eyes when Jericho grimaces at him, ignoring him completely.

"I brought lemon water to soothe your stomach, Little Chaos." Leaning down, he gently hands me a large glass bottle filled with water and lemons in the center.

"Thanks," I say, setting it beside me. I'll drink that later. You know, when I can move.

"Yeah! You have to stay hydrated, Kitten. If you don't, I'll strap you to the bed, put an IV in you, and not let you move until you give birth to my baby." Every word he speaks sends shivers down my spine as his breaths roll over my flesh. He grins, running his fingers under my eye, lovingly tracing my freckles.

He has this effect on me, making me shiver at the stupidest promises.

"If you touch me with a needle, I'll poke your eyes out," I whisper my threat and kiss the tip of his nose.

No more Miss Nice Girl.

"You act like I won't turn you over and fuck you right now. Your dirty talk is my brand of crazy," Arrow chuckles, pulling me into his arms with a sigh, forcing my leg to drape over his, giving his boner more access to my center.

Yeah, that ain't happening, pal.

"Unless you're into vomit," I murmur, nuzzling my face into his neck, aching for comfort when I hurt so badly.

"I draw the line at vomit. Sorry, Kitten," he quips.

"And pee," I hum with a smile.

"That, too! See! Our boundaries are important in this relationship. I'm good with blood and stabbings. But no other bodily fluids." I wrinkle my nose but don't offer any words.

"Are you feeling any better?" Jericho asks, plopping on the ground near my feet. His finger gently tickles my ankle, drawing circles over my flesh.

"No," I whine softly, sighing into Arrow's neck. "Feeling like I did earlier."

"Hmmm," Jericho hums. "Perhaps when we return to Briar Cove, we should find a doctor and have an ultrasound to check-in. Make sure my future heir is cooking appropriately. I've read they have medication for pregnant women to aid with morning sickness."

My breath stalls. Excitement I haven't felt in so long travels up my spine. An ultrasound. A glimpse into the baby growing in my belly. The one currently trying to kill me with vomit.

More footsteps enter the bathroom and pause in the doorway.

"Um…" Shepp whispers, clearing his throat.

"Welcome to the meeting, Sheppy Boy! Journey was detailing our deaths for knocking her up. Don't piss her off. She said she'll cut our dicks off," Arrow stage-whispers.

Concern laces Shepp's eyes when he stares down at me, entangled with Arrow on the ground to Jericho leaning against the wall with his hand on my ankle.

It's a party in the bathroom, and I'm the main attraction.

"Do you need food, Little Tempest? I've made something light for you. Soup, cheese toasties, and crackers." He softens when he looks me over.

I nod, attempting to pull away from Arrow, who holds tight, clinging harder.

"Arrow, you'll make me puke again if I don't go eat," I grumble through a breath when he squeezes me one last time before untangling himself from my body.

"Fine," he huffs, getting to his feet and holding out his hand. "Let's get you fed, Kitten."

"Then we can prepare for tonight," Jericho says with a frown.

Arrow leads me out of the bathroom, straight into the kitchen, and sits me down. Shepp hurries with the bacon, cheese, and potato soup with cheese toasties and crackers.

I'm almost too afraid to eat it, but I do. I have to. This is for my strength, but I'm also growing a tiny human who depends on me to eat. Now, let me eat, tiny human.

CHAPTER FIFTY-THREE

Journey

"GOD, JOURNEY WEST! IT'S SO DAMN GOOD TO SEE YOU again!" Jenni squeals, pulling me into a tight hug. "We didn't really get to say hi at my wedding," she murmurs in my ear.

I hold back my tears. She still thinks of me as a friend. Someone trustworthy. And I'm not. Guilt eats at me the moment I look into her tear-filled eyes. She's so damn happy to see me.

"It's so good to see you, too! You guys are all good after that?" I ask, thinking back to the explosions and gunfighting that almost took us all out.

"Beyond good. That was just a blip on the map for us." She smiles, waving it off. "Come on now, let's catch up while they plot," she giggles, pulling me to the couch until we're plopping down and facing each other.

"Be good, Little Chaos," Jericho hums, kissing my temple. "We'll be mourning the loss of Thomas Mondelli." Sarcasm drips from his words when he pulls back and takes a few steps from me.

AKA, they're going to view the body they haven't cremated yet. He told me he promised Elias a bit of Shadow to seal their alliance and start on the right foot. Too bad Shadow is no more.

"I'm always good," I snort, earning a smirk.

"Define good," he says with a pointed look, knowing full well I'm always up to no good.

I shrug, feeling lighter than I have in a long time. I'm finally under my own damn thumb. No one else's. Sure, Jericho is my demanding husband. God, that's so fucking weird to hear. But the moment Mikhail uttered Mrs. Viotto, I knew it was fitting.

I am Mrs. Viotto.

No man will ever rule my life like Gabriel and Shadow did. I am no one else's pawn. I'm the fucking queen of the castle.

Arrow straightens when another solid knock bangs at the front door. I know they were nervous to have such high-profile leaders in their secret safe space, but it was the only way for all of them to come together undetected.

"Is that the child?" Arrow stage-whispers with mischief in his eyes.

"Arrow, this won't work if you don't show respect. Like it or not, he's the head of the Bratva," Jericho states in a steady, lower-pitched voice. He lifts his chin, daring Arrow to argue with him.

"Ugh. Fine," Arrow snarks, crossing his arms.

"Well, that'll be an issue," Elias chuckles, raising a brow when Jericho huffs, opening the door.

"Mikhail," Jericho greets, waving a hand for him to enter.

"Jericho," he says pleasantly, waltzing into the living room. "Elias." They each give each other a respectable nod, acknowledging their points of power. "Journey." Mikhail turns to me with his face softening. "Sunshine sends her regards. You've been making her so happy with your texts."

A soft smile passes over my lips at the sound of her name. "Good to see you again, Mikhail. You've been keeping her safe. How's her recovery?"

"Still recovering. Rest assured, she's taking the proper medications to ensure a successful transplant and resting until necessary. I have a doctor on staff tending to her every need. My brothers sit beside her bed while I'm here on business."

"Brothers?" I mutter. "You have brothers?" Maybe that's the company Sunshine has been keeping when Mikhail works. But I could have sworn he was an only child.

How odd.

"Come by when you'd like. With a call so we can alert our guards." Mikhail stands straighter when several footsteps sound on the porch and stops outside the door. "But you're always welcome in Miami."

"Yours?" Jericho asks, nodding toward the shadows looming outside, no longer moving.

Mikhail inclines his head. "Can never be too careful. My guards will keep watch outside until we're finished."

"Why? You think we're going to slit some throats?" Arrow grins when all attention slides to him. He only grins wider at our expressions. Yeah, he's going to get us all killed at some point. "What? It was just a question." He shrugs.

Shepp huffs at him, rolling his eyes. Out of habit, he signs something to him quickly with jerky movements. Arrow waves him off, signing something back with a frown. Mikhail smirks.

Of course. Everyone knows sign language well. I've only learned the basics. It's a new language I'm eager to know more of.

"Thank you for keeping my sister safe," I say, clearing my throat of my emotions. "The threat still stands, though. Don't fuck with her. Or else." I drag my finger across my neck with confidence.

Is it smart to give this tiny psycho a death threat? No, probably not. He could take me out like he took his dad out. But I won't tread lightly with my sister ever again. She's too important.

Mikhail grins, exposing his teeth. "If I harmed her, I'd harm myself, Journey. Sunshine is my past, present, and future."

Jenni swoons beside me, tilting her head with admiration. "Wow!" she says dreamily, earning a scowl from Elias.

"Well, you're just putting us all to shame, aren't you?" Elias shakes his head, leaning down to kiss Jenni's lips. Its ownership. Love. Everything.

"Dude, you're like fourteen." Arrow gapes from the kitchen, now holding a small knife in his hands.

"Arrow," Shepp sighs, holding out his hand. "We're not a threat, remember?"

Elias, Mikhail, and Jenni instantly still at the sound of Shepp's voice echoing through the room. The more he speaks, the less rasp comes from his throat.

"You spoke," Mikhail observes, tilting his head. "No more silence?"

Shepp shakes his head. "It ended with his death."

Mikhail nods, an eerily sense of understanding crossing his face. "Understandable."

"You may not be a threat, but I have a baby mama to watch over and two gang leaders standing in my house. Although I am the most superior," Arrow cuts in, puffing out his chest. "Touch my woman..." he trails off, dragging his finger across his throat.

A true threat through and through.

"Holy shit, he's touch her and die," Jenni swoons again. "I've read about that in books."

"Woman! Would you stop swooning over other men," Elias hisses with pure jealousy ringing in his eyes.

Jenni smirks, patting his hand. "You didn't mind last night. Sharing is caring, if I remember right..." Jenni is cut off with Elias' lips locking around hers in a heated kiss.

"Jennifer," he murmurs. "You've broken so many rules tonight. Consider this your warning. When we return home..." he trails off, smirking when she turns beet red.

Interesting...

"Fine," she says with a shrug. "Wait... Baby mama?" Jenni

practically screeches from my side, leaning in with a grin. "Please tell me you're pregnant. Oh my God!" She claps her hands a few times.

"On that note, gentleman. How about we have a drink in the basement and toast to our new arrangements?" Jericho waves a hand toward the basement door.

"Good to see you again, Journey," Elias says with a respectful nod as they all walk down into the basement with Shadow's body to shake hands.

"Okay, well. While the boys play, we're going to gossip. Give me the tea, Journey West. You're pregnant and living here?" She looks around wide-eyed, taking it all in with an open heart.

That's the thing about Jenni. She's always been a true friend. A good person. Me? Not so much.

I snort, turning to face her on the couch. "I'm pregnant." I think it's the first time I've ever said it out loud without feeling a tugging inside me threatening to tear me apart. "And hiding here until we go back, I guess."

Jenni grins, sighing with happiness. "I can't believe you're pregnant. God, you're going to be the best mother." She taps my hand a few times. "Elias and I are trying, too. So maybe our babies will grow up and be besties. Just like us."

Just like us. Besties.

"Jenni," I breathe, swallowing the burning sensation in my throat. "You were such a good friend to me in high school. I had so much fun going out with you and going to parties." She beams again, telling me without words that she believes the same thing. That she trusts me.

And I'm a fraud.

"You know, you were my first real friend," Jenni says softly. "I never had anyone like you because of the organization my dad was a part of. Even if it was only for a few months. I know when I took off with Elias, we lost touch. But seeing you at my wedding and…" She offers me a sad smile.

"I'm just sorry you got mixed up in that life. You know Leighton ran off, too. Got hitched to that Chloe Satin bitch." She scoffs at that with a shrug. "Good fucking riddance, if you ask me. Such a sleazeball."

I cringe at his name, wishing he wouldn't have found his happy ending. He doesn't deserve it after forcing himself on me at Jenni's party. I mean, Arrow took his finger, and I destroyed his car, but still.

"Don't worry, they had to go into hiding. His daddy is looking high and low for him. Even though they would be a good alliance, she was offered to Jericho first." My eyes bug out. Seems my husband has been keeping secrets from me since we reunited. Granted, it's only been a few stressful days here. "Not to mention Chloe's dad has gone nuclear about it all. It's kind of funny."

Good. Fuck them both.

Silence consumes us for a few minutes as I digest her words. Jenni takes sips of water, grinning at me expectantly. I know the second I open my mouth, that'll be wiped away. She'll run from me forever.

Here goes nothing.

I suck in a breath. "My sister was taken from me when I was sixteen. I hurt someone..." My voice quivers at the memories. Every time it enters my mind.

The screaming. The blood. The knife. It knocks me back. Steals my fucking breath. No matter how many years. It's always there, eager to haunt me. I could be the strongest person in the world, and I'd still fall to my knees a few times a year. I break down. But I build myself back up time and time again.

Jenni leans her chin on her hand, listening to me. Even when I get quiet and lost in my thoughts, she stays still without interruptions.

"I stabbed someone to save her, and it was used as blackmail to get me to do stuff. Hurt more people." My eyes focus on the wall behind Jenni's head, staring at the pristine walls, beautifully painted. I can't take the pity in her eyes. Or the disgust when she learns of my past. "He kidnapped me. Locked me up. Tortured me." My fingers play with the scar above my heart. "And when he set me free, I was programmed to do his bidding. Spying on people..." Jenni's figure weaves through the tears shining in my eyes and spilling over my lashes.

There's a reserved look on her face. Like Jenni knows exactly what I was up to, and she's been waiting for me to spell it out for her. Maybe she's been waiting for me to say something and admit that our friendship was a complete farce. It wasn't. Jenni was truly the best friend I had ever had. She accepted me for me. Saw me in a light no one else had, except the guys.

Jenni was a good one, and I was about to decimate that.

"Who was it?" she murmurs sadly.

"Gabriel Viotto." His name feels heavy on my tongue, like the burden of carrying around my crimes forcefully committed by him. "I had no say in my life. It was either make friends with you and..." I roll my lips together and blow out a breath. Who knew clearing the air and telling your truths could lead to heart palpitations and vomit in your throat? "Your dad. He wanted information, and he said you were the ticket in. And then, after that was done, I had to spy on Elias and learn everything I could."

There was nothing more to admit. I had gotten her father killed. It was all me. She had to run because of me. I did it all. The catalyst in her life.

"So when I introduced you to my dad, you already knew who he was?" There's no accusation in her voice. No disappointment. Just her.

I nod, offering her a sad smile. "I'm sorry..." I trail off, moving my eyes to the floor.

She pauses for a second, taking me in with fresh eyes. I expect this is the end of our friendship.

The final wave goodbye.

"But you were real, right?" Jenni whispers, staring at me with shiny eyes. I nod. Of course, I was. Not at first. But our friendship was a pleasant surprise. "Then what's the issue?" A tear drops from her left eye, cascading down her cheeks. She nibbles her bottom lip. "Journey. You never hurt me. My dad was a good man to me in some ways but bad to the core. He was up to no good all the time, like everyone in the damn crime family. I mourned him. But I had Elias to pick up the pieces. My mom ran off."

"No issue then," I say, holding back my tears. "I hated working for him. I hated those jobs and missions." I shake my head, attempting to shut the door on my past. But it's ingrained in me. The deaths and break-ins. They're a part of me now. No turning back. "I hated that version of myself." I did. I was simply existing for the sake of my sister, living every day with her health and life on my mind.

But today? I have myself.

She's safe, and her health is on track. The guys truly love me. They've shown me time and time again. Fuck. I feel like I've been tossed in a boxing ring and have gone five rounds. My head pounds, rattling my skull.

"Oh, Journey," Jenni sniffles, pulling me close and wrapping her arms around my shoulders.

For years, I went without hugs. I was starved of touch and love and everything in between. A cage was my home. My prison. Even when I stepped out into the sunlight for the first time in months, no one touched me. Not until I let the Devils in.

This hug is everything.

"Thank you, Jenni. I'm sorry." About everything I did.

"All water under the bridge," she whispers and pulls back. "Besides, we're going to be meeting like this from here on out.

Sounds like our boys are going to be in cahoots with each other." She grins wider now, and she winks.

"Seems like it. You think they'll all be able to get along?" I eye the space of our kitchen, not hearing anything coming from the basement.

"They're all very business-motivated," she scoffs, rolling her eyes. "They'll do it for that, but as friends? Doubtful." She giggles at that, sitting further into the couch.

From there, we converse for what seems like hours. Talking openly about anything and everything. I give Jenni more pieces of myself than I ever thought possible. Here was this girl I was using for information, and she turned out to be one of the best people I had met along the way. I guess through my forced venture into the family, I discovered my tribe.

My family.

I have Sunshine—always will. She's my blood. But I also have my non-blood family. Jericho, Arrow, and Shepp. And now, Jenni.

Jericho emerges from the basement as Jenni and I sip our drinks. Me with Sprite to settle my churning stomach and Jenni with a beer.

Jericho's face sags the moment he sees me. Relief spears through me when they pile into the living room with slumped shoulders and satisfied expressions.

"All settled?" Jenni bravely asks, sipping her beer.

"Yes," Elias replies, sauntering toward her. "All good."

"Then the plan stands, gentlemen." Jericho raises his brows, and the men nod. "Tomorrow night, we'll be back in Briar Cove."

"And we'll be on standby," Elias says, helping Jenni to her feet.

"To raid your father's businesses," Mik says with his hands in his pockets. "Such an odd thing for him to sign over everything to your mother."

Jericho grimaces, running his hand down his face. "What an unexpected development. But of course, she did that."

With that new information, they all say their goodbyes with handshakes and head out the door, leaving us in silence.

"Your mother took over your dad's businesses?"

Jericho nods once, coming to sit beside me on the couch. He groans when he puts his head back, sighing heavily.

"She's taken over," he says with a tinge of sadness. "Everything. Somehow, she's manipulated the deeds to every business my father owned and signed them to herself. Elias looked into it."

"It's money, right? Is that all she wants?"

"Revenge," Shepp rasps, sitting down across from us. "She wants to destroy everything he's touched for making her marry him."

Right. The letters he found. The evidence of their long love affair with each other, long after they had married others.

"You know what we need?" Arrow asks with his arms spread wide. We stare at him until he pouts, not waiting for our answer. Instead, he turns on the first season of *Game of Thrones* with a grin. "Blood. Mayhem. Dragons." He wiggles his brows.

Jericho sighs but doesn't say a word of protest. Not even when Arrow sits on my other side, putting his arm around my shoulders as Jericho takes my hand.

In the silence of binge-watching *Game of Thrones*, our future gets closer and closer. The key to our doom pressing down on us harder.

Tomorrow, we'll meet Arrow's father and spy on the family meeting.

CHAPTER FIFTY-FOUR

Jericho

TENSION ROARS THROUGH MY ENTIRE BODY THE MOMENT WE enter Briar Cove. A war zone. Only, there's no sign of a struggle or fight. Buildings still stand untouched. Minus my father's fallen tower. Now, nothing more than rubble where it stood.

I half expected more signs of distress from our citizens: blood on the pavement, fires in the sky, and people running with fear in their eyes.

But there's nothing. It's untouched and perfect on the outside. But how are the inner workings?

It gives me hope for the future. That my father hasn't taken from them. Or my mother hasn't concocted some fucked up plan to destroy the town that betrayed her so badly.

Taking down the man who ruined her.

It seems Gabriel Viotto made it his mission in life to piss off as many people as he could. Well, he's succeeded. And now, his retribution is on its way.

Us.

My fingers curl at the thought of wrapping them around his throat and watching the life drain from his eyes. Excitement thrums through me. I'm so close I can't practically taste the victory. I'll track him down. Watch him and then strike when he least expects it.

After we spy on his meeting with all of Briar Cove's most prominent family members, that is.

Our truck cab has been silent the entire way back through the mountains and down to our hometown.

"And the priest has ensured our safety throughout this entire meeting?" I ask offhandedly, unable to drag my eyes away from the blurring images.

He could be a traitor. It's been a thought of mine from the moment Arrow confided in him. I trust my brother's judgment of people. He can sus out someone not revealing the truth. But this? It's his dad. He's always had a soft spot for the man who raised him with morals, giving him the sliver of humanity still lingering inside him.

But I grew up in the mafia. I trust no one but the people in this vehicle. Anyone can be tainted by money or pretty promises.

Even a priest.

Arrow shrugs casually. "It's nothing we can't handle, Daddy Jer."

He has a valid point.

We're the Devils. We can take anything head-on. Even a woman hellbent on making my father pay for the marriage she did not want. She's angry. Rightfully so. Taking back what she thought was hers.

And I'm eager to put my eyes on her again. To see the mother I never knew as the monster she's become.

"If it all goes sideways, we protect Journey at all costs." Shepp looks at me through the rearview mirror, nodding in agreement.

"I'd slice so many throats for you, Kitten," Arrow says, looking at us from the front passenger seat with a grin. "Spill all their blood. Soak the ground. All for you." His body practically vibrates with the prospect of the carnage he will inflict.

If he has to.

Deep down, I'm hoping this meeting we're going to spy on

doesn't provoke him into doing something stupid. Even though we took Shadow down in a bloody inferno, Arrow still itches for more. More destruction. More kills and blood.

He's insatiable at the thought of it. And we're here to keep him grounded.

"You're so romantic," Journey quips, snuggling into my side with a sigh.

My poor wife. She's been feeling the effects of her pregnancy. So much so that she's barely able to keep anything down. If I had my choice, I'd lock her in the cabin, call a doctor, and tend to her every need.

But going back to Briar Cove was always inevitable.

My fingers rub up and down her arm, gently soothing her from the motion of the vehicle. The moment we win this battle and take out the dictator attempting to steal my throne, Journey visits the doctor in town. I will not allow my child to siphon any more of her life force. It's weakening her, pulling her into the bathroom every chance it gets.

If I could fight a baby for my wife's health, I would. But in any case, the baby is ours, and I cannot harm what we purposefully made with our foolish notions to get her pregnant.

Perhaps we should have waited. Although, I'm ecstatic to see her plump with our child.

"I can get more romantic, Kitten," he says, wiggling his brows. "You name it, and I'll do it."

"If you mention soaking your cock in me one more time, I won't touch it for nine months." She scowls at him, huffing when his face falls.

It's exactly what he was thinking about. It's all he thinks about. I swear he's had a permanent boner since we fucked her at the wedding.

Arrow's lips pop open and close several times. "Fine. I won't talk about cock warming and how my cum could benefit your pussy and help with all the pain. Not to mention the baby. I won't mention anything, Kitten." He winks, turning to look at the road ahead of us, leaving my wife groaning and gaping at him.

"You can plot his abstinence," I quip, keeping her close. "Force him to watch as we fuck like rabbits for hours on end and not let him take part."

AKA a taste of his own fucking medicine. I still haven't forgotten the feel of the straps around my wrists and ankles, watching them fuck my wife as a punishment for marrying her with no one knowing.

She gives a breathy laugh, snuggling further into me without a word.

"We will not discuss that! And I'm truly offended, Daddy Jer! I didn't do anything to deserve a show and no wet dick," Arrow huffs with a frown, digging into his pocket and pulling out his phone. His lips pop open like he wants to say something, but he stops himself when it beeps again, deepening his frown. He taps a few times and sighs. "Dad texted and said the coast is clear, so we can park down the block and then come inside." The more words he speaks, the softer he gets, losing his normal fire.

When speaking about his father, a light sits in his gaze. He's like a god in Arrow's eyes. But right now? He dims slightly, succumbing to the dark demon in his soul like he's preparing for battle and death.

A strange silence engulfs him when he puts his phone away, even when he looks out the window without returning to our argument.

I know he's feeling the pressure of this meeting. We have to stay hidden wherever the priest puts us so we can listen in on what my mother has in store for Briar Cove. No matter what happens, we must remain quiet and stay in place. We chance death or worse—more imprisonment. On a long list of things I want to happen, being held at gunpoint by my vindictive mother is not at the top.

I shake myself out of my thoughts. The closer we get to parking near the church, the worse my thoughts become.

Why did my mother come back after all these years? Why does she want to inflict revenge so badly when she could have stayed gone? Run off to somewhere better and become someone else.

Instead of running away forever, she started her own gang. Entering into the same world, she so quickly walked away from—the family she so casually abandoned without a second thought. She was so damn close to me. Yet, so far away.

How can the woman who birthed me simply walk away, leaving me within my father's tortured grasp? She knew what he was capable of toward other people.

So, how was I so expendable? So replaceable?

I take a deep breath, blowing away all the rage brewing in my thoughts. If I let them, they'll consume me. And if they take me over, doing something stupid will be inevitable.

Killing my father will be a piece of cake. One slice and he'll be done. The joy it'll bring me to see his life drain away is something I'm looking forward to. For me. For Journey. For anyone he's fucked over.

My mother, though?

The woman who tucked me in at night, reading stories and taking my nightmares away—I can't envision shoving a knife through her heart despite the damage she has done.

Fuck.

I shudder a breath when the truck comes to a stop near a curb—a building obscures our view. The sidewalks are empty —devoid of life. Like everyone in this town can feel the war horses who have rolled into town, ready to take their newest queen by surprise. At least, I hope so. This whole thing could go belly up in a heartbeat.

We could all die in a blaze of glory.

"I can see the thoughts you're thinking," Shepp rasps,

using his fucking voice to knock me out of my spiral. Shit, I didn't even notice we were on this side of town.

"Oh, yeah?" I quip, raising a brow and loosening my muscles.

"Yeah, you look fucking constipated, Daddy Jer." Fucking Arrow.

Shepp grunts, slapping Arrow in the back of the head. "Ow! God, you assholes and your violence toward me," he huffs, rubbing his head.

"You're thinking about this meeting too hard," Shepp says, shaking his head. "We can't go into this with preconceived negativity."

Is he right? Yes. But I can't fucking help it. My confidence has been rocked. Every step of the fucking way has been one booby trap after another. Our only solace was at the cabin, but that's exposed now, too.

"I'm aware," I say smoothly, taking a deep breath. "We remember what we talked about." I send a pointed look at Arrow, who scoffs at me.

"You all act like I haven't hidden in the rafters of a fucking building and taken down ten men with a broken knife before. I can be a good boy and stay quiet." He mimics zipping his lips shut and throwing away the key.

Shepp nods. "I've texted Elias and Mikhail, giving them the one-hour warning. Once we're in the basement and we have eyes on Grace, they're taking down the businesses."

All part of our plan. We're spying on Grace, soaking in her movements while Elias and Mikhail's men raid her newly acquired businesses.

From the moment I woke up from my injuries in my bedroom and found out my father's businesses were being shut down for renovations and mysteriously opened back up better than ever, I had my suspicions. Why would they shut down? Why would that get renovated? But most importantly, why were the deeds signed over to someone else? Gabriel Viotto would never.

Unless it was her.

His sick obsession led him down some shitty roads, but this has to be the most volatile one.

Destruction.

It was all her. She took over the deeds, somehow getting them from Gabriel without a fight. It was too bad all those businesses were so far in the hole that there was no way she could have dug herself out of them. But she did with her organization.

"Brandon's on board, too," Arrow hums, staring at his phone. "He's on standby with our loyal soldiers, waiting for instruction."

"Then everything is ready to go." I offer them a tight smile. "Shall we?" I gesture to the door.

"Let's go kick some Shadow ass," Arrow whoops softly, climbing out of the car.

"You're going to be okay?" I ask, looking down at Journey, who slowly lifts her head. I'm taken aback by her ashen cheeks and glazed-over eyes.

She nods unconvincingly. "I'll be fine. Let's do this and take the rest of Shadow down."

Leaning in, I plant my lips on her cheek, soaking in her warmth for reassurance. For who? I'm not sure. Her. Me. All of us.

"You'll stay behind me if anything goes bad?" I question, looking deep into her eyes. "Don't fucking be a hero, wife." I cup her cheeks with desperation.

The last thing I wanted to do was bring her here in this delicate condition. But I couldn't risk leaving behind her, either. Safer by our side than falling into the enemy's hands. Shadow's men are still on the loose. The ones who weren't on the island.

"Not a chance," she whispers, leaning up to kiss my lips

before slipping out of my grasp. "I have a gun for a reason." She gives me a lop-sided grin, gaining more color in her cheeks.

Right.

I knew I shouldn't have given her a weapon. She'll stand there and fight with everything she has, even if it means putting herself in danger. But I wanted her to be able to do this. To point a gun and protect herself. Not giving her a weapon was not an option. If she didn't have something, then she wouldn't be able to live.

My only hope is we don't have to use them.

CHAPTER FIFTY-FIVE

Arrow

A HUNTING WE WILL GOOOOO! A HUNTING WE WILL GOOOO! Something, something, blah blah blah. A hunting we will go. Fuck. I forgot the words.

I stop, cocking my head with pursed lips, singing the song to myself repeatedly. Oh, well. No matter. I got revenge on the mind in the form of a bloody fucking meeting. Nothing gets my heart pumping and blood flowing like thinking about taking out a sadistic asshole and his minions. Or not his minions. Jer wants to woo the other bosses onto our side. Fat fucking chance that will happen. Those assholes will slice and dice straight through our tendons without a second thought if we show our faces after Gabriel's untimely death.

It's a good thing I like violence, death, and blood.

Jer's the heir. And I'm the spare. Shepp's the beware.

Because you better beware of the giant mother fucker who looks like a bear. Wait. Bear? Beware? I rub my chin in contemplation. He could be either. Shepp's the big old teddy bear you should beware of. Oh my God, I'm a fucking poet. I should write this down and publish it. I should…

"What in the fuck has you twisting your face like that?" Jericho hisses, jamming his elbow into my side.

Rude.

"Stuff," I say, waving a hand and fixing my face before we enter my dad's church from a secret side door in an alleyway.

Ah, I remember this door. Little me had to go in and out of it so no one would know I existed. It was either outing my father for fucking a drug-addicted hooker and producing me or Jesus.

You see who he chose in the end. The big man in the sky who watches over us. Sky Daddy, if you will.

I guess Jesus is a good choice for him. I never met the guy, but I believe in him. Somewhat. I mean, he made me like this, right? Dad used to say that God made me the way I was supposed to be, but the devil sunk his claws into my soul.

Whatever that's supposed to mean.

My dad was a good dad. He did what he had to do. Sure, I may have been a little bitter after he handed me over to Gabriel Viotto and exited my life as a parent. I still saw him every week for dinner in his small apartment, which was devoid of anything about me. And... Well, okay. Deep down in the depths of my feelings, I'm still a little hurt that my dad just tossed me into the arms of a maniac. Granted, that maniac helped me hone my skills, but his humanity was lacking. I guess that's where my dad came in. We spoke every week when I saw him for dinner, and he helped me work through things.

"You're doing it again," Jericho says, stopping to watch me as we approach the door. "You can handle this, correct? There won't be any reckless mistakes on your end? You understand that we have to be quiet. Invisible, Arrow. No murdering people tonight." He raises a brow with that stern, stuck-up expression he loves to give me.

Yeah, he'll make a great daddy one day. Good thing we have one brewing.

"Yes, Daddy Jer. I know I have to be a good little boy and zip my lips. No matter what." I grin at him, and he rudely scoffs.

"You will contain that murderous rage, Arrow. No matter

what they do in that meeting. They could string someone up and disembowel them, and you're not to move."

See? Such a goddamn daddy.

"Aye, Aye, Daddy Jer. I got it." I point to the side of my head.

"That goes for us all. We're invisible."

"Invisible, got it," Journey says sluggishly.

An ache breaks my heart at the sight of her pale face and glazed-over eyes. When I envisioned my woman plump with my baby, I didn't expect this.

"Kitten," I mumble, pulling her into my side and kissing her forehead. "After this, I'll take care of you and..."

"If you value your testicles, please don't talk about cock warming," she grumbles into my chest with a sigh.

"Nope. Wasn't going to say it." I totally was. She's very misinformed about the positive results of pre-cum and my cock just hanging out in her pussy for hours on end. "I was going to say we're going to find you a doctor and get those morning sickness pills for you." I grin, really trying to sell my words. See? I was thinking about her health with my brain. Not my cock.

Those deep moss-green eyes peer up from my chest, narrowing on my grinning face. "Sure," she mumbles, shaking her head.

"All right, let's do this," Shepp rasps, sucking in a breath.

Every time he speaks, I swear his eyes bug out of his head, much like mine. It's odd to hear my buddy's deep voice after talking with our hands for so damn long. God, I'm so proud of him. I could kiss him. I won't, of course. I cock my head again. Unless...

"Stop it," Jericho barks, pounding on the side door with his fist. "You're doing that, getting lost in your head, thing."

"Oh." I shrug. "I was just thinking about kissing Shepp." I don't elaborate when the door cracks open, and my dad's head pokes out.

"Good. You're just in time. Let's get you in position."

I grin when Shepp eyes me suspiciously and doesn't say a word. He can mull that over while we're in hiding.

My dad pulls out his pocket watch hastily while swallowing a thick lump in his throat. He's being extra fucking suspicious right now, and I can't figure out why. It's been gnawing at me since he pulled us into the empty church and took us into the basement via a secret staircase.

"This has been here the entire time?" My voice echoes through the small stone stairway.

"I, um. Yes," my dad says with wild eyes.

"Cool," I say with a shrug.

"Looks like this was the original setup," Jericho remarks from behind me, looking around at the stone stairwell and taking it in—no doubt memorizing it for when we need to escape later.

"It was." My dad keeps his comments suspiciously short without giving us too many details.

All right, I'll ask him later why he hid it from the family. I'm sure he has his reasons, like spying reasons. He's already admitted to listening to our meetings from a secret spot. How far down the rabbit hole has my father made it?

Dad stops at the bottom of the stairs, standing before a door. He shoves his hands into his pockets before looking at the four of us with a pained expression.

"This stairwell will be open for you to come through once the meeting has commenced."

"And where are we hiding, Dad?" I ask with a grin.

"It's a place no one will know where to look." He offers me

a puzzling expression, one I don't know how to decipher. "If you'll follow me."

And we do, straight into a closed-off room with several couches.

"This is where you'll be able to view them through," my dad says, pointing to two vents on the wall.

"This is how you spied on us?" Jericho asks, looking around the small room with furrowed brows.

"They'll be here in less than an hour," my dad says, looking at anything but me.

"And how often did you stand in the darkness of this room watching what my father did?" Jericho asks, with no heat behind his words.

A noise bubbles from my dad's throat, and he shakes his head. "I'd rather not discuss that."

Reading between the lines, I conclude my dad has watched every meeting since he struck up the deal with Gabe. Interesting. I'm not mad. But it makes me wonder what I've done under his hidden, watchful eyes. Not that I haven't done crazy shit in front of him before. With Gabe, though, I was protected. Kind of.

"Thank you for helping us," Jericho says without protest.

My dad licks his lips, giving Jer a sharp nod. "Of course."

"What is this place?" Journey asks, looking through the vent on the wall with furrowed brows.

Stepping up beside her, I lean down and grin. In front of us is an up close and personal view of the stage Gabriel likes to parade around. It's only slightly raised off the stone floor. Oh, what good times we've had here, fighting for our territories. Even pledging ourselves to the family. It feels like yesterday that Gabriel sliced into my chest and made me bleed.

How unfortunate that we're now the traitors in our own damn crime family. Oh, well. We'll take out the trash when the time comes.

"Our meeting and initiation room," I say quickly, gazing into her eyes.

Journey nods, rubbing through the material of her shirt right where the scar lies on her chest. The same one we have. So, she gets it. I wonder if he dragged her down here, too? Or if she was sliced in the basement she was kept in.

Whatever the case is, I'll slice and dice through Gabriel in the name of hurting my fucking girl. Of course, he's mainly Jericho's to torture. But I'll get my hits in, too. And stabs. And burns. You know, the usual.

"You've had a hidden room all this time?" Jericho hums, slowly pacing around the room and taking it all in with his devious, dark eyes.

"My intentions were selfish," Dad says grimly with a frown. His fingers fiddle together in front of him, and he sighs. "It had to be done. I had to ensure the organization my son was going to be under was as safe as possible."

"Yeah, and how'd that work out for you?" Jericho snarks, shaking his head.

My dad raises his chin. "In the beginning, good. Your father treated him the way I asked him to be treated. He helped Arrow hone his skills and sate his blood lust. Something I was unable to provide for him. But your father..." he trails off, running a hand down his face. "Things seemed to go too far, too fast. I wanted a front-row seat to see what my son was going through. So, if I had to run with him and hide, I would know when to go."

I swallow hard at his misty eyes. Nothing gets me in my nonexistent feels more than my dad. We've been in a strained relationship for many years, but we're finally coming to an understanding. I love the guy, which seems to be a new feeling inside me.

A chaotic black hole filled with nothing but hearts, rainbows, and ponies has opened inside me. It started with Journey. She helped me to understand that I was feeling more than an obsession with her. Sure, I climbed in her window, stole her panties, and took pictures of her sleeping. That was a deep obsession consuming my every move. But the man I am now. The one who will no longer drug her for safety or have to slip through her window to watch over her—that's a man who is in love.

At least, I think.

"So, Daddy-O. You've been watching all these years?" I quip, quickly shaking off the black hole of love consuming me.

"Every meeting. Every initiation. Everything," he says with a sharp nod.

"So, you've been spying on every word said?" Shepp asks thoughtfully, catching the priest off guard when he speaks from behind him.

Right. My Sheppy boy has his damn voice back, and he's using it all the damn time.

Dad stops in the middle of the room, smiling at Shepp. "You're speaking again."

Shepp blushes slightly and clears his throat. "I took back what was mine." That is all he says when he should have mentioned that he was badass and shoved a knife through his father's throat without a second thought, forgoing his fucking fear of blood and torture.

My little Sheppy Boy is growing up so fast. I sniffle, staring at Shepp with stars in my eyes.

"Why are you sniffling?" Jericho asks with raised brows. "Is he okay? You're acting weirder than usual today." He gives me that knowing Daddy look that I can't wait to punch off his face. Pfft. Weirder than usual? What an asshole.

"Asshole," I gripe, frowning at the man I call my best friend. "You're demoted to best friend number two. Journey, you're my only number one." I raise my chin in defense.

"For fuck's sake," Jericho grumbles.

"Number one?" Journey says at the same time with a smirk. "I'll take it."

"Is he ever?" Shepp quips quickly, whipping his gaze at me. "You good?" My dear old Sheppy is always checking in on me to make sure I haven't lost myself to the demon hiding inside. The demon is dormant. Well, for now. Right now, I'm high off the ponies and unicorns. Nothing can get me down.

"I'm always good, Sheppy Boy." I grin at him.

"Son," Dad says, stepping up to me. His hand finds my shoulder, gently squeezing me. "You'll promise to behave?"

There's something twinkling in his eyes when he looks at me—a knowing look. Like the big bad priest of Briar Cove knows something I don't. Maybe he does. But what is it? I can't put my finger on what he might be hiding. Bummer. I'll pick his brain later, after we've witnessed whatever this meeting is. Hopefully, Gabriel's demise. Or Grace's. She's up there on my shit list of baddies who need to meet their end. Only, I don't know if we'll be able to end her like we've done before.

"I will if you will," I say back, contemplating what might happen.

It's foreboding, pressing down on my chest. I've looked many enemies in the eyes, staring straight into their souls. They all give themselves away, clueing me into their deceptions. They all eventually break under my torture. But my dad? No. I could never watch him bleed. It would bring me... Sadness. I rub at my chest.

He softly smiles. "Of course I will, son." He slips away from me, moving to a spot on the wall. "This is an exit button, opening a secure door in the wall leading out into the meeting area. I'm hopeful you won't have to use it."

"Do you have any insight as to what we'll witness tonight?" Jericho asks, folding his hands behind his back. His head tilts, invading my father's mind with his cocked brow and knowing eyes.

Jericho senses it, too. I feel it in my fucking bones.

Dad shakes his head. "I was only informed of this meeting

right before you called. I assume it's important if it wasn't on the calendar beforehand."

"Of course," Jericho nods. "Gabriel is always prompt with the monthly meetings."

"He is," Dad says softly. "Now, if you sit back and wait, they should be here shortly. You can see everything through the false vents." He seems almost reluctant to give that secret away when his shoulders tense.

"Are you aware of my mother coming in tonight?" Jericho asks before my dad can scurry off up the stairs.

"She comes every time now, Jericho," he says with a polite bow.

"Every time," Jericho murmurs more to himself while nodding.

He doesn't show how it affects him on the outside, but I can see it from here. He's furious with her. Hurt. Fucking embarrassed.

"Be safe," Dad says before waltzing out of the secret room, closing the door to the stairwell behind him, leaving us in a secret hidey hole he's kept from me for years.

How odd.

"That was weird, right?" I ask the room.

Journey slumps into the couch with a huff, leaning her head on Shepp, who wraps his arm around her.

"He's hiding something," Jericho says, pursing his lips. "But what?"

That's the question of the hour, isn't it? What is my dad hiding behind his sinful eyes? It's a mystery to me. One I don't have to wait long to contemplate when the entire family waltzes into the meeting room with rumbling voices.

CHAPTER FIFTY-SIX

Arrow

THE LOUD VOICES OF THE FUCKERS CLOSEST TO GABRIEL leak through the walls. I grit my teeth as they whisper, begging for answers as to why they're there.

"Did the priest happen to mention if they could hear us from in here?" Jericho murmurs, standing directly beside me as we both watch through the false vents with a clear view of Gabriel's bosses standing around the large room with their thumbs up their butts. I wonder if they smuggled any weapons in? Seems kind of like a fish-bowl to me.

Come one, come all, grab your enemies, put them in this tiny room, and eviscerate them one by one. If I were in charge, I'd be down for a bit of death—*Game of Thrones* style. It reminds me of that one episode where they all gather for a wedding and get locked in. Immediate death. But no spoilers on my end. My lips are sealed. Especially to Jericho, who hasn't bothered to catch up after falling asleep during our last binge-watch. Amateur.

"Any ideas about what this shit is about?" one of his bosses grumbles, looking around the room with narrowed eyes.

Sucks to be that guy.

"Where's Gabriel?" another asks, shoving his hands into his pockets—the outline of his weapon presses against his suit pants. Oh, goody! They brought weapons to protect themselves. Smart men.

"They don't trust this meeting," Jericho murmurs, seeing the weapons on each of them hidden in their pockets and waistbands.

"Nothing, but come here now to discuss the future of Briar City and the promise of money." The third one shrugs with a huff.

"It's fucking suspect, is what it is," the other one hisses through clenched teeth.

"Indeed," Jericho answers back with furrowed brows. "They weren't clued in as to what was happening. Strange right? Father always sends a briefing as to what's going down." He may not be a good man, but Gabriel Viotto can run a business like none other.

"Right," is all I can say when my lips twist.

"Good evening, men!" Grace's voice rings out through the room, instantly silencing them.

"Good God in a fucking rainbow," I say with my jaw dropping. "It is your goddamn mom."

Jericho levels me with a look like he is completely done with my shit. "Did you think we lied about her return?"

"Wouldn't put it past ya," I quip, shoving at his shoulder.

Of course, I knew she was alive after what they told me. But to see her alive and in action, walking across the stone floor with authority, has my hackles rising. Guards follow behind her, helping a stumbling Gabriel find a seat on the stage. They dump him in the chair without care, letting his pliable body slump. His beady eyes remain closed, and his breathing seems off. And is that vomit on his suit? Ew. Has she not changed or bathed her husband in a while? Maybe he was poisoned or something.

Jericho shakes his head, turning pale at the sight of them both. "Fuck. He looks..."

"Like shit." I finish his sentence with a grin. "Looks like she's been taking care of your daddy."

"You call that taking care?" Jericho raises a brow.

"Obviously not hygienically, but morbidly. You know, she's been slowly killing him. I recognize it." I point to his father confidently.

Knock-out drugs aren't my only specialty. I enjoy a good poison here and there. Shit, I even left some in the basement of the mansion after interrogating a man for several days. It's a painful one. It makes your hands and feet tingle while a cough forms and slowly drains you until you're a blob.

"Interesting," Jericho says, rubbing at his chin before stiffening. "Look." He gestures to the main stairwell of the room.

"Cool. More victims," I quip, leaning in to examine the men piling into the room. "They look rugged. Manly men. Gross, too."

"It's Shadow's men," Journey says, standing beside me with panic lacing her gaze. "It's..." She covers her lips.

"Shadow's men, you say?" Jericho murmurs, rubbing a hand up and down her back. "We're all right. We're safe."

He's not that convincing, but she must believe him. She leans her head on his shoulder, still looking like she might throw up.

"A fucking trap," I hum more to myself than anything.

"She lured them all here," Jericho asks, confirming my thoughts.

"We should go then," Shepp says warily. "Something is about to happen, and I..."

"No," I bark. "This is a fight we don't step back from."

"We're hidden," Journey says shakily. "We'll be okay."

Famous last words, am I right? We're safe. We'll be okay. We won't get chased by a man with a chainsaw while hiding behind a wall of chainsaws. Or something like that. Do I think we're safe? Nah. But we're safer hidden here than sneaking out of the church with possible watch dogs roaming outside. And I tell them that much.

"He's right," Jericho says, looking pained for needing to say that.

"I am!" I say gleefully. "So, we stick it out here no matter what happens."

Shepp just nods, staying behind us with worry in his eyes. What's the worst that could happen?

"Good evening, family!" she says, waving more of Gabriel's inner circle into the room. It's packed with his men in suits. Business owners. Alliance members. Everyone essentially sits within ten feet of Gabriel and stands there with furrowed brows. They have no fucking clue why they were called to a meeting.

"Why are we here, Gabriel?" They snub Grace, turning their attention to the man in the chair gasping for breath. His beady eyes scan the room. Wide-eyed now. Begging for fucking help from the men who are supposed to be his most loyal.

Something shifts in the room. It's subtle. The business owners and Gabriel's bosses adjust to their rigid stances.

"You are here because he called you here!" Grace grits out, an angry red taking over her face. Her fingers dig into Gabriel's shoulder, looking like a devoted wife, except she's anything but.

An excited flutter blossoms in my stomach, seeping through my veins. She's taking over. This is a historic event within the family. Something I get to witness and then decimate.

I eye Jericho, who peers through the vent with a blank expression now. Devoid of everything that makes him Daddy Jer. He's Business Jer now—or Asshole Jer. Whatever I call him, he's not himself. But it's fun to make up so many nicknames in my head as long as I don't say it to his face. He already hates Daddy Jer enough.

"This is fucking weird," Jericho hisses, shaking his head. "She's..." he trails off, taking in his mother as she shifts, puffing out her chest. Her chin lifts, and only a smile a fellow psycho could recognize crosses her lips.

"Gabriel has gathered you all here today to witness history in the making." Her fingers dig into his shoulder again, curling her blood-red nails over his suit.

He doesn't fucking budge. Not like he could. If the poison has worked its way through his veins, then it's taken everything from him already. He lost his voice and strength a long time ago. Probably from the time Jericho said buh-bye and left them in the dust at the mansion.

"History?" Parker Sullivan, owner of a trading company within the city limits, scoffs. "We've been waiting for word from him for weeks. He's been MIA, and word on the street is he's sick. You sick, Viotto?" He raises a haughty brow, shoving his hands into his suit pockets.

I wonder how he fits his balls in those pants? Read the room, asshole. You're about to die. Now, where's my popcorn? I'm always in the mood for a salty treat when blood spills. After that, I can have some pickles and orange juice when they take their last breaths. Peace out, bros.

"Yes, my husband has been quite sick these past few weeks, as you know. That's why I'm here. That's why..."

"You?" A wrinkly old man steps forward, dragging his cane as he slowly approaches the front of the group. Ronald Thompson. Classic businessman making millions by embezzling. Of course, he hasn't been caught because Gabriel helps him and vice versa. A little tit for tat between the men for keeping their mouths shut. "What about him? He looks..." Ronald tilts his head. Stupid fucking idiot.

My skin practically buzzes with anticipation at the murder about to happen. I hope it's Ronald first. He's always been a cunt to his employees, family, and mistresses. The amount of times I've wanted to storm his castle and help him drop dead has been plenty.

"You feel it, Jer?" I whisper giddily, bouncing on my toes.

"Feel what?" he says, rubbing his chin, attempting to figure out what's happening. How can the ever-observant Jericho Viotto not realize that the Red Wedding is about to happen?

I lick my lips, taking the scene in. "You remember that *Game of Thrones* episode we watched?" I hum, straining my ears as the door at the top of the stairs shuts hard, and more people file into the room, surrounding the businessmen. Axes, hammers, swords, knives, and every exciting weapon hang on their shoulders. The businessmen take a nervous step back, shaking their heads.

"What the fuck, Viotto?" one shouts as they huddle together, attempting to fish out their weapons from their pants.

Fucking pussies. Did they not learn their lessons from before? Always bring a damn gun or knife to a meeting and have it in hand. Duh. You never know what you're going to encounter. Like now. They're about to meet their makers, but there's nothing they can do to stop it.

"We're going to discuss *Game of Thrones* when this is happening?" Jericho snaps, running out of patience.

"Yeah. You know. The episode where the family gets invited to that wedding dinner, and they get locked in and murdered as revenge?" I raise my brows, not taking my eyes off the disaster preparing to unfold. "Oh right, you fell asleep." Jerk. Can't even pay attention to my beloved show.

Jericho jerks straight, watching the excitement lighting up my face. "You're saying..."

But poor Daddy Jer doesn't get the chance to finish his words when chaos unfolds. Grace's words splinter through the air like a fucking whip.

"That's why we're here, boys. Your reign as kings of this city is over. Welcome to Shadow's grasp."

Jericho swallows hard, forcing all his emotions into the pit of his stomach.

Grace points a small knife at Gabriel. "You stole my life. You stole my future. Now, I'm ending your useless life. You're a pig." With that, she drags the sharp end of the knife over his throat. He weakly fights it off, flailing his limbs. The guards hold him down.

Her guards.

They're all there for her. The other half of Shadow. The woman who had a mission in mind.

"Well, I guess we know for sure why she came back to Briar Cove," Jericho says with wide eyes, watching as the rest of the guards slaughter every man in the room with vicious cuts and stabs before they can ever fire off a shot from their hidden weapons. Their screams echo through the basement. Fear permeates the air. Until every man associated with the Viotto family lies motionless on the ground, painting the cement red.

But we knew she was bound to do something. Something corrupt and foolish just like this. But we never expected her to take out the entire Viotto family in one go. Well, they didn't take everyone out. Not us.

"Bring him in!" Grace shouts.

"Arrow," Jericho says with a tight voice, gaining my attention. "Arrow, I need you to look at me." His hand finds my shoulder, forcing me to turn and look him in the eyes. "We need to go. Now."

"What? Why? It was just getting good and..."

"That's right, come forward, Priest."

Okay. It wasn't getting so fucking good. It's getting bad. Very, very fucking bad. It's the worst-case scenario on crack.

"I want to get off the rollercoaster now," I say breathlessly, shoving Jericho off my shoulder.

"Arrow," he pleads softly, stepping toward me.

"No," I snarl, not watching my volume.

Every muscle in my body locks up at the sound of her voice.

"Arrow, we will die if you do not look at me again," Jericho commands, forcing my face toward him again.

Something hot and burning fills my eyes, and wetness coats my cheeks. What the fuck is happening?

"Arrow," Journey's sweet voice fills the demon's fog, taking over my brain. "You're crying," she whispers, swiping the wetness away.

"Crying?" I croak, shaking my head and forcing them away from me. "No. Fuck this..." I trail off, peering through the vent. No matter how hard they try to drag me away, I get tunnel vision. It zeros in on my father, kneeling in front of Grace without a care in the world. He smiles at her, offering something warm and inviting, and FUCK THIS.

My heart beats a million times a minute when a shuffling of feet in the main room takes over.

"Grace," my dad says softly. "So wonderful to see you again." Kindness rings out in his voice. The same love he shared with me on so many damn occasions.

"You're special because God made you that way," he whispers as he takes my hand. *"We need to control your impulses, Arrow. We need to channel this into something good for the people."*

"For the good of the people?" my little voice asks with confusion when he drags me toward the storefront we had just come from several minutes ago.

"Yes, love," he murmurs, kneeling in front of my face. *"You understand why stealing is bad, right?"* Not really. If I want it, I take it. What's so bad about that?

I wrinkle my nose. "But I wanted the chocolate." I want to cross my arms, but he grips my hand in his, squeezing.

"You wanted the chocolate, so you stole it from the shop?"

He cocks a brow but never raises his voice at me. "It's wrong to steal, Arrow. It's wrong to kill."

"Why?" I question with a shrug. "Maybe they shouldn't..."

"No, son," he whispers, holding the candy before me. "You'll walk into that store and return the candy you stole. Face the consequences of your actions."

So, I did. Returning to the store with a frown, I held the two candy bars. I stole the ones I wanted so badly when my father wasn't looking while we were shopping on a Sunday afternoon. At that point, I'd been living with Gabriel for months, and he let my impulses run free. Hell, he encouraged them. Not my dad, though. He gave me a moral compass and encouraged me to correct my wrongs. Stealing was bad. Murder—bad. But he knew I had to do what I had to do to feel whole.

I always wanted my father to look at me with those compassionate eyes filled with love and understanding. At all times.

I was his. His son. No matter what.

"Arrow," Jericho growls, putting his hands on my face, jerking my gaze away from the man who gave me life, kneeling on the ground with his hands folded in front of him.

Now, it all makes sense.

"He knew," I whisper with defeat. A feeling I don't know creeps up through me. Desperation? Sadness? Rage? I can't decipher what the hell it is, but it claws me—digging in through my flesh and palming my heart. It squeezes so tight, turning into rubber bands and stealing my breath.

"Arrow," Jericho growls. "Don't do anything stupid. Don't..."

"Don't tell me what the fuck to do," I snarl, stepping away from him. Anger seizes me. Pulling me under into the abyss of my rage. The familiar anger I've come to know and shake hands with. It's my friend. My passenger. It fuels me. "Don't tell me to stand the fuck down when my dad, the good guy, is about to sacrifice his life for what?" I hold out my arms. "For what?" My voice nearly chokes up, but I stop because I can't stop anything right now.

I'm a fucking rollercoaster running off the tracks, heading straight for a life-ending crash. I can't stop the steps I take toward the door. I can't make myself stand down, no matter how many pairs of eyes are on my person. Their voices ring out, begging me to step away.

It doesn't penetrate the fog encasing my mind, driving me to do stupid, reckless things like exposing us to a room full of murderers.

"Arrow," Journey whispers, stopping me dead.

My sweet Kitten. The love of my fucking life. Her fingers graze my arm. I soak it in. Let it become me even when I step away from her. If she touches me now, she'll only be touching a monster. A monster who needs to unleash on the fucking bitch holding his father hostage.

"Don't," Shepp whispers desperately, stepping up. He could easily pick me up and hold me down. I'd fight against him. "Arrow, if you open the door, you'll expose everything."

I lick my lips, looking between my family. The ones who accept me for who I am. My dad did, too. He accepted me, flaws and all. He gave me life and reason. He gave me Gabriel to hone my skills he could no longer contain. The urges I couldn't keep under control. I killed animals. I wanted to kill people. Gabriel gave me the tools, but my dad gave me the morals to think of.

I turn my back to the ones I love. I shouldn't go out there or expose the room. But my dad wanted me to see this for a reason. He knew he was going to die and sacrifice himself for what, though? Why? Why let us view this if he knew he was going to perish?

I guess I'll find out.

"Arrow," Jericho says with a pained expression. He must see it. Read me like he reads everyone else. Shepp, too. Journey's pale face looks between us with popped-open lips. Frantically, she shakes her head, knowing exactly what I'm about to do before I can.

Grace's voice filters through the vents, spilling her hate. She's so vengeful against Gabriel despite already ending his life. The entire family has her hate and rage. But so do I.

"It's time to make amends with your God, Priest. You've done things no holy man should," she says confidently, holding up the sword used for initiations.

Something cracks inside me when all her guards gather around her. No doubt, people loyal to Shadow and only her and Thomas. They were a team, creating a weapon to take down the Viotto family. The family that so callously tore them apart.

They tore my father and me apart, too. Dad gave me to them with good intentions. Sure, I saw my father weekly, but Gabe always had words to say to belittle the time I had.

"Your dad has good intentions, son. But don't mistake his kindness for what your life is going to be like. If you value him, you'll do as I say. Learn your lessons and kill when I say kill."

I was six when he uttered those words.

Without a second thought or letting their whispers follow me, I slam the button, opening the secret door. I step out into the chaos, tearing my shirt from my body and tossing it back into the room. My mind is nothing but static. The need to kill pulls me forward like a piece of thick thread tightening around my rib cage and forcing me to move. I immediately shut the wall behind me. My impulses jump—my demon shrieks.

And chaos fucking reins down.

"Arrow, no," my dad gasps, kneeling before the she-witch holding a sword in the air. She grins at me.

"Oh, another one, huh? Were you hiding and watching the show?" She raises a brow, evil transforming her face into a thick mask of bullshit. I see right through her. She'll spare no one to get what she wants. And all she wants is the power Gabriel held and took from her.

I don't say a word. I can't when I stand among my fallen comrades. They worshipped Gabriel and his power. And look where it got them? On the ground, dead.

I lick my lips, cracking a smile. "You have something I want," I say, pointing to my dad. "He has nothing to do with this." I wave to the room.

"He's provided a venue for the Viotto Family to assert their bullshit rules," she says through clenched teeth. "He is as compliant as you are, Arrow Armour. Not to mention, he's been leaking information to the feds. " She cocks her head, looking me up and down. "Now, what are you going to do about it?"

My heart shudders in my chest. The feds? What the fuck does that even mean?

"I am no traitor to you!" my father shouts in my direction. "Only to the man that took you."

His words don't register. Nothing does at this point. There are a lot of things I want to do about Grace. I want to squeeze her head off and watch as her eyeballs burst. But I don't think Jericho would appreciate me murdering the mom he lost for so long. Would he be upset with me? Probably.

Fuck.

The devil inside me rears his ugly head, screaming in my mind to fight for my dad—the man who defended me my entire life. I can't let him die in vain. Without a fucking fight.

I don't think rationally when it comes to this moment. The little voice inside my head shouts for revenge. It demands this woman go down to the pits of hell where she belongs because she doesn't belong here. Not in the mafia world Gabriel so carefully curated.

She smirks, swinging the sword up further in defiance.

"Then you came out of hiding, just in time to watch the life drain from his eyes. You'll be next. Every person associated with Gabriel Viotto will die tonight. Blood in for the family. Blood out for freedom."

The roar that fills the room comes out of nowhere—vibrating my vocal cords when I march forward. I give into my demon, letting his vengeance free.

Kill them all. Kill Grace. Save my goddamn father. Everything in that goddamn order.

I don't feel the wood beneath my fingers when I pick up an ax on the ground. I don't see the heads roll when they tumble from their bodies without having a chance to react. Their screams fuel me until I'm tackled to the ground, thrashing under their hands.

"Son," my dad says, breaking through the fog. "Son, come back to this moment," he says with more authority this time.

Something snaps inside me, sucking back into the abyss that had opened inside me. Taking my demon from the front of my mind to the back, where he gets to cause more damage.

Heavy breaths leak from between my lips as the cool floor of our meeting space pushes into my cheeks.

The only thing grounding me are the eyes staring back at me in the same position.

"There you are, son," he whispers with a sad smile gracing his lips.

All the chaos around us ceases to exist. All the noise. It's gone into a vacuum as I stare at my father.

"I've always loved you, Arrow. Carry that with you with every breath you take. I'll always be with you. I taught you so well. Everything I did was for the good of you."

Grace says something above us, but I don't listen. I only watch as the sword penetrates through my innocent father's skull, cutting straight through the bone into his brain. Again and again, I watch as a sense of nothingness takes me over as he bleeds out. From his mouth. From his eyes. Ears. It's everywhere. Soaking into my clothes.

My brain doesn't register the moment I'm pulled on my knees, facing the bitch herself.

"Such love from a man who gave you to a maniac. Tell me,

what did Gabriel teach you?" She cocks her head, eyeing the red staining me now.

My father's life force. His blood.

Numbness takes over every molecule when I look into her cruel blue eyes, sparkling with revenge.

"Violence." It's odd to hear my voice so lifeless and devoid of everything that makes me... me. "Torture. Cunningness. He taught me to be the perfect mafia man." My eyes fall on my dad's body. His soul left its shell the second she thrust the sword into his soul. "That man taught me morals. He was innocent. You killed him for nothing."

The pointed end of a guard's knife sits against my throat. Pain. It envelops me, giving me life. I cock a smile, fighting through the fucking numbness begging to drown me.

"Innocent? Pfft." Grace waves a hand, leaning down to stare into my eyes. "None of you are innocent. You're born and bred to become him." She points to Gabriel, slumped in his seat with blood soaking his white shirt.

Lifeless.

She's taking everyone in this room and killing them quickly.

"Weren't you born into this life?" I ask, raising a brow.

She was.

Grace Viotto, formerly Grace Contelli, was an East Coaster until her father aligned with Thomas' father and Gabe's. But that's the extent of what we know now.

She doesn't answer me. Simply looking me over with narrowed eyes.

"Boss." A deep voice clears his throat from behind us, but I'm unable to turn my head because the knife continually digs into my flesh.

"Do you feel that way about me, Mother?" Jericho's voice booms throughout the echoey room. "That I'll turn out just like him?"

Grace's face softens when she takes him in. Her eyes move up and down his body, as he advances on them.

She tilts her head. "The sad truth of it all is yes. He molded you into the perfect little heir."

"Because you left." His words ring out like a whip, reeling her back a step. Her lips pop open. And is that hurt I see crossing over her face?

"Jericho," she says, lifting her chin and shaking off the vulnerability.

Of course, she can't show how she truly feels right now. She has to remain a stone to stay in power amongst the men following her orders.

"Mother," he retorts coolly without missing a beat. "Could you possibly remove the knife from my brother's throat?" I can practically hear the taunting in his voice and the lift of his brow.

He's strictly business Daddy Jer right now.

"No," she says, tilting her head the other way. "I don't think I will." She steps forward, and my eyes follow as much as I can until she stands before Jericho. He towers over her, staring down at her. He's cleverly wiped every emotion off his face, leaving a blank canvas. "You look so much like him, Jer." She licks her lips. "It's such a shame." She lifts a hand, and the men around the room close in on us, putting us in the middle of the circle. All their weapons draw as they wait on pins and needles for her command.

"It's never a compliment to look like him," Jericho says with a straight face. "You think I enjoyed being in his presence? That I liked being thrown in the basement and left for hours on end? You left me with a monster. So, I am a fucking monster now." Out of the corner of my eye, I observe as his arm moves, shielding Journey between him and Shepp, who covers her back. Shepp's wide eyes look around the room with breaths heaving his chest, ready to attack anyone who lays a hand on her.

Hook. He got her. Grace's face falls further as her finger works up and down his jaw. "Oh, my son," she murmurs with a loving expression.

She traces the stubble on his jaw, going over his nose like she's memorizing his face. Tracing it so she can't forget what he looks like when she slaughters us, killing off the last of the major players in the family. There are still small people. The other business owners simply owe us money, and we collect. In return, we offer protection and weaponry.

"You left me defenseless. I'm curious, was it worth it?" Jericho asks in a broken voice, his voice cracking with emotions he never lets free. But for her. The woman who discarded her child like he was nothing—he'll do it.

"What you went through pales in comparison to what I went through at the hands of your father." Her eyes harden. "Eradicate them," she softly says, stepping back. " Let this..."

"Do not fucking touch her," Jericho growls with venom dripping from his voice. "Do not fuck with my wife. Do not fucking touch my baby."

My spine stiffens at his words, bringing me back to reality. We're trapped in this room with these psychos. That's all fine and dandy, but my goddamn woman is here. My baby in her belly. And yes, it's mine. I can feel it in my fucking sack.

"Well, this has been fun," I murmur, reaching up without effort and yanking the knife away from the man behind me.

I could have done it all along, but I sort of wanted to be stabbed. Maybe just a little bit. Blood gets me going. And I wanted to feel the burn to know I was still alive. He yelps and puts up a small fight. Well, until the tiny knife that was once at my throat sinks into his neck. A pity, really. Such a waste of space. I grin as blood squirts all over my body.

"That was for my fucking father," I grit out, trying not to look at my dad on the ground without life in his body. It tears me up inside, begging my demon to go free again and murder every fucking person in this goddamn room.

Grace holds up a hand, momentarily stopping the advance of her men in their tracks, even after my little slip-up and murder of her men. She looks between the four of us with raised brows.

"A baby?" she breathes. "You're going to have a baby, son?" A creepy smile breaks out on her face. "How far along are you?" She peeks around, looking at Journey and holding eye contact with her.

"We're not entirely sure yet, Mother. We've been a little tied up and on the run from him," he says, gesturing to Gabriel's body. "Thanks for taking out the trash." His performance is applaudable. He's holding his chin up high, but I know the threat of murdering Journey has his fingers curling at his side.

"Stand down," she shouts, lowering her hand. "There's a change in plans. I'm going to be a grandma."

Seriously? This is what stops the psycho bitch in her tracks? Being a grandma? I won't question it, though. It saves my Kitten from witnessing my wrath. Again. And saves her life. I can't have my baby mama dead. Fuck that. I've already lost my father. I can't lose anyone else so soon.

"Let's escort you home, Jericho. You and your friends," she says with a weird smile twisting her lips.

"Home?" Jericho asks, cocking his head. "You want to take us back to..."

"The mansion, son. Let's go home and have dinner. We can get reacquainted. Then, you can tell me about my baby," she whispers, looking between them.

Her baby.

My heart rate spikes at her words.

"The four of us will go to the mansion with you if we have your word on our safety. My wife. My brothers. Me."

"Oh, we'll have use for the four of you, son," she says with a smile resembling so much of Jericho.

I always thought he got his psycho tendencies from

Gabriel. Every inch of him was evil. But Grace? She's slowly climbing up the ranks as the number one psycho. But I hold that status, and I'm not one to let that go.

I'll keep Journey safe until we walk into the mansion, but I can't let her see me fall apart more than I have. I lost my father.

And that's just something I don't know how to process.

CHAPTER FIFTY-SEVEN

Journey

It's odd to be back in a house that was the first place that truly felt like home. My trailer was a war zone—a place I could never relax in. It had my bed and a pillow, even my clothes, but it was not home. Not without Sunshine. Or security. My mother made sure of that with her drug use and letting men in and out.

But this place? The mansion. It's a home. This place may be filled with possessive idiots who only show love through handcuffs and barely legal contracts, but it's where I first felt safe. Even after they chased me with masks on and fucked me in the mud. I shudder, looking out the window at the trees behind the mansion blowing in the slight wind, signifying the changing seasons. I expect Arrow to be over my shoulder with a grin, asking if I remember when I stabbed him. Or when we jogged through the rain and fell into the mud together.

Much to my disappointment, though—he's not. He's nowhere.

And hasn't been since we returned to the mansion earlier.

The moment we stepped foot onto the property, Arrow withdrew. From me. From Grace. From everyone. His eyes clouded over, turning him into an empty shell. The first moment Grace left us alone, he kissed me and whispered a soft goodbye.

"Be good, Kitten. I'll be back," he murmurs against my temple, sucking in a breath.

"Arrow," I plead, shaking my head when he backs away, exiting the dining room Grace instructed us to stay in, and leaves out the back door.

It feels like a piece of me walked away.

Grace's guards yell at him to stand down and come back. They raise their guns and fire in his direction multiple times. My heart sinks in my stomach at the sound of the bullets ricocheting in the woods, echoing back in my ears. So much for the safety she promised.

I watch from the kitchen window with a slack jaw and Jericho at my back, pulling me against him.

"He'll be okay, Little Chaos. He needs time to process what happened at the church." His father's death. "He'll most likely barricade himself in with Max and Nova. They won't hurt him, but will hurt the guards if they try to enter their domain. He'll be fine..." he trails off when Arrow's figure completely disappears through the trees.

"It's such a long walk to the enclosure," I gulp, staring into the nothingness of guards chasing after him, weaving through the tall trees until they disappear.

"Arrow knows this property like the back of his hand. He'll be okay," Jericho murmurs, kissing my temple. "Why don't we sit back down?" I want to scoff and pull myself away from him. My eyes stray to the window again, aching to see Arrow with that familiar smile on his face.

But it never happens.

"We play this like you played Shadow. Understood?" Jericho whispers directly in my ear at the sound of high heels tapping against the floor and marching our way angrily. I nod in compliance.

We play the game until we're free from this hellhole.

It's only been a few hours since he escaped out the back door. Worry gnaws at me. Is he alive? Dead? Did they fucking catch up to him? God, I hope not. Arrow is...well, Arrow. I know he can survive a lot. I mean, I stabbed him, after all.

But he's still human. No matter how unstoppable he pretends to be.

"Little Tempest," Shepp says, drawing my eyes away from the window overlooking the vast property. His large hand engulfs my shoulder, gently squeezing. A heavy sigh rocks through me when my back collides with his front, and he traps me in his warmth. My eyes close. Oh, my silent giant. My rock. He's always made it his mission to be there for me when I'm spiraling down the drain, even when I wasn't aware of his presence.

I sink back into him, soaking up his comfort. Despite my mind twirling in the darkness of Arrow's absence. The barred windows of Jericho's office block slivers of the scenery below —beautiful gardens, manicured lawns, and the tall forest I want to get lost in. I suddenly miss the sunshine on my flesh and the warmth of the wind whipping through the property.

I'm tired of being a trapped bird caught in a cage of bullshit.

First, my monster. Then Shadow. Now, Grace. It's a relentless cycle repeating itself.

Eventually, we'll be free. But that day is not today.

My pity party falls flat when heels click against the floors, coming our way hurriedly.

"Incoming," Jericho mutters sullenly, stiffening in his chair. His fingers tighten on the glass between his fingers, and the melting ice clinks together as the amber liquid swishes with his jerky movements.

It's the most uncomfortable I've ever witnessed him to be.

We smell her perfume before she enters Jericho's office, throwing the door open hastily. She grins, lifting her chin as she takes us in with a sparkle in her eyes.

"Oh, Journey! Your doctor's appointment has been set for this week," Grace states with a twisted expression.

An expression that promises nothing good. It sends shivers down my spine. You know, some would say Jericho inherited his ruthlessness from Gabriel. But I'm here to tell you, I fucking disagree. Grace is ten times worse than my monster ever was. Only, she's subtle. Not as hands-on and more cunning than him. She could look you dead in the eyes and gaslight you into doing as she pleases.

And you'd never know the difference.

"I made sure Doctor Ellis would do an ultrasound so we can see my baby!" She practically squeals again.

I take a deep breath, attempting to wipe the words–my baby—from my mind. I'm here to play a part. I'm a good little captive, unable to stab her in the jugular like I want to do. But every time she refers to my baby as hers–I want to snap at her. She's obviously got something cooking in her demented mind that involves kidnapping my tiny human and possibly disposing of the mother—AKA—me.

Every time she looks at me with those glossed-over eyes, excited at the prospect of having a child—I want to shrink away and protect the innocent life inside me. My fingers run the length of my flat stomach, catching Grace's eye. She watches, mesmerized by the movement. Never taking her eyes off me. Fuck. It makes my skin crawl to have her focus all on me. Like I'm some lab rat she can't wait to dissect.

I shiver at the intensity, flicking my gaze to Jericho, who discreetly shakes his head. *'Don't worry, Chaos.'* he mouths so no one else can see but the three of us, leaving Grace out of the equation. Shepp continues to stand stoically at my back.

Jericho clears his throat, drawing Grace's misted eyes, knocking her from her stupor. "That was awfully nice of you, Mother," Jericho says soothingly, lifting a glass of amber liquid and taking a long drink. "I'm assuming you'll be accompanying us to the viewing?"

Of course, she will. Any time she can, my pregnancy is brought up. She gushes about the baby for hours, promising to be the best grandma on the planet. I call bullshit. She wants to play mommy, but I won't allow that to happen. I'll sneak my happy ass out of this mansion and escape. With or without my doting husband.

She lights up. "Of course, I will! I wouldn't miss it." She claps her hands a few times. "Now, if you kids will come downstairs, we've whipped up dinner. You think your friend will want to join?" Her brows furrow, and she stares out the window. No doubt trying to devise a plan to bring him back to the mansion.

Too bad she's failed twice already in the short time we've been here and lost guards to the lions' claws and jaws. Idiots. Who marches into a lion's enclosure only armed with a gun? Her guards. I guess they weren't that smart on the island, either. The more that go to the lions, the better.

"He's mourning, Mother. You had his dad murdered right before his eyes," Jericho says, setting his empty cup down on his desk with a loud thud. "Leave him for now." Jericho stands, rounding his desk until he's in between her and me. "He's where he needs to be. Unless you want blood on your hands?"

She scoffs confidently. "Like one little monster could take down my new headquarters."

Did she not see the damage he inflicted at the church? She's down at least seven men because of Arrow alone.

"Headquarters. Right," Jericho says, placing his hands behind his back. "This?" He raises an eyebrow, looking around the room.

"Yes," she says, lifting her chin.

Tension leaks off him in waves, filling the room with his festering rage. He's been silently plotting all day, sitting at his desk and drinking without uttering more than a few words to us. Shepp and I have spent our time reading the many books collecting dust on the shelves and attempting to entertain ourselves since our phones, tablets, and any sort of electronics were confiscated.

"I'll explain more over dinner; it's ready for us," she says, escorting us to the dining room without saying another word.

Walking with Grace is like walking toward the guillotine, hanging over our heads and ready to strike. One wrong move and we're toast. Every step we take within the mansion walls, eyes are on us. Her guards hang in every shadowy corner, eager to kill. Or maim. I'm not quite sure. It's like the promise of safety she so happily spewed back at the church no longer exists. Grace seems giddy to have Jericho back in her life. As for me? I'm pretty sure I'm an incubator and nothing more. Shepp and Arrow? Dispensable. They're only here because they haven't fucked up enough to be murdered.

Such a comforting thought.

As we take our seats around the table, the tension only amplifies. I swear my fucking chest is about to cave in and shrivel my heart. I shift in my chair, attempting to get comfortable despite the uneasiness.

My darkness looms in the back of my mind, eager to eat away at all my feelings and make me numb. But I don't let it. Not today. I need to be on my toes around Grace. Not an emotionless robot.

People bustle into the room, carrying trays of food before sitting them in front of us. Reminding me of the island hell Shepp and I went through. My gaze connects with his from across the table. His lips roll in.

"I'm curious, Mother. How did you become Shadow?" Jericho doesn't bother stalling to eat the food presented to him, shoving in several small bites while keeping his eyes locked on the woman sitting there.

"Many moons ago, Thomas Mondelli and I were madly in love," she says dreamily with a sigh. "Then Gabriel ruined our future union, forcing me into this marriage." She practically snarls at the thought of marrying Gabriel. I don't blame her. He was a monster of epic proportions, doing anything to get what he wanted. "The only good thing it gave me was you. Even if your birth was forced upon me." Disdain sits in her eyes when she glares at him.

Jericho's body stiffens, but he quickly lets it go. "Of course." He doesn't say anything else to the woman who birthed him. He shoves food between his lips and hums at the taste.

"And when Thomas came back?" I ask quietly, earning her sparkling gaze, which lights up further at the sound of his name.

She doesn't grin like I expect her to. Or give me heart eyes like I thought she would. No. Grace stiffens, licking her lips. "Well, if you must know. Thomas and I had been secretly seeing each other for years. He was the only one to know where I had gone. Then, we became Shadow together." The way she spits each word out infused in her anger, makes me wonder why she struck up an arrangement with him in the first place.

"You wrote him letters," Shepp rasps, slowly eating his food with apprehension.

We saw what Shadow did to people he didn't like. He poisoned them. Just like we suspect Grace did with Gabriel. Like Thomas did with Naum; poison is their M.O. I can only hope they won't do that to us. Grace has prattled on about our new jobs in her organization. Jericho is going to be the face of it like Thomas was. Her son. Her pride and joy. She wants to use his cunning nature to lure the family into her organization. As of now, the Viotto Crime Family has been eradicated in Briar Cove.

Shadow rules it all.

"For years after I left," she confirms with a nod. "I wrote to him when he was gone. He visited me and kept me company as I built our new home and helped build an army. That's the thing about men. They don't like to take orders from someone like me."

"A woman," I whisper with furrowed brows. "So, you..."

"Created a new entity, and he helped me build an army of people who could take down this," Grace says, gesturing to the mansion around us. "That's what Jericho will do for me now. And if not..." she trails off, sending each of us a warning glance.

If we don't follow what she says, she'll murder us all without a second glance, even though she needs us.

"We understand, Mother," Jericho says, sipping the glass of red wine. "We'll freely help you establish yourself in town."

"I already have," she says smugly. "Your father so generously welcomed me back with open arms."

And what a moron move that was. My fucking monster was so intelligent in so many ways, but the moment his missing wife came back into the picture, he didn't have a suspicious bone in his body. Maybe his obsession ran so deep that the red flags flying in his face weren't warning enough.

A server walks by, refilling her wine glass, and does the same to everyone but me. I look at my water with a sigh. Oh, how I'll miss drinking and eating whatever the hell I want. Like more than water. But according to Grace, I'm not fucking allowed. No soda. No juice. Just fucking water. I want some root beer or Sprite to settle my stomach. Is that too much to ask? Apparently. Ugh. At least I'm keeping food down a little better right now.

"And what did he give you?" Jericho asks, taking another bite of his food.

"Everything," she says with a shrug. "I vowed I would return and wreck everything your father built when I left. Nothing is in his name anymore. The bars. The clubs. The everything. Even this home was signed over to me one night without a fight. All my dreams are coming true, thanks to Gabriel Viotto. He finally gave me what he promised on our wedding day."

A part of me thinks their love became transactional instead

of from the heart. It became about what we can do for each other to get bigger and richer.

"Everything," Jericho says with a nod. "Of course. You wanted revenge on him, for taking away Thomas and giving him to Aurora. Where is she really, by the way?"

Shepp's spine stiffens as he listens in. I'm not sure how he feels about his mother. I haven't heard much. From what I know and have seen, she was an empty space who didn't give a rat's ass about Shepp and his safety. If she did, then his tongue would be intact, and his trauma wouldn't exist.

Grace laughs. "Aurora got what was coming to her. All through high school, she was a fucking pain in my ass, chasing after Thomas like a thirsty whore. So, I gave her the grave she deserved. Let her rot beneath the rubble of the tower." Grace's expression turns colder and colder, pulling down her features in her rage.

"You had inside help that night? Father made an exchange with Shadow for Journey and her sister in return for you..." Jericho trails off.

"Oh, yes. That was the premise of the deal. Let Gabriel think I've been locked away on his island all this time. We convinced him so thoroughly that he'd do anything to have me back. My torture on video. Shadow taunting me. Gabriel ate the evidence up, and with a flick of our wrists, he scrambled to regain his obsession."

"So, you manipulated Gabriel into playing right into your plan? Smart," Jericho quips, taking another bite of his dinner.

Grace grins. "It was the right time. The perfect time. I tried to get there before you were forced into a marriage you didn't want to be in, but..." Her brows furrow.

"I love him," I rush out, blushing instantly.

My eyes stay low as I push around the food I'm desperate to consume. But I can't bring myself to do it, not in the current atmosphere. Or with my turning stomach that can't manage to keep anything in it. I'd probably yack on Grace's favorite rug and earn my death.

Jericho makes a noise in the back of his throat, drawing my gaze to him. His face remains stern and business-like. It's a façade he presents to the world. Only the twinkling in his eyes lets me know he returns the sentiment. *He loves me.*

"You were too late, anyway. She is my wife," Jericho says, sitting back in his chair. "And my life." He raises a brow, discreetly threatening her without saying a word.

"Interesting," Grace says, tilting her head. Her lips purse when she shoves a small bite of food through her lips and swallows harshly. "You love her?" She scoffs at that. "Even Thomas didn't love me enough to keep his dick to himself over the years." Her gaze instantly drops to her plate, shame coating her reddened face.

Right. Sunshine resulted from him flouncing his dick in every direction when he was supposedly seeing Grace on the weekends. Apparently, she wasn't enough to hold his interest. Well, not until he died, at least.

Jericho stiffens at her remark, but once again seals his lips. He's all too aware of what's at stake here. She could end us with the snap of her fingers. Although, she doesn't seem too eager to get rid of us. Not yet, at least.

"After dinner, I'm going to take Arrow a plate of food. If he'll eat." Jericho leaves no room for arguments.

"He can rot in that lion's den, son. If he wanted to survive and eat, then he'd be here. You will go nowhere near that fucking cage!" she sneers, pounding her fist into the wood tabletop. More guards enter the room, holding guns at the ready until she waves them off. "No one leaves this mansion without an escort. He can die where he hides. No matter if he's mourning the loss of that disgusting priest. You're lucky I'm letting him live. He'll come in handy, though. When I drag him out of there." She rolls her eyes and stands tall. "Now, if you'll excuse me."

She marches out of the dining room with her chin held high, marching up the stairs and straight into the room she's been staying in. Her guards aren't too far behind her, watching her every move like hawks, ready to protect their newly found queen.

Four guards stand tall against the wall of the large dining room, watching as the three of us take tentative bites of our dinner. We don't utter a word. We can't. Instead, we sit in silence and soak up our time here until the guards escort us back into our bedroom and lock us inside.

Jer sits on the edge of our bed, stiff as a board, intensifying the anxiety building inside me. Jericho always has a plan. It never fails. He's the leader of the Devils, after all.

"Any plans?" I whisper, sitting beside him and taking his hand in mine. His fingers curl around mine, holding me like a life raft in a storm on the ocean.

Shepp stands beside us, staring down at Jericho with imploring eyes, begging him to have a solution to all these problems that seem to keep coming.

"You love me?" Jericho rasps, burning me with the intensity of his gaze.

I blink. "Yes," I whisper. How can he even question that? "I love all of you."

Jericho squeezes my hand one last time before standing and pacing before us.

"I love you too, Little Tempest," Shepp murmurs, taking Jericho's seat. My head falls onto his chest, and he wraps a tight arm around me, pulling me close. "We'll get out of this." But I don't believe it. Not an ounce of his tone indicates he thinks we'll run away from here unscathed.

My stomach drops into the nothingness, twisting with uncertainty. If we can't escape this prison, then we're bound to repeat this until I give birth. Only then will I know my true fate.

"We will," Jericho says, holding the confidence we don't

feel. "There's an answer out there. Our allies. Or anyone. We need to get a hold of them." His hands rest behind his back as he walks the length of the room. Back and forth he goes until he huffs, throwing himself onto the bed beside us. I've never seen him look so childlike. "No matter what, I'll protect all of us." His hand finds my stomach, stroking it. "All of us."

His pointed look lets me know he means it, but deep down inside, a helplessness claws at me. We're trapped in this mansion with eyes on us, locked in a bedroom that we don't have the key to and barricaded by steel bars on the outside of the windows.

We're sitting ducks. Once again trapped under the true Shadow's mercy.

Heaven help us all.

CHAPTER FIFTY-EIGHT

Journey

IT'S BEEN TWO INTENSE DAYS UNDER GRACE'S SCRUTINY. TWO days of getting sick, eating lunch and dinner, and then being escorted to our room when the time comes. Two days after Arrow left the mansion to check on his lions and never came back.

Two days of utter hell. Two days of rinse and repeat. I'm afraid to think of our future under Grace's hand. Something tells me she won't be as forgiving or nice.

"You think he's all right?" I murmur, staring out the window of a room overlooking the back of the property.

The large trees sway in the wind, losing their leaves.

"He's Arrow," Shepp murmurs, pulling me back into his front. "He'll survive whatever the fuck he's doing."

"They haven't eaten him, have they?" It's been my main worry since he disappeared. Previously, when he took me out there, he told me how he had slept with them. Never specifying where and how. I can only imagine his bloodied and clawed body lying in the open field after they attacked him or worse, ate him. I shudder, my stomach turning at the thought of losing my little psychopath to something as simple as a lion attack.

"No," Shepp mutters softly. "They see him as their parent. Even though they're wild and the zookeeper would disagree, they'd never harm him. Now, other people who tried to get him out. Yeah. They'd bite their faces." Case in point: the guards she sent to retrieve him after he didn't come back. Well, they're lion food. It was stupid of them to even go inside. That has my nerves on edge.

"We'll need to retrieve him," Jericho says from my other side, looking out the window with a pensive expression. "He'll be fine, Little Chaos. It's Arrow, after all."

"And your mother will let us go out there?" I question, raising a brow.

She hasn't let us out of her sight since we arrived. It's like she's afraid of losing us. Mostly me and the baby, I fear. She's been oddly happy about the baby and begging me to pick out nursery designs. Like she's living her life through me and eager to get her paws on my damn baby.

I sigh when the sound of the lock clicking filters through the air.

"Show time," Jericho mutters, taking my hand and leading me away from Shepp.

That's another thing. She doesn't understand the relationship we have with each other. All four of us being an item. So, we have to pretend, since I'm Jericho's wife, that it's just him and I.

"Darling," Grace says, entering the room and hugging Jericho. "Journey. Shepp," she says with a bright smile. Well, bright might be too kind to the vibes she's giving off. She's something akin to Arrow in his darkest hour. Only, she doesn't hide it very well. Or try to tame it.

"Mother," Jericho says, stepping back.

"We have got something exciting to do today," she says with a grin, pulling me out of the room by the hand. "Right here!" She pulls me in front of Shepp's art studio, the one room dedicated to his pieces he cherished. Oh, the memories of him painting me after our night in the woods. When the paintbrush smoothly descended my flesh and painted my scars. "We're going to use this as the nursery. So, near both our rooms." She grins, shoving the doors open and revealing an empty space.

I suck in a breath. It's empty. Everything. It's all gone. Bare walls. No tarps on the ground. My heart sinks into my churning stomach at the implications of Shepp losing everything he's worked so hard on over the years.

No. No. No.

Shepp's hard breaths ring through the air, stifling the sobs threatening to break through.

"Shepp," I whisper, wheeling around to stare into the devastation wreaking havoc in his ocean eyes misting over. All the color has disappeared from his face, leaving him ghostly white.

He shakes his head, taking a small step back from us. Those wide eyes take in every inch of the empty space.

"Mother," Jericho says in a low voice, attempting to mask the anger building in him. Attempting being the keyword. I read Jericho like a book. The tic in his jaw lets me know he's about to strangle his mother with his bare hands. But he's restraining himself so well. "Where have all the art pieces gone?"

I hold my breath. Everyone has taken from Shepp except for Arrow and Jericho. They nurtured him into the man he is. Accepting him for who he is. Learning sign language so they could communicate easily with him. When no one else did anything to step up.

Now, someone has taken from him again. His voice when he had none. Through the pictures he created, he told the world of his anguish without having to utter a word.

Grace raises her brows. "What art, hon? Maybe your father had something to do with it?" There's a breeziness to her voice giving away the actions she conceived.

I step forward, ready to pummel her fucking face in for ruining something so special for Shepp. Something that meant everything to him in a world of silence. But Jericho stops me by putting a hand on my upper arm and gently squeezing.

"My father, hmm?" he grits out, blowing out a breath. "It would be a shame if someone say—you—did something so heinous to beautiful pieces of art. Especially pieces worth millions of dollars."

Grace stiffens at the amount of money hanging in the air. "Well, we'll have to try to track those down now, won't we?" she says, stepping forward.

"If you'll excuse me. I need to..." Shepp's haunted voice rings through the air, choked by the emotions he's desperate to hold back. Tears swim in his eyes, drowning out the light once reignited in him.

He stumbles back, falling over his feet until he pushes from the room. Grace watches him with interest, quirking a brow at the guard behind us, silently encouraging him to follow Shepp. The sound of Shepp's heaving breaths has my heart in a vise. They echo through the hall.

"Good God! Take him outside and make him control himself!" Grace hisses to the guard standing in the doorway, flicking her wrist.

"Yes, boss," the guard grumbles when he leaves the room.

I hold my breath when they turn away from us and are out of sight. I want to reach for him. Beg him to stay with us so we can tamp down his anxiety. But I let him go off with the guard, hoping the fresh air would help him recover from such a great loss. Their retreating footfalls echo through the halls. A door slams somewhere downstairs, and silence engulfs the mansion.

"Perhaps it would be in everyone's best interest if we found the missing pieces," Jericho rumbles, pulling me close.

I can almost hear what he's thinking. Grace is playing a very dangerous game right now, taking away the simple things she knows each of us loves to destroy us inch by inch. She wants our foundations to crack, and then the rest will follow.

"The soft lighting in here will be perfect for little eyes. We can get blackout curtains and hold off the sunshine. What color were you thinking, Journey dear? I was thinking something neutral, like yellow or a soft green." Grace turns to me with a hopeful expression, folding her hands in front of her. "Or maybe we should wait until we find out the sex of the baby. That'll be soon! Then we can really work on a color." She sighs happily, staring around the room as dreams blossom behind her eyes of how this will all work once my baby comes.

I'm about to retort something sarcastic like, go to hell, bitch. But I'm interrupted by a burly-looking man standing in the doorway with a heaving chest. Sweat trickles down his forehead when his utter fear pulls down his features.

"Boss," a deep voice echoes through the room. "He... took off. Should we..." he trails off with a wary look, gesturing to the gun strapped to his hip.

The hairs on my arms stand on end at his implication, but Jericho gently squeezes me. He knows how this game works, too. We have to remain calm even if they're talking about gunning Shepp down. We have to trust he makes it to wherever.

Grace purses her lips. "So, you let him out of your sight? Let me guess, a fucking butterfly flew past and took your attention off the massive man throwing a fit in the backyard?"

"No, boss. I...." He rubs at his reddened cheek with a frown. "He sucker-punched me, and I lost consciousness for a second, and he got away. The other guards..." he trails off when Grace loosens her stance and sashays to him, swinging her hips.

Her painted nail traces over his jaw, down to his chin, and around his lips. "You had one job, Jerry. One fucking job to keep them in your sights, and you fucking..." She grins maniacally when Jerry's lips pop open and blood spurts from his stomach. A small knife protrudes from his flesh. Where it came from, I haven't a fucking clue. Jericho protectively holds me tight. "I'd suggest you walk it off and see the doc about your affliction." She flicks the small knife and then yanks it out harshly, spraying blood onto the carpet. "Oh, sugar. Looks like we'll have to add shampooing the carpets to the list." She shrugs, waltzing back into the middle of the room as Jerry staggers out. "That's a reminder for you two, as well. Don't fuck with me or leave the premises. It'll only end in your death."

My thoughts float to Elias and Mikhail. What has become of them? Were they able to complete their mission with Gabriel's many bars and restaurants? But I don't dare ask and tip her off.

"Why don't we pick some paint colors for the walls? I can't wait to fill this room with the sound of a baby." She sighs, turning back to us with a light smile. "Can you believe in just nine short months the little one will be here?" She rubs her hand over my stomach, inching closer and closer until we're a breath apart. "Soon," she murmurs, looking directly at my unborn child.

I stand rigidly, attempting to keep my composure. Harder than it sounds—might I add. If I had that knife, I'd stab her through the throat and suffer the consequences from her guards. Jericho and I would run to the others and fucking get out of this mansion. Shivers roll down my spine at the look she gives my stomach again. Not letting go. Like she wants to reach in there and take the baby for herself.

"We're thrilled about the arrival of our firstborn," Jericho comments, keeping me close to his side and watching her like a hawk.

"As am I," she coos with a grin, finally stepping back. My muscles don't relax when she claps her hands excitedly. "Now, let's go down for lunch and look at the magazines I found."

"Magazines?" I mutter when she walks out the door and heads down the stairs, leaving us to linger in the room that will now be our nursery. Or not, if I can fucking help it.

Jericho halts my steps, stopping to stand in the middle of

the room. Leaning down, he kisses my lips softly. "We need a plan here, Little Chaos." There's an odd sense of desperation in his eyes. He knows we're nearing the end of our ropes.

How much more can we take at the hands of his mother? With my monster, he was predictable. Hell, even Thomas was. But Grace? She's off her damn rocker, and there's nothing we can do to escape this hell she's thrust us into, especially with our baby's life in danger to her wicked ways.

"Where do you think Shepp went?" I whisper against his lips, staring deep into his dark eyes.

"No doubt to find Arrow. He won't be thinking straight." Jericho's heavy breaths whoosh over my flesh, warming me when he pulls me closer. "Let's be mindful of what we say in front of the psycho, yeah?"

"Yes," I whisper. "I'm worried now."

"Are you two coming? Your lunch is getting cold." Grace breaks up our fake kissing fest with a soft smile. "It's so beautiful to see the two of you so deeply in love." She sighs wistfully. "Reminds me of Thomas and I in our heyday... How was he?" She quirks a knowing brow.

"Before or after Sheppard put a knife through his throat?" Jericho goads, stiffening when she giggles manically.

"That man always did what he was told, didn't he? Such a shame he had to be sacrificed for the greater good. Oh, well. He served his purpose for our enterprise. Tell me, did he have anything fun to say? Any gossip to let loose?"

"Quite the contrary." Jericho shrugs, weaving his fingers with mine again. "He didn't have a lot of things to say. Although, the letters we found were quite telling. I'm curious, did you plan it all along?"

Grace takes a small step back, putting her hand on her chest. "Plan what?"

"Your escape from Gabriel? Leaving me here to suffer under his hands? I'm just trying to piece it all together." His voice remains devoid of emotions as he steps toward her with me in tow.

She frowns. "You would have, too, if you had been through what I had," she sniffs, shaking her head. And when I think she's showing her genuine emotions, her back straightens, and she claps again. "Lunch. Now. And then we'll discuss all things baby. None of this history talk." With that, she narrows her eyes, waiting for us to exit the room so she can follow us down the stairs.

I have a terrible fucking feeling about all this shit. Not only is she being forceful with the baby stuff. But Shepp and Arrow are on their own, doing god knows what.

CHAPTER FIFTY-NINE

Arrow

DESPAIR DOESN'T EVEN TOUCH THE MOUNTAIN OF DARKNESS gnawing my insides and taking my brain for a murderous ride. I want to take fingers, toes, and some goddamn ear lobes. Especially the ones of the guards I've been avoiding for the past few days. Grace insisted we stay locked up in the bedroom we created for Journey. Trapped like rats, that's what we were. But I'll be fucked if I follow those rules. Ever. Hopefully, they think I've been eaten by lions or something by now. I mean, it's a possibility for anyone else who wanders in here. Not with me, though. These cats are like my family. My babies. They recognized me the moment I walked through the gates with a sullen expression and numbness tingling in my fingers.

Numbness.

It's an odd feeling. It sucks all the emotions I should feel into a vacuum of nothingness. Like a black hole sitting inside my chest and absorbing everything. Even my beating heart.

I rub at my chest as it aches. Slowly, feelings have been coming back in small waves. Mostly anger and destruction. Worry, too. My people are inside that mansion, left behind because I couldn't stand being locked away and forgotten. My brain wouldn't let me. Memories of my dad's dead eyes staring through me—haunting me. Every night when I close my eyes.

Is that how death truly feels when it's someone so close to you? Yes. The answer is yes.

Fuck.

For two days, I've been wallowing in my secret room, which I built into the cave of my lion's enclosure. Only I was privy to the building of this secret apartment. Fit with a kitchen, bed, TV, and anything else I could possibly need when I craved solitude. Sometimes a guy just needs a little privacy when he's rubbing his cock. Here I'm free to come anywhere. And that's the freedom I thought I would crave.

So, here I sit, curled up in my secret room, contemplating what I should do next—besides slit throats and take some fucking names. I whistle to myself as I make coffee and put some cream in it. Bummer. I'm going to run out soon if I'm not careful. But if the devious little plan I've been cooking up comes to fruition, I won't be here much longer. I hope Daddy Jer won't be too mad at me for planning without him. He gets all angry and snarly when shit is out of his control.

Oh, well.

This is my show now.

I grin when the flip phone I had stashed in here comes to life, blaring some snarky song I selected just for Olivia.

"Oliviaaaaaa," I sing-song, plopping down in the recliner near my secret door. "Any news?"

"You're awfully cheerful for a guy stuck in a lion's den," she huffs—no doubt shaking her head at me.

"Don't insult them. They love me," I chide, sipping my hot coffee with a smirk. "So…" I trail off, setting my steaming coffee cup down.

"One day, they will, without a doubt, eat you, Arrow. I swear to God," she grumbles under her breath. Her heels click against the floor, echoing in my ears. Oh, so she's at the office. A door shuts, and then, it's just me and her. "We've got eyes on Grace and her movements. It seems all her businesses were raided. Any ideas?"

"Nope," I say, popping the P. "That's news to me." No way in hell am I telling a government agent we have new awesome allies who stepped up and knocked down some doors at our expense. Well, theirs, too. Semantics and all that.

Whatever.

"Well, since you're playing innocent, and I have no idea what I'm talking about. Masked invaders raided thirteen out of twenty businesses newly signed over to Grace Viotto. They left no survivors. Surprisingly, they didn't burn the buildings down. Any idea why?"

"Could they be holding everyone by the short and curlies for future business ventures?" I question in a hum, giddy with the success of our little takeover. Now, if they'd invade the damn mansion and take Grace and her minions out, I'd be a pleased boy.

Ah, well. That's what Olivia is for. My big, bad, Veritas agent, looking into every possibility for me.

"I'm guessing that would be the reason," she sighs, probably pinching the bridge of her nose.

"Maybe, maybe not. Who knows with those criminals; they get themselves into trouble. Something I'm not, by the way. I'm a good Catholic boy." My heart sinks at the reminder of my dad. Fuck. Why? Stop feeling like this. If I just had someone to murder, I'd be feeling just a little better, damn it.

"Anyway, I'm ignoring that, too. We're getting a task force together, Arrow. But we need a plan. If Grace remains at the mansion with her guards around her, she'll never surrender. It puts Journey, Jericho, and Shepp in harm's way. You understand what I'm saying, right? You need to either get Grace out of the fucking mansion and by herself, or collect your merry band of psychos and hide out in your cave." By the time she's done speaking, heat rests behind her words. "Despite me being in the government, you're all still my family. Ya got it? Don't fucking die."

"Aw, Liv. You warm my little black heart. Family?" I say,

holding a hand on my chest. "But I'm on it. I'll go collect my Kitten and the others." Although, if I don't, Kitten could be all mine. Nah. I shake my head. I love her too much to take her away from Jer and Shepp.

"Yes, family," she sighs. "I'm getting things in order, but I need you to do your part, too, Arrow. Okay? No funny business. We need to get this done ASAP." I can only imagine the stern look she's throwing my way.

"Got it, boss," I quip. "I'll get the gang into my cave, and then we'll…"

"No! Do not finish that disgusting sentence. Family, remember? Family doesn't discuss butts and stuff," she shrieks, cutting me off.

"You're rude, Liv. I was going to say we'll be safe. Nothing about fucking and…" My nose wrinkles when the line goes dead. I pull the phone from my ear and shrug, closing the flip phone. "So rude." I shake my head, relaxing further into the chair while sipping my coffee. I'll need all the fuel I can get to retrieve my beloved and her extra dicks—my bros.

I slump a little. I miss them. This mourning period has been lonely and dark. I need Jer to pull me from the brink of everything. That's why he's my Daddy Jer. And… I tilt my head at shouting coming from beyond the cave. Oh, please tell me they've sent someone else in here to retrieve me. I love a good bloody show. AKA when Nova and Max tear her guards to pieces as they shit their pants and slowly die. Lions-2 Guards-0.

That's solid entertainment that I can't miss.

When I stroll out of my secret door, making sure the rock slides back into place and covers my secret room—I head out to the mouth of the cave. Ah, what a beautiful day to watch another guard die. Or so I thought.

I instantly perk up at the sight of my silent giant making his way through the enclosure with… My face twists at his expression. Fresh tears stream down his cheeks. Well, now I will have to kill someone. No one makes my Sheppy Boy cry except me. And not even me. I hate to see the big man sad.

"Arrow!" I may have the emotional range of a centipede, but I can feel the utter devastation in Shepp's voice from here, even if I hadn't seen his face first.

My fingers curl at my side when I step out into the cool sunshine, watching my babies get to their feet. Their eyes watch Shepp with curiosity but don't approach.

"Stand down," I say, waving a hand at Max and Nova, who promptly plop down into the grass again, yawning and cuddling together.

Aw, they're so damn cute.

Guards shout Shepp's name with deep authority, but he ignores them while searching for me. His eyes are wild and unsure right before he makes it to the cave.

"Howdy, Sheppy Boy. Did you come to join the party?" I grin when he stops in front of me.

And I halt.

All the jokes I have on the tip of my tongue dry up at the look in his eyes again. I've never pretended to understand any sort of emotions. We've all been put through hell. Him, especially. I was born this fucked-up way and kissed by the devil. But Shepp? He was transformed into the man he is through the trauma his stupid fucking dad inflicted.

"You're alive," he murmurs with glassy eyes, shaking his head.

"Of course I'm alive. Don't tell me Daddy Jer thought I succumbed to my lions' teeth?" I grin again, putting a hand on his shoulder. "Now tell your favorite Arrow what happened because you look like Grace stomped on your favorite dog and threw him to the sharks."

"Worse," he mumbles, sucking in a breath.

"How can that be worse?" I ask, tilting my head and immediately going on alert. "What did she do, Shepp?" I'm deadly serious. I'll go to bat for this man. He's my brother. Even if I joked about leaving him behind so I could have my Kitten's pussy all to myself. I wouldn't have. Maybe I'd lock them in a cage for a few hours so I could have my fun.

But still....

"She fucking took my work," he whispers, squeezing his eyes shut. "They took my room and cleared it out, and now it's going to be a fucking nursery," he grits out. But just as quickly, he shakes off the anger boiling under the surface and hides it from me. I still see it, though. It's right there in his expressive eyes. "So, I came here. Hoping to find you still in one piece. Were they even fed this entire time?"

"Grace, in all her wisdom, continued to let the zookeeper keep them fed and alive. They would have torn her apart if she hadn't." I grin at that, imagining her lifeless body on the grass, along with her stupid fucking guards.

Fucking Shadow.

I can't wait until she fucking dies a miserable death at the hands of Jericho. He's the only one who will be able to do it. I'd be happy too. But, it's owed to him. She took so much from him. Time. Love. Everything. Blah. Blah. Blah. Fuck her. Fuck this. I'm so ready to unleash on all of them, but I hold myself back. If I hurt someone out here, then my Kitten pays for it in there.

"She always loved the animals..." Shepp trails off, running a hand down his face.

"You know what, Sheppy Boy? We'll find them, okay? Even if I have to kill everyone to get the answers. There will be blood! But there will also be a damn victory." I grin confidently. I will not let my brother down. Those paintings meant a lot to him. Just like the toes I keep in a jar in the basement. They're my trophies—my toephies, if you will.

"Thanks." He clears his throat. "So, what have you been doing for two days?" Right. My guy doesn't know about my secret escape.

"The usual." Thinking about how I can take Grace down.

Keeping my Kitten safe. Contacting Olivia so she can get her ass here and help. "Nothing special." I shrug.

Shepp blinks a few times. "Right," he mutters, looking back at the lions sprawled out on the lawn. "They'll be okay with me in here?"

"They love you and Jer and, of course, our girl. They wouldn't harm us. They'll protect us from those morons." I nod to the man standing in the middle of the den, pointing a gun at us, threatening our lives with his snarl.

Shepp turns, eyeing where I'm looking.

He's just in time for the bloody entertainment.

"The boss wants you both back in the mansion," he growls without fear.

Idiot.

"Come and get us then, big boy!" I say, waving at him. Shepp stares at me like I've lost a few screws in my mind. Maybe I have. Two days of solitude will do that to a guy. "I'm a little desperate for more action." I grin when the idiot puts one foot in front of the other. Well, slowly. Max and Nova make their move, standing on either side of me protectively. Who needs guard dogs when you have lions? Pfft. "You should see the way they sink their teeth into the enemies," I whisper to Shepp, hoping the dummy trembling in his boots hears me.

"Arrow," Shepp growls when I move him behind me in the cave, shoving him back.

"Have no fear, Sheppy Boy. He won't have time," I say, waving a hand when the man stays back. "Step behind me," I murmur to Shepp as the tension rises.

"You both need to come back right now. She won't give you another chance." He narrows his eyes, gripping his gun firmly. A small laser shoots from the handgun, pointing directly at my chest. Usually, they don't make it this far without being torn to shreds. They're smart, though. Not one of their bullets has injured my babies.

"I'd be careful there, Einstein. My babies don't take too kindly to threats." I grin, tilting my head.

"Then do this the easy way." He shrugs, not giving a shit what happens to him. But he will when his intestines become lawn decorations.

"What's the easy way? We come with you while you continue to hold a gun to our chests? Or..." I give him a knowing look when Max and Nova bare their teeth at the threat, continuing to march forward. My fingers run through the fur on their heads until they're practically purring under my touch. All it will take is one word, and they'll be on him like fresh meat for dinner.

The man looks terrified, staring at them with such fear I'm hopeful he'll piss his pants. Ope. And there he goes! It's running down his legs and forming a wet spot on his pants. God, I love this part of scaring people.

"That really won't deter them from biting you, you know that, right? They don't mind the smell of piss from a scared man," I say, shrugging. Max looks up at me, practically rolling his eyes at my statement. Okay, maybe they hate the smell of pee from their victims, but still.

"The easy way means the both of you leave this enclosure with your lives!" he shouts shakily, fixing his posture. One wrong move and his finger will slip on the trigger, and I'll be a dead man walking. Bummer. I have more to do in this life— like meet my baby.

"Besides, did you really bring a gun to a pussy fight?" I ask, lifting a brow.

"I'm not afraid of your domesticated lions. They wouldn't..."

"At the ready, babies," I hum when they instantly listen. "You know, I trained them myself? Everyone said getting them to listen to me was impossible, but I proved them wrong. You should ask your pal over there. He got a front-row seat to the show."

The man shudders, looking around at the carnage he stepped over. Who misses intestines on the fucking grass? That guy, I guess. Wouldn't that be red flag number one? Blood, guts, and body parts on the lawn? These aren't Halloween decorations, pal. His eyes whip to a group of guards outside the gates, shaking his head.

"I..." he quivers slightly, showing his fear.

And then he makes his fatal mistake.

His eyes dip, staring each of my babies in the eyes, basically waving a red flag in front of them and priming them for the attack. He shudders when they both take a few calculating steps together and bolts in the opposite direction.

Good luck with that.

"Well, now you've done and signed your death warrant. I'd say you can outrun them, but..." I smirk when he's pinned down and screaming. It's like music to my ears when he gurgles under their claws and teeth. "Good Max and Nova," I chirp. "Have fun with your new chew toy. Maybe another one will walk in shortly. By the way, boys! They don't take too kindly to threats." I grin when the guards back away from the fence and run toward the mansion, whimpering like kicked dogs. One of them even stops to vomit on the grass. Gross. They saw the carnage from the other two. Why are they sooooo surprised now? Amateurs.

"Jesus," Shepp grunts, turning his back on the carnage.

That's the difference between him and me. I watch with glee, loving when they rip his damn leg off and toss it in the air like a toy. Fucking brutal. And I love it with every fiber of my being. It mutes the despair of my dad's death. Finally. A little, at least. Maybe they'll send more guards in here, and my babies will have their way with them. But if they shoot my lions, the real beast will come out to play.

Me.

No one will be left breathing.

"Let's have a seat in here, Sheppy Boy. Take a load off and

enjoy your new getaway for the time being," I instruct, taking Shepp back to a secret part of the cave.

"What the fuck?" he asks, all slack-jawed and in surprise at my fully furnished apartment.

"Welcome to my second favorite place in the world," I say with arms wide open.

"What's your first?" he breathes, taking in space.

"Journey's pussy, of course." I shrug, pulling him to the bed and forcing him to sit. "So, tell me everything."

CHAPTER SIXTY
Shepp

When I marched into the lion's cage with guards frantically shouting threats, I knew I was in a safe space to escape their watchful eyes. Grace has made sure to put them on us so we don't run from here or retaliate.

But this?

"How in the fuck do you have a fully functioning studio apartment in your goddamn cave?" I mutter, sitting on the edge of a king-sized bed in the middle of a secret room I had no idea existed.

How the hell did he hide this from us? I look at him. I mean, really look at him, and shake my head. What other secrets is he hiding in that brain of his?

"Oh, this old thing," he quips, waving a hand. "Had it built for me. It's a getaway."

I don't even have to ask what from. It's a getaway when things become too overwhelming for him. When his demon makes too much noise in the back of his mind. Normally, he loses himself in the violence of everything. And sometimes, he holds it back.

"Well, it's come in handy, hasn't it?" I mumble, rubbing my gritty eyes, swollen from the tears I couldn't hold back.

My paintings have disappeared without a trace. My only hope is they're safely hiding somewhere deep in the mansion. I know it was her who removed them. She's been desperate for this baby and making a space for it. She took them to hurt me. Or maybe she didn't even realize how much they meant to me. Grace wasn't here when my father took my tongue. No. She was lost on some island, playing mistress to him and building an army to take over this place.

"We'll get your paintings back, Sheppy Boy. I promise." Arrow tilts his head, getting onto his feet. "How about a snack or something?" He waltzes to the small fridge in the tiny kitchen and cracks it open with a hum. "Well, I have pickles. You want a glass of orange juice?" He peers over his shoulder with sparkling eyes.

"I think I'll pass," I mumble, shaking my head. "Is this your goddamn murder sanctuary?" I grumble, taking in the tiny apartment-like room. It's fully functional, with a kitchen and a door that leads to a bathroom. No wonder he's been missing for two days. Staying here is like a retreat.

"You wanna know the best part?" he asks, biting into a large pickle, dripping the juice down his chin. He smacks his lips a few times, humming at the taste.

"What's that?"

"This," he says, pulling out an old flip phone and tossing it at me. I barely catch it when he sits beside me on the bed. "I've been holding Olivia off for two days. Well, I'm trying to come up with a plan, at least. Now that you're here, part of our plan is in action." He shrugs, looking pensive. "We need to separate her from Jer and my Kitten. Any ideas?" He bats his eyelashes at me with a hopeful expression.

I stare at the flip phone with awe. A lifeline. Something we can use to contact the outside world. It's like getting your one phone call from prison to the person meant to bail you out.

"Yes, Arrow," I whisper in awe. "You need to call her back."

"Just hit that button right there," he hums, pressing the number one. "There ya go, it's calling." He grins, pressing the speaker button. "You tell her whatever. I've had my fill of disappointed Olivia today." He shrugs, biting into his pickle again.

"I swear to God, Arrow. I have a damn job. You know, the one plotting to get you all to safety," Olivia snarks. "What do you want? Have you gathered your idiots into the cave yet?"

"You're so accommodating, Liv!" Arrow shouts, biting his food again and loudly munching in my ear. "Besides, that's insulting! What if they were all here to hear you call them idiots? You'd make Jer cry."

"Jer cry?" She scoffs. "My cousin hasn't shed a tear. Not since he saw my dad's eyeball get forcefully removed from his skull."

"Forcefully removed, you say? I remember that. It was epic," Arrow hums until I whack him.

"For a guy who told me to call, you sure are chatty," I grunt, sending him a death glare.

He waves me off, giving his pickle his full attention. I guess any sort of bloodshed on his doorstep is means for a celebratory pickle.

"Olivia," I rasp out with a trembling voice. "Arrow said you were waiting for Grace to leave the mansion?" I get straight to the point. Time is not on our side. At any second, Grace could snap the fuck out and take us all down with her. I don't want to be around for that. Jer and Journey are still inside those walls under her rule.

There's silence on her end until a small sob comes through the phone. "Shepp?" she questions softly.

"Yes," I say, holding back the tears in my eyes again. "It's me."

"Wow. Fuck. Holy shit. You're speaking. You're..." she trails off, sucking in several breaths. "Yes. Um. Arrow mentioned getting you all into his bat cave—his words, not mine—and hiding you so we could invade the mansion. I can't have you all in there and compromise your lives."

"What if I told you she's taking Journey to a doctor's appointment tomorrow at noon? Grace, Jer, and Journey will be there."

"I'd say that's the perfect opportunity to get shit done. Holy shit, I need to tell the team what the plan is. What's the doctor's name?" I quickly relay his name and the time again. "Okay, perfect. And you'll be…" she trails off.

"I'll be stuck here with Arrow," I say, looking back at him as he watches me speak into the phone. I swear the smile he's wearing never falters.

"Good. I can't have any of you interfering and getting in the crosshairs. I have a plan. A plan that's going to get them safely back to you both. But you have to stay put. You got it, Arrow? No hero shit!" she quips authoritatively.

"Hero? You've mistaken my role in this enterprise, Liv. I'm the fucking villain," he cackles to himself, shoving the rest of the pickle into his mouth, humming with satisfaction.

I shake my head. "We'll stay put."

"Stay put? But Journey's going to see my baby!" Arrow whines.

"Fine," Olivia sighs. "We're swooping in as soon as Grace is MIA from the mansion. I'll inform them of your whereabouts."

"In the lion's den! Make sure they have a code word like big dicks come out and play or something clever like that," he says into the phone.

"Yeah, sure, okay," Olivia huffs. "Listen, I'll call you back. Charge the fucking phone. I can't lose communication with you two."

And with that, Liv hangs up, leaving us with an empty cave.

"Wow. We're going to see our baby," Arrow says with amazement. "This is means for a celebration!" He jumps up from the bed and grabs another large pickle from the fridge, biting into it with a crunch.

"Are you pickle drunk?" I ask, shutting the flip phone and finding the charger beside the bed. Jesus. How much has he used this space? It looks well-loved and lived in.

He stops dead mid-bite and shakes his head. "For the first time in two days, I hope that we're on to a better future." His brows furrow as he takes another bite. "Two days ago, my dad died," he whispers in a low voice, almost catching with emotions.

"I'm sorry about your dad, Arrow," I say genuinely, coming to stand before him. "He was a good man."

"He was. You think I'm a good man?" he asks, tilting his head.

"One of the best," I say with a soft smile.

"Thanks, Sheppy Boy. I knew I could count on you." And with that, he plops down in his recliner and consumes his pickle like our conversation didn't happen. "So, what do we do now?" Arrow asks, licking the juice from his fingers.

"We wait for instructions," I sigh.

It's the only thing we can do. And pray that Jericho and Journey are okay in Grace's clutches for one more night.

CHAPTER SIXTY-ONE

Journey

"You're going to love this, Journey. You're going to see the baby and how it is developing," Grace coos as we sit in the empty doctor's office.

Jericho gently squeezes my hand a few times with reassurance. Something I don't feel right now. We're deep in the clogs of Grace's kingdom now. Unable to leave whenever we want.

"I'm excited," I say with a tight smile, trying not to show how truly exhausted I am.

"Me too," Jericho rumbles in a monotone voice.

If I didn't know him as well as I do, I'd suspect he wasn't excited. But I know him well now. He's attempting to hide the agitation and bite to his voice by remaining neutral in front of Grace.

"You look so tired, dear," Grace says, tilting her head with that creepy grin. "Perhaps the doctor can prescribe something for you so you can get some sleep." She nods a few times like that's the answer, humming to herself.

Jesus. You know, Arrow is out of his mind sometimes, and he shows it. Grace, on the other hand? This bitch is one of those quiet ones who strikes when you least expect it. I'm still shocked she's allowed us to live under her roof. I think the baby and Jericho are our only saving graces. Since Arrow and Shepp disappeared into the lion's enclosure, she hasn't tried to extract them again, claiming they'll starve or return to the mansion. But I don't understand how she's so confident they won't sneak away in the middle of the night to get help or go to Olivia's. She has mentioned stationing guards all around the perimeter to keep it secure.

"They'll be hungry soon enough and come out." is all she'll say while crocheting a blanket or whatever it is she's doing with those giant needles that I want to stab her with.

Sometimes, I wonder if Jericho would be mad if I took his mom out and we made a break for it. He's on edge with her. Rightfully so. But I can still see how conflicted he is. She's his mom, after all. I'm sure I'd be the same with my mom. Even though she fucked me over my whole life. Whatever. I'll be a better mom than any of these bitches combined.

If I make it out of this alive.

"Journey Viotto?" a nurse shouts from the open door, holding a small chart to her chest. Her green scrubs hang loose on her body, and a mask hides her facial features. The only thing visible is her dark brown eyes, taking us all in.

"That's us!" Grace chortles, clapping her hands. "Let's go look at my baby." She gleefully gets up from her seat, standing before me with her hand out.

I don't say anything as Jericho helps me up, and Grace retracts her hand with a huff, apparently disgruntled after my disrespect. Well, she can disrespect this ass because I'm ten seconds away from telling the damn front desk lady to call the cops and take this bitch out in a blaze of glory.

If only I could get away with it.

That would only endanger Shepp and Arrow more and put a target on their back.

"All right, Mrs. Viotto. I'm going to need you to lie back on this table and roll your shirt up to expose your belly. The doctor is going to take a peek and measure the little bean. You'll be able to listen to the heartbeat, and we'll get some pictures for you to take home."

I nod, swallowing hard when Jericho helps me onto the table stiffly. There's something in his demeanor that puts me on edge. My nerves tingle with excitement or fear. I can't tell.

Grace settles beside me, even being so bold to take my hand in hers. I want to recoil at the clamminess of her touch, but I hold my composure. Jericho, though? Not so much. He practically pushes her out of the way, forcing her hand out of mine and replacing it with his warm grip. There's something so soothing about the way he gently squeezes my hand with reassurance.

"Jericho," she reprimands. "Let me see," she protests, trying to physically remove him from my side.

"Of course, Mother," he says respectfully, gesturing for her to move beside him for a view, but far from me. "But I will be here holding my wife's hand as we look at our child together." He stares down at her sternly, not offering an ounce of warmth.

"Well, of course you will be," Grace says patronizingly, patting his shoulder.

"Let me go grab the doctor for you all," the nurse says slowly, looking Jericho up and down. Something seems to pass between the two of them, and Jericho relaxes with a deep breath.

"Thank you," Jericho says politely with a nod, squeezing my hand again. "Are you excited to see our little one, Little Chaos?" he hums, kissing my cheek. "It'll be okay," he breathes.

"I am," I say with a tight smile, imploring with my eyes for more information. How can he be so damn sure we're going to be okay? His mom is a goddamn psychopath, who I'm pretty sure is going to kidnap our baby the moment he or she is born.

All he does is offer me a hopeful smile before standing tall at my side.

The nurse steps back as the door opens, and a tall woman walks into the room with a mask on her face. "Hello, everyone! Are we excited to see the baby? I'm Doctor Ellis. I'll be giving you your ultrasound, and then we can discuss your concerns and give you a check-up. We'll need to get you started on prenatal care and taking precautions with lifting." I can hear the smile in her voice when she sits down on a rolling stool in front of the ultrasound machine. "All right, let's check this baby out. You're in luck; this gel will be warm."

I blow out a breath when the gel hits my stomach. True to her word, it's warm and soothing as she spreads it around. Nerves eat at me before she even begins. The only evidence of this baby existing is the pregnancy tests Arrow forced me to take. What happens if they are wrong? Or if the baby isn't there? Will Grace take us out then and rid herself of the burden of extra people?

My mind whirls when the machine comes to life, and the doctor grips the wand. "All right," she says, placing it on my belly. Let's take a quick look around, and—Oh, there it is!" She beams at me, taking a quick picture of the tiny little bean in my belly.

I lose my breath at the sight of the small flicker on the screen. Moving with the sound of the heartbeat thundering through the room. It's music to my ears. A piece of each of us I didn't realize I'd ever want. But there it is. It's real.

Our baby.

"Holy shit," I whisper, with tears in my eyes. "It's real..." I trail off when Jericho kisses my cheek, sucking in a breath. He lingers there, burying his face in my neck as he composes himself.

"And would you listen to that strong heartbeat?" Doctor Ellis hums, taking another measurement. "Looks like a good healthy baby growing in there! Congrats, Mom and Dad."

Tears take over my vision at the sound of that word—mom. I want to live in this beautiful moment for the rest of my goddamn life, watching as the life I unknowingly created with my three men grows into someone real—a baby. Holy hell, I'm going to be a mom. Arrow, Shepp, and Jericho are going to be dads. Dads! My mind attempts to wrap around those facts. Images of them getting up in the middle of the night to tend to the baby fill me with warmth and love.

"And are you Grandma?" the doctor asks, taking more measurements and capturing pictures on the screen of the blob.

"I am!" Grace coos with tears shimmering in her eyes. "I'm here to help them every step of the way."

We'll be okay. Jericho's words ring through my mind, but doubt settles in. Will we? How can I protect this baby from Grace when I can't protect myself or Jericho?

"Oh, good. Well, I'll print out the pictures for you, too. Grandma's gotta have a copy."

The doctor prints out pictures from every angle for us to see. It's just a tiny blob with no defining features, but my heart is so full of love. I know at this moment, I'd do anything for this blob. It's my baby.

"We're having a baby," I whisper to Jericho, who beams at me for the first time in several days. Light lives in his eyes, mixing with hope for our future. It's like all the tension he held onto fades into nothing.

"We are, Little Chaos. We're getting our happy ending," he whispers, leaning down and staring at the pictures I'm holding. "This right here is our future." He kisses my temple gently.

"We'll need to sit down and discuss the nursery more!" Grace interrupts with a clap. "And plan your home birth."

"Home birth?" the doctor asks, tilting her head with concern etched on her expression. "That's…"

"Of course," Grace sternly says, putting her hands on her hips. "Journey will not be coming to a doctor when the time comes. She will have it in the privacy of our home, where she can be relaxed." And murdered.

This bitch is on a whole other level of delulu if she thinks I'm skipping out on the epidural and medical help. That's a no from me, dawg. No matter what, we're getting away from Grace long before she can drown me after the baby is born.

"We can provide home birth care," the doctor says, straightening her spine. "It's perfectly natural to stay in your safe space and deliver. We can offer assistance and..."

"No," Grace scoffs. "No one is permitted in my home. Especially not you. You will monitor her throughout her pregnancy, and then I'll be the one helping when the time comes."

"If that's what the patient wants," Doctor Ellis says with furrowed brows. I almost want her to ask me to blink three times to see if I'm safe at home. The answer is hell no! Not with Grace in the picture.

"Then it's settled," Grace says with a grin. "Let's go home now."

"Miss..."

"Grace," she says with a nod.

"Miss Grace," the doctor says politely. "I would like to give Journey the full workup, check in on her blood pressure, and make sure she's doing alright."

"I can't stop vomiting," I interject quickly. "I've been so sick, and I feel very weak." Please give me drugs so I can eat again.

Doctor Ellis nods. "That's a cause for slight concern, hun. We'll get you a prescription to help with the morning sickness. Hopefully, you'll be able to keep food down and regain your strength." She swallows hard, her eyes darting toward the door as several loud footsteps scuff against the linoleum.

Grace's face turns beet red when her gaze furiously whips toward the doctor with a scowl. "I booked this entire practice to come here! How dare you?"

"I apologize, Grace. It seems some of my staff have come back from their lunch break." She checks her watch and nods. "Yes, it's just past one now. It's just more nurses," she offers with a trembling voice. If I could see her mouth, I'd bet her lips were quivering under Grace's stare.

"I can help with that," the nurse says in a chipper voice, moving determinedly toward the door. But before she can make it, she stops beside Grace and pulls down her mask, revealing her familiar face.

"Olivia," Jericho says in greeting. "I thought that was you." Relief soars through his tone, and his shoulders slump an inch.

She grins. "Of course it is. I tried to tell you," she sing-songs. "But you were never good at eye contact communication."

Jericho scoffs, shaking his head. "Eye contact communication," he mutters mockingly. "I have two guesses as to why you're here."

"Yes, and yes," she says with a grin. "You should really look into what Arrow builds on your property. He's a slippery little fucker, but I'd say this came in handy."

"Olivia?" Grace asks, looking her up and down with a skeptical eye. "Aren't you dead?"

"Hi, Aunt Grace. It's been a while. And by a while, I mean years since you disappeared. You did that, right? Fell off the earth for no reason? Funny seeing you here," Olivia snorts. "A lot of people used to think that. Funny how that works out. Fire didn't kill me. The knife didn't kill me. Nothing can kill me."

"Don't get too cocky," Jericho mutters, running a hand down his face.

"Why're you even..."

"Aunt Grace, I'm going to need you to put your hands behind your back now. You've been a bad, bad Shadow. You're under arrest." Grace doesn't move, standing there with a stunned expression. "I wouldn't advise running either. All your cohorts have been apprehended, and your home is being raided as we speak."

My eyes float to Jericho, who slightly frowns. "Raided? You didn't fuck up anything, did you?" he grumbles.

"Don't worry, Dear Cousin. We'll have that talk later," Olivia quips with a chuckle.

"Wonderful," Jericho says, sagging into me.

"There is no way in fuck I am letting you arrest me," Grace

snarls, stepping back. "You're a child! And you're not the authorities."

"Sorry, Aunt Grace. It's nothing personal. But you've wrecked a lot of lives." Olivia doesn't look apologetic at all as the handcuffs swing in her fingers. "And I am the authorities. Veritas, to be exact. You know Uncle Johnathan, right? Well, he handed it down right to me."

"Jonathan," Grace hisses, stepping back again, shaking her head. "I'll never let you shits get me."

"Don't worry, Mother. I'll help you," Jericho says softly.

"You will?"

"Why wouldn't I help the woman who abandoned me and then held me prisoner in my home, threatening my pregnant wife and my brothers?" He smirks at her, standing at his full height. "Better let Olivia do her job. Or I'll help in her very creative ways. You more than fucked me over to last me a life-time. I won't let you continue to do it to our future. Plotting to possibly hurt me or my wife was the final straw of our rela-tionship." He tucks his hands behind his back like always when he gets down to business.

"No! That's my baby! This is my chance!" she shrieks with tears streaming down her cheeks. "You back off, or I'll... I'll." Grace doesn't get the chance to enact her threat when Olivia pounces on her, pushing her against the wall forcefully. The door opens, and a tall, blond man saunters in with a smirk, tsking at Grace.

"Need some help, Livs?" he quips, coming to hold Grace's wrists behind her back.

"Yeah, could have used the help like fifty seconds ago, you asshole," she grumbles, shaking her head when the cuffs clink into place.

"Ah, welcome to the Veritas family, Grace Viotto. There's a special place for you." The blond man grins and then loses it when he sees me. He stiffens completely, blanching like he's seen a ghost. "Holy shit, another one?" he asks, whipping his gaze to Olivia, who chuckles.

"Yeah, Jordy. Another one. But you knew that," Olivia says, pulling Grace off the wall. She shrieks and protests, digging her heels into the ground. But it does nothing to stop them from taking a few steps.

I frown. "Another one?"

"He's referring to you being a West," Olivia says sympathetically. "You Wests seem to pop up all over the damn place," she chuckles.

"First Seger and Zepp. Then River. Then Rush. Now you? Let me guess, you're named after a band or something," Jordy asks, narrowing his eyes at me like I asked to be the chosen sperm of Corbin West. Fucker.

Jericho stands at his full height, crossing his arms. "I'd watch it, Veritas Agent." He raises his brow.

"Don't worry, Cuz. He has his own little West to keep his hands occupied," Olivia quips.

"Don't fucking talk about her. She's not mine," Jordy grunts, shoving Grace through the door.

"Another sister?" I ask, sitting up from the bed, feeling slightly woozy.

"He doesn't like to talk about how he fell in love with a criminal." Olivia grins, earning a middle finger from Jordy before he disappears into the hallway filled with more Veritas agents dressed in uniform.

"Wait," Jericho says urgently, walking out the door, clinging tight to the ultrasound photos. I only hear the words he utters. "For you, Mother. Something to stare at while you sit behind bars."

Grace sobs hysterically. "It was going to be so perfect, darling. I was going to have a baby again and..."

"Again?" Jericho asks.

"You had a brother," she whispers. "He was so tiny and precious. I kept him so safe, and then he just stopped breathing one night. My poor baby." She sobs harder, filling the doctor's office with her wails of pain.

My heart almost breaks for her. I can't imagine losing a child that was so innocent and small. But she's done so much damage to the people around her to feel sorry for her.

"We'll come to visit," he murmurs almost brokenly, despite wanting her out of our lives.

"We can allow that," Olivia says with a sharp nod. "Bring the baby," she says softly. "Come on now, Aunt Grace. Let's get you on your way." Olivia reappears in the room with a sheepish smile, waving off a few of her Veritas agents. Jordy follows her inside, shaking his head.

"When will the trial be?" Jericho asks, shoving his hands into his pockets.

Jordy snorts. "Trial? There's no trial, dumbass. This is Veritas. She's going straight to the fucking island to live out her days." He shakes his head with a cocky smirk. "Trial," he laughs.

"No trial?" I ask, coming to stand between them. Jericho seems two seconds away from strangling the idiot.

"This is Veritas, Little West. We do justice in our way. All the world's worst criminals are ours to fuck with."

"Even your West?" Jericho asks.

Jordy huffs, shaking his head. "No comment," he grumbles, walking away with his head held high.

"I have a little present for you two," Olivia beams. "Doc, you ready?"

My brows furrow when the doctor nods, sitting back on her stool in front of the ultrasound machine. "Why don't you come back and lie down again, Journey? A little birdy told me that there were more people who'd want to glimpse the baby."

Olivia grins, thumping Jericho on the shoulder. "We'll reconvene at the mansion, yeah? We've got a lot of fun stuff to debrief you on."

"You said Uncle Johnathan handed Veritas down to you?"

Jericho asks, catching Olivia by the arm. "What do you mean? I thought he was gone."

Olivia's lips roll in, and she sighs. "We'll talk about it later, okay? There are two idiots in the hall waiting for their signal."

"Was that the signal?" Arrow's voice booms, followed by frantic footsteps marching into the room. He grins at me, looking me up and down with light in his eyes. All the demons have left him.

"It's nice to see you actually showered," Olivia quips. "Wait... does your man cave have a shower?" She raises a brow.

"My secret space has everything," Arrow says, shrugging a shoulder. "Kitten," he says, ignoring Olivia when she goes to say something else.

"Arrow," I yelp when he advances on me and pulls me into his arms. "Can't breathe," I wheeze when he squeezes his arms around me.

"I was worried, Kitten," he pouts, shoving his face into the crook of my neck. "All I could think about was you." There's a hint of vulnerability in his voice when he pulls back and places his forehead on mine.

"Are you okay?" I ask, winding my arms around his neck.

"I've been worse," he says, kissing my nose. "I missed your touch and your..."

"Arrow! We're in public," I hiss.

His brows furrow. "I was just going to say your butt." He grins, setting me on my feet. "Now, let's see my baby!"

"Yours?" Shepp grumbles, walking into the room. "I tried to hold him back, but he's like a dog with a bone." Shepp pulls me into a hug, kissing my cheek.

"A dog with a..." I quickly cover Arrow's mouth, knowing exactly where this conversation is going.

"The doctor is still in here, patiently waiting," I say, giving him a pointed look. His eyes float toward the doctor sitting on her stool with a smirk.

"Sorry, Kitten. I'm just so excited to see you and this," Arrow grumbles behind my palm, rubbing at my belly.

"If you all would like to gather around," the doctor says brightly, leaving her mask off. "We can hear the heartbeat and see it in action."

Shepp gently helps me onto the table, and Jericho lifts my shirt like before. Arrow takes my hand, watching with hawk eyes as the doctor puts the warm gel on my stomach. The moment the wand touches my belly, she immediately finds the little bean.

"I did that!" Arrow beams with pride, pointing at the baby. "Wow..." Genuine awe hangs in his tone as the heartbeat echoes through the room, thrumming quickly at 145 beats per minute. "I can't believe it," Arrow murmurs.

"It's incredible," Shepp says, kissing my cheek.

"It is." I grin, not taking my eyes off the baby growing inside me.

The guys help me off the table once our second ultrasound is done, and I adjust my shirt.

"Well, congrats to all of you on the new bundle. I have the prescription ready for you, Journey. It'll help with the nausea you've been experiencing. I would like you to talk to the front desk and set up a time next week so we can do a full pelvic exam and talk some more. And I would like to see you once a month for checkups to monitor your vitals," the doctor says, getting up from her stool and handing me a piece of paper with the prescription.

"And no home birth," I say, taking the written prescription. "I need all the drugs to push a watermelon out."

The doctor chuckles at me. "Not the first time I've heard that. Everything looked good with the baby and you. Just take it easy and try to stay stress free." She gives the guys a stern look, alternating between them.

"Stress-free. Got it," Jericho mutters, pulling me out of the room with Arrow and Shepp happily on our tail.

How could I be stress-free?

CHAPTER SIXTY-TWO

Jericho

My home is tainted. Laced in hate and greed. Brought on by the people who granted me life, Grace and Gabriel Viotto. They were two people on the same side of the coin, chasing power and holding it in the palm of their hands. Never doing an ounce of good for the people who got them into that position. For my father, his last name thrust him onto the throne, allowing him to rule over the innocent and take advantage of them any chance he got. As for my mother, she was merely a pawn in his obsessive game, but she still ended up the same.

They both wanted power over Briar Cove. One died for it. The other went to prison. So, who is the real winner here?

Me. And I fucking hate it.

Everything my mother has touched. Every inch of this mansion makes my lips curl, and disdain takes me over.

She ruined everything.

My life. My joyful memories of her. Even her return is ruined by her actions.

I stare at the mansion that was once ours. A home away from Gabriel's tower and watchful eye. Our refuge from everything. A place where we could be ourselves and unmask from our public personas.

Now, she's put her hands on everything. Taking Shepp's

paintings and sitting in our chairs around the dining room table. Nothing is sacred in our former home—even the grounds we loved to walk.

"Looks like Olivia is already here," Shepp murmurs, standing stoically beside me.

A dark black, nondescript van sits in the driveway. But we all know it's Olivia's.

The four of us stare up at the mansion looming over us. Almost mocking us with the memories locked within its walls. It's a hellhole for all of us. My gaze slips to Journey, leaning against Shepp's side. Exhaustion weighs her down. I'd give anything to crawl into bed and hold her for eternity.

But not here.

Not in this ruined building that holds nothing but our nightmares.

"Indeed." I nod, lost in the thoughts running rampant through my mind. "She has a habit of making herself comfortable in my spaces." My voice barely lifts above a whisper.

"Jericho," Journey mumbles, forcing my hand in hers.

"Once this is over, we're vacating the premises," I say, gently squeezing her hand in mine. "But first, it seems a government agent wants to have a discussion with us."

Without hesitation, they all follow behind me as we walk through the front door and stall near the foyer. Rage boils through me at the sight of my things thrown around. Broken vases. Plates. Damaged paintings.

Fucking Veritas.

A tic forms in my jaw. It's just another piece of the fucked-up puzzle driving me away from the mansion. Grace fucked it up. But so did Veritas.

"Welcome home," Olivia says, greeting us with a smile and stepping out of the dining room. Her eyes sweep over us and then the space. "I tried to keep this as civil as possible with minimal damage, but you know how criminals are. They all think they can run from the law. Jokes on them." She waves her hand at the mess. My jaw tightens. "Anyway, should we sit down? I think we have some important things to go over."

"I'm sure your agents had a field day going through my belongings," I chide, looking down at her.

Her eyes narrow. "Like I said, why don't we sit and talk this through before you try to rip my head off?"

We follow her into the untouched dining room and sit around the table. It's eerie to think that just a few days ago, we were here with my mother, and her guards watched as we ate. Arrow, in all his clinginess, pulls Journey into his lap and wraps his arms around her with a sigh. After being pulled away from her for so long, I don't think he'll ever relinquish her to us.

"It's funny seeing you here again." Many years ago, we spent many days here before her father was ousted from the family. Although she was older than us and often hated being trapped hanging out with us—she was here. It wasn't until we met with Journey's brothers to discuss her money that Olivia finally made it back.

Something softens on her face. Going from the hardened Veritas agent to the cousin I looked up to as a child.

"It's strange being back. Especially after that," she says, shaking her head.

That I don't doubt. If I ever made it back to the home she grew up in until they were relocated to Greenwood, I'd have the same mixed emotions.

"Now, what did you want to discuss?" I ask, hoping she'll get to the point of this impromptu meeting. I'm sure she has other things to attend to.

Olivia stiffens, recognizing our moment is over. Her face hardens back into the woman she wants everyone to see, hiding the pain and everything else she shoves into the back of her mind.

Olivia sighs. "Oh, so many things, cousin. So many goddamn things. Your mother, for one. She's going to be locked away for a long time, along with everyone who was here and the other stragglers. We're still trying to locate more of her minions lost in the wind, but we're coming up empty right now," Olivia says, leaning back in her chair with a frown. "Fuck these Shadow assholes," she groans, rubbing at her temples.

A sentiment I can get behind. Fuck those assholes, indeed. They went unchecked for so long. How they remained undetectable will forever haunt me. My own mother was behind all the destruction toward Briar Cove.

"Listen, we need to have a pretty frank discussion about the past and the future." Her eyebrows raise, and we all nod. "I've been in your business for a while now, and I know what you do and who you are. I also know who your allies are and what their business is. I know it all, folks."

"This seems like a threat." I sit up straighter, eyeing her with a new appreciation.

Do I think my cousin would turn us into her superiors? No. Olivia has always been on the more trustworthy side, keeping secrets and never telling a soul. Hell, for the longest time, I never knew how bad her father, Raphael Viotto, was toward her. He was a pleasant man on the outside, but within the walls of their home—he was the devil.

It must be a thing of the elder Viotto brothers, treating their families like extensions of themselves, resulting in abuse.

"I don't take threats very well, Liv," Arrow playfully quips back, narrowing his eyes at her.

Even Shepp watches her closely, assessing our surroundings. I'm sure there are some Veritas fuckers hanging around.

"God, it fucking is, okay? But not in the sense you're thinking. You guys have your shit, and I have mine. I'll leave you alone and let you do your thing. Run your mafia. God knows I know about all our uncles and their less-than-legal shit. More than I care to know," she grumbles, eyeing us sternly.

"Does the rest of the family know of your existence?" I ask, folding my hands on the table.

It's something we haven't discussed. My father knew. Somehow. I'm sure he didn't keep it to himself. Or it's possible he did. Storing away information for a rainy day was his MO, anyway—anything he could use to have the upper hand on the rest of his brothers—the better.

"I'm a miracle, don't you know? Coming back to life after years off the grid," she snarks, rolling her eyes. "Anyway. All I'm saying is, I know your shit. So, keep your noses as clean as possible. And for the love of God, don't contact me again," she smirks and winks, getting up from the table with a huff.

"And how do you keep that from your organization's higher-ups?" I ask with intrigue. Surely, she can't keep our relationship from the agents working above her.

Olivia grins. "Didn't you know, Dear Cousin? I am the fucking boss. Remember when I said Uncle Jonathan handed Veritas over to me? Well, this is it."

I cock my head. "The boss, huh? Like..." I trail off when she grins, showing me exactly what she means.

"That means I'm covering for your asses the best I can by sticking my head in the damn sand every time a body shows up in Briar Cove. For now, it can be written off as Shadow's fuck ups. Or a random murder. But for God's sake, when a body floats on shore and looks like an animal attacked them," Olivia grumbles, eyeing Arrow with a knowing look.

"Well, it wasn't me! I buried those suckers in the back-yard!" Arrow yelps, pointing outside the house.

"And I didn't hear that." She grins.

"Whatever happened to Uncle Jonathan?" I hum, eyeing her when her shoulders stiffen, almost rocketing toward her ears.

Ah. Something happened there. The man who saved her after her best friends sliced her throat and left her to die, dragging her into Veritas as a form of protection. He was once an angel to her, but it seems like he slipped up and disappeared.

Olivia smirks. "Wouldn't you like to know?"

"I would, that's why I asked, Brat," I quip, tilting my head.

Arrow stiffens, realization smacking into him a few minutes too late. "Wait! Hold the pickles! You're the boss?" he asks with wide eyes. "Well, shit. That explains a lot."

"Yes. I am. And as much as Carter wants to hack into your phones and computers and put you behind bars for eternity, I won't let him. Got it? So... just... don't be stupid." She shakes her head. "Now, I need to get home, soak in a bath, and do all kinds of things with my husbands to wash away the shitty investigation that took way too fucking long to accomplish."

I shudder at the imagery. "On a list of things I didn't need to know, that was one of them."

She smirks. "I could go into gory details. Do you think keeping up with three of them is hard? Try five. It's tiring. But the orgasms? Totally worth it," she quips when I gag.

"Olivia," I grumble, running a hand down my face. "I do not, under any circumstances, need to be privy to your bodily functions. In fact, after you leave, I'm going to bleach my brain."

Olivia chuckles. "On that note, good fucking bye. I'm sure we'll meet again. Seger and Zepp are trying to set up a good time for all the Wests to get together and have dinner. Expect a call," she says, pointing a finger at all of us. "And congrats, Journey. Don't let my cousin smother you." Olivia turns on her heels, taking a step or two before she stops again. "Oh, and Shepp?"

He jerks his gaze at her, waiting expectantly. "Yes?"

She smiles at the sound of his voice. "In the search of the mansion, my officers located some paintings stored in the basement. My officers found the paintings covered in sheets and apparently well cared for in the basement.

Shepp deflates. "Thank you," he breathes.

Olivia waves without another word and leaves the house, softly shutting the front door behind her. For a second, silence descends on us. Olivia's words hang thickly in the air.

It's finally over. Olivia is going back to East Point, and we're here. Gabriel is dead. Thomas is dead. Grace is in prison. The majority of my father's bosses are dead after being killed in a massacre at the church, leaving the four of us to pick up the pieces with our new allies and get Briar Cove back into functioning order.

I get to my feet and reach the bar nestled on the other side of the dining room. Many thoughts flash through my brain. Plans start forming, and excitement settles in. I may not have wanted the throne passed down because of my last name, but I'll do right by it. Not just me. Arrow. Sheppard. Even Journey will assist in our new future.

I hum a tune to myself as I get a glass of whiskey, filling it until it's full. I have no patience or need to sip it tonight. I want it all to wash away the past few days' events. I quickly gulp down the drink until my throat burns and my headache starts to fade. Turning on my heels, I face the others who absentmindedly stare at me, watching my every move.

"I want to make a proposal," I hum, refilling my glass.

"Oh, do tell, Daddy Jer! Does it have to do with explosives?" Arrow wiggles his brows with a manic look crossing through his gray eyes.

I cock my head. "Well, not initially, but it could."

"What are you thinking?" Shepp's levelheaded question breaks through the imagery of blowing this blasted mansion to smithereens and starting fresh with a clean slate.

New house. New blueprints.

Our future.

"We need to move forward. The empire is ours." I take another sip, forcing myself to slow down.

"And Mikhail's and Elias'," Shepp reminds me with a nod.

"That, too. Now that Briar Cove is secured from Shadow's grip, we can return to normal."

"Normal? What's normal?" Journey sighs, rubbing her temple.

"Meaning we take back everything we did before. Arrow, you'll continue your father's work at the church with the townspeople." I lick my lips when he nods enthusiastically. Although I can tell he's still reeling from watching his father die, he'll do what he's always done. Persevere.

"You bet, Daddy Jer," Arrow hums, nestling further into Journey's neck and breathing heavily.

"We'll work out the details with Mikhail and Elias. But first..." My eyes dart around the room, taking in the carnage from Olivia's agents. "Let's get everything we need out of this hellhole and move to Rave. Then..."

"Can we light this place on fire?" Arrow asks with hope in his tone.

"Yes. We can blow this place to hell where it belongs," I agree with a nod. It wasn't my first choice. Hell, I would have left this place to rot and fall apart on its own. But blowing up? Yeah, that sounds like what this place deserves.

"No fire for you," Shepp interjects, shaking his head.

"Always such a party pooper, man," he scoffs.

"Then we can build a proper home for the four of us..." I trail off when Journey grins.

"The five of us," she corrects, setting the ultrasound photo on the table.

"The five of us," I correct myself, staring at it with awe.

"Shall we head to Rave and settle into our temporary apartment?"

They all nod, getting to their feet, and we meet in the foyer.

"Tomorrow, we'll come back for the rest of our belongings and begin moving things out," I say, lifting my chin to take it all in one last time.

And with that, we all pile into our SUV and make our way to Rave.

"So, is this your new headquarters, Viotto?" Elias asks, looking around at the small VIP with pursed lips.

It's been about a week since we moved ourselves into the small space, but it works. For now, at least. Besides, it's not as small as it seems. Shepp, Arrow, and I have spent many nights here after the club closed for the night. It accommodates us and works for now while we draw up blueprints for the new home we will build on the land of our former mansion.

"For now," I say, standing beside our bar. "Care for a drink while we wait for Mikhail?"

Elias nods, sitting across from Arrow and Shepp, who lounge on the leather sofa. Arrow, in all his glory, holds a knife, cleaning the thing repeatedly.

I return to Elias and hand him a drink as I settle into the leather chair, facing the three of them. "Cheers to our new partnership," I say, lifting my glass, and we clink them together.

"So, how goes the recruiting?" Elias asks, sipping his whiskey with a hum of approval.

I smirk. "It's going well. We have plenty of allies within the city to fill all the shoes of the deceased corrupt bastards." Every single ally in town stepped up to fulfill the necessary roles. "And your new establishments?"

Elias smirks. "Running beautifully now. New products are shipping on Monday and should hit the clubs and streets."

"Clean, I hope," Arrow says, pointing his shiny knife in Elias's direction.

"Always. They're my customers. I want to keep them as

happy and alive as possible. It's good for business," he says, lifting his glass in Arrow's direction.

"Good." I nod, tossing back the rest of my drink.

"Excuse me, sir," Brandon says, opening the VIP door and stepping inside. The noise of the club filters through, filled with all the citizens hungry to get back on the dance floor and drink our booze.

"Yes?" I raise an eyebrow.

"Mikhail and Sunshine Antonov have entered the building."

"Any trouble?" Shepp asks.

"No. They're headed on up," Brandon replies.

"Let them in immediately," I say, rolling my wrist.

"Of course, sir," he says, bowing his head slightly and stepping back through the door. Only momentarily, though, when Mikhail and Sunshine step through the door hand in hand, looking as cozy as ever.

"Sunshine, this is quite a surprise," I say, standing to greet her. "Journey is just through those doors there. She hasn't been feeling too well today. I'm sure your presence will cheer her up." I pat her back gently and pull back.

Journey's pregnancy has been rough on her. Despite having morning sickness pills to ease the nausea, she's still feeling the effects. Lucky for her, she has three doting men willing to do just about anything for her. That seems to please her. For the most part, though, she's been in bed, resting as she grows our future in her belly.

"Thank you, Jericho," she says with a perky grin and turns back to Mikhail, kissing his cheek. "Have fun," she squeals, taking off toward a set of doors leading to a massive bedroom with a king-sized bed. The place we've been laying our heads until we can finally burn the mansion to the ground and reclaim our lives.

"Mikhail." I offer my hand and firmly shake his. "It's good to see you again. Thanks for coming all the way from Miami."

He grins. "Business is business, Viotto. We have plenty to discuss. Besides, we'll be in town for the next month as we set up our shops and hotel."

"Right," I say, nodding. "You were able to obtain the remnants of the hotel."

Mikhail smiles. "All ours now. It'll serve as our headquarters here in Briar Cove."

"Good to hear." I lead Mikhail toward the couch, and I retake my seat and slink down into the leather chair. "All right, men. How about we get started with business?" I grin when they nod in agreement, and our meeting commences, solidifying the alliance we concocted out of desperation to save our hometown.

Now, three different walks of life with the same goal in mind will lead this town and prosper from new business ventures. From restaurants, bars, hotels, casinos, and beyond.

Our future is bright.

CHAPTER SIXTY-THREE

Journey

"THAT IS PERFECT!" JENNI SQUEALS THROUGH THE VIDEO CHAT with more enthusiasm than necessary. Actually, that's her entire personality. But I'm used to it by now. We've officially been best friend status for what feels like weeks now.

"You think so?" I nibble my lip with uncertainty. "I want it to be perfect."

"Girl! They're going to love every single thing you give them. Have you seen the way they stare at you?" Jenni scoffs at me, waving her hand. "You could give them a piece of string in a box, and they'd tie you to the bed and fuck your brains out in thanks." She giggles at that, laughing louder when my face turns red.

"God, you're too much," I laugh, covering my eyes. "Thanks, Jenni."

"Girl, I got you. But I have to get packed! Elias is taking me on a vacation. About damn time. I'm ready for wine, sex, and the beach all wrapped into one." She shimmies in the camera, showing off her beautiful smile. "Once he gets back from his meeting with your husband, we're off to the airport."

"Drink one for me!" I say, settling back onto my pillow with a sigh. "And have fun."

"You know I'll be texting you every hour of the day with

pictures. I can't leave my bestie out." She winks at me, and we say our goodbyes.

I sigh, staring up at the ceiling of our new bedroom. It's nothing permanent. So, it'll do for now. But I'll be glad when we have our own space again. A house to call our home. Not some nightclub with horny twenty-somethings gyrating on the dance floor. *That was you at one point*—my mind chides me snarkily. Reminding me of the time Jenni and I danced our assess off. Well, until she went and tossed her cookies down the toilet, and I got my rocks off between the three men I'm shacked up with.

Ah, this is the life.

Things have settled down over the past week since we got here. Everything we wanted was removed from the mansion, which wasn't very much. Shepp found his paintings and moved them into storage. But if I have my way, they won't be in storage very much longer. They'll be on display in Shepp's private building and maybe open to the public one day. Whatever he wants, I want to give him.

I have twenty million dollars to blow. Okay, not blow. I'm investing in our future. Jericho said he has enough funds to float us for the rest of our lives. But what's the point of having so much money—with more on the way from my inheritance —if I can't spoil my men? And myself? I'm paying off debts left and right and giving to the citizens I helped harm in Briar Cove. I've given Arrow the funds to add to his Wednesday night confessional meetings. Anyone who needs to get away from an abusive mom, dad, husband, or whatever—will now have more than enough to get started. No questions asked and no loans to repay.

Picking up my phone, I stare at the violin with a smile. Marked as shipped straight from Italy. It even includes a different version of his rare bow. I can't wait to see the look on Jericho's face when I hand him an exact replica of his old violin. The one he informed me that Gabriel smashed against his desk to get under his skin. He didn't deserve that. Shit, he didn't deserve half the treatment he got from Gabriel. So, this is me giving back to him and thanking him for pulling me away from the horrors of my life and treating me to something better.

My eyes stray to the bookshelf he installed a few days ago across the room. It's filled with so many great reads I can't wait to sink my teeth into. He explained he bought them for me while we were hiding at the cabin but knew I'd want them here. So, he had them shipped, and I've had fun arranging them between feeling run down. Most of my time has been spent resting in bed, reading books, and caring for my body.

I smile, reaching over to my end table, pulling out my newest read, *"Lyrics That Burn"* by Leah Steele, and placing it on my lap. Seriously, a girl could get used to this. When I'm hungry, all I have to do is text the guys, and they'll grab me whatever I want. Or, if I'm feeling not-so-lazy, I meander into the VIP room and go into the small kitchen to snack.

Just as I'm about to dive into chapter two of my book, the door to my bedroom swings open, and I drop everything.

"J!" Sunshine squeals, running toward me and diving onto my bed.

"Sunshine," I squeak, throwing my arms around her and holding her close. "What the fuck are you doing here?"

Sunshine and I have kept up regularly. We're always on the phone or video calling one another to talk. She's been getting so strong and healthy living with the Antonovs, and it shows in the color of her face and the energy radiating off her body.

"Came with Mik! We're here for a month, fixing the Grand Hotel and making it special." She grins, pulling back. "Besides! My sister is pregnant, and I needed to hug you in person!"

After we were settled and out of danger, I called Sunshine to inform her she was going to be an aunt. She was so thrilled to know I was going to have a baby. She promised to be here as much as possible. And now, it looks like she'll be able to visit often.

"I wish you would have told me you were coming." Not that I'm not happy she's here. But damn, I need a shower.

"And ruin the surprise?" She scoffs, waving her hand. "Fat chance, Sis."

I grin. "Well, that's true. So, how are things? You're doing good?"

She nods and tells me about her time in Miami with the Antonovs and what they've been up to. It seems like she's settling into her new role as mafia queen over an extensive empire. I don't know how she does it, but she slipped into it quickly.

"Have you heard from Mom?" Sunny asks, settling in beside me.

I wrinkle my nose. "Not for a few days or so. I think... I think she fell back into it, Sunny. So, prepare yourself for..." For what? I'm not entirely sure. My mom could get back into drugs, take up her old life, and ride off into the sunset like she always wanted. Or she could continue to get sober in rehab. Only time will tell.

"Yeah, I hadn't heard from her either. I was hoping she was getting better." Her face crinkles.

"She's an addict, Sunny. It happens, okay? We can only hope she goes back for the help she needs. We can only do so much," I say, blowing out a breath.

One day, my mom will be clean. But she's still fighting it, from what I can tell.

"I know." Sadness pulls down her lips, and tears glisten in her eyes. "It's hard, J. I feel like I should care what happens to her, but my whole life..." She shakes her head, sniffling.

Putting my arm around her shoulders, I kiss her cheek. "I know. It's hard to wrap your head around it. She's still your mom, but she's done so many bad things over the years. I understand. You can still worry about her and want the best for her, but also, you can keep your distance. We don't have to see her or track her down. She's an adult." It hurts to say those words. Even though Sable ruined our lives over many years under her roof with her drug use, she's still our mother. I'd hate for her to end up in a bad way. But on the other side of things, I'd rather not have her in my life anymore.

"Thanks, J. That actually helps. Mik mentioned something about making sure she was still in rehab, and then she'd be off to a halfway house to continue her treatments or whatever. I just…" She shakes her head, leaning on me. "It'll always just be me and you, right?"

"Pinky swears and promises?" I murmur, holding up my pinky.

"Pinky swears and promises," she retorts quickly, wrapping her pinky around mine.

Sunshine and I lie around for a few hours, catching up until it's time for her to go to dinner.

"I love you!" I say, holding her tight.

"I love you, too!" she whispers, dragging out of our hug. "I'll see you soon!" She smiles, waving as she takes Mik's hand.

"We'll be around more often," Mik offers. "As always, it was a pleasure," he says, nodding to each of us before he takes his leave.

"You know, I was skeptical about all this," Elias says, looking between the four of us. "But I can see this alliance will work wonders for this city. And our pockets." He smirks, shaking our hands before taking his leave, too.

"Have a good vacation!" I shout, waving a hand.

Elias smirks over his shoulder. "I'm sure my wife will let you know every single thing we do. I do hope she keeps some things private."

I smirk. "We're best friends, Elias. Nothing is sacred."

He shakes his head. "Have fun blowing up the mansion." And with that, he leaves through the VIP door and disappears.

"Now, how about our special event?" Jericho asks.

"Let's fucking do it!" Arrow whoops, throwing his fist in the air.

I grin. "Let's go blow up the mansion."

"Okay! Everything is all set," Arrow says, beaming and coming to stand beside the three of us a good distance from the mansion. "Now, if we press this button, it'll fucking blow. Bigger than that asshole who strapped a bomb to himself and blew up on our lawn," Arrow chuckles, handing the black remote with a large red button to Jericho.

Jericho stares at it with furrowed brows. "I don't think it was ever a home," he says, squaring his shoulders. "It was a house of horrors, courtesy of Gabriel and then of Grace's abandonment.

It was a prison for Journey," he grits that part out before blowing out a breath to calm himself down.

"It was never a home," Arrow says, shaking his head. "It was where I landed when my dad thought he was doing the right thing. The only good that came out of this was all of you."

"How sweet," Shepp quips. "It was a place I was brought to after my dad died. Fuck, I think I spent more time here as a kid than at home. In a way, Gabe saved me. But fuck him. Fuck this place." Shepp holds up his middle finger, waving it in the air.

"Fuck this place!" Arrow hoots, throwing up both his middle fingers.

"Fuck this place." I grin, holding up my middle fingers.

Jericho stares for a millisecond before hitting the red button hard. "Fuck this place!" he shouts over the boom of the explosion, eradicating the place that made all our lives hell. He tosses the remote to the ground, holding up his middle fingers.

The blaze takes the mansion quickly, burning through the walls and whatever we left behind. When the fire smothers away, all that stands are the ashes of a place two evil people resided in—a place that was never a home.

"Now, onto our future," Jericho says, taking my hand.

"To our new future," I whisper.

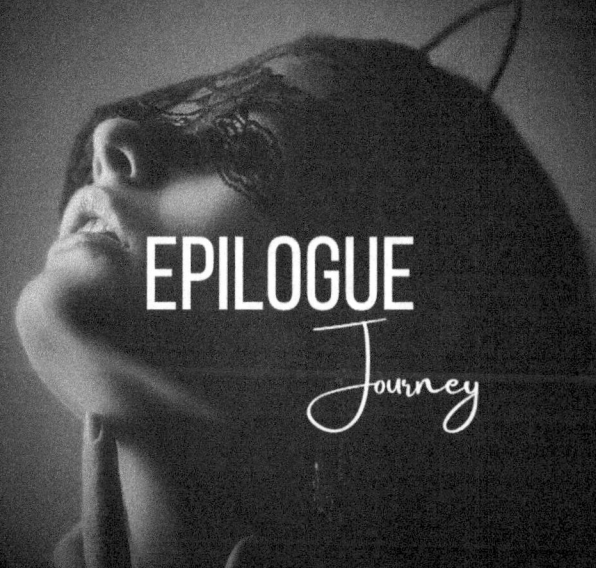

EPILOGUE
Journey

NINE MONTHS LATER

> You haven't popped yet, have you? *frowny face*

My face twists at the message, but I chortle at his words. He's been so anxious about our first dinner together that he's been texting me every day leading up to the event to see if I've had the baby yet.

JOURNEY

> No. Rude question, though.

"Who has you laughing like that, Kitten? I'm the only one who should see your teeth," Arrow says, narrowing his eyes. I swear anger blazes through his gray eyes.

"It's her brothers and sisters," Jericho hums, snatching my phone from my hands and eyeing the group chat.

"Ugh, give it back," I grumble, attempting to reach for my phone, but my enormous belly holds me back.

Jericho smirks. "I let him know he shouldn't be asking my wife those questions." And with that, he hands it back to me carefully, with glee.

> **JOURNEY**
>
> Do not speak to my wife like that.

> **SEGER**
>
> I see the mafia douche got a hold of your phone again. Bro. She's my sister. This is how we roll.

> **JOURNEY**
>
> Ignore him, please.

> **RIVER**
>
> I can't wait to put a face to the name. *laugh emoji*

> **JOURNEY**
>
> You say that now until you meet them. They might lock me up until I have this baby.

> **RIVER**
>
> Well, I'd come to rescue you. Tell them to be nice...

"I could," Arrow quips, putting his ear against my large stomach after peeking at my screen—invasive bastards. I swear I can't have a moment to myself. Let alone to pee. "Come on, Buddy. Give Daddy a kick." He blinks a few times, grinning when the baby does just that. "See? That's mine." He grins more when the baby moves, pushing against my stomach and into his face. "Ah," he sighs, relaxing into me more.

I sigh. This fight again. Here we go...

"You're highly confident that your sperm beat mine," Jericho says calmly, raising a brow as he rolls up the sleeves of his white button-down.

"You're highly confident it's even yours. May I remind you, Daddy Jer, you were tied to a chair while I got a total of five orgasms. Count that! That's five counts of spermies making their way to her egg." Arrow grins proudly, puffing out his chest.

Great. The last time this happened, they legitimately had a

fistfight. Of course, Arrow laughed it off with a black eye, begging for another round. And Jericho? The asshole came out of the fight unscathed. Like always. I swear he's invincible when it comes to fights against Arrow.

"Shepp," I whine, slumping my shoulders. "Contain them."

He snorts at me from his spot across from me in the recliner. "You say that like I can."

"You have before," I argue.

"There's no containing this, Kitten. We're uncontainable and shit." Arrow grins up at me before sitting tall on the sofa.

"Just don't break anything like last time." I give each of them a pointed look, trying to remind them of the mess they made before. Broken art—thankfully not Shepp's. Broken vases. Hell, they even put fist marks into the newly finished drywall. They're reckless as fuck, and it drives me up a wall.

"It's okay, Little Chaos. Arrow and I will take this outside and let off some steam." Jericho gestures for him to follow him out the back door.

"Whoop!" Arrow says, whipping off his shirt and jeans and throwing them on the couch.

"You're going to fight in your sneakers and boxers?" Shepp asks, rolling his eyes.

"Why not?" Arrow huffs, running after Jericho.

"You're seriously not going to stop them?"

"Stop them? Why? Let them beat the shit out of each other, Little Tempest. And while they're doing that, I can eat a meal." He grins, popping off the chair and falling to his hands and knees.

Shudders instantly go through my limbs at the feral look in his eyes as he crawls to me. "Shepp," I breathe when he forces my legs open and lifts my dress to my hips, exposing me.

"Shh. You don't want them coming back," he says, diving into my pussy and wrapping his lips around my clit.

"Fuck," I breathe, throwing my head back against the couch, getting lost in the feeling of him between my legs and bringing me to orgasm. Twice. While the others fight through their differences.

I could get down with this princess treatment any day of the week.

JOURNEY

We're on the way!

ZEPP

Good luck with the drive. Hopefully, you don't have the baby in the back of your SUV.

SEGER

Been there! Done that! It was magical.

ZEPP

And terrifying, especially when you're the one to catch him.

JOURNEY

I'll see you guys in a few hours.

RUSH

I wish I could be there to meet you guys. But it's so hectic here right now.

SEGER

One day, bro. You'll be able to make it. Tell her to quit busting your balls.

RUSH

laugh emoji Bro. I'll let you tell her that. She'd hang me by them if I even uttered those words. No thanks. I like the boys intact. **peace emoji**

SEGER

My fucking funeral, I guess.

RIVER

> I'll see you guys in a few hours. I'm so
> excited for this! We finally get to meet after
> months of texting! <3 Lyric is thrilled, too!
> She can't wait to meet her new aunt.

I never had a true family growing up. Sunshine was all I had. Even then, when I look back, I was more of a mother to her than our mother was to us. I took care of her from the moment she was born until she was kidnapped.

SUNSHINE

> Have fun at your dinner tonight! The boys
> and I are doing all right! How's my nephew?

I sigh, staring at her text message. A few months ago, before I became as big as a whale, I went to Miami and visited her and Mikhail and his secret brothers. It almost blew me away when the man who greeted me in the massive hallway of their Miami mansion wasn't Mikhail himself because he looked exactly like him, down to the damn moles on his face.

But I guess that's a secret to the world. One I promised I wouldn't talk about.

JOURNEY

> I miss you so much! You're still doing all
> right?

She's still so young to be living so far away and taking on the role of wife to the Bratva leader. She says she's fine, but I can see the yearning in her eyes every time we video chat. Although they come to Briar Cove often, I know she misses home. Health-wise, she's done amazing. Her body accepted the new heart immediately, but doctors are still monitoring her every step of the way.

SUNSHINE

Of course! I love you! G2g!

JOURNEY

Love you too!

"Now, if you feel any contractions, you'll let me know, right?" Jericho asks, snatching my phone from me again.

He and I will end up having a brawl if he doesn't stop taking my phone from my fingers. He claims it's to keep me stress-free, but I'm calling bullshit. He's an attention whore who wants my eyes and thoughts on him. I don't mind that, though.

"No, I'll sit here and stew in it myself," I grit out, holding out my hand. "Of course, I'll say something. It's your hands I need to hold when I push this watermelon out of my vagina, because it's all your fault!" I huff, wiggling my fingers for my phone.

Fucking jerks. First, they take my IUD without my damn permission and impregnate me. Impregnate me! Like some medieval breeding bastards. Ugh. Now, they're trying to be overbearing and possessive. Although it may turn me on. I won't tell them that tidbit. Ever. It still gets on my damn nerves. I'm a grown-ass woman now, and I deserve my phone and their fingers to crush whenever their son makes his grand entrance.

Soon. So fucking soon, and he'll be out in the world. I can't wait to see what they're like as fathers.

"So sassy, Kitten. You can hold my hand. You won't break anything." Arrow beams at me from the passenger's seat, winking when I scowl.

Wanna fucking bet? I raise a brow, challenging him, but he doesn't back down. Okay, he asked for it. I'm taking all my pain out on him when the time comes. Broken fingers are coming right up!

"Oh, I'll break a lot of things. Balls. Penises. Toes. You

name it, and I'll break it. Besides, you're the main culprit."
Am I dramatic? Yes. Am I excited to hold our baby? Double
yes. I'm so fucking excited to have him in my arms and be the
mother I always wanted to be.

Peace fell over Briar Cove the moment Grace and Gabriel
met their makers. Thank fuck. They were ruining this city with
their war and tainted drugs, killing their citizens. Our allies
have taken their places, moving into their new businesses.

All their allies took their pieces of Briar Cove and, for the
most part, we've been living in peace. Mikhail often visits to
check on his venues—with Sunshine. Other times, not.

"Main culprit?" Arrow acts innocently, putting his hand on
his chest. "I would never…"

"Drug me? Pull my IUD out without permission? Throw
me in your lion's den and leave a knife in my pussy? Yeah,
never." I roll my eyes at his theatrics.

"She has a point," Shepp mutters from the driver's seat.

"No one asked you," Arrow gripes, staring hard at him.

"Exactly. Now, give me my phone," I grumble, smacking
Jericho in the chest.

A blaze of fire crosses his dark eyes, and he smirks that
sexy smirk he knows makes my panties melt into a puddle of
goo. "What will you do for your phone back, Little Chaos?"

Well, so much for melting into a puddle of horny goo.
Now, I want to whack him in the back of the head until he
rethinks his words. Listen, I'm pregnant. Like forty-thousand
weeks pregnant. I want sex. I want food. I want to chop my
husband into bits when he's an asshole. And currently? I'm at
that last one. He thinks I'm going to offer sexual favors to
obtain my phone again? Fat fucking chance. He's the one who
needs to drop to his knees and suck my clit until I'm satisfied.

"I am nine months pregnant. If you think I'm bending over
and slobbing your knob in the car, you're mistaken. Give me
my phone, or I will let Arrow cut off your belly button."
There! That threat always makes him slightly stiffen. So

discreetly that I'm the only one who seems to notice every time I threaten the life of his stomach.

"I will, too!" Arrow hoots, pulling out a large knife from his jeans.

Where the fuck did he get that? Is what I would think if it were anyone but Arrow. That psycho always has some sort of weapon stuck down his pants. I don't know where he stores it or how it's remotely comfortable.

"You've got to stop encouraging her threats, Arrow. And why did you have that big thing in your pants?" Jericho grumbles, staring at the knife like it might actually cut off his belly button.

Arrow shrugs. "If it fits, it fits. Now, give my Kitten back her phone."

Jericho huffs, not bothering to argue when he hands me my phone.

"Thank you for the backup. You deserve a blowy later," I say with a grin, rechecking my group chat as my mouth waters, eager for food or dick. I can't tell right now. I swear my emotions are constantly all over the place. Thank you, pregnancy.

"Hear that, Daddy Jer? Looks like I'll be the one with her mouth on my cock later. Oh, Kitten! Can I tie him to a chair again?" He wiggles his brows, waving the knife around. "He'll have so much fun in the handcuffs."

"You may not," Jericho growls. "Now, put the fucking knife away before you stab yourself or Shepp. I've got some business to attend to." Jericho pouts, putting his nose in his phone, doing God knows what to avoid the conversation.

Arrow winks at me, sliding his knife back into its sheath and putting it back in his pants.

After three miserable hours in the car, we finally pull up to a large fenced-in property and make it through the gate. My eyes widen at the enormous house with even bigger garages sitting behind it. Yes. Plural garages. Like at least three with four car garages in each.

"Holy shit," I wheeze at the sheer size of the house looming before me. Granted, there are a million people that live inside. My two brothers, their wife, and the other two men in their relationship. Plus, their four kids. I wonder if it's something that runs through our blood, making it impossible for us to settle into monogamous relationships.

Whatever. We're here. Poly. And fucking happy. Get the fuck over it, haters.

"Why're you gawking? The mansion used to be as big as this," Jericho hums, putting his phone away with a head shake.

"Yeah, Kitten. You want me to build you something bigger than this?" Arrow asks, turning to look at me.

"No," I groan. "Our new house is perfect." And it is. Beyond fucking perfect. It's everything I had ever dreamed about when I was lying on my shitty mattress, aching for a real home with four walls and love inside it.

I got what I wished for. And more.

We designed it ourselves, laying out the blueprints. It may not be an enormous mansion like before, but it suits us. It's a one-story ranch with a basement, a multitude of bedrooms, and plenty of space to grow our family. Only this time, Arrow doesn't have a killing room down there for torture. Jericho and Arrow wanted a separate space to take traitors and anyone else who stepped out of line. I'm not privy to the location and don't really want to be, but I know it's hidden on the property.

"Okay, the baby is starving," I groan as the door swings open, and Shepp stands with his hand out. "Such a gentleman," I murmur, taking his hand and sliding out of the car.

"You okay?" he rasps, pulling me close.

No. Do I look fine? I'm bloated, gassy, and I want to lie in bed all day watching those stupid reality shows Jericho insists he hates but actually loves. Does Gavin love Bianca, or will he cheat on Tracy on the *Island of Cheating Love*? Neither. That Gavin bastard will take his dick to anyone who will listen to him.

"I'm fine," I say, smiling sweetly and tilting my head.

Does he buy it? Absolutely not. I can tell by the lift of his brows and the downturn expression on his lips. Shepp doesn't ask again, though, sending me a knowing look that I can read all too well. This conversation isn't over. And if he has to torture me sexually by telling him why I'm so bloated and down, then he will. Of course, it won't be actual torture. Oh, no. He's sucking my clit again and giving me orgasms. Oh, God! What a damn tragedy!

Shit.

I shift my legs while leaning against him. I've gone and made myself all horny again. What is it, pregnancy brain? Do we want to eat, fuck, or sleep? Or all three?

"You've got a horny look about you, Kitten," Arrow quips, shoving his nose against mine. Shepp huffs, attempting to shove him away, but it doesn't work. "Your cheeks are flushed, your legs are crossed. Do you want me to bend you over in your brother's bathroom? I can make it quick and quite satisfying." He grins when I groan.

"Brother and bending over don't belong in the same sentence," I huff, shoving him away and standing tall. "I'm starving. My stomach hurts. I want to go to bed. But I also want some D." I give Arrow a pointed look. "We're having a nice dinner with my siblings. So, no funny business."

Arms wrap around me from behind, gently resting his hands on my large stomach. I groan in relief when he raises my bump with his hands, taking the pressure of the massive baby off my hips and legs. Fuck. I wish he could stay here all day long and keep that up.

"Don't worry, my Little Chaos. We'll take care of all those needs after we have a nice, civilized dinner with your siblings. Then, I'm not letting you out of the house. Not until Jr. is born." Jr? I snort. We haven't decided on a name yet, but there's no way I'm naming our son after these three. Nope. Not a damn chance. That would be like setting him up for a life of craziness.

"Have you been pooping, Kitten?" Arrow asks, breaking my thoughts.

I blanch. Why, though? No clue. Arrow has this knack for asking the most random questions not pertaining to the conversation.

"Arrow," I groan, leaning my head back against Jericho's shoulder with exasperation.

"What? The book says constipation is normal! Besides, I can..." I quickly cover his mouth, stopping whatever words are about to spill out. I can sense exactly what's about to come out of his stupid mouth.

"Something, something with your dick. No, thank you. Now, if I remove my hand, will you be a good boy?" I raise a brow when he nods, mumbling about getting treats afterward.

"A reward would be nice if he behaves." Jericho's warm breaths spread over my flesh, strengthening my desire.

Damn them. They've conditioned me to love their warm breaths and mouths and dicks. Ugh. I'm completely obsessed and need them.

I remove my hand from Arrow's mouth. "Yes, a reward. For both of us. If we make it through this dinner and get back home. I'll let you rock my world."

Arrow wiggles his brows, swooping in for a kiss. "You got yourself a deal, Kitten. I call the back door with lots of lube!" he shouts, taking off toward the house. "What, what! In her damn butt!" He shrieks a weird song, making my face heat with embarrassment. There are children present inside that house, and here he is singing his favorite butt song.

Lord, help me.

"We can just leave him here," Jericho whispers, rubbing my belly with a chuckle.

"No. No. He'd end up showing back up, anyway. He's like a puppy who always finds his home." Besides, I kind of love

him and would be sad without his wild antics. Fuck. I'm hopeless. "Can't leave him," I quip, pushing off Jericho. No matter
how much I wanted to stay in his arms and let him rub my
belly. "Let's go meet my siblings."

"You nervous?" Shepp asks, side-eyeing me as we begin
the walk toward the house. Well, they walk. I fucking waddle.
Slowly.

"Very," I say without hesitation, nervously rubbing my
fingers together with every step closer to their home.

"You'll be fine, Little Chaos. It's the brothers you've met
before and a new sister." He smiles down at me, taking my
hand in his.

"I know. I'm just... It's weird," I murmur. "I haven't had a
family before. Just my mom and Sunshine, and that was a shit
show. Now I have all these brothers and sisters who accept me
for who I am and... God damn it," I hiss, wiping away the
hormonal tears rolling down my cheeks.

Shepp stops our progress near the front door and wipes my
tears for me. "I'm happy you found them."

"Me, too," I say with one last nod as we catch up to Arrow,
talking with Seger and Zepp on the porch. He grins. They
frown.

"Hey, Journey," Zepp says in greeting. "How's the baby?"

"Hey. I'm ready for him to evacuate ASAP," I chuckle,
taking Arrow's hand as he helps me up the front porch steps.
Jericho gently presses my lower back, supporting me from
behind.

"I bet you fucking are," Seger says, nodding his greeting.
"Come on, guys, everyone is here."

I smile when the warmth of their home envelops us. We
step inside the massive foyer leading to a family room on the
right. Loud voices echo through the space. Kids play. Adults
talk and laugh. I can't help myself. It feels like walking into a
place that holds all the people I love in life—which, I guess, it
does—even the siblings I didn't know about until this year.

"So, when do you think I'll meet Rush?" I ask, following Seger and Zepp toward the massive living room.

Rush is another of our brothers who lives locally with his wife and her other husbands. See? It runs in our West blood. He's always busy, though. I don't know that much about him yet. So, I'm eager to meet him face to face.

Seger snorts. "You've met his wife." Yes, I have. Multiple times. And she's a damn trip.

Technically, I think Jericho, Arrow, and Shepp have met Rush, too. Of course, he didn't go by his given name until Seger and Zepp found him years ago to hand him his inheritance.

Zepp rolls his eyes, shoving at Seger's shoulder. "Don't be an asshole. Rush is very busy maintaining a casino he inherited from his father in Greenwood. It's hard for him to get away. We've had them all down for Christmas and other holidays. Something you all are invited to now. We'd love to have a big West family gathering."

"Of course." I try to keep my voice monotone.

Seger smirks at me. "We get it, ya know? We only had Dad growing up and an evil stepmom—no other family. We knew everyone existed, but we were too young to know where or even understand all the circumstances. So, this," he says, gesturing to the living room filled with adults. "Is all we've ever wanted, too. You fucking got it? You're family now. Just don't fucking put us on a hit list or something." He tosses a nervous look in Jericho's direction.

"Why? You done something to be put on one?" Arrow asks with too much enthusiasm while leaning in toward Seger, who grimaces.

"Fucking nope," he mutters, taking a step back.

"You're my wife's family," Jericho says, reaching out and letting his hand hang in the air. "Anything we can do for you, we will."

"Fuck it. To family," Seger says, clasping his hand and

shaking it.

"To family," Zepp says calmly, taking Jericho's hand.

"You're Journey," a female voice says, quickly approaching me.

I suck in a breath, staring her up and down. Same green eyes. Almost the same facial shape, minus her eyes. Same brown hair with little waves throughout. She's my goddamn twin.

"We told you it was uncanny," Seger quips. "Journey, this is our sister, River, and her daughter, Lyric." The little girl grins up at me from behind her mom, clinging to her legs.

"Hi," I croak, holding back the emotions threatening to spill over. Again. "It's so great to meet you after all this time."

"You, too," River says, pulling me into a big hug. "Lyric," she murmurs, pulling back. "This is your Aunt Journey." She pulls the little girl, who can't be more than two or three, into her arms. Her mismatched eyes take in every inch of me, and she grins, clapping her hands excitedly.

"Nice ta meet ya, Aunt Joney," she says in a small voice, unable to enunciate her words.

"Nice to meet you, too." I can't help the smile that crosses my lips when Lyric bends over and copies what her mom just did, giving me the biggest hug.

"All right, Fam. Let's go eat some dinner," Seger says, gesturing to another room behind us.

We all pile into the large dining room and take our seats. Seger and Zepp's family is here—their wife Kaycee and her two other husbands, Chase and Carter, with their four kids. River is here with Lyric.

Laughter rings out throughout the evening as we indulge in pizza, wings, breadsticks, cinnamon bites, and everything in between. We catch up and get to know one another better. And by the end of the night, I'm feeling more complete than ever. I can't wait to bring my sister Sunshine into the mix and introduce her to everyone in our new extended family.

After where I came from with just my drug-addicted mother, my sister, and I, I've grown so much. Even being kidnapped and forced to live with the Devil's of Briar Cove. But I wouldn't trade it for the world. Jericho, Shepp, and Arrow gave me the much-needed stability I needed to push through my shitty life. They've slayed my dragons while standing beside me.

And I couldn't thank them enough for the things they brought to the table.

THE END

AFTERWORD

What's next?

Olivia's story! If you've read every series of mine, then you've collected the breadcrumbs of her life. Even when she was undercover as Espie. But let's go back to the beginning. Let's go back in time and see what made her who she is. And let me tell you, you'll be surprised.

To keep updated on cover reveals, release dates, series and book titles, join my FB group! It's the best way to keep up to date with me. Aly Beck's Reader's.

Curious about the other groups in this book? Well, you're in luck.

·Seger, Zeppelin, Carter, Chase, and Kaycee—Web of Lies.

·River, Kieran, Callum, Asher, Rad—Second Sets Omnibus

Acknowledgments

Behind every writer is a team of people who keep them in line. And for me, that's my amazing team of my alpha, betas, developmental editor, moral support, my besties, my editor, and my readers.

Thank you for all that you do, I literally couldn't do this author thing without you all!

Thank you for reading Journey's story and if you enjoyed, please leave a review.

www.ingramcontent.com/pod-product-compliance
Lightning Source LLC
Chambersburg PA
CBHW072345030726
47505CB00015B/1906